Book 2

The Confessions Series®

Ringside Confessions©

Apryl Butler-Bennings

Prayer and Confessions
Change Things

Imagery Publishing
Atlanta, GA

Library of Congress Number: 2017901617
Imagery Publishing, Atlanta, GA
ISBN-10: 1940681014
ISBN-13: 978-1-940681-01-6

Printed in the United States of America

*"The picture you paint
on the canvas
of your imagination
will one day
hang on the wall
of your reality.
If you keep thinking it,
it will come to pass."*

Dr. Luke S. Hall
Lukeism

THE CONFESSIONS SERIES

1. Confessions of a Church Stalker
2. Confessions of a Fighter in Training
3. Ringside Confessions
4. Confessions from a Builder and a Boxer

<u>Special thanks to The Confessions Team</u>

Alice Alexander
Chris Quarles Branding & Design
Dream Publishing - Susan Blackmon
Irvin Productions
J. Z. Alex Editing - Juva Alexander
Lori Hanes
Maleka Watson
Raquel Pam Singleton
Scott Bennings
Sheneita Astin
Syreeta ShaNee
Weather Proof Designz
Willie M. Smith II

TABLE OF CONTENTS

WEEK 17...1

WEEK 18...81

WEEK 19...108

WEEK 20...144

WEEK 21...184

WEEK 22...221

WEEK 23...263

WEEK 24...307

WEEK 25...361

WEEK 26...391

WEEK 27...423

WEEK 28...442

WEEK 35...457

WEEK 36...459

WEEK 37...503

WEEK 17
Tuesday

At four forty seven PM, my phone chirped indicating I had a text. It was from Randall. My heart was racing.

> It's final! She signed!

I pulled over on the highway. A lump rose in my throat. I quickly sent an email to my big sister Paige. She signed the divorce papers. How do I respond? She is always so eloquent in these matters. I changed directions and stopped by the house to change clothes. I did not; instead, I grabbed a red dress and shoes. *We are celebrating!* I picked up a bottle of low calorie nonalcoholic champagne. *I didn't know they made such a thing.* Then I headed over to Randall's.

I was shaking all the way over there. I had no idea what to say. I didn't know how to feel. *Was this really happening?* Paige had to be in a meeting if she did not respond right back. I am sure as soon as she reads my message there will be a group text or conference call. I was so nervous. It was as if he was immediately a different person to me. I dialed his phone. I was shocked he answered.

"Hello."

"Can you open the gate?" I asked.

"Are you there?" He ran to the monitor to check. Then I could hear the buzzer allowing me access.

Before I could pass the call box and drive the distance to the house, he was already standing outside. I got out and walked up to him. He did not say a word. He looked different; relieved is the word. He looked revived. He had bags underneath his eyes but he seemed like a weight lifted off him.

"CONGRATULATIONS," I screamed.

"Hey, I am so shocked to see you here. What are you doing here?" he asked.

"Am I not invited?" I asked.

"You do not need an invitation," he said confused.

"I came to celebrate if that is okay with you?" I told him.

"It's great," he said with excitement.

I pulled out the champagne. He hugged me. "Nonalcoholic and low calorie. Whatever," I read the bottle with excitement.

"You are so thoughtful. Today I will drink alcohol. It has been a long time coming and a long two days."

He escorted me in the house and to the kitchen. He placed the bottle on the counter. I could tell he was sitting outside by the pool before I arrived. I walk over to the door and glance at the pool. My bag still hanging on my arm. "Let's celebrate," I sang.

"I'll get dressed," he replied.

I pulled my bikini out of my bag and held it up.

He was shocked. "What in the hell is that?" he questioned.

"Swim suit."

"Says who?"

"Shut up. Says Victoria Secret. We are going swimming. Change your clothes." I instructed.

"Why," he said walking through the kitchen to the pool and jumped in with all of his clothes on.

I did not even give it one thought and followed suit. When I rose from under the water, we were face to face. He leaned his forehead on mine. Our lips gently touched.

"Can I kiss you?" he barely whispered.

"Do you have to ask?" I said as we kissed for the first time.

RINGSIDE CONFESSIONS

The kiss was intense and very passionate. Yes, it was long overdue but well worth the wait. It ended too soon.

I could not believe this was happening. It felt surreal. I felt as though I wanted more information. I needed more details. Sure, I knew he was not lying, but at the same time, I could not believe it was true. Tears ran down his face. It was finally over. I kissed each one of his tears as they fell.

"This is why I care so much about you Danielle," he said while looking me in the eyes.

I asked, "Why?"

"I can be myself. I can laugh. I can cry. I can pray. I can be weak. I can be strong. I can be transparent."

The more his tears fell, the more I kissed them away. Slowly my own tears began to fall.

"Why are you crying?" he asked while wiping my tears away.

"I don't know," I said barely above a whisper.

"Tell me please." His voice and his eyes pleaded with me for an answer.

"I am happy. I am very happy for you."

He gently placed his lips on mine. We were breathing each other's breath. Our lips touched and separated. They touched then separated again. Finally, he kissed me beyond passion. It was a forceful kiss. A kiss that said I want you desperately. A long over-due kiss indeed.

Before I knew it, my back was up against the wall of the pool. We were engulfed in each other. Our bodies were not only wet from the water. I had not been kissed in years. It was just like riding a bike, and let me tell you, I had not forgotten. Our breathing was extremely labored. My heart was beating so fast, hard, and loud until I swear I could audibly hear it. His was too, as I felt it beating on my chest.

No matter how hard I tried not to moan, I was not successful. There was no way it could be contained. It was a soft, gentle, and erotic moan. He groaned following a long, exasperated moan. The way we were going at it, you could tell neither of us wanted this moment to end.

He kissed my lips, neck, ears, and my chest. My body fell limp. I leaned my head back while he kissed my chest. The back of my head was in the water. Pool and shower romance is without a doubt the best. It was indescribable, sexy, provocative and irresistible. In order for him to keep my balance, I wrapped my legs around him. He pulled back instantly. I thrust my pelvic into his pelvis area. He groaned and immediately let go of my waist. Thankfully, I had my legs around his waist and my arms around his neck. He put his hands in between us in order to readjust himself. The back of his hand slid down my pants before he was able to gather himself. This caught me by surprise. I inhaled and held my breath as I was temporarily paralyzed.

He was fighting his body and mine. I kissed his neck and forcefully grabbed the back of his head. He gave into me; his body parts touched my body again. This time more powerful than the last time. He grabbed my buttocks and pulled me in closer to him. Wet cotton and air were the only things in between us. I was overwhelmed. Overwhelmed with his statue and the situation at hand. This morning I never suspected my day would end like this. He thrust himself back into me again. I made a loud moan as I gyrated in response. At that point, we were still fully clothed, but no doubt, we had just made love. Mentally, emotionally, and practically physically. I think we both climaxed.

"Danielle," he manage to murmur.

"Yes," I said out of breath.

With his eyes closed he whispered, "I need you."

I was holding his face. My lips on his neck. His lips on my ear. He was out of breath. We were in the twelfth round and today our ring was his swimming pool. I really could not tell who was winning, but it was damn sure a good fight. It didn't matter too much to me if we were being taped or filmed. At this time, I was only aware of my utter happiness and it felt so damn good.

"Danielle," he said again, this time moaning.

"Yes." I said as if it was the last breath I would ever take and his life depended upon it.

His voice pleaded, "I love you. Do not ever leave me."

He shoved me back to the wall of the pool. He tightened my legs around his waist. He took his shirt off. Wearing only his wife beater, I kissed the parts of his chest that were exposed. He placed his hands under my shirt. He rubbed my back, caressed my breast, but did not touch my skin as he ran his hands all over my body over my camisole. Our kissing was extremely forceful, aggressive, and passionate. My moaning was light and continuous like a nonstop whimper. He gyrated and I matched him with my own movement.

"DAMN," he pulled back. My ankles crossed around his body and snapping him back. His fist were balled up. I took my hand and tried to pry his fingers loose. Finally, when I got them open our fingers interlocked. He laid his forehead on mine. I could feel his body tremble. Not a sexual tremble, but more like a nervous tremble.

"We promised," he was out of breath. He said repeatedly. He was obviously trying to convince himself.

My phone had been ringing, buzzing, and chirping throughout this entire event.

He became rational, "We need to stop."

"Why?" I whispered. "Why?" I said again not wanting this to ever end.

"We promised. I have longed for you. But. But I have to stop," he stammered.

I moaned indicating I did not want him to stop. My moan and my body begged without me saying a word.

"We still have a line in between us. The line is a different color today than it was yesterday. Let's soak that in first."

"Deacon." How could he manage to be moral at a time like this?

Calling him Deacon seemed to ignite something in him. I think it turned him on even more. "Marry me today," he said.

In the heat of the moment, he asked and I responded. Both of us knew our passion was speaking. "Yes," I answered.

He babbled aloud, "Do not do this to me."

In between kissing his skin, I managed to ask, "Do what?"

"Tempt me like this," he replied breathless.

"I am trying not to," I said honestly. He was not alone in feeling this way. I understood because I felt it too.

"Well I can tell you now; you are not doing a good job. I am not as strong as you may think I am Dani. I am still a man. Please let me have you."

Oh my goodness, this man! All I could do was nod my head yes as if I were in a trance. He had taken all of my breath away. I felt like I was going into cardiac arrest. I was caught me off guard and truly excited.

"I am serious." He gave a small version of the laugh I love. "Let me have you."

I said, "Yes," wanting him to take me now.

"Not physically. Do not get me wrong I want you physically right now more than I have ever wanted anything in my life." He paused, looked away shyly then back at me again. "I think you can sense and feel that to be true. Nevertheless, let me have you. Permanently and forever."

I was overjoyed and speechless. All I could do was kiss his nose and lips repeatedly. The moment was too intense for me to speak.

"I love you Danielle Jade Rose."

I have never told him my middle name. He was more of a stalker than I was. "I love you too." I didn't need convincing. I knew he loved me and I loved him too. However, from that moment those three little words seemed to change. It was different. This time there was nothing and no one holding us back from the way we felt for each other. Whether our bodies technically met or not, we crossed the line and we would never be able to return. It took half an hour to do something we could never undo. Sure, we were not intimate physically, but there is no denying it, we were mentally. My mind raced with the thoughts of how much I wanted this and how much I needed it, and now, how much I couldn't have it. I hoped that after this initial encounter we would be able to control and contain ourselves and enjoy a proper relationship. I wanted to take it one day at a time.

The boundary lines were removed. He grabbed my neck and pressed his body so close upon mine until I swear he was in me and his body was pressing through me. My mouth was wide open like a fish gasping for air out of water. It was as if he penetrated me and I was trying to relax my body. My back was arched. Suddenly, he let go and stepped back. When I opened my eyes, I saw his eyes were still closed. His fist were balled up again. It was as if he got his and backed off.

He exhaled hard and stood there for a moment. You could tell his mind and his body did not agree. He was motionless. Finally, he gave up the ghost. His body lost the fight as he decided to go with his mind.

"Let's go." He pulled me out of the water. "Get dressed. Why would you jump in the water anyway? You are crazy you know?"

"Crazy about you." He hugged me tighter. Wet clothes were heavy. They weighed me down. *Wow, I think everything I am wearing is dry clean only*, I thought. I knew the clothes were not going to be salvageable, but I wanted to keep them anyway. I smiled at the thought that immediately came to my mind about a girl who kept the clothing she wore during her escapade that became a presidential scandal. I was keeping them anyway scandal and all.

I picked up my phones and bag as we headed through the house leaving a trail of water puddles.

Randall stopped in his tracks, "I did not even ask if you have clothes other than those strings in your purse?" He shook his head disagreeing with my swimsuit.

"Yes, I have clothes in my car."

"Where are your keys?"

"At the bottom of the pool," I said with a straight face.

"Seriously?" he yelled. As if neither of us was capable of getting them.

"No, silly in my hand." I laughed at the panicked look on his face.

He took my keys and went to the car. I followed behind him and stopped to wait at the door.

"Hey get that dress," I yelled out to him.

He gave me a mischievous look. He appeared surprised to see I was so well prepared. He gave me a look as though he thought I intentionally came with the plan to seduce him. I did not, but I cannot lie and say that I had not been wanting to for months. He held my bag and walked me upstairs. "You can shower and change in here or would you prefer my bathroom?"

"I should be fine," I said as he handed me the bag.

"Help yourself to anything."

"Thanks." Just that quick we were back to where we were yesterday. Friends. The pool scene was in the heat of the moment. The moment ended. As I got ready to turn to go into the bathroom, he snatched my arm and pulled me towards him and we started all over again. As quick as our little venture ended was as quick as it began again. We ended where we began.

Our bodies tossed around like ping pong balls from wall to wall. Front to back. Wall to floor. All of the stuff I had in my hands was scattered across the hallway. My phone rang and rang and rang. I could tell from the ring tones who was calling.

We rolled all over the floor like two animals in heat. I was not going to be able to take much more of this. I was either going to give in or pass out from exhaustion or anticipation. My phone continued to ring back to back to back.

Annoyed that my phone was continuously ringing but content that he was saved by the bell he asked, "Do you know who that is?"

Brushing my wet hair out of my face, I answered drained, "Sade."

He lifted his body up off me and searched for the phone. "Baby girl are you good?" he spoke quickly in his deacon daddy tone.

"Yes Uncle Hooks. Where is Auntie D?" she spoke back forceful.

"She can't talk right now. She will call you back later. Maybe tomorrow." He kissed me again while he held the phone up to his cheek.

"Is she okay? Why can't she speak to me? What is wrong with her? I need to speak to her NOW. This is urgent," she finished her sentence by yelling.

He took his time speaking in between kissing me. "Not one thing is wrong with her and Sade it is not urgent. You just said you were fine baby girl. She will call you later I am sure of it."

"UGH! Tell her to say something NOW! I am not playing! I am for real!"

He held the phone up, "Speak," he said to me.

I was so choked up I almost could not speak. "Hey girl. I will call you back." He hit the button to end the call.

"Where were we?" he asked with a look of mischief in his eyes. A look I must admit I liked.

"Right here," I said and I rolled over on top of him this time. I had no power, no will, and no hope left to stay strong. I think he knew it. He did not either. He tried to push me back. I took his hands and extended my hands the length of his arms above his head. I made up my mind. I was going all the way. There was no need in stopping now. "Tell me to stop if you want me to stop," I said seductively.

He opened his eyes. I had given him a choice. One of us was going to have to be strong and it was obviously not going to be me. He closed and opened them again trying to fight this feeling. "Danielle, do not do this to me."

"Do you want me to stop?" I sternly asked kissing his neck giving him no other option but to say no.

"NO," he moaned through wiggling trying to escape the sinful pleasure I was providing.

I tried to relax his arms a little as I continued kissing him.

"We have to immediately," he said strongly in his deacon daddy voice. "Let's do right," he said, but not so strong this time. "Please," his voice was now extremely weak.

I rolled off him onto my back, bent my knees, and threw my hands over my face. Not out of embarrassment, because I could not believe I made it this long and was willing and ready to give it up.

"D."

"Yep."

"I told you to trust me once before. Be patient and trust me like you did previously." He was now referring to us being intimate.

I guess I was supposed to respond. I didn't.

"Did you hear me?"

I sadly mumbled, "Yes."

"The mall is still open. We can get the ring tonight swing by Hunter's and be married and legal before the night is over." He made himself laugh. He stood up, shook himself off, leaned over me, and said, "Grab my neck."

Before I could get my arms around him, he pulled me to my feet, escorted me to the bathroom I was going to use then went to his master bathroom. He locked the door and immediately called Trevor.

I stood in the bathroom trying to take everything in. I stared into the mirror not believing this was happening to me. How was this? I texted the group.

> Hey, I am at Randall's. All is well. Stay up. Family meeting.

I turned my volume down because I knew one of them was going to text right back. Sure enough, before I could even get my volume silenced my phone sounded an incoming text.

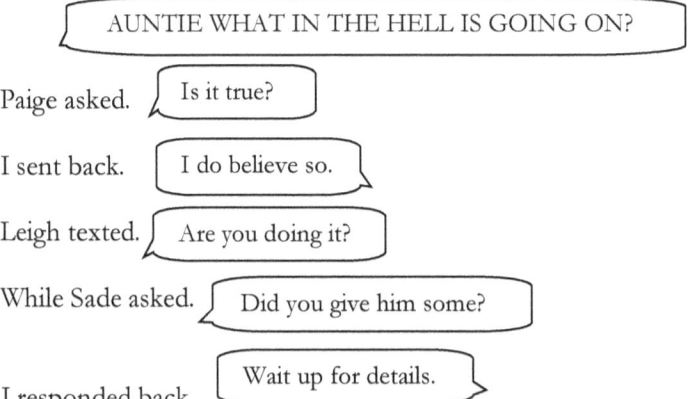

> AUNTIE WHAT IN THE HELL IS GOING ON?

Paige asked.
> Is it true?

I sent back.
> I do believe so.

Leigh texted.
> Are you doing it?

While Sade asked.
> Did you give him some?

I responded back.
> Wait up for details.

I held in my laugh. They were funny. *Here it is I am telling them the man is officially divorced and all they want to know is if we are doing it. The answer is no.*

However, I wanted to. DESPERATELY. *Intimacy would be a nice topping to end the day for him and for me. Accidents do happen. God will forgive us of our transgressions. It is not the first time.* I had to shake myself.

"Danielle get a grip," I spoke aloud. *The flesh is weak.* I quickly hopped in the shower in order to regain my composure. I let the water fall all over me. Then I realized I had to wash the chlorine out of my hair. I stepped out and got the hair products from my bag. I showered, washed my hair, checked a few messages, and got dressed. There was no hope for my wet hair at this point so I pulled it in a ball. *I need hair care products here,* I thought as I ran my hands over my hair. I lotioned up, sprayed perfume, looked in the mirror, and thought o*h well; this is the best I can offer right now.*

I looked nice with the exception of my hair. *If we go anywhere, I know people will assume something has popped off today by the way I looked. Regretfully not.* I opened the door. With my shoes in my hand, I walked down the hall to where I saw light and stood outside the doorway.

Without looking up, "Come in," he said.

I did as instructed. I could not observe the room because I was too busy looking at what he was doing.

"Is this your panic room?"

"You will thank me for this," he said unapologetically.

"What is it?" I questioned. I did not have a clue as to what he was referencing.

He stood up, turned around, and gave me a CD. "You look nice," he kissed my neck and kept walking. "I'll take care of your hair tomorrow," he said unruffled looking down as he buttoned up his shirt.

My eyes were now fixated on the screen and realized it was us. Not only us, but also us in the pool. "What the hell?"

"You have a CD of this. You have my permission to black mail me if you should feel the need. I have a copy too," he winked his eye.

"Oh really?"

"I was going to delete it but it is as close as I will ever get to a XXX tape," he chuckled.

"You need help," I said with laugher although I had to admit he was right.

Shaking his head, "Besides, I am sure I will need evidence and proof for Trevor."

"Well I certainly do not think this is it."

"You are right. But I think it shows you seducing me more than me seducing you," he spoke proudly.

His statement may have very well been true but I had to rebuttal, "Whatever."

Blowing my comment off, "Where do you want to go to celebrate?"

"Where ever. You pick. It is your day."

He was wearing jeans, a crisp white shirt and a sports jacket. I was wearing a nicely fitted red dress. Johnny Gill's song, My, My, My came to mind. He set the alarm and we walked to what he called a garage, but truth be told, it was more like a luxury car showroom. We headed to town. Once he stopped the car in front of the restaurant, the valet raced to open the door. You could tell they were shocked to see him pulling up. Stunned was more like it.

We walked in as if we were now a couple. "Good evening," the maître d' said.

"Hello."

"Hello Ms. Rose. I didn't know you had reservations for tonight."

"I am sorry I do not. Is that going to be a problem?" I questioned hesitantly.

Randall chimed in and looked at both of us like we were idiots. "The reservation is under DR Washington." Hooks spoke as if he had everything under control.

I looked at him and smiled, "When did you make reservations?"

Smiling that vibrant smile of his, he replied, "Do not ever under estimate me."

"That is amazing."

"What?"

Raising my eyebrow, "How did your mouth get so fly overnight sir?" I teased.

"Oh you know how. If not, I will gladly show you again. However, we do not have a pool to fully enjoy the moment."

Out of curiosity I asked, "Are you going to eat something here?"

"I picked the place correct?" he smarted.

"There it goes again," I said referring to his smart mouth.

"You have a problem with it?"

"One more time and it will be in the restroom getting washed out with soap for you mister."

"I doubt that very seriously," he laughed the laugh I loved.

Two can play this game. "One thing is for sure, it won't touch mine again."

He quickly corrected himself. "Okay, okay, you have my attention. It is under control from this moment on." *However, my thoughts are beyond kissing your mouth*, he thought.

"Thank you." I felt as if I defeated him even if I did cheat by using my girl power.

"Now Danielle, how often do you eat here for them to know you by name?"

"I would eat here every day if I didn't think it would make me gain twenty pounds a day."

The waiter promptly came over to greet us. "Ms. Rose. Mr. Hooks. So nice to see you this evening."

"Thank you friend same to you," I responded to waiter.

"What can I start you off to drink?" he asked.

"I will have my usual, a De'lite."

The waiter nodded, "Your norm. Grapefruit juice with a splash of cranberry."

Randall looked at me as if I asked for a gallon of hot prune juice.

The waiter turned his attention, "And for you Mr. Hooks."

"A bottle of your best champagne." Randall replied gaining my attention.

"Any particular occasion?" The waiter looked at me expecting a response.

Gazing into my eyes Randall answered on my behalf, "Yes. We made history today. Three times over thus far. I am going to try to push my luck and go four for four."

"What luck Mr. Hooks. How do you plan on doing that?" the waiter asked.

He was gazing at me before responding seriously, "I was thinking of asking Ms. Rose to change her name to Mrs. Washington."

I continued looking at him, "Wishful thinking," I spoke aloud. However, inside I was turning flips with excitement. Yes, I hoped it would happen one day.

"I hope that works out for you Mr. Hooks. Is there anything we can do here to assist you?"

He looked at me and said with all sincerity, "Pray she says yes."

I shook my head smiling on the inside. The waiter cheerfully walked away.

"Let me get this right," I said. "You are eating a steak and drinking champagne?"

Without hesitation, he replied, "Yes."

With disbelief in my voice, "I don't believe it."

"You will see. Keep sitting right there."

In deep thought and reflection of what was happening, I placed my hands under my chin. "Do you drink?"

"I have not in ten plus years. I have never been much of a drinker because it can affect your weight and athletic ability. Tre on the other hand. He opened the club up and shut it down daily. You have not a high priest that has not been touched by your infirmities. However, this is an occasion I want to celebrate. I want to remember this night always. I have two things I am celebrating. The Omega and the Alpha. My old life and my new life."

"You told the waiter three things."

"Yeah I did."

"They would be?"

Confidently he said, "Divorce, kissing you, and the ability or opportunity to date you."

This was amazing. A few short hours ago, I was pushing back and he was watchful of what he said to me. Now, a few hours later and he is out of his shell, so to speak. I knew he could talk, but tonight he is talking my ear off. I am sure he is excited and rightfully so. I am too. Right now, I couldn't be happier for him.

I interrupted, "So Randall, tell me how you feel?"

"I think I am still in shock. I got a call late last night to show up at Khrittyleberrg's office. I had no clue why. Tameka was far from my mind."

"And?" I needed more details.

"I showed up and found out she wanted to seal the deal. We went back and forth until she gave in. I was not and I did not give in. She and her attorney finally stopped haggling."

"So?" I pressured further.

"I did not ask any questions." He quickly changed the subject, "I heard you called and gave my trainer a hard time."

The waiter returned. He popped the cork from the bottle of champagne. It seemed as though we already had the attention of everyone in the restaurant. Now with the cork popping I was embarrassed. To embarrass me further Randall tapped the glass with his knife. If we did not have everyone's attention before, we sure do now. "Wait a minute," he said. "Waiter I need two things."

The waiter stood at full attention, "Yes sir Mr. Hooks."

"Champagne for everyone," he announced.

My idea of covering the tab flew out the door. "Stop it," I said. I was sure this one bottle was more than I wanted to spend and now he just bought the bar.

He looked at me and rolled his eyes. "Have the valet bring in some of the photos from my trunk please," he said to the waiter.

The waiter jumped at the instruction. "Yes Mr. Hooks."

"You do not have to do this," I kindly said.

He was now standing up. He leaned close to my face and placed his forehead on my forehead. "Danielle, please let me enjoy this moment babe. I am officially on cloud nine. I am loving life and most of all I love you," he said with sincerity.

At that, I swear, I could hear the rapid beat of my own heart. All I heard was my heartbeat and the continuous noise of bottles popping.

"Does everyone have a glass?" He held his glass up in the air. "I would like to toast to history in the making. A toast to love." He looked at me. "A toast to friendship and new beginnings. Life is short. I say, live hard, love hard, and laugh hard." He clicked my glass, "Cheers."

I clicked his back, "My sentiments exactly."

He sipped from his glass. This was unbelievable. I was celebrating his divorce with him. I could not believe he ordered the largest steak on the menu. I promise this was not the same person two days ago. I don't know if I like him more or less. Today he was truly a different person. He was free. The shackles were removed and he was one delighted person. You could see it in his eyes and read it on his face. You could hear it in his voice and you could detect it in his actions. Truthfully, I was as ecstatic as he was tonight.

I felt selfish and did not want to share him with anyone right now. I only wanted these next few days to be all about him with me. I had no idea how that would occur or what I would do if given the opportunity, but I was going to figure a way to make it happen.

He was so jovial. He passed out his pictures and socialized with the other patrons. He ordered more rounds of champagne, which he never drank. I did not indulge either. He was not about to get me tipsy. Oh no, I was not going to fall for the okie doke. I needed to be alert. I had too many more questions and I needed answers.

When our food came, he sat down, removing himself from the spotlight. He was no longer Hooks. He was back to the person I came with. He was Randall again. "King is going to kill you," I smirked.

He laughed trying not to admit the truth. "No he is not."

"Yes, he is," I replied earnestly.

Not sure why I made the comment. He asked, "Why?"

"Are you supposed to be out alone?"

"I am grown," he smarted off again.

"Are you allowed to have beef and alcohol? And surely you are not supposed to be passing out photographs?"

He looked surprised that I cared enough to question, "Whose side are you on?"

I looked up from my plate, "Does it matter?"

"Yes."

"Why?" I questioned.

"From this day forward you are supposed to cover me like King covers me and Keith covers you."

I frowned.

"What are you frowning at? King or Keith?"

"Both," I said matter of factly.

"Do not act. They are both your BFF's," he laughed sarcastically.

"Sadly you may be correct. Keep your friends close and your enemies closer. If that is the case then I am in line."

Between his laughs, he managed to let out, "I think you all like each other."

"Yes, you're absolutely correct. As much as a cat likes water."

"Why don't you like King or Keith?" He truly desired to know the real reason.

"Me?" I played coy.

"Yes you."

"I think it is the other way around." Truthfully, I think we all feel the same way about each other. The feelings are mutual.

He still needed clarification, "What do you mean?"

"I do not think they like me either," I said. The word either confirmed I did not care for them.

"What makes you think they do not like you?"

"King is being protective. He does not want anything to happen to you. He is not going to let me slip at all. I hope he checks you the same way he checks me."

I was under the impression King was very tolerant and accepting of Danielle. "You think so? You think he checks you?" he asked.

"DUH." *Did he really ask me that? Is he that unaware and unobservant?*

"Okay. What is up with you and Keith?"

"I am afraid to answer that?" I wanted to avoid going back to the conversation we had a few days ago.

"Why?" he continued.

"The last time we discussed Keith, I thought we were going loose friendship."

He knew she was telling the truth. "Danielle, you and I will never loose friendship. I hope you agree and understand that. I promise to listen this time."

I wanted to make sure he was not calling my bluff. "Is the champagne talking or are you talking?"

He gave up his robust laugh. "No the champagne is not talking for me yet, and I am not drinking again until we get to the club."

I overlooked the fact that he said he was not drinking again. I also ignored the club statement. I continued, "I think Keith is concerned he is being punished by being assigned to me."

He knew Keith was not happy about his assignment. "Why do you think?"

"What, other than him saying it?"

"He said that?" he asked in shock.

"On every occasion," I answered truthfully.

"Why do you think he feels this way?" Randall desperately needed to know the answer.

"Because you stuck him with RJ and now me."

"And?" This was ridiculous to Randall. Keith was not stuck. He was paid to do a job, he expected him to do it, and do it well.

"It sucks," I said referring to the job. "I know I am a handful."

"Why?"

"You put him on kid and girl detail."

He took a sip of his champagne. He looked over at someone in the restaurant and held his glass up as they returned the gesture. "You all do not get it?"

I agreed, "No, I guess we don't."

"Do I need to speak to Keith?"

"No. I do not want to get him in trouble."

Randall did not want to be argumentative, "I think I do."

"No please don't say anything," I pleaded.

"I try to do everything in decency and in order. There is a reason for my madness. It is truly a valid reason and unfortunately I am not changing for you, Keith, RJ, or King." He wanted to add, 'Live with it', but he took the safe route.

I raised my eyebrow. I didn't know if he was stating a fact, checking me, or getting pissed. I took a sip of my champagne and responded. "What is that supposed to mean?"

"King is with me."

"We all can see that."

"Watch your mouth Mrs. Washington. No need for sarcasm."

"More like smarty pants," I replied mocking his earlier behavior.

He slid up real close to the table. He cut more of his steak, shoved it in his mouth then gave a sarcastic laugh. "What don't you all understand?"

Why is he saying y'all? "Keith you mean?"

"You too. I am baffled. You spoke it yourself."

"What?"

"I *assigned* Keith to you and RJ," emphasizing the word assigned.

"You did. I thought we established that."

He took my glass. "No more for you smarty. I cannot send King to anyone else. We work well together and I need him. If I have to I will, but I really choose not to. You and RJ are the most important people in my life. I have assigned Keith to my two lifelines and he considers it an insult and punishment. In my eyes, it is the highest honor. Sure, it is a heavy burden, but I pay him extremely well for his services when he is with you two. Not because I think you all are more trouble. Actually, you are less trouble. He should not have any trouble with either of you. Well, hopefully, not with you. Both of you should be easy. I pay him handsomely for a reason. Much more than I should because I want him to take this position serious. As far as I am concerned, he can kill if necessary. Working with me is just that, work. You get up early, work late, be the bad guy to the fans, to the media, to the public, to my friends, to my family, and sometimes even to me. Whether you know it or not, King has to be the bad person to me many days. Keith does not want that. He had better watch what he asks for. To whom much is given, much is required. I require a lot of time, physical, and mental ability from King. I am sure that is not what Keith wants. King has been doing this a long time. When I move, he moves. When I eat, he eats. When I go to the restroom, he goes. If I do not, he does not. You get the picture. It is a big responsibility."

I couldn't help but to laugh. I heard those same exact words coming from Keith.

"Not that I am all that. If I work out eight hours, King has to work out eight hours. Keith does not want to be bothered with me like that." He paused, "Why are you laughing?"

"You really want to know?"

He took my glass and smelled it? "There must be something in here that I did not have," he looked perplexed.

I placed my elbows on the table and leaned in, "You know what little man?"

He raised up as if he was going to talk trash.

"Your little attitude has been atrocious today. You may want to check it."

He took note to what I said by nodding his head, but did not comment. He wanted to wait until a different time. However, he was curious as to why I made the remark.

I continued, "Back to what I was saying. Those things you just mentioned is exactly what started the fight Friday."

"I am glad you mentioned that. What was that all about?"

"Friday?" I asked playing dumb.

"Um yeah Danielle." He was not going to let this go until he had an answer.

"You all tried to let the Rottweiler loose on me but little did he know I am a Pit Bull. Don't let the smooth taste fool you."

He looked surprised, "I did nothing."

"Well someone did. We were having a simple conversation that went bad very quick. He made it known for me not do anything to betray your trust. He also informed me he eats when you eat, pees when you pee, etcetera, etcetera."

"And that was it?"

"Basically."

"I have a feeling you two said a little more than what you are claiming," he accused.

Shyly but defensively I said, "What makes you think that?"

"I thought you two were going to fight. You both looked like a couple of wolves showing teeth."

"Whose teeth were the biggest?"

"So you did respond?"

"No," I said innocently.

"Oh yeah," he gave with sarcasm.

"Yeah. It wasn't a response. He attacked and I attacked back. It was simple."

"Champagne makes your mouth a torture chamber young lady."

I made a facial gesture. *Look who is talking,* I thought to myself.

"Okay, what did you attack back?"

I was ready to close this subject. I do not like them and they do not like me. "Does it matter at this point?" I asked.

"Yeah it does. I need to see if I need to have a word with King too."

"Are you speaking to Keith also?"

In his stern voice, he responded, "Yes. I told you I would."

I made a body gesture like a child throwing a tantrum. "Why you got to go and do that?" *Now Keith was going to be mad at me too. We were finally starting to get along.*

"I need for Keith to change his attitude before he ends up at the high school volunteering to help the wresting team on my behalf."

"Now that is punishment."

"While I am doing all this talking, tell me what do I need to talk to King about?" He sat up on the table giving me his full attention.

"Nothing," I said shyly.

"What else was said the other night?"

I laughed remembering what I said. "I politely told him that if I became the sheriff he would be downgraded to Barney Fife. That's all."

He sat there with a blank expression for a few moments. I could not tell what he was thinking. I made an unhappy facial gesture. *Oh no, I am in trouble,* I thought. "Randall."

He excused himself from the table. My eyes followed him as he walked away. He went to the men's room. Little did I know, he stepped away to make a phone call.

When he returned I asked, "Everything alright?" before he even had the chance to take his seat.

"Of course. I am trying to figure out what can I do about you all," he said as if it was a bad thing and too much for him to think about at this time.

I continued to probe, "What are your options?"

"You two have none. Either you amicably decide to get along or I get to make the decision of who is the sheriff on which day. Trust me; you all do not want me to do that. It will probably be me every day."

"Hmm," I mumbled dryly.

"I am going to repeat what I said the other night. I suggest you two work it out." As far as Randall was concerned, this was the end of the Danielle and King not getting along conversation.

I noticed he took another sip from his glass. We continued talking during dinner. He sent desserts to every table in the restaurant. Once we were done, he ordered the car, paid the bill and extended his hand for me to stand.

He thanked the waiter and maître'd then handed me the leftovers. The night was still young. He talked as we drove along the highway. We pulled up to the garage at Heavy Weights. As he clicked the garage door open, a security guy I did not recognize came running in our direction to greet us.

"Hooks, what's the occasion?"

"It is still my name on the building, right?" with sarcasm in his tone.

"Yes, I do believe so," the guy said apologetically.

"I thought so," realizing his earlier tone, he took it down this time.

"We were not expecting you."

"I didn't know you took reservations," he joked.

His mouth was off the chain today. I have never heard him speak so flippant.

"Who is with you?" he asked, referring to personal security, not me.

Hooks looked over at me while holding my hand. "Who else?" Looking to his left and then right, "The same crew that is always with me."

The guy looked around and said, "Is King in a different car? I don't see him."

"I was not referring to King. I was referring to the Father, the Son, and the Holy Spirit," Hooks replied.

I let out a giggle. They both glared at me at the same time. I looked up like a lost puppy.

We exited the car and stood in the hallway behind a metal door. "Any more questions or am I allowed to enter my club now?" He looked down at me never letting my hand go. "Are you okay?" he asked without expecting a response.

"I am. Are you?"

"I have never been better." He smiled and so did his eyes as he asked, "Do you need anything?"

"Not at the moment."

"Record it as being so. From this day fourth you never will need anything again. Not as long as I shall live." From the way he looked at me I knew he meant it.

His comment caught me by surprise. All I could do was smile.

He slid his finger down the bridge of my nose, "I love your smile."

Immediately Shanice's song from the 90's came to mind and I sang *I Love Your Smile*.

He laughed hard. "You are so random and I love it. With your old school self," he said as he leaned in my ear and kissed my neck. The door was not open yet. He yelled, "Open the damn door!"

"Hey, hey, hey." I took his chin and looked him in the eyes. "Take it down," I said with my eyes pleading with his.

"What?" he quickly responded obviously still a little hyped.

"Calm down," I replied, realizing all of this was new to him. He was excited like a child on Christmas morning.

He closed his eyes trying to contain himself, "I am calm."

"No you are not," I snickered.

After taking a few deep breaths, "Okay, maybe I am a little excited," he admitted.

"A little? You think?" My voice was high pitched through my laughter.

"Just a little," he said while motioning his fingers to indicate something small.

"It is final. No one is going to reverse it. You have the rest of your life to be excited."

"I'll admit it, I am beyond ecstatic."

"That's fine," I said looking him up and down. "But if you don't calm down I will never allow you to drink again and I will be calling King."

"Who let the dogs out," he sang loudly. However, it confirmed he thought of King as a Rottweiler just as I did.

I shook my head as the door finally opened. "How long are you going to be crunk?"

"Just for a few days maybe until I realize it is really over. Know what I mean?" He looked back, "Sammie, Black, you two are up." He motioned for the two guys to come over. "You have Ms. Danielle for the night." I didn't know Sammie so I extended my hand and gave my normal strong handshake. He looked down as our hands clasped together.

Randall broke them apart. "This is not work for you Danielle. Only for him," he clarified.

Little did he know every day and every hour was work for me. I was never off. Even if I was not working, I was thinking about work or mentally working.

He looked at both guys and continued with his instructions. "No one near her. Check anything she eats or drinks. She is never left alone."

Black leaned into his ear, "What's going on Hooks?"

"We will all meet this week. Expect an email before the sun comes up."

I shook my head at him.

He caught me and asked, "What?"

"Do you boo," I said at him giving orders. Not even a second ago, he was the one informing me of how I was not on the clock, yet he was working.

Black and Sammie escorted me to the same booth where we sat at the last time we were here. I looked around and realized Randall was at the bar. *What is he doing now?* I continued to observe the room. It was a Tuesday. Not too empty but definitely not crowded like it was the last time I was here.

I then took notice of two guys approaching us pulling a hand truck. They were very muscular and wore black tees with silver monogrammed hooks on the front. They walked up to the table. Sammie and Black did not move but they allowed them to get thru.

"Excuse me ma'am." I stood up immediately. "Mr. Hooks would like to know which you prefer."

They each pulled out a bottle from the selection stacked on the hand trucks. Krug, Cristal, Bollinger Blanc, Moet & Chandon. I was impressed he kept such a selection, which made me wonder who the buyer was. I replied, "Neither."

"We have more. Would you care for a different brand? Please name it." He rattled off some other names, which sounded slightly familiar. I opened my bag, took out my phone and began to call him.

"Yeah babe," he said looking directly at me from across the room.

Before I could step down from the booth Sammie asked, "Where are you going?"

"Follow me." I went and stood on the side of the bar where he popped about ten bottles and poured glasses. "What are you doing now?"

"Working," he said non-chalantly as he walked to the other end of the bar. We both still had our phones to our ears.

I hung up the phone and stepped inside the bar.

"You hung up on me," he said grabbing my waist as he walked by me. "Which do you want?" He held a bottle in each hand.

"Neither."

"Let's stick with Dom since that is where we started. I do not want you to be hung over."

He leaned down and kissed my forehead. *Who was this person?*

He took his phone, dialed a number, and said to someone, "Bring my crystal from my office."

"I do not want anything else to drink." *Was he not listening to me?*

"One last toast," he winked.

"I want you to take it down," my voice pleaded with him.

He grabbed my arm and turned me around so no one could see him or read his lips. "Danielle, on a scale of one to ten this is a hundred for the best day of my life. Learning I would be able to fight again was a fifty. It was big, but this is huge. It rocks the scale. Do you know how long I have waited for this day? If they told me no to fighting, I would keep working out and ask again in three hundred and sixty five days. I have been wrestling with Tameka over half of my life. The fight is over I hope. If only you knew how I have prayed for this day. How long I have laid prostrate. How long I have fasted. How long I have pleaded."

"This is not my character. I am aware," he continued. "But tonight is such a different kind of night until I want to be out of character. You know it is unusual for me to drink and I am sure I will pay for it tomorrow. Do one thing for me tonight. Allow me to enjoy you, enjoy the moment, and let a brother shine," he kissed my forehead again.

I said nothing. One of his guys now had a camera. I thought, *oh Lord, now we will have pictures to reflect on this nonsense.*

The DJ made an announcement. "Champagne is being served by the Champ, Hooks Washington. The bar has been bought out on a Tuesday. You will be given a glass do not drink until the toast is made."

He started passing out glasses. I felt bad so I began to help him. The wait staff attempted to help but he shot them down. He wanted to do it himself.

Once everyone had a glass he took the microphone, passed me a glass, and made a toast. The camcorder and the cameras were on. He and I were also plastered on the monitors. He had the microphone in one hand, the other holding his Waterford Crystal with his arm was around my neck.

"Good evening. I wanted to take a moment and thank you all for patronizing and supporting me. It means a lot to me. I am not who I am without all of you. My friends, my fans, my family, my staff, and crew. I love you all. I wanted to share this moment with you tonight as the Alpha. Today marks the beginning. My life has taken a shift. My first life ended and the second part of my life began. I did not think it would or could happen. When life throws you hard blows, when it hits below the belt or it serves you a TKO, please know you can begin again."

"Tonight I want to toast to us," he said looking at me. "New Beginnings," He raised his glass, "CHEERS MY FRIENDS."

He emptied his glass before I even had the opportunity to turn mine up. As soon as I did, he snatched it from my hand and swallowed it too. He then took my face and kissed me so passionately until I lost balance and nearly fell. We were on the big screen for everyone to see. *This is going to be a mess.*

He let my face go. The DJ began to play Earth Wind and Fire featuring Raphael Saadiq, *Show Me the Way to Your Heart.* Just as I began to walk away, he grabbed my hand. This rarely happens, but I was embarrassed.

"I love you," he said still holding the microphone, which echoed throughout the speakers.

I was so discombobulated until I could not speak. I reached for my empty glass. He handed it to me after he refilled it half way. Then he commenced to tilt the bottle to his head. Still on the screen, I yelled, "Don't you," but before I could get the word dare out, the bottle was to his mouth and he was taking it to the head. I yelled, "Where the hell they do that at?"

"Yell at me tomorrow," he said. "I hope I remember this night," he laughed.

"It's on tape in case you don't." At the rate, he was going he was not going to remember a thing.

He smiled.

I spoke to the camera and video men, "I will take those cameras with us when we leave tonight." I immediately began to question myself and wondered if I should have said anything at all. For all I know they could easily download or switch out on me. If they did, no doubt, there would be hell to pay. I went to the DJ and made a request.

"Ms. D where do you get this old stuff from?" He said while shaking his head.

"You are playing Earth Wind and Fire but you call my request old?" I teased.

Before I could get back to the booth. I heard the beat. I looked on the screen and it was playing the video for *I Love Your Smile* by Shanice.

I went back to the dance floor. He was still standing there holding the microphone. I serenaded him. The more I sang and danced the more he smiled. I did a come here motioned with my finger. He passed the microphone, bottle, and glass to someone and came closer to me. We slow danced to the fast song. No one was on the dance floor but us. Right when the song was close to ending. I said, "Let's go home." A grin spread across his face from ear-to-ear. He looked like it was going to be his lucky night.

"Sorry, you missed your chance earlier," I said.

"Well damn," he said wondering if I was serious.

As we walked off, I took the camera and the recorder as both men stood speechless. *Bet they did not see that coming.*

Once behind the metal door he asked suspiciously, "What's up with the cameras?"

"I am editing these photos and videos before I see you on the news with a Dom bottle up to your mouth."

"Thanks. In addition, thanks for celebrating with me. The next celebration will be our engagement party."

"Yeah, yeah." It was always something about the sober person's attitude towards the drunk person. He was not drunk but probably as close as I would ever get to see him in a lifetime.

"Hey, someone drive us home," he yelled as we both stood there looking at the two-seater. "We have a problem," he said.

"Yeah. You should never drink," I said pointing to the Land Rover next to the two-seater that he apparently overlooked.

"That is why I keep you around. Do you need to get anything from my house?"

"Yes, my car. My computers. My stuff." *Duh.*

"Are you working tonight?" he asked as if that was the craziest thing he ever heard.

"Um, no. Not tonight," I admitted truthfully. I had too much on my mind to work right now.

"Can I bring it to you in the morning?"

"I guess so."

"What time are you going to the office?"

"Five." *I hope the champagne does not hinder me.*

"Your car will be at your house before then."

As he pulled me closer to him, I laid my head on his chest. Before I knew it, I heard the snores. He was asleep. When we pulled up to my gate, I gave the driver the number to dial. It dialed my cell phone and I clicked the gate open. When we got to my house, my intention was to sneak off and exit the car without waking him. He woke up as soon as I moved.

"Where do you think you are going?" he asked me smiling as if we had just had a one night stand.

"You were asleep," I whispered.

He exited the car with me. "Wait," he said to the driver.

As I keyed in my garage code he walked in the house behind me.

Seriously, he asked, "Are you good?"

"Are you good?" I asked in return.

"Yes."

"You are going to have a terrible headache in a few hours."

"Nothing like the one I have had for the last twelve years."

I laughed aloud.

"Thanks D."

"For what?"

"For being Danielle."

For the first time all night, the air was heavy. It was a different kind of air, yet familiar.

"Good night."

"Good night Randall. Congratulations. I am glad you are happy. I hope the happiness you have today remains with you the remainder of your life. I pray nothing or no one attempts to steal your joy. You deserve it. It is promised to you. Successful, happiness, warrior, champion is your name and covers you."

"I receive it Prophetess. Now, go to bed," he swiped his finger across my nose.

"I know you purposefully tried to get me tipsy so I could not work. But it didn't happen," I said in the attempt to lighten the atmosphere.

"More like to take advantage of you."

"Get out."

"I will now but I will be back in a few hours," he winked.

"You know what to do when you get to the house."

As soon as I closed the door and turned on the alarm, I sent a text.

MEETING – 9:30 AM.

I dozed off. He texted when he arrived home.

> Thanks for celebrating with me. You are crazy for jumping in the pool. I will rebuke any cleaner's bill. Have a good night.

---

2 Corinthians 5:17
Therefore if any man be in Christ, he is a new creature: old things are passed away; behold, all things are become new. Today I became new. The old me passed away.

He was supposed to be asleep but he blogged at two sixteen AM.

I looked at his message again and started to text. Instead, I called his house.

"Hello. What's wrong?" he said quickly.

"Go to sleep."

"Good night my love."

"Good night."

Wednesday

I got up at four forty five, dressed, and forgot the fact I did not have a car. Well, I had a car; however, I was missing the main one with my computers. I have a laptop in my office so I will be fine for the day.

At five thirty seven, I was ready to leave. I gathered my things and headed to the garage. Normally, I never open the door until I am in the car and ready to leave. Today I opened it before opening the car door. "What the?" I said startled.

He came right in as soon as I opened the door.

"What are you doing?" I was trying not to panic.

"I told you I would bring your car before you left."

"How long have you been out here?"

"A few minutes," he looked at his watch. "Seven minutes to be exact."

"You are amazing. Let's go," I shook my head.

He smiled, "I love this car."

"Thanks. It is nothing like the Phantom though."

"You are not ready for the Phantom."

"Are you scared to give it up?"

Sternly he informed me, "Ain't happening."

"Well, if that is the case, where am I taking you?"

"I am going to work with you."

Through my laughter, "Oh no you are not," I yelled.

"Why? Is your boyfriend going to be there?"

"Cheap shot," I smacked my lips.

"What?" he asked playing innocent.

"You can ask me if I have a boyfriend. There is no need in beating around the bush." I did not know where he was going or what he was alluding.

"Do you?" he spoke sincerely.

"Do I what?" I asked, playing with his words.

"You know," he said shyly.

"Do you have a girlfriend?" I asked him squarely since he was not being direct with me.

He looked as if he had to think about the answer, "Not exactly."

I came right back, "What about a boo?"

"It's complicated."

"Are you married?"

"No, I am not! Thank God!" he said it as if he had finally been asked a question he could answer with confidence.

"Hi, my name is Danielle. My friends call me Dani," I extended my hand.

"Oh, no Ms. Rose?" he questioned sarcastically.

"No, not today."

"Well if that is the case then hi, my name is Randall. My friends calls me Hooks."

"Why do they call you Hooks, Randall?"

"I am a boxer and that is my fighting name."

"Interesting. Nice to meet you Randall," I winked.

He gave that radiating smile, "Nice to meet you too Danielle."

By the time our courtesies were over, we were pulling into the gate of his gym. I was glad we introduced ourselves. It gave the feeling we were meeting for the first time. We were officially starting from scratch. It was truly feeling like a new beginning.

"I will pick you up at six," he said as he jumped out of the car.

"Hey! Hey!" I yelled while he ignored me. I jumped out, "Six?"

"Yes," he confirmed.

"Pick me up from where?"

"Where did I pick you up from earlier?"

"Home?"

"Sherlock," he used my word being sarcastic.

"That is early. I will still be at my office."

"Today you will not," he said. "And no other Wednesday for that matter," he added.

"I will meet you at the church at six forty five," I backfired.

He walked over and leaned his head down over my face. His nose touching my mine. "I will pick you up at six from your house for Bible Study." It was not a question or up for discussion. He spoke and that was the end.

"UGH," I shouted and stomped off.

"What?" he asked affectionately.

"No fair," I said in temper tantrum mode.

"What?" he said as if he might entertain my tantrum.

"You are using proximity to persuade me." He knew what he was doing getting close to me.

"Six Danielle," he walked away as if nothing happened. I could not speak for him, but for me, I was in the middle of an inferno.

Leigh showed up at seven forty five, which is early for her.

"What is going on?" she stormed in asking.

"I said ten thirty," I reiterated.

"Correction, you said nine thirty," She gave me the look of death.

At nine twenty three, the line was lighting up. All parties were on the call. "Good morning ladies," I said casually.

"Cut to the chase Sissie," Paige demanded.

"Pushy," I said joking and trying to buy myself some time.

"You made us wait all night then you want to take your sweet little time. Spill the beans," Leigh yelled.

Not to my surprise, the child gave her two cents, "Did you give him some or not?"

"Sade!"

"What? It was a sincere question. You are past the getting to know you stage. It would have been girlfriend approved," she said referring to them approving.

"Stop pussy footing around," Sissie demanded.

"Okay. Okay. The divorce is final," I spat. "Although I have no written proof at this time, I'm pretty sure he was not being dishonest. I was on my way to the gym to figure out what was going on when he sent me the text. I went home and grabbed a bag so I could treat him to whatever he wanted to do. I got my red Tadahi Soji dress. Just so happened the bag I grabbed had my bathing suit in it."

Sissie sang, "My, my, my, my, my, my. You shoul' look good tonight."

I forgot how well my sister could sing. I had not heard her voice in so long. "Shut up! I picked up a bottle of non-alcoholic champagne," I continued.

"What a waste," Sade barked back.

I cut her short before she started her soliloquy, "Are you going to allow me tell the story or not?"

"Go," Leigh said.

"I drove over to his house."

"Did he know you were coming?" Sade asked.

Leigh asked at the same time, "Was he expecting you?"

"No. I pulled up to his gate and dialed his home phone. Can you open the gate? You could hear the excitement and shock in his voice. He opened the gate and was at the door when I pulled up. I walked in with the bottle and my bag. We went to the kitchen. I said we are celebrating whatever you want to do. I could see he was sitting out by the pool. I reached in my bag and pulled my Victoria Secret bikini out."

"Not the VS Auntie? Trickie Vickie. That is like a stripper costume. You are scandalous as hell. Wait until Hunter hears about this. You will be on scandal patrol."

In the middle of laughter, I kept speaking, "He quickly informed me that was not a bathing suit and he dived in the pool with all his clothes on. Therefore, I jumped in right behind him."

"What the hell? Sade crooned. "Ratchet."

"You did what?" Sissie asked in her mother voice not knowing if she should be appalled now or wait until she heard all the details.

"Have you lost your mind?" Leigh spoke loudly.

"From there the rest is history. Then we both showered and changed."

"Together? Why did you all have to shower?" Sade asked.

"No, Sade we did not shower together. He showered in his bathroom and I showered in mine. We showered because we were wet."

"I bet you two were," she mumbled under her breath. "Your bathroom and his. You are claiming a bathroom there already. Ratchet. I never thought I would see the day Auntie, but I love it."

Once she took a break I spoke up, "Wet from the pool and we had chlorine in our skin."

"How did it get in your skin if your clothes were on?" she rattled on as if she was going to catch me in a lie.

I ignored the child, "He was in one rest room and I was in another. After we got dressed, we went to Ruth's Chris. That is where he chose to celebrate."

"Did he eat?" Leigh questioned.

"Did he? Yes." I was surprised. He can really eat if he chooses to.

"What?" Sister commented as if she could not believe it.

"Then he bought champagne for everyone."

"What the hell?" Sade said again. "Let me get this right. You went to Ruth's Chris wearing a Shoji dress with your hair wet and standing all over your head. He bought out the bar while I was not there. Ghetto fabulous and extreme ratchetness. That is what I am talking about Auntie. Y'all straight hood. Hood rich. Both of you are hood and holy."

Ignoring her I continued, "We left there and went to his club and had a champagne toast there." Sade interrupted me.

"He bought out a second bar Auntie?"

"Well not exactly. He already paid for the second bar."

"Y'all doing it big for the man that does not eat or drink. Do we have footage?" Sade confirmed.

"Yes we do."

"You keep mentioning champagne. Did he drink any?" Sissie asked.

"Did he? He got tipsy. One of the guys took me home and then took him home. My car was left at his house all night and when I opened up my garage this morning and he was there with my car."

Silence covered the phone. I turned in my chair.

As expected, Sade was the first to speak. "So you never answered the question. Did you give him some?"

I rocked in my chair, allowing the suspense to linger a little longer.

"Say?" my sister pressured.

"I have footage of that too," I said stirring them up even more.

"What the hell?" Sade yelled.

"That's three times Sade," I said reminding her of her vulgar mouth.

"Say what? You gave it to him three times?" she smarted back at me.

"You have said what the h-e double hockey sticks three times. Enough."

"This is serious business," she recapped.

Instantly you could hear the dinging sound of the incoming emails. I sent them the first piece of footage with us intently swooing each other in the pool. The second email was of him making the toast.

"What the hell," Sade said again.

"Leigh almost tore the hinges off my door. Roll the complete footage," she demanded.

"I can't kiss and tell everything," I said in mocked modesty.

"Yes hell you can," she said. "And you better."

"No."

"You will."

"I did not give him any," I confessed.

"Let me get this straight," mother hen added. "His divorce is final?"

"Yes."

"You jumped in the pool with all of your clothes on?"

"Yes."

"Y'all had hot, steaming, wet, bumping, fully clothed grinding?"

"Check."

"Randall ate red meat and drank champagne?"

"Yes."

"Then you went to his club where he bought the bar out for the second time?"

"By George she's got it."

"Bull crap."

"What?" I said in my innocent voice.

"You are sitting on this phone calm as if nothing happened."

"I am excited."

Leigh stood there staring at me and said with all the attitude she could muster, "I am looking dead at her and she looks calm as can be."

"Whatever. That's all folks," I said with sneaky laughter in my voice.

"So what's next?"

"We really didn't talk much last night. Considering what was happening, I let him baste in his excitement. He was different. Oh and his mouth was ridiculous," I laughed. "He was moving in fast motion and all over the place. He was so excited. It will probably take a full week for all of the dust to settle and for him to think clearly."

"I am happy for him," Paige added.

"You can see the difference it made in his life immediately."

"How do you feel?"

"I have not had the chance to really think about what this means. I do not want to get my hopes up and he comes back with let's just be friends Danielle," I said mimicking his voice.

With skepticism in her voice Paige said, "Do you think he would say that?"

"You have to remember that was his only girlfriend. This maybe the break he has been waiting for to cut loose. Do not forget he plans to fight soon. Groupies will be everywhere."

"I beg to differ," Leigh said.

"I agree. I think Randall is too rooted and grounded," Paige noted.

The question was is he rooted and ground in me.

"We will bow all those hoes off. Besides Hunter is not about to let him go out like that. You can bet that," Sade added.

"I hope you all are right."

"I think you are going to be booed up real soon," Paige acknowledged.

"I don't know," I said hesitantly. "You all are still my boo's."

"We love you too boo," Sissie said.

"You all are so gay gay," Sade moaned.

"Bye girls. I got to go get my mind right and try to work."

"Tootles."

I humped it all day. I was slammed or maybe I slammed myself to avoid the thoughts of last night. Not only the thoughts of last night, but also the next few nights to come. I wondered what they would bring.

It was a struggle for me to leave work and be home by six. I will never agree to this again. His ring tone rang my phone. "I am almost home," I answered.

"What is almost?"

I said nothing. *Why was he harassing me?* Was I sure this was the right person for me? *Heck yeah.*

"You hear me Danielle," he said knowing I was ignoring him.

"Seven and three quarter minutes." I was trying to be funny.

"I will see you then," he said checking his watch to time my accuracy.

I beat him there, but as soon as I walked inside my phone rang from the gate. I won. Does not matter by how much. The point is I beat him there. I opened the door and ran down the hall to get my things before he got to the driveway. He stepped in the door. I could smell him from down the hall.

"Hey," I said making my way back down the hall towards him.

"Hey."

Once I reached him, he pulled me into his arms. *Wow. I forgot we are officially allowed to touch.* He hugged me a little tighter then kissed me. *Oh my goodness, I do not know how much longer I can go like this. We may have to go back to the non-touching rule.*

"What time are you on duty?" I asked, breaking the hug.

"I am not today."

I could not believe what I was hearing. I turned around, "What? Seriously?"

"Nope."

"Why not?"

"I want to sit next to you and enjoy service. First time for everything."

"What do you mean?"

"I have been on duty since the first day Hunter started preaching. Even when there was only twenty three of us meeting, I was there serving."

I thought for a moment in amazement. "Wow, look at Hunter now. For those that did not like him then, I am sure they hate him now. Nevertheless, it is all good. Let all the glory be to God."

"Besides," he said, "The next few weeks are sure to be full of many firsts and I want to enjoy them. For example, yesterday was the first time I have had a female caller at my house. You were the first person I have kissed other than the last person. It was the first time I really made out, not to mention, in a pool. I experienced my first real date and today will be the first time you and I can enter the house of the Lord together as two single people. So, I took tonight off."

We pulled up to the church. King opened his door right away as Keith stood outside mine but did not open it. He waited until Hooks came around and as soon as he stood directly in front his hand and Keith's hand touched the handle at the same time. He helped me out of the car.

"Phones in the car," he ordered.

"Yes sir." I obliged only because of his soft tone.

"Good job," he winked.

We walked in the church hand in hand as a couple. He spoke to all the other deacons as we entered the building. My favorite usher looked confused. He approached the isle where I normally sit. Typically, this is where he drops me off and runs away; however, today he did something different. He directed me to the same seat I sat in Sunday and he sat in Keith's seat. We sat next to each other. Keith and King sat where he normally sits. I do not think they needed to have him under praise alert today but they were there just in case. I assume his prayers have been answered.

As all the other deacons walked passed him they all shook his hand as if they did not just speak to him ten minutes ago. He was here Sunday. He was going to be back serving Sunday. He was not gone or going anywhere.

Hunter preached on Omega to Alpha. I swear they spoke about this. Randall blogged Omega to Alpha last night. I made a mental note to ask him about Hunter's sermon. Everything was moving so strangely. It may have been sheer coincidence or maybe Randall really was at the right place in his life.

He wrote on his offering envelope and handed me his check book with the check signed and nothing else completed. "Fill this in please."

I said, "okay," but continued to pay attention. A little after I began to fill it out, I paused for just a second to do a double take. Written on the tithes line of the envelope was $100,000.00, love offering $ 25,000.00 and every other line he wrote $5,000.00. The total was $150,000.00. I waited to get myself together before I commenced to write a $150,000.00 check on the behalf of someone else. I didn't want my hand to visibly shake.

I completed the check then passed it over for him to review. He did not. Instead, he ripped the check from the book, stuck it in the envelope and handed it back to me.

I took out my own completed envelope and he took them both and laid them on the altar. When the baskets were passed he stood up out of habit. I was surprised he made it this long before standing to serve. I do not think he realized he was working. However, as soon as he did, he sat down quickly.

"I do not think I need your approval or Schlossenbloum for tonight's tithes," he whispered. "But just in case, is that alright with you?"

"Not a problem." *Am I hearing things or did he just ask my permission to write a hundred and fifty thousand dollar check for his tithes?*

I appreciate the way she did not hesitate. Yes, I believe it is safe to say she has my interest at heart. Granted, I am not able to spend one hundred and fifty grand on a car, but she has no qualms with me tithing. She did not flinch while she wrote the check. I promise it was not a test when I asked her to do it. I trust her and I want her to be a part of my life and handle the tasks I hate. However, when I think about it, if this was a test, she passed with excellence. Not to mention she also wrote her own tithe check and has never asked me for anything. Well, technically she has asked me for two things. The Maybach and the Phantom. I could not imagine giving those two up, but for her I would in a heartbeat. I think she knows it. Besides, I tried to leave one of them in her possession and she refuted. The one time, in which, I left her with a car, she only drove it to church and not a place further. When she was done, she left it in the garage and sent it back by Keith.

She wrote the check proving she can write checks with a whole lot of zeros. It is impressive and confirms she is the wife for me. She never mentioned it. She simply handled business and kept it moving. I must admit, I have been afraid of gold diggers. Maybe that is why I never attempted to date. I do not want anyone to see me as a bank book readily available.

Danielle has a great job. If I was not a fighter she would probably make more than me. I have no idea of her finances but from her lifestyle it appears she has done well. I would not say she is flashy. Wait. Yes, she is flashy. However, I think she has it under control. She likes nice things. She works hard and she buys what she likes. I think if she were out of control she could easily have anything she wanted. She does have self-control. She controlled what she ate. She controlled how she behaved. She was in total control. I do not know if she will be willing to let me in her space but I sure as hell planned to try.

Who I am and what I have is not impressive to her. She loves me for me. Up until last night, she never asked to come to my house or visit. When she finally did come, she wasn't impressed. I am blessed I was on duty the Sunday she showed up for worship. I am blessed she was feisty enough to not park in the designated area. I was blessed we did not pave the field a day earlier. Everything has a reason. There is no such thing as coincidence.

***

The collection was gathered and once again, out of habit, he stepped right up and took the baskets. I closed my eyes and put my hand over my mouth to hold in my laughter. King looked at me like what is he doing? I raised my eyebrows. He put his hand over his mouth too and dropped his head. Then I saw Keith speaking into his wrist. Everyone around seemed to notice this except Deacon Washington.

As he took the money back to the accountants, I turned my head sideways patiently waiting for him to return. He must have walked five feet behind the door when someone mentioned he was supposed to be off duty. By the time the door closed all the way, he was coming back.

He plopped down, leaned up on his knees with one elbow resting and looked over his left shoulder. "I am sorry. It is a habit."

I snickered.

"I know," he said laughing at himself and shaking his head. "Charge it to my heart."

I touched the hand that was on his knee and said, "It's all good."

He reached for my other hand. We locked fingers. Hunter glanced in our direction. In fact, he had been watching us all night. At one point he stood in front of us so long I counted the stripes on his shirt. Then he stood on Deacon Washington's side with his hand on his shoulder.

We were no longer out of order and I was ready for Hunter if he had something to get on us about today. After the benediction, we hung around to fellowship. He struggled hard not to be Deacon Washington. Tonight he was trying to be Randall.

As anticipated, finally we were face to face with Hunter. Hunter spoke first, "Psalm 27:14. Wait on the LORD. Be of good courage, and he shall strengthen thine heart. Wait, I say, on the LORD. Look at you too. Looking like the Ebony couple of the year. As if you just stepped out of a photo shoot."

Deacon gave up the laugh I love. I was too busy rolling my eyes at Hunter. "There are people waiting to speak to both of us."

"Wait now, you two can't have my job. Tell your folks to pull up. How are they coming to my altar to speak to you two? Let us pray." Right there he prayed and covered us. Randall held onto my left hand tightly as Hunter came in closer to us. He put his hands on our foreheads. My right hand raised and Deacon raised his left. After a few minutes, he pushes our heads until they touched and then he laid his head on ours.

It was at this moment I knew it was serious. I gained a deeper appreciation of their friendship. He wanted the best for his friend and wanted him to make the right decisions. I felt in my heart this time of prayer was just the beginning and not an occasional event. He covered him like this weekly. In all honesty, there is nothing wrong with prayer and intercession. As long as you have the right person praying with and for you. Actually, this was a good thing. After last night, I know I am going to need some extra help and a whole lot of prayer.

Hunter poured himself and I was grateful. Then it dawned on me the power of having a pastor as a best friend. Sure, it may have been a little uncomfortable at times, but when you needed him, he was the best friend to have other than the Father Himself.

I did not open my eyes but I could feel body heat. I am sure the crew and Hunter's security covered us. Once Hunter finished he laid still on our foreheads and did not move. He was still where we needed him to be. In that special place with the Master. He waited to make sure he was not missing a word from God. He kissed my forehead first. Then he kissed Randall's head. He led me to the pulpit. I sat in his seat and Pastor Hunter sat in Elders chair. He and I received a counseling session right there in the pulpit. He stood and went to the steps and sat Randall down. Hunter counseled him too.

Hunter was brilliant for this. Get to the people where you can. Do not even bother with an appointment. Stop them right where they are. I am sure Randall told him about our passion last night or he could have possibly assumed. I was not embarrassed nor regretful.

"I don't know what to say different to you two. All the same rules, covenants, and commands remain in place regardless of the freedom the law has allowed," he said.

I nodded.

He looked at Deacon who was clearly in another world and asked, "Understood?"

"My loves, go in peace." It was as if he did not want us to leave. It felt like he was sending two teenagers out to the prom unsure of what would happen.

I leaned into Hunter's ear. "Thank you Pastor. We love you. We need it and we receive it."

Happy to hear this he smiled and replied, "In the name of Jesus."

Deacon might have been in another world but he knew he missed something. "What's going on?"

"Let's go," I said shaking my head.

"Be good. Behave. Be safe," Hunter called out.

"I'll hit at our normal time," is what Deacon said but I did not know what that really meant.

He tried hard not to do anything other than leave. I was convinced there would not be many days he would sit in church with me. He enjoyed serving too much. I was fine with him serving weekly. Either way we would still be here together. That would be enough to make me happy.

We drove home. It was not a hard departure for him tonight. I think he was truly tired.

"Good night Dani."

"Good night Deac."

"Get some rest young lady."

"You know what to do once you get home."

Thursday

It was four eighteen AM. I immediately checked my phones and emails. There were no missed calls, emails, texts, or blogs. I did not miss anything because he did not blog. *Something must be wrong*, I thought. *For the last four months, he has blogged every night but last night he did not. I will call him once I am in the car and ask him if everything is okay.*

I laid there soaking it all in. Although the time was finally here, it still felt surreal. I guess I never really thought the day would possibly come and we would have a chance of dating. That day was here. I pinched myself to make sure I was breathing. Then I closed my eyes tight and opened them again. The scenery was the exact same. Nothing moved. Not even me. I didn't know where to start. I could not hold my breath any longer.

I reached over again. It was four twenty eight. This time I called him. He answered immediately.

"Hello," his voice was groggy.

"Are you asleep?"

"Yes, what's wrong?" he replied with concern in his tone.

"Nothing. I am sorry to wake you. Call me later this morning." I made sure I specified this morning and not later today.

"Are you sure you are okay?"

"Yeah, I am wondering now if you are okay."

"Why do you ask?"

"Well, number one you are asleep. Number two you are not running. Number three you did not blog last night. Number four."

He cut me off with that raspy robust laugh.

"Need I go on?"

"I think you have made your point Danielle."

"That would be?"

"I am out of character. Please keep me in check. If I have you and Hunter riding me I should never go wrong."

Riding you? *Well, well, well, the thought has crossed my mind on numerous occasions.* "So what's the deal Randall?" I replied gathering my thoughts.

He laughed again. It was such a harsh robust sound and oh so sexy. I wanted to hear that laugh at this hour for the rest of my life. I am sure my questions sounded abrupt and out of line but I was caught off guard that he was asleep.

"What?" I asked in an attempt to find the reason behind his laughter.

"I think all the excitement has gotten to me. I literally passed out last night after I got home."

"Did you stand King up?"

"Not exactly. I texted him around three when I took my clothes off and rolled back over."

That was all I needed to hear. My spine tingled. I did not need to know he was naked or close to naked.

"Dani."

I said nothing. I was too busy thinking of him naked.

"Dani?"

"Yes," I said ever so calmly.

"Are you on the way to work?"

"I should be but believe it or not I am still lying in bed."

"Huh?"

"I know right. I am getting up now. I wanted to talk to you and make sure everything was okay."

"Thanks Dani. Everything is fine. I really appreciate you checking on me and your concern."

"Go back to bed."

"I am. Call me when you get to work. I think I am going to be here all day soaking this in. I cannot believe this is real. I wish it happened ten years ago but in all actuality, I am glad it happened when it did. Perfect timing."

"Well good."

"Umm. Umm," he stammered. "What I am trying to say is I am glad we met."

I will admit, it takes a lot for me to become speechless, but for some apparent reason this man always managed to do this to me. He made me nervous. There was an awkward silence.

He broke the silence, "Get dressed babe. Be safe. Do not work too hard. Have a wonderful day. I will be around here all day. I will call you later."

He took my morning and changed it to later today. "Get some rest," I said softy and then I hung up the line.

I got dressed and rode all the way to work with my head on the headrest and the music off. All of my thoughts were on him. Surprisingly my workday turned out rather productive.

Before I realized it, Leigh was asking about lunch. I wasn't sure I wanted to leave. I needed to complete what I was doing so I could make it to the hair salon. It was mandatory I go today. So much for leaving early as Leigh was successful in convincing me to get a quick bite.

On the way to the hair salon, I called him although I was reluctant to do so. After all, he told me last he would call me.

"Hey Danielle."

"Hey you."

"I know."

"You know what?"

"I told you I would call you back."

"Well?"

"I am being lazy and sleeping all day. I don't think I have ever done this before."

"Have you eaten?"

"Yeah. Umm."

"Umm what?"

"No."

"Why not?"

"I guess because I cannot get up."

"Can I do anything for you?"

"Sure."

"Name it," I said.

He chuckled and then let out my laugh. "Maybe later."

I smiled to myself but I didn't pester him for an answer. My mind went there too. "So you promise you will eat?"

"I will. I am going to check all of these messages, respond to texts, and lay back down. Do you need me to do anything?"

"No, just relax. I am on my way to the hair salon."

"Let me get up. I owe you. Where do I need to come to pay?"

"Go to sleep. Call me later."

"Thanks," he really did not want to leave the house anyway.

"Goodbye."

It troubled me that he wanted to sleep all day. I didn't understand how he felt. We all cope differently. I think I would have been partying as if it was nineteen ninety-nine. Randall instead slept it off all by himself. He enjoyed the moment. This is probably why he was a boxer. He played well by himself. He threw the punches. No team members to rely on. No one else to blame. He was a one-man operation just like me.

I arrived home after eight PM. I started to work as usual. He texted around nine and then called. He had not eaten and was still chilling in bed. I wonder if he felt this was a good thing or a bad thing. I had so many questions for him. I decided to save the interrogation for another day. After our early goodnight, I worked until I began making errors. In other words, until I was falling asleep. I knew then it was time for me to get in the bed also. Although I didn't want too.

My phone chirped at one seventeen alerting me he blogged. I texted.

PATIENCE: Know that tribulation and the trying of your faith worketh patience; (Romans 5:3/James 1:3) But let patience have her perfect work, that you may be perfect and entire, wanting nothing (James 1:4) and you might receive the promise. (James 1:3) Have patience.

I pray your patience has worked in your favor and you receive the promise.

He responded right back. Why did I think he would not? If I recall correctly he once told me he didn't text much. I think he lied.

Thank you for your patience. I hope our lives are perfect, complete, and blessed.

Instead of texting, back I dialed him. His line was busy. Now I see why, he was calling me. "Yes sir," I answered.

"Go to bed," he ordered without addressing me first.

"Excuse you? I am going now."

"That was together."

"Huh?" I said loud and country.

"Our lives are perfect together."

Oh, wow. I hope he could not hear my smiles.

"Good night. I love you," and he hung up the line. I held the phone until it fell on my chest. My phone chirped again. *What now,* I thought. I could not figure out the notification. Then I saw it. His status changed. It went from married to single. His interest went from boxing to boxing and roses. This was very big. I cannot believe this is happening. I laid still until I drifted off to sleep.

Friday

I had to be at a jobsite today. They were remodeling my high school. My beginning. A lot of my life was engraved in those walls. It was there in art class I made the decision to become an architect instead of an accountant. Granted, I loved numbers more than drawing. However, as an architect I had the ability to be much more creative. Besides, the engineer route would make my father proud.

I took this free assignment more serious than I did projects a hundred times larger. My name was on the line considering the fact I designed these drawings at no charge against the will of the firm. Therefore, I sent the bill along with a personal check to pay it. As far as I was concerned, a donation was a donation. I was determined to donate these plans. I understood the firm's perspective. If we all designed for free, we would go bankrupt. However, give and it shall be given to you. When it was given to me at this very same school, I didn't know what I was receiving. All I knew at the time was a teacher was down my throat insisting I could do better. Reiterating what I drew was not the assignment. Since I did not follow instructions, I was staying after school to complete the original task. Forcing me to draw paid off. Oh how I would love to go back and say, "Look, now I don't have to draw at all, I point and click or speak into an earpiece and it comes to life right before my eyes."

Truth be told, I missed the drawing. I find myself sometimes doing it just because. The old heads in my firm still draw. More than likely, they probably do not know how to operate the software. In fact, it's very possible it is not even loaded onto their computers. I know this is true of one of them for sure because I am the one who logs into his computer every morning. I bet all he does from there is check emails. Maybe type a few letters, but surely no spreadsheets or pivot tables. I think my skills are a plus to the firm. Hmmm, the way I easily switch between free styling and voice command digital drawings deserved my name on the building alone. Although my opinion may be a little biased.

Either way it went, I was hand holding this project as if it were my newborn baby. I want this school to be perfect. I want these kids to have the opportunity to learn all they can. From the second they walk into the building they should be excited and ready to learn. I want to create such an atmosphere of learning to which they have no choice but to crave it. The foundation was laid. I can't help but smile at the thought of how society has separated government and religion, but I have brought it back together. There is always more than one way to skin a cat. God will be the foundation of the building as He is with any foundation I build. If I can get to it. I will cover it. I have prayed, anointed, and left scriptures all over the building. Bibles are sealed in the concrete, the beams, and between the walls. Pages of the bible have been sealed under stairs, in concrete, lockers rooms, and everywhere we have started. We still have months of work to go and you better believe the other areas will be covered as well. I have fingered scriptures in the concrete. "Lord, bless these kids," is my ultimate prayer.

***

After I spent time with the Master, I started my day. I was glad it was Friday. It had been a long week. A good week but a long one. It was almost a sweet relief to be at the jobsite all day.

I got up and got dressed. I put on my True Religion jeans, my firms monogrammed V-neck, and my Tory Burch Lyle Kiltie ankle boots. It was too hot for boots but they were mandatory for the jobsite. So if I had to wear them in eighty or ninety degree weather they might as well be cute. It is very possible I will be asked to take them off since they have a heel. If so, it is cool because I always have my Good Year, my Tims, and my Gore-Tex in the trunk of my car or truck.

I guess I will stop by Krispy Kreme and pick up a few dozen donuts. I had better grab a few cases of water from the garage too. It is too hot for coffee; although I am sure the guys would drink it.

I was dressed. Hardhat check, safety glasses check, safety vest, computers, drawings and water, check.

I pumped my volume and headed to the school after I picked up the donuts and a smoothie for myself. I made sure to bring snacks with me because days like this were long and hard.

Most of the time they hated me on the jobsite. It was my job to ensure what I drew was being built. That is what the owner paid me to do. This time I was not being paid, nevertheless, this building was going to be as I designed. Me showing up was like having the inspector onsite. There was always a list of to do's, do over's, and notices of rejected items.

Oh, I also have a portable office I bring with me. It is just that, a computer, printer, table, and chair. We can do whatever we need to right there on site. No need to meet again, email, fax, or talk later. I can type anything I need a person to have. They can sign it right there then scan it, fax it or whatever your pleasure from the tenth floor of the open building. We do not need to go in the construction trailer. What is that? Trailers are for slackers.

I greeted the crew as I entered the building and brought the donuts in. I dropped the ice in the cooler, put my PPE (personal protective equipment) gear on, grabbed my plans, clipboard, and iPad.

The superintendent got word I was there. I never like to tell them when I am coming. They would be on their best behavior in advance.

"Ms. Rose, good morning."

I was kneeling over my drawings measuring something I thought was not up to par. I threw my hand up. Of course, he walked over immediately.

"Can I help you?"

"What's up with this wall here? What are we doing?"

He explains while we walk the building. We get all the tradesmen together and I go over with each of them some things I see that should be different. I was not leaving until I knew we were all on one accord.

The day was passing by. I spoke to Leigh an infinite amount of times throughout the day. I am sure she was sick of me. The other two ladies and I exchanged multiple text back and forth about Deacon Washington's blog last night. I finally ended the communication.

> I am in an unsafe environment. I will text you later.

It was true. However, I explained further.

> I'm working on your Al Ma Mata. Leave me alone.

I haven't spoken to him. What is the deal? Just as I was thinking it, he called.

"Excuse me guys." I saw some eyes rise at the ringtone. Especially since I said excuse me. Typically, when someone else called I took it right there or ignored it.

"Dani Ro."

"Hey babe."

"Hey there."

"How are you?"

"Good what about you?"

"I am good. I have not heard from you all day."

"Technically you have," I corrected him.

"Watch it young lady," he warned me.

"I was racing to pick up stuff to get to this jobsite."

"How is it going over there," he asked

"Humph."

"Is that good or bad?"

"You tell me."

"I do not know that's why I am asking," he chuckled.

"It's like. Umm it's like dealing with King sometimes."

He gave it up. He laughed so heartily until I had to move the earpiece from my ear. "What is that noise?" he asked.

"I am unwrapping a bar. I am about to starve to death."

"Why haven't you eaten?"

"I have been too busy getting excuses as to why this or that has not, cannot, or will not be done."

"Can I bring you lunch?"

"No, you don't have to do that," I answered being modest but smiling my heart out on the inside.

"Too late. I am bringing it. Besides, I may need to show up to break down the barrier you seem to be facing."

"I need you to help me with King and not these chauvinistic jerk faces."

"King loves you."

"I guess next you will tell me pigs fly?"

"You should see how he treats Tameka."

I was squatting when he said it. I laughed so hard and loud until I lost my balance.

"Ms. Danielle," one of the guys screamed ready to help me if I fell over.

I waved I was okay and kept laughing.

"Oh it is bad. You are laughing but I am serious. I am glad they did not have to encounter each other too often. He loves it when he is assigned to pick up RJ. I think if I said the word he would knock her off."

"Shut up."

"No for real," he said calm but serious.

"Really?"

"Seriously."

"Why does he dislike her so much?" I asked out of curiosity.

"He feels like Tameka has held me back from being who I could really be. I'm going to tell you now; he is going to give you a hard time until I prove you different."

"Nice. My future with King depends on you. Great. That's just great."

"Trust me," he said sincerely.

"Next you will tell me to have patience."

"Have patience. Lunch will be there shortly."

I continued to work. What seemed like ten minutes was in actuality forty-seven minutes. There was noise from below. I could look over the railing to outside since there were no walls or windows. As I begin to walk over to the future window. My phone rang. I immediately knew what was going on. The Champ was on the premises. Other phones in the room began to ring. Bodies moved to the window. I started down the stairs clicking my alarm to my truck. The guys were racing down the steps behind me. Once I hit the dirt, or Georgia clay as we call it, there was an entourage before him checking him out. No one was saying anything. I was the only girl on the premises. So quickly, they figured out why he was there holding a Whole Foods bag and what looked to be a newspaper.

"Alright. All right guys break it up. Let's get to it," I said in my Dani Ro tone.

"Is that?" someone began to ask.

"No," I said calmly to the voice behind me. I was in arm's length of Randall. I licked my tongue out at him. As I approached, he hugged me. I went to the back of my truck, let down the tailgate, and plopped down. As soon as I took off my hard hat, he leaned in and kissed me.

"Where is yours?" I was referring to the bag of lunch he gave me.

"One of the Arden's Garden is mine."

"Which one do you want?"

"Either one."

"You really didn't have to do this," I stated again although glad he did.

"Look at you," he said while giving me the once over look.

"What?"

Shaking his head, "I should have known."

"What?"

"You blinged out your safety vest, pink hard hat, and I told you your boots had heels."

"Shut up," I said and playfully punched him. Right then a camera flashed. I pointed my finger and said, "I will have your money here in thirty minutes. Try me. I will pay you out of my pocket and send you home."

Randall frowned at my tone and comment, "You are rough on the jobsite."

"You have to be to run with these guys or they will run over you. I hope you have cash because I may have to send a few home."

"They will not bother you any longer. Not after I have shown up."

My phone rang. I looked and saw it was the superintendent. I put the phone down.

"Hey you are on the front page of the news section of the Atlanta Journal Constitution."

I looked and read the title. "Humph. Coincidental. I am here today." I sent a text to Leigh.

Call AJC and order 100 copies of this morning's paper. Go buy ten copies now and put one on each guys desk opened to the Local News and Education Sections. Pull it up on line and call me. Thanks.

"You are at lunch. Eat your lunch. I have one hundred copies in my car."

I blushed while I stuffed my face.

"King bought them. He may have one thousand copies by now. I think he bought a few stores out today."

I voice texted Paige.

> Sissie, you slipping. I am in the Local News and Education section of the AJC today.

I thought she was the only person in the world who still read the newspaper in paper form. I was surprised she did not see it and call Mama Rose. Each time they acted as if it was the first time my name appeared in the Atlanta Journal. They were both proud of me. I often wondered if I would have made my daddy proud too. I reached for my phone to see if I missed a text from Paige as my phone rang again. It was the superintendent again. I held it up in the air and clicked ignore. I am sure he was standing over the window.

"So how is your day going?" I asked Randall giving him all of my attention.

"I thought it was going well until I received a call on the way here informing me I needed to go over to Scholossenblum's. This is unexpected. The last time I went, it was good news. I hope I am not pushing my luck."

Giggling I said, "Randall they can't take the divorce back. Stop worrying."

"I have come too far for something to go wrong."

"No, you have come too far not to trust Him."

"You are right. So what are you doing with this building?"

As I began to tell him I stopped mid-sentence, "Did you read the article?"

"Yeah I did. Humanitarian."

"I am far from a humanitarian. All I did was give back to the place that rooted and grounded me. No big deal. You do it daily."

"Yeah and people call me a humanitarian too."

"Don't put me in that category. I am nowhere near your scale." He grabbed me anyway and gave me a nuggie.

"Excuse me Ms. Danielle, Champ."

Didn't they see I was in the middle of something? "What is it?" my tone was harsh.

"Well, I called you twice."

"I saw," I shrieked.

"The guys wanted to know if they could come down and meet the Champ."

"No. I am having lunch with him. Right now he is not the Champ." Randall looked at me with those puppy dog eyes. He smiled, as I yelled, "NO," I cupped my hands over my face and screamed, "Ugh. Y'all make me sick. Blow the horn and bring em' down."

"Hey thanks Ms. Rose. You are the greatest," the superintendent said genuinely.

Yeah, yeah, yeah. Is this what dating him will be like?

Randall interrupted my thoughts, "Do you have photos in your truck?"

"No, I do not," I said regretful. Not regretful that I didn't have photos but regretful I had to share him with everyone right now. I cannot recall a time a guy brought me lunch to the jobsite and when one finally does, I am forced to share his attention.

"I will have Vickie give you some to keep with you."

I still did not have anything signed from him myself. "Where is mine?"

He did not know what I was talking about, "Your what?"

"My signed picture?"

He looked as if I said something bad. "Why would you want a picture when you have the real me? Besides, you have blogs, presents, and cards from me. I would say all of those things are worth more than a glossy 5 x 7. Let me go to my car." He walked away unaware as to why I cared about a photograph.

I handed him my keys, "Here you want to drive?"

"No, I will walk."

Why did I think any differently?

One of the tradesmen jumped in, "I will take you in the golf cart Mr. Hooks."

When they returned, he had a huge stack of portraits. He has to spend thousands upon thousands on these photos. These were not copied at the nearest photo booth. He stood directly in front of me. I would not look up or make eye contact.

He sensed what I was feeling, "D?"

"Un huh?" I muttered sorrowfully.

"Are you okay?"

"Sure," I added as much sarcasm as I could.

"No. You know what I mean."

"Yeah," I knew exactly what he was talking about.

"Are you going to be upset?"

"Nope. Even swap ain't no swindle," I dished out.

He raised both eyebrows, "What is that supposed to mean?"

"If you get to work all the time then I get to work all the time."

"This is different," he tried to correct me.

I stuffed more vegetables in my mouth. "How so? I certainly do not see how. Seems the same to me. You work. I work." I threw my hands up.

"Not the same D," he was about to get annoyed.

"We will see," I said proving a point to him.

The super came over and quickly broke up the little banter, "Ms. Rose works a lot?"

"Does she?" he asked him while looking directly at me.

"So when are you fighting again Champ?"

He took his focus off me and directed his full attention towards the superintendent, "Do you think I should?"

They went into this long dragged-out dialogue and before I knew it he was signing autographs and writing notes to little such and such. I think the guys were happy because I was off their backs and Randall was beyond thrilled to be in his element. I could tell he liked it just as much as they did. He was preparing for the new beginning. It was now only days away. As soon as he publically made the announcement this would be his life.

"I have to go," he said looking at me.

"Okay," my face and tone said it all.

"What do you have planned for this evening?" he asked.

"I don't know yet."

"I will call you as soon as I leave the meeting."

"Okay."

"Be safe babe," he spoke as if he was concerned.

"Good luck," I said trying to eliminate his concern.

"Thanks."

Saturday

I woke up in the four o'clock hour. I had a restless night. I do not know what had me so wound up. Okay, I do know what but I do not know why. I was freaking out. They cannot reverse a divorce. Why was I so uptight? He did not seem too overly concerned at the jobsite about why the attorney wanted to meet with him.

I could not take it any longer. I jumped up, got dressed, and headed to my track. I was there before five AM. I think I startled the group. They didn't expect me that early.

I went upstairs, plugged all my gadgets in and started walking. I sent quite a few messages to Leigh and myself in reference to electronic devices I needed to get to allow me to work while working out. We would need to plan to spend an afternoon over here trying to figure out what exactly I needed and how to get it to work. I may even have to bring my IT person to assist. I should have done that yesterday while Randall was busy. I certainly did not need him here during the technology installation. He would not approve of working while working out.

It was a little after seven when I heard the commotion. It sounded like a troop entered the building. I heard the pitter patter of feet running up my steps. No one is allowed up here and they all know the rule.

"Danielle," his voice was stern as usual.

Uh oh. I'm in trouble. I have only been here two hours.

He stood at the top of the steps. I acted as if I didn't hear or see him. He waited until I came around to the other side. As I approached, he spoke.

"Let's go." It was not a question.

"Good morning to you too sir," I said as cheerful as I could.

"Morning." he gave the same level of sternness as the first time.

"I am going to have to ask you to leave my area if you can't behave better. Do I need to get my security?"

He looked at me with the fiercest snarl and said, "Are you done for the day?"

"Not yet," and I ran off.

He caught up with me and tackled me. I yelled out of instinct. He laid on top of me and kissed me.

I heard Keith yell, "Ms. D, are you okay up there?" I could not respond at that moment. Keith ran up the steps, "Ms. D." Then he spotted me on the floor with Hooks on top of me. He walked over. Randall began shooing him away with his hand. Keith leaned down and said, "You two are nasty. N-A-S-T-Y. Do I need to have a bed put up here?"

"That will be nice," Randall said between kissing more to annoy Keith.

"I have one thank you," I barely got out before he kissed me again.

"Where?" Keith asked in shock. I pointed to the bed. He said, "We have not been allowed to go over there." He looked amazed at everything else in the loft space.

Randall rolled off me. Keith gave him a hand to help him to his feet.

"Remember who signs your check. Running up here checking on her?" he said laughing at Keith's immediate reaction to my scream.

"It's my job," Keith backfired.

"I guess it is your job to CB too?" Randall whispered the word cock block.

"Comes with the territory. Protecting her includes from you too. I will have a chastity belt installed on her tomorrow for back up. I'm watching you," he scowled pointing at Randall.

Keith reached down to help me up. Hooks slapped his hand and pushed him away like a five year old. "I got it," Randall yelled at Keith's attempt to deny him his chivalrous duty.

I then took the time to give Keith a tour. I'm positive it was probably much more than what he was interested in, but he was in charge of me right. Randall sat on the couch watching CNN while the tour went on.

Once we were done, I thought he would have forgotten. He didn't.

"Are you ready?" he asked.

I slowly gathered my things buying me some time while pretending I was not submissive to his orders. The more I took my time the louder the television got. "I get it. I am packing up," I rolled my eyes.

"Do you need me?" Keith asked before leaving. "We are going to get cars washed. Ms. D do you want the Porsche cleaned?" he asked as if he was leaving me with a stranger.

"I'm good," I replied as I stood with all my things now waiting on Randall.

He did not move. You would think he had ten kids how well he did the ignore but answer parent strategy like Mama Rose. "We will drop it off on the way to breakfast," he said referring to the Porsche.

Keith asked, "What are you driving to church tomorrow?"

No one responded. I turned around and Randall was still in the television. Keith looked at me waiting on my response. "My Sunday car I always drive to church. The BMW," I replied.

He then looked at Randall as if my answer was unacceptable. Randall did not move his eyes. "We will take the Phantom," he finally looked at me realizing I was ready.

"I am ready," my tone let him know I was now waiting on him.

"Thank God."

Rolling my eyes, "I was not taking that long."

"You were trying to work. It is Saturday, which means no work. Breakfast time."

It was amazing how his personality went from calm a few days ago back to forceful and demanding. He was Dr. Jekyll and Mr. Hyde going from calm friend status to boyfriend status making decisions. I was not going to get used to it because I still did not know his intentions. Neither was I going to ask. Not now at least. I decided I would give him thirty days to see how the chips fell before I mentioned anything. We drove in two cars. We dropped the Porsche off at the car wash and headed to Mikey's.

"Hey, hey, hey," I sang walking in disturbing all the other patrons.

"The Queen of the dammed and The Champ," Mikey called out with his back turned.

"What's going on Mike?" Randall said initiating a handshake.

"I am trying to figure out how you got hooked up, tied up, and tangled up with trouble over there. You are ruining your good boy reputation."

"Well it is about time I am considered a bad boy," Randall admitted.

"Just give it a few more days."

"I love you too Michael," I grimaced.

"What are you eating?" he asked as he leaned over the bar and kissed my cheek.

"I am not jealous," Hooks said with envy in his voice.

I turned and kissed him on his mouth. Immediately, Mikey leaned over the counter again. "What in the hell is going on?" he demanded throwing his bar mop down.

Randall looked me in my eyes, "My divorce is final," he said.

Mikey high fived both of us. He then looked very serious, "When is the wedding diva?"

"Soon," Randall said before I had the opportunity to answer.

"That is what I am talking about. Be careful. Hooks is Hooked," Mikey said speaking to Hooks but winking at me. "What will you have Baby D?"

"Egg whites with spinach and mushrooms."

"No meat?"

"Not today."

"Are you sure?" Randall asked confirming my breakfast choice.

"Yes."

"Give her some wheat or raisin toast with no butter. I will have a fruit plate and a large tomato juice."

I frowned. He looked up from his newspaper to Mikey who was looking at me. "What's wrong with your face?" Randall asked looking at Mikey.

"Your radar does not pick that up?" Mikey laughed at my response to Hooks and walked away.

We ate, left and went to pick up the freshly washed Panamera. We dropped my car off at my house. I did not go inside. I threw my bag with my clothes in the garage, got my laptop bags, and jumped in the car with him. We headed towards his house. I could have driven my own car but he insisted. It was still early, close to eleven AM on a beautiful Saturday morning. We chilled with him sitting on his end of the couch and I sat on my end.

"Come over here please," his voice and eyes pleaded.

I moved in closer and laid my head in his lap.

"I need to talk to you." I heard hesitation in his tone forcing my heart to flutter.

I rolled over on my back, looking up at him and gave him my full attention, "Yes."

"I wanted to speak to you, ask you, or for you to consider."

He was stammering over his words. I must have looked cross-eyed.

"Well, I am sorry. I am nervous. I have never had to do this before."

I got startled. *Do what? What is he talking about? What is he about to do? OMG what is he about to tell me?* Thoughts ran wild in my head. *I knew I should not have gotten involved with the church boy. Oh Lord here we go!*

"Danielle."

He paused for a long time. I was not sure if I was supposed to speak during his silence or not, "Yes."

"I really do not know how to say this. I am so nervous," he gave a light version of his laugh.

I touched his hand. It was shaking and so was his leg under my head.

"You can think about it. You do not have to answer right now. Will you consider dating me?"

I sat up and looked at him face-to-face and eye-to-eye.

He took his time before he spoke. "I think I am doing this backwards. I think I should have asked before I fell in love but I wanted to and intended on doing this in decency and in order. However, love beat me to the punch. I cannot let that go. I cannot turn back now. I do not want to go another day of my life without you and loving you."

At that moment, I knew he was a man. Human I mean. He was truly nervous. I paused for longer than I intended deep in thought. *I cannot believe he is this nervous or asked me if he could date me. He fights in front of millions of people. His bank account laughs at mine. He makes me look like I have not done anything successful. Women gawk when he is in their presence. He smiles the most beautiful smile I have ever seen and he is nervous to ask little ole me to date him. Come on! This gets stranger and stranger daily.*

"I have never asked anyone before," he confessed.

Only as Randall would, he puts a spin on it making it even more special. I felt the tears welling in my eyes. I knew as soon as I blinked they were going to fall rapidly. I also knew when I spoke my voice would crack. Therefore, I punked out and turned my head.

He held my hand. His was sweaty and shaking. "Danielle, I want to see you exclusively. Not that I am seeing anyone else now but I want you to know how serious this is to me. I want you to be the only person in my life. I hope you feel the same way and I am the only person in your life. I still want to continue in the precepts of God. I want to be with you intimately more than you know, but I think we should do His Will."

He continued, "I want to laugh with you. I want to hear your voice the first thing in the morning and the last thing at night. I want to shower you with roses, gifts, and love. Other than God, I need you in my life. I want you in my life. If only you knew how much of a blessing you have been to me. I never would have done this without you. I never would have ventured out to fight again. I was dying on the inside. My faith was low, my heart was weary, and my burdens were heavy. Today, I am full. I am full of joy, love, and faith. Most of all, my burdens are light. "I made a promise to you that I want to make good on."

He was talking to my back. I wanted to turn around. God knows I did but I could not bring myself to face him.

"I promised you I would tell you what was bothering me. Everything was bothering me. I was at the weakest I have been in my life. I needed to get out of that situation. I came to the realization I loved you and needed you. I knew I could not go on without you and I could not go on the way we were. My strength and faith were both low. No one other than God could help me. I prayed and He gave me a path to get out. I prayed and He gave me an answer. I laid prostrate on the altar for days and nights that you do not know about. King, JJ, Keith, and the other disciples taking shifts watching and waiting. Of course, Trevor has been there through my travail. They are the greatest friends."

That is one of the reasons King is hard and rough on you. He does not want you to hurt me as she did. He saw my pain. He heard my cries. He has been there for me. I know they are glad that part of my life is over. I would not say it was drama but it did not feel good. I never want to go through foolishness like that again. I had to fast and stay on bended knees to get through the turmoil."

He was still nervous, speaking at a whisper, soft, and gentle. "They know it was you who brought me here. Your presence silently pushed me. You changed my life. I think they are all happy about it. Someone has to be the gatekeeper and that happens to be King. I know you dislike him, but I think you both are doing what you should do. He is protecting me and you are standing up to him letting him know you do not intend to hurt me. You are showing him that you are going to be you and I love it. Not that you two are passing words but the fact that you are not backing down. Now, if you had shied away, he would have immediately thought you would not be able to handle the lights, the camera, and the action. He would have advised against this relationship."

"What I do is difficult. It is a fight no matter how you look at it. You have to be prepared. If by chance I am getting my butt whipped, King has to know you can take it and so do I. If you cannot I need to know now. I do not want to be in the situation I was in before. I think King is over the gold digging stance. No one thinks that is your motive. You can handle your own. You have proven this. I think it is safe to say they have taken a liking to you. All of this is new to all of us. I expected a lot of push back. I expected everyone from Trevor, to King, to JJ, to Vickie, and the others to veto our relationship. To forbid, prohibit me, and even be disrespectful to you. It has yet to happen. Unless it has and you have not mentioned it. I have not witnessed any disrespect."

"They have all adapted well which was one of the reasons I knew this was right. I knew you were the one. No one fought it."

"King is not fighting?" I asked amazed.

"No not at all."

"Pastor?"

"Is being Pastor. Like he told me, not on his watch. We will behave. He said, of all people in my congregation I cannot let you fall. If I have to hold you up myself. If I have to give up sleeping in my bed and sleep on the couch to keep an eye on you I will."

"I have no doubt he will not do it too. So far he has been a man of his word and done everything he said he would do." He exhaled deeply, "God knows my heart. It has been difficult to hear His voice during this time. It took days for me to hear His response. Nonetheless, He was the faithful God that He is and fixed my problem. He restored my soul."

"I am in awe at how everything worked in my favor. I did not have to call Schlossenbloum. I did not have to argue with Tamika. I got a call to show up and it was done. I am glad. It troubled me for a long time and now it is as if a weight has been lifted. I am grateful you noticed my struggle. You noticed it immediately although you have known me for a short time. You are in tune with me. You feel me," he chuckled at himself.

I cut my eye at him because I knew where his mind drifted.

He continued to laugh when all along his manhood was erecting at the thought, "Well not yet."

Immediately something touched me that should not have.

Laughing in order to hide his embarrassment, "What?" he said innocently.

"What size shoe do you wear?"

"That is not true."

"Well, tell me what size," I persisted.

"Thirteen," he said chuckling. "Sometimes fourteen depending on how the shoe is made."

"Oh," I said with my own excitement brewing.

He noticed my excitement, "Why do you say it like that?"

"Never mind." *He said it wasn't true. A size thirteen shoe. It should be true. Well maybe not for him.* I thought to myself. *I may need to rethink this through. If it is not true, it is a deal breaker.*

Although I tried to lighten the mood, as did his body parts. He could still see the tears rolling down my cheeks.

"Please do not cry."

I held my head down ashamed to allow him to see me this emotional.

"Why are you crying?"

Now, I was breathing hard. "I don't know," I managed to say. I really didn't know why I was overcome with such emotions.

"Yes you do. Tell me please."

"They are tears of joy. I cannot believe this is happening to me. I do not know how to feel. I don't know if I should feel happy, lucky, roll with it or feel like a husband stealer."

He took my face into his hands and held it extremely close. "You are not a husband stealer. It was over ten years ago. You helped me remove myself from my misery. You wonder why I do not eat or sleep. Misery forced me to stop eating and sleeping years ago. You did nothing. Don't you dare blame yourself for this."

I nodded.

"I mean it. That is BS." Just like that, he reverted to the stern Randall.

He did not curse too often and when he did, it came as a shock to me. I knew this was a serious matter. I opened my eyes.

"I'm serious. I do not want to hear you say that again. Do you really feel that way?"

"I don't know how to feel is what I said."

"You, me, we deserve to be happy. Maybe you already were but I certainly was not. I have not been happy in so long until I did not miss it. I almost forgot what it feels like. Then you showed up out of nowhere. I was not looking for you. You astounded me. You came with a problem. The parking lot guy called me out of all the other Deacons to come rectify a problem. Then your car approached and when you exited the car, my life changed immediately."

He paused. It was as if he reflected. I sat there holding onto his neck like a sick child holding onto daddy for dear life. He hugged me back just as tightly. He sighed. You could tell he had said some things he had been holding back and needed to say for a long time. The fear was now over. He was no longer nervous and was back to himself.

"Let me have you. Let me love you. Let me spoil you. Let me be a part of your life. Let me in your world."

I said nothing. I could not believe it. These were big requests he was asking. I looked up to the ceiling through teary eyes. "Is this being recorded?"

He looked back at the camera I saw. "I will have them disconnected if you think we should. I am not use to anyone being here but me. I will give you a copy of the tape before I delete."

He tried to move. He could not because I was straddled around him. "Lift up for a minute."

"You don't have to do it right now."

"No, I am going to do something else." I got ready to stand up.

"No you don't have to go anywhere. Just lift up."

I did. He reached in between his legs and pulled out two boxes. "Here. Please accept this gift."

"Is it breakable? After the rising of the events it may be broken," I raised an eyebrow.

He laughed embarrassed.

"Well is it?" I asked with my eyes wide at the surprise of now receiving an unexpected gift.

"I don't think it will break that easy. However, I do have the power. If that is what you are asking."

"Hubris and cocky. Take your clothes off and let me be the judge."

He was now lost in laughter, "Can't do it."

"Why not?" I asked as I gave him my meanest look.

"You won't even be my girlfriend but here you go telling me to take my clothes off."

"Chicken."

"I do not want you to get yourself in any trouble. My clothes are not coming off. Woman, do not try me."

"What is this?" I asked as I took the box.

"Open it," he demanded.

I did. It was a bracelet with a diamond hook and rose dangling from one circle together. Gazing at the beautiful charm bracelet, "Wow. This is nice."

"I want to give you this as a token of my love. If you accept this gift, I will wear one like it also. To me it symbolizes us from this day forward. I pray it is the beginning of uniting a hook and a rose. Basically, this bracelet is the check box. If you accept it I will assume we are in an umm, a relationship. A covenant." He opened his box and it was the same bracelet on a much larger scale.

"Like dating?" I asked.

"Exactly like dating."

"Like you will be my boo," I said laughing.

He gave up that robust laugh I loved. "Yeah, I will be your boo. Will you be my boo?"

"Well, I guess we all booed up then," I giggled. "Now, that's what I'm talking about Deacon. Go get you a boo."

He laughed as I handed him the bracelet to put it on my right arm. I took his bracelet and slid it on my arm too. As soon as I moved my arm, it slid right off. Instead, I extended my leg for him to put it on my ankle.

Frowning while putting it on my ankle, "Are you going to take mine too?"

"Maybe," I smirked.

"That is fine. I will order me another one. I will do that only for you."

"You know a lot comes with being booed up. Especially with me. Why do you think I am single?"

His confidence kicked back in, "You were waiting for me."

"You think? It is not easy dating me. You have seen me work. I have high expectations."

Smirking back at me, "Like what Danielle?"

"Attention, honesty, monogamy, friendship, fun, and love. Just to name a few."

"I think I can handle that."

I held my finger up and touched his nose and said, "Don't let me down Deacon."

Staring in my eyes, "God knows I will try my best not to."

"We shall see what happens."

He whispered, "Thank you."

"For what," I asked as he hugged me tight.

"Accepting my proposal."

"Thank you for asking. How do you feel?"

"Right now, I feel like I can conquer the world. Taller than any building you could ever build. Stronger than anything imaginable. Kryptonite could not stop me. I have everything I need and everything I want. I feel like I have the wind in my fists." He looked at his tightly closed fist. "To God be the glory. I owe Him my life. No man can stop me right now." He squeezed me again, "How do you feel?"

"Happy. Happier than I have ever been in my entire life and far more than I ever thought I could be. I feel like a million bucks." I am sure a million bucks was small change to him, but he knew what I meant. "Randall Hooks Washington," I said aloud.

"DeWayne."

"Huh?"

"My middle name is DeWayne."

Being sarcastic I asked, "Oh. It's not Hooks?"

"No, sorry to disappoint you."

"Well damn," I laughed. He knew I was joking. "I can see that hitting the tabloids."

"Headline news."

"Jade."

"I know. Danielle Jade Rose Washington. That is going to be a long name."

"Can you handle it?"

"Can you?"

"I am sure I can."

"DJ. Does anyone call you DJ?"

Shaking my head, "Nope. Never. Just D."

"Not anymore DJ."

I smiled. *Aww, he gave me his own name. No one else will be allowed to call me that. I do not know what I will call him. Should I give him a nickname too? All of this is moving so fast. Well technically, it is not, but because of the situation, it is. It's hard to believe tomorrow will be exactly four months since I met him. Just to think, when I met him I had no clue who he was. Now here it is four months later, he is divorced, preparing to fight again, I am lying in his lap at his house, wearing God knows how much this bracelet cost and we are dating.* So many thoughts ran across my mind. I had to close my eyes to make sure I was alive. I could see another camera from another part of the room. I stared at it as if it was going to flash a light that said I was being punked.

Danielle is dating. I have not done this in four years. I am elated. Right then it hit me. The reality was neither of us had been in a relationship, kissed, nor been intimate in four years. This is weird. *This dating and engagement may only last thirty days. What the hell Dani. You waited this long you might as well push it to the limit.*

There was a long moment of silence. We both took it all in. It was new, different, and exciting. I felt like a sixteen year old with my first boyfriend who just gave me his class ring to wear.

"DJ you want to do anything?" he asked as he stroked my hair wanting to commemorate the moment.

"Nope. I just want to lay here like an old couple."

He lifted my body up and stretched his legs on the couch as I laid there in his arms. Now I could do that legitimately and it felt perfect.

"Come let me show you the house then we can pick out something for church tomorrow."

"You are not serving tomorrow?" I asked surprised.

"Nope, I am on my pre-honeymoon. I am going to enjoy this one more day and sit next to you."

"Deacon?"

"Yes babe?"

"We sit one aisle away from each other," I reminded him.

"Too far. I will see how I feel next week and decide if I will be on duty Wednesday or not. I like sitting next to you."

"Don't get me in trouble with Hunter and the other Deacons."

"Do not worry. I got you. Believe me; they are not going to let me chill for long."

I gave him the side-eye, "Not like you really chill. You still think you are on duty even when you are not."

"I have never been there without being on duty."

"Don't let me be the one to switch it up."

Right when I was about to doze off. I heard what I thought was Elvis Pressley, but when I looked at the television, Elvis wasn't on the screen. Then I heard BB King and Michael Jackson.

"What is that?" I asked.

"King calling. I need to take it." He reached over and answered, "Yeah? Yeah. I did not make it yet. Yeah. I will before the night is over. Yeah." He threw the phone on the floor. "King is coming in the door."

I said, "Okay," but I thought *oh goodness*. Then I got it. King's ringtone was BB King.

When he walked in, I did not move. We were lying in each other's arms on the sofa all comfortable and cozy.

King did a double take, "Ms. D."

"Yes."

"Are you good?" he asked.

"Yep."

"Do you need anything?"

"I think I am fine."

"Do I need to get Keith to get that chastity sooner than Monday?"

"You are too late." He was shocked. I successfully left him speechless.

Randall gave up the laugh I loved. My face stayed the same, never looking in King's direction.

"Do I need to run the tape back?" King grumbled.

"Do what you do. Don't get shocked. You may learn something," I replied cool, calm, and collected.

He glanced at my ankle. "I see you got a new piece there hanging from your leg. What's up with that?"

"It's a token from someone special."

Randall fell out laughing. He laughed more than any man I knew. I could not tell if we were comical to him or if he was embarrassed.

"Oh yeah?" King's tone revealed his hesitation of us dating.

"Yeah."

"Why do you have it on your ankle? Was it too big? It should not have been." This let me know King was with him when he purchased it. Therefore, he had already seen it.

"That's mine. Hers is on her wrist," Randall interjected before King was worked up and held my wrist up so King could see the other bracelet.

"Oh that explains it. Just like a woman. She will take hers and all of yours too."

"Watch it! We were doing well," I warned.

Randall leaned down, kissed me and got up without moving me. My phone was on the table ringing.

He picked it up and passed it to me, "Paige is calling."

"Thanks babe," I answered.

"Babe, excuse me. I will be outside for a few minutes. Do you need anything?"

"No," I answered smiling from ear to ear.

He winked.

"Hey girls. What's going on? I am sending you all a picture right now."

As the pictures came in, "What is that monstrosity," Sade yelled.

"Charm bracelet," I replied.

"Oh we can see that," she barked back.

"You have two?" Leigh asked.

"One is mine and I have his on my ankle for the moment."

"Dang," Sissie said. "What does that mean?"

"It means we are officially dating," I said proudly and smiling.

"Danielle's got a man at home," Sade sang.

I laughed so hard. "You all make me so sick."

"So did you do it yet?" Sade just had to ask.

"Sade," Leigh and Paige both screamed.

"Sade we are not doing it," I replied

"How lame," she responded.

"Whatever!"

"We should celebrate now that you officially have the hook and rose attached to your ankle," Sissie said.

"We can but it is not necessary."

"Oh yes it is," Leigh interjected. "You work us like slaves and then you get the man of all our dreams. Oh heck yeah, you better believe we are celebrating. So you might as well start brainstorming about what you'd like to do."

"Okay, let me think about it. I will call you all on my way home." He came back inside shortly after I got off the phone with the girls. I was still chilling in the same spot.

He came over closer to me. "Sorry to keep you waiting," he said as he bent down and kissed my lips.

This man amazed me. It was hard to believe that someone so powerful, strong, and brutal was also genuinely nice, gentle, romantic, and Godly.

He lift me up. "Come on we have to pick out clothes for tomorrow."

"Oh yeah."

"Let me show you the house," he said excited like a little kid.

As we walked through, he showed and explained every detail, every award, every plaque, and every picture to me. He walked directly behind me holding me at my waist the entire tour. There were no other pictures of anyone other than himself, RJ, Hunter, his crew and his parents. No signs that a woman was there or had ever been there. I think he told the truth about her never living here. The house was beautiful. It was not overdone or overstated at all. It looked as if a decorator may have followed his instructions. Sometimes less is more and it left room for the imagination. There was nothing gaudy, outrageous, or questionable, until we got to the master bedroom.

Randall never came across as a flashy kind of guy. Not even from the first encounter. Sure, he likes cars and now I see he is just as impressed with electronics as I am although he would never admit it. His bedroom is reflective of what it is called. A master bedroom, fit for a king. *I can imagine him and me in this room in a different capacity than we were right now.* His closet was ridiculous. I stepped into Neiman's, Ralph Lauren, Brooks Brothers, Mark Shale, Foot Locker, Bally's, Sean Jean, Jos A Banks, and Gucci all at once.

The jeans and white tees were unlimited. Then there was his hat display. There had to be every baseball cap in every color imaginable. I swear I have never seen anything like it in my life. There was a lot of jewelry around; however, I do not recall him wearing much jewelry. No doubt, he had a good jeweler on staff. Monitors displaying his security cameras were everywhere. I stood in awe.

"You need a bench or chair in here so I can have somewhere to sit," I said looking around realizing he was not there. I stepped out the door and he was standing there awaiting a response from me. "You should be ashamed. If I recall correctly, you made mention of my closet."

"I know that is why I am out here," he said shyly while giving me puppy dog eyes.

"Get your tail in here and find a suit among these five hundred. We only go to church once a week."

"Actually, I am there more than that."

"I'm sure you are sir, but you are not suited and booted in a five piece ensemble. Don't you ever disagree with me about color coordination again."

"Most of them are black. We wear a ton of black."

"Liar."

"We do wear black."

"Liar that most of them are black."

"You may want to do something where I need a wear suit," he said as if trying to make up some type of justifiable excuse.

"Hush," I did not let him finish the lie.

"What color do you feel like?" he asked sliding hangars from side to side.

"You are picking this time. How do you normally decide?" I asked while looking at all the suits lined up.

"Normally, you tell me what color you are wearing and I match it. Easy."

"Okay, pick something." I sat on the floor Indian style. Then I laid on my stomach. In the course of ten minutes, he had five options.

"Which one?" I asked him. We settled for the taupe with a matching shirt and golden color tie. "Nice."

"What are you wearing?"

"Heck if I know. I will pull something out." I had a particular suit in mind; however, I was not very sure it would be the right color.

"Why are you on the floor? Do you want me to get you a chair?"

"No silly. I am good." He sat on the floor next to me. Just as I began to doze off for the second time, his phone rang again.

"Hey. No, I have not made it to the barbershop yet. I will." It was after six o'clock. "Let me take you home," he said.

"Now?"

"Yeah, are you hungry?"

"Not quite."

"I'm not trying to rush you. But being in my bedroom with you all alone is making me real nervous and uncomfortable."

"Uncomfortable?" *What did he mean?*

"For lack of a better word."

"You can handle it," I said in an attempt to encourage us both.

"I am glad you trust me and have faith in me. For I am weak and then I am strong. You are making me weak. The spirit is willing but the flesh is weak."

I rolled over and said, "I love you too."

"Danielle, you make me weak. Please. "

"Please what?"

"Let me take you home," he begged.

I texted the girls as I started to gather my things. We had time to celebrate after all. It was still early and the sun had yet to go down. Deac and I spent the majority of the day together. I think that was too much time for us alone. I didn't want to leave; however, I didn't want to pressure him. As far as I was concerned, I was under control. He said he felt weak though, so I agreed for him to take me home. Besides, I wanted to scream my excitement in private.

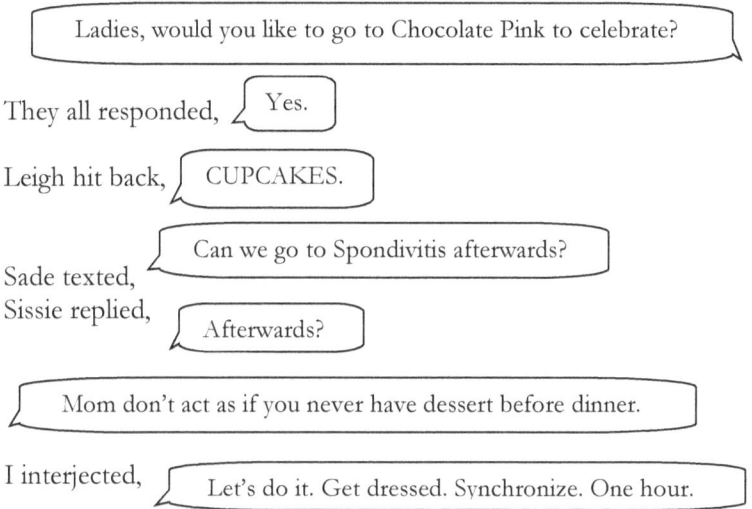

Ladies, would you like to go to Chocolate Pink to celebrate?

They all responded, Yes.

Leigh hit back, CUPCAKES.

Sade texted, Can we go to Spondivitis afterwards?

Sissie replied, Afterwards?

Mom don't act as if you never have dessert before dinner.

I interjected, Let's do it. Get dressed. Synchronize. One hour.

It was a day for me to remember. He dropped me off. He pulled up and then sat there in thought for a minute. I was not sure if he felt the same way I was feeling so I asked, "What's wrong?"

"I do not know," he admitted.

"Are you sure?" I wanted to confirm.

"I am sure."

"Remember before we were supposed to always be honest. This policy is really in effect now," I mentioned.

He responded, "That goes for you too. I want you to talk to me about any and everything. If you feel as if I have done something wrong please let me know. If something bothers you let's talk about it immediately."

"Let's talk about what is bothering you now?" I pressured.

"DJ, I am overwhelmed, over joyed, ecstatic, and downright happy. To be honest, I am having a hard time containing myself," he confessed.

He does feel the same way. My shoulders relaxed. I laid my head back on his seat and picked up his hand. "ME TOO," I screamed. "Now I hate to rush you off, but you made me come home and now I have a date planned with the girls. I need to let go of some of this excitement."

He rumbled.

I laughed too, "You know what?"

"What?" he said thru this laughter.

"Your laugh alone makes me happy. I hope I can always make you laugh."

He leaned over and kissed me. It was a very sweet and gentle kiss at first. The next couple of seconds I thought he was going to jump in the seat with me. He practically touched my esophagus. I felt his passion. I understood why he asked to bring me home. We could be dangerous together. Addictive.

He was able to stop himself; however, he did not open his eyes. He leaned his head down, "Have fun sweetheart. Keep your locator on. Do I need to send Keith?"

To my surprise and to his I gave in and said, "Yes." This was a no win battle I was bound to face anyway so I figured I might as well start now.

He opened my door, walked me inside, and never once looked up. "Have fun. I will see you in the morning my love."

I reached up and held his face. He did not make contact. "Everything is going to be just fine. Have faith Randall."

"That's why I love you."

"I love you too." He ran down the steps and pulled off. Ten minutes later, he called.

"Hey babe."

"Keith will be calling you."

"Thank you."

"Did I tell you to have fun?"

"No." We both knew he did.

"I think I did but have fun."

"I will call you in a little while."

"Great. Be safe."

"Bye," I said miserably.

Keith called next, "What's the deal Ms. D?"

"The girls and I are going to dinner. We need an escort."

"I am on the way."

"Sorry for the short notice," I got in before he hung up.

"It's cool. This is better than what I had planned for tonight anyway."

"Thanks."

Everyone arrived ready to go, even Keith. I looked outside and decided we were not riding in that Limo tonight. I threw Keith the keys to the Cayenne and we did exactly what we said. We got dessert first. I think Keith had the most to include a variety to go.

We behaved all night. We were home early. It was in the ten o'clock hour.

As we pulled up to my gate, Keith said, "So he is your boyfriend now?"

I smiled.

"Nice choice," he agreed.

"I think so too."

"I was speaking of you. Hooks has done well. You were worth his wait. I am in agreement."

"Well thanks Keith. That means a lot. Now, if I can get King to agree."

"What you see is what you get with King. If he did not agree you would not have made it this far. King and Tre are very powerful in his life. Get used to it. Everything is cool though; looks like you are ranking high on the scales with both of them. Good job Ms. Danielle."

I appreciated Keith's conversation.

"Good night ladies. Who all is riding in the morning? Do we need one or two cars?"

"Just me," I said absorbing Keith's conversation.

"Hooks will tell you what time we will be picking you up."

"We?" I said sounding a little confused. *Who was we?*

"He and I. Make sure you call him."

That was strange, "I will. Good night."

"Ladies are you leaving too?"

"We are," Paige answered on behalf of the group.

"I will follow you out," Keith advised.

I stood on my porch watching them leave. Today was a good day. I pulled my phone out but before I could get back in the door, he was calling. "Hey."

"Are you home?"

"You know I am home," I giggled like a schoolgirl.

"I do not sit around and watch your monitor."

Full of sarcasm, "Really?"

"I have a life."

"I have seen your life and it encompasses a recliner and a wall full of monitors. That's lame."

She had room to talk, "Oh well that might be true of my old life but I do not live like that anymore."

"Seriously?"

"Yes, seriously. I do not have time. I am dating and preparing for a fight, if it is any of your business," he scolded.

"Yeah, it is my business and don't get your girl's butt kicked."

"She can handle her own, and whatever she cannot, I can."

"Trash talker."

"Where is everybody?"

"Gone home."

"Can I come over?" he asked in a mischievous tone.

His flirting pleasantly surprised me. My initial thought was *hell yeah*, instead I responded, "Humph. Are you spending the night?"

"You are trying me. Where is the baby?" he said referring to Sade.

"She is supposed to be going home but that could change at any minute."

"Are you letting her go out at this time of the night?"

"She is grown."

"Humph."

Curiously, I questioned, "What are you doing?"

He admitted, "Thinking about you."

"Watching the monitor," I accused.

"I was not."

"Whatever," We talked for a little while longer.

"Good night sweets."

"Good night Randall."

"Good night DJ. I will see you in the morning. Do I need to bring you anything?"

"No babe I don't need anything other than your beautiful smile."

He laughed.

"I love you Randall."

He was quiet. Almost too quiet. I instantly became afraid I might have said something wrong.

"DJ, DJ, DJ. I wish you knew how much I love you back."

I laid on the bed with all my clothes on until two eighteen AM when I assumed my phone was alerting me he was blogging. That was not the case. He changed his Facebook status. Earlier it was changed to 'single' and now he changed it to 'in a relationship'. "That is with me," I said aloud to myself.

I texted.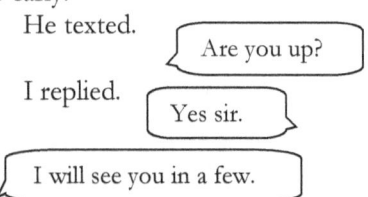

Close your eyes and get some rest sir.

Sunday

Is it morning already? I slept the night away. He was picking me up earlier than my normal time and I was going to make sure I was ready. Even if it was too early.

He texted.

Are you up?

I replied.

Yes sir.

I will see you in a few.

I managed to get ready on time and before I realized it, Randall was at my gate. He was standing on my steps when I opened the door. *Oh my goodness, this man is so, so, so sexy.* He was wearing his pants, his shoes, cross necklace and white tee. As we rode to church, he read his paper and I responded to emails. I noticed when he was at my door he had a fresh cut and shave. I asked without looking up, "When did you go to the barber shop?"

He did not answer. I knew why. It is because I made mention once before of how he always had a barber on duty. I think someone in the crew must be the barber. "I was speaking to you," I said knowing he heard me the first time.

"Yeah, I know."

"Well?"

"A few minutes ago."

"You failed to show me the barbershop." He knew exactly what I was referencing. I was referencing the barbershop obviously in his house.

"Next time," he winked.

We pulled into the parking lot. He quickly put his shirt on and tucked it in his pants. He tied his tie then looked over to me for approval. When he got out of the car, he put on his jacket and walked over to my side where Keith opened the door. I looked up and realized Hunter was standing there. Hunter was never here this early. This was a production. This was just the beginning. There would be a lot of red carpets and photos. His life could easily be a production daily.

He extended his hand. I sat still. He leaned his body inside the car and said, "Are you okay?"

"Yeah."

"Are you sure?" he asked for confirmation.

There wasn't anything wrong; I was trying to soak all of this in. *How did all of this happen?* Hunter said something to get his attention. He turned around and started talking to him, which distracted him from me and gave me a brief moment to think.

He leaned back inside and asked, "Is there anything wrong?"

I took a deep breath. *Okay Danielle get out of the car.* Immediately, I slid my legs out. He and Keith reached for my hand at the same time. I handed Keith my handbag.

"Hooks and the Royal Court," Pastor Hunter had to say.

Then I noticed he was standing outside in his white tee also. He was either waiting, being nosey or both, "Good Morning, Pastor."

"Danielle," he said nodding with approval and leaning in for a hug.

"Why are you standing out here almost naked Tre?"

"Waiting for you."

"I am off duty today. What do you need?" Deacon Washington asked knowing Hunter needed nothing.

"Nothing. Can I greet my best friend?"

"A messy Pastor. Where they do that at?" I mumbled.

"Nosey. There is a difference," he corrected me.

"Get your clothes on," Deacon Washington ordered. He looked around as if trying to figure out whom he could send with Hunter. He must have realized it was just him, King, Keith, and me. There was no one else to send.

He reached for his phone. I snapped my neck at the phone in his hand. He got the message. "Who is with you today?"

Hunter turned around, "Everybody is on point."

"Except me? You all will be just fine. Go do something. I will see you in fifteen minutes," he barked. I was elated Hunter was the one being chastised for a change.

He could not do it. He could not walk from the car directly into the sanctuary. He stopped and talked to the people, the deacons and others who were serving. However, he never let my hand go.

I think King finally felt like enough was enough. King was smooth. He never said a word. He was the type that did not have to speak but you understood the message loud and clear. He started moving towards the door. Deacon Washington kept nodding in King's direction. Finally, King had indeed had enough. He opened the door, which Randall knew meant move now.

We got to the door and he whispered in my ear, "We are on. I love you Danielle." We walked in hand and hand. Fingers locked. We went to my row and took a seat while King and Keith sat in Deacon's normal seats.

Praise and worship went on. It was off the chain as always. We had done what we were supposed to do. We ushered in the Spirit of the Lord, which makes preaching easy.

Hunter came and delivered his message. He was on point removing his jacket in the first fifteen minutes. Deacon Washington did not allow Elder the opportunity to assist him. He stepped right up, took his jacket for him, and placed it on the back of his chair. Hunter's armpits were sweating. You could visibly see how wet his shirt was in the front and back. He always gave the people of God what they needed. We needed a word from God of hope, encouragement, and instruction. His energy level was at an all-time high. It was transferrable. I could feel my energy rise and Randall was just as hyped as he was. I understood more and more why he kept Pastor Hunter close to him at all times. They fed off each other. You could tell they were each other's hype man.

It was clear as to why they were friends. I wondered if Randall and Hunter both saw what I saw in Deacon Washington. Better yet, in Pastor Hunter too. I saw Bishop Hunter and Pastor Washington when I looked at these two. I am not sure what either of them was waiting on. I guess Randall had to get his personal life together. However, God did say come as you are. Funny thing about it is we never do. We want to come to Him perfect. Is there really such a thing?

The energy in the sanctuary was so high. It was mad crazy. I am surprised the county was not called to see what the commotion was. I am sure the roof was vibrating off the rafters. This building cannot handle us. Hunter was sweating so badly and Deacon was busy trying to motion for someone to pass him some water. No one paid Randall any attention. He was getting a little irritated. You could tell by how he fidgeted. Finally, he must have had all he could take and could not take it any longer. He took my hand and squeezed it. Then he stepped to the side of the pulpit and grabbed Pastor's water and handkerchief. Then quickly came back to his seat.

By the time Hunter ran down to our side of the altar Deacon Washington held his finger up as if it was not an option. Hunter grabbed the handkerchief from his hand and continued running. He wiped his face quickly and continued back and forth preaching. He walked down the aisle. He came back up. "Sit down. Sit down," he said out of breath. "That was the introduction. Y'all are making me nervous. Stay with me. I am going somewhere. Give me five Baptist minutes." Everyone sat except for Deacon Washington, the Ambassador, security, and the crew. He stood next to Deacon and exhaled. Randall handed him the glass. He gulped it and got his second wind. He ran up the steps long enough to run back down and he kept going as if his life depended on it.

The place was rocking. I was sweating and so was Deacon. I do not think I had ever seen him sweat. Not even at the track or while he was working out. Well maybe yesterday when he asked to date me. I looked over and handed him my handkerchief. Judging by the look on his face, you would have thought I gave him a kidney. At the exact same time King was handing him his too. He held mine up not caring lace was dangling down. When he held it up, I saw his bracelet shining from underneath his sleeve.

I must admit, it was a banger. He may not have been flashy per se, but he sure had darn good taste. Finally after jumping up and sitting down, jumping up and sitting down again, I decided to stay down. Hunter was not about to make me have a heart attack. My blood was pumping, my heart was racing, and I was sweating like a run away slave. I could feel sweat running down my back. I sat in my chair, placed my elbow on my knees, and watched Pastor Hunter run from side to side. All I could do was shake my head. HE WAS PREACHING today!

I cut my eye at Deacon when the offering began. I watched as he went and got the envelopes from the pulpit. Then he passed them to the other Deacons.

"It's just one day. They can handle it," I whispered to him.

He put one arm around my waist, pulled me closer, and held my opposite hand while Pastor Hunter gave the benediction. I was exhausted and could tell Pastor was too. He almost did not have the strength and energy to close us out.

"I'm tired y'all. Bye. I am just kidding." Everyone laughed. He gave a proper benediction after preaching what I would say was his best sermon ever. There was not a soul in the building whose heart was not touched.

Everyone should have been revived and ready to conquer the world outside those walls. I knew I needed it and so did Deacon Washington.

You could tell service drained him. He turned and looked at the crew. "Let everyone move out before we move," he ordered. I sat still while he stood to let the crowd clear.

Pastor Hunter came over to us first before he greeted anyone, "Meet me in my chambers before you leave," he stated. It was not a question.

I looked up at Randall. I must have appeared nervous. "I do not think we are in trouble," he said to relax me.

"Thank God." I mumbled but loud enough for him to laugh.

Keith came over. "Let's go," I said to Keith.

Deacon Washington knew something was up, "Where are you all going?"

"Ladies room," I answered like a teenager about to get into trouble.

"Okay, I will meet you in Tre's office," he had to add.

They were both there when Keith opened the door. You could tell he was dropping me off and escaping. No one ever wanted to be in Hunter's office. Keith got ready to pull the door behind me.

"Come in Keith," Pastor Hunter said before he could get away. "Beloveds. I saw something this morning I want to talk to you about."

"What's up?" Deacon Washington asked.

"I think you two would be a great addition to the Singles Ministry. We need you all to jump in right now while the relationship is fresh and new. Show the youngsters how it is done."

"That's it?" Deacon asked surprised. Here he was mentally ready to fight with his best pastor friend.

"Shall I sign you up? It will be great. I think you all could teach and be a good example for the singles."

Randall answered for the both of us, "We will think about it and discuss this week."

"What is there to discuss? You both are single?" Hunter added.

"We do not plan to be for long," Randall replied.

My head snapped. Keith saw it. He was too observant at times. *Why do they invite me to these closed-door sessions? I never get a word in.*

Deacon got Hunter's attention also, "Really?" Hunter said disapproving.

"Really." Deacon Washington stood up and extended his hand. 'I will holler at you later dawg. Get some rest. You need it. Good job out there Champ." They pounded and hugged. "Seriously, good job man. I almost gave you a love offering."

"By the way, thanks," Hunter said referring to the handsome offering Randall gave on Wednesday night.

"Keep doing what you do," he said as he gave his friend a pat on the shoulder.

"You too. Let us pray before you leave."

Once prayer ended and as everyone began to leave the office, Pastor Hunter called out, "Ms. Danielle."

"Yes Pastor Hunter?"

"I see what you two are working with," he smiled while nodding his head in the direction of my bracelet. He extended his arm towards me gesturing to take a closer look. I instantly became embarrassed.

He looked at Hooks. "They turned out nice Bro. He was so concerned they were not going to look like he anticipated. He thought his would be girly."

Deacon Washington shook his head at Hunter telling on him. "Any other secrets you want to tell before we leave or do you plan to tell them some other time?" Randall asked his friend.

Hunter shook his head no.

"Good. I will deal with you later," Deac threatened.

We made it to the car with just a few interruptions. He only stopped once and began to help someone before King interrupted him and pointed to me.

"Do you mind?" he asked King perturbed.

"YES," King answered back.

Deacon Washington looked around, "Can you handle it Deac?" he asked one of the other Deacons.

"We can. Enjoy your day off. Whatever we cannot figure out we will leave here until Wednesday. Are you back on Wednesday or are you still relaxing?"

He looked at me. I gave a gentle nod.

"I'm back on," he said like an excited little kid.

When we got in the car, Keith turned around in his seat and casually asked, "What was Hunter on today?"

"I don't know but I need some immediately," I interjected.

"He was crunk up on Jesus baby." Randall said while texting still feeling Hunter's energy.

His phone alerted a few times in a row. Surprisingly I realized I did not have my phone. I was too busy thinking about Hunter's message and his request of Randall and me to head up the Single's Ministry. I was stuck on Randall's response of how we would not be single long. *This is moving faster than a speeding bullet. I am not sure if I like it or know if I'll be able to keep up.*

Keith handed me my phones over the seat. Randall reached for them and hesitantly passed them to me one at a time. His eyebrows were raised for some reason.

"Don't look at me in that tone. You jumped in this car and your phone has distracted you. I do not want to hear it. Not one word from you sir."

King looked in the review mirror and smirked.

I had seventy-nine texts. "What in the world?" I looked and noticed a few were from Randall. My neck snapped in his direction.

I picked one from Leigh and read it first.

Then I scanned the next one. What do I need to bring?

From Sissie. I will be there. YEAH BABY.

I went to the next text from Sade.

I looked at him and rolled my eyes hard. Then I went to the first one from him.

Dinner today at five at Danielle's.

"What do you think you are doing?" I probed.

"Huh?" he said dumbfounded.

"You heard me you jerk." I squeezed my eyes at him.

The car stopped. King and Keith both looked back.

"It's cool man," he laughed heartily. "We good. What babe?" He pulled me over to him. "I have everything covered. All you have to do is open the door."

"I hate you," I pouted.

"Hate is such a strong word Danielle."

I leaned up to Keith. "Can you tell him I quit him?"

"She just quit you." Keith gave my response, reached in his pocket and gave King a hundred dollar bill. I didn't know what that was about.

"Ain't ever happening. And you surely can't quit me thru Keith," he laughed snatching the bill from King and throwing it back at Keith.

Then it dawned on me, "Y'all bet on me? Jerks!"

I took my phone and sent a text to everyone.

I QUIT YOU HOOKS!

Paige responded back. That was quick.

Leigh hit. Long term for Dani.

Sade texted. Dang Auntie, he didn't make it twenty-four hours. Uncle Hooks, I still expect dinner at five.

We pulled up to my house. Keith and King both jumped out and opened our doors. I did not move until he came around to my side. I noticed that was important to him. He would not allow anyone to help me out of the car when he was present.

"Thanks guys," I said nicely to them.

"See you Ms. D," King said.

"I will talk to you later," Keith replied.

"She will not need a ride today."

Rolling my eyes and walling away from him, "How are you going to be jealous of the help you provided?"

"I am not jealous," he tried to convince me.

"I can't tell."

As soon as we entered the door, I immediately took my shoes off.

"I will bring everything. Is Italian good?"

"That will be fine," I smarted.

"Sweetie, do one thing for me."

"What?"

"Be naked when I get back."

I raised my eyebrows and thought to myself, *why leave? I can do that right now. Right here in the foyer on the floor.*

"Just kidding. Think about Tre's question though. I am sure I will have to respond to him no later than tomorrow morning."

"I think it is a trap. Hunter is clever. I love it."

"Why do you say?"

"You can't see through that?"

"No. What is up? What are you thinking?"

"Ray Charles could see through this."

"I missed it."

"Come on. You are a smart guy. If we sign up for the Single's Ministry, especially as leaders, then we are committed to following order. He knows you and I will both do the correct thing. It takes the pressure off him. He does not have to chastise us any longer. He has trapped us where we are now accountable for our own actions and not him. He took the stress off himself and threw it back on us. He is clever. That is how he can preach messages like those that he did today. This is the reason he has a double-digit thousand-member congregation. I love it."

"How did you get all of that from a ten minute conversation?"

"I deal with men all day. Now you think about it."

His jacket was unbuttoned. His head was skinned. He pulled me closer. My back arched. He leaned down over me. I knew he wanted to kiss me but he was trying not to. His eyes locked with mine. Our lips were inches away. His mouth slightly opened. He moved his head. Now his breath was my breath. He tried to fight it but he could not take it anymore. He kissed me. He stopped and then could not resist again. He pushed me up against the wall and laid in on me. I gave it back to him. He took his arms off me. I could feel them moving but I did not open my eyes. He put them behind his back. He was fighting the temptation to touch me. He slapped the wall with both hands making me jump. His face was next to my face. His eyes closed. His hands above my head on the wall. There is no denying it; I wanted him as bad as he wanted me.

Furious with himself he said, "I just left church and I still cannot control my flesh."

"Keep your eyes focused and set on him. We can do this. We did it long before we met."

"Alright." he furiously walked out the door. Then he came right back. "Sorry. I am not sure I can handle another kiss or hug. I do not think I can be around you alone." He hugged me, kissed my cheek, and walked out the door closing it behind him.

I locked the door and took my suit off. He walked right past the car.

King jumped out with him. Keith took the driver's seat, followed behind them close and slow. They walked by a few houses before he said a word. King was used to this. He knew him like he knew the back of his own hand.

"Get Tre on the phone," he ordered.

"Pastor Hunter," he answered.

"Man, I can't do this!"

"Whoa. What's wrong RW? Where are you and what happened?"

"I am walking in Danielle's neighborhood. I just dropped her off. Man when I get close to her I feel like a vampire. I have to have her. I need her to survive. When I touch her, I get weak but other parts of my body get strong. I cannot control it. Last week I could because I had legal constraints. This week she breathes and it makes my you know what do you know what? I cannot do this man. It is killing me inside out."

Tre said very calmly, "Yes you can. You have done it for four years. You can make it another year."

He snickered, "She just said the exact same thing. I cannot do it. I am telling you I cannot. I did not have anyone around me for four years. Why is this happening? Bro I can't be left alone with that woman."

"Get your head together man. It is lust right now and it is coming at you strong because in the natural you know you cannot handle it. Tell Satan to get behind thee. You have fought bigger battles than this. I mean that literally. Keep in mind what your mission is and remember how far you have come. You have a kingdom goal. Don't fall short now bro. You can do this. This feeling too shall pass. You can do it," he encouraged. "How is she handling it?"

"I think she feels the same way. We kind of flip flop. She has a moment and then I have a moment. So far, we have been able to check each other when needed. But what happens when we both are weak at the same time?"

"I have prayed for you that your faith does not fail. That you are strengthened my brother."

"Tre it is going to take a little more than prayer."

"What do you think it is going to take?"

"I don't know," Randall said sounding discouraged.

"What problem have you ever had that prayer didn't fix?"

"Come on Tre." He knew his friend was right although he did not want to hear it right now.

"Answer the question. Last week you knew how to pray when you needed strength and He came through for you. Now a week later you have forgotten." Shaking his head, "Nah, I don't think so. Maybe He did not make all of this happen sooner because He knew you could not handle it. You have to get control of the inner man. What you two are feeling right now is not what is important. Get to know each other. Have fun. Enjoy. You wanted a woman of God and He provided. Now here you are trying to take the God out of her. You cannot do that man. It will all be in vain. Keep the faith son. Do not allow yourself to fall short. He loves you and I love you too. In fact, He and I will love you even if you fall short. The blood will cover you but I cannot let you go out like that son. I am going to be watching you man. Therefore, you might as well go ahead and get mad with me now. I am not going to let you go out. You hear me?"

He did not speak.

"Get it together Randall."

Trevor did not call him Randall too often. Not until they were in front of people that only knew him by that name. He knew it was serious when Trevor said it.

"Man this is too hard," he moaned.

"Hooks, I can see. She is nice and nice looking. She is a cute little honey. But be right and do right."

"Why did you ask us to be leaders in the Single's Ministry?"

"For this reason right here."

"She said that."

"Did she now?" he asked with raised eyebrows and a slight smile on his face. "I want you all to hold yourselves accountable to the kingdom and too each other."

"I am going to have to ask her marry me," Randall said with determination.

"Take this time to really get to know each other by spending quality time together. If God is speaking to your heart and telling you to marry her, you know I got your back. Wouldn't it feel great to marry her and anticipate that special night? Don't take that away."

"Easier said than done."

"I know it has been a long time but."

"Go to hell Tre!"

"What did I say? Man you better keep doing what you been doing thus far."

"I HATE YOU MAN!"

"Let me call First Lady, go change my clothes, then I will be over to help you get your mind right."

"Thanks bro."

"No problem. You will be fine."

***

I took a cold shower but it did not help. I laid across the bed. After two hours of lying there I texted him.

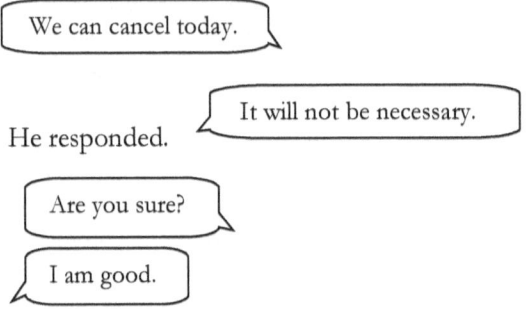

We can cancel today.

He responded.

It will not be necessary.

Are you sure?

I am good.

"Now look," he hands Trevor the phone. "She does not think I can sit still to have dinner."

"Well, you did seduce her in her foyer and punch holes in her wall. What are your plans over eggplant parmesan?"

He gave his friend a look as if to say shut up. "Why are you my friend?" he bid Trevor.

"Hooks, I think she did the right thing. She is being sensitive to your needs. She does not want you to be uncomfortable. She is concerned about your feelings. Can't you see that?"

"I guess," he lied.

"Stop thinking like a nineteen year old."

He did not say anything immediately, but he knew Tre was right. "If I ever needed you before, I really need you now man. I am faced with some strong challenges I was not expecting."

"I am here for you. What's on your mind?"

"I thought I was ready for all of this. Now here I am having second thoughts. I have been asking myself do I really want to fight again. Physically I am about ninety percent ready. I thought I was mentally ready but how will the fans, the people, and the world see me? Do I have to be in the camera's eye?" he paused. "I thought I could date her. I was so confident. What do I know about dating?"

"I am glad you asked. You want friend talk or real talk?"

Hanging his head low, "Give it to me real."

"Remember Philippians four and thirteen. I can do all things through Christ, which strengthens me. It is an important scripture for you and is going to be your basis for this season in your life. You can and will fight. You can and will date. Therefore, you can go ahead and get those thoughts out of your mind right now. I realize all of this is new and a lot is happening at one time. However, I am excited for you because I can see the bigger picture. I cannot wait until we get past the fight and the wedding. All of this will certainly be a testimony. I am going to hold you accountable for sharing it. You believed, you asked, you prayed, and He provided what was lined up according to His will. Now it is up to you to give back to Him. He answered every one of your prayers and now you want to turn your back because they all came through at one time? He has equipped you for what you need to get through this and I am going to do my part to help you. Do you really think I am going to watch you fail? Do you think I am going to let you get out there and leave you? Do you think I will allow you in the ring unprepared? You really think I am going to let you be out there in love, booed up, stripped down butt naked, and not cover you. He said He would never leave you nor forsake you and neither will I. Now that was friend talk. Are you ready for real talk?"

His head was spinning from everything his friend said. He was not sure if he could handle any more of this conversation, "I think that is enough for today. We will get to real talk another day."

"So what's the deal?"

"Other than physical, I guess I am scared."

"Why?" Hunter asked trying to console his best friend.

"It feels like this is a dream."

Smiling as he spoke, "Dreams have a way of becoming reality my friend."

They talked further and Hunter left a little after two. He had two hours to get himself together, pick up dinner, and head over to Dani's.

■ ■

It was four thirty when my phone chirped. A simple sentence.

> On the way.

His on the way meant he was more than likely around the corner. I immediately texted the girls.

> Be on time. He is scared I will seduce him and he just might be correct.

Now I had ten minutes to figure out what I was wearing. I settled for cargo Capri's, a studded tee and studded flip-flops.

Of course, he buzzed the gate at ten before five. I waited for him at the door. I decided I was going to flow with him and follow his lead. The last thing I wanted was for him to be uncomfortable. I was going to try everything within my power for him not to be. I had already made a step in that direction by making sure I did not have on anything low, revealing, or provocative.

I opened the door and he had bags upon bags, "Let me help you," I said while grabbing one of the bags.

Trying to contain himself, "Hey babe."

He had so much stuff. Enough for a full week instead of a day. "What are we eating?"

"You will have to wait and see," he smirked.

"It looks like you did a lot of cooking," I said sarcastically. We set the bags down. He leaned on one cabinet and me on another. I felt the heat rise in the room. I reached in the refrigerator and got us both a water. He pulled me to him, took my water, opened it, and handed it back. We both took a big swallow at the same time.

"DJ?"

"Yes," I said with a mouth full of water.

"What do you think you are doing?"

I almost choked, "Huh?"

"Why are you over there and I am over here?"

"Oh no," I was not falling for that trap.

"I swear I am good," he chuckled.

"Are you sure? I don't want to start anything we can't finish."

He laughed but I was as serious as a heart attack.

"I am not that kind of girl anyway. You have not even taken me on an actual date since we have been dating."

"I have too," he disputed my accusation.

"No you have not," I barked back.

He pulled me between his legs. "I took you to church."

"Church does not count. Besides, you had me in the Pastors chambers. Try again buddy."

He let my laugh out. He leaned his head on mine and kissed me.

"No wonder you two can't be left alone," Paige said bursting in the house like a hurricane.

"Down tiger," Sade said smacking her lips and rolling her eyes.

"Leave them alone," Leigh said. "They are cute."

"It's good," he said and pat my rump.

I held my finger up at him, "Watch it buddy."

He laughed. "I can do that," he said trying to be funny.

"Good one, but no you can't," I informed him.

He quickly corrected me and pointed at my arm, "As long as you wear that watch and that hook hanging from your wrist I can."

"Newsflash, put a ring on it," and I flashed my hand at him. We all high fived.

"Let's eat if I am going to be double teamed," he retreated.

We all sat down to eat as he blessed the food. I stole a glance and opened my eyes to watch him while he prayed. The food was excellent. He promised to take us to the restaurant he picked up from one day. We enjoyed each other's company and conversation over ziti, fettuccini, cheesecake, cannoli, and tiramisu from Il Bacio while he ate fresh fruit.

"Ladies, can we talk?" he said out of nowhere gaining everyone's attention. We all looked at one another not sure what to expect.

"Dani, do you mind? I do not want to be rude. This is your house."

I extended my hand. "Go right ahead," I said having no idea what was about to happen. I placed my hands under my face.

"Well," he said as he made perfect eye contact with everyone in the room. "As you all should know by now I have asked Danielle to date me. Exclusively that is. Considering the fact I have never really dated before I am not too sure what this all means or entails. All I know is she will be the only person I am seeing. I am going to do a lot of things differently for a change." He looked over at Sade, "As you may have discovered, I do not spend a lot of time in the public eye. I think that standard maybe about to change." He said it like it hurt to think about it. "I realize I have no choice but to get up close and personal for the next few months or at least until the first fight. I have to get the people and the fans back on my side again. I must gain their trust and confidence in me as a fighter."

"Danielle mentioned, and according to her interaction with King and Keith, she is not crazy about traveling in an entourage. Unfortunately, for safety reasons it is the only way I can travel most times. With that being said, this means it is the only way she can travel as well. In addition, it is the only way you will be able to travel. I do not want to startle you all but I would rather have you safe. I can fight or kill any man with my bare hands but I have not tried to stop bullets. Since I am unable to do so please understand there may be times you are required to wear protective equipment. Or there may even be times you cannot travel or attend because I prefer to keep you out of harm's way."

"I am having Vickie book my schedule now. I want to include you all as much as possible without interfering with your daily lives. I know Danielle wants to avoid the crew as much as possible so I need your help."

There was complete silence. "I need you all to support her as she supports me. I need you, Danielle, to always be truthful with me. If you do not like what I do tell me. If you do not want to go tell me. If you do not want me to go, let us talk about it. If you and King cannot get it together, you two are grown, work it out. I do not want to get involved."

Everyone looked at me. I threw my hands up.

"Her happiness is of the upmost importance to me. If there is anything I am doing to cause you pain, travail, or unhappiness let me know immediately," he said looking at me. "Ladies, if she mentions she is unhappy I need to know. If you think she is I need to be informed. If you see something I am doing wrong or should do differently please tell me. I am human. There are going to be things I miss, I mess up on, and I flat out slip. There are things I do not know; therefore, I am asking for your help. Rest assured, I will never hurt her or you all." He glanced back in my direction, "Do you understand me?"

I nodded my head.

"Never," he reiterated. "Your family is my family. We have to do this together. I am going to call on, rely on, and need you all just like I need my crew. It takes a lot to do what I do. It is not as easy as getting in the ring and fighting. A ton of work leads up to the day by others not just me. I need you all there right behind me in the ring. I must have her support and in order to have it she will need to have yours. This means I need you all to be there. Everyone plays a part. Sade, I need you to help her get dressed for events. Leigh keeps her schedule organized and ensures she is on time, is where she needs to be when she needs to be there. Paige, I need you to hold her up when she grows weary. You become her strength and backbone. I already know she is a strong woman. She may not need it, but I would rather her be prepared if she does. I hope not but there might come a time when I am getting my butt tore out the frame. I pray not. If this is the case, she has to remain calm. It is my job. I need her to stay calm so I can remain focused. The last thing I want to do is look over the ring and see her crying, panicking, cursing, or acting a fool. It would not be good for my opponent. I am going to say this again. I can kill with my hands. However, it is not what I should do. In other words, if she freaks I am going to freak so her remaining calm is very important. I would rather have her stay in the box or wait for me in the room. Somehow, I do not foresee that happening. I think she can handle it and I believe you all can too. Although, we have to work on it and prepare in advance."

Giving me his attention, "You cannot get me disqualified. Danielle, you cannot fight for me or with me. There will be no tagging. If I did, no offense, but I would tag King for the fight and you for your mouth. I hope we have that understood."

"Before I go further, I hope I have your blessings on dating Danielle?"

They all looked around the room. The two of them looked at Paige as if she was the spoke person.

"I do not think we have a problem with that? D, are you okay with that?" Paige asked.

I nodded.

"Shall we take that as a yes?" she confirmed.

"Yes."

"Good. You did accept his present. Now, Mr. Hooks, we will not issue credits or refunds at any time under any circumstances."

He gave a little laugh, "That's fine."

"Now, let us give you our rules and stipulations," Paige said.

Somehow, I knew it was not going to be that easy, but he asked for it, I thought.

"Okay. Run it," he said while he leaned up closer on the table.

I was intrigued. *Did they practice this?*

Looking him square in the eyes, she said very calmly, "You will not hurt her. If you do, we will be on your a** like stank on sh*t. Don't think we are just four girls. We are a posse. A clan. A mob. A female mafia. Our goons got goons. Our undisclosed coterie lineage is powerful. You do not need to understand it. All you need to know is we will F you and the twelve disciples up and think nothing of it. One call is all it takes. To you she is Danielle. To me she is my baby sister." She pointed, "Her auntie, her friend, mentor and boss. Do not ever get it twisted. We don't give a damn about who you are. At the end of the day, she had better go to bed happy. If not, you had better not be the reason why. The most you need to do is make it right. I do not expect and neither do I want any BS from you. Your job is to do all you can to make her happy. As long as you are doing that, we will make sure she is doing her job to make you happy. We are not asking you to do anything we do not expect her to do. The same way we plan to check you if you step one baby toe out of line is the same way we will check her. You do not want to piss her off or get on her bad side and you really do not want to piss me off. EVER! Every Rose has a thorn! Are we clear?"

"Wow! I am going to hook you and King up. Both of you are pit bulls." He pointed at Paige and me. "Nevertheless, I have it noted."

Paige was not accepting his answer, "Not what I asked. My question is are we clear?"

"Yes," his eyebrows raised.

Looking around the room she asked, "Anyone else care to add anything?"

"Uncle Hooks how many kids do you have and how many baby mamas?"

He laughed. He shook his head, held up one finger, and twisted it around.

"One kid and one baby mama, or ex-wife."

"Are you sure?"

"I am sure," he looked at me. "I am positive. I am positively sure."

I threw my hands up. I made a mental note in my memory.

"I have had one girlfriend, had sex with one person and Danielle is the second person I have kissed in my life."

He embarrassed me forcing me to cover my face.

"Y'all are a couple of dorks for real," Sade said shaking her head. "Humph, no wonder you can't keep your hands off each other. You are horny as hell. This will be interesting. When nerds fall in love," she teased and laughed. "Please do not embarrass me by telling anyone else that story. He said it with pride too. Don't be boastful. It is an absolute shame," Sade looked like she wanted to puke.

We all looked at Sade as if she was about to cry us a river.

"Now, so that I don't bore you to death, let me tell you all what I need from each of you," Randall said. "Sade, you are in charge of social networking. Facebook, Twitter, Instagram, etcetera. You will work with Vickie and me. Her hands are about to become too full working publicity so she will not have the time to focus on that. However, it is important that it be maintained. You are also in charge of helping your Auntie and me stay on point as the Fashion Coordinator."

"Leigh, you seem to always have a camera attached to the other end of your wrist. I think you would make a great addition to the team as the photographer/videographer. You will work with my photographer on staff."

"Paige, you are the temperature gage. It will be your job to know what is going on in her head at all times. You are to her what King is to me. You are to keep her focused and grounded."

"Danielle, your job is to tell me what ever is bothering you. To be honest with me. To love me."

There was silence.

"I am done," he said causally.

"Well on that note we are going to clean up the dishes and let you all spend some time together." In other words, Paige was done with threatening the man.

"Ugh," Sade said as she got up dragging her feet into the kitchen.

They cleaned up the dishes then we walked them to the door. We closed the door as if it was our home together. We went and sat back down outside. This time instead of sitting across from each other, we sat side by side.

"Let's talk," he said.

"Okay," I agreed.

"Whatever you wish to talk about," he instructed.

"Feel free to start."

"What is on your mind?" he asked.

"Somehow I get the feeling this is being switched back on me."

"I think you know more about me than I know about you."

"It's true. What do you want to know Randall?"

"Everything."

I started with my favorite color, sports, food, clothes, travel, hobbies, celebrities, movies, books, cars, and restaurants. Turns out, I did not know him as well as I thought, but I did know him better than he knew me. I thought I would clam up and not talk about myself; however, the opposite happened and I shared openly. I was both surprised and proud of myself.

There were a few things I did hold back but for the most part, I was open and honest.

He pulled my leg a few times I think. He told me his favorite books were the Bible and "The Danielle Rose" Book as he has so named it. The first part of the sentence may have been true. The second half is only true if he has not read a book in twenty years.

We laughed, sighed, and shared personal and confidential information. We talked about regrets, failures, hurt, pain, and disappointments.

"Can I ask you something?" he asked sincerely.

'Go ahead."

"Do you feel I am doing the right thing?"

"In regards to what?"

"Everything. King, Keith, fighting, Trevor, and you?"

"I think you should be you. Do what you feel is right. Do what is in your heart. At the end of the day you have to make you happy."

"Do you think I am pursuing you the correct way?"

"I don't know."

"I am new to this. Tell me," he pleaded. "Do you think I might have overstepped my boundaries today? Is it too soon for me to be dating? Am I wrong for asking Keith to protect you and not allowing him to do what he wants to do? Should I be disciplining King for his behavior?"

"Oh boy. I can't tell you how to deal with your employees. Remember they have been here years before me. You never know, they could easily be here years after I am gone."

"So you think?"

I hoped not. "As far as the girls go I think you spoke how you felt. I also think they appreciated your honesty and sincerity. They did not hesitate to share with you their sincerest feelings as it relates to the two of us. I do not think it was inappropriate from either side."

"Umm yeah. I thought for a minute that I was going to need back up. I began to think this conversation was a bad idea. I was waiting to get slapped any minute."

I laughed.

"What are you laughing at? You did not say a word. After tonight, you know I am never stepping in between you and King."

"What did I do?"

"You left me hanging."

"I did not."

"Yeah you did."

"Oh man up! They are girls."

"You talk a lot of trash," he said as he tickled my feet making me laugh until my stomach hurt.

There was a brief awkward silence and then I said, "I do have a concern I want to talk to you about?"

"What babe?"

"I hope I am not the flavor of the month, the rebound chick, or the starter girl."

He frowned. "What does that mean?"

"Just like it sounds."

"Explain please."

"I hope after all the dust settles you don't forget me."

He looked like I stabbed him with a knife. He did not move. He did not blink. He did not swallow. I could not even tell if he was breathing.

He stood up. "Walk me to the door please," he said.

I was startled. *I thought we were sharing. I told you how I felt.* I stood up and exhaled deeply. Then I began to walk to the door. We got there and I really did not know what to say. *This is bad.* I stood in front of the door. He stood behind me so close I could feel his breath on my neck. He reached around me and opened the door. I never moved. He stepped on to the threshold. I didn't know what to say. He stopped.

"I'm sorry."

"For what?"

"I don't know. Upsetting you." I threw my hands up and shrugged my shoulders.

"You did not. I am not upset. You told me how you felt. You are right."

I jerked my neck back ghetto style.

"You are the flavor of the month, the rebound chick and the starter girl. To answer your question."

I rolled my neck and my eyes this time. *What in the hell did he just say?*

"Good news for you, I like the same flavor every month. You have helped me rebound my life to start over again. Therefore, you are the rebound and starter girl."

I dropped my head. *Thank you Jesus, I am not going to have to cut him after all.* I put my hands over my face embarrassed while he hugged me.

"Good night. We will not make this long, drawn out, and painful for me."

"Don't wear this cologne anymore," I said in the middle of our embrace.

"You don't like it?" he asked sourly.

"Just the opposite." He stood on one side of the threshold and I stood on the other. We embraced, kissed, and he left. He had to be just crossing the gate when he called. "Hello."

He admitted, "That was so hard for me." I could hear it in his voice.

"Excuse me?"

"It is extremely hard for me to leave you. I do not ever want to leave you. Danielle, I want to spend my life with you."

Every time he spoke, he made my heart melt. "Promise you will feel like that forever."

Breathless, he said, "I promise."

"I'm holding you to it. Good night."

WEEK 18
Monday

To say the least I was refreshed at work. I tried my best not to act so excited. The way I behaved like someone who had the pleasure of getting some early in the morning right before they came to work. They are always chipper and you can't help wanting to put them on blast. For that very reason, I tried to stay in my office because I was sure someone would check my behavior. Besides, it wasn't even true. I had not had any in so long I would be a dead giveaway if I did.

After work I went right to the gym. I noticed my weight was slightly up since I slacked the last few weeks on working out and watching what I ate. Just when my rhythm was good, and my mind was clearing, I heard my name being called. "Yes."

"Can you join me for a moment?" Randall asked.

"Now?"

"Yes please." I grabbed my hoodie and met him at the top of the steps. He held my hand as we walked down the stairs. We entered into a conference room. Everyone was seated except him, King, Keith, and me.

The room was full of people I had never seen. He walked over and stood at the top of the table. King stood at the side like the secret service and Keith stood on the opposite end. As I approached the room, he moved to the middle of the room expecting me to follow. I held my hand up letting him know I was cool where I was. I was not moving any further. I needed to be close to the door. I wasn't expecting anything to pop off today, but just in case I would be ready to leave.

"Hooks Gym," he said with excitement. "Thank you all for joining me this evening. This will be brief. I will not hold you long but there are a few things we need to discuss. Is every one doing great?"

As everyone responded, I quietly slid to the back by the door.

"Any issues or topics we need to discuss?"

A few hands went up. There were some sports related topics, a parking lot, and a monogrammed towel issue. They resolved or delegated all of those.

"Anything else before we begin?"

I kind of slightly held my finger up. He gave me the preacher come to Jesus response. He pointed, "I see you in the back. You can have a seat or move to the front if you would like."

I gave a hand motion that relayed I was fine.

"Well, since she raised her hand we will start with her. For those of you that don't know, that is Danielle Rose in the back of the room. She has quietly reminded me, and I am sure this will come as a surprise to her that I would remember we need to discuss a safety tip. I have observed her at her firm and she starts every meeting off with a safety topic. Does anyone want to volunteer one?"

He looked around the room as everyone looked back at him and one another. No one spoke. "Do not all speak at once."

Then of course the true Ambassador he is, JJ provided the safety tip. Afterwards everyone was more relaxed and the meeting officially began.

"Well, let's get to business. I am sure many have been gossiping, have heard, want to know, have been asked, or wondered what is going on. It is true, as of last Tuesday my divorce became final. Hence the change in my demeanor. I am very happy and I pray I remain like this always."

"Secondly, Danielle is my female interest. To say it mildly." Everyone looked back at me. I closed my eyes. *Oh great. He did not prepare me for this and I am looking a hot mess.* Observing some of the faces I could see hope shatter right before my eyes. One in particular but she was too young for him anyway.

"Sorry. I didn't mean to call you out," he said throwing his hand in my direction. I made a facial gesture back at him.

"As many are already aware Danielle has a track above. Therefore, she will be here a lot working out. Daily probably. Early and maybe late until I can get her to conform."

"Conform?" I said in my Dani Ro tone.

"If she is here too long at any given time call me. I do not want her here working out for long extensive periods of time. I also do not want her here working a lot either. The sole purpose for her being here in the first place is to reduce work related stress. She somehow manages to incorporate work into everything."

"I guess that is why we are complimentary of each other. She loves her job and I love mine. By the way, I noticed some of your facial expressions. I am glad you asked. The answer is no, we do not live together. We live in and pay for our own respective houses, which we had before we met one another. Let's clear the air now. Besides, I do not think she will have it any other way. Anything else I need to touch on?"

He thought for a minute. "While I have all of you, let me prepare you if questions should arise. Who is she? Those questions should be directed to me, Keith, King, or Vickie. If you feel you must respond to the media. You have my permission to say none of your business. I know some of you will not so I'll help you out with a response. Danielle is my love interest."

"I can't label it more than that right now because I have not spoken with her to formally change her title." My facial expression must have changed drastically because he said, "No worries D. I will give you time to be the girlfriend and fiancée before I have your name changed to Mrs. Danielle

Washington. I like that. It has a nice ring to it." There was commotion in the room. It was my opportunity. I walked right out the door.

Did he really stop me for this? To embarrass me?

"Get her please," he laughed while I did not see anything funny.

Keith came right behind me. As we re-entered the room Randall bowed. "Sorry. I will behave. As I was saying she will be here a lot. Keith has been assigned to her. When she moves he moves."

"We all will respect her and treat her like a family member. Do not let her fool you. The cliché do not judge a book by its cover applies to Danielle. She is smooth on the outside but fierce on the inside. I think King can attest to that," he roared a laugh. "We are going to pray and work on those two. They will eventually get it together. I think right now they have a love-hate relationship. Stretch your hands to them now and let us take a moment to pray." They did and he prayed while I sighed and rolled my eyes. I looked over at King, he frown, and folded his forehead together. "Amen. For those of you that do not know, she is in line to be the next partner at a well-known Architect Engineering Firm here in the Atlanta. You have seen her work and do not even know it. She designed the track upstairs. I bribed the firm to let me have the plans without her knowledge. She is the designer of Plaza Overlook. Holy Cathedral of Christ, which is the largest Catholic Cathedral in the United States. The Nineteen Building, the Hartsfield–Jackson Towers, numerous other buildings, schools, hotels, and malls in and out of Atlanta as well as overseas. She is preparing the plans for the new Mayors Mansion just to name a few. DJ did I miss anything?"

I closed my eyes and shook my head. He missed a lot. That was just the first few pages in the book he has, but I was not about to add to what he had going on right now.

"Vickie, while it is on my mind order a few more of those high dollar Danielle Hall of Fame books and we will display them around the gym. Have three dismantled and framed for the lobby, my office, and my house. I think she may even autograph them for us."

"Keith, you are probably wondering how you got stuck with the girl. Well long story short. I cannot move King from where he is. Believe me, you would not want me too. King has to be everything. My eyes, ears, voice, feet, and my thoughts. He has to cover me from the crown of my head to the soles of my feet. Not that he is God by any means, but he is a King. He has to cover me at all angles. He cannot blink if he wants to. Then after all that he is up working out with me, training, eating what I eat and doing what I do. All day every day."

"Believe me you do not want to be bothered with me full-time. You have; however, been given a much larger task in the grand scheme of things. King protects my mind and body but you are protecting my heart, my love, and my future wife. I hope you take that as an honor and a privilege. I do not take this position lightly."

"Okay, enough of that. I think Danielle is going to barf back there. Sorry babe."

"Get ready! Get ready! Get ready! I am about to do something I have never done. I am going to start promoting and attending more functions. Vickie is working hard organizing these events. Award shows, sporting events, premiers, you name it. It is a lot of work involved. We are going to try to stay local first. This means keep your suits, dresses, and tuxedos ready. You may be asked to work at any given moment. I am working with Leigh. You may or may not know her, but she is the one who always has a camera attached to the end of her arm. She is Danielle's wonderful assistant. She will be the one to coordinate our schedules. Leigh and Vickie will soon be BFF's. They will communicate a lot."

The group made whispering noises. They all knew who Leigh was.

"Today I will begin my rigorous training. We all are aware they accepted me back into the association. King, JJ, and I have decided we will grind it out for a few months before the public announcement is made. I have a gut feeling once the announcement is made there will be no turning back. I need to be ready as well as get Danielle ready. I am sure the fights will be lined up. We will cross that bridge when we get there but I want to be prepared."

"I am mentally ready. I am hyped. I am happy. I am spiritually ready. I can always use more preparation. Now I just need to enhance the athletic side of the puzzle. JJ and King are the ones who make sure this is done. They will not let me make this public unless they know I am ready and we are all ready. Their names are on the line just as much as my own. We all have to be ready because it will move fast."

"A couple of points we need to take away," he said as he walked to the board and made a list. After he was done going over his list he asked, "Questions?" then paused and waited. When no one responded, "Let's get busy!" There was commotion in the room. "Thank you for all you do every day. I am not who I am without each and every one of you. From the person who washes the towels to the one in the ring punching with me. You all may not know it but the towels are important. If they are spoiled I can have a bad day. Imagine, you are in a good rhythm and then you wipe your face with a dirty spoiled towel."

That broke the ice. They all chimed in laughing and commenting. "Do we need to cover anything else?" he asked. "Vickie, Keith, King, and DJ?" he said pointing to me. I could tell Keith relaxed and felt much better once he heard the reason it was important to be assigned to look after me. I felt good about his decision also.

"Meeting adjourned."

I ran from the room and up the stairs. He arrived shortly walking right beside me. I did not remove my buds from my ear as I spoke, "Good job handling Keith."

"I prayed about it."

"You did well."

"Sorry to put you on the spot. I needed to lay down some ground rules and nip the chitter chatter in the bud before it had a chance to start. The main thing we needed to go over was the fact that we are about to be grinding. I have prayed about this. I feel like this ride is going to ramp up one hundred miles per hours instead of cruise control. I want them to realize it is not just me, JJ, and King on the ride. All of us will be on the ride, including you." He looked at me lovingly.

"I gotcha."

"Are you ready?" he asked concerned.

"As ready as I will ever be," I said.

He walked around the track with me. "Good answer. Let me know if anything should change."

"I will."

"How long are you going to be here tonight?"

"I just got started. The owner distracted me."

He smirked and looked down at his watch, "You have one hour," he ordered.

I did not have the courage or strength to argue, "I will call you once I am done."

"I was planning on running up here with you for a little while if you don't mind."

"Help yourself," I said not showing my excitement. After I was done he walked me to the car. He promised he was going home. I was for certain he was going to stay there all night. If I have the strength I will drive by after midnight and instruct him to go home. When midnight came, I really wanted to drive back to the gym. I was not sleepy but I did not want to bring temptation to him so I called him instead.

"Yes DJ," he answered. He sounded annoyed to be busted.

"I am not sure I like your tone."

"I think I know why you are calling," he said.

"Oh yeah? Well, I think I know where you are mister."

"Give me thirty minutes and I will call you from the car."

"Ten minutes Randall."

He sighed. He did not like to take orders as well as he gave them. "I will call you back once I get in my truck."

"Please do not make me come up there." I clicked off and checked the clock. I was giving him ten minutes no more or less.

He had not called in twelve minutes so I called him back. The phone answered. I could hear his robust laughter in the back ground.

"He is leaving now," someone blurted while he remained in silence. I did not respond.

"I am trying to get to my truck," he finally said.

"Umm hmm," not believing that was true I disconnected the line.

In five minutes he called me back. Dryly I answered, "Hey."

"Hey babe."

"I will talk to you until you get home."

"Why aren't you asleep?"

"Too early and I am waiting for you to get home. Why aren't you home?"

"I have to train. Do I need to buy you the Rocky Series? This is serious work."

"You need to eat and go to bed."

"Negative."

"Say what?"

"Babe, I need to get two more hours in."

"Come on Deacon."

"Seriously. I have to," he said gently in a begging tone.

"I'm calling you in two hours and shutting it down."

"Please don't," he said. He knew I would. "You have to understand this is important for my success."

"I fully understand but so is food and sleep for the nourishment and strength of your body."

"I will get a few hours in. I am pulling into the gate now."

"Don't try me Deacon. It does not count that home working out."

"Yes ma'am. Good night." He knew from her tone she was serious.

"I will talk to you in two hours."

He sighed and hung up.

I laid down and set the alarm on my phone. At 2:40 when the alarm sounded. I called he picked up before the finishing of the first ring.

"You are a minute late. Do you hear the shower?"

"Good night."

"Danielle?"

"Yes."

"I love you."

"I love you too. Thank you for your obedience. It will make this so much easier for us. No blogging tonight."

Tuesday

"Good morning beautiful."

"Morning."

"How did you sleep?"

I smirked, "Good and you?"

"Horrible without you."

"I slept like a two year old."

"Liar. I have had the pleasure of watching you sleep a few times. You sleep like a zombie-vampire. Not much and very lightly."

"Not fair," I barked back. He was correct again.

"I have a meeting today at Schlossenbloum's office."

"Oh, why?"

"I am not sure."

"Who is going with you?"

"King. I do not think Khrittyleberrg will be there."

"Do you need me?"

"Was that a question? Of course I need you. I know you have things to do at work. We can handle it. I think." He was not sure himself.

"Okay, let me know."

"I will. I hope this does not interfere with my training. We have a full day planned and I am already side tracked on the first day before it ever begins."

"It's cool. Handle your business. You will not be at his office all night."

"I hope not. DJ, have a great day."

"Thanks sweetie, you too."

"I love you."

"I love you back."

My day was good. Leigh and I got some things accomplished. We had a productive day. I went over to the track and worked out. I had not heard from him since our conversation this morning. I was kind of worried but I was not going to show it. I wasn't sure if I should call or not. I was hoping when I walked in someone would mention his where abouts. That did not happen.

I walked for over two hours while no one said a word. I hung around and worked buying time for him to show up. A phone rang. I looked around and it was the land line.

"Dani Ro."

"Ms. D."

"Hey Keith. What's up?"

"In case you are wondering, they are still at the accountants office. Do you need anything?"

"No, I am good."

"Let someone know if you do."

"I will. Umm, by any chance did he say how much longer he was going to be?" I asked trying not to sound overly concerned.

"No he did not."

"Where are you?" I asked wondering why he called me instead of walking the stairs.

"Downstairs."

"Okay thanks." I decided to kill another hour and take a shower at the gym before I left. I came down the steps to the juice bar while on a phone call. The usual for here please," I said in between my call.

I drank my smoothie and ate some fruit and nuts while talking to the guy behind the bar. Once I was done, I ran back up the steps and did a few more things before I shut down my computers. I was installing some software on the laptop and desk top that remained there. Once it was done I had nothing else to do so I packed up to go.

I walked to the bar, "May I please have a plastic bottle of water to go?"

"Sure thing Ms. D."

"Oh, and will you buzz Keith and let him know I am leaving?"

Keith met me at the door. "You calling it a night or did you give up waiting?"

I was busted. "Yeah. I will call him on my way home."

"You work this late every night?" Keith was trying to be funny. He knew I did. He was also fully aware I was waiting on Randall.

"Yes sir. This is kind of early for me. I will go home and work for another hour or so."

Shaking his head, "I do not know how you two are going to do it. Overachievers and work alcoholics," he spoke as if his words were insulting me.

"Wa wonk, wa wonk, wonk wonk," I mumbled.

He laughed. It took a lot to make Keith laugh. He walked me to my car and watched as I pulled off. As soon as I got to the curb Randall's truck pulled up. JJ stopped the truck and Randall jumped out of the passenger side.

"Hey babe," he said exasperated.

I put the car in park and got out. "Are you good?" I questioned looking him eye to eye.

He sighed heavily confirming he was not with bloodshot eyes, "Yeah long day."

"I can see. You came back with an Yves Saint Laurent handbag on your shoulder. Should I be worried?"

He looked at it like he had no clue it was there. He kissed my forehead. "How embarrassing."

"I must admit I am a little concerned. You are dressed nice and carrying a designer handbag."

"This is some of Tameka's mess." He opened the bag. It was full of jewelry, credit cards, watches, and papers. "She returned items I requested and items she deemed she no longer wanted."

"Who gives back jewelry?" It was a rhetorical question.

"Apparently, she does. I am taking it to the jeweler tomorrow and selling it. I mean what am I going to do with this anyway. I thought about giving it to RJ when he gets older and let him give it to his girlfriend, wife, or daughter but I'm not even going to bother. I cannot see myself lugging this baggage around with me for ten years or more."

"Put it in a safe deposit box for him," I suggested.

"Good thought, but I am getting the money and paying her with it. Trying to be a butt she messed around and shot herself in the foot. Today we settled on a financial number. The number was much less than I anticipated on paying her. I threw a number out and she took it. Oh well. I am not changing it. The house she is in will be placed on the market tomorrow. I will give her a few options for a new home. I will offer $280,000.00 but no more than $350,000.00. I will have a flatbed pick up whichever two cars she decides she wants to let go of and sell those. I will even be nice and take all three and trade them for one new one if she prefers. I figure with the proceeds of this jewelry, the furs in the truck, these bonds, the cars, and the house, I will have her alimony money for the next six years. I will even pay for her to be moved from one spot to the next," he said. "You will have all of this in a written version sometime tomorrow once Khrittyleberrg has it all typed up," he added.

"So how was she with all of this?"

"She voluntarily brought this stuff back. I didn't ask for any of it. Majority of it she bought on her own anyway. The other half I don't even remember. I asked for the cars, credit cards, and the bonds. I am sure she is pissed because she cannot have two cars and her alimony stops if she remarries. Either way after RJ is eighteen she gets nothing. If she is smart, she had better have a plan at hand. I cannot believe she sold herself short. I could have easily added another zero to the amount she settled for, but she cut off her nose in spite of her face."

"How do you feel?"

He put his arms around me and kissed me a few times. In a low voice he replied, "Free and happy."

I blushed, "I am glad."

"Go home," he instructed.

"Huh?"

"Help me help you."

I knew what he meant. We were too close to each other again. I got into my car and proceeded home. He didn't want to be tempted and neither did I. I texted to let him know as soon as I made it home.

Wednesday

Before the day even began Randall called early issuing directives, "I will meet you at your house at 5:30 this evening."

"That is too early. You are pushing it," I yelled still with sleep in my voice.

"Somehow I figured you would say that. Keith will pick you up. That way we will have one car to drive home from church this evening."

Now fully awake I raised up and said, "You think you are so slick."

"Not really but is it working?" he laughed.

"Heck no."

I had to bust my tail to get everything done for the day, be home, and changed by five thirty. *Who does this? Who in the world is really home and changed at this time of the day? This is crazy*, I thought to myself. Nevertheless, I followed instructions against my judgment. When Keith arrived I was ready and in place. We went directly to our seats once we got to the church. I allowed my mind to drift off and thought of the millions of things I could be doing instead of sitting still. Then I checked myself. This was decompression time to prepare for the Word. Once the Deacon entered the room and took his post I smiled without looking in his direction. I was present, accounted for, and ahead of schedule. There was nothing he could say. All he could do was smile back. Wouldn't you know it; as soon as he did, Hunter busted him.

After service I waited patiently. No, I was not patient. I was like a kid made to sit still for too long. My ADHD kicked in. I was trying hard to people watch so I would not get distracted and pull my gadgets out. It did not work. I was fully engulfed in work on my iPad when the shadow appeared.

When I looked up he was shaking his head, "Not even for twenty minutes Danielle?"

"Try fifty two," I corrected. I had been waiting fifty-two minutes. That was a very long time for me to sit still.

"Better than I thought," he said proud he finished within that time frame. He was deep in thought as we walked to the car. "I am still waiting on an answer about the Lambo," he said seemingly out of nowhere.

"Hi Danielle. How are you? I am great Randall. Thanks for asking. Pastor taught the Word tonight. Yes he did. I love you. I love you too."

"Hi Danielle and all that stuff you said. What about the Lambo?"

I gave him the side eye. "I gave you the answer and it remains the same as it was the last time."

"Will you think about it?" his voice pleaded.

"For you, sure," I paused and took the time to look at my watch. "Umm, the answer is still no." He switched lanes like a contrary kid.

"Still no," he said like he was trying to comprehend being told no. Then he sighed in disgust.

"This behavior might be the reason why. If you drove this car with responsibility, then I could possibly consider. Be a wise and faithful steward."

He looked super perturbed. I gave a fake smile back. He did a double take. He really wanted to say something instead he opted not to. "All I did was ask a question and here you go bringing the Word into it."

"We did just leave bible study right?"

"You are riding back with Keith next week."

I have no problem with that. "I detect a little hostility."

"No, you said you were going to think about it."

"I did," I scowled.

"All of one second."

He was wearing me down, "I tell you what. Let's get through this first fight and revisit this conversation at the beginning of next year."

"NEXT YEAR," he yelled, unable to believe what he was hearing.

I pulled out my phones. Yes, I was ignoring him and his temper tantrum. He continued to snarl in my direction. I never moved or gave him my attention. "I can see you," I informed him while sending a message.

"DANIELLE, WHY BE SO DIFFICULT?"

"Mental note, never ride home with you on Wednesday nights. I will do better walking," I said.

He was sort of upset. This was all new to him. Apparently, no one ever told him no from the looks of it. He has had free reign to do whatever he wants whenever he wants. Truth be told, him wanting a Lamborghini was the least of my concerns. This was obviously a big deal to him because he didn't seem to get the fact I was holding onto my original no. If we were going to be in a relationship he is going to hear no a lot. This is a matter of him gaining self-control and learning discipline in his spending and his physical emotions. He is not going to be able to continue to punch my walls either. He is not allowed to thrust himself or his fist into my walls any longer.

Then I thought about it. *Who am I to talk? If I take one more cold shower I will shrivel up like a prune.* I surely felt the same exact way he felt. This was going to be a long courtship. I found it difficult just sitting next to him without thinking and wanting him intimately. *This is purely lust of the flesh.*

You could feel the tension rise in the car. I told him no and now I was not giving him any attention. I typed with one hand and rubbed the back of his clean shaven head with the other hand. He reacted just like a kitten. He relaxed his head in the palm of my hand and I could literally feel all the worry, anxiety, stress, pain, and heartache transfer to my hand. I knew then the real issue was not the car at all.

As we exited the highway he spoke softly, "Danielle."

I did not look up, "Yes."

"Please I beg you. Whatever you do please do not do that."

I shifted my body in the seat to give him my attention, "Do what?"

"That," he gave no indication as to what that was.

I put my phones down. "Satisfied?" I naturally assumed he was talking about me being on the phones.

"That is not what I was referring to?"

"What then?" I had no clue.

He pressed his head in my hand. "That," he said again.

My hand stopped moving immediately.

"That would not be good."

"Sorry."

"It's all good," he said and then sighed heavily. "No it is not. Don't ever do that again. If so there will be consequences and repercussions. You are making this extremely hard for me."

"We will be fine. I won't do it again."

"That is the problem I want you to but I would hate to humiliate you and myself by pulling this truck over and ruining the future right here on the off ramp."

I laughed. I had touched a spot. It was good information to know; however, right now it was useless information. *Hooks had a spot.*

"I'm serious. Pick up your little toys and keep playing. When I pull up to your door jump out and keep it moving. Do not look back. Are we clear?" his tone was serious.

"We are clear, but FYI, Keith had the chastity installed."

We both laughed. When we pulled up he left the Rover running, walked me to my door and barely touched or kissed me. I knew why and was not the least bit offended.

Thursday

I walked into Leigh's office and stood in front of her desk. She was busy working on something and did not look up to notice I entered the room. "Leigh," I said.

"Yes," she replied as she finished what she was doing and finally looking up at me.

"We need to make arrangements to spend a day over at the track. The office area needs to have a few upgrades so I am able to properly work while I'm there."

"Oh okay. Exactly what do you need to have done?" she asked in an almost sarcastic tone.

I rattled a list.

"No problem. I will get what I need on order and contact Vickie to find out the particulars. Speaking of Vickie, Hooks has a very busy schedule you may want to take a look at before I confirm your attendance to any of these events."

"What?" I practically yelled.

She shrugged her shoulders and said, "The perks of having a balling boo." She laughed and redirected her attention on her monitor.

"Perks or downside?" I rattled back at her walking back to my office.

"You tell me in thirty days," she mumbled.

Say what? I stopped and turned around. "What's happening in thirty days?" I was now confused.

"Check your new calendar," she perked up.

"Great!" I replied full of artificial enthusiasm and walked around Leigh's desk.

Leigh pulled up her calendar. It was so colorful I almost could not read it. "What in the hell is that? We need to go back to day timers. Paige would be ecstatic."

She gave a detailed explanation of everything on the calendar. Listed was his Deacon schedule to include colors, attire, church events, workout regimen, and training schedule. Also listed were financial particulars, birthdays, notes, memos, and then a color chart of engagements. There were at least three to five appearances a week.

"The ones in pink are ones you are asked to attend. The ones in purple are the ones he desires you to attend."

"Maybe I am slow. What is the difference in him asking and desiring?"

"From the looks of it, the ones you are asked to attend are not considered mandatory so to speak. The ones he desires for you to attend are ones in which he must have a date, so you need to be there."

There was just as much purple as pink. "This is too much. There is no way he is attending all of these events."

"Yes, it is. All I can say is block your evenings."

"It's already blocked," I said referring to my work life.

"Call it however you choose."

"Am I supposed to respond today?" I asked in panic.

"You have a few days.

"How do you want to handle these day time events like photo shoots, commercials, and press conferences?"

"I don't know. I guess I will need to look at them against my calendar and check out the locations. What is the process here? Am I able to decline or accept them all now then show up to the ones I'm able to attend?"

Leigh looked at me as if I was crazy, "I don't think Hooks works like that."

"What have I gotten myself into?" I made a mental note to speak to him about this as soon as possible.

"You can handle it," Leigh reassured."

I suddenly felt stressed. "Let's call it a day. I will talk to him and see what we need to do about this. I think he is trying to cheat by appearing places that are work related for him, but to me he's calling it a date."

Leigh took his side, "Hooks would not do that. He is trying to promote himself for the fight."

"I will get with Sade and have her to go through these dates and generate two calendars. One is a Hooks calendar and the other will be a Dani and

Hooks calendar. She can coordinate my wardrobe. Besides, this gives her a job to do." *When will we have time to date?*

We both walked to our cars. I drove directly to the gym. I didn't waste any time. I parked in my spot, jumped out, walked in, and went right to the ring.

He looked over, "Hey babe."

"I need to speak to you in private," I said immediately. It was not a question.

"Now?"

"Take your time," Although I am sure my tone and body language stated otherwise.

I went upstairs to my track. I plugged in, logged on, changed clothes, and began walking. Nearly forty minutes later he came up. His hands were still taped.

He ran over to meet me and kissed me. "How was your day?"

"Informative." His delay in urgency forced my behavior but gave me time to calm down a bit.

"What's up?"

"What is up with the schedule you sent over?"

"Those are the events I have been invited to."

"And?"

He gave me the puppy dog eyes, "I am begging you."

"Whatever," I snapped and rolled my eyes.

"I am going because of you," his tone was sincere.

"Come again." His statement caught me off guard.

"Please," he begged.

I gave in, "Let's see what we can work out. First we will need to look at these dates together."

Pleading he asked, "Tell me what would be better for you?"

"It would be better if you were to attend one event a week. Maybe two if they are simple and easy."

"Example?"

"If the event is like the one at the Georgia Aquarium and it's an all-day event, then you can do one of those a week. If it's something like reading to the third grade class for an hour then we can squeeze in two or three a week."

"I will look at the calendar again with Vickie," he agreed.

"So, when are you going to date me?" I asked politely trying not to be selfish.

I could tell my question got him thinking. "I will let Vickie and Leigh know to cancel all the engagements. This way I can be with you by myself."

"Can you handle it?" I sneered.

"Heck no," he said firmly and proudly.

"Then we are back to the schedule I guess."

He walked around my track with me. I could not ever force myself to simply say the track. It was not the track. It was my track. We did not say a word the entire walk. I was thinking about the future agenda with him while he was avoiding thoughts of being alone with me. To clear his mind he would run a bit and walk a bit.

JJ called him to come down. He screamed back, "I am running up here." I had a feeling he was breaking the schedule. JJ was much less fierce than King but his seniority was much firmer than King's disposition. He politely came up the stairs. He never left from the second to the top of the steps as he handed him a jump rope.

He squatted down and waited for him to begin. Once he did I could hear the timer ticking.

When I circled back around I spoke, "Way to go JJ. Can't bring the horse to the water then bring the water to the horse. I love it."

Randall looked back at me while jumping.

"Watch it. Do not get in trouble on my account. You are still working," I smirked.

"Stay focused Hooks," JJ said with a soft but stern voice.

I snickered. JJ and King were so opposite. I guess having a perfect balance is what made them work so well together. There was a good cop and a bad cop.

I walked around once and Randall said, "How much longer are you going to be?"

"Stop," JJ shouted.

Randall looked over to me as if I had gotten him in trouble.

JJ simply said, "Start over. Forty minutes."

"Forty minutes? I was almost finished." He was braver than I thought to question JJ.

"Yeah, you went thirty two minutes and you got distracted. Now start over."

"Why am I starting over?" his tone was calm.

"Why did you get distracted?" JJ's tone was calmer than his was.

He said nothing. I was afraid for him. I was going to call it a night as soon as I got around the bend. I didn't want to get him in anymore trouble.

"Get prepared. If she is distracting you now just wait. You got to block, fight, train your mind, and condition your body. Do we have to start over with the basics?"

"No sir."

I started to run a little to hurry up and finish. "I'm done."

"Keep walking," JJ said to me. "You have forty more minutes in you too. What, he didn't tell you? You are in training too. Everyone is going to be ready once the date is set."

I didn't argue back. I was praying for him like he was in the middle of a fight. He was, except this fight was more mental than physical. The closer it got to forty minutes the harder it was. At about thirty five minutes JJ called out, "Ten more minutes." JJ then came over and walked with me.

"What do you have to do once you are finished?" he asked.

"Nothing really. I was going to check some messages before I left."

"Oh." JJ left his comment at that.

I picked up on the unsaid message, "I guess I will be checking them in the car."

"Good girl. Get your stuff together and I will let him break free. You have five minutes. He has an hour in the ring and another hour on weights."

"How long has he been going at it?"

"Off and on all day. Today, tomorrow, and until we fight."

"Wow," I was amazed.

"Yeah," JJ said as if this was an ordinary day.

We walked right past him. He didn't even notice us. I gathered my things as JJ watched him from the other side of the room. I took a few minutes to watch JJ watching him although I didn't know what I was looking for.

JJ looked over at me and nodded. I nodded back. He hit is stop watch and Hooks stopped instantly.

"Good job. You have five minutes to be back in the ring. There is a water on the steps. Good night Ms. Danielle. I will see you at this same time tomorrow.

I noted it was not a question or a request. "Good night JJ," I replied.

We acted like the principal was watching us. Hooks stopped by the bar and ordered my smoothie and gave instructions to bring it outside to my car.

"Hey," I said sympathetically.

"Hey babe," he was drained and his night had not begun.

"Are you tired?"

"Not at all."

"Sorry I got you in trouble," I looked down.

He lifted my chin, "You should be," he said with a wink.

"Hey wait a minute. You came in my domain," I frowned stating the facts.

"I will not be coming back. You get a brother in trouble. If you don't hear from me tonight know JJ is still working me. He just got here too. I already know he is ready for a full night."

"What do you mean?"

"I train in the mornings with King. They overlap in the afternoon and JJ has me all night."

"All day," I said to make sure I was understanding correctly. Was he training for twenty-four hours?

"Around the clock."

"Wow, that's unbelievable," I said.

"You could do it."

"I am glad you have confidence in me." Not that I wanted to ever do that. "Well, I am going home now. I do not want to distract you."

"Training is one way I do not have to worry about my flesh," he proudly added.

"You are going to be too tired and exhausted to do anything else."

"You can never be too tired," he winked.

I laughed.

"You have to wait on your smoothie. Call me when you get home."

"No sir, I don't think so. I am not getting in trouble with you."

"Yes, you will. I get in trouble for you all the time. I will be on weights for an hour. I am sure JJ has the night planned." They brought my smoothie out to him. He took a sip then handed it to me. "I will call you as soon as I get in the car. Promise!"

"Cool."

"Bye," he kissed me and took off running.

I texted him as soon as I got home. He called me when he got in the car. He was exhausted. I could hear it in his voice. We both said goodnight.

Friday

TGIF. I was so glad it was Friday. Not like I had big plans. Or shall I say we? I did have a boo now. From the way the schedule looked the other day I may need to relax and enjoy this weekend. It might be my last quiet one for a while. Forever. I hoped someone was going to occupy my weekends from now on. I hoped that someone was Deacon Randall Hooks DeWayne Washington.

Just as I was entering the highway my phone rang. I could hear the wind blowing through the ear piece before I ever spoke, "You are late."

"I know. Good morning babe," his voice showed his Friday was weary one.

"How are you feeling?" I asked knowing he was exhausted.

"I would feel better if King let up a bit," he answered with honesty.

I could not believe what I was hearing, "No, you didn't say that?"

"Yeah, I did. He is looking at me crazy too. You two were home while JJ punched me to death last night," he said hoping his ribs were not broken.

"You can handle it," I tried to encourage him when I really wanted to help him. "Call me later."

"I love you D. Have a great day."

"I love you too. Train well."

My office door was a turn style all day. One in. One out. I was exhausted. *Did they save all their questions for the week and spring them on me at once?*

I looked at Leigh and she looked just as rough as I did. Her hair was standing on top of her head. "What is up with this day?" I asked beat.

She threw her hands up. "Hell if I know. I have had just about enough of this nonsense," Leigh admitted.

"It's done. Let's go. Shut everything down quickly."

"Where are you going?" she asked as we walked to the car.

"To the gym if I can stand up long enough to walk."

"Don't forget ten tonight."

"I haven't forgotten," I lied. I completely forgot. "What am I wearing?" She rattled off some options. "I am going because?"

"He is your client and you promised three months ago you would be at his fiftieth birthday party."

"Do I have to do anything, say anything, or bring anything?"

"Your present is already there. Just show up, smile, and play like you are having a blast of a time. Oh and bring the boy if you can."

"Did I RSVP for a guest?"

"As a matter of fact I did and it is already on his calendar. Vickie called for the dress code and I think the car has been cleaned and driver arranged. Hooks is a date and a scapegoat. Mentioned you have another engagement but would not dare miss the party. I will see you at ten. We are getting cake, some lobster stuffed something's, and bouncing."

Realizing how blessed I was to have Leigh around I asked, "What would I do without you?"

She looked at me with all seriousness and replied, "Be just as crazy as you are with me."

I laughed because she was right. "Love you to the moon and back. I'll see you at ten," I said as I jumped in my car.

I arrived at the gym and noticed the guys were already there. I leaned over the ring. JJ and King had the chance to observe how Hooks responded with me being there and away. I waited patiently until he was free. He came over and greeted me with a kiss. "Why didn't you tell me we have a date tonight?" I asked.

"I just found out. I guess you booked my calendar before I was able to book yours. Be home and ready by nine fifteen."

I looked down at my watch. It was only a quarter till four. "Okay, I have plenty of time," I said.

I went upstairs and plugged in, changed clothes, and came back to check emails before I got started. Once I was done, I headed back upstairs to my track. Out of nowhere, I felt a body standing over me. I opened my eyes and Hooks was standing there.

"Are you okay?" he asked.

"Why do you ask?" I was deliriously confused.

"Apparently you have been asleep for two hours."

"ASLEEP?" I looked around, spotted a clock, and sure enough it was six PM. "What in the world?"

He jumped, "Is something wrong?"

"No."

"Are you sure?" he questioned.

"How did I fall asleep?"

"I do not know," he laughed. "I imagine you closed your eyes."

"Dang."

"Can you come downstairs?"

"Now?" I asked.

"Yes. If you can please."

I got up and tried to shake it off. As I began to walk with him, I realized I had nothing with me. So I turned back to get my phones, water, and iPod while he waited patiently. Quickly I headed down the stairs after him. He stepped back into the ring. No one told me what to do or said anything. I didn't know what he wanted me to see therefore I stood there watching him throw punches quickly into Kings hand. JJ and Keith stood really close to me. I looked to my left and right like what's up.

"Flow with me," Keith said.

"What are we doing?" I asked since they were acting stranger than normal.

"Shh," JJ said.

Suddenly hands on my back were guiding me. We moved to the other side of the ring. They pushed me so close my toes were touching the base of the ring. I was too tall for the bottom rope, same height as the middle rope and the top rope was way over my head. At this point, I still had no clue as to what was going on and to top it off, I was still sleepy. Each angle he moved I was steered in the same direction.

King switched it up by handing him the rope as I stood directly in front of him then King took his place behind his computer.

"We will try this again tomorrow," JJ said.

Yeah right, I thought to myself. *Try what tomorrow? I wasn't planning on coming here tomorrow.* I looked at JJ and headed up the stairs to try to figure out what I needed to do. I decided I should go home and get ready for my date.

On my way out of the door, I watched as King punched him. Something about it bothered me. In fact, I did not like it. I wasn't sure if I didn't like the fact he was getting hit or because King was the one doing the hitting.

I did not know if I should speak or not. I took my chance, "DW."

"Yeah babe?"

"I'll see you in a little while."

"Are you leaving?" He said in the middle of getting punched and shaking it off.

"Yeah."

"Just like that?" he said as if nothing was going on.

"Just like that."

"Pull up King." When King backed up, he came over and gave me a kiss.

For some reason today his kiss made me feel different. Why, I do not know. What I do know is I rode home on cloud nine. It seemed as soon as I got home and got half way dressed the phone rang from the gate.

He needs to not be prompt all the time, I thought to myself, "Yes."

"Hit the gate."

"Please. You are welcome." I corrected his behavior as I opened the gate.

I ran and opened the door and ran back to finish getting dressed. When he rang the doorbell I called his phone.

"DJ," he answered sensing I was not ready.

"It's open."

This girl insists on tempting me, he thought. "Danielle, are you ready?"

"Yes I am. Chill please. I'm almost done." He was so impatient and prompt. It drives me nuts sometimes.

I came around the corner dressed and ready. I could tell from his expression he was pleased to see me. It was amazing how we both transformed in a matter of seconds.

"Need I say anything?" he said impressed that I was truly ready.

"You can," I encouraged.

"No need."

"What is it?" I questioned.

He leaned in my ear whispering as if the room was full, "You look beautiful."

I blushed, "Thank you."

"Do we have to go?" he asked snidely.

"Sorry and yes," I mumbled as he nibbled my neck.

"You cannot fault me for trying," he said pointing towards the door.

I stepped outside the door. I was not expecting security. Why? I guess I had not put much thought into it. Security and I were going to get tired of each other very quickly.

He could tell from the look on my face I was surprised. "What's wrong?"

"I wasn't expecting Men in Black."

Laughing and shaking his head, "Behave D."

"Ugh," I was disgusted. They officially ruined my mood.

"Promise," he ordered.

"I promise," I mumbled only to pacify him.

"Let's roll," he smiled.

"I can get use to this," I teased.

"What?" he replied.

"Three dates at one time," I said to purposefully annoy him.

"Oh hell naw. Do not get it twisted. You are on a date with me only," he declared pointing to his chest. "They are here working," he pointed to his guys.

"So you say. My story and I am sticking to it."

He looked at the guys, "You all are staying home from now on."

I knew it would work. "Are you hating?"

"I am not. I am just making sure no one else gets it confused. Hey make sure it is clearly evident who she is with tonight. We are good tomorrow and Sunday. Take the day off guys. I appreciate each of you."

I couldn't help myself. I bust out laughing while he was so serious. It sparked conversation the entire ride. As we entered the party people began to speak to us. We agreed earlier we would not be there all night. Everything was beautiful. The food was great and the people were super nice. It was a great party if I must admit.

We sang happy birthday, which was our queue to exit, but it didn't turn out that way. The birthday fellow himself took the microphone and began speaking. He thanked his family, friends, and colleagues. "Now one of my colleagues who continuously adds to my success is Danielle Rose," he said putting me on blast.

Everyone knew I was embarrassed. Randall let me drop my head into his chest. I made a mental note to discuss this with my client later. That was not enough. He continued, "I also want to thank Danielle for bringing a superstar with her to share my birthday."

Bam! Just like that, the heat was off me and turned up on Randall. He threw his hand up to wave at the crowed then threw his hand up like stop it.

"Danielle, how many buildings have we built together?" he asked.

"Nine," I replied with a smile.

"Wow! Nine! Danielle designed my very first building when she was still a student. She has designed every building I own since then. She should have her own building."

"Thank you," I said vey shyly.

"She is awesome. We are much obliged that she brought a date with her tonight to celebrate with me."

He blushed as I leaned in. "I am glad I am not the only one embarrassed," I whispered.

"This is the last function," he said without moving his lips.

"I present to some and introduce to others Hooks Washington. Only Danielle would be the one to bring a Champion Boxer to my birthday party."

"Only the best for the best," I said.

We enjoyed the night. We did exactly as we said we would do. We stayed briefly then left. We all talked the entire way to my house. "Good night DJ."

"Good night sweetheart. I'm sorry you were put out on the spot."

"It's all good. I am use to it," he frowned.

"Get some sleep."

"I love you Randall."

"I love you too," he smiled.

Saturday

I was at the gym by seven AM. Randall and King were running on the treadmills next to the ring. I mumbled, "Good morning," and headed straight upstairs.

"Where are you going?" King shouted. "You are working down here this morning."

"Do not get too comfortable babe. We will not be here long," Randall yelled.

I followed instructions and stayed downstairs. It was a little over an hour when King allowed him down from the treadmill. The entire time he had him running backwards. Once he let him off, he handed him a jump rope. I raced upstairs. Before I could break a sweat Hooks was yelling up the steps.

"Babe, are you ready?"

"I guess so, what's up?" Although I was not. All of my workout plans were disrupted.

"I want to take you to Mikey's and to your friend's new movie."

I laughed aloud. "You can say his name. It's okay. He will not get mad at you. Say it with me, T.I. T.I. TIP. See it is easy. Now you try it."

"I'm taking you to see the movie. I am not saying his name too," he said with disgust.

"YEAH BABY. Today is a good day. TIP here I come."

"Watch yourself. Keep it up and you will find yourself watching some animated PG movie."

"HATER. Can you say that with me? HATER."

He rolled his eyes at me.

"You really do not like TIP huh?"

"I like TIP. I think he is the King of the south. I love his music."

"But?"

"I don't like the fact that you like TIP as much as you do."

"Now the rubber meets the road. We are getting somewhere. I will arrange therapy for you beginning next week," I laughed.

"Yeah right. That will be the last time I am honest and express my feelings to you."

"No worries. I love you more than I love TIP."

He nodded his head, "Now that is what I am talking about. I was a little concerned. I was about to arrange a meeting with TIP to find out if he was your last boyfriend and plan an arm wrestling match."

I reached my hand to touch the back of his head. He jerked it back and smacked my hand.

"Watch it. Don't start with me."

"Sorry, I forgot." We sat and watched the movie hand in hand. There were a few times he covered my eyes. Then the one time he glared at me. "What?" I asked.

With his eyebrows raised, "Why are you looking at the screen like that?"

"Like what?"

"With passion," he whispered.

"Passion?" I asked.

"You are all into it too. You never look at me like that," he said with mock jealousy.

"Sure I do. All the time," *you just do not see it.*

"No you don't," he squeezed my hand.

We continued to watch in silence. I think we both enjoyed the date as much as the movie. Although, he will never agree he was into the movie as much as I was. Afterwards we stopped for smoothies before he took me home.

"Babe, I do not want to leave you but I have to get back to work."

"Aww," I whined. "I would say don't go but I think that would be tempting and torturing you."

"Yes it would," he agreed. "But you can offer and I will let King and JJ wait."

I cut my eyes, "You sure know how to ruin a thought."

"What does that mean?" he asked puzzled.

"You mention King, JJ or Hunter and it ruins every mood."

"You are crazy," he said as he let go of that robust laugh.

"What are we wearing to church tomorrow? I was thinking you would choose."

"Black and white," he said with confidence.

"Done," I agreed. *That was easy*, I thought.

Not wanting to leave he said, "Call me if you need me."

"I will. Have a good workout."

He kissed my neck with passion and said, "I love you D."

I moaned deeply and my breathing became extremely heavy. My neck flopped as if it were broken. In just an instant I lost control. "Hooks," I moaned. I never refer to him as Hooks when speaking to him directly.

"Huh?"

"You need to leave," I managed to say.

"Are you sure?" he uttered while he continued kissing my neck and now my ear.

I moved my arms from around him. "Come on now," I panted.

He laid his face on my neck. Then abruptly he pulled away. "Bye," was all he said.

He got in his car and for the first time I heard him rev his engine up. He sat there for a moment and then hastily backed out of the driveway.

It was still daylight. I watched television for a few hours and then called in an order for a pizza. I caught up on some much needed me time. It was after eleven when he texted.

> You and me tomorrow chilling.

> Is that a date or a command?

> Call it what you want.

> Why don't you call me and ask me?

I did not have the chance to sit the phone down before he was calling. It made me blush. I felt like a fifteen year old again.

"Hello."

"Babe, I know you are going to think I am lying but as much as I enjoy our conversation I am going to lie down."

"Yeah, I do think you are lying. Are you going to the club? Is your boo on the way?"

He laughed. "I knew you would think I was lying. They are killing me and I am truly tired. I am going to not only get in the bed but go to sleep."

Get in the bed? "Is that something unusual?" I asked.

"For me it is. I cannot remember the last time I slept in a bed."

Randall! I screamed on the inside. "We are going to change that real soon."

"I like the sound of that. I am going to try to keep my mind clear right now. I do have to open the church in a few hours," he said.

"Have it your way but I was not speaking in a sexual connotation sir. Your mind is the only one that lives in a gutter."

"Hmm, I do believe I recall someone having a weak moment earlier and asked me to leave. Am I correct or did I misunderstand?"

"Good night Randall."

"Oh, I am back to Randall. Earlier I was Hooks," he laughed. "Good night. I will see you in a few hours."

"I love you," I said quickly.

"Danielle."

"Yes darling."

He sighed, "I love you too."

"No blogging," I ordered.

"Alright," he said without putting up a fight.

I stayed up a little longer watching television but remained on the couch all night. Before I knew it my phone was ringing at 5:00 AM.

Sunday

"Hello," I said in a soft and groggy voice.

"Sleepy head."

"Yes," I whispered.

"Do I need to send Keith?"

"No."

"Are you sure?"

"Yes."

"Are you going to wake up at all today?"

"Yes. In an hour."

"I will call you back then," he said in a hyper tone.

Sure enough in one hour he was calling. "I'm getting up now," I said as soon as I picked up the phone.

"Thanks."

"For?"

"Being patient with me, loving me, being on time and not asking me to snooze you again."

When I arrived at church, Keith met me at the door. I looked around and Deacon Washington was nowhere in sight. For some reason it made me nervous. I had the same feeling I felt a month ago when I would see him. I knew he was there. I knew he was fine. Most of all, today, I knew he was mine. The thought put a smile on my face.

I went to my seat with Keith sitting next to me. I looked around and noticed Deacon peeking in the door soon as praise and worship began. The glimpse of him made my heart flutter. Keith nudged me to get my attention for him.

Without redirecting my attention, "I see him."

"Please acknowledge," he said.

"He will be fine." I could see him out of my peripheral vision. I wondered at that moment if men had peripheral. If so, they never acted like it or used it.

He came down the aisle behind us. He darn near knocked Keith over trying to reach for me. Keith moved up a step, maybe two. Once he was able to get to me, he came in for a hug.

"Good morning beautiful."

"Hey handsome."

"Excuse me," he said to Keith. Keith did not budge. "Switch with me," he said.

Keith shook his head no.

Furious, he walked to his seat. After we sat down Keith spoke through his teeth. "He is angry with me."

I snickered. It got Deacon's attention. He leaned up on his knees.

After service I proceeded directly to the car. Right as Keith's hand touched the door to open it I heard him, "Ms. Danielle," his tone was direct.

I turned around and at the same time someone was calling him. "Deacon Washington."

"Wait a minute," he said not acknowledging the person.

He came and looked Keith right smack in the eyes. "I got this." If looks could kill today would be Keith's death.

"See you Keith," I said.

"You two get real cohesive and think it is funny," he spoke to me but eyeballed Keith.

"That is what you put us together to do. We are trying to be like you and King." I winked at Keith.

"Funny. Wink Keith and you will wear a black eye for a year," he threatened. "Why don't you drive this car much? I love this car," he confessed as he scoped it out.

"I don't know. It's my Sunday car."

He looked around the back to confirm the tag. He shook his head. "Who goes with you when you buy a car?"

"I go by myself," I said frowning.

"Humph," Randall reluctantly replied.

"You are not the only person who likes cars."

Impressed, "I see," he responded. "Remarkable," raising his eyebrows.

"What?"

"It's remarkable you have four awesome cars and a truck you picked out yourself. As much as I love cars, I have none of these in my collection. I do not own a BMW or Porsche and yet you own two of each."

"What? You don't think a girl can go to a dealer and pick out a ride? A car that will pull the brothers and make me look hot and cool all at the same time?"

"I am not worried about that."

"About what?"

"That was your last time picking out a car alone and I will be the last brother you pull."

"Or else what?"

"I will break his legs and knock his eyes out of the sockets," he said calmly.

"Deacon, you are on sacred grounds. Why are you so violent?"

"I am serious. This is what I do you know."

"Seriously, you are crazy and arrogant."

He ignored my statement, "We have a date today."

"Are you asking me or telling me?" He was telling me for the second time.

"I am confirming."

"If that is the case, then yes," I confirmed.

"Three o'clock."

I leaned up and kissed him really quick and suave. He laughed. I was planning on telling him one day how much I love his laugh and I never wanted him to stop laughing.

I laid my clothes out. One thing was for sure, he would certainly be punctual. At 2:53 my home phone rang. I opened the door and noticed immediately he was in the Spyder. He walked up to the door with his hand behind his back. He hugged me with one arm. He gave me a single white rose and a box. I sat them both down and embraced him properly.

He guided me to the couch with our arms still wrapped around each other. He sat on one side and I sat on the other. We talked for hours enjoying each other the entire day. Before long we had grown to know more about each other than we did when he first arrived. It was a fun, simple, easy, and cost free date.

"DJ, I am going to go now."

"Oh," I was surprised.

"I want to be respectful. You know I am on a strict schedule since I am officially training."

"Okay."

"Speaking of training, I will talk to you more in depth this week about it."

"That will be great."

We hugged and solemnly said our goodbyes. As I closed the door my attention was drawn to the rose and box. I put the rose in water and came back to get the box. I opened the box and to my surprise it was a rose and a hook key chain. Not only a keychain, but also the box was full of random keys of all shapes and sizes. I called him immediately.

"What's wrong?" he answered sounding panicked.

"Turn back around."

Not hesitating for a second, he quickly turned around making an illegal U-turn. He ran up to the door leaving the car running. He seemed startled to see me standing in the door.

"What is this?" I asked.

He looked at the box, then back at me, and smirked. "Keys to all my possessions. My heart included."

That did it. I fell on the floor and the keys spilled everywhere. He jumped, thinking something was wrong. Truth is no one had ever been so generous to me. He was not embellishing. These were keys to everything he owned. Every car, his house, his businesses, and I assumed the gym. I stood up and walked in the bathroom. I closed the door. Without hesitation, he followed me.

"I cannot accept this."

"Why?"

"This is serious."

"Yes and I want to show you how serious it is. I could buy you ten cars or ten houses. I could shower you with gifts every hour of every day. But what would that show you? I love you and I want to share what I have with you and show you how much I love you."

"I do not know," I said overwhelmed.

"Tell me Danielle. What do I need to do to show you how much I love you? How do I prove how for real I am? How do I explain how serious this is to me?"

"Just be you. You don't have to buy me anything or give me anything but love, honesty, faithfulness, happiness, and respect. With those things your heart will become audible and speak volumes. It will not only speak to me but to the world." I began to cry.

"DJ; please, tell me why you are crying."

"I can't recall a time I have ever been this happy. I don't want you to ever go away. Don't change. Always have that hearty laugh you have. I love it."

He pulled me up to my feet. "I will do everything in my power to make you happy. Even if it means denying my own happiness as I leave right now so I do not have to torture myself. I do not want to ruin it."

"Go," I said. I was not a man. I didn't understand their physical disposition. What I did understand was being too close to me was too much for him.

"I need to leave before I get in trouble. No working tonight."

"Good night."

WEEK 19

Monday

Today was cool. Not bad for a Monday. It was not too busy and not too slow. Leigh and I had the opportunity to catch up.

I spoke to him only a couple times, early this morning and then before lunch. I knew he was training and wanted to be respectful of his schedule and not blow his phone up. Leigh sent alert reminders of my upcoming engagements. He was doing something at an elementary school this week and I was invited to attend. I was still considering and had not confirmed yet. I left work at an absurd time as usual and went straight to the gym.

As soon as I walked in the door Keith approached me, "Can I talk to you Ms. D?"

He always looks so serious. "Yeah sure," I replied walking past the ring. "Excuse me."

"You are late," he barked.

I gave him a quick up and down glance over. "Do I know you from somewhere?"

"Don't play."

"Yeah, yeah, yeah."

I walked up the stairs, put all my things down, and turned my attention to Keith who was now standing there. "Go ahead."

"King and JJ need your help."

"For?" *They better not start with some silly BS like stay away from him, pull up or back up crap.*

"We have noticed something in his behavior. He is a different person when you are close to him."

"I am not following you."

"When you are close he is calm and much more laid back. When you are not around he is extremely brutal. We have observed his pattern and levels, both are from one extreme to another. We would like to try something to see if we are right. When we are training, we need you to keep him calm. Then there will be times we need you to disappear. We want to record what is happening starting today throughout the rest of this week. This way we will be able to confirm if our theory is correct."

"So what do you want me to do?"

"We need you to sit outside the ring today. Read, send emails, do something. Then we will get you to stand up to the ring and pay close attention. We want to see how his pattern changes."

"Is he aware we are doing this?"

"Not yet. We are trying to confirm before we get him involved."

"Run it," I said glad to be of assistance.

"Okay. Get dressed and do what you need to do up here. In thirty minutes come down and take a seat. Maybe speak to him. We will give you instructions as we go."

I came down forty minutes later. I stood next to Keith. I had my phones and iPod. I had a feeling helping him was not going to get me any exercise this week.

"Check the time on your watch," Keith said.

I looked down.

"Take a mental note of the current time."

"Okay."

"Go stand closer to the ring, but don't say anything. Just observe."

I did it for what seemed to be forever.

JJ came over. "Okay. Now go back to the other side of the ring."

I did as I was instructed and Keith motioned for to me to look at my watch. I looked down and then back at him. He motioned for me to remember. *Will I remember?* I thought to myself.

JJ came over, "Speak to him."

"Hey babe," I said as pleasant and normal as possible.

"Hey."

"Are you good?" I asked.

"Of course."

"Okay. Looking good," I said encouraging him.

JJ led me over to some trainer guy I had never seen before. He was training with someone else when JJ brought me into the middle of their session. Hooks could clearly see me. The guy talked to me and then worked with me for over forty minutes. Every now and then Keith would motion to check the watch, smile, and give a thumbs up. I was probably just as confused as Hooks was. *Am I helping him train or making him jealous?*

Keith called my phone. I looked around the room like why is he calling me.

"Dani Ro."

"Talk. He does not need to know it is me." Keith and I talked like we were not fifteen steps away.

"Laugh hard," he instructed.

I did. I laughed so hard I thought I broke a rib.

"Excuse yourself. Thank him and run up the stairs. Check the time."

I followed the instructions I was given again. Shortly after I arrived upstairs Keith came up carrying a laptop.

As I was watching the monitor Randall's levels definitely showed changes. He worked out differently when I was around. He had the same intensity, however, he was a lot calmer. This revelation was going to require me to train with him all week. Right now, they were finished with me for the night, although, I didn't want to leave until he was finished.

When I managed to get his attention, I motion that I was leaving. He asked for a five minute break. JJ looked at King. King would have said no but I think too many people were around.

"Five minutes only," he snapped.

He had just enough time to walk me to my car and race back inside to abide by the rules.

Tuesday

I'm not sure what was going on but for some reason I felt out of it. I got plenty of sleep and I did not work out yesterday. Call me an emotionalist but I felt drained. All I did yesterday was stand while he threw punches and I am the one drained. What happens when he says come in the ring with me?

I knew exactly what to do to get my blood pumping again. *Stop and get some liquid nitrogen.* It always makes me feel good. It was like a good Word. It could change your mood in a matter of seconds. It worked my soul. I needed it to jumpstart my battery. Today was one of those days.

On my way into the office, I stopped and got Leigh and I a caffeine cocktail. The day was business as usual busting our butts. What other choice did we have? We were crunk up from grande coffees. He called a few times during the morning wanting to see how I was doing. He was good. All I wanted was to see his face and that beautiful smile.

At four Leigh said, "Please, let's call it a day."

"Are you sick?" I asked.

"No, but I am trying to avoid it. I want to get some rest. We have been going and going nonstop. I am going to go have some Leigh time in my bed with a remote tonight. There will not be a laptop nor cellphone.

"I can't believe it."

"I suggest you do the same," Leigh encouraged.

"Well I am on duty at the gym."

"What do you mean?"

"They have discovered Randall trains differently when I am there."

"Ahh, I see. He puts on for his boo. That's what I am talking about Hooks."

"No actually it is the opposite. He is calmer when I am there, which is what they want. They are trying to get him to train at calm levels. Use his head and not get over excited. If you think about it, it makes perfect sense. You don't want to exert too much energy at the wrong time. If you come right out of the gate and fight like crazy in the first three rounds then wear yourself out, you cannot produce for the next nine rounds. King and JJ have his training regimen very organized and technologically enhanced. The watch is monitoring him and other monitors like those he wore at the Georgia Aquarium. They also record everything and are able to decipher his levels at any given punch. It is real interesting. You should come by one day and check it out."

"Has he scheduled a fight yet?"

"No, remember he has not announced it yet. He said he was going to train hard for two months then announce. They are expecting a quick fight immediately afterwards."

"OMG! I cannot wait. I am bound to find a boo in Vegas."

"Bye," I laughed. "I will be at the gym. Call me if you need me."

I walked in the gym with what looked to be enough stuff to move in. I had my workout bag, my handbag, my bag with my computers, and a set of plans under my arms.

Keith greeted me, "Ms. D you are early today. Do you feel okay or did you come to help us?

"I came to help."

Hooks looked around Keith smiling as he hit the punching ball a few more quick repetitions then spoke. "Hey."

"Hey," I responded back.

But he wasn't talking to me. "King," he called out.

King never stopped reading his paper.

"Can someone help take her stuff upstairs since I cannot move."

"You can move. You'll just start over again," King announced from behind his newspaper. "I suggest you help her. She is your girlfriend."

"I got it," I yelled as I got to the steps not wanting him to get in trouble. I took the first set of my things up the steps and left the rest at the bottom.

As I walked back down the steps I heard him ask, "Can I stop?" he confirmed with King.

"Yeah you can and you will start the timer back over." He ran like a four year old who had just been given the okay to leave time out. He had no care that the clock would start over. He met me on the steps and helped me take the rest of my things up. Once we reached the top of the stairs, he gave me a kiss. It was sweaty and salty, but I still liked it.

"Five minutes," King shouted from below.

"That's all I need. I am a three minute man," he yelled back. I raised one eyebrow. He looked at me as if I wasn't supposed to have a problem with his three minutes. He further explained, "I am a three minute man right now but I will get it together. With practice that is. Do you want to practice now?"

I slightly pushed him away and said, "No thank you. You have a date with a hot punching ball."

"Keep me in line," he gave a slight version of the laugh. I am sure he was grateful I did not oblige. "How was your day? It looks like you left early."

"Leigh has had enough. So we left."

"That is a shame she has to tell you when enough is enough."

"Umm, watch it. I do believe the Terminator sitting downstairs has to tell you the same thing."

"So, he's the Terminator now?"

"Sure is," I said with confidence.

"I love it. Speaking of which let me go before he rips the steps off the wall."

"Bye," I sounded like he was never coming back.

"I am not going far."

Once I finished walking, Nate came and got me. We operated the same way. I followed their instructions while they observed, recorded, and compared his levels. Since I arrived early we were able to work out for five hours. I thought this was a considerably long time for both of us, especially when you consider he had been doing it for over ten hours already. If the shoe was on the other foot, I'd be exhausted. However, it was his passion and he did it effortlessly. He loved it. I on the other hand, hated working out. I did it as a way to relieve stress, relax my mind, and subsequently mentally prepare to work harder. I was prepared to leave. As I came down the stairs, I told everyone, "Good night."

"Wait," he ordered.

"Five minutes," King mumbled again.

"I will be back when I get back," he smarted off.

King rose up as if he had the last word. Truth is, he did or he would before the night was over.

"Text me once you get home."

"What time are you leaving?" I asked.

"I may stay here all night. But I have to be asleep by midnight. I have training at three AM."

I frowned at his response, "You know I don't like you staying here all night."

He knew but asked anyway, "Why?"

"You need to get in a bed."

"I have one upstairs. Can I sleep in your bed?"

I rolled my eyes. "Humph. Yeah, I guess so."

"Then that is what I will do."

"Can you get in?"

"I have a key."

"Okay," I said. I took a few seconds and stared at him, "How do you feel?" Knowing he was bruised and possibly with broken bones.

Honestly, without holding back he replied, "I feel like I have been in a fight."

"DUH!"

"My arms are so tired," he said as he rubbed them.

"I will kiss them for you," I said sweetly. He laughed. It made him nervous at the thought. Since I distracted his mind from his sore arms, I quickly left before I aroused other parts of his body. I went home and he, just as he said, stayed at the gym all night.

Wednesday

I called him at four fifty AM. He answered, "Hey babe." His breathing was hard and you could hear the air blowing through the earpiece.

"Hey handsome. How do you feel this morning?"

"The same as last night."

"What can I do?"

"What you said last night will be just fine."

I laughed.

"Are you on the way to the office this early?"

"And you know this. It's meeting Wednesday."

"What does that mean?"

"I give my one on one updates with all departments. Today I am meeting with IT, graphics, and my person that builds my replicas. Leigh and I go over meeting notes, make quick calls to the city, the general contractors, and the owners. I receive updates on where we are, what they need, and the overall progress. It is a time to encourage the ones that are in progress, offer help, or upsell myself if necessary."

"It sounds like a busy day?"

"It is busy but nothing compared to your next few months."

"Thanks for the encouragement."

Why was he thanking me? It was my job to encourage him. "No problem babe. I am going to change these meetings from Wednesday. I find myself saying this every month, but they wear me out and I have got to do something about it. By the time I get to Bible Study I am too pooped to pop. Sometimes my voice is going because my anger is through the roof and I have yelled and cursed everyone I could. Then there are some days so smooth, I don't feel I have done a hard day's work."

"Why do you feel like every day should feel like a hard day? We are going to have a discussion about your career."

He said career. Umm, what did that mean? "Now?"

"Nice try. You know I cannot talk now. Maybe this weekend on our date day."

All I could think of was, *what is this conversation going to be about.* I really didn't need this on my one-on-one day. Besides, that is how my daddy raised me. I remember how hard he worked daily. "You can call me if you need me," was all I replied.

"I will not disturb you."

I was already disturbed with your last comment. "You can. I may need a little help."

"If that is the case, then help will be on the way."

"What time are you picking me up for service?"

It caught him off guard. Normally, I said no to him picking me up. He paused everything. He didn't say a word as he stopped running. King looked back at him standing still. He was trying to understand why, while reminding himself this was the reason he did not want him to get involved with Danielle. Hooks threw up the finger. "What time will you be ready?"

"You tell me what time to be ready?"

The submissive responses absolutely made his day. However, he knew not to get accustomed to it. "I have to be there by six."

"Okay, it's a date. Pick me up at five thirty?"

"It's a date?" he asked trying to remain cool.

"Yep. It's a date."

"How about five fifteen?"

"Don't push your luck buddy."

"Good bye babe."

It went just as it always goes with these one-on-one's every time. You win some you lose some. One of my big projects in Belize was behind. Jamaica was flat out not going well and we won't even discuss the Bahamas. I loved these overseas projects but they were difficult to stay on top of. I could not ride over there and check them out in the middle of the day. The list of stuff was enormous from these three alone. I was disappointed that I did not receive good news from any of those projects. The ones furthest away always seemed to be the ones I cared for the most. I could not hand hold them like I wanted or needed to. I always have a camera on site so I can review the results, but you could not see everything from a camera shot. If it were up to me I would live out of a suitcase until they all were finished, but then I would be neglecting my babies here. Not to mention my Boo. He needed me more than any of these buildings. They could manage without me. He could but did I want him to was the question.

I dropped my face in my hands in an attempt to recharge myself just as the phone rang. It was his ringtone. I hit my earpiece, "Hello."

"What is that tone about?"

"You name it. Engineer hell! Project behind, failed inspection, can't get permit, the structure is incorrect, concrete will not be poured today, the chiller is out another four weeks, the custom air handler would not start up, and the inspector failed the smoke alarm system," I rattled off. Frustrated, "I can go on and on."

"So what do you have to do?"

"Try to fix them."

"You can handle it just not today. We have a date at five fifteen."

"Nice try slick. Five thirty is what I said," I reminded him. "I promise you will be on time," I added for reassurance.

"You are pushing it but we will roll with it today and if I am late then it will be five fifteen from now on."

"Deal." I half-heartedly agreed.

"And what else?"

"Belize is behind. Jamaica and the Bahamas are somewhere in left field."

"They will catch up."

"I know. I am just concerned about when they will catch up. I hope not at the same time you are ready to announce you are fighting. Then my plate will be completely full." Mentally, I was on overload.

"We will cross that bridge when we get there."

"I am afraid it will be more like travel back and forth when the time comes," I continued.

"That's cool too." He could not understand why she was making such a big deal over this.

"I don't want to miss anything. But I may have too." I felt very conflicted at this point.

"Life and death are in the power of the tongue."

"Thank you Deacon. I don't want to miss your big moment and these other moments either."

"If it means that much to you then I won't let you. I promise."

"How do you plan to do that? Stop time Superman?"

He laughed to himself. He never tried to stop time but he did not foresee it being a huge ordeal. "I can coordinate my schedule to match yours and if that does not work, remember I do own a jet." That was as close as he could get to freezing time.

"Oh how could I have forgotten?" I said sarcastically.

"Now that we have all of that taken care of what else is on your mind?" he asked as if he was now her problem solver. He hoped he was anyway.

"I guess all minds and hearts are clear."

"So you say."

"What's on your mind?"

"Let me lick you up and down until you say stop," he sang.

I hollered laughing.

Embarrassed, "Did I say that out loud?"

"Yeah, you did," I was still laughing.

"How embarrassing," he said while putting his head down in mock shame.

"Yes, it is Deacon."

He looked up, clapped his hands together and said, "All minds are clear now that I got that off my chest."

"You need help."

"I know. I have some big fighter dude in my face right now. Let me run. I have a busy day. I will see you at five."

"Five thirty," I yelled. "Tell the Pit Bull to sit it down," I added referring to King.

"Love you."

"Same here," I said.

"Don't do me," he uttered with an attitude.

I knew exactly what he meant, "I love you too."

I left at four fifteen. I did not want to be late. I knew he would be on time as always. Besides, I was thinking of changing my clothes.

I beat him to my house. When he arrived I was changed and ready at five nineteen. *I knew he would be early. Those four minutes probably killed him.* He came in with six roses and tons of baby's breath. He did not even hand them to me when he walked in the house. Instead, he dumped the old ones and replaced them with new ones. *Who told him? Someone is whispering in his ear. Hmm, looks like they have given him Danielle's instruction and how to manual,* I thought. Whoever it was did a good job. He was a quick learner.

"Dani, how was the rest of your day?" he asked.

"How much abuse can one person voluntarily take?"

"You may not want to ask me that," he pulled up his shirt and his body was literally bruised. His entire chest was black and blue. It never dawned on me what he looked like underneath his clothes other than ripped. He was ripped but right now, my focus was on the purple bruises. There was no way you could tell me his ribs were not broken.

"What the hell," I screamed before I knew it.

He put his finger over my mouth, "It's my job babe."

I kissed his finger passionately. He realized where this was going and snatched it back. "I'ma kill them all," he said referring to his team.

I took his hands and observed them. They were bruised and tattered also. His knuckles were as bruised as his chest.

He lifted my chin to look at me, "As long as I know you got my back it is well worth the fight."

I gathered all my stuff as we walked out. He was in the Benz this evening. He popped the trunk while I commenced to getting in the car still visualizing the bruises.

"Danielle."

"I got it," he said.

I knew what he meant. "I will keep them up here with me," referring to my computers.

"Danielle," his tone was soft but it still said don't try me.

I stuck one leg out the door. He came over and held the door open so I could get out and place my computers in the trunk.

We talked all the way to church. When we pulled up he asked, "What time is it?"

"Six o'clock," I said proudly.

"Danielle. Are you going to lie at church?"

"It is," I said smiling and laughing.

"You are correct. It is six but it is also after six. Next week I will be picking you up at five o'clock."

"The devil is a liar. We would have been on time if you were not disputing with me about my bags."

He looked at me with the side eye, handed me the keys, gave me a quick kiss, and ran inside. For a moment I wondered, *do I have time to run down the street to the mall and get perfume.* I did. But I didn't want to push my luck. *What am I going to do for an hour? This is too much idle time for me.* I fidgeted around for a brief moment but I am sure you can guess what I did next. I popped the trunk and walked around to the picnic table and got busy. I realized there was no receptacle. I made a mental note. *The church needs to add some outlets out here.* It was code anyway. Therefore, I took it upon myself to send my electrician over tomorrow.

Twenty minutes later I heard a door move behind me.

"Relentless. Resilient. Unyielding. Irrepressible. Need I go on?"

"Nice vocabulary for a jock. Impressive. I think I got it?"

"This table will be gone next week."

"Mean Deacon. Meanie," I frowned.

"What are you working on?" he leaned over my shoulder to look at my monitor. His breath was on my neck. We were not at the right location for this proximity.

"Trying to see what I can do to get these three projects on the right track. They are hurting me," I griped.

"Hurting what?"

"My brain."

"Relax. They will be fine," he tried to convince me. "You have done your part. No let the tradesmen do their part and God do His part."

"Watch the words you speak," I warned.

"I am a big guy. I can handle it," he smiled.

I laughed, "You are not a big guy." He barely weighed two hundred pounds and it really did not count if fifty of it was sheer muscle.

"We are at church do not make me say something inappropriate."

"Do you boo."

"You continuously try me Danielle. You have twenty more minutes." I was moving my lips mocking him as he spoke. He walked back in the building as he made a mental note to get with Leigh.

Service was good. I had another hour before he was done. I went out to the car and then came back inside. This time I went in the sanctuary and made my way over to a corner on the floor with my laptop plugged in and quickly started working. He found me and shook his head. On the way back to my house, he picked up a smoothie for dinner before he dropped me off.

When he pulled up he got out, opened my door, and said, "Good night."

"You didn't pick me up from the driveway," I reminded him.

Shyly he responded, "I know."

"So why are you dropping me off in the driveway?"

"Trust me."

I got the point. I kissed him good night and walked towards the door.

"Do not forget about tomorrow," he reminded.

"It is on my calendar."

"There will be an entourage. We will pick you up from the office."

"You mean us."

"You are not going to be working?"

"It is a work day?" I challenged.

"We will talk about this on our weekend date." He shook his head and walked back to his car in disgust.

Thursday

I made it my business to be in the office at five. If I was spending the majority of the day out of the office I need to get an early start. I called him on my way.

"Why are you in the car?" he said without a hello, questioning me fiercely.

"I have an event this afternoon; therefore, my day must start a little earlier than normal."

He sighed heavy. He despised her behavior and the lack of safety this early in the morning.

Wait a minute, I thought, "How did you know I was in the car?"

"I know ALL things."

"How is training and running going this morning?" I asked. I really did want to know, but I also wanted to take the focus off me.

"Brutal." *Not to mention you just made it worse by calling and annoying me being in a car at four o'clock in the morning*, he thought.

"It is a piece of cake for you," I encouraged.

"I hope it is worth it."

"Shake that loose."

"I will," he said sourly. "See you at ten fifty."

"Eleven. Good bye," I said quickly before he could respond.

At six thirty AM I called Paige and Sade. We talked until the breath of fresh air arrived. I told Leigh to arrive at her normal time. She came in at seven with an attitude. I knew not to bother her. I didn't understand how people were not morning people. It was puzzling to me.

At about seven twenty eight she finally came alive. She was now a different person from the one that arrived less than thirty minutes prior. It was business as usual and rapid. The velocity was abnormal. We both knew we had a lot to do and a short time to get there.

Leigh's phone rang as she stepped out to take the call in private. *Probably a sales call. She will do anything right now to get away from me which made me chuckle.*

Before I knew it a handsome, I repeat a handsome, young man walked into my office bowing. He was so well trained in such short time. Once again, he had a bundle of roses, removed the old ones and replaced them with the new.

"Are you ready Ms. Rose?"

"I better say yes," however, I was not.

"That would be my advice."

He knew which bags to grab.

"Do I need anything in particular?" Leigh asked me.

"Chargers and water," I told her.

He interrupted, "We are in the van. You do not need anything."

"Does she need to have anything? I am not prepared if so," Leigh informed him.

"She is there for support and encouragement. Why would Vickie let my first event be a speaking engagement to impressionable kids?"

"Second event," I said moving like lighting. "Fight for the cure was the first event," I reminded them.

"Someone is keeping tabs," he joked.

Leigh was frazzled for some reason and I didn't understand why. She also had way more stuff than what I thought we needed. *Sometimes the assistant knows best.*

As soon as we were all settled in the van and entering the freeway he said, "Leigh can you prepare a speech for me really quick?"

She shot a look in Vickie's direction. We all bust out laughing. Her anxiety intensified. "You all are jerks," she said in a don't F with me tone and rolling her eyes.

We enjoyed the hour long ride to Reinhardt College. It was opening day for sports camps. There were over five hundred kids there for the week to enhance the sport of their choice and over ten different sports groups were represented. Wrestling included. He promised he was going to interact with each group individually. He spoke at what I would call a meet and greet pep rally in the gymnasium. We stayed for lunch but of course he didn't eat a single thing. He went to the van and ate. His lunch consisted of nuts and carrot sticks. It was humorous to me. My phone rang uncontrollably. I was glad he got to see it first-hand. When they broke off into their groups we all became interactive. Luckily, Leigh and I are always prepared with our flats.

Keith finally caught up to me. "You will probably need to get a bag to travel with."

"You will not catch me slipping again," I said.

Leigh ended up with the girls and boys track team. I had the cheerleaders, the girls volleyball and boy's and girl's basketball. Everything was well organized to include activities where the kids could win prizes in their group. They loved it. He did as promised and interacted with each group. He did however spend the most time with the football team and wrestlers. He came prepared with a change of clothes so he could physically work with the kids. When he got to my group I was with the girls volleyball team.

"You owe me big time," I said without moving my lips. *Is this what his life is like?*

"I know Vickie texted me last night to tell you to bring a change of clothes. I forgot."

"Dead meat!"

"Sorry. Thanks for your help and support."

I rolled my eyes as I growled at him.

"If this is any consolation prize, you look sexy," he said then quickly ran away.

Dinner was at five. I could not believe they were going to ask me to sit down and eat dinner after I had been sweating. Thank God I always wore a tank top. I had taken my blouse and jacket off during the group activities and played in my tank. So at dinner I took the tank off and washed under my arm pits in the ladies restroom while Keith held the door for me and Leigh. I spray perfume, remade my face, put my blouse and jacket back on and sat at the designated table. He spoke to the kids again while everyone ate except him.

He put me on blast a few times. Well both Leigh and me. He talked about the importance of high school and college while referring to me. He then publically thanked us for getting physical in our suits. "That is what humility, friendship, long suffering, joy, loyalty, patience, and meekness will do. Always work in these fruits of the spirit in every aspect of your life," he continued on. I was impressed. I wanted to ask if he prepared this or if he was speaking off the top of his head. Either way it was on point.

On the way back the crew was hungry. Leigh and I clearly did not follow the rule, if he does not eat then no one eats. Up until now, we had not even noticed that not one person in his crew ate the entire day.

We stopped and broke bread. We were having so much fun I forgot our cars were still at the building. *After a good day like today I just want to be dropped off, cuddle in bed with my boo, and read a good book.*

We got to the building. "DJ get right in the car," he ordered.

"I need to go up. I wasn't expecting to be gone ALL day. That wasn't in the meeting request," I snarled at Vickie.

"You are one hard headed child." He kept walking. I assumed he did not want his crew to see him kiss me.

"What are you doing?"

"I'm going up with you. You have five minutes."

"UGH," I snarled.

"Umm hmm."

Leigh laughed. "Thanks Hooks. Otherwise, we would be in here another hour."

"I hate y'all."

"Hate is such a strong word," Leigh said.

"Oh you're right. I just have strong feelings about what you two are doing to me. Why won't anybody just let me be me?" I questioned not expecting a response.

"Right about here is the where the attitude and tantrum comes in," he announced.

I cut my eyes so tight at him on the elevator. I swear I was momentarily blinded and used ten percent of my brains capacity by confusing it.

"And the horse I rode in on," he snapped back insinuating my look said F you.

Leigh laughed while I stomped off the elevator.

"All the time," Leigh told him referring to my tantrum and feet stomping.

"It's cool. I can deal with it. If this is as bad as it gets then this is gravy. Eventually it will subside."

"I can hear you two you know."

"We know. All of this is repercussion or lack of," he said with pride.

I turned around. "Lack of? UGH! Never mind! Freak! Pervert!"

"It's okay baby. I will fix it for you one day. Be patient with me please. I haven't had any either."

"Deacon! TMI!" Leigh said laughing at the both of us.

"Sorry Leigh you will notice the change immediately. Tongue tied, speechless, coming in late, leaving early, long lunches, smiling all day, and the whole nine yards."

"Talk is cheap," I yelled out interrupting his brag session.

"Get your stuff," he ignored my comment.

"You just make sure to make good on your bragging and be able to back it up," I challenged.

Calmly, he said, "Let's make a deal."

"Run it," I hyped up.

Raising his eyebrows as if he was up to something, he said, "If I do make good then you cut work short at a reasonable hour every day?"

I frowned. "Nope. Don't like it. No deal."

"If you scared then say you scared."

"I'm not. I refuse to compromise work over intimacy."

Confidentially, he said, "We will see."

When we reached the parking deck I drove him around to the front. He got out and came over to my side and kissed me passionately. It was like he was putting on for the cameras. If kisses were rated this one was XXX times two. I do not know if that was for me talking trash or for the cameras that continuously snapped. I think they were all out of the car taking shots. The kiss was just that long and passionate. I will admit I needed a wet wipe after that one.

"Get a room," Vickie shouted.

He stopped. I think I was breathless and my eyes were still closed. "Show is over. I love you go home," he said with pride. "DJ?"

"Huh," I responded coming out of my trance.

"Close your mouth babe. Go home."

I mustered enough energy to say "K," but that was about it.

I drove home in a daze. *What was that about?* He had never kissed me like that before. If I had tonsils he would have touched them. The way he went in, I think he checked my esophagus and cleared my lungs of any particles all at the same time.

He texted first. I forgot to text when I got home, still dazed.

> Are you home?

The noise from the phone startled me and made me jump.

> Yep, in the shower.

I lied. I was on the couch in the dark. The couch was as far as I managed to get.

> What does your day look like tomorrow? I want to do something for you and Leigh.

I agreed.

> Okay.

I thought about it and texted again.

> Oh tomorrow is my jobsite day. I will be there all day.

> We will work it out. Good night.

> Nite nite.

Friday

I jumped up and dressed. Since I was going to be on site all day I could get away with wearing jeans and a tee or tank. I had to get to Krispy Kreme donuts. That was probably the only reason contractors want to ever see me arrive to an unfinished jobsite. The good thing was the sugar rush I will have for the next few hours. The bad thing was I always found flaws and things to be re-done. In the middle of placing my order at Krispy Kreme, he called.

"Hey Champ."

"How did you sleep?"

"Good and you?"

"Brief."

"Why?"

"I had to hit the gym babe. This is grid time."

"You mean to tell me I had to go home and you went to the gym."

"I am training," he smarted.

"Don't smart off mister."

"How is your disposition this morning?"

"About to be the same as it was last night."

"Sensitive or sensual?"

"Shut up!"

"Are you coming by the gym tonight?"

"Don't I always?"

"Cool. You have an appointment when you get there."

"Is it on my calendar?"

"It will be."

"What is it?"

"Can you date me tomorrow and Sunday?"

"So you are going ignore my question?"

He did. "Great. It's three dates then."

"The gym is not considered a date," I scolded. "It is more like work for me and brutality for you."

"Are you sure you are okay with this boxing thing?" He stopped running.

"I am as long as you are healthy and unharmed."

"You would tell me right?"

"I sure would. You did have bruises the other day right?"

"Yes," he regretfully admitted.

"Okay then."

"It's settled, one appointment and two dates. What a great start to the weekend."

Other than earlier this week, he was always so positive. I hope to get that optimism in my spirit. I needed a double portion of what he had.

He called around ten when he had his first break. "Dani Ro."

"What guy is looking at you?"

"No one here. These guys aren't making eye contact with me. They are all too afraid I will fuss, make them change something, or go off. This is the last place you have to worry about someone trying to holler at me. They run from me around here."

He laughed.

"What's up?" I asked taking a break for a second.

"Just finished running and wanted to check on you."

"I'm cool," I said. "Wait a minute. I will have to call you back before I snap. I am looking at some drawings closely."

"I am glad it is not on me."

I worked like crazy. I am not sure which place I worked the hardest. At home, the office, or the jobsite. One thing was for sure, I worked too much. I was glad to be having some sort of life lately though. I smiled at the thought of it. I let down the back of the truck, changed my shoes, and took my shirt off right there on the site and drove off in my tank.

I pulled up to my spot at the gym. I looked at my rose and reminisced. *Who would have ever thought this would be reality?* I sat there daydreaming before getting out of the car. "Enough of the sentiments," I said aloud. "Hey," I greeted as I entered the gym.

"You are needed in the conference room," Sol said.

"Oh yeah?"

"Yes ma'am."

"I will be there once I speak to my honey and put my stuff down."

"I will let them know."

I put my stuff down right then and leaned over the ring. "Excuse me sir, are you here with someone?"

"Ma'am I am busy."

JJ helped me climb in the ring.

"Heels off," King shouted like Oscar the grouch.

I took them off without responding or batting an eye. "Sir, may I speak to you?"

"Ma'am, I am going to have to ask you to leave the ring. My girlfriend will be arriving and I need for you to go."

"I am not interested in your girlfriend. I am interested in you."

"I am not interested ma'am."

I leaned my body up against his. Danny was in the ring with him and immediately backed up. I then kissed his neck and said, "Are you interested now?" He didn't respond. I kissed his ear. "Now?" He didn't respond. I proceeded and kissed his lips over and over and over again. "How about now?"

I broke him. He laid in on me.

"Get a room," King yelled. "Not in my damn ring! He is sweaty and salty. Have some respect for yourselves. You two are disgusting!" Someone snapped a picture. I felt the camcorder in our face. He pushed it back without looking up.

I let go, leaving him hanging. "I thought that would get your attention," I said. By now, I was imagining us intimate on the floor of the ring. I am sure that will encourage him to work hard daily by remembering a moment like that.

"Hey babe," he finally acknowledged me.

"Hey," I said joyfully.

"How was your day?" he snickered.

"Busy and yours?"

Looking at me as if I were naked, "Where is your shirt?"

"I worked like this."

"That's a lie," he mumbled in furry.

"It's in the truck. Why am I needed in the conference room?" I asked frowning.

Matter of factly he said, "I told you that you have a meeting." As if to say, I have already discussed this with you once and will not do it again.

"Really?" I replied to annoy him further.

"Seriously," he cut his eyes sharply at me while I acted as if I missed it.

"Well I will be back. Are they inquiring about the specifications on my Bentley?"

"In your dreams," he held back his laughter.

"Dreams do become reality." I threw my hand up and rolled from under the rope. I gathered my stuff and began walking up stairs.

"You left something in my ring," JJ mumbled almost inaudible.

"What?" I responded letting him know I heard him.

He looked up shocked I heard him and even more shocked I questioned him. "Your shoes."

"I'll be back. Maybe King can borrow them," I threw in.

"Low blow D," Randall jumped in to diffuse the fight which was about to take place.

"Tell him to man up," I insisted talking trash all the way up the stairs. I dropped my things off and came back down to the conference room. I had no clue what I was walking into. It looked like a testing facility.

"Ms. Danielle?"

"Yes," I extended my hand for a handshake.

"I am here to fit you for your earpiece and teach you how to use it."

"Earpiece?" I said louder than anticipated.

"Yes."

I raised an eyebrow.

"We decided we will allow you to have one also," Keith added so graciously.

"Wow. Allow. That is so kind of you all," I said sarcastically.

"Which ear would you prefer?"

This went on for over an hour. It had to be molded and then we had to wait for it to dry. They showed me how to insert it, the hand piece, the battery pack, and then how to use it. Until now, I did not think it would be so difficult.

I pushed the button before given instructions. "Testing one two three testing. My mic sounds nice check one. My mic sounds nice check two. Microphone check one two one two. Here we go. Here we go. No, no, no, no, no, no he didn't."

"We can hear you," King yelled in total disgust and irritation.

I jumped. It was in my ear. "My bad." I held the button down on purpose. "He is always so contrary. Never mind him. He is like all the people on the yellow brick road. The lion, tin man, and the scarecrow. He has no heart, no brain, and no courage, but he is real strong."

"I can still hear you," he warned.

"I am learning how to work it." *Checkmate*, I thought to myself. I knew he could hear me and I said it purposefully. Keith motioned for me to stop playing. After we perfected it I insisted on keeping it in. I walked back out to the common area.

"Are you ready babe?" Randall said as if we were on a secret mission.

"Yep, I feel like Men in Black. Do I get to wear it in church too?"

"Sorry to disappoint you," his voice was stern as if there was no way I could convince him otherwise.

Relentlessly I continued, "Where do I get to wear it?"

"Here."

"Here?" I shouted.

"I don't know. It is only if you need it. We will see."

"Well that's no fun."

"From what I understand you are having fun with it, but it is not a toy Danielle," he said then punched the ball extremely hard. All I could hear was the ball rapidly moving back and forth from his one punch.

"Not yet," I said. I was waiting to really see what this gadget could do.

"I heard you were in concert."

"The headliner has not begun."

I ran upstairs and got my iPod. I plugged it in the sound system and scrolled down to Dougie Fresh. I blared it over the speakers. I do not think those speakers had ever heard such volume. I was getting crunk. As soon as the words sang, I sang right along with them.

You could tell they were all physically tired. They were each taking turns with three minute drills in the ring. There was no boxing going on however. Even I could see that. There was a lot of holding and dancing around and then holding again.

"Y'all finished dancing yet?"

"Not yet," Randall said leaning on his opponent.

"Well what are you all doing? Dancing or playing because it surely is not boxing?"

"Come in and join us," he smarted back.

"I could knock all of you out right now."

"Let's see," he encouraged still resting his weight on the man in the ring with him.

"Nope, I am going to enjoy my music."

It played and played and played over again. Finally someone yelled "Ms. D!"

"Tell them to stop playing," I pointed to the ring. "Otherwise I am going to keep playing the same song over and over again and singing out loud." Most of them had their earpieces hanging down from their ear by this point. It didn't matter. I was still singing loud enough for everyone to hear me. I was loud, wrong, and off key but I knew all the words and that is what mattered.

JJ climbed out of the ring and tried to explain to me what they were doing. I looked so uninterested. "Help me in," I sighed. JJ did. "Excuse me," touching Danny on his shoulder. "I got this."

"Your hands are not taped and you don't have on gloves. If you attempt to punch me you will break your hand or wrist."

"I don't need any. Neither of you are throwing punches. Let me show you what you are doing." I showed them what I saw. "I see one of these things. An inexperienced fighter, a scared fighter, a tired fighter, or a weak fighter. Which one is it?"

Hooks was insulted, "NEITHER!"

"Well piss or get off the pot."

Danny stepped back up. Randall swung and laid him on the mat immediately. Nate swung next. He ducked, swung back, and Nate was down. Finally, King jumped in and down he went.

I threw my hands up. "Can we go now?"

"Bye," King said as if he was putting us out.

"I have been kicked out of better places. At least the people are standing when they put me out." I leaned over him and repeated in my best Chris Tucker voice, "You got knocked the hell out." I wasn't going to ever win King as a friend or fan so what the hell. Why not? My mouth had gotten me in trouble with him again. He jumped up like he was going to kick my butt.

"Alright kids," Randall said as we tap danced on his last nerve. "Let's find somewhere to take you." He pointed at me, "Out of the ring."

"Checkmate," I said as I was being pulled backwards pointing my finger at King as if we had really been in a fight with each other.

"Enough," Randall said to break up the taunting. "Where are we going?"

"I do not know." I pointed at King again and Randall slapped my finger down giving me a stern look.

"Where do you want to go?"

"You can go home and get some rest."

Exhausted, he did not put up a fight. "I will pick you up tomorrow for breakfast and we will hang out."

Still side eyeing King, "Cool."

We got in our cars. I decided to go and hang out with Sissie and the niece for a little while. I did not stay too long. I did have my stand in hair appointment in the morning after all.

I texted him when I got home. He was not asleep and immediately responded.

> I love you.

I tried my best not to work. No such luck. Before I knew it I was logging on. I forced myself to stop and relax. *What is good for the goose is good from the gander.* I thought to myself. Finally, I drifted off to sleep on the couch.

Saturday

I was at the gym at five AM. I was going to get some weights in and maybe thirty minutes of walking before I went to the salon. I had been there over twenty minutes when BJ walked up.

"Ms. D, Hooks is going to be upset when he walks in and you are here this early."

"I will be gone by the time he gets here."

"You better be. I am not taking the heat. Why are you here anyway?"

"Working out," as if he could not see that.

"You have one hour."

"K," I replied, although I was tired of being given instructions and ultimatums.

Nevertheless, I finished walking the track and jumped in the shower. As I was pulling off the lot he called.

"Hello."

"Hey babe."

"Hey you."

"What time will you be leaving the salon?"

"Can I call you when I am on my way? I am guessing after eight."

"Okay, I will pick you up from the house."

He said THE house not your house. "Okay babe."

"Miss you."

"Oh my God," King chimed in.

"HATER," he snapped back.

I was at the salon and just about to lay my head back in the bowl when he called again. "Heller."

"Danielle," he said extremely stern.

"Snitches get stitches," I said forceful knowing his tone meant someone ratted me out.

"Goodbye."

"Bye babe. Love you."

"Umm, Dani did I just hear you say you love someone?" Tammy, my stylist checked.

"No you did not. Mind your own business."

"Oh mami. This is my business. Come on and give up the details girl."

"You of all people. Child please. Never!"

"Why not D?" she whined.

"You talk too much that's why."

She smacked her lips in disappointment. It would be on headline news if I told her. I was on schedule just as I figured. I was walking out of the door at fifteen after eight. I called him while moving towards the car.

He answered, "Yes hard headed."

"You are wrong. No one said anything about not going to the gym today."

"I thought it was understood."

"Yeah me too. That I would work out first."

"I beg to differ."

"Oh, it is neither here nor there. Shall I see you shortly handsome?" I asked trying to get the heat off me.

"Clever."

"You are handsome."

He gave up the laugh I loved so much. "Yes, I will see you shortly. By the way, your BFF is not happy. I guess I should have cleared it with him before I asked you on a date. He is pissed we did not finish yesterday and now I am leaving early. I cannot make everyone happy at the exact moment they want me to."

"It is hard being married to the mob."

"I do not know what to say about you two. I am going to stay out of it. You two be respectful, hands off, and above the belt then I will let you two bicker as much as you want."

"Thank you."

"What? That is not the response I was expecting. I see now you two like this
nonsense. You like insulting him and he likes pushing your buttons. You all will not drive me crazy."

"Does it bother you?" I sighed, "If so I will suck it up and behave. Even it if kills me."

"Bother me? I am not sure I would describe it as that but I do want you two to get alone. You will be spending a lot of time together. I cannot understand why you do not. The bickering comes out of nowhere and I do not know what to do. I can talk until I am blue in the face, send you two to your corners, or point you to scripture but it would be like preaching to the choir. I try not to get in it. It does not seem to bother either of you a bit."

"It doesn't bother me. I do feel like he doesn't particularly care for me, but at the same time, I don't think it is personal. To be honest, I do not think he would care for any female in your life. Male either for that matter. Male as in a guy friend like Trevor," I clarified. "I think he wants your mind clear. I'm not sure if he irritates me intentionally thinking it will make me go away or to see how much I can take. To see how tough my skin is. But please be advised if I felt he was going too far, being disrespectful or out of line, you would know it. Because then my blows would certainly be below the belt."

"No blows below the belt. If you think you need to then get me involved."

"Yes Big Daddy."

This put a smile on his face. "Big Daddy will handle it."

Shortly after we disconnected he was buzzing from the gate. I was standing on the steps by the time he pulled up. He pulled up like he was about to do a drive by. *Is he on the phone with a broad? Did I catch him off guard by being outside? Or is the Dani stance putting him in a trance?* Yep, I had the stance on.

He pulled up. I did not move. I let him get out the car to walk around and greet me. I pecked his lips.

"Are you ready?"

"Yes." We rode and talked all the way to Mikey's. Once we got there, we did our courtesies, ordered, and went to our booth.

"By the way, I need to talk to your guys about this security project I am working on."

"What about it?"

'I need to brainstorm some ideas. The company is a security technology company. They have leased previously but now are in the process of building their first building. The building will also serve as a showroom for their customers. I have a lot of information from them already and also from the Casinos I have done. However, I was thinking you have experience with a lot of security because of your profession, the church, your home, and family. I also know your guys are a wealth of knowledge."

"Can we talk about it tomorrow or once we are back to the house?"

"Yes, that is fine."

"Do you love your job?" he wondered.

"Kind of."

"Understatement," he retorted.

"You might be right. I love it. I want to be partner one day."

"Why?"

"Because I have worked hard. I have bust my butt. I give two hundred percent. I deserve it."

"Why not own your own firm?"

"You have to have money and clients," I answered sincerely.

"I think you have enough of both," he laughed.

"I am glad you have confidence in me but I do not have enough of either. Money, clients or confidence."

"Yes you do. You have all you need. You have the good Lord and me. Tell me why you like your job?"

"I have drawn my entire life. I think my mama has every drawing I have ever done."

"Speaking of which, when am I going to meet your mother?"

"Oh no! You are not ready to meet Mama Rose yet."

"What?" he asked sounding surprised.

"She knows about you."

"I didn't ask you if she knew about me. Why can't I meet her?"

"You are going to catch HE double hockey sticks. I would do better bringing a thug home."

"I could have easily been one. Tre and I barely escaped that option."

"A fighter? I bring a heavy weight fighter home. Come on! You know you are getting the lecture of all times. My Mama ain't nothing nice."

"Really?"

"HECK YEAH!"

He laughed sarcastically, "Imagine that."

I was serious. "You would get a lecture for hours. I would leave you there and come back later to get you. It would go something like this. Let me tell you one thing Mr. Hooks. You lay one hand on my baby and that will be one fight you will lose. I will kill you. That may very well be all she says. If so, stay on guard cause I can tell you now, it ain't over until Mama Rose sings. You will know when it is over because she will then try to feed you. Oh my goodness, I just thought of something. I don't know how on earth you are going to turn her down because that would definitely be rude and unacceptable. Maybe I can use that as the excuse. You can't eat because of your diet and training restrictions so therefore I can't introduce you. Does that work?"

"I may need to meet her on the side of the ring so I can get hyped up before the fight."

"You may be right." We both laughed at me being so terrified to introduce him to my Mama.

"Why won't you do it?"

"Do what Randall?"

"Open your own firm."

"That is a major dream. I am working towards the goal. Thank you for your
support and encouragement."

"I offered more than words of wisdom. I offered the opportunity to start your own firm. Give me an approximate number and Scholessenbloum and I will make it happen."

"Thanks for the offer but my rule is if I can't pay for it I wait for it. I want to be in decency and in order. He will send and set me when the time is right."

"Call me first when you are ready."

Is he really serious? "Will do."

"I thought you had some really big project going on?"

"I do. I have some big jobs going on right now local, out of state and out of the county. But when they are over, they are over. They may not need me again for another year, five or ten years. Who is to say they will come with me if I leave and not stay loyal to the firm?"

"Step out when you are ready. I am sure they will follow you."

He was not going to let this go. "Thanks."

"So tell me how do you feel about marriage and kids?"

I laughed. "Overrated." He wasn't expecting that answer. "I'm kidding. I think it is beautiful as long as it is with the right person."

"Do not look at me. I am not a good example," he said ashamed of how his first marriage turned out.

I tried to encourage him. "It can be used for good."

Confused, he asked, "Like what?"

"Umm. Don't know?"

Wishing he could erase his past, "Yeah tell me. Help me out please. I need clarity on this goof up."

"Well, now you know what not to do."

We both laughed.

"I think I have learned enough to know what to do the next time."

I snuck a question in, "Would you ever do it again?" He didn't look up from his glass. I was wondering if I said something wrong. There was a long strange silence, almost like the silence surrounding death.

"I plan too," he finally mumbled continuing to look down.

I missed what he said, "Say what?"

"Yes."

"Yes?" *What is he talking about?*

"Yes, I plan on marrying you," he said like the confident Hooks I know. I choked on my water. Now the silence was like double death.

Uncomfortable at the silence, "Only if you are interested."

I smiled.

"Did that surprise you?"

"Kind of," I confessed.

"Why?"

"Because you are serious." I knew from his tone he was indeed serious.

"Yes, I am. I would ask you to marry me today but I am afraid you may say no."

"Really?" *Was he serious? Did he think I would say no?*

"Yes."

"So what's your game plan?"

"I am planning on dating you until I think you are ready."

I am ready! I thought to myself. "Ready for what?"

"For me to propose."

"How will you know?"

"Once you are comfortable I will know."

"Comfortable with what?"

"Me, boxing, my world, everything."

"Then what?" I asked.

"That will be my confirmation. It will be time for me to ask for your hand in marriage," he said.

"How will I know you are ready?" I asked curiously.

"I think you knew it the moment you met me," he said with confidence.

I hated the fact that he was right. "Did I miss something?" I questioned.

"Yeah, how desperate I was when you met me," he noted.

"You still are."

It was the perfect ice breaker needed for the moment to get us to laugh.

"There is some unfinished business we have also," he said sharply.

He was springing too much on me at one time. *What next?* "Like?" I asked.

"Like you need to meet my son," he waited for my reaction and continued, "Besides, you won't let me meet your mother."

Financing me a firm, meeting my mother, marrying me, and meeting his son? None of this is happening any time soon. "Not ready," was all I said.

"I'm not ready or you are not ready?"

"Both," I was really feeling nervous now.

Sincerely he asked, "When do you think you will be ready?"

"I am not sure but I know it is important to you."

"I do not want to force you. Let me know when you are ready," he said hoping it would be soon.

"I don't know when that will be," I replied honestly.

"What will be easy for you?"

"I don't know." I placed my hands over my face both embarrassed and uncomfortable.

"You tell me when you want to meet him. Whatever makes you at ease. You can meet at church, at my house, at the gym, at your house, or wherever. You name it."

"Tell me about RJ."

He instantly lit up with excitement. I have never seen him shine other than when he found out he could fight. This kid was his world. I liked that it made him light up like this. I let him talk as long as he wanted.

"We can meet out," I said.

"Huh?"

"I will meet him out." How could I refuse? He wanted me to be a part of something that was special and important to him.

"DJ, do not push yourself because of me. We have nothing but time." He was excited she reconsidered.

"Make the date," I said with confidence although I wasn't feeling so confident. *Come on Dani, he is a kid. How much damage can a kid do? Oh goodness. Why would I ask that? Sade is a kid and she can wreak havoc in one sentence. This might be a bad idea after all. A very bad idea,* my mind raced.

"Now that we are on the subject of kids. How do you feel about them?" he probed.

"They are bad, stinky, whinny, hardheaded crumb snatchers."

"Don't hold back. Tell me exactly how you feel."

"They alright," I said raising my shoulders.

"Seriously?" he laughed knowing I was joking.

"Danielle, loves the kids. Especially, when you can give them back."

"I will ask you again. How do you feel about having kids?"

"Of my own?"

He laughed my laugh. "Yes."

"I will order one of each, potty trained, decent hair, polite, high IQ, athletic, and healthy. I will make a list for the other details."

"You do know it does not work like that right?"

"I know the stork does not deliver them. DUH! I draw them up and they get incubated at the baby incubation center I designed. When they hatch into potty trained three year olds you'll be notified to come pick them up," I retorted proudly.

"DJ," he yelled.

"Oh, you have to write a check to get them released," I added.

"Danielle!"

I got serious, "I guess I never thought about it."

"I am asking you to think about it."

"Okay," I said reluctantly.

"I want to know if you want to have kids. That is an important conversation we need to have."

I knew the answer then. However, I was not about to freely give up the information right now. It was too soon. I wanted kids. More than two. I wanted his kids but I could not muster up enough in me to reveal this to him. Not yet anyway.

"Think about it," his voice pleaded. I knew this was a serious matter to him.

"How does it feel to have Hunter as your best friend?" I asked. "A prominent pastor of a mega church. He has grown and done so much in so little time."

"He feels it is as difficult as I feel."

"What do you mean?"

"He feels the heat of pastoring a mega church just as I feel it for him and from him. It is not as easy as people think it is. There are times when I have to make an appointment to talk to my best friend. It is crazy because he also feels the same of my career. Sometimes he has to make an appointment and has even had to travel across the country to talk to me. It is a small challenge, but we both love and respect what the other does. His warfare is not carnal, however, mine is."

Digesting his response, I broke the awkward silence, "What are you wearing?"

"We are wearing our black suits, white shirts, and deacon ties."

"So how will I know which one you are?"

"I will be the one staring at you," he said sweetly.

"Watch it. My boyfriend is the jealous type who likes to fight."

Sunday

He looked extremely handsome. I do not know if I liked him better in a three piece suit or in his boxers. It was a tough decision. Once he sat down, I noticed it. *What in the whole wide world?* I could not believe my eyes. He was wearing a ten carat ring that was blinding everyone on my side. Immediately it pissed me off. I could not concentrate. I kept thinking, *Danielle get it together. Why is he wearing his wedding band? What was he thinking?* I was angry and my emotions were getting the best of me. *If it were not for knowing Keith would be on my heels following me, I would walk out right now. What in the hell is that on his damn finger? I knew I should not have gotten involved with anyone at church of all places.* Then a Deacon. Deacon James flashed back in my mind. My inside laughed but on the outside I remained the same.

Keith shrugged my shoulder to get my attention. I looked up furiously with my arms folded across my chest and slouched in my seat pouting like a five year old.

"Sit up and unfold your arms," Keith muttered reminding me of Mama Rose.

I sat up tall, sighed, and smacked my lips. Years ago that alone would have gotten me pinched and popped in the mouth.

Keith spoke out of his teeth, "Is there a problem?" Rather rudely I must admit.

"Yes there is."

"Hold it until Hunter is finished preaching," Keith demanded.

I crossed my legs and turned my back like a defiant little kid. I sat like this during the entire message. *"Get behind thee Satan,"* I said to myself and closed my eyes but it was too late I had let him in.

Keith nudged me throughout the entire service. I never looked his way other than to look at the beautiful ring sparkling on Deacon Washington's ring finger. It was lovely but I did not want him to wear it ever again.

Deacon Washington stood to pick up the offering from the steps. As he approached me he purposely knocked my legs from being crossed. Keith pinned his elbow in my arm as punishment. No one knew what ticked me off. Deacon smirked. He didn't know what was wrong but he knew right now he had the best of me.

Normally Keith did no touching in service. He was on duty. He did not hug, hold hands or close his eyes. Today, he quickly took my hand. Almost too quickly. As we held hands for the benediction it felt like he tried to break mine. I did not squirm at all. However, my squirm meter was off the chart. Once he let my hand go it was numb. All I could think was, *did this dude just break my hand.* At that point, I really did not care I was glad he let it go.

"I don't know what your problem is but get it together now. Act like you have some sense. You have been a butt since service began," he said like he was somebody's daddy looking me dead in the eyes.

I huffed, "Good day," and I walked off going directly to my car. I was pulling the gear into drive when someone or something almost broke my glass. I looked over and it was Randall with Keith right behind him. Keith was speaking into his wrist. I rolled down my window. They were double-teaming me.

Keith hopped in the passenger side, "What is your problem?"

I looked at him with the ghetto girl look. "Honey you might want to back up this ain't what you want," I babbled to Keith.

"Danielle, what's wrong?" Deacon asked calmly.

"I have a problem with you," I said pointing at him with much attitude.

He squatted down on the side of my door. I could have choked the crap out of him right then, right there, and then drag him out of the parking lot for good measure. "Let's work it out." It was not a question.

"Can we talk alone?" I looked at Keith.

Randall pushed my chest back with the hand wearing the ring and looked at Keith who looked like he was not going anywhere. "I think I have this under control."

Keith opened the door but never stepped out of the car.

Annoyed, I asked, "Can we talk when you are done?"

"Sure," he said in an even more peaceful tone than before. "I will be right over."

"Fine."

"Be safe. I love you my dear," he leaned in and kissed my cheek while the ring sparkled on my steering wheel so vibrantly. I literally felt sick.

I began to pull off when Keith tapped my window. "Ms. D do we need to talk?"

"No!"

Looking around making sure no one was witnessing, "I think we do."

"I need to speak to him first," I barked.

"I expect a call. FYI today will be the last time you will have bad behavior in service. We should have discussed what was bothering you before we entered the sanctuary. We could have resolved the issue. Now I am going to get my butt chewed because of your nonsense this morning." He looked pissed.

"FYI, it didn't happen until we were already in the sanctuary. Do not worry about it. I will handle your butt chewing. I will take one for the team. Or the so called team, the ex team, or whatever you want to call it."

"I have gotten half of it already," he replied.

I felt bad. "I will take care of it. I'll call you later." I made it a few feet down the street and had to pull over quickly. I got sick right there on the side of the road.

He ripped Keith a new one as soon as I pulled off. "What is wrong with her?" He asked while standing in Keith's face demanding an answer. An answer that Keith certainly did not have.

"I do not know."

"What do you mean you do not know? It is your job to know these things. You are supposed to be able to handle her and know what she is thinking at all times. JJ is reviewing her levels to see exactly when they elevated."

"She said it happened in the sanctuary," Keith informed him.

"You were with her."

"She was fine when we entered." Thinking to himself, *you were with her too.*

"What do I pay you for? To be her BFF. Do you go get nails and feet done together and go shoe shopping too?" He waited for a response from Keith. There was none. "Now I have to go do your job and mine too. I leave you two alone for ten minutes in the sanctuary and all hell breaks loose. I am taking you off." He was pissed rattling the change in his pocket as he slowly walked back in the church trying to cool down.

"Off what?"

"Duty!" he said not looking back. "Indefinitely!"

Keith did not panic. He remained calm. He stopped by the tape ministry and purchased ten DVD's. He threw the cash on the counter. He went to the video room, King and Randall were both already there when he got there. They were playing and replaying the sanctuary scene. They could see when her demeanor changed but they could not determine the reason why. They played and rewound several times to no avail.

"We are not going to figure it out. Let's go cross the line of fire," Deacon said.

"Do you need me?" Keith asked.

He walked out of the door ignoring Keith. He instantly thought, *how rude,* then turned back to respond to Keith. "If this doesn't get right your tail is on the line. Stay here until I get back," he barked.

He drove directly over to her house. He rang her at the gate. She did not speak as the gate opened. He sat there for a moment. *What was going on?* This was the last thing he wanted to deal with period, much less on a Sunday.

When he got to the door it was open wide. He walked in calling out, "Hey babe." She did not answer.

She could hear his feet as she took her pearls off. He went right in the bathroom and helped her. Then he placed his arms around her waist and turned her around as he sat on the counter. "What's wrong?" his tone was soft and gentle.

She took her earrings off.

"You promised Danielle," he stayed focused although he was annoyed.

"Promised what?" she asked calmly.

He thought, *this is good. Her tone was right.* "You promised we would never keep secrets. You would talk to me."

"What are you wearing?" She could not believe it herself. Just that quick she was transforming back into the person she put away a long time ago.

He raised his eyebrows. It caught him off guard. He was not expecting that. He looked down at himself and could not figure it out. "I am not sure I follow you."

She tried to pull his arm from around her waist but he would not let go. "Let go!"

"I will not."

"Fine! F it then!"

He let go with both hands and held them in the air as if he was surrendering.

She placed his hand in front of his face, "What?"

"What is that on your finger?"

"My ring."

"No sh*t Sherlock. Ray Charles can see that. From another country I might add."

"Watch your mouth Danielle," he had enough of her profanity.

"Why are you wearing it?"

"What?" he asked clueless.

"The band?"

"What band?"

"Are you crazy?"

"I'm a guy. I can't keep up. This is spinning out of control. I do not know what you are talking about Danielle. You have to speak clear and direct to me. Otherwise I do not get it."

"Alright," I took his hand. "Why are you wearing this ring on this finger on this day?"

What? "I am still confused DJ?"

"Why are you wearing your wedding band?"

He laughed as she walked away. He took the ring off and placed it in her drawer.

He caught up to her in the hall, "Is that what this tirade is about?"

She did not respond.

He held his hand up. "That is not my wedding band. It is a ring I bought when Tre and I turned thirty along with this cross." He pulled a chain from under his shirt. "I gave him one too. We wear them on first Sunday. He had his on his right hand. I would normally have mine on my right hand too but my knuckles are swollen from training and I could not get it on that finger this morning. If it bothers you I won't wear it again. You can watch the DVD and see Tre has one just like it. I am surprised you didn't notice it. You are much more observant to have missed it. But I guess you were too busy pouting unnecessarily about mine to notice his."

I relaxed my shoulders.

"Do you think I would ever wear a band again that might be representative of my marriage to Tameka?"

I dropped my head.

"Answer me?" he asked calmly.

"I don't know?" I said in a harsh tone.

"You don't know?" he raised his voice. "You should. Why would I need to wear a band? Am I married? What would I be proving and who would I be proving something to?"

"Those were the questions I wanted answers to."

"Look DJ, you do not ever have to worry about me reliving that era. I love you and I'm not interested. I am not looking for, looking at, or pursuing anyone else."

"Sorry." Now I am embarrassed.

"Do you love me?" he tilted my head up so he could see my face.

I nodded.

He leaned in. "What did you say baby?" He spoke in the tone I normally use.

"Yes I love you Randall and I am sorry. I should have stayed calm and asked you but I let my emotions get the best of me."

"Trust me Danielle. Have I ever hurt you before?"

"No." *No, you have not but someone else surely did.*

"I do not plan to ever hurt you."

"I'm so sorry."

"Who loves you?"

I pointed my finger at his chest as he kissed me.

"I have to go back to the church. They are waiting on me," he snickered, shook his head and then laughed. "I will be back. Rest your nerves. Your levels are high. Getting me all worked up and making me curse Keith out. Now I have to apologize and hire him back. Women are emotional troublemakers."

"You fired him?" *Oh boy.* I just shook my head.

He looked at me while running down the front steps like that was the dumbest question he had ever heard.

"I will call Keith."

"You do that. Tell him it is your fault and he is still responsible for you, crazy and all."

I laid my head on the wall and laughed at myself while pulling out my phone to call Keith.

"Ms. D," he answered on the first ring.

"Hey Keith."

"What's up?"

"I think the coast is clear."

"So my head is off the guillotine?"

"I do believe so."

"Should I expect him to come in and blow up on me again?"

"No. I think you are fine. It is my fault you have received a tongue lashing. I do apologize."

"Should I even ask why I was lashed out on in the first place?"

"You can ask him. I am sure he will tell you."

"Is he pissed?"

"I think he is fine. He didn't seem to be when he left."

Hesitantly Keith said, "I shall see in a few minutes."

"It is all my fault. I over reacted. Sorry."

"As long as you all have this straight and I can show up to work tomorrow."

"I am positive you can show up tomorrow. I am sorry I got you fired even if it was for a few hours." I really felt bad. *This is why I do not need anyone to be my sidekick. There is no telling what kind of madness I will get them into. I am dangerous enough alone. I do not need any help.*

"So you know the rules from now on?"

"I do not, but I am sure I am about to find out," I said.

"We will set some later, but for now let's just agree to try and stay on the same page. Before you lose it again we can discuss what is going on. I may have the answer to squash the issue before it is full blown," Keith said in his monotone.

Cheerfully I replied, "You are absolutely correct. You could have squashed this in one simple answer."

"You will learn."

"The hard way as always. That's the Danielle way." I said chirpy as if it was a good thing.

"Don't we all."

"Call me if you have any problems from the raging bull," I referred to Randall.

Deacon Washington ran back in the church. "Deac."

"Yes," he looked and saw it was Keith calling out to him. "Walk with me."

"You mean run."

"I am walking it is just fast. Really fast."

Wondering why he was still moving so fast, "Are you good?" Keith asked.

Shaking his head, "Yeah. Women."

"Is that good or bad?"

"I think I forgot. They are…They are…I do not know the word. Sensitive. Over reactive. Hard headed. You can't tell any of them anything. Women."

"So what's the deal?"

Hooks held his hand up to answer Keith's question.

"What?"

He flashed his hand again.

Confused Keith stated, "I am not getting it."

"The ring."

"What ring?"

"The thirty ring."

"Where is it?"

"At Danielle's."

"What about it?"

"She assumed it was my wedding band."

"And?"

"She took offense to it." He was busy moving around the church, always about his father's business.

Shocked Keith asked, "Oh yeah?"

"Yeah."

"Why would she do that?"

"She thought it was disrespectful?"

Keith was really expecting an answer. "Or she has deeper feelings. Or maybe the relationship is going to a different level. What's the deal Hooks?"

"We are simply dating? Nothing like what you are thinking."

"Is that what you say? Or is that what she says?" Keith probed.

"We both agree."

"It seems a little more than that to me."

"Who asked you?" Hooks wondered if Keith knew more coming directly from Danielle.

"No one had to ask me. For Ms. D to get that pissed and make an assumption over a ring. Say what you want but it sounds like a serious relationship to me."

He stopped moving around and engulfed himself in thought. He did want it to be more. He hoped it was more. He had not really had a chance to think about it but Keith did have a good point. Maybe she did have stronger feelings than he realized. Maybe this was a positive sign. Was her reaction a call for more? Was she expressing deeper feelings? Was this a sign he overlooked? Should he make an assumption or should he read it the way she gave it? Why was she so upset? What did this really mean? He felt the sudden need to spend some time thinking.

Keith waited for Hooks to respond. "Back to earth," he said.

"I heard you man. I am ignoring you." He really was not ignoring him. He was caught up in his own thoughts.

They finished up at the church and prepared to leave. He decided not to go to the gym. He wanted to go sit and think. The gym was always there and he could go there any time of the day or night. After all it was his gym. Right now, he needed private time. "I am about to take it to the house," he said just as his phone rang. "Yeah," he answered.

"Wow, that's how you greet me now?"

"Never. I am sorry. Hold on a minute. I'm jetting dudes. I'll hit back later."

"Love calls?" The guys snickered.

He ignored them and their smart comments and walked to the Phantom while unloosening his tie. Once inside the car he unmuted the line. "Sorry about that." He took his jacket off and laid it in the backseat and threw his tie in the seat next to him.

"You think you are so slick. Why do you insist getting on my bad side today?"

My words were like a punch to the face. It caught him off guard. Up until this point, he had been trying his best to remain calm. He laid his head back on the seat. He wanted to scream, *what are you talking about now?* Thankfully, he was wiser than his instincts and simply replied, "What did I do this time?" In his mind though he was thinking, *you have gotta be kidding me, again. Twice in one day. All I did was show up to church. Am I having déjà vu?*

"What is this in my drawer?"

He closed his eyes. He was happy he wasn't being defeated. "Come again?" Although he knew what she was talking about.

"Funny. Very funny."

"Call it a present."

"What am I supposed to do with it?"

"Wrap it up and give it to me as a wedding present."

"Why, I have not even received my invitation yet," I said playfully.

"They have not been mailed. They will be hand delivered and you will be chauffeur driven to the secret wedding location."

"Oh wow, how disappointing. I was expecting to be driven via carriage pulled by twelve white horses or Clydesdales. I thought you would go all out for me like Princess Diana." I sighed, "I guess I was wrong. Seriously, why is your ring in my drawer?"

"I do not have to worry about any confusion. The ring is at your house."

"I am giving this back to you. Are you on the way to get it? I do not want to be responsible for it." *This ring has to be worth at least a million dollars,* I thought to myself.

"Not right now."

"Okay. Fair enough. Do you want to call me later?"

"I will babe."

"Bye sweetheart."

WEEK 20

Monday

I woke up exhausted. You would have thought I partied all night the way my body felt. *This must be the result of too much sleep and relaxation.* This is why I didn't do it often. It wore you out. Rest assured, I had a cure for this system shut down and it came in a white paper cup. I called it nitrogen. The way Nitrous Oxide Systems made a car perform at high speeds, added energy, and reduced heat was the way Starbucks made me perform. It added energy and reduced heat while I performed at high velocities.

I made a mental note to call my stockbroker and question Starbucks. The way I saw it, if I was going to visit this establishment daily like we were in a deep relationship, I might as well reap the long-term benefits.

Of course, if I stopped for Batman's fix, I had to get my sidekick Robin, aka Leigh, a fix too. It was only the right thing to do. I called Randall on the way.

"Hey babe."

"Hey," I said rather dry.

Detecting something was off he asked, "What's wrong sunshine?"

"Too much sleep," I said with even less enthusiasm.

"You will be fine before the week is out."

I didn't know what that meant but I responded. "What is your prediction for the next hour?"

"It is going to be a challenge."

"Then I need to go with my first mind."

"That would be?"

"Stop and fuel up with the nitrogen."

"Humph?" He did not know what nitrogen meant.

Noticing the hesitation in his voice I said, "Go ahead and say it."

"Let me get you a substitute."

My mind went to the other side of the gutter. What is lower than the gutter? Well whatever it is, that is where my mind went and remained. Truth be told, I rather liked it. Reality hit and I remembered I was driving and talking so I could not drift away as far as I wanted.

"Excuse me, are you still there?" He noticed her silence.

"Yep," I said dazed.

"Are you narcoleptic also?"

I could hear King in the back ground laughing. "You tell the Tin Man I am not that tired. Okay."

"It's too early for this kids."

"He started it."

"I thought you were tired?"

"That might be true but I can rumble anytime. Tell trainer man he may need to up y'alls game if y'all can't rumble at a moment's notice." I felt myself get hyped. Maybe all I needed to begin with was for King to step on my nerves.

"You two are not rumbling. You two are just talking trash and a drunk man can do that. I do not know how many times I have to tell you all I am the fighter of the group."

"Wa wonk, wa wonk, wonk, wonk. Y'all got me hyped up now."

"So you are not getting coffee?"

"No."

He high fived King. "What are we going to do with your mouth?"

"Kiss it."

This time it was his mind drifting to the bottom of the gutter.

"Umm excuse you. I see you can go to lala land in a moment's notice. Can you take me with you next time?" I said getting his attention.

"Oh believe me you were there," he said referring to the fact I was in his thoughts. "I mean how am I going to fight if I have to be worried about your mouth? You are going to be on the side of the ring getting me disqualified or kicked out of the association."

"Unless it is King talking trash then I should be okay."

"You two are going to keep me on my toes. Is this what I have to look forward to?"

"Yes. Unless you make him behave."

"And?" he said as if more needed to be added to the statement.

"Oh, I already know how to behave."

"Who said you did not?" He knew how to pick and choose his battles wisely, so in this case he took the easy route out.

"You are taking King's side. You two are double teaming me. I will call you later."

"Dani?"

"Yes sir?"

"I love you have a good day."

"N-A-S-T-Y!" King shouted in the background.

"He can spell or was that a flash card?"

"Good bye," Hooks announced.

"I love you too."

He looked at King as if he had another victory under his belt, "Man, do that every morning until I can detox the caffeine out of her system."

"My pleasure," King graciously said.

"She is crunk to def right now."

"I can make it happen all day," King said with much confidence in his ability to work Dani's nerves.

"Why can't you two play nice and fair?"

"I thought we were," King said like he was really serious.

Randall took off running at King's comment.

I did not stop and get my fix and around six it kicked in. I should have gone with my first mind. I was getting tired. The caffeine would have fixed me for another three hours.

"Whew, Leigh I am getting tired."

"Getting? I was tired three hours ago. It is six PM. You have been up thirteen plus hours. Normal, insane people have called it a day already."

"Cheap shot. Point taken. Let's wrap it up."

"I vote for let's leave everything as is and run out the door," Leigh suggested.

"Five minutes to shut down and we are gone." We did exactly that. I arrived at the gym, "Good evening," I greeted.

He stepped away from the bag. "Hey. How was your day? You looked pooped."

"It was good," I replied. "I am pooped though so I will not work out too long today. In fact, I will be leaving in a little while. I only came because I wanted to see you."

"What's wrong?" he asked concerned.

"Humph, I guess I am a little exhausted."

"Can you wait an hour?"

"Sure. I will walk real slow."

"Good. I will take you to get a steak," he offered.

"I am not hungry. Food is the last thing I want right now."

"You need it," he ordered.

"Need what?"

"Nourishment."

"Why do you say that?"

"You always need it during this time."

"During what time?"

He put his head down and looked embarrassed.

"What?"

"Umm. Umm. This time of the month," he mumbled.

I folded my arms and rolled my eyes.

"Let me explain before you get upset." He pulled me to the side and sat me down.

Did I mention this to him? Ever? How did he know? This is about to be a scary response. "Go ahead."

"We have never monitored this watch on anyone except me. With that being said, we have no clue what all it is capable of doing."

"Umm hmm. Go on," I said, irritated.

"So the first month when your levels were extremely elevated we could not figure it out. You seemed normal and as far as we could tell there was nothing wrong. You did not mention one single thing. It was led to believe you and I had done something we should not have. After hours of denial, it was assumed you were doing something you were not supposed to do. It was not until we were all together and could see for ourselves what you were actually doing and your levels were still just as high. So I kept a very close eye on you. Nothing happened but in about ten days your levels were back to normal. Exactly twenty eight days later they began to creep up again. Then we figured out what was going on. You were cycling and then ovulating."

"What a group of geniuses," I responded more sarcastically than angry.

"We didn't know. I do not have that issue. I have been wearing this watch for ten years and we have never seen anything like it."

"So why didn't you ask?"

"Ask you if you were on your cycle?"

"Umm yeah."

"I don't think so," he said embarrassed.

"Why?"

"That would be inappropriate."

"So what are you asking me now?"

"Who said I was asking anything? I am telling you that you are on day three of your cycle. There is no question about it." This also explained the emotional thirty ring fiasco on Sunday.

I bucked my eyes. I had no rebuttal.

"So these next few days we can spend the night and sleep in the same bed and I will be fine," he said proudly as if he was total in control.

"Speaking of which, how have your levels raised in intense intimate situations over the past ten years?"

"What is your question?"

"I think you understand my question," I said direct.

"I'm not sure what time frame I am responding to?"

"When you are IN-TI-MATE what does the watch read?" I pointed to his wristwatch.

"I do not think I have ever been told or recorded my levels. If you give me some time I can get back with you on that. I would hate to not be able to answer your question."

"It's no big deal."

"Oh yes it is. Inquiring minds want to know," he winked.

"So what you have informed me is you know when I am on my cycle."

"Yes."

"Ovulating?"

"Yes."

"And?"

"Anytime your body levels change from normal range for any reason. Scared, working out, upset, and umm, umm, sexually challenged."

147

"And that means you and King can see this?"

"Well yeah," he stammered.

"Well?"

"And the multitude," he said hesitantly.

"I wear this watch because of what?"

"Safety," he responded.

That did it. "We will have to come up with a better arrangement," I said.

"Please do not be upset," he pleaded.

"Okay." *This is freakish and weird.*

"Are you mad?"

"Check the levels," I snapped.

"For real?"

"For real. You all could at least have the decency to inform me mother nature is on her way since you are invading my privacy and remotely violating my body. Now that's real talk," I said with much attitude.

He wasn't quite sure if she was serious or sarcastic. "So can you hold out an hour?"

"I guess so." *Do I have a choice?*

We went to dinner and after wolfing down half of my steak I was now sleepier than I was before. I wanted to suggest to him it would be a good night to drive me home. Instead, I sucked it up and drove myself. *Apparently, this monitor does not detect sleep deprivation*, I thought.

Tuesday

Today was a normal day in the engineering world. I hate to admit it but Randall's little cure worked. I woke up energized, recharged, and ready. I was still pumped when I got to the gym later that evening. I let the top up and stepped out of the BMW. I had been blasting the radio but when I walked into the gym it seemed liked I walked into a funeral parlor. It was so quiet. All you could hear was repetitions of beats and silence and then back again. Everyone appeared to be on one accord. The jump rope, the feet hitting the treadmill, the bag being punched, and the hits in the ring all collided at the same time. This time I came in, sat down, and observed. Not one person stopped what they were doing. A blind person could clearly distinguish all the movements. The silence was enough to drive me crazy.

I gave a general hello as I took my bags upstairs and while there I took the time to examine the Bose system closely. I could not determine if I was connected to the system down stairs or upstairs only. I changed into workout clothes and went back downstairs slowly.

The funeral must have still been underway because no other noise could be heard. I walked to the front desk and went behind the counter to look around. I saw what I thought might be a controller for the audio system but I wasn't sure.

"Is everything alright Ms. Danielle?" Mimi asked wondering why I was behind her desk but afraid to tell me to move.

"No. Thank you for asking."

I kept observing. *All of these televisions and monitors on the wall but where on earth is the volume? I have a big project ahead of me. This place is going to come to life regardless if they like it or not.*

He got into the ring and I started climbing in to join him. Someone came over to help me get in. I walked right up and I jumped in the middle of him and the opponent. As soon as he swung I grabbed his glove in mid punch. I was shocked it didn't break my hand. I guess I never thought about the velocity and the power behind his punch until I got in the line of fire.

He spit his mouthpiece out, "Danielle, what are you trying to do? Get yourself killed?"

"No, more like get my hand broken or amputated," I said while shaking my hand.

"What is wrong?" he shouted. He was pissed I was there but even more pissed no one stopped me from getting in the way.

"I need to ask you a question."

"What is it?" he said as his frustration turned to concern.

"Where is your controller for the monitors and the overhead system?"

He stood up straight putting both hands on his hips. He leaned in and kissed me and said, "What did you ask me baby?"

I repeated the question.

"In my office."

"Thanks," I said as I prepared to walk off.

He snatched me back harder than anticipated. I looked down at his hands not understanding how he was able to maintain a grip with those gloves on.

"You stepped in the ring in the middle of a punch to ask me that? You could have asked anyone?" *You could have been killed,* he thought.

"I know. But I wanted to ask you," I said sweetly and sincerely.

How could he get any angrier? "Let me make sure I have this correct," he said. "That was your only question?"

"Yes," I tried to walk away again and he pulled me back again.

"You are crazy. Do you know that?"

"Thank you. I have had years of practice." I smiled then I rolled under the ropes. I walked to his office to find the door closed and locked. His door was equipped with a key lock and a key pad. I had no other choice but to go back. I climbed in the ring. Again, no one stopped me. "Excuse me," I said as I stepped in the middle. He looked slightly annoyed.

"Yes baby?" *Someone is about to lose a job if she enters this ring one more time.*

"May I have the key or can someone come unlock your office."

He fell down on the mat. I leaned over him. "That is a nice trick," I said like he was a puppy performing a trick for a treat. "Good job. Key please."

Annoyed and biting his bottom lip, "DJ what planet do you come from?"

"I am not of this world." *Doesn't he know I am from Daniland?*

"I am aware of that. Does anyone else live in that world with you?"

"If you ever want to you will retract that statement."

"I do not want to know what you are up to."

"Thank you." As I tried to walk off he grabbed my ankle. "Hey, man what are you trying to do?" I yelled almost falling over.

"Get low," he said.

I leaned down. His tone and disposition changed. "Do not you ever get in this ring again unless we know you are entering. I do not want you to get hurt. Are we clear?"

"Can you add a doorbell?" He let my ankle go in frustration as I rolled out.

"Forget it. I tried. King, tag, you are it. I have no clue what she is up to or talking about."

"Don't put your crazy girlfriend off on me," King replied uninterested.

"Help me Lord."

"Help is on the way," I yelled back waving my hand.

I went into his office. It was a nice office. I thought that every time I entered. It was more like a condo. I found the controller. There was no place for a disc or iPod. *Who installed this dinosaur*, I thought to myself. *Oh Lord! I have some work to do.* I found a decent radio station and blasted it. Then I grabbed all the remotes and headed back to the floor. As I turned to close the door I heard King's voice behind me.

"What are you doing?" he asked.

"Minding my business."

"You are making noise."

"No I am not. The radio is playing music. I know those are too many vibrations for your animal ears to comprehend at one time."

He gazed directly at me. If looks could kill then you might as well add the dirt because I was dead.

"Are you going to just stand there and look stupid or help me with these?"

Considering he did not respond right away his answer was initially no, but finally he took some remotes. "Why aren't these televisions programmed to use one remote?" I asked.

"We do not use them," he barked.

"Why are they on the wall?"

"In case we decide to."

"What is the rationale behind not using them?"

"We are busy working."

"Yeah, busy working my nerves," I smarted off. I held the remote in his direction hoping it would make him disappear but I had no luck. He was still there.

"Right now I think it is the other way around."

We had an audience. "You know what King? I am sick of your S-H-I-T. In the ring now! Let's handle this like two ladies. Are you ready to rumble?" I held up one of the remotes like it was a microphone. "Good evening ladies, gentleman and King. Coming to you live from Atlanta, Georgia at the Hooks Arena. On the left, we have Danielle in the black and to your right we have King in the pink. This fight is for the respect of the game. The winner will be respected from this point on. This will be a fair and clean fight. No hair pulling, mudslinging, or bra popping. Come in the ring King and touch pounds and let the fight begin."

He didn't move. Everyone looked at him as if to say, she is challenging you.

"I don't fight girls," he replied.

"Lady," I corrected. "Cool then help me."

He sighed, "What do you want crazy?"

He gave in. Then he and I went through the televisions and figured which remote went with which television and labeled each one. I asked him a hundred questions about the set up. Everyone else went back to what they were doing while I people watched. The momentum in the room changed. The music made everything seem to go faster and created an intense atmosphere.

"King we have some work to do," I said.

"What exactly are we doing?"

"A couple of things. We are going to bring this system up to speed and get some noise in here. The televisions and the radio."

"Why?"

"Music is for the soul."

"Who's soul?"

"Trust me and work with me on this."

"You ask for too much," he mumbled in disgust.

"Umm hmm. I love you too."

"Don't ever say that in public again," King said embarrassed.

"Whatever. I am going home and taking some time to figure out what I need to order. This was not on my agenda tonight."

"You can postpone it forever," he whispered.

"You wish," I retorted. "I will not. We are going to knock this out. I am going home."

"Hooks take a break. Walk your girlfriend out. Take your time."

Hooks was at the bottom of the steps when I came down. "Hey babe."

"Hey trouble," he replied.

"Am not," I frowned.

"What's going on?"

"I have work to do," I smirked.

"What are you trying to do?"

"Bring this place to life. Call me when you get home." I jumped in my car, went home and surfed the net finding all the pieces needed to get the job done. I then emailed Leigh with the order confirmations. Be on the lookout for this at the office. It is for the gym. We will need to spend some time making all of this work.

Over the years I learned to be my own everything. From plumber, yard man to IT specialist. It was not a matter of being independent, but rather when you are single, you learn to swim or sink. I knew just enough to either get it working or in some cases get myself in trouble.

I got in bed with my laptop, a pen, and paper. I thought about what I wanted to do to make this work with what he already had. It wasn't a hard job but could possibly be more than I could do with a few screwdrivers and wire cutters.

Wednesday

I woke up confused. I still had a computer in my lap. I think I have a problem. I was addicted to something. Work, computers, projects, the internet, or something. This was a serious addiction. Or was I addicted to the man in the ring? I pushed the computer to the side and rolled over. I didn't look at the clock but suddenly realized dude didn't call or text to say he was home. I immediately reached for my phone and peeked out of one eye. Nope, he had not called. I rang his phone.

"Why are you up?" he answered.

"Why haven't you called me?" I remarked.

"Do you want me to answer that?"

I did not respond.

"I am not home yet but I am not working either."

"What are you doing?"

"I am watching television."

"What are you watching?" That was strange. I had never heard him say he was watching television before.

"I, I, I don't know the name," he stuttered. I knew he was lying immediately. I didn't think it was a trick question.

"Why are you lying?"

"Because you are going to be mad."

"What are you watching?"

"A video?"

"What kind of damn video?" I snapped. Triple X rated is what came to mind.

"Not like that."

"Well, answer the question."

"Of me training."

I rolled my eyes. "Good night honey. Don't ever talk to me about how much I work again."

"I am going to lie down right now."

"I will talk to you in a few hours," I snarled.

"DJ."

"Go ahead."

"I will do better. I would be able to sleep if I were there with you. What I am trying to say is I wish I was. I am going to make it happen. Mark my words."

"We will see," I replied then hung up.

Three hours and forty-seven minutes later, I was in my car and dialing his number.

"Good morning D."

"Did you go to sleep at all?"

"You are not going to be mad are you?"

"We will have a discussion."

"Why?"

"How in the world do you plan to be on your A game and be in the best boxing condition if you can't even lie down to get some rest. Come on now. Use some form of common sense. Matter of fact, let me speak to King."

He said nothing but followed instructions and handed King the phone.

"Yes Ma'am."

"Good morning."

"Good morning. How are you?" King said shocking me.

"I am a little perturbed right now."

"What's the problem?"

"Who is the problem would be more accurate," I said.

"Who?"

"Your little boxer is my problem."

He stopped jogging. Hooks stopped too. "Keep going. I will catch up." Hooks lingered around anyway.

"What's up?" He was expecting to hear something Hooks had personally done to directly affect her.

With all seriousness she asked, "Are you aware he does not sleep?"

"Maybe not to the degree you are aware. Please discuss. Keep running son!" he demanded.

"I do not think he ever gets sleep, much less decent sleep or a good night's rest. I am not a boxing expert but I do think he should at least try to get some sleep. Sleep is important and even the fighters sleep on 24/7. There is a difference between sleep, rest, relaxing, winding down, and in my opinion he needs to do all of them."

"You are absolutely right Ms. Rose. What do you consider as never sleeps?"

"Well last night he did not sleep or go home. I think that qualifies as never sleeps."

"How do you know?"

"I called him at two AM and he was still at the gym watching himself train. Sure, there is a bed there for him but something tells me he was not in the bed. Even when he is home, I do not think he gets in the bed. He is probably in the chair all night. He falls asleep there, wakes up, and does it all over again. I just want him to be safe and healthy."

He frowned. "Ms. Rose I am aware he does not sleep a lot but staying up all night is unacceptable. Before now, I thought he was stressed about his situation so maybe that is why he didn't sleep but now there should not be any excuse."

"He needs to go home and lay down every night at a decent hour. When he is at the gym no one knows what he is up to because he is behind closed doors. I do not know what I need to do other than be the enforcer. He is not going to like it but someone will have to be with him all day and night."

I responded, "If he is not going to eat then he certainly needs to sleep. Besides, if he eats like he should he would probably fall asleep."

"He will be mad but he will get over it," King said without hesitation.

"I'm sorry," I offered.

"No, you are good. Let me know when you see him or his behavior inappropriate. It is impossible for him to train like we have been without sleep. We both need to make sure there are not any other issues keeping him awake."

"Do you think there is an underlying reason?" I asked with concern.

"I do not know. It's possible. I didn't know he wasn't sleeping. I would probably never have known if you didn't tell me. You check on your end and I will check on mine. I really appreciate this conversation. Keep me posted and I will do the same," King softened a little.

"Will do. Have a good one King."

"You too Ms. D."

I rode into work feeling like a snitch. Where I am from snitches get stitches. I can only hope he understands I am looking out for his best interest. I pulled over to the shoulder and prayed for him. I went to work starting my day worried about him.

At lunchtime he called, "Hey DJ, what time shall I pick you up?

"Don't you try it. You will have me there at four o'clock if I let you. No sir. I will come alone."

"If you do not want to go with me just say so, but just so you know, I will be hurt."

"I am not going to be there opening up the church with you this week and shutting it down. My days of opening and closing went out when I left the club."

"Why not? It is our midweek date," he said.

"You are so cheap. You want to date me at a place you know I am going any way."

"Not true."

"So true. You can't even feed me that early or that late. Cheap skate."

"Take it back."

"No can do. I will see you right at seven. I may take my time." I was not riding with him so he could chasten me for tattle telling.

"Do not play DJ."

"See you."

We spoke several more times throughout the day. At three he called, "Are you sure you do not want me to pick you up?" he asked nicely.

"I am positive," I quickly replied.

When I pulled up to the lot, it was a quarter before seven. I called his phone but there was no answer. I called Keith's phone next and he didn't answer either. *Oh well.* I was a little caught by surprised that no one was waiting on me and no one answered their phones. I walked in and saw Jon Jon at the door. Immediately he spoke into his wrist. Then I saw Nate who yelled down the hall. I could see Randall's head a mile away.

Nate yelled again, "Deacon Washington."

I swear everything stopped. Everyone turned around including him. Time was frozen. It was clear he was speaking to a female and he was being warned I was approaching. *Who does that?* I felt like the po-po pulling up to the trap. I walked up making sure I made eye contact with everyone.

"Deacon Washington," I purposefully said his last name in three syllables.

"Hey babe," he replied as cool as ever.

I got real close to him. I took my finger and held it as straight as I could and just a hair from his nose. "Try me if you want too. This is not what you want. Remember when you were playing house I was running game. Don't do me," I warned. I looked at the rest of them and said, "You simple silly punks."

He put his finger over my lips. Not that I was loud but he didn't care for the words I was speaking at church. I walked off. He caught up to me. "DJ that was a member I was having a brief conversation with."

"That would have been fine until your boys blew your hustle. Maybe you need to explain it to them because they seem to have felt differently." My back was to the crew. He gave an awful look past me. By then Keith and King walked up. "Wow, now here comes dumb and dumber," I said out loud.

"I do not have a hustle. And that was not nice. Take it out on me. I am the one you have an issue with."

"Maybe you should let them know that this is not a hustle for you. But don't think I don't see all. As soon as I stepped in the door one commenced to speaking into his wrist while the other one yelled from across the way. Sounds like a hustle to me. Game recognizes game." I gave him a glance over.

"I think this has been up played for no reason. We both need to take this down a notch and sort it out like adults."

"Let's step outside then. All of us," I said giving a look to the crew.

"I cannot right now. "

"Why?"

"Because I am serving now."

"I guess you were serving when you didn't answer my call too. Oh and I guess Keith was serving and protecting you when he could not meet me at my car nor answer his phone." I looked over at Keith who was standing straight and firm. I could not tell at this point if he was on my side or Randall's. I looked him dead in the eye and winked. "Good job Keith. I will make sure you get The Cover Randall's Butt Award at the awards ceremony this year. As for you Terminator," I said looking at King. "You may want to check your brigade. They have turned into a group of BI's. Now, check my levels on that." I bucked my eyes.

Randall laughed. He was definitely not laughing at my insults. This time he was confused. Most of the time, well all of the time, I hated Keith being by my side and the first time he was not there it sparked a debate.

I started to walk off. Not one single soul moved. I did not realized it but the entire battalion surfaced and Randall and I were in the center. King and Keith were defending him and all the others behind me. You would have thought it was a standoff. It looked like him and his two and me and my crew. However, the whole group was his crew. I ran alone. I didn't need any help. I fought my own battles. Me and this two edged flaming sword in my mouth was ready for war but no one wanted to step outside and go to war with a no limit solider. It was in their best interest not to. Therefore, I shook it off and went to do what I came to do--be in the army of the Lord. I walked in the sanctuary alone. I heard him say in a stern, forceful voice he frequently used, "Meeting in my office now!"

He was careful to show no signs of stress in front of me. But I could hear in his tone he was perturbed with them. I was not angry. I think he knew it. His boys handled something minor inappropriately. Regardless, he needed to check that with the quickness. It could have been a bad situation. I knew he was doing his job. I have been with him long enough to know he does not flirt or do a lot of contact so it was no big deal to me. Tonight his crew thought it was huge.

I sat in my normal seat and told the usher, "You can fill this seat next to me." I forced Keith off my row. I refused to make eye contact the entire service. Then to top it off after the benediction I escaped via a different route. I got to my car and called Sissie.

"Hello."

"Hey."

"Hey girly. What's up?"

"I am coming over."

"Great!"

As soon as I walked in the door I was asked a thousand questions about bible study.

"Auntie, tell me you two are not showing out in the house of the Lord?" Sade asked.

"I wasn't," I immediately defended.

"Umm hmm," Paige muttered in disagreement.

"Wait until Pastor Hunter finds out. You two are going to make a public apology in front of the congregation and be baptized in acid." Sade looked as if she enjoyed the thought.

"Shut up!"

"I am telling the truth and I want front row seats."

My phone rang, "Hello."

"That was rude."

"I know. You should check your boys." I knew he meant my escape route.

He laughed. "If you had come with me none of this would have happened."

"Yep, that's classic. Switch it up and blame it on the girl. Is that what your meeting was about?"

"There is no win for me right now is there?"

"Umm, let me think." I paused, "NO."

"It was handled incorrectly I will admit," he hated to confess but it was true.

"I thought we came to that conclusion three hours ago. I am out right now," I said as I quickly turned my watch off. Then I realized he could probably track my last where abouts to the precise moment. "I am out. Can I call you back once I get in my car?" I was pacing the floor as I spoke. It was a habit I did when I was dealing business. I needed to do so now to keep my tone strong and stern.

The girls were in the back ground like here she go. I was on good behavior. I just wanted him to know I wasn't going to roll over and play dead.

"Humph. Alright Danielle. Call me when you get in your car. I will probably be at the gym." You could hear the reluctance in his voice. He wanted to say more.

The girls and I continued on. Not even ten minutes later, he called again. We were laughing so loud I didn't hear my phone ring. I do not know why we always got together and acted like we were twelve years old. We all thought we were the same age. Whose age I do not know. Paige's, mine or Sade's.

In the midst of a laugh Sade noticed my phone and said, "Auntie your phone is doing something."

"Okay," I replied but I didn't reach for it.

Then the house phone rang. Paige looked at the caller id. "What in the hell? Yes," she answered.

"Paige, good evening this is Randall, give Danielle the phone please." He was nice and rude all in one.

"I am fine thank you." She gave him nice nasty back. "Here," she said handing me the phone.

Sade reached for it instead.

"Not you."

She took it anyway and looked at the caller id. "Oh crap." She dropped it in my lap like it was stolen merchandise.

"What chumps?" I looked at the caller id. It read RDW Inc. I looked around the room. They both glared back at me. I got it together. I was shocked. "This is Danielle."

"Cut the watch back on." I did not respond. "Now."

I cleared my throat and pressed the button on the side of the watch.

"I do not play games. Neither am I playing with you. Thank you and I will be waiting for your call," he hung up the line.

We all sat in silence until I broke the awkwardness. "What are we going to do?"

"I am not in that mess," Paige happily yelled.

"Mom, think."

We collaborated for another hour or so. We came to the conclusion that I accepted the watch before knowing all it was capable of doing. What a dumb mistake. It was now clear if I wanted to cut it off I was going to have to do it differently. I was also going to have to be aware of my travels if I didn't want them recorded. I was considering returning the gift. I do not think I have ever given a present back. Especially not jewelry. That was a cardinal sin. But was this really considered jewelry? Nope. It was a tracking device. It had powers. Powers that allowed other people too much access to me.

I decided I was going to first ask for the rights to his device like he had to mine. If that was a no then I was definitely returning the gift. An hour later I prepared to leave my besties. You would have thought I was going off to a foreign county to fight a war at how dramatic our goodbye was.

"Good luck Sissie," Paige called out.

"You can do it Auntie," Sade chimed in.

I am sure his monitor informed him I was in my car moving and the direction I was headed. I purposefully waited to see if he would call me first. I waited almost twenty minutes before calling him myself.

"Yes," he answered sounding as if I was disturbing him.

"You wanted me to call you," I said in my polished business tone.

He sighed, "Go to bed. I will talk to you in the morning." This dating thing was beginning to wear him out. He realized it required far more work than fighting.

"No need putting off until tomorrow what we can handle today."

"Okay. Go ahead," he replied exhausted already.

"I do not have anything to say. I thought maybe you did."

"I really do not know what to say."

"What do you think you need to say or should say?"

"I am not sure."

"All I want to say is I did not wait this long to involve myself in nonsense. You asked me to wait. Believe me, I would not have waited for BS. I hope we are clear."

"We are clear," he confirmed.

"Great. Good night,"I said then clicked the line off.

Thursday

Work was long. Well, in actuality it was no longer than any other day. It seemed long because I was anxious to see him. I could not get the Cayenne to move fast enough. *This is supposed to be a Porsche,* I thought to myself. "I better let up off the gas before I get a certificate," I said aloud. Certificate was my little nickname for speeding tickets. I have had enough to know many presents, rewards, and surprises came with driving my car to the limits the speedometer and tachometer said it could go.

The way I saw it, if carmakers really wanted them to only go fifty-five miles per hour then the engine would not allow higher than fifty-five. If the speedometer reads one hundred and sixty, how am I supposed to ever know if the car I purchased can produce as it describes? I have yet to figure that one out. The conversation I was having in my head would be the perfect one for Randall and me. He likes cars. All of which seem to have speed in common. Today however was not going to be a day I inherited a ticket, so I pulled up and pumped the brakes.

I arrived at the gym. I spoke to everyone, looked, and saw him lying on the mat of the ring. I walked over. "Hey." He did not speak back. "Hey," I said a second time. Nothing. King, JJ, and Tony were all standing there in the ring leaning over him. I dropped everything in my hands. I tried to figure out how to get in. Keith helped me up. "MOVE!" I yelled. "Randall, what's wrong?" His eyes were closed. He looked horrible as he shook his head.

Something was definitely wrong with him. He moved his head so I knew he was alive, barely. "Open your eyes!"

He tried. He was too exhausted. Keith handed me a water bottle. I was handing it to him then I realized his eyes were closed and he was wearing his gloves. I squeezed the water in his mouth.

He opened his eyes, "I am good."

"No you are not," I yelled in distress. I started trying to take his gloves off. I was either too upset, too emotional, too wired up or I had no clue how to get them off. His hand literally flopped out of my hand. He was on the mat damn near in the fetal position.

"Take these off his hands,"I bellowed. No one moved. "Take these f'ing gloves off his hands." They moved but it was a little too slow. "NOW," I screamed.

When I tried to lift him up, he moaned as if he was in excruciating pain.

"That's it." I noticed one of the girls picking my stuff up and putting it back in my bag. I knew Keith was going to make some noise about that. If my bag had been zipped nothing would have fallen out. Right now I could care less about the contents of my purse or the cracked screen I was sure my iPhone received from the drop.

I leaned over him, "Sweetie, can you hear me?"

He said nothing. His hands were now free from the gloves but still taped. He moved slightly. Someone was wiping his face as he squirmed like a newborn baby seeing light for the first time.

"Randall, can you hear me?" I asked again.

He nodded but he did not open his eyes. "Can you stand up?" He shook his head no.

"Baby, tell me what hurts?" He tried to sit up and speak and then collapsed. I looked over at King and JJ. They had the nerve to be on their damn computers as if this was normal. Lord knows I wanted to go off but I didn't. *I will handle them tomorrow. They do not know who they are f'ing with.*

"That did it we are going to the hospital," I announced.

"I am fine," he managed to say.

"Well get up and show me," I ordered.

He tried to stand to his feet but stumbled back down. I then tried to help him and we both staggered. With all of his weight shifted on me, he felt more like three hundred pounds verses what he actually weighed. Keith came in the ring to help me. He attempted to let him stand on his own but finally decided to pick him up.

"Where are we going?" Keith asked.

"To my truck." I handed him the keys. I , at King, JJ and Tony. Tony walked away. "What happened to him?" I tested.

"We were training," King answered as if this was acceptable.

"Training? Training?" I said louder the second time.

"Yes," King shouted back still facing his laptop.

"Don't F with me," I snarled through my teeth.

I opened the passenger door. "Randall," I screeched. "Are you okay?"

"Yep," he lied. He was happy he was alive, could hear, and somewhat see.

"What hospital am I taking you to?"

"Home is fine." He reached for my hand. I was afraid to touch his. I didn't want to hurt him. His hands were swollen and bruised.

Keith came back with a bag. It contained his clothes, keys, phones, laptop, and a few other things. "Do you need me?" Keith asked me.

That was a dumb question I thought. Randall mumbled, "No," continuing to keep his eyes closed.

"I think we have it," I said in rage and fear. "Thank you. Text me the doctor's number. I will call you if I need you. Thanks for your help." *The others just sat there looking stupid.*

"I really think I should take you to a hospital," I reiterated as I pulled off.

"I am good. It's all in a day's work. A few cracked ribs, a concussion here and there. I will survive," he responded nonchalantly.

"What can you take?"

"I do not need anything. I will be fine in the morning."

"What can you take?" I questioned again forceful.

"Tylenol," he mumbled. I looked over and his mouthpiece was hanging out his mouth. I put my hand up to his mouth like I use to do to Sade when she was sick or didn't like something. He spit it in my hand. As with Sade, it didn't seem nasty. I placed it on a paper towel and put it in the cup holder. I knew then I really loved this man. I didn't care he was in my car with just his shorts on, hands taped, covered in powder, with a bloody face, and spitting in my hand. All I wanted to do was make sure he was okay and nurse him back to health.

I stopped at the grocery store for a few items. I got fresh fish, vegetables, Epson salt, witch hazel, Tylenol, heat patches, Pedialyte, Ensure, and Gatorade.

We pulled up to his house realizing I did not know how to get in his gate. "Randall, what's the code?"

As I drove towards the house I asked, "Where are your keys?"

"You have your own," he reminded.

I looked at him and rolled my eyes. If he wasn't half dead in my seat I would have snapped back. I searched my purse and then looked at him and asked, "Which key is it?" He took them from my hand, opened the car door and threw one leg out and sat there. It was a struggle to help him out the car. We walked through the door of his house as the alarm blared. He struggled to get to it in time to cut it off then sat down in the first chair he came to. "Don't sit down. You are getting in the tub."

I stared towards the bedroom. He followed slowly holding himself up along the wall. I drew him a bath full of Epson salt, green alcohol, and witch hazel.

He came in and sat down in the chair. He unsuccessfully tried to take his shoes off after I unlaced them. "Can you take your clothes off?"

"No, I need help," he tried to snicker.

"Even on your death bed you are still being bad."

"You would not deny a man on his death bed," he said with his head hanging low. As much pain as he was in he was still joking. Maybe this was normal. I didn't know, but nevertheless, not on my watch.

"Get in the tub," I giggled and walked out leaving the door open.

"Get in with me?" I heard him reply.

"Not tonight," I said while continuing to walk away. I went to his kitchen and figured out how to cut the oven on and found what I needed to start cooking. I put the liquids in the freezer. After thirty minutes or so I had not heard one peep from him. I went to check. He was alive and laid back. I stood in the door. Luckily, the tub was far enough away that I could not see anything. I do not think he cared who saw him right now.

With his eyes closed he spoke, "I can see you."

"I see you too. You need to go to the hospital."

"I am feeling better already," he said. He was feeling temporary relief from other parts of his body, which let him know he was still alive, and some things functioned very well regardless of how much pain he was in now.

I was thinking to myself, *if he wasn't in pain I would jump in that tub with all my clothes on and let him peel them back one layer at a time.* I moved to distract my thoughts. I went back to the kitchen and got the Pedialyte. "Drink up." I rolled the bottle across the floor. He laughed knowing why. He downed it in one swallow and rolled the bottle back to me.

"You can come closer," he said not sure of himself.

I walked over and popped another bottle open. I then heard a noise as his wet hand took the bottle from my hand.

"Ms. D, Hooks, can I come in?"

"Yeah. Bottoms up and here comes security."

Keith came in. I was sitting on the edge of the tub. I was still in my suit. If it wasn't for the bubbles the tub was making I would have been able to see all of him.

"Hey," I said.

"Man, how do you feel?"

He did not speak. "I am leaving you in charge," I said as I walked out and checked my food. Twenty minutes later, I came back and they both were in the same place. "Keith can you help him out and make sure he gets dressed?"

"What do you want me to do with him?" Keith said as if he was a dead body we were trying to hide.

"Put him in the bed." The next thing I knew he was sitting at the breakfast bar across from me. "I thought I said to get in the bed," I said without turning around hearing his moaning.

"I know."

"That presents a problem," I said as I placed a plate in front of him. "Keith, do you care for some dinner?"

"No thank you."

"It's okay man. Take mine," he said shoving his plate to Keith.

"You eat it," I growled.

"I am not hungry," he defiantly spoke back.

"Eat it or go to the hospital." Immediately he proceeded to eat. I fixed Keith a plate and when I turned around King and JJ were coming through the door. "Anyone care to tell me what went on tonight?"

"First night of rough housing," King said proudly which lead me to believe he was the main contributing factor in this fiasco.

"Why?"

"It is training," the ring leader said.

"It is torture," I yelled.

"Danielle, it is how I train," Randall tried to interject.

They all started trying to speak at once.

"This was the first day of hard core blows. They all punch from one side to the next. It is getting my body used to taking blows. It prepares me for the ring. You came in on the tail end."

"Yeah, tail end. Your tail ended up on the damn mat barely breathing with God knows how many cracked and broken ribs." I took my bags and went to the other room to get all my things back in order. I could hear him slowly coming back to life.

"Ms. D, may we get a plate?" King shouted.

"Yeah," I mumbled.

"Babe did you eat?" Randall yelled.

"I'm good," I yelled back from the other room. I was too frustrated to eat. I looked up and King was bringing me a plate anyway. I was scared to eat it. *Is he trying to poison me?* I took it back to the kitchen and broke a piece of fish off of it.

"Ms. D do you need us to do anything before we leave?" JJ asked.

"Yes put him in the bed for me please."

King got ready to pick him up and he yelled in pain. King held up one shoulder and Keith the other and slowly walked him to the bed. "We are leaving," JJ informed me.

I walked them to the door."Ms. D don't worry, he will be fine. It is the first day. Each day he will get stronger and stronger until the blows bounce back. In a few weeks he will not feel them at all," King said.

"He said he can have Tylenol. Is that correct?"

"Two," JJ quickly agreed. That is when I noticed King and JJ were on motorcycles.

Keith came up to give me a hug and whispered in my ear, "Good job."

"On what?"

"I think you passed the test. You have shown yourself approved. Not only to him but to all of them as he looked back at King and JJ on their motorcycles like two little boys. You made a huge statement to us all. Hooks included. He has been very concerned that you would not be able to take him in his weakest form. Tonight was not planned, but God made it happen that you walked in when you did. You have confirmed to everyone you will not be fragile and afraid. But we will have to work on toning down that attitude and mouth of yours. With us it is fine. I need to see how your mouth responds when the blows are from the opponent. Otherwise, we may be ready to fight soon."

"I thought training would be for two months."

"We can get him ready in two days if his mind and health is right. His mind should be right now. I think he was waiting on you."

Confused I asked, "On me?"

He kissed my cheek the way a father or brother does. "Yep, we have been waiting on you. Don't be surprised at how fast things start to run. Let me know when you have trouble with anything. It is my job to keep you safe and protected. That means mentally too. When you are not right, he is not right. Get used to it. I don't think it will change unless you initiate the change. Good night Ms. D."

I threw my hand up and waved goodbye speechless.

"Close your mouth and do not take advantage of my boy. I am not sure everything is working well tonight. You may be disappointed. We would hate for him to be left looking like a punk. Just keep waiting. The time will come," he snickered.

I closed the door and went back to the room. He had the remote in his hand. I sat on the edge of the bed and handed him the two pills and a Gatorade. I leaned over, "Get some sleep."

"AWW," he yelled.

"Sorry."

I got my Mary Poppins bag out of the truck which had a few extra sets of clothes. Around midnight, after taking a shower, I went to check on him.

"Danielle."

He shocked me, "Yes," I replied.

"Why are you still here?" he asked.

"I am watching you. Are you okay?"

"Yes. Why are you up?" he questioned.

" I heard you making noise," I responded.

"Do you need anything?" he asked.

"I have everything I need. Get some rest babe."

"You can lay up here with me. I am too tried to even touch you," he painfully confessed.

I laid on top of the cover upside down and sideways and to my surprise I fell asleep before I could figure out what was on the television. Soon after I heard him turn the set off which I hoped meant he was asleep also.

Friday

At three thirty AM he was up and getting dressed. He was a different man. Not the man he was less than eight hours ago when I scraped him up off a rubber mat. Amazingly, he had been a good patient. He was already outside waiting when King arrived.

"Damn man," King growled knowing it was about to be a rough morning.

"You can't keep me down even when you try." He cut his eyes at King since he was the main puncher yesterday, although he would never confess to Danielle. He did not want to give her any more fuel than she already had to dislike King.

"Are you sure you feel good?"

"Incredible. I hope you are ready," Hooks warned.

"What happened?" King looked perplexed that he felt this great knowing for certain he was badly bruised.

"I have a good nurse."

Not really wanting to know the answer, "What else did she give you?"

"I think you all made certain nothing else was popping off. Speaking of which did anyone call Tre?"

"JJ called Tre and Doc. They will both see you today. Are you sure you didn't hit it?" They tussled and wrestled like two five year olds in response to King's question.

"I need to stay close so I can run back and make sure Danielle is up for work by four thirty or five."

Not believing what he was hearing, "Look at you. What's up? We have cellphones."

"Nothing man," Hooks said with a big grin. "She was and is good to me and I want to be good to her. She supports me and all I can do is support her back."

"Is she going to continue to work?"

"Huh?" he slowed giving King his full attention.

"When we start travelling? Is she going to continue to work?" King wanted to know this for a few reasons. For starters, he was concerned he was going to have to worry about a female being around and disrupting his fighter. Lastly, he couldn't help but wonder if she was really after a pay off?

He laughed, "Danielle, umm probably so. I do not foresee my work stopping her work. I will have to buy a diamond mine and go hard in the paint if you know what I mean. It has been four years. I don't even know if I still got it like that. Besides, we are going to take this one event at a time. Girlfriend, dating, events, boxing, etcetera."

"It's like riding a bike once you get back on, it will all come back to you. Literally, back on it. Trust me. We will see," King said as if he was truly giving words of wisdom. They both laughed.

"No we won't see. This will not be broadcasted and recorded. The monitors will be disabled."

"So I know when they are no longer working then you are working it out in the Kings chambers."

"Hopefully after Tre has pronounced us husband and wife."

"Stick to the plan. I got you right where you need to be right now. I do not need any more interruptions. If she brings it hard in bed like she did last night we will not be able to handle you."

"Keep up," he said and took off running. He did not want to think about Danielle in bed this morning. He had already thought about it enough over the last few months.

As they sprinted back to the house at four fifty eight he said, "I'll be right back. Get some water or something."

"Let me ask you a question before you go in."

"What's up?"

"Do you love her?"

He got his breath together. He dazed into space, wiped his face with his shirt, and checked his monitor to be sure it would not give him away. He looked King in the eyes, "Yes I do. I have never felt this way in my life. I would give this all up if she asked me to. Everything. The cars, clothes, money, fame, and boxing. Just let me keep my God and her and I will survive."

King looked like he really did not know how to respond. Was that good news or bad news? He dropped his head in disgust. They stood there shoulder to shoulder for what seemed like hours.

This was a moment of truth. Hooks was honest with him and he had to be truthful back to him. "I like her too." They man hugged. "You deserve her man and I won't let you mess it up. We will work this out for the good of everyone. Trust me."

"I'm counting on you and holding you accountable to holding me accountable." He ran in the house to avoid getting emotional. What King said meant a lot to him. He needed to know that King liked and trusted Danielle. However, they had an awful way of showing it to each other.

He looked over at her sleeping. He laid across the bed and moved her hair. She moved slightly, "I can see you Randall."

"No you can't. Your eyes are closed." He kissed her face, her hands, and her neck.

"Where have you been?"

"I ran to Boston and back?"

"Shut up!"

Kissing each finger individually, "I did." He wished every morning could be like this.

"Where is the Terminator?" He gave up the laugh I loved.

"He is outside waiting on me."

"Tell him I am going to kick his a-s-s."

"I think he is aware of it. Are you going to get up?"

"Nope, I am calling in. I had a rough night."

"Yeah right. I will be right back. Get up," he said as he kissed me again.

He came back in five minutes with a smoothie. Now he was kissing all over me. *I cannot believe this is the same guy. What happened?* I was embarrassed of my morning breath, "I haven't brushed me teeth."

"So what."

"You can't kiss me or see me until I am washed up and dressed."

"Remember I saw you when you were sick and I don't think you cared."

"Well I do now. Good bye," I demanded.

"I am not leaving."

"Yes you are."

"You cannot kick me out of my room at my house. What are you going to do once we are married? Hide every morning?"

I was speechless. I have not thought about marriage in years. Here he is speaking as if we are in the planning stages now. *Oh my God! Maybe it is in his planning stage*, I thought. I stared directly at him not knowing how to respond.

"Do you have clothes for work or do I need to go get you some?"

"Randall, where in God's name are you going to go get me some clothes from at this time of the morning?"

He grinned. 'I don't know," he said thinking about what he said.

"You got it bad."

"Concussion. I hit my head yesterday."

"Shut up liar."

"I have enough to cover what I need today. I think I am going to look at some jobsites. I am not going to stay at work too long."

"Surprising."

"What does your day look like?"

"I am sure someone has arranged for the doctor to look at me and then for
Trevor to come oil me down. It wouldn't surprise me if he gives me a lie detector to discover what happened here last night."

"When are you going to see me?"

"At the gym when you get there."

"Are you going to be coherent today or will I have to roll you off the mat again?"

"I will make sure they kick my tail before you get there and you do not have to see me like that again."

"Are you coming back here before I leave?"

"How long will it take you to get ready?"

"Normally I blink and click my heels three times and I am ready but this morning I think it may take one click. I don't have much I am working with."

"We can go get you some things today to leave here. That is if you want to. Please feel free to do so. I do not want to step out of bounds," he said nervously.

You could tell he had never done this before. I wanted to assure him. "Is that an offer?"

"Umm yeah it is. But only if you want to."

"Mr. Washington you know I am not that kind of girl."

"No, that is not what I mean."

"Well, what do you mean sir?"

"I was just. I was just saying in case you are here and need to change clothes you will have whatever stuff you need. Girl stuff. I mean Danielle stuff," he corrected. "You know if plans change or we decide to go to dinner or swimming or something. Oh never mind. Forget it." He was flustered. He could not get out what he wanted to say. "It's cool. Forget it."

"No it is cool. I just may do that. Sounds like the two of us might have quite a few dates to look forward to."

"I am hoping so. You name it."

"I should be ready to leave at six if you want to come back and lock the door?"

"You got it."

"Got what?"

"Locking up."

"What do you mean?"

"You have the key to this door on your key ring."

"You are so smart. I am going to keep you around. What do I need to do special?"

"Tell me you love me."

"I love you. Now tell me, will I need to cut the alarm on and if so how?

"I will give you a lesson for both here and the gym. In the meantime text me when you are heading out and I will enable it from my phone."

"I do not have that feature?"

"You have not because you asked not."

"You are correct. How do I get this option?" I asked.

"Ask and it shall be given to you. I will take care of it."

"Is it that easy?"

Agreeing, "Yep. That applies for anything. Ask and it shall be given unto you," he said while walking out of the room.

"Can I get the phantom?" I lifted up and yelled.

"You have the key. It is in the garage."

I had to do a double take. *Did I hear him correctly? He must have hit his head hard yesterday. I don't remember having the key. I do not know what I have keys to. I have keys*, I thought. I rolled over on my back. I looked to the ceiling and laughed. I was so happy. I rolled all over the bed laughing and grinning. I was lying in Randall Hooks Washington's bed. Deacon Washington. I did nothing to get there and nothing to be left here. It felt so good. There were thousands of women that would have done a lot to get here. Or she would have done them all. I hoped I could continue to walk this same faithful walk.

Immediately, I heard his voice. It scared the heck out of me. "DJ, you do know I can see you right?" he advised watching from the kitchen.

CRAP! I forgot he could see me. Why was he still here anyway? "You do know I don't care either, stalker!" Truthfully, I was busted.

He went back to join King. He was happy that I was happy. I took my time getting dressed wanting to savor the moment. I gathered all my things from the guest bathroom making sure I did not leave anything behind then returned to his bedroom. If you want to call it a bedroom. It was more like a condo. I made up the bed and checked both rooms two, three, four times. I wanted to make sure I was not leaving anything. I did not want to leave one strand of hair. I could not give him the idea I was purposefully leaving anything behind. I toddled lightly after I had packed my bag. I didn't want to leave. I tried not to make any unnecessary movements or motions knowing I was being filmed, although I took my time. Once I got to the door and gathered all my things I called him.

"DJ, are you good?"

"I am walking out the door now." I closed the door behind me. A few seconds later as I walked to my truck I could hear the alarm activating.

"Babe turn right outside the gate and you will see me so you can give me a kiss before you leave. That is if you brushed," he joked.

"Too late. I am turning left."

"Ah man. That is jacked up."

"So was your little smart comment. Jerk."

"You lied I hear you coming behind me." King turned around. I flashed my lights. "Race you." He took off running. It took me a second to realize he was really racing me but I was stopped. I finally pulled up close to him. He came over on my side still moving in place. I rolled down my window and gave him a kiss and handed him two waters. He threw one to King.

"I will see you this evening correct?"

"Of course," I smiled inside.

"Have a good day babe. Be safe."

"You too. See you King."

King mumbled without looking in my direction. "Go build something tangible and leave his ego alone."

"Kick rocks mush mouth."

I stopped by all the sites I needed for the day then headed to the office around two. As soon as I stepped out of the elevator, I was chastised immediately.

"Where have you been?"

"It's Friday Leigh."

"Not today. Last night?" she questioned.

"Huh?" She looked me dead in the eyes without blinking. "I spent the night at Randall's," I confessed.

Not believing what she heard, "YOU DID WHAT?"

"I stayed at Randall's. He wasn't feeling well."

"How is he now?"

"He is fine. Thank you for asking."

"You are not a nurse. Why does he feel good?"

I had to explain to her and of course she got the girls on the phone to relay the details. I yelled into Leigh at five. "We are not staying here all night."

"Yes we are. Just because you got a boo now does not mean we can just leave when we get ready."

"I think everyone is against me," I whined. "Bye Leigh. I will see you later this weekend. I will be here for a while longer." Right at seven my phone rang. I knew it was him even before the tone sounded.

"Once we are married, are you going to work early and stay late every night?" he asked.

"I do not stay late on Wednesdays," I corrected.

"So it has to be a church related event for you to leave at a decent hour?"

"You will need to be the preacher."

"You are pushing me Danielle. I guess I will be a preacher then. Instead of calling you Ms. Rose they will call you the Preacher's Wife."

"A man's gotta do what a man's gotta do."

"Go home. Dress comfortably. I will be by to pick you up."

Dress comfortably. What did that mean? Let me call my fashion consultant.

"Hey Auntie."

"What's up?"

"Nothing. What are you doing?"

"I just walked in the house."

"What?"

Disgusted, I said, "I know right. Randall made me come home."

"Wow! To his house or yours?" she flipped out of her mouth.

"You know what I am not going to take this. BYE!" I hung up and then realized I didn't ask the question I called her for so I called right back.

Sade sang the lyrics to an Usher song as she answered, "You got it bad. When you are on the phone, hang up and you call right back."

"I didn't know you were so poetic and lyrical. Randall said to dress comfortably. What does that mean?"

"It is a nice way of saying, please do not wear a three piece suit, anything shiny, sparkly, or fancy. No heels. And whatever you do, no blazer! Can you do that?" she asked sarcastically.

My answer of course was a big fat 'NO'. I sat on my chaise and popped open a water while I gazed into my closet. "What time does the mall close? I have nothing that meets the requirement."

Sade laughed out loud. "Auntie, just put on your uniform."

"I hate you.com!"

"It's cool. Throw on the tennis shoes and take a bag with the bare essentials."

"Overnight bag? A Mary Poppins Bag?" I almost choked on my water.

"No crazy! A purse, hipster or something. Did you ever date?"

"Who asked you? I'll call you back in a few minutes."

"Do I need to come over there?"

"I am not that helpless." Either I really needed help or I was more clueless about dating than I realized. Maybe I was making this bigger than what it was.

"Helpless, no. Lame and nerdy, yes."

I really needed her help. However, I guess I could handle it by myself. She said my uniform. Casual to me consisted of jeans or khakis with a boo beater or white tee. She said tennis shoes. Literally, she did not mean for me to wear tennis shoes. They all should know that was not happening. She was referring to the greatest sandal ever made. A Tory Burch thong. I didn't like flat shoes either but these were awesome. I opted for the jeans with stones on the back and a tank with stones. I really wasn't sure. I think this was more difficult because I had no clue as to where we were going. It was a Friday night. I tried to think of what entertainment or sporting events were in town, but couldn't come up with anything.

He was there in an hour as promised. He rang the buzzer and I opened the gate without saying anything. He kissed me as soon as I opened the door.

"You know what?"

"What babe?" he said with so much enthusiasm.

"I missed you."

It startled him. He was not expecting that. He blushed and squatted down and grabbed my legs. "Get dressed."

"I am dressed."

He stood up with a disagreeing look, "I said comfortable."

I gave him the look over. He was comfortable. I guess for a guy. He was wearing his Nike gear. "Fine. Where are we going?"

"Change. Comfortable. You will be walking. A lot."

"Are we going to the track?"

"NO. We are on a date."

I was walking down the hall, "Walking? You get cheaper and cheaper. I can tell already I don't like this date." I changed to my Under Armour gear and broke down and put on my Air Max. I didn't feel good about this date. I had no control. I hesitantly came out of the bedroom still unsure of what was going to happen. With Randall anything goes.

"What are you doing?" I asked looking at him lying on the floor.

He looked in my direction. "Good job DJ," he said in approval.

"I am ready." He didn't answer why he was laying on my floor.

We walked to the door, "Are you missing anything?"

I looked around myself, "No."

Shaking his head, "Get it DJ."

I quickly ran and got my bag with my computers, iPads, and cameras, "Let's do it." Wherever we were going I had my essentials. Even my original outfit was in my bag just in case he pulled a fast one on me. He was in the Aston tonight. As he closed my door I asked again, "Where are we going?"

"Relax. Just ride."

We rode and talked the entire way. We were downtown when he pulled over

and parked the car. He unbuckled and got out. He came and opened my door. I looked suspect. This did not look like a date to me, "Are you getting out?"

"I guess so? Where are we going?"

"We are walking," he said again.

"Where?"

"Down the street."

"Where?"

He pointed. "There. You are going to introduce me to your world. Close up."

"What do you mean?"

"I want you to walk and tell me about these buildings. The ones you did and the ones you didn't do. What would you change? What should you have changed? What do you like about them? You see me working every day. You have been learning and experiencing my world. Teach me your world. I want to understand why you love your job so much."

I looked puzzled, but nevertheless, I got both bags, took his hand and started talking. We walked for hours as he listened closely. He asked great questions and seemed genuinely interested. He was impressed that I was licensed to be both the architect and the architectural engineer. I could literally design every aspect of a building. I was capable of designing its foundation, heating, electrical, plumbing, structure, cosmetic appearance, and held licensure to design, coordinate, and furnish its interior. Most people could not. Actually, the only other person I knew who held as many licenses and degrees in this field was Rose.

Randall quickly realized I loved talking about architecture. I liked it even if it wasn't my own work. As we walked people looked. They did double and triple takes but all were reluctant to ask if he was who they thought he was. I was very pleased that not one person stopped him. He had become so immune to the attention I do not think he noticed them watching. I was glad. I was the one on the date with him and I wanted all his attention and yes I had it.

"Let's stop here," he said while admiring a hotel we were passing. It happened to be my favorite hotel. *Did someone tell him?*

"Why are we stopping here?"

He laughed, "To have a drink and a bite to eat. No caffeine."

We sat down after placing our orders. I leaned up on my elbows on the table, "How did you know?" I asked.

"Know what?"

"Out of all the places I have and have not done this is my favorite of them all."

"I did not know."

I nibbled on a salad while he pilfered some of my vegetables. Once we finished we walked back to the car. We took our time enjoying each other's company along with the view. I continued explaining in detail as we passed each structure. As we rode back home I did not want our date to end. "Randall."

He took my hand. "Yes," he replied.

"This was the best date ever"

His heart melted. "I agree." He took my face and kissed me.

I gasped, "You are driving."

"Sorry. This is what you do to me. You make me lose all train of thought." While walking me to my door he asked, "Will I see you tomorrow?"

As if it was a strange request, I responded, "Do you want to?"

"Danielle, I want to see you every day for the rest of my life. Good night," he said quickly kissing my lips and racing back to his car.

Saturday

I did my normal Saturday routine before I meet the girls at Mikey's. It was brunch for me and an early breakfast for them. All three of them headed to the salon after we ate. I left and went home to change and go to the gym to gain control of my thoughts while working out.

I walked in the gym and spoke, "Hello."

"Hey gorgeous."

"Hi handsome."

"This is a gym and not a meat market," King barked.

"It must be a difficult job to always be disgruntled," I barked back.

"Come here girl," Randall intervened while refraining from laughter.

I walked over to the bag he was punching and tried to get close in between punches.

Not looking in my direction he said, "Your hair looks nice."

"Thank you."

Continuing to punch the bag repeatedly ignoring how close I was standing, "You are not about to work out are you?"

"Yeah."

"And mess up your hair?"

"It's just hair."

"If you give me the chance we will have plenty of time for me to mess it up

later."

"Meet me upstairs," I winked and pursed my lips.

He corrected me, "I will meet you at the house in two hours. I am getting in the sauna and then showering."

"We have a sauna?"

He laughed my laugh while I looked serious. "Yes babe. We do."

"Well why didn't anyone tell me? Is it just for boys or something?" He paused with a mischievous look on his face.

There is no way Danielle will never be allowed in the sauna as long as I am in the building. She generates enough steam within me by standing a few feet away from me. Just thinking about it arises me.

I walked away. I went upstairs and walked for a little while to calm my thoughts. Once I felt refreshed, I left. I did not see him on my way out. I had too much on my mind to question it. I continued deep in thought all the way home. I changed clothes and just as I became engulfed in putting my ideas on paper my phone rang his tone.

I opened the gate. When he came in the door he could tell I was working. "Danielle, what are you doing?"

"Looking over plans."

Afraid he was disturbing me he had no choice but to ask, "Shall I come back?"

"Anytime but you are not leaving if that is what you are asking."

In his serious tone he requested, "Can I speak to you for a minute?"

He obtained all of my undivided attention, "Sure."

He took a deep breath, "Thanks for rescuing me the other night. They would have left me there all night until I could get myself together. They would have left my hands taped and gloved."

"No problem. That's what friends are for."

Disappointed in the use of the word, "FRIENDS?"

"Ah crap. My bad," realizing what I said.

Needing immediate clarification, "Friend? Are we just friends?"

"We are friends but you are my boo." I grabbed his neck and put him in a choke hold hug.

Not settling for my response, "Back up. Back up. I do not want to be your boo."

I could hear his seriousness, "Huh?" I let him go.

"You refer to TIP as your boo."

"Ah he is jealous. The big heavy weight is jealous of little ole TIP." I laughed. This was cute.

"I'm glad you are aware he is little. I will crush him with the palm of my hand."

"Okay, baby, sweetie, sweetheart, the love of my life, the greatest Deacon, and fighter to ever live. My boyfriend."

"That's a little better. Not much," he said trying to sound disappointed.

I grabbed his cheeks and laid one on him. "How is that?"

"Not quite."

I kissed him longer and more passionately. "Now?"

"Close."

I knocked him down and laid on top of him kissing him. I felt him rise at the same time he pushed me off.

"That was over kill," he admitted. "I am going home now."

"I was just following orders."

"Yeah you did," as he punched my wall again.

"Mental note. Have these walls double lined with metal."

"You do not want to do that babe. I will break my hands. That is how I make my living remember. With my hands," he held both of his fists up. "These hands are worth millions and one day I hope to make them worth billions. They are the resource for our happiness. You and me that is. They are the beginning of our life together, the help that will make our world go around, and the resource for all of your needs and wants. Next to God and me they are the only thing you will ever desire. If they get hurt then you hurt. Others will hurt. I have a lot of people's lives riding on these hands. I think about it and pray about it daily. I hold people's lives in the palm of my hand. Everyone on my payroll depends on these," he said as he stared at his hands.

He rolled over on top of me and laid his forehead on mine. He waited and took his time before he spoke. "I have really been concerned about you. I hope you can handle this. I've been down this road before. I do not want to lose you over me fighting. You are more important than fighting."

Flattered, "No I am not."

"You are the only thing that makes my world complete. Do you understand me?"

"No."

"Danielle, what don't you understand?"

"I don't want you to put me before boxing. That is your passion. Boxing is your life. That is what you have worked hard for all of these years. I could not come in between that. I would walk away before I allow you to place me before boxing."

"Listen to me and listen well. I have done this for twelve years. There will be a day when I can't do it any longer. The Association will say, my mind will say, my body will say, the fans will say, King and JJ will say, God will say, and you will say. If the day you say comes before all the others then it is a done deal. I still have tons of other things I am involved in and can do. Who knows maybe we will have a little crumb snatcher or two who I can train. Maybe I will make movies. Maybe I will help you build buildings. Maybe I will referee, commentate, or even broadcast. Who knows what the future will hold? It will not be the last of Hooks, but rather the start of Randall Washington.

"Maybe you will preach. Reverend Washington. One thing is sure, whatever you do it will be your decision and not mine, Pastor Washington."

"I receive it in the name of Jesus. As I lie on top of this fine woman and keep my composure it has got to be the Lord."

"I really do not think your composure is all together you are just handling it well," I said insinuating his statue pressing me.

"I got this. Mind over matter. We do need to talk. I think we should have one more conversation on how you feel about this. "

"Tell me how do you feel?" I asked.

"I am sort of nervous and a different person from when I started this. I am a man now at a different stage of my life. I seem to be much more calm, meek, humble, single, and older." He took a deep breath. "I am concerned about drama and women. No one ever noticed me just like you did not and I hope it stays that way. I am not programmed to deal with groupies. In my earlier years, I was hyped, not cocky, and just young. I craved it. I wanted it. I would have done anything for it. Now, I still love it. I still want it but my focus has shifted. I crave God first. I am hungry for Him. You come next and then a list of other things like health, peace, and family. I want to win. That is the entire purpose but if not I deserve a safe and fair fight. Truth be told I am worried about letting all of you down more than anything else."

"Let me stop you right there," I said as we laid on the floor of my foyer. "I did not notice you. I was not looking for anyone. Yes, I desired a mate but I was not looking. You know how I am. I was into my work. When our paths crossed I was so preoccupied with where I was and why until I was not looking. But that is how God works. He satisfies your needs and wants without your help when you least expect it. Then when we began to talk. I never thought about it.

You are different. Not what I would have expected. I do not know what I expected. I surely did not expect to be worshipping with a boxer, much less dating one. Your stature seems different. You are larger than four years ago when I would have watched you and I guess the added weight makes your height appear different. Although, I know it did not change.

As far as letting us down, you do you," I wanted to make this point clear. "Don't worry about us. If you get in there and give all you have then that is all we can ask for. You are the one that will have to take and give those punches. None of us will be in there with you. None of us will feel the blows and pain. We will not have to mentally or physically endure the ring. Do not do this for us. Do this for yourself. Promise me you will not worry about us. We all will love you the same. I could care less whether you win or lose. I want you to be the same man once you step out of the ring. The same physically, mentally, spiritually, and emotionally."

"Thanks for your support, but you do know I want to win."

"I know. We all want you to but it is okay if you don't."

"Do you know RJ has never seen me fight? He has never seen me train. I am not sure how I feel about him seeing me."

"Ask him how he feels and then you make a decision. He is a big kid now."

"His mother hated it. I hope she has not corrupted his thoughts."

"You can easily find out." I paused waiting on him to respond. "What else troubles you?" I asked sensing there was more going on with him than he was telling.

"What if no one wants to fight me?"

"Then you pick someone and challenge them. Someone will take the bait."

"How do you know?"

I looked at him with raised brows, "Money is involved. Right?"

"Not if people do not show up to the event. What if people don't want to see me fight again?"

Why was he being so negative? I felt fear in his tone. "Then we hope they come for the opponent."

"How does that help me?"

"Why do you care who they come to see as long as the arena is packed. You came to win. Who cares who is there to spectate. We all will be there right?"

"If you are asking if you will be there then I would hope you would like to come."

"Do you think I would miss it?"

He asked unsure, "Are you spending the week in Vegas?"

"Umm. We will have to see about that."

"I will make sure Leigh is there too if that helps."

"Bribery gets you nowhere."

"What about Paige and the baby too?"

"I do not think you want all of us in Vegas for a week. We will be of no value to your preparation. Then you will have to worry about how all of us will behave in the city of lights."

He regained his confidence, "That week I will assign King to you. This will not be a party week. This is work. When I work we all work."

Yelling at his remark, "That ain't ever happening."

He laughed my laugh.

"First off, King will not leave your side for a minute that week and secondly, you do not want us to kill each other. You need him."

"You are absolutely correct. Which means you will not leave my side either. And all the more reason you all will not kill each other that week. It will be too important."

"From what I understand you are extremely concerned with me and your fighting and will not announce it until you feel confident in my ability to witness."

In disgust he barked, "Who told you that?"

"Is it true?"

In a calmer tone, "Somewhat?"

I changed my expression at his lack of honesty.

"Well possibly. I am not sure how fast this will go. I need you to be okay and most of all trust me. I do not want to be in Vegas and you think I am doing wrong. The last thing I need is for you to be upset about some BS and not speaking to me the day or week before I fight. This is why I asked if you are able to be there the entire week."

Jovially, I gave him orders, "Make the announcement. I will be fine. I will walk in the fruit of the spirit. Worst case scenario, if I have something to discuss I will hold it until we get back home and we can discuss it then."

He scowled at my response, "Wrong answer. I do not want you to hold anything in either."

What was he so concerned about and afraid of? "Why do you think something will happen?"

"I hope not. Better not."

"How about this? If something jumps off. If I feel uncomfortable I will talk to Keith and King," I said as reassuring as I knew how.

He was not convinced. "I guess that will work. However, I still do not like it."

"How about we journal to each other. For two weeks. You journal your thoughts to me and I journal mine to you. Then at the end we share with each other."

"I can do that but it seems a little cheating to me."

"Why?"

"You know I will surely be blogging during that time."

"You will be blogging to the world."

"That is true but lately all my blogs have been about you and to you." *Does she not see she is my world*, he thought to himself.

I blushed and quickly changed the subject. "So what's next?"

"DJ, I have so much going on it is amazing."

"Are you holding back from me?"

"No. You know everything," he reassured. "I am preparing to fight and need to decide when to make the announcement. I also need to talk to RJ about you and then about fighting. I have not figured out if it would be best to do it all at once or a little at a time. I have a lot of battles to conquer before I even get to the ring. The guy in the ring is easy. I am prepared for him. It's Mama Rose who concerns me."

"You can handle it," I lied. Mama Rose was going to chew him up and spit him out. I would do better bringing a thug home than a boxer.

"I can handle her as long as I have you on my side."

"I say send out a blog and an email. That way you cover the press, fans, RJ, family, and friends."

Nervously he said, "Write it up for me."

"Don't be nervous. Pray about it. You know what to do."

Cautiously, he said, "You are right." We chilled and talked the rest of the afternoon until early evening.

"Babe, do you want to do anything before I leave? Maybe dinner?"

"No, I am good. I am going back to my office."

"I know you think I did not notice but I appreciate and I am proud of you for not texting, emailing, or working while I was here today."

"Does my work bother you?" I had to ask since he has mentioned it on a few occasions.

"That is not what I meant."

"Elaborate please," I was prepared to wait patiently.

He paused and gave half of a laugh. "I had some serious subjects I wanted to discuss and I think if I was interrupted I would have changed my mind. I hope and pray we are on one accord. I do not want to jump out here and make this announcement and you jet on me."

I could not believe he was so nervous and concerned about my response to his fight announcement. I tried forcing him to relax. "Honey, make the announcement. I am good. I promise," I reassured.

"It feels like proposing at the dome in front of thousands possibly millions of people and the girl says no. How embarrassing."

That is a strange analogy. Why did he pick proposing? Danielle calm down he is not about to propose. "I would not say no. Not right at that moment anyway. I would say yes then take the ring and change my number." I laughed to myself although he did not find it funny at all.

He gave me a look like WTH?

I gave one back. "What? At least the guy won't be embarrassed," I said clearing up his confusion.

A barrage of thoughts came to Randall all at once. *Why did she say the guy? Does she not know I am referring to myself? I am the guy. Does she not know I have been contemplating proposing right there before or after the fight? Wow, it went right over her head. I will play it out and see what happens.*

We kissed and he left. A few hours later Leigh called. "Your package arrived."

"Cool. On Monday let's check to see when we can put this on the calendar."

"What are you doing?"

"Working," duh.

"You make me sick you over achiever. Find something else to do. Go polish your nails. Make flowers with toilet paper. Count rice. Do something other than work. How about this for a change? CHILL."

"What is that? People still do that?"

"Umm, yes we do."

"Lazy folks," I teased.

"Call it what you want," Leigh teased back.

"I call it utilizing my time."

"Whatever nerd," she insulted. "Good bye."

Randall called after his work out. We coordinated for tomorrow and called it a night.

Sunday

I arrived to Keith meeting me in the parking lot. The watch told them my location before I arrived. Once he escorted me inside, I greeted them all as I entered the vestibule. Deacon Washington had a strange look on his face.

"What's wrong?"

He leaned in, "Nothing."

With a grimace on my face I whispered, "Liar."

"Shh, don't say that in church."

"Then tell the truth."

Doing a double take, he looked around as if he wanted to make sure no one was looking. He guided me by my waist as we begin to walk. "I love you." I looked up and he ran off.

Keith followed as I walked in the sanctuary and sat down. He looked nice until I looked down and almost fell out. If he was ten I would have pinched him and pulled his ear. His pants were wrinkled from the cleaner's hanger. That was a major pet peeve. Sure, we all might have been guilty of it at some point in time. Nevertheless, I made a mental note to get to church earlier from now on to review the guys. I was going to have Deacon put an iron and board in his office immediately. Keith always stood in a protective stance.

He was directly in front of me. When he was in protection mode, he was a different person than he was on an ordinary day. King was next to Deacon Washington when they came in the sanctuary. Hunter followed right behind them.

When we got ready to sit down my bible was in Keith's chair. The way he looked you would have thought it was a bomb. His eyes quickly turned to daggers as they stared at me. I snickered, "Sorry."

He ended up knocking my arm shortly afterwards. "Sorry," he said.

I knew he did it on purpose, "You are good. Tight neck."

He cut his eyes.

"You look like you have on a neck brace and you can't move," I jokingly whispered trying to mellow him out. He rolled his eyes. When he sat his back to the chair later I whispered, "Why are you sitting up so straight? Does your back move?"

I was annoying the crap out of him and enjoying it. I could talk as much trash as I wanted and he could not nor would not give it back to me. Deacon looked over and caught me taunting Keith. He stared at me waiting for me to look in his direction. I knew he was watching. I could feel his eyes on me but I refused to make contact. The next motion we stood up at Hunter's request. When Deacon prepared to sit down he inconspicuously swapped seats with King. It was smooth. I did not see the switch coming. His move gave me ammunition to talk smack to Keith.

I mumbled, "You are trying to get me in trouble. Snitch. I thought we were cool."

Right then Pastor said, "Everyone with you may not be for you."

"Preach on it Pastor," someone yelled out.

Then he gave an illustration. He called for Deacon to come to the pulpit and a few other Deacons. Of course when Randall moved King and Keith both stood and moved. "Sorry Bro. This is a football illustration." He did a spectacular job on getting the point across. We all appreciated and received it. Then they did it to me. Keith and King changed seats. Before I knew it King was next to me.

"UGH," I sighed heavily in disgust. So much so until the woman next to me shuffled.

He spoke into his wrist, "Ms. D needs assistance."

At the same time I frowned Keith and Randall both looked. I did not know Randall had an ear piece in his ear too.

"King, why can't I wear mine if he has his in?" I pouted and folded my arms as he continued to ignore me. Right when church was about to dismiss he said, "Because I said so."

I rolled my eyes again. He was responding to my question from thirty minutes ago. I knew right then he was certifiably insane. I made a mental note to research him as soon as I got home.

After service King mumbled, "No talking in church Wednesday."

"You all put on full conversation with animation every service."

"You heard me," he shouted without shouting.

Deacon walked me to my car hugging me. As soon as I took my seat he said, "Pull your skirt up so I can see your legs."

Like an idiot I did. He sighed as if my pale legs took his breath away. "Let me have you."

"I can be bought with a price."

"Name it," he said with confidence.

I held my ring finger up.

He laughed, "Check me girl do not allow cheap thrills."

"Then you know what you must do Deacon."

To him this was confirmation he could go through with a proposal. "Watch what you ask for. You have not because you ask not."

Buying a diamond ring was nothing to a guy like Randall. "I still did not ask," I sassed.

"You have eluded enough." That was all he needed to know she was or would be interested in accepting his marriage proposal.

"Eluded what?"

"Let me do my job."

"Whatever honey. Bye," I continued to sass knowing he was not serious.

"You say that like you don't like it."

"Do you like it? Whatever it is?"

"I love it," he glowed as he spoke.

"Then that is all that matters." He kissed my cheek right before I pulled off. I looked in my review mirror and as always he was running back inside. Between running and laughing I was not sure which he did the most. I did nothing but think about him. *I wonder what the change will be after he announces his return to boxing.* I was happy but the selfish side of me made me very sad. *Where will this place me in his life?* Then I remembered the week he went to Vegas. I was neglected. *I don't know if I can stand for another week like that,* I thought.

He called after three. "Hello," I answered.

"DJ."

"Hey babe."

"What do you want to do this afternoon?"

"I am cool."

He picked up on my tone, "What's wrong?"

"Nothing."

"That is not what I sense."

"Now here you go." Something was bothering me but it was no need for discussion. "I am working that's all." I hated lying to him. I was normally lying that I was not working. Now I am lying that I am working.

Reluctantly he said, "Carry on. I am going to the gym then. Call me once you are done and I will come over if you do not have a date."

I rumbled with laughter, "I think my schedule is free today."

"It better be free from dates everyday unless they include me," he mumbled just loud enough for me to hear.

"Excuse me?"

"Nothing."

"I heard you."

"I know you did. I meant for you to hear me."

"We are going to work on that bipolar stalkerish attitude."

"We can but it will remain the same."

"We shall see."

I finally got up, dressed, and went to Mikey's for dinner. I needed some best friend conversation, advice, and love. After annoying Mike and him annoying me, I came home and called it a night.

He blogged at one fifty six AM.

My life changed overnight. Well, not quite overnight. It was a long time coming. Now that it has come it is moving rapidly. I must admit, it was worth every miserable moment. I am excited. I can't wait my love. I will see what the end shall be.

I rolled over once I heard the phone chirp. I did not realize I fell asleep. I read it and sent him a text.

What do you want the end to be?

He texted back.

I thought you were sleep. I want the happy ending. I think you know the desires of my heart.

I text back.

You have the power to write the story to end however you wish. Remember that.

> What does that mean?

> As long as you do what you are supposed to do the ending will be happy. The story is in your hands. Good night.

WEEK 21
Monday

As planned, Leigh and I showed up to the gym to work. I had been there since five thirty this morning. Of course, I could not beg, bribe or demand Leigh to arrive that early. She made it in around seven. By the time she arrived, I had all the tools and ladders out of the truck. I could not move any further because I was waiting on the equipment. I knew there was at least two to three hours to get started before he arrived. He was going to have something smart to say; therefore, I was already mentally prepared. My IT help was there and so was the Muzak Company. I was not only going to run voice through the entire place but data also. I never knew when I might want to present or televise from my laptop. So, now if I did, or in case he wanted to televise for that matter, the gym would be equipped to do so.

No one had yet to ask me what I was doing thus far. This was a good thing. It seemed like it was going to be an easy project. The easy ones are the ones that usually turned on you. I hoped I could get enough started before Randall arrived and shut me down. We had already started pulling wire when Leigh joined us.

She came in rather chipper for it to be a Monday morning. "Hello," she sang. "Dani?"

I yelled, "Yes ma'am," from the ceiling never looking down.

"I need some help."

"Yeah, I know."

She ignored m sarcastic comment. "There are some guys out there just pull one. Anyone will be fine."

That she did not want to do. She looked around the room for the longest time before she decided whom to ask.

***

We were getting into the groove of things and working hard when I heard the commotion. We had been at it about three good hours. Everything was looking good and on target. Nowhere near complete but a good place nonetheless.

"Is that Danielle's truck outside?" he asked as he entered the common area. I did not hear anyone respond as I was buried deep in the ceiling. Maybe they nodded. I am sure someone answered. There was deadly silence. Suddenly, the room roared, "Danielle! What are you doing?"

"Working," I answered calmly.

"On a ladder?"

"Yep."

"You work at a drafting table," he shouted.

"Not today."

"Come down immediately," he expressed his frustration.

"Not yet." I was pulling from a box of wire below me.

In a fierce tone, "Do not make me come up there," he threatened.

"Do what you need to do," I thought but said aloud.

He could not believe my defiance, "Say what?"

"Handle your business." I could feel the extra weight on the ladder as I stood on the highest rung inside the ceiling tiles. "Get down." He was now making us a safety hazard.

"Not until you come down."

"Wait a minute," I said to him and yelling, "pull it," to my IT guy on the other end. "Do you have enough?"

"Barely enough," he yelled back through the ceiling.

"I have plenty. Pull some slack. We are not counting cost. We are spending Mr. Hooks' money. I want it right. Keep pulling." After that pull, I came out of the ceiling. I would have assumed he would be gone. As soon as I looked down, he was standing there looking me in the face.

"Yes sir?"

Never knowing what to expect from her he asked, "Danielle, why are you in my ceiling?"

"Working."

As calm as he could he then asked, "On what DJ?"

"Music."

In disbelief at her response, "There is music in here."

"No there is not. Y'all need some hype music. It is dead around here like a funeral parlor. How are you going to train to fight in sheer silence? The arena will be full of noise. You will have to learn to tune it out. How are you going to do that? I'm glad you asked my dear. With practice my dear."

He had not considered any of this and it pleased him that she thought enough to want to help, although he would never confess it. "I can train without music."

"Nonsense. Do you want me to tell the people they can leave we are done?"

He walked away not wanting to admit she won the fight and the battle was over.

"Hey. I am speaking to you."

"Have it your way DJ. Whatever makes you happy," was the best response he could give since all eyes were on him. She knew how to make him weak.

"You sure know how to make me happy. Thank you babe. You can thank me later."

Even though he felt defeated, walking away was easy. After that, he thought about it, this is what you would call a win/win. He really did not know what that meant up until this point. In his profession, there was no such thing. No runner up. No first place. There was a winner and a loser. However, today it was a win/win for him although it appeared he loss. He was happy she was thinking of him and she was happy he was leaving her to do what she wanted to do. "Yeah right," he said.

"You will. Eighteen hundred television stations, iPod connection, data ports, premium sound, satellite, and much more."

"Come down."

"Say what?"

"Come down off the ladder please."

"No."

"Why not?"

"You are going to make me stop."

"No I am not."

It took a minute but he was finally able to convince me to come down. He kissed me and said, "Let me handle this."

"Handle what?"

"This catastrophe you started."

"I got it."

"Move girl before you become an OSHA hazard for me. You are already a liability."

"Why?" I asked as he started to climb the ladder. "Randall, do you know what you are doing?"

King laughed from across the room.

"What's funny?" I asked. It was as if they were in on a joke and leaving me out.

King shook his head.

"Say?"

Randall spoke from the ceiling, "You can tell her."

"Tell me what?"

"This is basically what he did when he worked a job."

I was in total shock. "Hey! You had a job?"

"I told you that," he yelled from inside the ceiling.

"What did you do?"

"IT," he laughed.

"No way."

"Yes way."

"Get out."

Coming down from the ladder, he replied, "For real."

"Shut the front door. Explain to me why I am paying someone for stuff you could do and should have already done?"

"From what I understand, I am paying. Either way, let's get it done."

"I hope you all heard that. Hooks is paying. Guys get your money from him." I looked over at Leigh, "That includes you too. With that being said, we will run the works. Spare no expense people. I want only the best for my Champ."

He let go of my laugh. "Babe that is not quite what I said."

"Well that is what I heard."

"You could not have."

I leaned into his lips. I touched mine on his. I blew my breath into his mouth and said while my lips touched his, "Well what did I hear?"

Trying to turn his head, "You will not turn me into a punk."

"I am not trying to. I am simply showing you how to help me make you happy."

"Where does the music come in?"

"It feeds your soul. It tells stories. It gives you life. It picks you up when you are down. There is so much music does for you. When you cannot do anything else. When you do not know what to do listen to the music. Music makes me lose control."

I began to walk off. He grabbed my arm. "Why are you doing this? You have music upstairs."

He still did not get it, "This is not for me."

"What is it for?"

"Who is it for is the question. It is for you. You will see. I bet your performance, training, and overall attitude will change simply by having this noise in the background. You may not play it all day, but when you do, you will notice a change in your speed, intensity, and mind. Trust me."

He was giddy on the inside, "What am I going to do with you?"

"Love me or leave me baby," I said as I threw my hands up. "What are you going to do?" I looked at him and asked.

"Does it look like I am going anywhere?"

"Well then, let's get busy."

"Why were you sneaking and doing this?"

I gave him a knowing look and replied, "Because I knew you would have something to say. I am here explaining why I want to do this. It was easier for me to do it myself since I knew what I wanted and why. Now you know so let's make it happen. I promise you will love it," I reassured. "Not to mention, as much as you love music, I am surprised you have not done this before now."

"I kind of like to concentrate when I am training."

"Okay. Don't cut it on then, but at least try it to please me then let me know how you feel. It will be interesting to know what King and JJ say about your performance afterwards. If it sucks then I will face the fact I was wrong and we won't play it. If it works then we will pump up the volume."

He thought aloud, "So all I have to do is try it to please you?" This was an expensive attempt.

"That's all I ask."

"You are so easy."

"Watch it buddy. You will ruin my reputation if other people hear you say that."

"My bad. I do not think anyone would ever think you are easy."

I rolled my eyes and stomped away. I drugged my ladder to the position needed and got back in the ceiling. Before long, not only was he helping but the others were too. King showed back up with more ladders and tools.

"Ms. D," he said.

"Yeah."

"What do you need me to do?"

I came out of the ceiling and looked. I was shocked King wanted to help. *Was this also his previous career? Did I touch a soft spot with him too?* It made me wonder why we dog each other so horribly. Then I could not hold it any longer, "Who let the dogs out? Woof. Woof. Woof. Woof," I sang aloud.

Everyone stopped what they were doing. Randall was sitting in the floor splicing wires and making taps. "Danielle," he yelled.

"OKAY," I replied to Randall and then looked at King, "You and I can run that side over there," I pointed. I got down off my ladder and King took it to the other side for me. For the rest of the day we teamed up.

I ordered lunch and when it was delivered, we took a break, sat down, and ate together. Everyone except for Randall of course. I got up and nodded for King to follow me. Randall noticed. I proceeded up the stairs with King right behind me. I could hear Randall's footsteps coming behind us. I closed the door and locked it right away. I made sure to stand further from the door so he could not eavesdrop.

"Why doesn't he eat?" I asked concerned.

"He does."

"No he does not." I tiptoed away and snatched the door open. He was standing there as if he rang a doorbell and was waiting for a response. He was busted, "Yes," I said.

"What are you two doing?"

"Can you send JJ and Keith," I asked without answering his question.

"What the," he said confused.

I closed the door back. A few seconds later, I heard the tap and opened the door again. He commenced to come in with them but I put my hand in his chest and pushed him right back out. His chest was like steel, unmovable, but he got my drift and backed up.

"I am going to ask you all the same question I asked him," I said pointing to King. "Why doesn't he eat?"

No one responded. "I see where this is going. Look, King asked when I have an issue for me to discuss it. He also said if it is something I cannot discuss with him then to ask you all. I am asking a valid question. Why does he not eat?" I repeated. "I think that is a fair and acceptable question and I need an answer."

As always, JJ was once again the spokesperson for some reason. "He feels like food is to the body like gas is to a car. All it does is keep it running. Fuel is all your body requires. You need nothing else."

Are they for real? "Umm, I am not sure if anyone has notice, but he is not a car. In addition, I hate to be the bearer of bad news but a car runs off more than gasoline. It uses petroleum oil, transmission fluid, radiator fluid, brake fluid, friction between sparks plugs, and numerous other components to make it function. Why does he think he can just run off of fluids?" No one spoke. "Do you think this is healthy?" Again, I received nothing but silence. "Does his doctor think this is healthy?" I continued. Still more silence. I looked at them and pretended to retreat. "I guess this is none of my business," I said.

"We give him what he needs in his fluids. As you are aware, he is very conscious of his health. He does not want to ingest anything harmful to his body and has opted to eat as little as possible."

"It looks to me like you have muzzled the ox."

"We did not do it," King said. "He chooses to."

"So you want him to stand twelve three minute rounds getting punched just off of liquids? Do I understand you correctly?"

"Ms. D it is not a problem. As long as he remains healthy and holding his own we do not press it."

"Well I am pressing it. If he eats French fries all day he may remain healthy, but would you let him do it?"

"He is not going to change," Keith said.

"Why not one meal a day?" They all just looked at me. "What about protein?"

"Supplements," Keith said.

"Are they safe?" I asked.

"Yes," JJ replied.

"King I need to make an appointment with his doctor."

"Okay," King said. "He will not change. We have worked with him for years on this."

"I will take care of it." I opened the door. He was sitting on the steps.

"What are you saying about me?" he asked offended he had not been included.

"If I wanted you to know I would have invited you. I will talk to you about it later."

"Why do I have to wait?"

"Trust me," was my only answer.

We all went back downstairs and finished eating then we jumped back into workflow mode. It was a long day but I will admit it was fun. I did take some calls and read some emails but nothing that constituted true work. I think he was pleased. By the same token, I came up with my trade off.

A few hours after lunch I told Randall and his crew, I knew they had to train so we were getting out of their way. Their assistance cut my schedule down by a full day, which I was greatly appreciative. We then went up to my area and did what we needed to do there. Once we had everything lined up there were only a few minor tweaks and programming issues. These would be addressed later. Besides, I really wanted to play with everything to get all my tweaks done at one time.

At seven I called in dinner and told the crew, after we ate we were done for the day. Of course, I ended up staying around plugging in laptops, iPods, and software to see what worked and what did not. At ten Randall made his way upstairs. I was sitting on the floor trying to figure out why something was not working.

"Do you need some help?"

Exasperated and ready to give up, "Yes," I replied and explained the problem.

"Why don't you go home and let me troubleshoot this?"

"Thanks but I will stay and help you."

She is trying my patience for one day, he thought. "You will go home. Remember we have a function tomorrow and you have been here since five this morning." He made sure his voice was soft. If he had not learned anything over the last few months he did learn it was more in his tone than in his words. "Danielle, please call it a night."

I wanted to refute but I knew I would soon be battling him on his eating habits so I went ahead and submitted to him. I had taken my shirt off earlier, exposing my boo beater. When we sat down for dinner, he had given me a Hooks Gym shirt to wear. I took that shirt off, picked up my original one, and continued to walk out with my boo beater on. He had my truck sitting at the front door waiting. JJ had already placed my tools and ladders in the truck.

He opened my door as I stood toe to toe with him, "Text me when you get home."

"I will call you," I said. I knew what he was up to and was not having it.

He lowered his head knowing I was about to blow a fuse.

"Oh hell no Randall."

"Babe, I have to. I have been working with you all day."

"You should have stopped and completed your training routine."

"I needed to make sure you were good."

Anger quickly set in, "Something has to change."

He panicked, "What do you mean?"

"You are not going to train like this day in and day out without eating and sleeping," I barked.

He began to speak but I shut him down.

"Stop. Pick and choose your battles carefully," I warned. "The same way you asked me to come down off that ladder is the same way I expect you to respect my request now. I am being nice and requesting this time, but the next conversation will not be a request. Let's play fair. You know damn well you cannot go without eating and sleeping and anticipate on being in a ring for forty minutes and fight well."

"How do you think that is healthy?" I asked not really expecting an answer. "You can think about it and tell me later how you plan to change your eating habits. From now on, you will get some sleep. Not in a chair, not here and not on the couch. You will get in the bed every night. I will take as little as four hours but you will give me something. Randall do not kill yourself trying to get ready and then get there and be no earthly good because of lack of care," I pleaded. "There is no need in being prepared to fight if you are neglecting your health. You do not want that. I must admit I am very disappointed. You are doing yourself a disservice by enhancing one set of skills and neglecting your daily health. I also believe your guys know you are but have grown accustomed to your choices and accept it to avoid fighting with you. There is something you can eat that is not bad for you. Do we need to get a nutritionist involved?"

He lowered his head. I could tell he did not want to hear my conversation. "I hear you," he barely mumbled.

"That is not an answer to the question I asked."

"I tend to disagree."

"It's cool."

"I appreciate your concern."

Now I was livid. "It is still not an answer. I see this is going to be a fight for us. Bring it." He knew I was serious and had an issue with him. He also knew I was going to be relentless. What he did not know was he started a war. I was not going to back down.

"We have it under control," he said trying to blow me off again.

He knew he was trying to blow me off. I was concerned about his health and safety. I would be happy with fruit and vegetables, but he only had liquids today from what I witnessed.

He reluctantly gave me a kiss and I pulled off without either of us exchanging further words. I texted him when I got home. I was not upset;

nevertheless, I was not wavering on what I said. I do not think I was asking anything unreasonable. He texted.

> Good night.

I was following my own orders and got in the bed around midnight. At one he texted me back.

> I am home. I will get in the bed. Sorry but I will only achieve three hours of sleep if I can even force myself asleep.

I felt the sarcasm through the screen.

> It's a start. Thanks for your obedience. It is required in a relationship. Just do it for me. I would like you to make a doctor's appointment so we can discuss it before we meet with the nutritionist.

He immediately got pissed off. It took him a few minutes to respond.

> Thanks for telling me how you feel. It has been acknowledged.

ACKNOWLEDGED. This is not an agreement. Moreover, he purposefully made no mention of the doctor. I debated on responding. Instead, I called his home phone. Not to check to see if he was home but just because I wanted him to see how serious I was about his health.

"Hey," he answered dryly.

"If they say what you are doing is healthy then you can keep doing what you do. But if they suggest you need to change then I would hope you'd change."

He still did not like my response, hence the silence.

"Come on baby this is not for me. It is for you."

"Good night," he disregarded the conversation.

"Oh no. I do not think so."

"I'm good."

"Why are you upset?"

"I am concerned eating will weigh me down and make me sluggish. I do not want to do it Danielle," he emphasized do not.

I wanted to cuss and yell but instead I held my silence. There was no need right now. I think we both understood how strong the other felt.

"I will call you in a few hours. I love you," he hung up before I could speak.

I debated on calling him back. Then I quickly remembered he was the one who asked to be my boyfriend. As far as I was concerned, that gave me the right to call back.

"I'm sorry," he answered. He knew he was being a pain.

"You are out of line Deacon Washington." That stabbed him. "You asked me to share how I feel. I do not feel you can work out six to ten hours a day, every day, on liquids. You burn a lot of energy. What you do is strenuous and you need more substance in my opinion. Good night and I love you too. Another thing, if this is the attitude you are going to take, then from now on I will keep my feelings to myself. Sleep well." I did not wait for a response. I hung up. I was angry and my feelings were hurt.

He blogged at four thirteen AM.

> To have things you have never had before, you have to do things you have never done before. This will be challenging. I can do it. I refuse to lose this joy. Most of all I refuse to lose her.

Tuesday

I checked his blog and smirked. *He is such a boy* I thought and rolled over. *Why couldn't he have been nice last night?* *Why did he have to blog everything?* I decided I was going to snooze another thirty minutes. However, I needed to get up since we were going to be out of the office for over half of the day.

***

On the other side of town, Randall was meeting King at the gym. They ran different routes daily. King had a method of how they were scheduled. This was done so no one knew his routine. Some of the routes were hilly, flat, red lights to stop and go, asphalt, grassy, and scenic. Most all of the routes had the local city's police officers aware, as safety was necessary for King. He always made sure security was on point. Randall's health and security ranked equally for him. Randall never knew which route King would select from day to day. After sending out his morning inspiration, he closed his eyes as they drove to today's destination. He was not happy about the strenuous route as they slowly started at a jog. "King," he said.

"What's up boss?"

"Can I ask you a question?"

"What's the question?"

"Do you think my eating habits are unhealthy?"

"Ms. D got to you already?"

"Yeah."

"She is fast."

Randall removed his ear buds, "I take it this is what your closed door meeting was about yesterday?"

"She is concerned," King replied in honesty.

"I have done this for years," he reminded King.

"I know that but she does not, and neither does she care."

He signed deeply, "What did you all tell her?"

"We did not tell her anything. We are planning on accommodating her request."

"Which was?"

"Scheduling a meeting with the doctor."

"She asked me to do the same. Have him come to the gym since she is not going to let this go."

"I will but from my observation she is not going to take the opinion of Doc. She will think he is on your side. Be prepared to be seen by a different physician."

"Did she say that?"

"No, but be prepared."

"Why is so she independent, professional, and always about business? Can she ever relax?"

King could not believe Hooks used the word relax. "You picked her," King frowned. "You are asking me as if I prearranged this."

"Right now I feel like you did."

"If I had a choice I would pick her too. She is the total opposite from the road we previously travelled."

"Road? More like a dead end cliff with no signs ahead," Randall agreed referring to Tameka.

"She wants to make sure you are healthy. There is nothing wrong with that."

"Do you think I am unhealthy?" He asked now feeling concerned and unsure.

"I think I have grown accustomed to it. I eat what you eat. Which in the big scheme of things is not much. It is energy, vitamins, and minerals to sustain us and keep us healthy. The point she is trying to make is whether it is enough to absorb ten hours of training and twelve rounds of boxing. Do you have enough protein? Do you have enough to have good levels of cholesterol? To be honest I think she has some valid points. I also feel this is a good sign that she is observant. She is not asking you to eat a buffet daily. A piece of fish a few times a week will not kill you. I think it is because she does not see you eat and when she does it is from a cup. True, everything in the cup started as a fruit or vegetable, but when she sees the cup, it is liquid. Maybe eat the vegetables whole instead of pureeing everything. It is the same concept. The only difference is it requires chewing. You can eat celery, tomatoes, cucumbers, carrots, squash, broccoli, strawberries, and bananas whole and not in a liquid form. You like them."

He listened without speaking or acknowledging but thinking to himself, he was not eating carrots or strawberries due to the natural sugar.

"Your blog today said you refuse to lose her. If this is true then you will eat solid food. If you are going to proclaim complete vegan then now is the time. Do you not want meat or solids? Do you think they will make you sick?"

"I have not really thought about it until she said something. She has referred to it and so has Sade, Paige, and Leigh but it never crossed my mind. It must be extremely noticeable. I do not know if it will make me sick or not. I just do not want to change my habits right now. They are working. I am at my ideal weight and I feel great. I feel healthy. I am afraid if I started eating a little at a time or every now and then, I may develop bad habits. I have gotten my mindset that if it still tastes great in a cup then it is healthy for me. I really do not know what to do," he said with honesty.

"I suggest you give it some thought if you want this relationship to work out."

"I gave it a lot of careful consideration last night and I still do not know what to do."

King was getting annoyed that he was making this difficult. "You have a lot of thinking to do. Think while you run."

"I need help," he cried out. "It has taken me years to get to where I am."

"Now it is time to sacrifice. I suppose it is time to die to self."

"I do that daily. How do you think I gave it all up years ago? I had to die to my flesh."

"That's true, you did. Nevertheless, when you died back then you died to self for self. Now you have to die to self for someone else. It is to make her happy. She isn't asking for you to eat a cow a week."

"King, I am not sure I can do this."

"Were you sure you could wake up every morning and let your flesh die before?"

Shaking his head, "You are right."

"Just do it."

"I don't think I have any other choice but to carry this cross."

"Make the appointment and let's see how it goes. Explain to her what you have explained to me. Tell her your fears and hard work. You may even want to let her see the ingredients before it is blended. That may make her feel secure."

"I hope you are right."

"Now what are you going to do about the sleep issue?"

"Oh God. I did not even think about it. I was so concerned with the food issue."

"Put some thought into it. She is adamant about that too."

"SHE DOES NOT SLEEP," he yelled.

"That may be so but she doesn't fight either."

"Whose side are you on?"

"Unfortunately, I am the mediator."

"Why do you feel so inclined?"

"Because my fighter and I have been jogging at a snail's pace and having great conversation for forty minutes. It leads me to believe he is stressed. Something is on his mind. I do not think we are going to be able to change her mind so our best bet is to change your mind."

"I feel like you and the enemy have teamed against me."

"Again, she is concerned. You do not eat enough to fight. Her next concern is you do not sleep. This is easy. Lay down and you will eventually go to sleep. All she wants to do is make sure you are well rested."

"I foresee this turning into hours and days of sleep."

"That is what normal people do. Hooks we all need some real sleep. None of us gets it. Her included," he added.

"I know when I need it."

"You do not. Listen to her man. This is important."

Hooks knew King liked her although he would never admit it. *King thinks she is good for me. The truth of the matter, she is. Why does she care? She is not trying to change me. All she is trying to do is help and support me. The least I can do is try. If I do not like it, I can say I tried and I gave it my best.* They picked up the pace. They were a little behind for the morning but Hooks needed to clear the air. Clear his mind rather. At six, he motioned for King to slow up as he dialed Dani.

"Hello Champ," she answered.

"Hey. Are you at work?"

"Nope."

"What's wrong?"

"Nothing is wrong. I snoozed and slept a little longer. I know I should have gotten up since we have an event today which will keep me out of the office."

He motioned again to King and they both began to walk. "I am glad you mentioned sleep," he paused.

"What's up?"

"Well I have taken into consideration what you said last night and I am going to do my best to address your concerns."

I was surprised and didn't expect this conversation, especially after his defensive response last night. "Duly noted and greatly appreciated."

"I want to apologize if I was harsh, rude, or inappropriate." He knew he was.

"Apology accepted."

"From what I understand King is making the doctor's appointment."

That confirmed King stepped in. I wonder if King was asked or if he volunteered. "Tell me where to be and I will be there."

Desperately wanting to change the subject he asked, "Did you sleep well?"

I laughed.

"What is funny?"

"Nothing. I did. What time do I need to be ready?"

"King, what time do we need to pick up Danielle?"

"We can send Keith after lunch."

"I want her to arrive with me unless it is on her calendar after lunch."

"I am not sure what time is on my calendar. I think the entire day is blocked. Leigh and I were prepared for all day."

"King make note. Moving forward and for most events, I would like Danielle and me to arrive together in the same car unless there is a specific reason why she cannot."

I jerked my head. I was not expecting that. His request meant a lot to me. This was a sentimental moment for us.

King replied in tone of approval, "That is not a problem at all. We can make it happen."

"So I should be ready at ten?"

"Yes, I promise this will not be an all day and night event like the last one."

"It's cool. I will have my work with me and I'm sure it will keep me busy."

"Do you still love me?" he asked.

"Is a blue bird blue?"

"That is all I need to know. Everything else is secondary. Text me when you get to the office."

"Bye sweetheart. Thank you."

"For?" he questioned.

"Listening and being receptive."

"I was a little slow but I am getting it."

I got busy as soon as I walked in the office. I had a lot of ground to cover and a short time to get there. I sent some print jobs to the printer, banged the emails, and started drafting a set of plans. I had four screens going when Leigh arrived.

"Good morning," she muffled as she walked in the door. "What time to do we leave?"

"Around ten."

"I better get busy because ten for Hooks means nine thirty."

"I have some plans on the printers. Can you get all of those together and send to arrive tomorrow? I have some jobs to be booked. I placed the TIP sheets on your desk and loaded the information on both the A and B drive.

Check those out and tell me if you need anything else. Other than that, I think we are good unless you have something for me. I will have my files with me so I can work on these plans while we are gone."

Leigh looked suspicious. "You are moving fast this morning. What's the deal?" the sleepy non-morning person questioned.

"I am trying to stay on top of things."

"This would have nothing to do with a certain person's blog last night would it?"

"Get everyone on the line. Let me tell the story once."

Sounding like a four year old, as soon as Sade picked up the line she said, "Auntie are you and Uncle Hooks getting married?"

"Not that I am aware of why?"

"I just want to know in advance. I want to be prepared. I will have to hit the gym hard."

"If he asks you Sissie what will you say?"

All of this was catching me off guard. "I do not know."

"Why?" Leigh questioned fully alert all of a sudden.

"What are you all talking about? Do you know something I do not know? What is going on?" *Did I miss something?*

"We are just asking?" Sissie said.

"You all are making me nervous. I do not think we are at this level yet. We have not had a conversation about marriage."

After we got off the phone, I was a little perplexed. They made me nervous. *Did they know something I did not?* I went back and read the blog again. *What did I miss? This whole conversation was extremely weird.* It took over my thoughts. I could not shake it. *There was no way he is going to ask me to marry him.*

Time seemed to fly by me and before I realized it. The level of noise heightened which could only mean one thing. Hooks was in the building. He has been here enough times to where everyone should know him and it should not be as if a celebrity was in the building. More like Danielle's beau was here. Each time he came was like the first time. My mind wondered off. *I hoped that would be true. Each time for us would be like the first time.*

There was a knock on my door. "Come in Mr. Washington."

He walked in and took a seat. Just as Leigh predicted, before nine thirty. "What's up with the Mr. Washington?" he asked.

I never looked up. "That is your name correct?" I said in my business voice.

"It's babe to you. Or so I thought."

"Are you doing okay?"

"I am not sure." He stood up and opened my door as I looked over my eyeglasses.

Leigh walked in. "Are we ready?"

"Give me three minutes. Umm, where did he go?"

"Who?" Leigh asked confused.

"Y'all play too much. Please come in Mr. Washington. Randall." No one entered. I stood up and walked to the door. He was leaning on the wall outside my door. I folded my arms and placed my back up against the wall too. Co-workers walked by for no other reason but to speak to him.

"Are you ready for me now?"

I grabbed him by the neck and pulled him back in my office. One of the guys walked by. You could tell he wanted to speak but not quite sure what to say.

"She loves me man," Randall said with laughter.

Immediately Leigh said, "Get a room. We have to go. There is no time for this."

"You are so jealous."

Although she would never voice it aloud, Leigh confessed to herself that she was in fact a little jealous.

"You were talking to me like I was a complete stranger. You did not give me eye contact. You are hard on a brother."

"Brother was ticked off with me last night. Remember."

"Yeah, I was but I am cool now. Your point has been acknowledged and I appreciate the honesty and concern. Good looking out babe."

"I love you too." He grabbed my bags. I got my handbag, phones, keys, and shades as we left.

Once we got to the van the first person I saw was King. He winked his eye. It meant he and I were on the same page. I winked back. When we pulled up to the parking lot there were uniform officers waiting on us. It always seemed new to me. I do not fully accepted or understand his vast magnitude. I did not relate to this side of him. To me he was the Deacon from church, my boyfriend, and man of God. Superstar, boxer, and celebrity were not on the list as far as I was concerned.

We pulled to the curb. The officers blocked the flow of traffic coming in and out. He stood up in the van and reached for my hand. "Let's pray. Father, we thank you for this day. We thank you for all you have graciously provided for us. We thank you Lord for the ability to use our minds, limbs, and body naturally today Father. We know you that give us the capability. We do not take this lightly or for granted today. As we step into this place, not only walk with us but also help us. Do not allow us to see with the eyes of sorrow or pity but open our hearts, eyes, and minds to compassion. Father, we ask that you make this place your habitation. Cover everyone from the doctors, nurses, parents to the smallest of small patients. Father, cover them on every hall, floor, and room. As you state in your word by your stripes they are healed. We pray boldly for happy and healthy children. We pray for miracles for these children."

His prayer went on and on and on until he became emotional. The administrator and marketing person approached the van. The officer opened the door so they could join us in prayer. No words we spoken other than Randall praying. You could hear the fullness in his throat. You clearly understood the passion in his prayer. The prayer was very different from when he started. Leigh was snapping pictures. He squeezed my hand. He drained himself. If he had room, I think he would have fallen out or even kneeled. JJ shoved a bottle of water in my other hand. I was not sure if it was directed to me or to Randall. You could hear the tears from his voice. When he finished I held him and wiped his tears while everyone else went on with business as usual. I loved the way he had no fear. No shame. He was transparent whenever wherever.

"God has a calling on your life. Favor ain't fair but it's all over you. Keep doing what you do. Do not let anyone, not even me, stray you from what is right." Leigh took shots. He nodded each time I spoke. I had one hand around his face and the other on his face holding his close to mine while I spoke. I could feel the tears rolling down my hand. At that moment, I felt his energy transfer from him to me then back to him again. It bothered him to face sick children when there was nothing he could do to fix their problems. He could fight his heart out. He could sell all he had and deplete all his accounts, but he could not save these babies lives. It troubled him dearly and deeply. His emotions transferred to me. The life I kept speaking in his ear transferred my energy to him. He appeared to strengthen with each word. Why hadn't he expressed beforehand this was a struggle for him?

The words he spoke were for all of us, but we could have tackled this last night. The administrators waited. No one moved. Besides, you could not start the party without the star. "God loves you. He is watching and keeping record. Do not believe for a second that your work is going unnoticed. You are being blessed in return right at this very moment. Stay faithful and remain who you are. As you continue giving and pouring into the lives of others, God will continue pouring into your life. Do you understand me?"

He nodded. "Randall, I love you so much." I had never told him by adding so much before. He nodded. I stood in front of him. I kissed and wiped his tears away. "We will not move until you are ready." I spoke aloud. Then I kissed a tear. Leigh snapped. He closed his eyes. "Do you want the cameras off?" I held my hand up like get back.

"The cameras are fine," he replied. He took my face and laid his forehead on my head. "Danielle, this moment right here is why I love you and need you in my life. We complement each other so well. Where I am weak, you are strong. I cannot live without you. How did I do it this long?" If he was prepared he would have proposed right then. A ring was not the question. She knew I could provide whatever ring her heart desired. I did not have permission from her parents, blessings from Hunter, and confirmation from my Father yet. However, I knew deep inside my soul she was the one. All I could do was kiss her forehead for now.

"I am not going anywhere unless you want me to." I whispered in his ear.

He shook it off. "King." King peeped his head in the door.

"We are waiting on you Champ." In that instant, something transformed. We experienced two-metamorphosis right before our eyes. First, he went from everyday Randall to a spiritual and emotional filled Randall. Second, he went from the spirit-filled deacon to the well renowned fighter. It was amazing to witness the change. To see such a great and strong man become soft and sensitive then change gears for the good of others fascinated me to the highest degree.

Vickie began to speak business starting with formal introductions. "Hooks Washington this is," she formally introduced.

I was so drained I missed it all. King stepped up in the van. "D."

"Yes." I looked up and sighed deeply.

"Good job baby girl."

I sat on the seat. I laid back and tried to get myself together. I had King's approval. Keith placed another bottle of water in my hand. I had given Randall the other one. "Take your time. This is a hard job. He will be worse once we leave."

My eyes rolled in the back of my head. It felt like an hour but I laid there for eleven minutes. To say this was a hard job was an understatement. It was a job millions of women wanted, but only a few could handle. Most women would have never expected his life to be this intense and still be able to deal with such a strong guy at his weakest moments. All they were concerned with was the fame, the lights, and his debit card.

I finally regained my composure and went inside. We found him eating lunch with the kids. In a matter of seconds, he was yet a different person. After lunch, he played games with them, drew, colored, signed casts, and passed out pictures. He even took individual pictures with each of them as he went from room to room visiting.

Once we convened back in the multipurpose room the Hospital Facilitator spoke, "Kids we have a surprise." The kids cheered. "Mr. Hooks has asked his doctor to come visit him here." They cheered even louder. "See Mr. Hooks has to see the doctor too as big and strong as he is."

I smiled. This was not for the kids. This was for me. He was clever. This was his response to last night's conversation. His doctor was there along with a Children's Health Care doctor. They did the routine check-up right there in front of all the kids. They let the kids listen to his heartbeat. They took turns checking his reflexes. After they checked him, they both came to talk to me. It was a complete physical with blood drawing, finger sticking, and the works.

It was something the children were accustomed to but had never witnessed anyone else receive, much less the Champ.

They felt like he was fine but stated it would not hurt for him to intake more. They passed me a written report with a business card and told me to call if I had questions.

He finally broke away and made his way over to me. Before he could speak, I spoke first, "You are a mess."

"What?"

"You know what."

In a serious tone he said, "No I do not."

"Mission accomplished."

"We shall see."

Around three o'clock they drove Leigh and me back to the office. I called it a night around seven to go to the gym. Once I made my way upstairs, I saw a few new iPod's on my table. I didn't think much about it. I changed my clothes and then it hit me. I leaned over the rail and called out. "Randall can you come upstairs please?"

It was a few minutes before he arrived. "D, what's up?"

"Someone was up here."

"Oh yeah? How do you know?"

"They left five iPods all in different colors."

"What? Why? Did they leave a note?"

"No, I am asking you why?"

"I bought an iPod for every location that is set for an iPod so you do not have to bring yours in every day. I hope you like it."

I hugged him. "Thanks." He was so thoughtful. When and how did he ever have time to do the things he did?

"Enjoy."

"Go finish training. I want to take you somewhere," I said.

"Where?"

"Hurry. It is a school night."

I went downstairs when I finished my workout. "Guys, can I borrow the Champ for a few hours?" You could tell they did not like the request. They were not use to it. Now I was competing with their time. Their time always consisted of training which was much more important than dating as far as they were concerned.

"You said two hours baby. I still have time," he said to pacify us all.

I went back upstairs and did a little work while I waited. Promptly forty-five minutes later, he graced me with his presence. "Are you ready?"

"Yes." He was wearing jeans with a big belt buckle. Instead of a white tee tonight, he wore a black V-neck tee and his chain. I did not know which one I liked the most on him, white or black.

"DJ are you working?" his voice was stern.

As he stood behind me, "No. I am shopping."

"Umm, shades. Cool. I am shocked. They are nice. Did you buy them all?"

"I haven't bought any yet. I was just looking."

"Whose are those?" he asked pointing to one of the pictures on the screen.

"Melodies by Mary J Blige."

"They are nice." he stated again, "Get them all. Are you ready?" he asked.

"Let's ride."

We walked downstairs. "Ay, I will be back. Behave," he instructed. He thought to himself, *I know she is about to take me somewhere where I will have to eat.* We walked outside where Keith pulled the Benz around. He opened my door and we both got in and drove off alone. We got to the end of the driveway. "Which way?" he asked.

Instead of answering, I opened my door and walked over to his side. "Switch." It was not a question.

He hesitated. Not that he was concerned about me driving his car. I had a key remember. He was letting go of his control. Once he stepped out the car, we heard Keith yell out. "What's wrong?"

"Nothing," he yelled back.

I got in on the driver's side and we pulled out. We drove down the highway talking and laughing the whole way. I exited the highway with him having no clue as to where we were going. Anything was still possible. I turned into the plaza. He was confused. I parked and said, "Let's go." He opened his door reluctantly. We went to the music store.

"It's Tuesday! New releases! We are getting them all for the gym."

He was in shock. A trip to the music store was not what he expected at all. He laughed and grabbed my hand. We acted like two children in a candy store. We bought much more than needed. Our selection consisted of old school, new school, rap, gospel, new releases, and stuff we never heard of. Sure, we could download music all day but it was something about having an actual CD.

We cashed out and of course argued over who would pay the bill. I finally won this time. I think it was because the cashier was distracted and amazed Hooks was in front of him until he just took a card. He had no idea whose it was.

"Thanks D." He was so excited over a few bags of CD's. It was a simple yet amazing date. He drove us back to the gym while I popped open the CD's. I didn't need anything inside so I jumped in the Porsche, handed him the bags and headed to the house. I texted him once I got home.

> I am home. Thanks for the iPods. That was a great idea.

He hit back.

> I am listening to one of the CD's now while JJ and I train. I am going home tonight. I will text you when I get there.

> I love you too. Go to sleep. Pick me up at five thirty for church.

He read the text repeatedly. JJ was getting irritated waiting. He wanted to make sure she typed what he read. She wanted him to pick her up for service. He was excited. She knew if he gave in to her then she must reciprocate and give in to him.

Wednesday

My phone sounded at four twenty eight AM. I was sleeping hard. I let it sound instead of checking it on the first tone. I knew it was him blogging. However, I had no idea what time it was. After ten minutes of snoozing, my eyes popped open. Curiosity killed the cat. I needed to know what it read.

> Tell me what you want. Help me understand what you need. Explain to me how to treat you. Show me the way to your heart. Teach me how to love you.

This guy is unbelievable, I thought. I never knew what to expect from him. Right now, the same way he was asking for instructions is the same way I needed instructions. He was no ordinary person. Not only was he not ordinary but I do not think he knew what he needed either. Although I was glad he asked I did not know how to answer him. I felt heavy. My heart was loaded. I could not explain it. I needed therapy.

Here the man of my dreams just shows up one day. He was called on a two-way radio to assist me. A man, now a divorced boxer, is asking me in front of the world to teach him how to love me. Here it is a Wednesday morning, hours before the city awakes and I have no idea how to answer him. I prayed for an answer.

I took my time getting up. I wanted to wait. I asked God for an answer and I did not want to move too fast. Finally, I got up. I dressed and I picked my phone up several times to call him but each time I decided not to. As I closed the door to my car, my phone rang. It startled me. *Where is his home training? Who calls someone this time of the morning? Besides, who is up this early other than me?* It didn't matter. I loved it and I was glad I was on his mind to call this early. I clicked the answer button but I did not say anything. I did not know what to say.

He sensed it. It was so easy for him to pour his heart out over the internet but difficult for him to do so face to face for some reason. He was not shy. He actually had a great way with words. I do not know why he had such a problem talking to me. We both held the line. From his breathing, I knew he was running.

"Are you going to say something?" he asked.

"You called me," I responded.

"You are supposed to greet when you pick up."

I paused then confessed, "I don't know what to say."

"Hello, hi, good morning, or even hey babe I love you would be an awesome start."

"I think you know what I am referring to."

"I did not ask you to respond."

"You most certainly did when you asked me to explain and teach you. That happens to requires response."

"I did not necessarily need it right now; however, the sooner the better."

"Randall, Randall, Randall," I said in mock exasperation.

"Yes darling," he said in a singsong kind of way.

"Please tell me what am I going to do with you?"

In all seriousness he replied, "Help me and guide me. Danielle I hope this is the beginning for us. I do not know what to say further. I have explained to the best of my ability verbally how I feel about you and there is really nothing left to say. Now, the only thing I need is for you to help me love you the way you need to be loved."

I could not speak. This was very serious and I was in awe.

He broke the awkward silence. "It's early. We have plenty of time to talk. Have a great day babe."

"Thanks babe you too." It amazed me how he called in the middle of a two-hour run, melted my heart as if it is nothing and continued to run off peacefully.

"Are we still on for five thirty?" he asked confirming.

"Stand me up if you want to," I barked.

"Do I need to start a countdown at noon?"

Laughing, I responded, "That would be helpful."

For some reason work was difficult for me today. My mind was so far gone until it was unfortunate. I needed to be home lying down in thought. At one, I decided I could not take any more. I went down stairs, used the gift cards he gave me and took advantage of my wasted time by getting a thirty minute massage. Afterwards, I went straight home. I knew right then I had it bad. I walked in the house, dropped my bags and did exactly what I said I was going to do. I laid down. The house was dark with no sign of light coming in anywhere. I put the phones by my ear then closed my eyes. It was two ten when I laid down; I did not hear anything until his ringtone sounded at three fifty. I answered on the first tone. "Hello," I whispered groggily.

"Babe?" he sounded as if he accidentally rang the wrong number.

"Huh?"

"Are you alright?"

"I think so."

"Do you need anything?"

"No thanks babe. I'm good."

He could not determine from my voice, "Are you asleep?"

"Yes."

"What's wrong?"

"Nothing."

"I will see you in a little while."

"Okay."

It concerned him that she was home asleep so he called Leigh.

"Hello," she answered.

"Leigh, this is Hooks."

"Hey friend."

He skipped the preliminaries, "What's wrong with Danielle?"

Now sounding concerned, "Nothing that I know of. Why do you ask?"

"Let me ask in a different way. Why is she home asleep in the middle of the day?"

"Oh that. I think she was having a rough day."

"Is that a good or a bad thing?"

"I can't determine."

"Is there any particular reason why you can't determine?"

"Yes, there are a couple of reasons. For starters, the past two days have been rather rough ones for us. Then today started much differently than normal so I think it was just too much for her to take. It seems there was a blog from some local fighter in what is assumed to be expressing his love for her before some ungodly hour this morning. I guess it was enough to make a girl have to lie down and get it together. A good morning like that for us requires shoe therapy, tequila body shots, or a nap. She obviously went with the latter. Hooks it is draining dating you and she needs reviving and replenishing. This is a hard job for all of us not knowing what will happen from minute to minute. You are full of surprises. Some magical and some mental."

He blushed from ear to ear. Leigh issued out way too much information. He gave up the laugh Danielle adored. "Okay Leigh. Thanks. Sorry to be so draining."

"Only for you Champ."

"Thanks." He was pleased with Leigh's response and he could agree. He knew it had to be draining to date him. He drained himself being Hooks. He could not imagine having to deal with Randall, Deacon Washington, Hooks, and Babe, as she had to do daily.

At four forty five, my eyes opened. My body wanted to continue sleeping but I knew he was coming and there was no way I would be able to call him and cancel. I wanted to though, just this one time. I needed to rest. My mind would be clear and I could think distinctly after I rested. Right now, I was lazy. Discombobulated was more like it. I slid into a pair of skinny leg jeans, a white shirt and my Ferragamos. I was plain and simple. I glossed my lips then I sat on the couch with my head back waiting for the call from the gate.

Like clockwork, he called precisely when he said he would arrive. By the time he made his way to the house, I was standing outside waiting. I was at the car door before he was able to get out and open it.

"Are you okay DJ?"

"I am fine," I babbled.

"I will not blog tonight."

"It is not a problem," I lied. The truth is I wanted him to blog because it was the only way I got out of him what I needed.

"Yeah it is." He did not move.

"Don't change you. I will have an answer for you, I promise. But right now I am still thinking."

"Let me know what you come up with," he smiled.

"I will." I had not paid him much attention for focusing myself. Once we got to the church, I realized I had nothing. I did not bring any computers today. I sat in the car with my head laid back on the headrest. He leaned over and kissed my forehead then went inside. At six forty five, I walked in and went directly to my seat. I do not know why but I was still in a zone. He came in rushed. You could tell he had been looking for me. Just then, I realized I had not seen what he was wearing. We both had on jeans and white shirts. I had on pumps and he had on Gucci loafers. *Great minds think alike.*

He looked over noticing how intently Dani was listening and paying attention to Pastor Hunter. He thought to himself, *she is as plain as she can get right now, but she is still as beautiful as ever.* Her lips seemed to shine like wet diamonds. All he knew was he loved her and she was his future.

Service was great. Hunter did his thing again. He was such an anointed man. I wondered if he really understood the blessings bestowed upon him. I waited for Deacon Washington not talking much to anyone. I still could not shake it. He finally arrived and we rode back to my house. He tried to make small talk but for some reason I could not get myself together. He kept at it persistently trying to make me feel comfortable. He could detect my weariness. It troubled me that I did not readily have an answer to his blog. A man was asking me what I needed and how he should treat me and I could not answer. I should have had a written response on ready.

"How do you do it?" I asked with my eyes closed.

"Do what?" He did not know what she meant.

"You see right through me. How do you do it?"

He looked over at her, "I am reading your heart. The heart never lies."

"I guess you are right."

"I'm picking up RJ this week."

"Do you have a weekend planned?" I asked.

"I was planning on talking to him about me fighting. After that I was going to talk to him about you."

My neck snapped. The trance was over. Now I was about to flat line. "ME?"

"I think it is time."

"WOW!"

"Is there any particular reason why YOU were asleep in the middle of the day?"

"I have some things on my mind."

"Work?" he asked knowing the answer to the question since he spoke to Leigh.

"Life."

"You need to do that more often so you do not work yourself to death. Do you want to elaborate on life?"

"If you eat more substance I will stop working so hard," I said eluding the question.

"I am going to do my best."

We said our good nights quickly. It was best. He was throwing too many big things at me at one time. I could not take any more Randall 'Hooks' Washington tonight.

Thursday

He did what he said he was going to do. He did not blog and I was proud. I called him as soon as my feet hit the floor. We said our good morning greetings and before we ended the call I said, "Have a good day babe."

"I am a little nervous," he confessed.

"Why?"

"I am going to talk to RJ today." You could hear the nervousness in his voice.

"It will be fine." *He is a kid* I thought.

"I hope so."

"Pray about it and ask God to lead and guide your tongue."

***

"Son, let's go look at a few houses I picked out for you and your mother."

"Are we moving?"

"Yes you are. I picked out a few but you have to tell me which one you like best."

"What if I stayed with you?"

His response was a pleasant surprise. "I would love that but I am not sure how your mom would feel?"

"Well you can take me to school every day."

"If I am in town," he eased in.

"Where are you going?"

"Well son that is another thing I want to talk to you about. I am thinking about fighting again."

"Really?" he said with excitement.

"Yes."

"For real?"

He laughed, "Yes, son for real."

"That's what's up dad," he pounded his dad.

"Are you sure?"

"Yeah dad! You seem much happier when you fight."

"I am son. It is my passion. I love it and when I tried to live without it I was very unhappy."

"Can I come?"

"We will have to see what your mother says?"

"Do you think she will say yes?"

"I do not know, but I have a rule. You cannot miss school."

"Come on dad. You do not want me to miss your passion."

He did not respond right away. "I am glad you mentioned passion. I want to introduce you to someone."

"Who?"

"My friend."

"A girl or guy?"

He laughed and had to remember RJ was not five any more. "A female," he answered.

"Is she your girlfriend?"

"Yes, as a matter of fact, she is," he said proudly. He then second-guessed how he might have sounded and hoped it was the right response.

"Does she have kids?"

"No she does not." He did not know if that was a plus or minus for Danielle.

"Do you like her?"

"Yes, I like her very much. This is one of the reasons why it's important for me to introduce you two."

"Does she know you fight?"

"Yes," he laughed.

"Does she like it?"

"I do not think she dislikes it. She says she does. I sure hope so. If not we have a big problem."

RJ got a real serious look on his face. "Are you happy dad?" he asked.

"Son, I am very happy. I have never been this happy in my life." Immediately he thought everything he said was inappropriate. He hoped RJ did not go away thinking he was not an integral part of his life. He felt as though he was botching up this father son talk.

"Dad, I want you to be happy. That is all I want for you. You deserve it."

"Thanks son."

"So this lady is your girlfriend?" RJ asked as if to gain clarity.

It caught him by surprise. He was happy his child felt this way. It seemed like everything in his life was finally falling into place. He was truly blessed. "Well," he stuttered, "Umm yes."

"How long have you known her?" he continued.

He thought for a moment. *Is this kid trying to figure out if I was seeing her while I was married to his mother?* Then he rationalized the fact that he was a kid. *Do kids really care? His mother and I were separated for four years. There is no way he could have thought we would get back together.* Then he pondered on the question. He wanted to look back and figure out exactly when he met her. It seemed like a year but he knew it was nowhere near that long.

He sent himself a message to check with the church secretary, King, and Vickie. He knew if she gave an offering on her first day it would be recorded. However, he also had given Vickie and King specific instructions on that day. He needed to mark his calendar for both occasions. The day they met and the day they officially started dating. Then it occurred to him he should have an email saved from both King and Vickie that same day. "I met her at church," he replied.

"What is she like dad?"

"She is nice, smart, funny, and keeps me in line."

"No dad. I meant what is she like?" He did hand motions illustrating her shape.

"Son, what do you know about that?"

"I know a little something."

"Boy, you better watch yourself?"

"So why do you like her?"

"Because she is cool, true, and always herself. She is not fake and does not pretend. She likes me for who I am and not for what I do or what I have."

RJ did the shape motions again. "So what's the deal? Everything is real?"

"What do you mean RJ?"

"You know what I mean?" RJ said being a mischievous little boy.

"RANDALL JUNIOR."

Ignoring his father's threat, "Are you going to marry her?"

He did not respond off the rip. God knows he wanted to. He knew he was going to propose one day. The question was what would her answer be? He had to respond to RJ as if he was a child. He was a child. He could not answer the way he really wanted. "It is too early for that," he said instead. He did not lie. It was too early, although he knew he wanted to marry her.

"Ahh man. You scared dad." They laughed about it and talked trash. He felt a little better. The talk went better than he anticipated. He desired to text her right now but he wanted to be a good example to his son and not text and drive. When he was situated, he sent the text. It read.

> Missing you. Girl you got me gone.

She texted back.

> That makes two of us.

He and RJ looked at the houses. RJ had a difficult time deciding and was torn between two of the houses. Overall, they had an enjoyable day. They had the chance to hang out at the gym and meet up with RJ's godfather, Trevor. The day was great. He missed his son a lot and wished the situation were different. He could enjoy being with RJ all day every day. Randall felt like he was living the best of all worlds' right at this moment. He had God, RJ, a great best friend, and the love of his life. Not to mention, he was given the opportunity to fight again with both his team and hers behind him. His life was falling into place perfectly.

He took a pause. "I'll be back," he said to RJ.

He went to his bedroom and laid on the bed with his feet still touching the floor. He paused and reflected before he dialed the phone. Everything was good except a few pieces he could not get to fit into the puzzle he called life. Finally, he realized it was nothing he could do tonight so he prepared to call. His heart started pounding quickly and his hands were sweating. *Why am I so nervous? Why does she do this to me?* He felt like a teenager. *RJ is supposed to feel like this, not me.*

"Hey sweetie," I said sounding more excited than I wanted when I answered. I wished I could take it back. My tone was over the top.

He gave up the laugh. My enthusiastic greeting actually made him feel a little better. "Hey baby."

"You sound exhausted."

"No I am cool."

"Babe?" I said in a questioning tone.

"I am."

"So what's the deal?"

Other than missing you nothing, he thought. "RJ had me eating junk," He admitted to her,

"WHAT? You are not going to purge are you?"

"I don't know. Can I?"

"Can you?"

"I am asking you?" he questioned.

"No, you cannot. So I see who can encourage you to eat," I said with a smile on my face. "RJ and I may be best buds after all."

"DJ I hope so."

Me too, I thought. "So how was your day?"

He shared every detail. Where they went, what they ate, and how they had an excellent day.

"I am so happy for you. Sounds like an exciting day."

"RJ and I are going to hit this game and then lay it down. Tomorrow I think RJ, Trey and I will go look at cars."

"WHAT?"

"Not for me," he said with a quickness then laughed. "I am to provide Tameka with a vehicle. I think I am going to trade the ones she has and let RJ pick out what he wants her to drive and be done."

"Okay. So what do you guys plan to look at?"

"I am not sure yet."

"I am positive you three will come up with something." I was asking because I felt it would be inappropriate for her to have something like a Bentley, Bach or anything along those lines. She was the ex after all. As far as I was concerned, she needed a Toyota or a Tahoe.

"I hope it goes as smooth as the house ordeal."

"I am sure it will." It amazed me that he sweated the small stuff.

"I guess I will check out some whips before I go to bed."

"You promise you are going to bed right?" I wanted verbal confirmation from him.

"I promise."

"See you later."

He blogged at three thirteen AM:

> I have missed my love. Who would have known one day would make this much of a difference? I never knew love like this before. I have all my loves. If only my four worlds could meet. I think my life would be complete.

I called him at three fifteen. He should have been asleep, but here he was obviously wide-awake. He answered, "Hi Sweetheart."

"I missed you too."

"If I have my perfect will there would never be a day I am without you."

"Who said you could not?"

He was known for eluding the question, "I love you," he said instead.

"I love you too," I replied while shaking my head.

"Good night."

Withholding my laugh I said, "Night."

Friday

I could not go back to sleep. He did not say if he could have his way, but rather, his perfect will. That was a deep statement. At four, I decided I was being unproductive so I got up. I figured the earlier I got to work maybe the earlier I would leave. It was a Friday after all and I did have a Boo now. Regardless, I knew I was not leaving work any earlier. Whom was I fooling?

I called him immediately. "What's wrong?" he answered.

"Nothing."

"Why are you up?"

"Getting ready for work."

"Now?"

"Yes."

"Why?"

"I could not go back to sleep."

"Why?"

"I am not sure," I lied. His blog had me as it did most nights.

"What is it?" he asked, sensing my untruthfulness.

"I don't know," I lied again.

"Do you want to talk about it?"

"I am fine."

"Do you want to talk to someone else about it?"

What does that mean? Hunter? A shrink down? I did not get it. "I will be fine."

"I am confused now. You are fine or you will be fine," although he thought to himself, *you are fine.*

He was very observant. "Danielle, I think you are playing a word game. Did you learn this from talking to someone?"

"I think you need to be getting some rest."

"Really? Wow. Now this contradictory coming from you of all people. The person who never sleeps."

"I have a lot on my mind."

The timing was perfect. I switched it up on him. "Do you want to talk about it?"

"Not right now," he admitted.

"Are you holding back?" I sounded curious.

"I need to get my thoughts and plans of actions in order," he stated.

"Then will you speak to me about it?"

He did not say anything.

"I take your silence as a no."

"No it is not a no. I am not sure what is on my mind." Now he was the one lying. "I do not think it will require a conversation. My mind is spinning out of control," he added.

"Why don't you go to sleep and relax it?"

"Have a good day," he ignored the question.

"Will you call me later?" I asked.

"Haven't I always?"

Quickly, I replied, "Do you want me to answer that?"

He rebutted, "Do you disagree?"

"I sure do."

"Then yes, answer the question please."

"Vegas."

That stabbed him. "You are right. It was a different set of circumstances but you are correct I did not call. I was not allowed to use the phone. Umm, it will not happen again. I am not sure what else I can say or do to make it right."

"Just call me later and I think we will be fine."

"Are you sure?"

"Try me and see."

He gave up my laugh. It was early but his laugh was still the same. I loved it more each time I heard it. I found myself thinking about him all the way to work.

He and RJ hung out all day. Although most of the day they spent looking at cars with Tre. After looking at the different car options, they finally were able to come into agreement and decided on the BMW X6. They all enjoyed another boy's day.

No doubt, the day had been long and fun. As they were riding back home Randall did not know if this was the right time or moment. He waited all day. He was not sure if it was better to do it alone or with Trevor. Each time the moment occurred it was cut quickly before he was able to speak the words. He decided to take a chance. He was talking to a child right. How hard could this be? He was the adult.

"RJ, I was wondering and hoping you would be interested in meeting my friend," he said nervously.

"You can say it dad. Your girlfriend."

"That is not true."

"The girls at my school will ditch you if you don't refer to them as your girlfriend."

"I am cool. I don't think she will ditch me."

"Bet she will." RJ teased.

"Will not," he bantered back as children do.

"Well I will ask Ms. Danielle myself."

"So you are going to meet her?" containing his excitement.

"Yeah."

"Are you sure?"

"Dad why are you so nervous?"

"I don't want to put you in a difficult situation. I do not want to make this complicated for you."

"Dad, come on. I know you are going to have a girlfriend. I am shocked you only have one."

"What?" *What did that mean?* he thought as Trevor's eyebrows rose.

"I mean you are a big time boxer. Right?" the kid confirmed more so than questioned.

He cut his eyes.

"I mean if I was a big time boxer I would have all the fine honeys bruh." RJ did the illustration showing the silhouette of a woman again.

"Man that is not my style to have more than one girlfriend."

"I know. You are lame," he said in jest.

He punched his arm.

"I was just kidding dad," holding his arm.

"You better not have a girlfriend, much less more than one."

"RJ is a player."

"Watch it son."

"I mean my dad is a Champion Boxer. So all the girls want me."

"You don't say," he said giving his son the side eye.

"It's true."

"That explains it all then. I guess that is why no one is interested in me because they are all interested in Randall Jr."

"Ms. Danielle is interested in you dad."

"Yeah, she is and that is the only person I need."

"Somebody is in love," the youngster joked.

He slammed on the brakes. He wanted to scream. Then he realized there was no need. He was in love with her.

"I am going to tell her about this too," the kid warned.

"You are such a snitch. You know snitches get stitches right?"

"We can rumble anytime you want to old man."

"Are you threatening me? As soon as we get to the house, get your boxing gloves ready."

RJ was not stopping, "Which way you want it? On the tube or in the ring?"

"Bring it. You do not frighten me."

"I don't but 'Ms. Danielle' makes you nervous," RJ mocked him while emphasizing Ms. Danielle while Trevor sat back, not able to hold it any longer releasing his laughter.

Once they arrived home, they wrestled and boxed for hours until he decided to take a minute to text Danielle.

> Hey babe. I am wresting with RJ. I will call you in a little while and then I can give you my undivided attention. I hope you had a great day. I miss you. I love you.

I got the text. I could not come up with a decent response. I was not sure if my bad day at work was carrying over. Therefore, I did the best thing I could in this situation. I did not respond at all. *I will wait until he calls me.*

I went through all my options and resolutions to get this darn Hotel's issues resolved. I researched and read until I felt like I was blue in the face. I was on construction overload. When I looked at the clock, it was a few minutes before midnight.

Now, I was pissed. *I specifically asked him if he would call me later and he said have I ever not. He did not call all day. Where they do that at? F it.* I called him.

His home phone rang. He jumped and answered. "I am so sorry," he said right away instead of hello.

I did not say anything.

"I am sorry. I messed up."

I said nothing.

"Are you still there?"

My voice was frightening, "Do you remember our conversation earlier?"

"Yes, I am ashamed to say I do."

"Un huh."

"Other than me forgetting to call what is wrong?"

"I am not sure which one is the number one issue I have today," I answered.

"Between what?"

"First, you promised me you would call. I really want to trust your word. Second, I can't sleep and third, I have a project driving me crazy."

"Tell me about the project," he said in a calm tone as if to soothe me.

Right as I was about to speak, I heard his cell phone ring. "Who in the hell is that?" as I did not have his undivided attention. Most of all, I believe I was upset someone was calling him this late.

He answered and I quietly listened to the one sided conversation. "Hey, what's wrong? Un huh. Yeah. I support you one hundred percent. It is your job. Why? You can do it. It is the right thing to do. Tell me why? Un huh. Look, I have Danielle on the other phone. Hold on DJ."

Then he muted me. I could hear nothing. *Is he really going to have another conversation while I am on hold? What is up with tonight? Is it a full moon?*

He continued his conversation while Danielle was muted, "Get dressed I will meet you at the church in forty five minutes to an hour. Stop and get the donuts. It is going to be a long night. I am bringing Danielle. She had a rough day and I did not call after I promised I would. You are married. Why didn't you say something? Tell me to check in or something bro."

"My bad. I will see you in an hour," Tre replied.

He unmuted the phone. I could hear him again. "DJ, get dressed. Get all the stuff you are working on. I will be there in thirty minutes."

"What? Who was that? What is going on?"

"It was Trevor. He cannot sleep either. He has a difficult subject he wants to teach on but is concerned how people will receive it. Get dressed." He hung up the line not giving me much time to respond.

"Son I am meeting Uncle Tre at the church," he told RJ.

"Lame dad. I am staying here so I can play my game. I am killing it right now."

I wasn't sure if he was serious or not. He did say he would call me earlier and he did not. I called him back to verify.

"I am about fifteen minutes away from you. Get some tea."

"Okay." I hung up. I threw on some jeans and a tank. *There is no telling where we will end up. He picks some of the strangest places to go*, I thought. Sure enough, he was there in fifteen minutes. I was still rolling up drawings. He came right in and got my bags from by the door. I had my printer also just in case I needed it. I would rather have too much of what I needed than not enough. I hope he was not planning on going to Mikey's. It was a Friday night and it would be too packed for me to work.

"Sorry, I messed up and I am not bearing gifts or a peace offering."

"Yeah," I said dryly. He noticed the attitude.

"Is this all work?"

"Yep." He reached for the plans. "I will hold them." He looked like most people do when I say that. The look said it is only paper. To them it is, but to me it is the making of life. I can make anything happen on paper. The same way he looked and felt about his fist was the same way I looked and felt about this paper. "Don't look at me in that tone. You use those tiny hands. I use paper." He continued to look at me in that tone anyway. He put my stuff in the truck as I held onto my plans.

"My hands are not small," he said as he checked them out.

"Actually they are for your height, structure and the size of your feet."

He continued to look at them as if he had never seen them before. "Ay, I got the feet and hands comparison. It is so not true."

"Most people that do not fall in the positive aspects of the theory always say it is not true."

"What do you know?"

"I know thirteen's when I see them."

He looked over and bopped me in the head. Then he took my hand and held it to his face. "I am sorry. I feel horribly bad."

I did not respond. I knew he was with his son, which was the reason I asked if he would call. I wanted to know up front what to expect when he was with his son. I also wanted to know where we were going. "Where are we going?" I asked.

"Relax sometimes. Let me take control."

We pulled up to the church. Hunter's car was there. He parked. I guess that is what you call it. We gathered all of my things and walked directly to the sanctuary. Pastor was there already sitting on the front row in the area I normally sat with a dozen donuts.

"Hey Pastor."

"I hear you can't sleep either," he said as if it was the middle of the day.

"Yeah, is this where the insomniacs go?"

"I guess so in RW's world."

"So Randall, what are we doing here?" I questioned now calm and relaxed.

"You are going to your corner and draw," he said to me. He looked at Pastor Hunter. "You are going to your corner and practice until you get your confidence up."

"What are you going to do?" Trevor asked.

"I am going to go back and forth between you two until you are where you need to be while jumping rope."

"Dang Pastor, sounds like he has turned your pulpit into a ring and he is the referee. How do you feel about that?"

"RW, what's up with that?" Trevor asked him.

"I am helping you both in the world I relate to."

I went to my corner and so did Pastor. I did not even notice he walked out until he came back in with tea.

It was three in the morning when I looked at the clock on the wall. My problem was not resolved but I must admit I felt better than I did earlier. I do not think Hunter's problem was resolved either. His topic was still a tough one, but he seemed a little more comfortable than he did a few hours ago. The situations had not changed at all, however, our outlook changed. I am not sure if this was his plan but these were the results, which worked for both of us.

By the time we loaded the truck back up he was only wearing his black jeans and his black wife beater. Now I had to decide if I liked him better in the black or in the white wife beater. The result, I liked him in both and preferred him in neither.

Saturday

He pulled up to my house to drop me off. Before he had the chance to put the truck in park I said, "To ensure we do not have a repeat episode of yesterday maybe we should agree we will talk tomorrow or Monday."

Confused he asked, "Why would you say that?" *My apology was not enough.*

"I know you will have your son and I do not want to interfere on his time. There is no need for you to be pressed with trying to call me."

He was hoping this did not go there. He was so engulfed with RJ; he missed the opportunity to contact her. He did not want her or RJ to feel like he was choosing between the two. This was new to him and he knew he would have to figure out a mutual balance. He was confident he could do it. "Today will be different," keeping his reply simple. "Do you have the salon today?"

"Yes. Then from there Mikey's. I am running to the mall and chilling the rest of the day."

"Are you really chilling?"

"I am sure I will find a way to work at some point."

We said our goodbyes. I laid across the bed for a few hours before starting my day.

He and RJ had another great father son day. He had the talk with him again in the attempt to get RJ comfortable with all of the sudden changes in his life. However, RJ's response did not change.

Sunday

Per our conversation last night, he was having Keith pick me up. We were spending the day together. He was dropping RJ off after church and the remainder of the day was all mine. I was so excited and could not wait. It had only been a few days but I missed him already. I do not know if he knew it but it was our five-month anniversary.

Not really but really. We had not been 'together' five months, per se, but it had been five months to the day since I met him. What a difference one hundred and fifty days made. I would have never imagined this. I was happier than I had been in a long time.

When Keith arrived, I had a change of clothes ready and my computers of course. I did not know the game plan. After service, I saw RJ leaving with Keith but no one introduced us. If RJ was leaving with Keith then that meant I was stuck waiting on King. Finally, I asked, "King can you take me home or to Randall's?"

To my surprise, King and I talked as if we had good sense on the ride. I opted to sit in the front seat. When we arrived at the house, he opened the door, powered down the alarm, and brought my things inside.

He talked for a few more minutes and then left me alone. I went and changed clothes and returned to the sofa. As I flipped the remote, I noticed a beautiful set of diamond earrings on the table. I knew they were not his because they were hoops. My phone rang. Before I could say hello he was speaking.

"Danielle."

"Yes."

"I need to make mention of something," he said with urgency.

"Go ahead."

"Where are you?"

"Sitting on the couch."

"Damn!"

I thought to myself, *did he just say a bad word?*

"Those presents on the table are for you. I have not been able to give them to you yet but I wanted to clarify before you got upset and think they belong to someone else. I did not know King was taking you to the house. I thought we were going back to your house. I am still tied up but I wanted to tell you those are your presents. You can open them if you would like."

"I'd rather wait on you."

"I will be there are soon as I can."

I was asleep when he arrived and didn't hear him come in. When he kissed my forehead, I barely opened my eyes. I could see his shirt was outside his pants and his tie was untied. He sat down on the side of me ruffling my hair back and forth. He leaned up and handed me the two boxes. I knew what was in one box because it was open when I got there. I did not have a clue what was in the second box. I was scared to open it. I lifted my head up and kissed him.

"You didn't open them yet?" he asked.

"No. Thank you in advance." I still would not open them. What was wrong with me? I was laying here holding two jewelry boxes and now hesitant to open them. He took one from my hand and opened the box himself. He took the chain from the box, lifted my hair and placed the cross around my neck. He held my hair up and kissed the back of my neck repeatedly making me weak internally.

"Happy five month anniversary," he said.

The tears rolled down my face. I turned around and dumped my head in his chin. "Thank you."

As he kissed my forehead, "For what?"

"Loving me."

"No, thank you."

"How did you know?"

"I have my ways," he said not wanting to admit to her he had been keeping track.

"I know you've been in the dog house since Friday. You may get out now," I said with a smile.

He smiled back, "I have wanted to give these to you and I guess today is a good day since it is the fifth month anniversary of us meeting.

WEEK 22

Monday

Today I was on cloud nine. I cannot believe he remembered and I was certainly not expecting gifts.

Work was crazy; however, I did not notice it. All I could notice all day was the sparkle from my earrings and pendant reflecting in my monitors. Not to mention the sparkle in my eyes. A phenomenal guy made my day a phenomenal day.

Tuesday

Work was just that today. Work. I busted my tail all day. I was annoyed and honestly wanted to tell them all to take these drawings and shove them. Instead, I pressed through the day and made my way to the gym afterwards.

From the minute I walked in King rode my tail. The last thing I needed today was another sucker riding me. My rump is a two-seater not a bus. I did not have room to haul any more passengers. I was not allowing anyone else to ride me for the day. King was about to be dealt with within the next few seconds if he kept it up. The others were able to bust on me since they paid me but King was not privy. Today was not a good day for him or his insults.

"King, up your weight before you buck at me boy. My goons got goons."

"Why you got to get your goons?"

"Don't F with me King."

"Is that a threat?"

"Nope, it is a promise."

"It is actually exciting around here," Sam said from the ring with Hooks who in turn punched him.

"Tape her hands," King yelled.

No one would so King taped my hands himself. As soon as he finished my hands, he put tape over my mouth.

"KING," Randall shouted.

"She gives everyone a hard time. Let's see her talk now since she can't get it off."

"No, she only gives you a hard time King," Hooks replied.

"I know and I am tired of it," King said looking at me as I frantically tried to get the tape off my lips.

I managed to finagle the tape loose from my mouth. "King you need a dog biscuit. That is part of the problem. You are hungry," I said seriously. "Eat some food sometime. If you eat, you will stop being so mean. Food is good for your soul. Haven't you heard of soul food? It helps you live. Come by on Sunday. I will fry you some chicken honey. Make sweet potatoes, macaroni and cheese, sweet water bread, and apple pie. Now, if that does not help you then a straitjacket it is."

"What time Sunday?" he asked calmer after the mention of soul food.

"Five."

"What do I need to bring?"

"Nothing, just leave that attitude in the bottom of the ocean honey."

"DJ, let's go," Randall said escorting me to his office where he and I chilled for the rest of the night.

Wednesday

I woke up today not feeling much better than the day before. At least not mentally. I tell you, one hard day has the ability to drag you through the mud. I made up my mind right then and there that I was going to leave work early. I planned to go to the hair salon and have Randall pick me up for church at five. *Good luck with that*, I thought to myself.

I called his phone. "Good morning sunshine," he answered.

"Good morning heavy weight."

"How is my girl?"

"Truthfully?"

"Real talk."

"Dreading the day."

"What kind of talk is this? Death and life are in the power of the tongue. Watch your lips. Guard your mouth. Now, command your morning to change," he instructed.

"Okay," I said like a child being chastened; although, I knew he was right.

"Don't just say okay DJ. Make it happen."

"Pick me up at five."

At that, he stopped running on a dime. "What happened?"

"Nothing."

"Why am I picking you up?"

"For bible study. It is Wednesday right?" I was confused for a minute.

"What?" he asked sounding even more confused than me.

"Don't ask questions. You said command the day. Just do it before I change my mind."

"Bye girl."

"See you later."

I made it my business to have a good day. Or rather to not have a bad one I should say. I left early as planned and made it to the salon. I was feeling good because so far everything was going according to plan. Then the curve came. Leigh called. *I knew I should have left my work phones with her.*

"Yes, Leigh. I am under the dryer."

"Good. You have just been requested to be on a conference call at five PM."

"I can't do."

"Yes, you can. You can do thirty minutes."

"Screw me Leigh. You know I am trying to be on time for church. I told Randall to pick me up at five," I said annoyed.

"I will call him and explain it to him."

"No. I will handle it." I hung up the phone and sighed. I lifted the dryer head and went outside to call him.

"Hey babe."

"Hey Randall," I said dryly.

"What's up?"

"Nothing."

"How is your day going?"

"Well, it was going good until a few minutes ago."

"What's wrong?"

"Leigh just scheduled me a conference call at five."

"You can take it in the car on the way."

"No. I do not want to do that. Besides, it would be rude. Don't worry about picking me up."

"Danielle. Are you still at work?"

"No, I am at the salon."

"Why are you changing plans?"

"Leigh dropped this on me," I said pitiful.

"Speaking of which," he said looking at his screen. "She is calling my phone right now. Hold on. Hey Leigh," he answered.

"Hooks, I am sorry. I scheduled Dani for a five o'clock conference call."

"She is on the other line telling me now. I am a little disappointed."

"I am sorry. It should not be longer than thirty minutes," Leigh ensured.

"Thanks."

He came back to the line disappointed. "I'll see you at the church," he told me. He took his time getting dressed. He was disheartened. It was not as if he had anything special planned. Being in her presence was special enough.

I joined in on the call right at five. The conversation was going as I figured. A lot of testosterone was being exchanged. *We could go all night at this rate.* Leigh was on my list. Nothing was going to get resolved. Promptly at five thirty I interjected, "Guys, this has been informative. Can we schedule this argument later?" I said sarcastically.

They continued as if I said nothing at all. It was now six PM and I needed to go. I got in the car and drove to the church. This was officially a wasted conversation. I was still where I was Friday night. Nowhere.

Keith had been out to the car twice to get me but I could not get off the call. It was seven fifteen by the time I clicked off the line and everyone decided we were done. I glossed my lips and made my way into the church. I looked at the clock on the wall as I walked in the sanctuary. It read seven eighteen. I wasn't expecting to sit in my same seat considering I was now a late, but the usher led me there anyway. I was next to Keith. I did not see Deacon Washington as I came up the aisle. I finally spotted him.

He looked at his watch and then turned back towards the praise team. I knew what that meant. Randall despised tardiness. I waited and looked over and again he looked at his watch a second time. This time he tapped it. I looked at mine to confirm I read the clock correctly. It was seven twenty three. I was not that late. *Why is he tripping? I have been on the property for an hour.*

His body language informed me he was pissed. He tapped his watch several more times and the facial expressions he gave were brutal. Then my phone rang in my ear. I kept my earpiece in my ear under my hair because I figured someone would call back. I walked out as soon as Hunter began to speak. I stood in the vestibule for a few minutes but after realizing this debate was going to be longer than anticipated, I stepped outside. I knew he would send someone.

After ten minutes, I could feel something overshadowing me, or rather, someone. I purposefully did not turn around. Once I began to speak, I turned and waved hello in the middle of my conversation. As soon as his face rose to explode, I held my finger up to signify one minute. I was caught off guard. I wasn't expecting him. I was really expecting the Terminator. Right now, I preferred King opposed to him.

When I was able to take a break from talking, I leaned over and kissed his lips. I could tell he wasn't expecting it but it didn't work anyway. His arms were folded as he shifted his weight from side to side. As angry as he was he was still sexy. Maybe even sexier. I did a double take and then looked him up and down.

He spoke in his wrist, "Everything is fine. Danielle needs to realize she is not at work."

I turned my back and spoke over my shoulder. "You look extremely handsome Deacon."

He said nothing.

"I am real close to having a horrible day. Please do not chastise me on church grounds."

I could hear his feet stomping away. I took my earpiece out of my ear and held it away from me. "Deac," I called out. He turned around. "I need five more minutes please. It's work. Sorry. The problem hotel. Be patient with me please." I leaned in to kiss him but he did not move. I have never seen him this upset before. I was working. Why was he so angry?

He stared with no response or expression. Then he walked away. I could see him running through the glass all the way around to the sanctuary. He was pissed because I was working. What was a girl to do? I knew right then I would eventually be forced to make some changes I didn't want to make.

Immediately, my defense came to me. *He asked me to be patient and wait for him. Now, it is his turn to be patient. I am here, present and accounted for. I can still hear the message. In the meantime, let me do my job.*

It began to rain. Therefore, I walked back inside the door and noticed Keith standing not too far away. I gave a courtesy smile. He checked his watch giving me the impression I had a time limit. I walked back out the door. He politely came, opened the door and held it as if I was expected to come in. Just that quick it started storming. All I could think was my hair was going to look like a poodle in a matter of minutes.

I was finally at a point where I could politely end the call again. Once I did Keith and I walked back inside the sanctuary. Deacon Washington fumed the remainder of service. His normal gunshot claps were like cannons today. He even turned his entire body in the chair to make sure his back was to me.

I nudged Keith. "What is his problem?" Keith did not respond. Randall stood right in front of me while waiting for the collection. He scolded me with his eyes and walked away. I waited and waited and waited for him after bible study. Finally, Keith came over and said, "I will walk you to your car." It was not a question.

I wanted to go off but instead I chose to remain calm. It wasn't Keith who was being a pain. He was simply doing his job just as I was earlier.

I stood there looking crazy I am sure. I snickered, "Is this how he is going to act?"

Keith looked uncomfortable and you could tell he did not want to be in the middle of it. "He said he will see you at your house when he is done."

"So he sent a message?" I asked disgusted.

Keith felt my temper rise. "Let's walk," he instructed.

We walked in silence. Once we arrived at the car he said, "Stay on your same behavior. Text him when you get home. He will be fine."

"I don't know," I said. He was showing me a different side of him tonight.

"This is new to him. He wants to and is trying to do the right thing. You know there are things he is serious about and that's God, boxing, and you."

"We will see what happens. Thanks." I hugged him. It was not his fault. His boss was being a jerk. I got home and started checking the emails and voice messages I missed by leaving work early. I wanted to stay on top and not get too relaxed since I did not know how his conversation was going to go. Working would keep me focused. After an hour, he rang the gate. I clicked the button to open it without say anything.

I saw the lights pull up and went to the door. He did not greet me or give me a hug as he normally would.

When he did speak, he literally cursed me out. "Don't say anything to me when you are sick. Why in the hell would you stand outside in the rain on the damn phone? Why would you accept a phone call in the sanctuary? On the front row nevertheless."

"The same reason you run in the rain," I retorted.

"It is my job Danielle."

"It is my job Randall." I bounced back. "Did you forget?" My words stabbed him.

Why was she so ambitious? Were all women like this? Were we an exception to the rule? We are both committed to our respective professions. I realized this was not going to change. I am going to have to accept it the same why she has to accept me fighting, travelling, speaking, and promoting. She is supportive of me. *Why can I not tone it down and support her?* "Not to be personal, but how much do you make a year?"

"What?" His question caught me off guard and in disbelief.

Then he pulled out his checkbook from inside his jacket pocket. "I will double it. Therefore, I will not have to worry about this problem."

I stood still. Now I was about to bust a blood vessel. My temper rose. My blood was boiling. I tried hard to control it. Before I knew it, I snapped. I slapped his hand with the checkbook in it. It hit the floor. "F you and the horse you rode in on. Who do you think I am? Do you think of me as a cheap trick? You can't buy me. I am not for sale. You got me twisted," I had to laugh a little to keep from crying or punching him. "Let yourself out when you are done and stop off on the way home and purchase you a few tricks. Ten would not be equivalent to my worth."

I walked off talking and fuming. "No hell he didn't come in my damn house and try to buy me. Who in the hell does he think he is? Pretty Boy Floyd, TIP, Diddy, or LL? Get on somewhere with that man. This is the main reason I have been by myself. Men need to make up their damn minds. You want an independent woman. Then when you get her, you want to turn her into a gold digger. Did he really just come over here and insult me with a check? All because I show up late doing my job. I am handling my business with a contact from across oceans he probably has never even travelled. What kind of crap is that? You want to buy me," I said as the ice hit my glass. "Pay me to build you a four hundred million dollar project. Repeatedly. Get my attention like that. Otherwise, you will have to have the Brinks truck deliver my pay. You are supposed to be just as much of a businessman as I am a businesswoman. You know I am never doing anything without a contract. Where you been handling business at? We would be in a boardroom with counsel. However, you want to show up with a checkbook and insult me. Do you know how to write a check on your own? What is your check number one hundred and two? Try over twenty thousand personal checks written. I wrote them. Not my accountant. Not my assistant. That is what you get Dani. Do not quit your day job. Back on the grind girl." I slammed my bedroom door. My house had never experienced drama. This door has never been slammed before.

I got in the shower and stood directly under the faucet. I wet my freshly done hair. I stayed there a long time trying to calm myself. I sat on the floor of the shower and cried out. *Why? How did I get right back to where I started? In a relationship with a person who discredits what I do. I bust my tail to get to where I am. Does he really think I am going to let it go? Come on dude. Really?*

I stepped out of the shower and walked to lock my front door. I wrapped my towel around me. I had to have been in the shower for at least forty minutes. I did not even check my monitors. I was sure he was gone by now. I stopped in the kitchen to make me some tea. I walked to the door and he scared the hell out of me when I turned around. He was sitting in a chair at my dining room table.

He was still there. I was naked and soaking wet. The only thing that separated us from becoming physical was a towel and a high level of pisstivity. He reached out, grabbed my hand and pulled me to his lap. Now, nothing separated us. My wet bare bottom half covered was touching his jeans. He pushed my wet hair back. He leaned his back in the chair observing me. I was sitting straight up. My face was stern. I do not know if he thought the tears were water from the shower. I looked him dead in his eyes. Why was he still here? His checkbook was on the table.

Finally, I broke the silence. "You need something else? More insults maybe?"

He did not blink.

"Don't push me away. Please do not do that. You will force me to build a wall."

He placed his hands behind his head. His eyes were closed. "I am not trying to do that. I f'ed up."

I did not respond.

His eyes remained closed. "Help me to understand why would you take a call during service?"

"I hoped they did not but I knew from the way the conversation ended they would more than likely call back. Unfortunately, I cannot say sorry people it's Wednesday. I have bible study and Deacon Washington hates when I am not on time."

There was a long silence. "Why is your hair wet?"

"I soaked it under the shower?"

"Why? You went to the salon today or did I misunderstand that too?"

"It is only hair."

"I have upset you."

"Is that a question?"

"No. It was really a statement."

"Why are you so concerned if I can relate to your job but you cannot seem to relate to mine?"

He opened his eyes long enough to know I was looking at him. *I have to keep my eyes closed* he thought. *Otherwise, I will realize she is wearing a towel.* "I can't answer that right now."

"You need to."

"I do not think I considered it a problem until this evening."

"So you do think it is a problem?"

"Yes as a matter of fact I do. You work too much. You stress too much over work."

"What is it you think you do?"

"It is different Danielle."

"Explain it to me then," I demanded.

He did not speak.

"Let me tell you where I have a problem. Not one time have you asked me if everything was all right. I am sorry I was late for church. I had all good intentions. I was there on the lot way before time. I am sorry I entered the sanctuary late. I am extremely sorry and rude for taking a call during service. But you know what, I am also sorry all I have done was try to please everyone except Danielle today."

"I started the morning changing my plans to ride early to church with you. Then those plans were changed to please a client by taking a conference call. Then I went back to appeasing you by showing up to church. Then changed to appease you by coming in the sanctuary. Not once have you asked how my day today was. You knew this has been on my mind since Friday. This was not a call to tell me good things. It was not to praise and give me accolades. This was a call to chew my butt. Any conference call from five until seven is probably bad. I was able to deflect some of it but the gist of the call was to rip me. Nevertheless, I still came to church."

He said nothing.

"I am sorry I had to change our plans. I am sorry I was late. I am sorry I was rude. This was a no win situation for me. If I took the call while you and I were riding together, I still would have been rude. So how was I to win? You fight in a ring, which is really a square; go figure, in front of millions of people. It is usually clear or evident who the winner is. Rather it is decided and calculated. I work on paper. Some days I have to fight. Today I did and it is not clear who won just yet."

"It is not just you anymore. It is not all about you. You have to be concerned about another person. You want me to be fair and understanding to you. However, you are not fair to me. We need to play by the same rules. I know this is difficult for you. It is different for me too. We can do it together. I know we can."

"Your behavior tonight was unacceptable. You were spiteful in the sanctuary. I knew I was late. You did not have to emphasize it by tapping your watch repeatedly. You were rude by not coming out from where ever you were at the church and then flat out disrespectful when you got here. I am shocked. You cannot buy everything and everybody to make them do what you want them to do. Let me make this clear. Don't ever insult me and play me cheap like that again."

He was quiet.

"I understand you are upset but do not ever treat me like you did tonight again. You were purposefully mean and that was jacked up Randall."

He remained silent.

"Look," I paused. "Some days will be my days and some days neither of ours. I love you very much; however, you have to let YOU go. I think you are the greatest and I pray you are in everything you do, but there is life outside of you. There are others of us that exist."

He sat still with his hands behind his head and his eyes closed.

"Say something."

He shook his head.

"What's wrong?"

He remained quiet with eyes closed. I stood up and repositioned myself straddling across his lap. I pulled his arms from around his head and placed them around me. I laid my head on his forehead. "Please talk to me," I said almost in a whisper.

He sighed as if it was his last breath. "All I can say is I f'ed up."

"Why do you say that?"

"I have boxing under control. I have training down. But when it comes to you, I have no idea how to treat you."

"It is okay. I understand this is new to you. Your experience in dating has been limited. How would you know? You best believe I am going to tell you how to treat me. You won't ever have to worry about that."

"I am worried." he sighed and dunked his head.

"Why? What are you struggling with?"

"Danielle, I am sitting here thinking I may not be as ready as I thought I was. Maybe I need to get Hooks together before I try to date you because I have no idea what I am doing. It is not as easy as I thought." He took a deep breath. "And now here it is I find myself apologizing for stuff I have done or didn't do." he paused. He was in deep thought and up until this point; he had yet to open his eyes. It was as if he refused to look at me. "I do not know what you need or how to love you. This is hard."

"First of all, I am not in a relationship with Hooks. I am dating Randall," I clarified. "Hooks is a part of you. He is a cool and nice person and I like him and all. However, Hooks is what you do not who you are. At the beginning and end of the day, you are Randall. When I say I do it will be to Randall and not to Hooks. When I met you, I meet Deacon Randall Washington. If you wanted me to meet you as Hooks, you would have introduced yourself as such. I am by no means an expert in this arena of relationships. I have the same experience you have and it is useless. What I do know is how I want to be treated. I am sure you know how you want to be treated as well. We can show and tell each other. I am not here to hurt you. I am here only to love and support you to the best of my ability. With you, I want to bring out the best in me. My best work is yet to come and your best fight has not even been planned yet."

"Why are you so upset because I was working? Do you expect me to tell an upset client it is Wednesday night, I cannot take your call. If that is the case then you will still be mad because I will be taking the call at midnight. It is a no win situation. Tell me what you think I should do about my job."

Randall thought long and carefully before he spoke. "I do not want you to quit. I need to understand it is not a traditional nine to five. Even if it were, you would still take it to heart and go beyond because you are an overachiever. It is not a bad thing. I like that about you but I guess I do not when it interferes with my time. Honestly, I have to ask myself if I was upset because you were working or because you blew me off. I think the latter more than the first. We had a date. It was my time."

"Babe, I am sorry I blew you off," I offered my most sincere apology.

"I was extremely excited to ride with you today and I guess from there it all seemed to have gone to hell rather fast."

"I apologize. I will try with all my efforts to have Wednesdays clear from this point on. What else can I do?"

"Can you teach me what you do? I mean, I know what you do. I have seen you work but I do not understand what would have you so worked up over the last few days. I am sure you do not understand all of what I do. Why I work out so hard and eat so little. However, you see me in action every day. Help me to understand you."

"Communication is the bridge to a successful relationship and unity. Right there we have started something." I lifted his face and kissed him. It was a passionate kiss.

He was out of breath. He had just enough passion to be slightly rough and yet he was mostly romantic. Instantly he stopped.

"What's wrong?" I asked.

"GET DRESSED. Please get dressed." He leaned his neck over the back of the chair.

"What time is it? Where are we going?"

"We are not going anywhere. You are about to explain in detail the problem with this job."

"Okay. I would love to do that. That is not a problem," I said full of excitement still sitting in his lap.

"Oh yes it is," he was referring to his lower internal excitement.

"Huh?"

"I am a man Danielle."

He only called me Danielle when the matter was serious. "I am aware of that," I said trying to kiss him again not realizing what he was referencing.

"Babe you are trying to kill me."

"Huh?"

"Dani you are naked and your female zone is in my man zone. Not to mention, my zone has been informing me that I am a man. I think I am going to have an asthma attack."

"Oops sorry. Do you have asthma?"

"No."

I tried to kiss him one more time before I stood up. "I love you."

"Um huh. I love you dearly and if you do not want me to knock everything off this table and show you just how much, you will get up immediately. I have held out for thirty or forty minutes. I cannot do it any longer. God is really trying me. I have never been tested the way he has tested me these last few months." He took a deep breath. His tone changed, "Girl, please get up or it is going to get ugly."

As I stood up, he yelled, "Hold up. Let me cover my eyes or something."

He put his hands over his eyes.

"You know I am the one that was in my house minding my own business and you were the one sitting here in the dark."

"Yeah I know and I won't do that again."

"You can uncover your eyes. Any other time I would have been completely naked."

He stared me up and down. "Let me have you," he said.

"Here I am," I replied.

"I am going to go to the kitchen and get some water before I go into cardiac arrest."

He went to the kitchen while I went and put on a pair of shorts and a tank. It was provocative and in hindsight a bad choice. When I came to the kitchen, he had taken his shirt off exposing his wife beater. His jewelry was lying on the counter. He poured us hot tea and milk while he was making my favorite, grilled cheese. He was expecting it to be a long night.

I laid the plans out on my drafting table. As I ate my sandwich I explained how all of this works via Danielle's version. Then I covered the specific parts of my issues.

It was now two in the morning. "DJ, I am enjoying our time. I hope we can do this often but I do want to let you go to sleep."

"I should be able to get three hours in. Luckily we have an event tomorrow."

"Crap. We sure do," he remembered. "I am sure they have blown my phone up by now."

"Where are your phones?"

"They are in the truck."

"You are going to be in trouble."

"It was worth it. They have located me and know I am at your house. I am sure they have assumed we are making love from my levels."

I choked, "What?"

"I think both of our levels were high. They are assuming sex. It will take a lot for me to explain this. Trevor will probably be involved with a lie detector."

"Leave it to Trevor."

We said our goodbyes and he left. His shirt was still on my chair and his jewelry on my counter. I was not mad at all. It let me know he would be back. I put his shirt up to my nose. It smelled of him. It was the closest I could get to him for now. I laid on the sofa holding it until I fell asleep.

Randall pulled out of the driveway with mixed emotions. How was he going to make all of this work? A few days ago, it felt easy. Now it was a challenge. She was a challenge to him. He decided he was not going home and went in a different direction. On the way he texted King.

No running in the morning. Meet me at the cross.

He parked and got out, "Good Morning." It was after two AM.

"Good Morning Deacon Hooks," the female security officer said.

"What time is prayer this morning?" he asked.

"Six."

"I will be in the sanctuary."

"Do you need anything?"

"Thanks. Everything I need is there," he said hoping to get the answers he needed.

The officer was nervous. She had a crush on Deacon Hooks. Here he was in the church with her alone wearing only his wife beater. She wanted to talk to him. She felt as though this might be her time to push up on him. She debated and debated. For years she wanted to approach him but never had the chance without others being around. Now she had all the opportunity in the world. She told herself to politely flirt while she made her rounds. However, when she entered the sanctuary she could not bring herself to talk to him. He was prostrate on the altar. She stood there impressed. There he was, a man of God, laid out worshipping late in the midnight hour.

Damn he is fine, she thought to herself as she watched him. Every female at the church wanted him and all had secretly confessed it. Now was her chance. Rumors were he was finally divorced. She was going to jump in headfirst. All he could say was he was not interested. She did not think he would be rude. He did not seem to be the rude type.

She sent her crew an email. She knew they were asleep but she had to let them know she was alone with the finest man she knew. Other than his best friend of course, Pastor Hunter, who was happily married?

She did her outside rounds and took a picture of his truck. Then she took a selfie with her and the truck to prove to them he was there. She sent the email with the pictures.

"Ladies, when you wake I will be at breakfast with Deacon Hooks. Details to follow," the email read.

Thursday

At four, the security guard could hear his phone ring and then ring again. He did not answer or silence either call. Finally, she went in to check on him. "Deacon Hooks, can I get you anything?"

He barely moved. "I am fine thank you."

"Are you sure? Your phone has been ringing."

"Sorry." He reached for the phone barely moving.

She leaned down and passed it to him. She got a glance at the screen in the process. Four missed calls from King.

He called the number back. "You got my text? Yeah," he clicked off.

"Are you sure you are okay?"

"Great," he snipped needing to be alone.

"Stop by before you leave."

"Sure," he said not thinking much about her request.

The officer was still plotting. She laid the foundation. If he stopped by then she could find out what she wanted to know and give him her number.

It was five AM when pastor pulled up. "Good morning beloved," he greeted the officer as he walked in.

"Good morning Pastor nice to see you this early." Pastor never arrived this early. She knew why he was there. His best friend had been there over two hours and needed him. Nevertheless, right now, he was interfering with her plan.

"Where is he?" Pastor Hunter asked as if he had a tedious job ahead.

She pointed to the sanctuary, "At the altar."

"How long has he been there?"

"Since a little after two this morning."

"When the intercessors get here do not send them in until you check with me to make sure we are ready. We may have to send them to the chapel this morning. Let me check on him first."

Trevor walked in and went right to Randall. He laid over him and began to pray with his friend. King had forwarded Randall's text to Hunter. Randall was blessed in ways he never knew. His crew kept him covered. Keith and King were planning to arrive soon as well. They knew he would not admit it but was having a hard time dealing with being in a relationship. It was new to him. Honestly, they did not want him to mess up. They knew he needed

Danielle. She also needed him and they were good for each other. No one knew how everything worked out last night, but they all were more than aware she was doing her job and he hated it. He may have said or done something to push her away. If so, they were prepared to intervene immediately.

King and Keith arrived at the same time. It was amazing how they were all so in touch with each other just like a fine tuned clock. They both walked in and the security chick was amazed that all the handsome men of the church were there with her alone. *What is going on*, she thought?

"Hey," King mumbled to be polite although preferring not to speak.

"Hello Mr. King," she replied.

"How was the night?" Keith asked trying to defuse King's behavior.

"Tough. I have had many visitors this morning. Something must be up?" she gently inquired.

"We have it under control," King said as if no further questions were needed from her. Sarcastically, "We know you will jump in and handle it if not." King was aware of all the vultures that preyed on Hooks. In addition, she was surely one of them.

"Where are the fellows?" Keith asked again attempting to lighten King's tone.

"Laid out on the altar," she replied rolling her eyes at King.

"A good place to be," King replied insinuating she should spend some time there too.

She thought to herself, *this atmosphere is getting crowded*. She knew then she might not be able to do what she wanted to do today either. *So close yet so far.*

They went in and automatically hit their knees. No one said a word. At five thirty, Hooks phone rang Dani's ring tone. He answered on the first ring. "Excuse me," he mumbled to them.

They all looked like WTH. How is he going to jump up from where he has been lying for the last few hours to answer her call?

"Hey babe," he said softy still respecting the sanctuary.

"Hey. What's wrong?"

"Nothing," he replied sourly.

"Are you alright?"

"I will be fine," he answered.

"You will be or you are?"

"Payback huh?"

"Yeah. Randall where are you?" she asked, sensing something was up.

"At the cross," he answered. She knew exactly where he was. There was always room at the cross.

"I'll be there in a minute." I clicked the line and pumped the accelerator. I took the next exit and jumped back on the highway heading in the opposite direction of the job. Before entering the highway again, I sent a quick text to Leigh while waiting at the red light.

> Start without me. I will be at the church.

It was not ten minutes before I arrived. "Good morning," I whispered to the security woman.

"Good morning," security hesitantly said back. Others were starting to arrive for prayer. She informed them to begin in the chapel just as Pastor instructed. However, this one did the opposite of the direction given and went to the sanctuary. *Why is she here? What is going on*, the security woman thought.

When I walked in, immediately they all smelt my perfume and knew it was me. I kneeled at the altar, gave a quick moment of silence then leaned over and kissed each one of their cheeks, including King. I got down next to Randall.

He took my hand, "Hey."

"You got it worked out?"

"Not yet," he confessed.

"What can I help you do?"

"I have it under control."

"Have you been here all night?"

He nodded confirmation.

"Let's get up Babe. We have a busy day."

The guys looked at each other. It must have gone better than they thought. In the past, they would have been there until he had to speak later this afternoon. He was speaking there at the church so at least he would already be in place. However, he was wearing the same clothes from the previous night minus a shirt. They were happy she showed up. This confirmed what they already speculated. She was the one.

He was sitting up. The guys were standing. I was still squatting. "You did not run this morning?" I asked concerned trying to discern his troubles.

He shook his head no. "I should have. I have been here all night."

"You are going home now?" I presented a question but it was a statement.

"I am here now. I am going to stay until prayer is over and then I am going to the gym."

"You do not have on a shirt."

"Tre has one. If not I have one in my car or in my office. Someone has one I can borrow."

"Don't make me come back up here," I warned as I stood up to leave. I looked all three of them in the eyes. I wanted to say something but I did not want to come off too harsh. Especially not this early and not in front of Pastor Hunter.

"We will take care of him," King said relieving her fears.

"I do not want any mess from you King."

He frowned and threw up the deuces.

As I walked out Keith followed. By the time we hit the door in the vestibule Randall was running behind us. I realized he had on different shoes than when he left my house. He was now wearing a pair of black air max.

"Keith I got it," he pushed the door open. He walked me to my car and I left for work. As he walked back in the building, the security officer stopped him.

"Deacon Hooks."

He slowed from running. He was like a two year old. He ran the majority of the time instead of walking. "Yes ma'am," he politely responded.

"Is everything alright?"

"Yes, just fine thank you for asking," he said in a hyperactive tone.

"No problems at home?"

"None, why do you ask?" changing his tone and facial expression.

"A married guy showing up at two in the morning sounds like problems on the home front," she said.

This was strange. He looked at her name badge so he could call her by name. "Melissa that is a strange way to ask, but I got the purpose of your question. No, I am not married any more. No, there are not problems at home. I live there alone. There are many times when I am here prostrate. Sometimes for me and sometimes for others. I appreciate you asking," he nodded as if the conversation was over.

She did not get the tone they were done talking. "I am sorry to offend you Deacon Hooks."

"Two separate names," he corrected her.

"Excuse me?"

"They are two separate names. Deacon Washington or Hooks." He normally never corrected people when they addressed him as Deacon Hooks. In fact, most people put the two names together. It usually did not bother him but for some reason today, it did.

"I am really messing up this morning."

Yes, you are, he thought to himself. "It's cool. We all have those moments. No offense taken. Give me a few weeks and hopefully I will be married again. I am definitely working on it." He wanted to eliminate any thoughts and hopes she or the other women in the church had immediately.

It stabbed her like a knife. Just when she thought she had an opportunity. Just when they had spoken enough for her to slide in he came back on her with that. "That sounds promising?"

"I hope so. I will let you know how it goes. You will get an invitation to the wedding. Maybe she will spare me and jump the broom in the middle of the night here and you can witness."

Now she was crawling in her skin. "I wish you luck," she said and faked a smile.

"Help a brother out. Tell her how great I am. What a nice catch I make. Hype her up when you see her. Okay?"

"I would not know who she is."

"She just left."

"I will remember to tell her. What is her name?" *I will remember her all right. How did she get so lucky?*

"Danielle Rose. Soon to be Danielle Rose Washington."

"Good luck Deacon," she said as she searched for Danielle Rose on social media to officially begin stalking her.

Hooks met up with Pastor and the guys in Pastor's office. "What's up?"

"Put this shirt on. We are on," Hunter responded as he tossed his friend a shirt.

Those who came participated in one hour of weekly morning prayer. Deacon Washington needed it. As soon as prayer was over Pastor greeted those that waited then Randall's team all went back to Hunter's office.

"Sit down," Hunter ordered. "What happened last night?"

He sat down, placed his elbow on the arm of the chair, rubbed his eyes and covered his face. "I acted like a butthole. I messed up. That is all I can say."

"Then what?"

"She checked the heck out of me."

"What did you do RW?"

"I kind of lost it."

"And?" Hunter probed.

"Humph. I umm…went off about being late and being outside in the rain on the phone. If that was not enough, I harped on taking a call, having the phone and earpiece in the sanctuary. But I think I really screwed up the worst when I tried to write her a check."

Perplexed Hunter asked, "A check for what?"

"I can't even talk about it."

Hunter rolled his hand in fast motion like carry on as he always does.

"Man, I know nothing about relationships," Randall confessed.

Trevor getting perturbed, "What did you do RW?"

"I f'ed up with a capital F. That's what I did."

Trevor's patience was wearing low, "We are listening."

"I asked her how much did she make and I would double her salary for the year."

"What? Stretch your hands toward him guys. What in H E double hockey sticks would possess you to say that?" Trevor responded in disbelief.

"Won't do it again, that's for sure," Randall admitted.

"What did she say?" King smirked. It felt good knowing she ripped someone other than him.

Randall quickly responded, "Man, what do you think? She cursed me out."

"Did you really think that was going to fly?" Keith asked while King rolled over the chair laughing his butt off.

"I do not know what I was thinking. I will never do that again. I thought she was going to punch me. She told me to let myself out. I think that was a nice way to put me out. She said it is not all about me. If I had not taken it upon myself to stay I do not think she would have ever allowed me back at her house, much less spoken to me again,"

"She would not," Tre said with confidence.

Randall slid down in the chair.

"I cannot believe you said that," King said shaking his head. "What in the hell were you thinking man? Why did you get angry about her taking a call? I will advise you to not start possessive behavior."

"Look, man. My wife is not always here. She has things she wants and needs to do for herself, our family, and the church. She is supportive. Most of the time she has heard the sermon beforehand. I would prefer her here but she does a lot of stuff behind the scenes that others do not see. You know this. You do too. First Lady may be in her office taking calls. There are times she is praying with members, stepped in for me by visiting the sick and the shut in, or taking food to the needy. She does whatever it takes. Sometimes after she has spent an entire day mentoring, helping me, making sure my mind and heart is clear and I am dressed appropriately, she is too tired to come out. I am walking in here dressed and ready but here she is in sweats. I will tell her, baby relax, and you can watch me from your office. It is all good. Get a grip dawg."

"You prayed and prayed for the right woman to come in your life. She has shown up and now you want to change her. If she did take your check and quit her job then you would think she is out to get you. She is independent, doing her own thing, and you are knocking her. If you were not fighting, she would probably beat you two times over in salary. She did right and I respect her for that. Once you marry her and have some kids then you can talk to her about quitting. She is not about to listen to that nonsense. This is Danielle we are talking about remember. She has worked hard to get where she is. Do you think little old you will come in and change her? She is running shop," Hunter advised.

"You are right."

"All minds and hearts clear?" Trevor looked at each of them. "Let's pray." Hunter prayed and after they said Amen he said, "Get out of my office and don't come back in here after doing stupid stuff."

"I have been put out of two places in twenty four hours. King, Keith do you have your stuff. We are running. I am going to my office to change and call Dani. You all can talk about me while I am gone."

He walked pass Melissa again. She remembered Hunters sermon that stated she could look and admire twice before it was considered lust. If she were not in church, she would take him from this Danielle Rose. Instead, she sat back. Nevertheless, she did admire and appreciated what she saw. She could not help but to wish it was her instead of Danielle.

She heard Deacon Washington say, "Hey Babe," interrupting her thoughts.

"What's up?"

"You keep me on my toes. Have you ever boxed before?"

"Where did that come from?" Danielle wondered.

"You keep me moving like I am in the ring. You shut down my entire strategy last night. You had me on the altar this morning then had my boys escorting me to the principal's office. You got me cursed out and put out and now I am sure they are talking about me behind my back."

"You will learn."

"So are we good?" he needed to know.

"Yes."

"I will see you at five?"

"Yes."

"Have a great day."

"Stay away from King. His temper is rubbing off on you," I joked.

He gave up my laugh as he walked back in the door returning from getting clothes out of his truck. He waved at Melissa and kept it moving. Once he got dressed, he went back into Tre's office. The guys were right where he left them. "Are you cackling hens finished?"

"No," King said with pride. "We forgot to ask you about these levels," he said pointing to the screen on his tablet.

"I do not want to talk about it."

Trevor looked up, "Oh you are going to. It was not an option."

"Did you sleep with her?" King demanded.

"What? Let's go," Hooks yelled, walking out of the door.

"Look," King called him back. "From three to eight you can see where her levels increase and decrease. After she came back into the sanctuary the final time, they stabilized. Right here," he said pointing to the screen. "It looks like every time you refused to look at her, her levels shot up again but came right back down. Then as she is walking to the car, she is up again. She tones down somewhere in between the parking lot and the highway. You on the other hand are up from about three o'clock and never go down until she arrived here an hour ago. Somewhere in between ten thirty and eleven, you are so elevated you should have felt a pinch on your wrist. The problem is she is completely calm during this timeframe. This is strange. Either you are sulking or she is. When you are at the peak of explosion, she is calm. We think you two were together, but then again, maybe not. What was going on?"

He looked at the screen and then back at the guys. "Let's go. I am not answering or entertaining this nonsense."

After prayer, he went for a run to relax his mind as soon as he got to the gym. He completed his normal workout routine and once he was complete, he went home at three to get prepared to go back to the church for the domestic violence seminar he was hosting. He did not call her. He called Leigh instead.

"Hey Hooks," Leigh sang.

"Hey. Make sure she is ready and in the car at five. We will be starting at six. No conference calls please. Yesterday's call got me in the doghouse."

"Friend, what happened?"

"No more conference calls. I may get dumped over the next one."

"Sorry friend she didn't mention it. I assume it is resolved."

"I hope so."

***

I made it my business to arrive at four fifty. It was a stretch. I made calls, texted and emailed all the way to the church. I did not wait for the others. I didn't want a repeat of last night. I found everyone in his office. I opened the door without knocking. "Sorry, I will come back later," I said as I noticed they were all talking as Hooks was writing.

"Come on in," King said motioning for me to enter. "We are going over the details."

"Where is Paige, Sade, and Leigh?" Hooks asked without looking up.

"I am not sure."

"Find out. They are models tonight," he ordered.

I reached for my phone.

He quickly checked himself, "DJ. Sorry. That was rude. Do you mind checking to see what time they will be here?" He smiled. "It is not about me," he said remembering our conversation.

I winked. He winked back. He walked pass me and nodded his head indicating to follow him. We stepped outside the door. I leaned against the wall while he leaned next to me. "How was your day?" he asked.

I smirked. It was obvious he listened to me last night. "It was good and yours?"

"As long as I still have a girlfriend it was a good day."

"It was good then."

By seven o'clock the house was packed. The turnout was much greater than I anticipated. Surprisingly, many men were present also. We all walked in the sanctuary together. Hunter, his Ambassador, JJ, Randall, and I entered with King, Paige, Leigh, Sade, and Keith behind us. We filled the entire front row. Hunter took the microphone and greeted the crowd, prayed then introduced Deacon Washington with an awesome introduction. The best part of his intro was he knew the information. He did not have to prepare notes. He spoke from his heart and it turned out to be a true heartfelt introduction. I was so moved I could have cried.

Randall stood up and bowed. "As it is customary in this house, all capable to stand please do so at this time. Stretch your hands toward Hooks. Blessed be the man who comes in the name of our Lord."

With open arms Deacon Washington said, "I receive it." He turned and hugged me. King and Keith stepped up and stood on each side of the pulpit. He was a different person up there. It was as if he belonged there. He spoke on violence. Violence for both receivers, pointing out the male and female perspectives. He showed a few short films then opened the floor for questions. He provided contact information for those who were victims and those who knew victims. He used Sade, Paige, Leigh, Jon Jon, Sam, Nate, and Sol for demonstrations. He ended the same way he opened, with scripture.

This was a seminar. Not a church service or bible study, but Hunter knew some of these people would never be in a church again until a baptism, a wedding or a funeral. Therefore, he gave a mini sermon based on what Deacon said and opened the doors of the church. A lot of questions and conversations were held after Hunter gave the benediction. There were people from other associations there to assist. They had pamphlets, brochures, and ready to counsel and encourage victims and family members.

"Babe you can leave me if you want to."

"I will stay a little while longer."

"Good. I want a kiss before you leave."

"Do you now," I said sarcastically and seductively.

"Do you think I deserve one?"

"It's something sexy about a boxer standing in the pulpit."

He laughed. "I wish you knew how much I needed you. It meant a lot to me to have you sitting on the front row wearing that beautiful cross. We have had a long twenty-four hours. Why don't you go home and I will call you when I get in the car."

"Are you rushing me off so you can holler at your girlfriend?" I teased.

"You know I am nowhere near that skilled. I cannot have two girlfriend's much less two in one place, city or state at the same time for that matter. I am having a hard time pleasing one girlfriend," he confessed.

Giving him a glance over I said, "Humph, those tend to be the best cheaters. I am not leaving."

"Come on. Round up everybody so I can walk you to the car," he said with authority.

We got to the car and stood there for a moment before he hugged me from behind, putting his chin on my shoulder. I had to remember we were in the church parking lot. I could not do what I really wanted to do. Instead, I turned around and simply said, "Call me when you get in the car."

The girls and I pulled off. It was after nine when I made it home. For me it was still early. I showered and ate an apple while I checked messages. I reviewed my computerized drawings repeatedly until all the lines began to look alike. Finally, my phone chimed his ringtone. "Hello," I quickly answered.

"Hey beautiful."

"Hey."

"Can I buy you a present?"

"A present? For what?"

"Because I want to."

"No," I answered sternly.

"Why not?"

"Because you are trying to buy me again, that's why not."

"I have learned from that lesson. This time I am trying to spoil you. There is a difference. Whatever you want. You name it."

I smiled. "You just bought me a present."

"No, I did not just buy you a present you are just seeing your present. Now what would you like?"

"I want you to be happy."

"If I tell you what will make me happy and you do it then can I buy you a present?" he asked.

"Umm. This sounds like blackmail to me," I answered reluctantly.

"Will you have dinner with me and RJ tomorrow?"

I froze. *How do I respond?* I was not going to be able to avoid this forever. Especially, if we are going to go any further in this relationship. "Tomorrow?"

"Yes."

I could not think fast enough. I would have loved for this to be a text. Even a blog where I had time to respond. I had no time. I had to give a reply now. "Umm okay."

With excitement he asked, "Okay what? You will go?"

"Yes," I replied trying to meet his same excited tone.

"DJ if you are not ready we can do it another time. It's cool I promise."

"I will be fine," I lied.

"There you go again. Will be?"

"I will. I am." I was stuttering.

"You can cancel tomorrow if you need to. However, will it make you feel better if we go to Cheesecake? Would that relax you?"

"Bribery gets you nowhere."

"Is it working?"

"Cheesecake is fine."

"I will not get too excited so if you change your mind I will not be disappointed."

"I will not be cancelling," I assured him. *God knows I want to though.*

"Thanks. It will make me happy."

"Good night."

"Good night my love."

This was deemed a shitty night. I was not going to be able to sleep at all. This makes two nights in a row. I could manage; I was accustomed to sleep deprivation. He sprung meeting his son on me so fast I forgot to tell him my thoughts. I called him back.

"You changed your mind already?"

"I forgot to tell you."

"Tell me what?"

"Rather talk to you."

"I am listening."

"What do you think about hosting a self-defense class at the gym?"

"I host or you host?"

"Umm you. I know nothing about self-defense," I answered.

"You will learn."

"I don't think so."

"Are you volunteering to host this program?" he mildly asked trying to avoid sounding as if he was giving an order.

"No, I am not," I replied.

"Sleep on it."

"I am serious," I said sternly.

"What are you proposing?" he asked in his business tone.

"After tonight's presentation I think you are a good person to teach these people. If you do not teach the class then someone at your gym will be able to handle it."

He thought about it for a second. "You have a point. It is not a bad idea. Get with Vickie and she and I will figure how to make it happen."

"Not to be rude but what will Vickie and I be doing?"

"I just approved the initial thought. Either you, or the two of you, will tell me how we promote it, who we market to, how, when, etcetera. I will help you go from there. This is your idea, your project so go ahead and own it. I am merely agreeing, approving and supporting."

"Are you teaching it?"

"I appears I have no choice. But I will teach you how to teach it also."

"Let me see what I can do." I mumbled.

"Good night."

"Night."

Friday

Just as I thought, I did not sleep at all last night. I was in the bed opposed to working but sleep was nowhere in sight. *This is going to be a long day. I do not know how I am going to make it through dinner,* I thought.

When Leigh arrived, I walked to my door and said, "Girls meeting now!"

"What's wrong?" she mumbled. "It is too early for Danielle and her antics."

"Get everyone on the phone. Quick," I yelled at her slow movement.

"Paige, its Leigh. She is on a rampage today. Get Sade on the phone."

"Sade get up and get on the phone. Auntie is having a crisis." Paige called out.

"Auntie D can you please have your crisis in the afternoon? In addition, not Thursday through Sunday. I am tied up those days," Sade grumbled.

"She is not on the line yet," Paige said ignoring Sade's comments. There was no need in dealing with two of them in crisis mode this morning. One was more than enough.

"Wake me up when she gets on the phone after two this afternoon."

"Seriously, Sade. Are you ready for me to get her on the line?" Leigh asked practically dreading what was about to occur. Paige and Sade were on the other side of town. She on the other hand, was the one having to deal with Dani all day.

"Do we know what is going on?" Paige calmly asked accustomed to her sisters' semi valid crises.

I was trying to control my impatience, "Leigh, are they not on the line yet?" *What is taking them so long?*

"Waiting on Sade," Leigh lied.

"Why does everyone feel the need to throw Sade under the bus at eighty five miles an hour?"

Leigh walked into my office and put the phone on speaker.

"Sissie what's up?" Paige asked as if nothing was going on.

"When is the baby due? Boy or girl?" Sade said annoyed and full of sarcasm.

"Go to," I said but was immediately cut off.

"Ladies. Ladies," Leigh yelled. "D, what's wrong?" annoyance brewing in her voice.

Exasperated and full of emotion, "I have agreed to meet Randall's son tonight."

"Oh. Yikes. Ouch. Umm ghee." Sade said fully awake now. "How depressing. Nasty kids. A boy kid at that. Oh, I feel sorry for you. This is out of my league. Call me later. Good night. Mommie you are tagged in."

"Shut up," Paige yelled.

"Thanks Sade," I said sarcastically and sorrowful.

"How did this happen?" Leigh asked looking as I dropped my head.

"I asked him what would make you happy."

"Hooks is such a family man, sensitive, and caring," Paige acknowledged.

"What do I do?"

"Have your spleen removed this afternoon and cancel," Sade said.

"Get off the phone Sade," Paige yelled. "That is your seed," she said to me.

"If I recall correctly, I was in my bed dreaming Trey Songz was begging me. Just when I was about to give in I had a nightmare. That is when I heard someone saying, "Wake up Sade. Wake up. Auntie is having a crisis." Now, I wake up from the man of my dreams. I get on the phone and listen that she is meeting some little funny looking snotty nose kid. Now everyone is mad at me because Auntie has to meet the man of her dreams offspring. Does anyone care I just lost the man of my dreams in my dream? Huh? Does anyone care? You heffas. You do not care do you?"

Everyone held the phone in silence hoping Sade's melodramatic episode was over. I finally broke the silence with a loud robust laugh. "What is she talking about? Is she high?"

"Our little drama queen needs help," Leigh managed to get out in between laughs.

"Okay, laugh all you want. I am not the one going on a date with a twelve year old. Neither am I stressed out about it. Oh and for the record, I am not going to be hiding in the bushes at Dixie Land either. Where are you all going? Chuckie Cheese?"

"Cheesecake."

"Oh we're coming," Paige shouted.

"Hooks is good. He sucker punched you with The Cheesecake Factory. How sentimental. Let me touch basis with Harold to make sure he is the server. I will let him know not to leave your side. What is the code word for tonight?" Leigh asked with concern.

I thought about it for a moment. "Banana split," I said.

"Girly, he is just a kid. It is not as if you have to be left alone with a three year old. He knows how to act. Hooks is his father," my Sissie encouraged.

Sade took pleasure in adding, "If not, do him like you would do me? Punch him in the mouth."

"What is wrong with her? You know darn well I have never punched you in your mouth."

"Nope, but you use to say you were going to," Sade reminded me.

"Well I should have and from the looks of it now would be a good time to make good on that promise," I jokingly threatened.

"It will be fine," Leigh reassured as she always does.

"Help me Lord," I said as we said our goodbyes.

The anticipation was killing me. After lunch Sade texted me.

> I am up. Are you nervous?

> Heck yeah, like I am going to the prom. What am I wearing?

> Jeans and Ed Hardy tee.

> He will not take me seriously.

> White V-neck.

> Denim capris, army green V-neck, camouflage Michael Kors bag and MK sandals.

> That will be cool. Do I need to come over? Do we need to hide out in the restaurant?

> Be on standby.

I was nervous all day. I could not manage to get myself together. The day was finally over. I got my things and as I headed home, my mind was out of control. *What am I going to do when I meet the parents?* I put on just what I said I would and nervously headed out to join him. When I arrived at The Cheesecake Factory, the valet opened the door and reached for my hand.

"Good evening, Mrs. Rose. Mr. Hooks is waiting for you." The same valet was there the last time we dined here. The one Hooks invited to the gym. Now that I think about it, I have seen him there a few times since then. He was a good kid in my opinion. I could see where Randall was going with him. He was setting him up for a future job.

"Hi. How are you?" I said glad he was greeting me to ease my nervousness.

"I am fine Ms. Rose."

"Great."

"Enjoy dinner," he winked.

I walked in and as soon as I stepped foot in the door Keith was knocking me over. "Ms. D," he called out.

"Yes."

"You are upstairs tonight."

"Upstairs? Not with the public population. This is serious. What have I gotten myself into?" I stated not a question expecting a response.

"All is well. He is a good kid. Did you really think you and the kid at would be in public view?" he stressed the word kid.

"Gotcha," I replied. Although, if truth be told, I really did not think it was time for me to meet the kid.

"Relax he is more nervous than the two of you. This is very important to him."

"I will be on good behavior," I prayed.

"Only if a tranquilizer gun is involved," Keith smarted.

"Low blow dude. All I try to do is be like you."

"You learn well grasshopper."

I bowed my head in response.

"By the way, you look nice."

"Kid friendly?"

"Yeah, everything is covered, cool, and kid relatable," he was referring to body parts being covered.

"Thanks," *I guess*.

"You always do. Cover up that is. There is no need in impressing the boss by showing what you have. He likes the thrill of not knowing and the anticipation of waiting. You already have your hooks in him. You do not have to do anything further. Leave that to the groupies he detest."

That was a huge compliment from Keith and one I knew he was not comfortable giving. I tried to break the ice, "So will you go shopping with me and help me lay my clothes out?"

"We are not that cool. We may need to put your crew on the payroll. This is where I draw the line. I will not be shopping," he said without making eye contact and scanning the room as we approached the stairs.

We were now walking in the area where they were. The entire upstairs area was closed. I looked back at Keith quickly.

"No worries. Harold is your waiter."

"Good job."

"Dad, is that her?" RJ asked in a surprised tone.

"Yeah son," he responded proudly.

"Wow."

They both stood up. They were sitting side by side at the table. *Why didn't they have a round table? I will talk to Harold about this. What was he thinking?* Therefore, I did only what Danielle would do. I went for the head of the table.

"Hey guys. Have you been waiting long?"

Taming his nervousness, "No, you are good," Randall said.

I extended my hand for RJ, "Hello. I'm Danielle."

He obliged. "Hi, I'm Randall. It's a pleasure to meet you Ms. Rose."

"Thank you kindly, same to you." I smiled looking at the replica of his father.

"Hey Babe." He went in for the hug then kissed my cheek very sensual.

"Hey you."

I proceeded to the head of the table.

"Oh Ms. Rose. I forgot. I got this for you," he said while handing me one red long stem rose.

"Oh my goodness. A young man after my own heart." I kissed him on his cheek too.

"Hey, watch it now," his dad said with mock jealousy.

We both snickered. "How did you know I like roses?"

"I kind of figured you did."

"Good assumption. I like that."

Harold walked up. "Ms. Danielle. A pleasure to see you tonight."

"HEY," I jumped up and hugged him.

"Why has it been so long since I have seen you?"

"You just saw me a month ago dude."

"I know, and a month is too long," he added.

"No it is not."

He leaned into RJ. "You make sure she is here every week and there is a nice piece of cheesecake in it for you."

Eyes big with excitement, "Yes sir," he replied.

"He doesn't drive," I said.

"Not yet," Harold replied and winked.

"He has a lot of time before we get there," Hooks responded dreading the thought.

"Not that far off Dad. You can begin teaching me now in the Ferrari. "

"More like your mom's truck."

"When can we start?"

"In four years."

"Wow," I said before I knew it.

"What?" Randall asked.

"Nothing." I shook my head. "Nothing."

Harold came back. "Ready to order?" I looked at the boys. Randall looked at me. "She wants the same thing as usual. Correct?"

I nodded. Of course I did.

Randall ordered first. Then RJ took control. "I will have the spinach dip, blue cheese BLT, French fries with cheddar cheese and strawberry lemonade please."

His father interrupted, "Harold, correction. He will have the turkey burger without mayo, sweet potato fries, and orange juice."

I wanted to say something but it was his child. There was no way I was getting involved. I thought to myself, *not everyone has your eating habits. Especially not children.* "We will keep the dip Harold." I decided to interject anyway.

Randall gave me an intense look but I winked in return.

"Don't start DJ," his tone was cold as ice.

RJ looked as if he knew he was missing something. Kids are very aware when grown folks speak over their heads.

I ignored his warning, "So guys how was your day?" I asked.

They both went into details about their day. I could not tell who was the most excited and emotional. Both were so animated about the day's event. We shared the starters. The girls texted during appetizers to check on me. On the second round, I responded then silenced the phone. I didn't want the boys to think I was being rude. RJ and I were getting along well so far. RS, Randall Senior that is, was barking orders, giving commands, and making corrections as usual. I was shocked he was such a strict parent. Very strict, I might add. If RJ slipped and said an incomplete sentence, he corrected him. To me it let me know the child's comfort level was increasing.

I had enough of his correction; therefore, I sent him a text. When his phone rang out Ne-Yo's 'One In A Million', I looked shocked. I did not know he changed my ringtone. He looked up at me before he ever checked his phone. I smiled and winked.

> You are a mean daddy. Let up. He is feeling comfortable. It is cool.

RJ and I were engulfed in conversation when he said, "I got it," very unexpectedly.

I never turned my head although I knew he was responding to my text. I kept my attention on RJ and as soon as RJ looked away, I winked at his father without looking. RS gave up the laugh I adore.

Harold brought our plates. "Ugh," RJ rang out in sheer disappointment of the food on his plate.

"Harold, can he change this please?"

"Sure D."

"What would you rather have?"

"Danielle," Randall Senior let out.

"Umm," the child hesitantly said. He was nervous to change his plate. He knew his butt would be in huge trouble later. "Thanks, Ms. Danielle. That is nice of you. I am going to eat what my dad ordered but I will need help on the choices of cheesecake."

I do not think he meant flavors. I think he meant help persuading his father to let him have a piece. There is always more than one way to skin a cat. Therefore, I texted Harold and asked him to prepare what the child originally ordered to go.

RS prayed over our food while the three of us held hands. For some reason, this moment felt so right. I texted him a few minutes later. It rang the same tone. *Busted* I thought to myself. The text read.

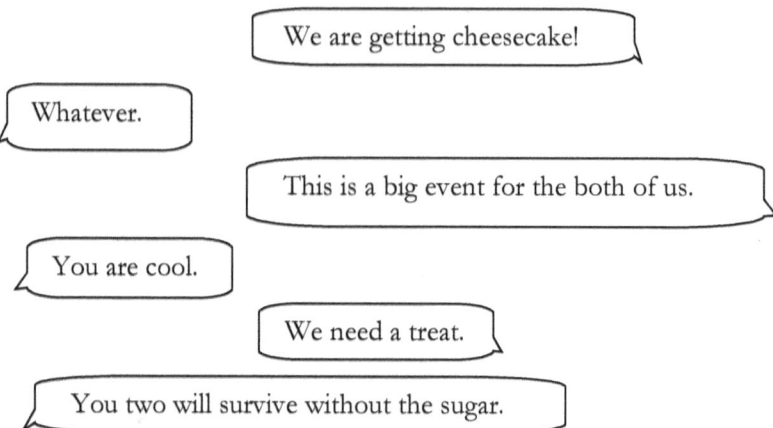

We are getting cheesecake!

Whatever.

This is a big event for the both of us.

You are cool.

We need a treat.

You two will survive without the sugar.

We ate our dinner talking and laughing the entire meal. We were in between dinner and dessert. The empty or half-eaten plates remained on the table. "Since you are drilling me we might as well have sixty seconds," I said to Randall Jr.

"That is fine with me. Dad time us."

"I am not. You two are silly."

"Drop top or hard?" RJ started.

"Drop."

"Old school rap or new school?"

"Old."

"Lifetime or Showtime?"

"Duh Showtime," I said frowning.

"CNN or Boomerang?"

"Boomerang."

"Concert or Opera?"

"Concert."

"Movie or Play?"

"I will take the movie on the couch."

"Icee or milkshake?"

I had to think, "Tough choice. Icee."

"Cupcakes or pie?"

"Cupcakes loaded with cream cheese icing."

"Too much icing. Dad would die."

We both laugh as Randall Senior looks up as if we were two idiots. "Hamburger or hotdog?" RJ continued.

"OMG. Hotdog," I yelled.

"Gelato or funnel cake?"

"Was funnel cake with ice cream a choice?"

"That is what I am talking about. Virtual game or board game?"

"Oh my, is Atari considered a virtual game?"

Randall laughed. It was so loud it startled both of us.

"RJ do you know anything about an Atari?" RS asked.

"Umm no," he gladly admitted.

"Danielle is showing her age bringing up an Atari."

"How old is she?"

"Whoa son. I have told you not to ask a woman her age. I still recall the day I asked her. I think I was verbally abused and my skin deteriorated from the flames from her eyes."

"I should not ask her then?" The kid questioned unsure of his father's sarcasm.

"I would suggest not. But, it is up to you?"

"Ms. Danielle, how old are you?"

"Older than you but younger than your dad. Way younger than your dad." I had to smile at my answer and the look on RJ's face was priceless.

He looked stunned as if he was now wondering how much younger.

"I think you guys are trying to change the subject. It is my time for the sixty second drill." Randall Senior laughed again. He has to be the happiest person I knew.

"RJ it looks like you are on," his father forewarned.

"Ms. Danielle. Are you about to drill me?"

"Umm yes. Are you ready?"

"Run it Dad. Get the timer going? By the way, I noticed Ms. Danielle wears the same watch as you do. You said I was going to be able to get one when I got older. I am older now. Twelve. That is teenage years."

"Twelve is not teenage son."

"Yes it is."

"What are you doing to justify teenage behavior?"

"What do you mean?"

"Like I thought," he said with his point proven.

He was a tough strict parent. I was shocked and impressed all at the same time. He was almost on the verge of mean. "Excuse me guys. I would love to entertain this tender father and son moment with you two darling handsome young men, but I am trying to conduct an interview. Hello."

"It would not be all about DJ right now would it?" Randall asked sarcastically.

"I do believe so. You all are not cheating me out of my turn. You can discuss this man talk in the car on the way home."

"Ready?" Randall Junior confirmed.

"Tims or Air Force One?"

"One's."

"Wife Beater or White Tee?"

"Tee."

"Nikki Minaj or Rihanna?"

"You would ask that. I do not know. Rihanna."

"I do not believe you."

"Not a fair question. I pass."

"No passes."

"You are right close your eyes Dad," he said. He then whispered, "Nikki."

"Madden or Manning?"

"Which Manning?"

"Like you know something about the Manning's. You have no clue about Archie and Cooper."

Randall's eyebrows rose. He was impressed that I knew a little about football.

"Who?"

"Like I said. This may need to be a lesson on the way home. Right now, either Peyton or Eli?"

"Manning. I like them both."

"LeBron or D Wade?"

"D."

"Humph. I will let you have that little bit."

"Do you disagree?"

"I sure do."

"Who are you with?"

"LeBron. However, in all honesty, I am old school. Therefore, you know I am a Jordan fan. However, you would not know anything about that. I think Jordan was crowned King for life and retired before you were born."

"Ms. Danielle," he yelled. Everyone in the room looked.

"Yes," I said calmly.

"I know who Jordan is."

"I did not say you didn't. You have not experienced him live and in action. I will see what I can do to get that experience for you."

"Dad, help me. Tell her I have seen Jordan."

"I am not in it."

"Dad," he pleaded.

"Let's move on," Randall Senior said as if he was anticipating the next question.

"Are you ready young man?" I asked as Harold walked over to the table.

"Who is on the date? Father or Son?" Harold instigated.

"Hate," I yelled.

"Are we ready for dessert?"

"Yes, bring my favorite and bring the cart."

"Will do Ms. D."

"Okay. TIP or Lil Wayne?"

"Low blow DJ," Randall laughed. "You are setting him up. Son, think about this. Really, think about this. This is a trick question. Everything is riding on this one. We will be dumped if you do not get this correct."

"Don't cheat Randall. You said you were not in it. You are tipping him off."

He turned his back. "See, I am not tipping him off. He can't even see me," he put an emphasis on tipping.

"I got it. I got it. TIP. Ms. Danielle TIP."

"You two are cheaters. I am not playing anymore. I will not play another game with you two ever. Cheaters."

We continued to enjoy dessert and fun. At the end of the night, I said my goodbyes to Harold and the staff. They pulled the 650 and the Ferrari around. All three of them reached for the door handle at once. I felt like a queen. I stepped all the way back and let them argue about who was going to officially open the door. Randall, big Randall that is, won. Of course, he would. I do not think the valet or RJ would have the balls to challenge him.

"Nice ride Ms. Danielle. When are you going to let me borrow the whip?"

Randall mushed him in the face. "Get back little boy."

"Let me say good night man." He gave me a hug.

'It was a pleasure having dinner with you."

"I will see you later."

Randall hugged me. He kissed my neck and then my cheek. "What the hell, I am grown." Then he kissed my lips. First a peck.

"Stop. You are embarrassing me," I whispered not able to see the child's face.

He kissed my lips gently again. "Are you embarrassed yet?"

"Yes."

He kissed them more. "What about now?"

"Yes," I giggled.

This time the held the kiss for a long time.

RJ yelled out, "Dang, dad she can't breathe."

"How do you feel now?"

"Like I need a cigarette."

"You do not smoke."

"I don't?"

"No. You don't," he laughed.

"Maybe I should take up the habit."

"Are you going home?"

"I think I should stop by Mikey's while I am this close. I am not staying long. I have a hair appointment and conference call in the morning."

"Conference call?" You could see him tense up.

"Yeah, I dare not ever have one scheduled on a Wednesday. The last time I did there was trouble in paradise."

He laughed slightly. "I am following you. Do not stay out too long, if I may make that request. Call me, not text, when you get home."

"Sir, yes sir."

"Will I see you in the morning?" he asked.

"It depends."

"Depends on what?"

"What you say tonight to convince me to see you tomorrow."

I sat in the car as he squatted down on the side. "Thanks for tonight. I know this was difficult and you were not ready. However, it meant and means a lot to me. I think it was extremely successful. I am not sure who was on the date as Harold said, RJ or me. I was almost a little jealous. I am glad it went well. I was not sure what to expect but I must admit I am glad it is over. Maybe I will get some sleep tonight and next week and I can decide on announcing my return."

Was he waiting on me to meet his son before he made his announcement? "He is a good kid or knows how to behave well in front of company. However, you run a tight ship."

"Yes, I do and I do not plan to change it."

"Point taken, noted, and recorded. We will see," I challenged him.

He took my hand and kissed it. He laid his head on my leg. We were holding up traffic. The valet did not have the nerve to ask him to move. Keith did what he is probably accustomed to doing. He went and redirected traffic out the entry.

"Where did Keith go?"

"He went down the driveway to send the outgoing traffic."

"Who is with RJ?"

"He is in Keith's car behind me. He is fine. I can see him in the mirror."

"Why did Keith move from right here?" he said in an angry tone.

"He was either going to have to direct traffic out or ask you to move. You are holding up traffic."

"I guess he did right then. I do not want to leave."

"We have to go."

"You know what to do when you get home," Randall instructed.

When we pulled off, they rode through the first few traffic lights in silence. I turned off and blew my horn.

"Dad?"

"Yeah son." He really was not ready for his comments.

"I could take your girl dad."

"What the what?"

"If I wanted to I could take her from you," he said with confidence.

"I am glad you do not want to."

"If it was anyone else I would take her. Since it is you, I will leave it alone. But know that I can."

"I take that as a good thing."

"Yeah dad. It is a good thing. I like her a lot."

"I like her too."

"Are you going to marry her?"

"I would love too. I do not think we are that far yet."

"How do you know when you are?"

"I am not sure. I am hoping God will tell me when I am or when she is ready."

"Wow. I hope He tells you. I think I asked you but does she have kids?"

"No."

"Has she ever been married?"

"No."

"Are you a lot older than her?"

"What's a lot?"

"Like five or ten years older."

"If that is the case then no."

"So she is like twenty five or twenty six? She looks twenty one."

"Son, don't ever ask a woman how old she is?"

"They do not like it?"

"Heck no," he shook his head.

He and RJ laughed and had guy talk all the way home. Once they arrived he texted me to let me know he was home. Thereafter, he and RJ played video games and chilled until I called two hours later on my way home. He took the call to the other room because RJ would not let him speak in peace. He thought that maybe this was a bad idea after all. Was RJ trying to take his girl? Finally, he demanded RJ to respect his conversation before he left the room. He knew Danielle was going to comment on his abrasiveness. Nevertheless, tonight he laid down and slept in his bed for a change.

Saturday

My phone rang out at five AM informing me he blogged.

The night could not have gone better. Not even if it was scripted. This cannot be real. My two worlds collided helping make my life complete. Everything is falling into place.

I did not feel like it but I got up and made my way to the gym. I wanted to be sure to get a work out in before I hit the hair salon. After eating a heavy dinner last night, God knows I needed to work out.

I could not believe I arrived at the gym before he did. *He must be running somewhere else or having a hard time waking up RJ this morning,* I thought. It was 7:20 when I heard the commotion. I don't know why he causes so much noise when he arrives.

Before I could finish my thought, he yelled up the stairs, "Good morning DJ. May I come up?"

"What's the password?" I yelled back.

"I did not know I needed one," he stalled.

With confidence I replied, "Yeah, you do."

He hesitated, "Please?"

"No. That is too easy."

"I give," he pondered.

"Butter pecan."

"That was going to be my next guess," he lied as he ran up the stairs. Before he could reach the top step and extend for a hug and a kiss, RJ was yelling.

"Dad, what is up the steps?"

"Do not come up," he ordered.

"Why?" the child probed.

"You do not know the password."

"Password?" he said sounding puzzled.

"Stop it," I said to Randall chastening him.

"Dad? Is that Ms. Danielle's voice?"

"No son. You are hearing things. I am glad I do not have another girlfriend up here," he winked.

I punched his arm as I answered the kid, "Yes it is."

He ran to the top of the stairs. "You do not have that much game neither are you that cool Dad to have two girlfriends. Leave that to me please." RJ took his time and looked around as if all of this was foreign to him. Technically, it was. He had never seen this area before. "What is this?" he questioned.

"It is Danielle's indoor track."

"Wow. Nice." The child took off running around the track.

"Guys, I would love to stay and entertain you two but it is Saturday."

"Are you leaving?" RJ asked disappointed.

"Yes, I have to go."

"But you just got here."

"Nope, you just got here. I have been here," I corrected him.

"Doing what?" he asked as he continued running around the track.

"Basically, what you are doing," I answered.

"Dad how did you build this?"

"Ms. Danielle designed it," he replied proud of my work.

"Cool. This is very cool. I can run my remote control cars up here."

"No son, you cannot."

"That's no fun!"

As I began to pack my things, RJ asked as if he and I were the ones dating, "Will we see you later?"

"I do not think so," I said reluctantly. Randall raised his eyebrows as if he was not happy with my response. I raised my brows back at him.

"Do you have plans?" the junior asked. He was already on the road to being a well-trained gentleman.

"RJ," his father scolded for questioning me. RJ turned around looking at his father oblivious to why he was yelling. "You can't push us off on her. Maybe she does not want to be bothered. Last night may have been enough of us. Maybe she has plans. Pull up son. You make it seem like I am desperate."

"All right boys. I am going to have to put you out if you two are going to fight."

"Excuse Dad. He has never had a girlfriend before," he said sincerely. Out of the mouth of babes.

I laughed. Randall smacked RJ in the back of his head without thought. "It is on for the rest of the day," he said as the smack rang out and RJ ducked his head a second too late.

"Boys. Boys. Walk me to my car please." They were just as bad as Randall was with King or Hunter.

"See what you did," big Randall said.

"You are the one," little Randall replied.

I left them there accusing each other. After the salon, I was planning my normal routine. I was going to Mikey's for a bite to eat, hitting Smith's for a suit for tomorrow and then my normal Saturday chores. The cleaners, the post office then I was going to head home. I had leftovers from dinner last night, the internet, and cable. I was set. I planned to chill the remainder of the day.

After I left, the boys had another eventful boys' day. RJ did not hold back any punches. "Man, do you love her?"

"I don't know," his father lied. He did know the answer to the question but what he did not know was how to respond.

"Come on Dad." RJ knew his dad was fooling him.

"Come on what?"

"You built her a track," he commented.

"And so what?" He knew the kid was right. He built it to have a reason to see her daily, to alleviate her stress and to avoid himself from worrying about her at an outdoor track all night.

"It sounds like love to me."

"Because I added a track to the gym? Besides, what do you know about love?"

"Indoor track," the junior corrected the senior.

Looking at his son, "How old are you again?"

"You know I am twelve."

"That is what I thought. Then why am I being questioned by a twelve year old?"

"I guess I should not mention the matching bracelets? It's levels to those bezels."

He knew the kid was right again. Since he did not have a response, he diverted his attention by playfully putting him in a headlock. From that point, they wrestled like two small children. After forty minutes of horseplay, he answered the kid, "Yes, I do."

"Do what?"

"I love her." It hurt him to say it but he knew he did and needed to confess.

"I already know you do."

"If you know it then why did you ask me?"

"I wanted to see what you would say."

He tackled him again.

"Does she know?"

"Know that I love her?"

"Yes."

"I hope so, and before you ask, yes I have told her."

"You are getting good at this."

"At what?"

"Dating. Hang around me pop and I can teach you a few things. I have had more girlfriends than you."

He thought about it and it was shamefully true. His son was right. If you count the two girlfriends he had in elementary and middle school he had three total. In thirty years, he only had three girlfriends. It would have been a good thing if the last one had been the one. She was his child's mother so he knew he had to deal with her but he could not help but to think what a waste of time she was. He had to have been the lamest person he knew. Then he realized something he had not thought about before. He was not lame by himself. Even Trevor only had three girlfriends. He was married to his high school sweetheart. The way he figured, they were the two lamest people he knew. It made him a little upset. Then he thought over the last ten years. He was not really where he wanted to be but he surely was in a good place. He was in a much better place than over ninety-nine percent of his class. The other one percent was Trevor. They may have been lame then but look at them now.

He found himself hoping the day would come where he could say; *I am happily married to the woman of my dreams. I am the proud parent of these children. I have won the title to every weight class. I have done it all and accomplished it all, not by my will, but by the will of God. His grace and mercy have been with me through this journey. There have been detours and roadblocks. Right now, it seems like I have been in the wilderness for forty years. However, the good news is I am coming out. In addition, when I do I will never look back, bringing others out with me, and I plan to never return.*

***

I did all I said I was going to do. Once I was finished working I texted Sade.

> I am chilling on the couch. No computers. All television.

She hit back immediately.

> Did you break them baby?

She makes me so sick. I can live without them. Well I did years before. I am sure I can now. Maybe. I had eaten dinner, spoken to Randall, laid my clothes out for tomorrow and there was nothing else left for me to do. I checked the list and checked it twice. What was I going to do with myself for the rest of the night? I was determined to force myself not to work. I was not going to surf the net either.

Therefore, I sat on the couch and propped my feet on the coffee table. I knew better but it was my table after all. I flipped through the stations. I was not in front of the television as much as I thought but I had seen all of these movies. *Maybe I am lamer than I think.* I finally reached the Showtime boxing station. I went past it. After ten more stations, I went back. I watched the preliminary fights before the show down between Juan Manuel Marquez and Michael Katsidis. I was excited. Hyped actually. I turned all my speakers on and sat on the couch anticipating the fight as if I was in Nevada. I had the TIVO set and ready.

The match began and I am so excited. *One day I will not be a spectator and will have an interest in one of the two guys.* I found myself observing the crowd just as much as I observed the fighters. I studied everything as if I am preparing for a test. From the music to the lights to the referee and the trainers. I want to be prepared mentally and emotionally. I do not want this to shock and overwhelm me when the time comes. This could easily be intimidating to me if I do not prepare for it.

Round one went a little different than I would have estimated. *Those had to be the longest three minutes in life.* To the average person three minutes seems like a few seconds. However, to those guys taking and giving a combined one hundred punches, whether hit or miss, these three minutes seemed like a lifetime. Then the one-minute timeout is just enough time to catch your breath, spit some water out and listen to a dude behind the rope barking orders at you.

Round two. The momentum is up but still not in the direction I was anticipating. I am trying to figure out what my strategy would be if I were in there. *Do I come out hard and wear him down or take it slow and blast him in the end? Hmm, maybe I would just stay with his approach and see what the end brings?* My first thought was go with number one, which would be to get in and get out. I was so caught up in the match when I realized I was not a boxer. Not only that but I had never prepared to be one so my approach may not have been the wisest of choices. I would make the strongest assumption that my approach would depend on my opponent's tactics. However, anything could change from minute to minute.

Round three began. Quickly one was on the mat. My adrenaline was pumping. I knew then I was going to need something to calm me down if I had to watch Randall fight live. I was standing in front of the television. I did not know either of these guys and my heart was racing. Suddenly it hit me for the first time what Randall really did for a living.

"Oh my God." I screamed out. I stood there in shock as I watched the replay. One guy was hit so hard I knew his face was reconfigured by the way his head spun around. Just then, the phone rang his ringtone.

"Hello," I answered loudly.

"What are you doing?" he asked quickly in response to my excited tone.

"Watching the fight."

"Oh yeah," he said overjoyed with a giggle to his tone. "What do you see?"

"Right now nothing."

"What are you learning?"

"Should I be?"

"Yes. You should be noticing patterns, techniques, speeds, and styles. Who are you going for?" he asked.

"I am not sure. The one I was going for looks like he is the weaker of the two. The fight is a great fight but I am concerned."

"Why?"

"I am wondering."

"I am watching it too. The crew is here watching and recording. I would have asked you to come if I had known you were interested. You and I will watch this over again and learn a few things. You have some homework to do. Tell me what you see. You said your guy seems to be the weaker. What makes him weaker to you? What fight are you watching? What's the class or title?" he rattled on excitedly. He paused for just a couple of seconds then asked, "Do you want me to come and get you now?"

"No. I am good," I lied. I preferred to watch it with him now but did not confess. "We can replay it tomorrow. I am sure you will school me."

"What are we wearing tomorrow?"

"I am wearing gray and white and you are wearing gray and white pin stripes."

"Yes, Ma'am. What is up with you and these stripes?"

"If I were you I would wear them," I said in a seductive tone.

"Oh, okay. I take it you like them."

"Good assumption."

"I will call you back once this is over," he rushed off the phone just as the fight was starting back.

He did just as he promised. He drilled me on the fight. We talked until I heard his guest leaving. "Go entertain. I will see you in a few hours," I told him.

"Can I come over?" he asked as if it was the middle of the afternoon.

"Heck no."

"Why not?"

"Booty call. That is why." *I would gladly give it to you*, I thought.

"Good decision," he agreed. "Good night."

I couldn't help but to think of him as I tossed and turned the entire night.

Sunday

When I was finally able to go to sleep, I kept waking up to check his blog. *Any other night he would have blogged by now.* Finally, at three AM I texted,

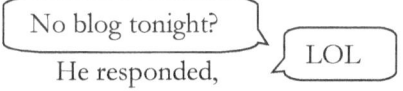

He responded,

I did not think it was funny. At three twenty, my phone chirped alerting me his blog posted.

> There is nothing more amazing than to find the love of your life. When you stare at her from across the room, she stares back at you. When you wink, she winks. When you see her, your heart races and then melts. Your blood pressure rises as your palms sweat and butterflies seem to dance in your stomach. Just the anticipation alone is so overwhelming it gives you a migraine. You feel faint. You cannot sleep. You toss and turn. Then you discover she feels the same. Her heart pants just like mine. Her palms sweat just like mine. I make her just as nervous as she makes me. It means the world to me.

All I could do was roll over and giggle. I asked for it. He was so vocal behind that keyboard. Afterwards, I slept like a baby. I almost woke up late. I should have been half-dressed by the time I awoke. However, I was neither stressed nor pressed. I still took my time. Not that I wanted to be late. That was the last thing I ever wanted to do, but I was in love. I was relaxing and remaining calm. There was the difference.

I spoke to everyone as I walked into the church. Deacon Washington was not in sight. I did not look for him or wait. I went directly to my seat. When he walked in you could see the relief on his face. However, I did not give eye contact. *I overslept waiting on your blog. There is no need for a staring contest.*

We took our seats while he purposefully stared. He looked at his watch. I looked at mine. I realized the date was wrong. I took mine off and started spinning the dials to correct it. The thought occurred to me that I probably do not know how to change the date.

I fumbled with it for a minute. I pulled the plug with my teeth and began to twist it. I could see Deacon Washington out of the corner of my eye. *He was about to bust a blood vessel.* I still refused to give him eye contact. He leaned up. He leaned back. He cleared his throat. *This is going to bother me that this date is wrong. I have to change it now.* I knew if I did not change it, I would not be able to focus the entire service.

"Acknowledge him," Keith said in a demanding urgent tone.

I nodded my head in response. He cleared his throat so hard I almost looked but I knew it was a set up.

Suddenly, Keith takes the watch from my hand. I rolled my eyes and mumbled to him. Randall reached out, took the watch from Keith and placed it inside his jacket pocket. *I wanted it fixed.* I said to myself mentally throwing a tantrum. I made a noise that should not have come from a person much less in church.

He gave me the evil side eye. It worked. I was attentive for the remainder of service. I was now dreading the lecture I was sure to receive afterwards. *It was not that serious. All I was doing was fixing my watch.*

Before Hunter could finish saying, "Go in peace," Deacon Washington held his finger close to my face and said, "Do not move," in a strict tone.

King walked him out and exactly eight minutes later, he came back inside. I knew the time from the clock on the wall. He removed my watch from his jacket pocket and handed it to me. "Don't touch this watch other than to put it on and take it off," he threatened.

"I know Keith already informed me."

"What were you doing and why did you pick now to do it?" he asked as if he was speaking to a child.

"I was trying to change the date."

He tried his best to understand, nevertheless, he had to admit to himself with Danielle he never could. "It could not wait?" he asked mildly.

"Keith has lectured me already."

"That was not what I asked. I anticipated an answer."

Instead, I said, "Let's go."

I went home, changed my clothes, and waited for him. He picked me up after he left the church. We hung out at his house all day. Any other time it would have been hard to be alone with him all day but today he was still dismayed with me so it was easy. He put some fish on the grill for me and after dinner, he dropped me off before seven so he could get his daily routine in. Clearly, today was an easy day for him too. Not once did he get too close.

WEEK 23
Monday

Before the rooster had the chance to crow, he was calling my phone. I was not in a deep sleep but not quite awake yet. "Babe are you sleeping in today?" he asked sarcastically.

"I was planning on it," I answered.

"Did you have a rough night?"

"The club was off the hook. I opened it up and shut it down."

"That's what's up," he said without acknowledging my lie. "Now go ahead and get up."

"I was planning on sleeping in and fixing eggs for breakfast," I said.

"Sorry to change your plans."

"They haven't been disrupted."

"Great, open the gate. You still have time to prepare my eggs. Do you know how I like them?"

"You know what, let me get up and get dressed since you are talking trash early this morning. You do not even eat eggs. Are you running?"

"Yes, I do. Yep, I am running. Call me when you get in the car." He knew he could not beat her at her antics so the best thing to do was to join her.

Work was good for a Monday. I received some good news from one overseas project. The building received the final certificate of occupancy. We worked hard for this, or rather, they did. I did a lot of communication and legwork but they got the job done. They assured me they would inform me when the hotel was opening for business. I wanted to be the first to book a room and sign in. Besides, we must have a grand opening party. It was great news. It was a long year getting this building off the ground. I told Leigh we were celebrating with sushi for lunch. I called Randall.

"Hey babe," he answered. I knew I was disturbing his training.

"Hey you," I said with enthusiasm.

"What's up?"

I gave him all the details of the project and how happy and excited I was this one was complete. I also informed them they thought they would be complete in a month and I was planning to travel there. I then suggested if he would like to join me, he was more than welcome to do so.

"Do I need to?" he asked.

"Well, I would like for you to if it does not cause a conflict, makes things difficult or confusing."

He was quiet for a brief moment. "I'll see what I can do. Please let me know the dates in advance."

It was not a definite yes but it was better than a no. "Is that something you would be interested in? I am sure Leigh would travel with me and a few others from the office."

"Are you going to be there?"

"Of course I will be there," I replied laughing at his question.

"Then yes, I am interested. You are aware I will need to bring King, Keith, JJ and at least two others, not including Vickie?"

"No, I did not realize this. Then cancel my request. It is not that serious."

'No, you asked me to come. I will come." Now his mind was spinning on how to make this happen.

"That will be expensive and more than my budget can afford right now. Do not worry about it."

In an offended tone he replied, "Did I ask you anything about the cost?"

"No you did not," I answered.

"I did not think so. Let me handle this. It is just money. There is no comparison to supporting you and making sure you are happy."

I blushed trying to remain calm. "Okay." I think he could still hear me blushing anyway. Later that evening I arrived at the gym speaking as I entered.

He leaned over the rope and said, "Once you are done holler down and get dressed. We are going out."

This was unexpected news on a Monday. "Sure," I replied. "RJ too?"

"Cool," he said without hesitation.

I went upstairs and changed. I was rounding my tenth lap when I heard feet running rapidly. "Ms. D?" RJ called out.

"Hey there."

"You feel like some company?"

"Sure. Can you keep up?"

"Try me," he challenged.

We walked and talked for six more laps. He had interesting conversation to be a young kid. Actually, he had better conversation than some grown men I knew. He seemed to be a good kid despite his parents being total opposites. From what he shared, anything goes with his mother, and then on the other hand, his father is the opposite. No doubt, Randall was about business. He was strict and wanted the best for his child. I could tell he kept him on a real short leash, which might not be a bad thing.

We ended up at his restaurant. It was early on a Monday so it was not crowded. The atmosphere was family friendly enough for a kid to be here. It did not matter either way. It was his club and his kid. Who was going to say something?

"I figured this would be fine with both of you and I didn't have to make reservations," he said. "We can go somewhere else next week, but you both seem to like it here."

"Do you like it here Ms. D?"

"I do. The question is does your Dad like it here?"

"Dad?" he asked.

He began to speak and then looked at me, "Yes, I like it here. It is my restaurant. Do I like it here? Of course, but in the back."

"You can go back there and leave us here," I smarted.

"Do not even try me Danielle Rose."

We hung out, talked, and laughed. Then RJ hit me below the belt.

"Ms. D we are going to the lake this weekend."

"Oh fun. You two will have a great time I am sure. I am so excited for you."

"I am glad you are excited. I was going to ask you to go with us."

The child set me up. "To the lake?" I asked loudly.

"Yes."

"Umm. I do not think I can do that," I stuttered.

"It will be fun. We will be fishing, tubing, and even volleyball."

"I regret to inform you but that does not sound like fun to me."

"Dad, help me out here," he pleaded with his father.

I rolled my eyes at him. *He knows I cannot go. He set me up. He brought me out and let the child do his dirty work.* We were not at a place where we can travel together. Although it was only an hour away, I couldn't help but remember Pastor Hunter's conversation. I surely could not travel with him and definitely not with his son. He knew that. *I will handle him later,* I thought.

"Danielle," he said as if I was supposed to change my mind. "I do not think she likes camping son. Is it too manly?" he asked looking directly at me.

"Something like that," I said coldly.

"What is it?" RJ asked concerned, obviously picking up my tone.

"It is too...It's too," I stammered. "Umm, woodsy, outdoorsy, distant, remote, and secluded. I can think of a hundred other words I am sure. Let's just say I am sort of accustomed to running water." Randall gave up the laugh. "What's funny babe?" I asked not understanding what he found humorous.

He grabbed my hand and kissed it.

Again, I asked, "Seriously. What is so funny?"

"Nothing sweetheart." He looked at RJ and shrugged his shoulders. RJ laughed too. They both laughed but I still did not get the joke.

Looking at the two of them, I felt a little awkward. "Okay. I am the only one at the table not laughing and I seem to have a problem with that."

"You tell her," Randall told his son.

"Nah, you got it Dad."

"You brought it up," he fired back.

"She is your girlfriend."

"You wanted to ask her."

"She said no," RJ reminded him.

"I told you she would," his father stated.

"Cut," I interrupted. "She is sitting right here," I said speaking of myself.

"Go ahead Dad."

"Our version of camping is not what you're thinking. It is a little more modern and includes running water. We also have telephone and internet service. There is a shower, cable television, and all the amenities of home. It is more like a house on a secluded lake."

"More like a five star hotel on a lake," I commented.

"Call it what you want," he snickered knowing I was right.

"Does this mean you will come?" RJ asked disregarding the debate his father and I were having.

"No, I'm afraid I can't miss work for that many days. Thank you so much for the invite. It means a lot to me."

They both looked so disappointed. I would have gone. Really, I would have. However, he knows Hunter has drilled me. I cannot travel with his child. I do not want any static for him coming from anyone including the press and surely not his ex-wife. Man, that felt good going through my mind. *His ex-wife.* I wanted to say something to make it up to them but I did not know what to offer. "Boys, I am sure I would not be much fun anyway. You guys are going to have a great time. Send me pictures and videos of everything. I am so excited. I am going to be bored without you two. When will you be back?"

Neither wanted to answer. "Maybe Saturday or Sunday," Randall mumbled.

"Yeah," RJ chimed in dryly.

"We may miss you so much we come back Thursday," he said and kissed my hand again.

I felt like crap. My heart fell to the floor. They both looked so pitiful. I knew right then I had a hard road ahead of me. It was one thing for one to look pitiful but right now I had them both with the puppy dogfaces. I could not take it. It was killing me on the inside. I wanted to change my mind right there but Pastor Hunter was in my head. *I have to stand firm on my grounds. I can do it. We will have a lifetime to spend at the lake,* I prayed. We arrived back at my car, "Are you going home?" I asked.

He smirked. "I was not planning on it." He gathered from the way I walked away that I was not happy with his response. "Will you give me one hour?"

"Good night. Call me when you get in the car. Randall," I sang. They both responded. I did not look in Big Randall's direction. "He has one hour friend. Make sure he takes you home."

"Yes ma'am."

He laid a hug on me while I whispered in his ear, "Take that baby home. I am not playing."

"Ms. Danielle. I am not a baby."

"You are absolutely correct. That is why I am putting you in charge as the time keeper."

"I heard you," Big Randall replied. "One hour."

I got in the car. He closed my door while RJ leaned in and said, "Hit us when you get home."

Which of them am I dating? Feels like both of them, I thought. "I will," I replied and pounded him.

Big Randall shoved him to the side in jealousy, "Move son."

"Hater," little Randal defended.

"Good night," he said then kissed me. He almost pulled me through the window. I have to confess, he is a good kisser. I rode home and did as expected by texting after I arrived. I showered, checked messages, and got my clothes ready for tomorrow. As soon as I got in the bed, he called me. I could tell he was in the car.

I answered, "I love you."

"Are you sure?"

"I would not tell you if I wasn't sure."

"Why? Because I followed instructions?" he asked.

"That was only tonight."

"Oh?"

"I am giving you a second set of instructions. Call me when you can talk."

His curiosity peaked, "Any particular reason why?"

"Because I asked you to."

"Should I be concerned?" he asked.

"No. Not at all."

"Wait up for me," he said before disconnecting the call.

As promised, he called as soon as he got home. "Hello," I answered.

"Sweetie what did I do wrong?" he immediately asked.

"You know I can't travel with you to your lake house, much less with you and RJ."

"Tell me why?" You could hear the concern in his voice.

"Hunter told me not to."

"What do you want to do?"

"The same thing you want to do. The right thing." Right there was where we said good night.

Tuesday

He blogged at three sixteen AM. *Does this man ever sleep,* I thought. Then I had X-rated thoughts. I am not sure which thought I liked more. *Either, he needs some desperately or he is going to be wearing me out all night.* I could guess it was a little bit of both scenarios. Neither of us have had intimate relations in years. *This is going to be scary. I am not even sure how you really start.* I shrugged; *I guess you just roll with the flow. Hmm, the pool event leads me to believe we can pick it back up quickly.* I sighed. *This is going to be either extremely eventful or extremely pitiful. For me maybe even painful. I hoped anyway. Lord, do not let me wait this long to be disappointed.* I wanted painful. Not just from the lack of activity. I wanted it from his over endowment. *I will take extreme over endowment please. Is this a prayer, a thought, or an important request?* My mind continued to move on. *Let him not only be overly endowed but also let it work and let him know how to use it.* "Danielle," I said aloud.

It took a minute to get my mind off the size and a few more X-rated thoughts before I went back to my original train of thoughts.

How do you get two people together that have not been intimate in four years? This was my confirmation he was the right person. I had been praying and asking God when the time comes to send me a companion that would understand, accept, approve and participate in my celibacy until marriage. *But my God, you didn't give me that. You gave me someone that is right where I am. Not a year ahead or a year behind.* I almost tore my bed up praising my God. I never had this revelation until now. I stopped right then and gave him all the praise and glory. Not just for Randall but also for carrying me, keeping me, and protecting me through the storm. God knows all. He knew Reginald was not the one for me. He had to let me go through what I went through with him and these four years thereafter so I could recognize this. I had to go through the fire so that I would have a reason to be at Victory Church. The Property Manager had to refuse to pave the lot; otherwise, I would never have required a reason to call the Deacon out. If I had not called him out I probably would have never paid him any attention. *God set me up and it was all for my good. He had to have a difficult divorce; otherwise, he would have already been dating someone when I showed up. OH MY GOD. I can see this clearly. It was all a set up and all in God's plan. He knows the plans he has for me and Randall way before we were ever formed in our mother's womb,* I thought.

I jumped up and started getting dressed. It was a few minutes before four. I had not read his blog yet. In the midst of dressing, I had a thought. I raced back to my computer. I got mad with myself. I searched my email. I received an email from Vickie a few weeks ago with his training schedule and one from King with instructions on how to locate him from his watch. I pulled them both up. It was Tuesday and according to his training schedule and monitor, he was right where he was supposed to be. The only problem, I was going to have to track him while I drive. *When are they going to make these cars with computers? I could sure use it right now. Whom do I need to contact to get on that design team? JD Powers maybe.* I made a mental note to contact them later today.

I opened the garage and initially went for the church car because it had enough front seat room to spread my computers out in order to track him. As I began to spread my stuff out I changed my mind realizing I may need the faster car so I went for the drop top.

I hit the on ramp and before I made it to the highway, I was doing one hundred. Or how we say it in zone three, ahunned miles an hour. By the time I was in the lane I was at one thirty. "Slow down D. What jerk face cop would be out this time of the morning on a Tuesday writing tickets? Some creep," I said as I pulled up off the gas. "Girl pump your brakes. The man ain't going anywhere." It was then I realized I had not read his blog.

I was using skills the Department of Transportation was trying to outlaw. I had a monitor up, I was searching my phone to find an email, and I was still traveling over eighty miles an hour. My philosophy is if the speedometer says it goes that fast then push it to the limit.

> I have a strong woman who sticks to her word. She is independent. She makes up her own mind. She leaves nonsense behind. This beautiful Rose of mine.

When I look up after reading the blog, I have no clue which lane I am in. It was not the one I started in. *This is exactly why we have a no texting and driving law.* I was glad no one was on the highway but love sprung me. However. I slowed my roll to under fifty-five.

"Oh crap, my exit. When you do a hundred Danielle you get there quicker." I had to cut across three lanes. *Thank God, no one is on the road. This is horrible driving.* I jumped off and checked the screen. It showed he was less than a mile away. As soon as I thought I was up on him, leave it to him, he turned the corner. *Who told him to do that?* I thought. "King." It left me with no choice. I had to make a turn in motion. You could hear my wheels screeching.

"What was that?" Randall asked. King removed his ear buds.

"Pull back," King said pushing Randall off the sidewalk and pulling out his piece as their pace slowed.

I was rolling so fast I did not realize I was pulling up on the opposite side of the street until I passed them. I saw them both look back in my side mirror. Then I saw King make what I thought was a grip move on his piece. I was the only one on the street other than them so I could not lie and say it was not my tires. As soon as I backed up, he covered Randall.

I rolled the window down. "Dammit Danielle," King yelled. "Only you would be up this time of the morning rolling up on folks. You almost had steel for breakfast. A lot of it."

Oh snap, he is pissed. I freighted him.

I parked right there on the street. I got out the car but quickly turned back around realizing I forgot the water I brought. I ran back across the street and handed King a bottle. "Good morning to you too pit bull," I said nonchalantly.

"What's wrong DJ?" he asked looking down at his watch. His tone insinuated something had better be wrong.

"Nothing," I said exuberantly.

"Why are you showing up like you came to complete a hit?" King interrupted.

I rolled my eyes at King. He was just as annoying at five in the morning as he was at five in the evening. "Can I speak to him please? ALONE," I added.

"He is not the baby's father. I do not care what you say," King demanded.

"Shut up jerk." *It is funny how Randall rarely gets in the middle of our spats. He always sits back and lets them play out. I wonder why?*

He grabbed my hand and started walking with me. "Watch the car King," he said mildly.

I looked back and stuck my tongue out like a kid. King opened his water shaking his head at me in return. "We are starting all over because of this little interruption," King informed his boxer.

"Punk," I yelled.

"Yeah, I gotcha," Randall replied unconcerned.

"Are you really going to have to start all over?"

"Yes, that is nothing. What's wrong?"

"Well, I," I hesitated. *After all that Night Rider, James Bond action I cannot believe I am speechless. He does this to me every single time. It is getting annoying. He needs to stop making me nervous,* I thought.

"If I have to start over running eight miles again I would at least like to know what is on your mind."

He was not even pissed about starting over. "That right there," I replied.

"What?" He looked up and down like what. His heart began to race. He looked at his monitor. It was higher now than when he was running. He held his arm up in Kings direction.

King pulled out his phone to check the rate. King was shocked at the results. *He is usually much calmer when she is around. What is going on? I hope she is not pregnant,* King thought. *What could be the problem? Do not tell me this is going to be some BS. Please do not be asking for anything. Money, co-signing, bail out,* King's mind continued to wonder.

"Just you," I said sweetly. Pausing for a moment, "I woke up this morning and I could not go any further until I told you how much I love you. How much you mean to me. How much I need you. How I prayed for you and asked God to send you to me. How I hope you feel the same way. I want to spend the rest of my life with you," I admitted. "You are all I think and dream about."

The thought of him brought a smile to my face. "I light up when I hear your ringtone? I get excited each time I see you have texted, emailed or blogged. You leave me speechless and my palms get sweaty when I am around you. You make me nervous and my heart races when I know I am going to see you. I radiate when I walk into the church and see you. I beam with joy and happiness when you walk into the sanctuary. I can't remain calm around you."

Looking him in the eyes, I continued, "Don't you see that? Can you feel it? Do you feel the same way? I am like a puzzle and every minute I am without you, I realize you are those missing pieces. It is no accident we met or why you were the one called when I was in distress. It's not by chance I was lost, arrived late, and then had to park in the field. Why wasn't another Deacon called? How were you chosen? Why did I leave my directions? Why didn't I think to use my phone or iPad to find where I was supposed to be? Why? How is it that for four years you have been dealing with this divorce and suddenly it is finalized? Not to mention she accepted less than what she originally requested. Tell me. Do you have the answers to these questions? Any of these questions? It is not a coincidence. It was all in God's plan. Am I dreaming this? Am I just imagining? Help me out here," I pleaded.

He stood speechless. Not a single word was spoken. The only movement he made was to drop his head. I felt dumb. I felt like a complete idiot. Here I was in the five o'clock hour pouring my heart out in the middle of what would normally be a busy street to a man who said nothing. *Maybe I felt too good this morning. Maybe I woke up a little beside myself,* I thought to myself. I stepped from in front of him and moved to his side. He did not move. I was beyond embarrassed. Humiliated is a more accurate description. Now I was just as speechless as he was. I had nothing else to say. I had given my confession, pouring every feeling out right there on the pavement. I might as well have been naked. I exposed all of me. I was completely transparent and he did not cover me. This was a very awkward position and I needed to figure out how to walk away with my dignity. Right then I did just that. I put one foot in front of the other. I lowered my head and said, "Hey, have a great day. I am sorry to have disturbed your training." The tears fell, "Call me later babe." I didn't know what else to say. I did not know if he would call. *I might have gone overboard.* I stepped off the curb. I wanted to look back but instead I took my time and crossed the empty street. There was not another soul in sight.

King picked a fine time to be a gentleman by opening my door. I sat in the car as he held my door open. "Let me know if you ever want to get rid of this car," he said. He must have then realized something was wrong and squatted down and asked, "Are you okay?"

I nodded my head yes, but that was a lie, I was not okay. King and I exposed different sides of ourselves to each other. He saw my sensitive side and I saw his affectionate side. I closed my eyes and cupped my hands over my face.

"Sit here and get yourself together before you pull off," he instructed.

"I will. I am okay. Thank you for your concern. It means a lot," I said through my tears. I reached past him to close the door. He stood still as I sat there motionless.

King walked across the street, walked up to Randall, and punched him in his chest. "What just happened?" he commanded.

"I do not know," he said while sucking air from his chest being caved in.

"What do you mean you do not know?" he demanded.

Randall stood there confused. He did not know whether to run after her or not. This was sudden and unexpected. He did not know what to say or how to respond. "I know nothing about dating," he confessed.

"You better learn fast. You do not have much of a choice."

"Stay here," Randall said then ran across the street.

My face laid in my hands and I could not put the words together on how I felt. He opened my door and scared the crap out of me. He spoke in soft and sensitive tone, "Danielle," he said as he squatted down next to me.

"Yes."

"Why are you crying?"

"I am embarrassed I suppose."

"Why? Do you feel what you just expressed?"

"Yes but I'm afraid you may not."

"Did I say I did not?"

"You did not say anything."

"I am sorry but you caught me off guard. I was not expecting this. I do not know what to say. I want you to feel the way you do so please do not take my silence as negative. I am thrilled and excited. Don't worry, I feel the same way." He pulled my arm. "Get out of the car please," he instructed.

He is the most polite demanding person I have ever met. When he spoke, it was usually a command more so than a request. However, the way he gently said it made you do what he commanded. He always spoke forceful with authority yet gentle and caring all at the same time.

He closed the door and leaned against the car. He pulled me close to him preventing me from leaning on the car too. "Do not get your clothes dirty. I will have these cars washed today," he said hugging me tightly. He positioned me in between his legs. It then occurred to me I was forcing him out of his blogging non-verbal comfort zone. He had no choice but to verbally speak to me face to face.

"Dani, I wish you knew how long I have longed to hear you say these things," he began. "This mean everything to me. You have confirmed my thoughts and brought sunshine into my life. I do not feel as if I can live without you. Can't you see it? Why do you think I am out here in the middle of the night running? It is because I am happy Danielle. It is because I want to fight. Because of you, I have the drive to get into the ring again. I want to give you everything you ever need or want. I want you to be happy and not worry about a thing. I will be there for you. I need you Danielle. I love you."

At the moment, my heart shattered in a million pieces in a good way. He was the only human that could melt my heart and mend it back again in a matter of seconds. It melted right there in the street but before he could finish the next sentence it was mended again. He said all I needed to hear. He felt the same way. *I cannot believe you God,* I thought. *Your powers. How You have moved. I love You. Your powers are miraculous and mighty. You are above all. There is none like You. All the trials and dead ends in my life brought me right here to this point. To this day. To this street. A normally busy yet dark street. They brought me here to realize Your power, Your grace, and Your mercy. They brought me here to my soul mate. He is my modern day Boaz. I did not find him. He found me. I had a need and You fulfilled it. You sent him.*

We parted while I went to work and worked hard all day. Although I could not really explain how I felt, I knew I could not wait to see him again. When I arrived at the gym, he was working on hand and eye coordination. They had him doing live exercises as well as virtual stimulation. I could not keep up. I observed momentarily then went upstairs intending to walk. Somehow, I found my way back downstairs on the treadmill. After an hour I could not concentrate. My eyes, heart, and mind were focused on him. More so on what he was doing. He was fighting against a computer opponent for hand eye coordination. It was playing on every screen. It gave the results immediately, verbally, and visually. King was totally engulfed in something else. After every round, King spoke instructions. Hooks never looked up. It was amazing to me. The virtuosity calculated his speed and timing. The opponent would not only move but also completely disappear in a matter of seconds, hence the hand eye coordination. I went upstairs and tried to concentrate and work. I was unsuccessful. I ended up bringing my drawings down and laying them on the floor so I could continue to watch him.

"We are not putting a desk or computer down here. You can cancel the thought right now," King yelled at me.

For the first time he was distracted, "What?" Randall answered.

"I am talking to Bob the Builder over there," King replied without ever looking up.

Randall looked back and quickly got punched.

King snapped. "This is one reason why. This is a gym not an office. My fighter is training not courting. You see, you looked back, and got clocked. Your day will end the same way it started," King bellowed.

"You are working on a computer," I said defensively to King.

"I am working with my fighter."

"Pay attention Randall," I yelled like a cheerleader.

Randall looked between King and me trying to figure out what was going on.

"Start it over from the top," King yelled. "This is the second time today. I have nothing but time on my hands we can do this all night if we need to," King replied.

"What a jerk," I mumbled under my breath while Randall laughed.

"What was that Ms. D?" King asked as if he did not hear me. "Keep it up and I will ban you from my gym and my fighter," he threatened.

I kept working as if I did not hear him. *If I wanted you to hear me, I would have said it loud enough in the first place. I am a distraction to Randall. Well I am not coming tomorrow. Oh yeah, tomorrow is Wednesday. Nope I am not coming. We will be at bible study.*

After an hour or so I was so intrigued with what he was doing I could have watched him all night but I decided to leave. King barked and yelled the entire hour. I did not understand how that did not annoy Randall to death. I guess that was King's job. It sucked. He got on my nerves so I packed up.

"Take your little crayons with you too," King said referring to a box of highlighters.

"They are highlighters but a caveman like you would not know that."

I think we were the entertainment for the gym. It always sparked everyone's attention when we attacked each other. I have come to grips with the fact that our relationship will never change. King would forever remain a thorn in my side.

"D. Where are you going?"

"To get my toe tags."

"Nice," he said unamused by King and I.

I got in the shower there at the gym holding out for him to finish. I wanted to talk to him before I left. As soon as I bent over to pull my underwear up, I heard a tap on the door.

"What?"

"Can I come in?"

"Can you do what?"

"Are you dressed?" he asked.

"Hold up." I threw my clothes half on and opened the door. "What's up?"

"Why did you leave?" Randall asked.

"It is getting late and my boyfriend maybe wondering where I am."

"Just let him know you are with your future husband. He can call me if he has a problem."

Smiling on the inside I questioned, "Cocky are we?"

"I guess you can say that. Do you have a second or are you rushing out?"

"I was rushing out. I do not want to get you in anymore trouble today."

"I want to talk to you about today," he replied.

"Go ahead please." I was surprised.

"You know you amazed me this morning. It was a great surprise. I was not expecting you to show up or our conversation. You kind of caught me off guard. I appreciate it. It made me feel good to know you went out of your way to express to me how you truly feel. I do not know how I conveyed the message but I wanted to make sure you know I feel the exact same way."

"Thanks. I was a little discouraged before I left," I admitted.

"Are we good now?"

I kissed his lips. "I do believe so."

"Let me walk you to the car."

As we walked out he said, "You know I am going to the lake Thursday morning?"

"Yes, I know. I will let everyone know the party will start Thursday and end Sunday night," I teased.

"I am not worried. We are not that far away."

Wednesday

I felt like I was leaving or forgetting something but could not figure out what. I looked around and still I could not put my finger on it. It was five o'clock in the morning and I was pulling out of my garage. I always backed in and followed the same rule. I never opened my garage door until my car was in drive and my seat belt was on. I hit the button to let the door open and looked down to check his blog.

Startled, I yelled, "Oh shucks."

"Good morning," he replied calmly as if I did not almost run him over.

I jumped out of the Porsche. "Why in the world are you standing in the dark in front of this door? I could have run your narrow behind over." He kissed me and politely walked away. "Excuse you?"

"Have a good day DJ. I will pick you up at half past five for bible study."

"That's it?" I asked.

"Yep. That is it," he answered.

He got in his freaking Ferrari, pulled off and went roaring out of my driveway and down the street. *What in the world?* I slammed the door and called him as I pulled off in fury.

"Hey babe."

"Randall Washington."

"Yes sweetie."

"What is your deal?"

"Thought I'd surprise you like you did me."

"I had a conversation. You did not."

"I think breaking in your gate, waiting for thirty minutes outside your garage, and kissing you good morning was enough said."

"You little punk."

"You love it."

"I will not be ready at five thirty."

"Yes, you will. I am leaving in the morning so you are dating me tonight. Whether you want to or not," he added.

"Randall you are pushing my buttons."

"I will see you in a few hours."

"Ugh," I screamed.

"Have a good day precious," and he hung up.

Of course, he was now on my mind as I drove to work. *What a jerk. He is very stern in everything he does. Now I see how people are always able to do what he wants. He really does not ask. Not that he has to. Then again, he probably had to be stern with me. I am a piece of work myself. Stubborn to say the least. If he were not firm with me, I would be running all over him by now.*

All day I tried to figure out a way to tell him I would meet him at the church. I needed that extra two hours to work. I could not come up with a decent excuse that he would fall for. Therefore, I began to push myself harder so I could get out and be home by the time he arrived. *This dating stuff was crazy, demanding, and required too much time.* I made it home just in time. As soon as I put my bag down the house phone rang.

"Yes babe," I answered.

"Can you open the gate?"

"No."

"What?"

"Use the same tactic you used this morning."

"Low DJ," he clicked the line.

Five minutes later, he was ringing my doorbell. I opened the door shaking my head.

"Are you ready?"

"You are a sick puppy. Let me get my things," I said. As we approached the gate I realized he left it open. He broke into it and left it open for anyone else to barge in. "Pull over," I demanded.

"I will fix it," he agreed.

"I got it. You can take a brother out the hood but you cannot take the hood out of the brother. Coming over here to my projects tearing up my gate. The neighbors are going to have a field day with this at the next association meeting."

"I hope they kick you out. Then you can move in with me," he said roaring his engine to help with the association forcing me out of the neighborhood for noise violation.

As we were riding and talking, he springs it on me, "Is there a way possible you can go to one phone and one computer?"

"No," I said sharply without a second thought.

"But do you really need three of each?" he asked.

"Yes." *I thought the first answer was the end of the conversation.*

"Give me a reasonable explanation why one phone or one computer will not do?"

"Ain't happening Randall." *He still does not get it.*

"Why?"

I gave him a scolding look.

"You did not even think about it."

"I would give up my heels before I give up my computers."

"So you would appease King and Keith over me?"

"I think that is probably just as much your request as it is theirs."

"Keep the heels and let the technology go." He paused having thoughts of the heels and nothing else. "They all do the same thing. Why do you need three of each? Besides, the heels are sexy. Humph," he mumbled under his breath.

"RANDALL."

"Never mind."

"Thank you. Let's not loose friendship on the way to church."

"We will never lose friendship no matter how hard you try. What about seven to seven?"

"What are you talking about now?"

"Can you work from seven to seven and not twenty four hours all day?"

"That's cool. Seven AM Monday until seven PM Wednesday."

"You know damn well that is not what I meant."

"You work twenty four hours a day too."

"Help me out here Dani."

"How many from your pit can you let go?"

"Come again?"

"Sorry. I was speaking a foreign language to you. I was speaking NASCAR. I forgot you know nothing about that."

"I beg your pardon. I know a lot about NASCAR, but how many NASCAR drivers know boxing? None. Boxing is not like getting in a car driving. There is a technique to boxing. NASCAR is getting in a car and going around and around and around." He went on and on and on.

He lost me. *I am sure there is some NASCAR driver out here who feels the same way about boxing,* I thought to myself. *Who would want to get in a ring for three minutes twelve times to be punched? I'm sure most people would ask what technique was there to boxing. I know because I watched him train, but how many other people know it is actually a skill. There are many techniques. I'm not about to add to or take away from this tirade, but for his information there is a lot of technique required to drive in circles.*

"I was asking are you going to get rid of some of your security. Cut back to four men."

"DJ you know I cannot do that."

"Why not?"

"I can't."

"That is not a valid answer. In fact, it is not an answer at all. Why can't you?"

"You know quite a few of them have a responsibility to help me train. The others have a responsibility to protect us."

He said us. I liked it. "Why can't you cut them? Why do you need them daily?" I was not disputing his need for his guys I was making a valid point. They were a part of his job and these computers and phones are a part of my job.

"We are totally on two different pages. You can use one computer for all of your needs. One phone. We can stop and pick you up a new phone and a new computer if you would like. However, the guys stay. No ifs, ands, or buts about it," he said making himself very clear. "You have to remember I cut a man and I change his life. This is a career for him. I will make personal sacrifices before I change my staff. We have worked hard to get to where we are. Nothing happens to the computer."

"No thank you. However, it was a nice offer."

"You still have not explained why you need three?"

"Number one they all serve a different purpose."

"Think about it DJ. That would be a nice gesture and it would make me happy. I would like my time to be my time. Not shared with gadgets. Am I asking too much?"

I took note of his request. However, I knew it was not going to cross my mind anytime soon. "You are fine," I said annoyed he would ask this of me. "You raised a concern you have. I will give it some attention. Why didn't you just say I do not like splitting your attention?"

"I thought that is what I just said?"

"What is the difference when I have to share you with an entourage? When I have King barking up and down my back daily? What then?"

"I will speak to King. He will back off. It is that simple. When you tell me what you need, want, or desire I will make it happen."

He shut me down. I used King and magically he said he would handle it. "I can handle King. When are you going to eat solid food and sleep?"

"We will deal with that later."

"Humph," I growled.

"Humph," he gave back out of sarcasm. "Are you sure you do not want to come to the lake?"

"Umm, I think I am positive, especially if I have to give up my gadgets."

"What about for the day?"

Here he goes again. The power of persuasion. "I will think about it," I opted to say because the last answer warranted the notion I did not give it any thought. This time I was going to give it thought before I said no.

"Humph," he said then laughed aloud.

He gave up my laugh. Oh my God. I love his laugh. I need to record it and make it my ring tone. However, the way he laughed is as if he knows my answer was going to be no. Now, I am really going to give it some thought. The lake is only an hour or so away. I could still do my regular Saturday stuff, run up there around ten and leave about seven or eight. I could do one even better. Hit up there for lunch then jet back. I have gone further distances for lunch with a client. Not to mention I had to pay. Hmm, I will check my schedule and consider it. I wish I could surprise him but I do not know where I am going and I would hate to get there and have to search the swamp, creek, or river for him and interrupt his tubing. By the way, what black people tube, I thought.

We were a red light away from the church. "Are you going to work while I go in?"

I felt like this was a Mama Rose trick question. I was being set up. I had not dated in a long time but I was wise enough to respond correctly. "Do you need me to do something?"

"Not really. Are you hungry?"

"I think I am good until after service."

We pulled up to the curb. King and Keith were both standing there. It was interesting how they coordinated. I thought, *I must admit they are always on point. I am sure two hours ago they were all scruffy in shorts and tee shirts working out. Now, here they stand looking handsome and debonair. Mental note, never refer to King as handsome or debonair again. Never ever. The only thing he is to be referred to is annoying.* JJ always stood off in the background. He was like the watcher of them all. Randall jumped out and opened my door as I reached to get my things. Keith pulled the car into a parking spot while we went inside the building. *I do not understand the purpose of someone else parking but whatever. If they like it then I love it.*

I heard him say that on occasion he had an office at the church. *Why, I do not know? I guess it may have something to do with the fact that his best friend was the Pastor along with the fact he just might be the heaviest tithing member.* Either way it goes, I had not seen it yet. He unlocked the door. Why was I surprised? It was picture perfect. *Does he ever come in here? I should have known.* It was now a competition to which office was the nicest, his or Hunters. This was a tough call.

"Plug in and do what you do. I want you out promptly at sixth forty five."

I could not respond because I was observing. Before I knew it he pressed his cheek up against mine, laid his head on my shoulder and kissed my neck. Then he disappeared.

I got busy working. I had less than an hour to catch up and get ahead. If there was ever such a thing. To my surprise, I actually got a lot accomplished. Then I thought about it. *He has this beautiful office and he had me outside on a conference call in the rain. We were going to have a talk about this.* I texted him immediately.

YOU ARE IN TROUBLE.

After forty minutes or so, I decided I had better use the ladies room before I enter the sanctuary. The last thing I wanted to do was not be in place after he gave specific instructions. Not to mention, I had to ride home with him. Besides, I was going to be the one doing the ripping tonight.

I was not sure what to do. I did not have a key to lock the office door. I stepped outside the door to check. The hall was empty. I must admit, I was a little turned around. I heard noise so I decided to follow the noise. I ran into the choir before I spotted the restroom. As soon as I made a dash to cross the hall, I heard JJ's voice.

"Where are you going?" he asked.

How does he always do that? JJ was like a super hero. He was always at the right place at the right time but no one ever sees him enter or exit. "The ladies room," I answered.

"Come on." He took me back to the office. He opened a secret paneled door and low and behold, there was a bathroom. "Here you are. I will be back to get you."

"Thanks." *What is up with the secret doors?* I walked in reluctantly looking around before I closed the door behind me. *Am I going to be able to get out?* As soon as I cut the water on to wash my hands I heard a knock at the door. I checked my watch. Technically, I had a few more minutes. I cut the water off to make sure I was hearing what I thought I was hearing. I opened the door. "Yes Deacon?"

"Are you okay? I just read your text."

"Why in God's name did you have me outside in the rain on a conference call when you have this nice office?"

"You did not ask to use my office."

"You are such a boy." I reiterated shaking my head.

Reluctantly, he replied, "I hope that is a good thing."

"What am I going to do with you?"

"Love me I pray." He kissed my cheek, forehead, and lips then ran out. He was always running, yet still clueless as to why he was in trouble. For him to be such a simple person he sure had elegant taste. This office was no different from the ones at the gym and club. And to think, he had the nerve to comment on my closet.

I sat back down to do a few last minute things wishing I had thirty more minutes. To avoid conflict I wrapped up working. I was sitting at the door when JJ walked in. You could tell he was shocked he did not have to wait on me.

"Are you done?"

"No but let's do it." I checked the mirror one last time. JJ opened the door as I walked out ahead of him. The corridor seemed long and quiet. As soon as we hit the end of the hall, I could hear the noise. He was all the way on the other end of the hall. He was not that tall but I could spot his head a mile away. When I did, he looked up and did a double take. He stopped in midstream and watched me approach. He observed me as if he had not seen me ten short minutes ago. The way I captured his eyes one would never have known we arrived together. It made me feel special. He was so engulfed in me the other Deacons turned to see what he was looking at. I smiled at them all.

As we got closer, JJ backed off and Keith stepped in. It was like a programmed event. I spoke, "Good evening gentlemen." I looked at him and winked my eye. "Deacon Washington," I addressed.

He sucked his teeth, "Girl, don't push me. Cause I'm close to the edge."

I winked again and threw my hand up brushing him off. Keith and I walked in the sanctuary. The other Deacons laughed as we walked away. As soon I crossed the threshold I heard him laugh. It was enough to stop me dead in my tracks. I can't really explain but there was something about his laugh that tickled me. I took a second to get myself back together. Keith looked at me and smiled as if he knew what just happened with me internally.

Oh my God. Bible Study was off the chain. I think First Lady must have broken Pastor off in his chambers or something because he was crunk to death. He was sweating before he finished the first scripture. I knew it was going to be a night I sweat out my hair but not the way I intended. Pastor Hunter kept the same pace the entire service. After he gave the benediction, the praise and worship team continued to praise while Hunter began to sing. He did not sing often, but when he did, it was always a treat. The next thing I knew we were in bible study part II. The sanctuary cleared out then suddenly it was getting packed again. This was the official after party. I put my handbag back down. Deacon Washington came in and out a few times. He was doing his duty. This was probably a stretch for him. He needed to be in too many places at one time. He was expected to watch the door, clear the parking lot, count the money, shut down the bookstore, assist and secure Pastor Hunter, and now he was in charge of clearing the sanctuary again. He was like a magician. He moved from one side of the room to the other. There was too much going on too fast for him and his crew. If this was the club it was lit and a perfect time for something to jump off. Every place he moved within the room he continued to make eye contact with me.

I watched him just as much as he watched me. Finally, Hunter was tired. "You all do not have to go home but you have to leave here," he said sounding a little winded.

The crowd kept hyping him up. Then when he stopped singing, they hyped the band up. Finally, Hunter gave in and walked off the stage. The crew and Deacon Washington walked behind him. He was perspiring as if he had been in a sporting event.

I went back with Keith to Deacon's office to get my things. I walked around looking for him but I didn't see him so I went to the car. It was easy to find now since most of the cars were gone.

He wasn't there and the car was locked. Therefore, I went back in the building. I was walking aimlessly when I heard him from behind me, "Excuse me Ms. Danielle. Do you need a ride home?"

"Actually I do, but I was expecting dinner also."

"May I make an offer?"

"I am not sure. I would not want my boyfriend to get upset." We had dinner before pulling back up to my house. I always felt like a sixteen year old who never wanted the night to end when I was with him. Apparently, he felt the same way because tonight he came in. I was going to ask him to but he did so on his own.

It was after midnight. "Babe, I have to go. Otherwise, the night is going to end differently," he said.

"You don't have to leave."

"Oh yes I do. I am going home and getting in my bed."

"What?"

"Yep. I am getting in the bed."

"I am proud of you."

"I am proud of you too."

"What did I do?"

"You were on time, no work, and ready when JJ came to get you this evening."

"Well thanks. What time are you leaving in the morning?"

"Before noon."

"Okay," I said sadly. "I won't see you. I am going to miss you. I love you."

He kissed me passionately and intensely for a long time. Then he left me. He could not have made it to my gate before he called me. We talked all the way until he got home.

Once he walked in the house he admitted, "I am sleepy."

"What?" I said surprised.

"You and Hunter have worn me out today. I have to get some rest. I have a few full days ahead of me. I wish you would change your mind and join us."

We said our final goodnights and went to bed.

Thursday

He called me at five AM. "Are you up?"

"Yep. I am about to walk out of the house in ten minutes."

"Okay sweetie. I will call you once we get on the road."

Leigh and I were on a teleconference in my office when there was a rattle at the door. *Now I know damn well they can see my light.* I paid out of my pocket for this light outside my door to let them know when not to come in but no one ever obeyed it. I wanted to scream but could not even speak now. I felt stuck and could not move. I motioned to Leigh to get the door. She stood and opened the door. I looked at my visitors and said, "Shh. I am on a teleconference."

Instantly they both sat very still. I was expecting for at least one of them to lose it. Before I could get the screen and phone line clear they spoke, "Hey Ms. Danielle."

"Hi friend."

"You look busy."

"We are sorry to disturb you. It was his idea," Randall said pointing at Randall Jr. as if they were eight years old.

"You two are good."

"We wanted to say bye and extend an offer again," Big Randall said as if it was all RJ's idea to come by.

"Good bye guys. I will see you two in a few days."

"Does that mean you are coming to the lake?" RJ questioned as if my no was not clear.

"No. Are you two staying forever?"

"Ms. Danielle please," RJ pleaded.

"You two will be fine. It is father son time. You do not want some girl interfering on your trip. You two go and have some fun. I will see you Sunday or Monday."

"We drove all the way up here, parked miles away, had to sit quietly while you were on the phone, and you are still saying no?" the kid reenacted.

I simply replied, "Yes." As I walked with them, Randall and I were locked arm in arm. I leaned in his ear and whispered, "That was a low blow babe. You put the kid on me. You fight dirty."

"It did not work so it doesn't matter."

I noticed his disappointed tone. Nevertheless, we talked practically his entire ride to the lake and all throughout the day. He must have called me more today than ever. He is not a big phone talker. I think he does it only to appease me. Then again, since he did not have a routine workout today he might have also been a little bored. On the other hand, maybe he really missed me. I must confess I missed him too. I was completely uninterested at the gym this evening. I worked out harder today than I have in a long time. I guess this is what happens when you do not have distractions. Now I understood what the guys meant about distractions. It was boring here without him and the mouth of the south. At ten o'clock, I heard my name but I didn't recognize the voice.

"Ms. D?"

"Yes?"

"It's time."

"I'm sorry?"

"Mr. Hooks has requested you leave for the night."

I didn't respond.

"Ms. D did you hear me?" the voice asked sternly.

"Of course I heard you," I said kindly, "Sorry to ignore you. Tell Randall to deliver his message to me himself." I was being my normal rebellious self.

"Is that what you want me to reply?"

"You sure can. Otherwise, I am in the middle of something right now that I can't stop. Shall I call you when I am ready?"

"Yes ma'am," he replied as he hesitantly walked away confused. They were not accustomed to objecting to Randall or disputing him. I could see him shaking his head as he walked back down the steps. Randall did just as I thought he would after my response. He called me. At least I knew the guy repeated me verbatim.

"Hi Randall," I answered.

"Hey babe."

"What are you doing?"

"Waiting for you to get home." His tone was not as relaxed as it had been earlier.

"Are you there?" I asked seductively.

"Say the word and I can be at your house. I will leave RJ here and be there in one hour or less."

"And what do you plan to do when you get there?"

"What are my limitations?"

"You tell me?"

"I want to personally make sure you are home safe and sound."

"I do not believe you."

"Let me come and show you."

"Tell me," I insisted.

"Danielle," he paused. "Trust me. It would be very illegal and disrespectful if I verbalized what I want to do to you." He paused again. "Please let me show you."

Laughing, "I think I will pass."

"You don't trust me?" he questioned.

"No, I do not trust me," I confessed.

With persistence he asked, "Are you on the way home?"

"Give me a little while."

"I'm calling back in thirty minutes. After that I am shutting down the power to the building."

"That is below the belt Hooks. Why are you so demanding?"

'Because I love you and I am not staying up all night waiting for you to get home."

"You are going to be up all night anyway."

"Yes I am, but for other reasons. Good night."

"What else are you going to stay up doing?" I asked.

He laughed my laugh ignoring my question and unsaid accusation.

"I will call you once I am in the car."

"I will call you in thirty minutes while you are in the car."

He was learning me. Just because I said I would call once I am in the car did not necessarily mean I would be there in thirty minutes. He was pushing me again. Besides, I needed more than thirty minutes to complete what I was doing. Once I finished I took my time walking to the car and observing all the faces. I was still unsure who the guy was that relayed the message and there was one particular man who caught my eye. I swear I knew him from somewhere but could not figure out where. We did talk once I got in the car although it took me longer than he allocated. He kept me on the line my entire drive home and up until I closed my eyes to go to bed.

Friday

I was crunk. I guess it was because it was Friday. Perhaps I was hyped because of the recent conversations I had with my boo.

Regardless of why I was hyped. I felt great as I arrived to the jobsite giving orders and calling shots. If I called Leigh back at the office once, I called her at least twenty times. I'm positive she was probably tired of me.

Once the day ended, I walked around my truck and took off my personal protective equipment. I put the truck in reverse and decided I could drive to the lake tomorrow for the day. I suddenly had the desire to surprise him.

I made a call to Tammy who said she could do my hair today instead of tomorrow. I avoided his call a few times again today. I did not want to call him until I was certain of the plans for tomorrow. Finally after I was home I was able to put a bag together, gathered all my gadgets, blueprints to take with me and laid out my clothes, I decided to tell him close to midnight or soon afterwards, otherwise he would get too excited.

"Randall?"

"Yes."

"I need to talk to you."

"Oh. Now?"

"Yes."

His heart began to beat rapidly, "Umm okay. Hold on let me go into another room."

"Don't say it like we are hiding secrets from RJ."

"Well are we?" he asked but was afraid of the response.

"No.

You could hear him closing a door. "Yes babe."

"I will be driving up in the morning."

"Huh?"

"I will meet you there in the morning. Can you give me the address?"

He wanted to clarify before he got too excited. "WHAT?"

"What is the address?" *Duh.* I thought to myself.

"Do you want me to pick you up?"

"No. That makes no sense."

"What time will you be here? Do I need to go get anything for you?"

"No silly. I will leave here between six and seven."

"DJ I can't wait to see you."

"Good night."

"Shall I wake you in the morning?"

"Don't you always?"

"Good night. I love you."

"I love you too Champ."

Saturday

I awoke at four thirty AM before his wake up call. I spent time with the Master before my feet touched the floor. I dressed, got my bags, and headed to the garage. As normal, I cranked the car then hit the garage door.

"What the hell," I was startled.

"What?" King said looking up from the Atlanta Journal Constitution as if I should not have been surprised.

"What is up with you stalkers? Why are you standing outside my garage door idiot?"

"Pay attention," he said.

"Good morning to you too."

"Yeah?" he snapped back.

"Oh great. Now I get to ride the entire way with you to the bug infested tubing place. Oh, what joy? How freaking fun. I knew this was a bad idea," I said.

"No different than NASCAR." He was referencing my near death experience.

"Nice. I get to ride with Mr. Sunshine and his happy go lucky attitude. I would rather wrestle with a bear."

"Say the word and I can make it happen."

"What is the deal with you two breaking in my gate?"

"How else are we going to get in?"

"I guess it does not really matter since I will more than likely get put out by the association because of you two."

"Look, I am only here to take you to the lake," he said in disgust.

"I thought I told him I would be there."

"You did. Hence the reason I am here."

"Don't you have something better to do like fall off a cliff?"

"I would rather be set on fire than ride an hour with you too."

Rolling my eyes in frustration, "How did I get stuck with the Terminator? Randall sure knows how to make my day."

"How do you think I feel having to babysit a two year old?"

"Make yourself useful. I was going to gas the cars. You can cut my time in half by helping me take two at a time."

King softened up although he would never admit it. He now had a different level of respect for Dani. Here she was a single, black, independent woman making it a priority to take five cars to the gas station to gas them for the week. It was evident she had been single for a long time. He realized right then she deserved a good guy like his boxer. However, those words were never escaping his thoughts.

As we got to the gas station, I walked up to put my card in and realized the pump was flowing. "Excuse me. What did you do?"

"I paid for the gas," he rolled his eyes.

"Why did you do that?"

"Hooks orders. I would not be paying otherwise. Believe me," he lied. Hooks did not make that order and neither was he using the company card. Today King was using his personal American Express Card.

We went and got the last two cars. King was driving the F350 when I called him. "Hello."

"King you can go a little faster. She will run."

Next thing I knew he was gone. The 350 was a big girl but she could move. Of course, I modified everything under her hood. You know big girls who can drop it like it is hot and scrub the ground too. That is how my big girl was. She could move something. Finally, we were ready to ride to the lake. Yippee.

As we entered the on ramp I notice something. "What is that?"

"What?"

"That noise?"

"The radio?"

"Umm yeah?"

"The radio."

"I am not. I will not and I refuse to listen to talk radio with you for an hour." I pulled out my iPod. We were in the Aston. There should have been a port for an iPod adapter so I could plug up. "How lame is that?"

"What?"

"You can't ride in this car listening to talk radio dude."

"What is wrong with talk radio?"

"It is for losers if you are riding an Aston Martin. It is so not cool. I do not like you but I like you enough to tell you the truth and as much as I would like to ignore you talk radio will not do it. What do you want to listen to?"

"Neil Bortz or Clark Howard."

"Nugatory. Let me handle this. Keep your eyes and your hands on the wheel. Again, how did I get stuck with you today?"

"That is a good question? One of us pissed someone off. Where is Keith? You are his job?"

"Why didn't he tell me you were picking me up?" I huffed.

"I guess you will have to ask him."

"Smart a**," I snarled.

"I do not know the answer to your question," he laughed being honest.

"You should have asked him when he delegated you to this assignment."

"I am off. You have ruined my day."

"Imagine how I feel. At least you had heads up. I came out of my garage and found you there. How disappointing and scary."

"You can drive yourself you know."

"I am well aware. I have been doing it for over fifteen years. I appreciate the offer anyway."

"Are you always this vocal?"

He had some nerve. "This is calm. You haven't seen vocal yet." I went directly to Afrika Bambaataa's Planet Rock. Everyone loves this song. It was and is still the jam. I did not hear King's phone ring. All I heard was him speaking.

"Yeah," he said as if he was pissed off. I turned the volume down on the radio. "Yeah, mouth of the south is in the car." Someone on the other end responded before he spoke back. "This is my last time. Believe that."

I didn't know his conversation was over when my phone rang. I let it ring until King looked over at me. He knew who was calling from the ringtone. I clicked my ear. "Hello."

"Good morning sweetheart."

"Good morning."

"How are you?"

"I was fine until an intruder was found standing in front of my garage."

He ignored the last comment. "Where are you now?"

"You mean us?" He was not addressing the issue of the Terminator. "You two."

"I think you know where I am."

"I will see you two in forty seven minutes."

"It may only be one of us."

"Behave."

"Bye," I said scowling at King. I clicked the line and pumped the volume back up.

"What you know about this?" King asked genuinely.

"You have not seen anything yet."

"Let me see that iPod girl. What are you holding?"

We rolled all the way to the lake jamming. I am not sure what I was thinking but I was truly misled. I cut my eye at King when we pulled up. He knew why. We rolled up to a mansion on the lake. The car was barely in park before I stepped my foot out. I did not waste time getting my things. I walked directly to the door and rang the bell. Nothing happened. King walked right behind me, opened the door and held it open for me to come in. I walked in and walked right to the patio door. By the time I got there and turned the handle I could see him, RJ, and Keith walking up the steps.

"Ms. D," Keith said greeting me.

"Hey RJ."

"Ms. Danielle. You came," he said with excitement.

"I told you I would." I smiled at the kid before I chastised the adults. "You two front porch now," I yelled.

"Man," RJ said.

Randall and Keith both looked at me as if they knew it was coming. We stepped on the porch. I stood there for a few minutes. No one spoke. King came outside. He was always intimidating. Nevertheless, right now he was the only one of them on my good side.

"Anyone care to explain?" No one spoke. "No need for you two to speak at once."

"Yeah. No need," King co-signed in humor.

"Explain what babe?" Randall felt obligated to respond.

I rolled my eyes.

"All I said was I have a house on the lake and you would not be roughing it. Did I not?"

"You did not say it was the Ritz Carlton. And you definitely failed to mention Oscar the Grouch was picking me up."

Keith laughed.

Hooks looked at King awaiting his response. He graciously replied, "I feel the same way about the Wicked Witch of the South."

Keith laughed again although he never laughs.

"Did you all not get enough of insulting each other on the ride here?"

"That was not the question." Keith snickered again interrupting me.

"Baby do we need an audience?"

I looked at Keith while I continued to laugh. "What is wrong with Tickle Me Elmo?"

Keith looked like he expected me to be on his side.

"Bye guys," Hooks said in his commanding voice. Keith obeyed the command and left but Oscar the Grouch stayed as if the order did include him. Hooks did not turn around but he knew King was still there. He hugged me, kissed my neck, my forehead, and my cheeks. I could see the disdain on King's face. As he hugged me, he spoke. "Baby, you were not coming. When you said you were coming I changed King's schedule to escort you here. Believe me I am in just as much trouble with him as I am with you."

"Why couldn't I drive myself?"

"You are supposed to have a day of relaxation."

"And you think an hour in the car with King is relaxing?"

"You seem calm."

Ignoring his statement, "Why couldn't you tell me King was coming?"

"You would have changed your mind Danielle and I would have had to track you down today."

"So you feel like what you did was right?"

"Bye King," he said just audible enough for King to hear.

"I am not leaving until she treats you the way she treats me. I rode with her for an hour, listening to her and her horrible tunes. I refuse to leave."

"What a jerk face butt hole," I said referring to King.

"Watch your language and tone young lady," Hooks whispered.

"I am glad you see him in the same light I see him in," King said walking away. He knew darn well I was referring to him and not Randall.

"Randall DeWayne Washington."

"My love," his tone was soothing.

"Why is everything a mystery with you and once the mystery is revealed it is always over the top?"

"Elaborate?" he asked as if he had no clue.

"I find out you are a Boxer. You show up to the track in a Phantom. You send me gifts to my job for weeks. You lay on the altar for weeks and become a hermit. You invite me to go camping and the tent is a 20,000 square foot glass tree house. What other examples do you need?"

"It is not quite 20,000 square feet. And it is not in a tree."

I looked at him dead in his eyes. He knew he was smarting off and tried to hug me. "Ugh," I walked in the house avoiding his embrace.

"Alright boys. It looks like I am the only girl and there is electricity so what is the game plan?"

"We have been waiting for you to get here to eat breakfast," RJ said with much enthusiasm.

"Are you all ready?" Randall asked.

"You do not have on any shoes," I stated. Then I immediately thought of Leigh. She always says, 'Danielle stop stating the obvious.' Everyone else walked out the door. I stood there eyeing him.

"Forgive me. Are you going to let this go today? We told you that you would like it."

"You know what?"

"You love me?"

"You make me sick." I didn't know what to think. *This house is beautiful*, I thought. *I would love to come here and relax.* Truth be told, I did not know the meaning of relax. I observed my surroundings more. *I could live here. It is definitely not what I was expecting.* I did not know if I should charge it to him being humble or to him hiding things.

As I snapped pictures he stood behind me asking, "Are you mad?"

"I'm. I'm," I laughed. *King would have to witness this moment. I am sure he is dying for me to be speechless.* Just as King came to mind, he blew the horn. Randall then quickly slammed the glass door. I was shocked it didn't shatter. He was so unaware of his strength. Speaking of which, he had no idea of many things such as his talent, his calling, his personality, how handsome he was, his sex appeal, his effect on me, nor his humility. "Randall, Randall, Randall," I said aloud while shaking my head.

Calmly he answered, "Yes my love."

"Help me."

"What do you need help with?"

"Tell me truthfully who you are and the things you like. I want to know what you truly love, the things you possess, your fears, desires, needs wants, and your goals. Help me to know you better. Help me to love you."

"I am trying. I will. I promise. Marry me and you will find out all of these answers." He looked in my eyes, "By the way, the key to this house is also on your key chain."

"If it's easier for you to express yourself in a blog, it's totally okay with me. I realize sometimes it's a challenge for you to discuss things directly."

He gave up my laugh although I was dead serious. He took my face and kissed my forehead. We walked to the truck and got in the back. King was driving. RJ was in the front. Randall, Keith and I were in the back. *Here I am expecting to eat potted meat and we are pulling up to a valet at the country club.*

We ate a lovely breakfast. Everything was scanned before it came from the kitchen of course. I could understand why King was pissed off. Technically, he and Keith were still on duty.

Surprisingly, Randall socialized with the patrons, signed autographs, and passed out photos. He promised to do a charity benefit at the country club soon. When we got back to the house, the boys decided they were going to go fishing while I relax on the deck. Unbelievably I did not work, check emails, or text. I came prepared with a magazine and my eBook to chill. I was not expecting to have internet or cell service. He told me I would but I thought that was a lure to get me here. I read my magazine. I could not remember the last time I was able to completely chill.

After an hour or two RJ ran up the steps, "Ms. Danielle we are going on the boat do you care to come?"

"No, I am good." Then I remembered he was the real reason I came. "Wait, sure I will come. Let me change my clothes." I changed out of my dress into my bathing suit and a pair of shorts.

King drove the boat all while giving RJ driving lessons. He was a jack-of-all-trades. He looked over at Randall and spoke, "Boaz do you want to teach Jezebel how to drive?"

"Look a here partner," I interrupted Randall. "The Bible says thou shalt not kill, but it does not say anything about pushing a ninja overboard and pulling off. Try me if you want to homeboy. You falling and drowning is not considered murder. I'm just saying."

"You would locate the most ghetto, the most boisterous, and the most rebellious woman you could find at the church. Is this punishment for me?" he asked Randall who opted not to respond or look in our direction.

This was a nice boat. What did he have that wasn't nice? No pun intended but he fought hard literally and deserved nice things. I feel like anyone and everyone who works for it and can afford, it should splurge on himself or herself. The key words are work hard, can afford and for themselves. Hence, me. Some may consider my lifestyle lavish but so be it. I am single, childless, and I bust my butt day and night. I pretty much buy what I want when I want. The only difference between Randall and I is where I spend $1,000 he might spend $10,000. Okay, his spending was more like $100,000. His pay scale is much grander than mine therefore his toys cost more. Right now, I felt like the Joker. My question is where does he get these toys?

I took a moment and thanked God for him. It is clear he has truly been blessed. It is the middle of the day and here he is on his boat, with his son, trainer, security, and me, his girlfriend, straight chilling. It must be a good life.

We enjoyed the lake. Randall and RJ gave details of every house on the lake as we passed by each one. Who owned them, how they look on the inside and every detail in between. They were both excited to discuss the details. I made a mental note to suggest he spend more time here with RJ. It was probably one of the only places he had his dad's full and undivided attention. I also noticed Hooks ate when we were at breakfast. *I probably should not expect it for lunch. That maybe pushing it.*

It was lunchtime when we arrived back at the house. He told RJ to go wash up for lunch and so did I. When I arrived back to the table, it was set and lunch was ready. *This was turning out to be an amazing day.*

After lunch, King and Keith excused themselves from the table and parked in front of the ninety-inch television. They left us three alone. I gave Randall a nod. He did not acknowledge. I nodded again. No response. I shot him a text.

> Let me and RJ have the table please.

He read the text and remained seated as if I didn't say anything. I sent another text.

> Can I have a few minutes with RJ please?

I wanted to make sure RJ did not feel as if I was intruding on his time with his father. I knew Randall would snap his head off if he ever did, but he needed to feel comfortable telling his father how he felt with all of this.

He read the text and continued in the conversation. In the midst of his conversation, he said, "No Danielle," and continued to speak.

I got up from the table and took the dishes to the kitchen. They both proceeded to help me. "Grown folks," Hooks said.

Immediately, without hesitation, RJ got the message, "I am going fishing."

As Randall and I shared the chore of washing the dishes I asked, "Why are you so hard on him?"

"I am not."

"Yes you are."

We finished in silence avoiding a disagreement on such a lovely day. We walked to the deck to find RJ struggling with his line. "You need help son?"

"I think so Dad."

RJ looked at me, "Do you mind?"

"No, not at all." I didn't. I saw his father every day. Most days we both had an agenda, but I was with him much more than RJ. I walked back in the house and sat on the couch with my eBook.

"What are they doing?" Keith asked.

"Fishing."

"Oh, let me get a line," he replied excitedly.

"I'm taking a nap," King said as if he did not want to be bothered.

I flipped the remote and found a movie but I am sure I was asleep within the first ten minutes. I peeked out of one eye to see King going outside too. After an hour or so Randall was back and on the couch with me. Before you knew it, they were all back inside we watched a movie together.

Midway through the movie King got up and went outside with Randall following behind him. I wondered what was up. Then I realized they were cleaning and grilling the fish they caught. Dinner was served. Without any doubt, one thing was for sure, I had eaten well this day. Maybe if I came up here once a week I would know for sure he ate at least three meals for the week. After dinner, we had cheesecake the guys prepared. I was skeptical at first to try it. To my surprise, it was delicious.

We all sat on the couch, chilling and watching the game. I had no recollection that I was supposed to be back home. I felt like I was home. Even with the annoying one here. Speaking of which, the Terminator spoke, "Let's pack up and ride out," he ordered.

We all jumped as if daddy spoke. When we got out side, I realized I had not checked my phone or emails the entire day. I followed behind Keith to the truck while typing.

"Oh no ma'am," King said. I stopped dead in my tracks. "You and your Boo will be riding back together. Take the day off tomorrow. Church has been cancelled," he falsely instructed. Clearly, he did not want to be bothered with me on the ride home.

"No it has not Ms. D. I will see you in the morning Danielle." RJ said.

"Danielle? That is Ms. Danielle," Big Randall corrected.

"Ms. D we have a date in the morning?"

"Bright and early," I confirmed.

"Dad, are you coming home tonight?"

I shot a look at Randall, "What nights have you not come home?"

"I meant he comes home every night. I was asking about tonight. Is he coming home tonight?" RJ tried to retract the statement.

"What does that mean?" I asked again.

"I don't know," RJ said defeated.

"Yeah you do. What is that supposed to mean?" my tone changed badgering the child.

Randall had the strangest look on his face. I could not tell if it was guilt, embarrassment, shame, or humiliation.

"The kid wants to know if he is spending the night at your house," the Terminator added.

I flinched.

"No sir," Keith said. "Ms. D does not play that."

"King ain't playing it," King said. "I am not babysitting all night. He is bringing his tail home or I am dropping the kid off on the doorstep.

"Son, I will be home," he reassured. "I have to finish whipping you on the game anyway."

The three of them pulled off while we stayed back to make sure everything was locked. Randall and I rode back home together. We could have easily blown them out but we were in no hurry to get back and leave each other's company. I started checking messages and sending replies. Instantly the phone chirped back responses. As I opened the first one, he slammed on the brakes. The first thing I did out of instinct was look in the mirror to see if anyone was behind us. I saw no one. I looked and there was no danger in front of us. I looked at him confused. *Why is he stopping?*

"We have had a very good day so far with just two of us. Can you leave your other man out? You will be home shortly," he said as he held out his hand for the phone calling it my man. Without hesitation, I handed it over. He ate three times including dessert. I could not dispute; therefore, I gave in and gave him the phone. "I want to talk to you about something," he said.

I was not expecting this. You never know when people said that if it was good or bad. "What's on your mind sweetie?" I asked.

"First off, I want to thank you for coming today. It meant a lot to RJ and me. Secondly, thank you for not killing King," he said with all sincerity. "You two have got to make this work and if bickering is how you plan on doing it then fine with me. All I ask for is a fair fight. Thirdly, I need your help."

"Okay. Help on what?"

"I want to have a party."

"What kind of party?"

"An 'I'm coming out' announcement party."

"Coming out?"

"Not divorce. I want a fight announcement party. This way I can tell everyone at one time. I do not have to blog it, Facebook it, text it or make hundreds of calls. You know how it goes. Someone is bound to get mad. You told her before you told me. Then this aunt is mad because I told her last. Just cut the drama and tell everyone at one time."

"Nice plan."

"Can you help me plan it?"

"Help you?"

"Help Vickie rather," he corrected.

"Oh ghee. We will discuss the details and your vision tomorrow if that is okay. Something tells me this is going to be a lot of work," I said.

"Sure, we can discuss it tomorrow. It will not be that big of a deal just close family and friends. We can even do it at the house if it makes it easier."

"Randall every time you say no big deal it turns out to be enormous, gigantic, and overboard."

"Simple D," he reiterated.

"I am holding you to it."

"You are the one doing the planning so whatever you do is what I will have to roll with."

"So what is the game plan from there?" I questioned.

"I may propose."

"Shut up. You play too much." I knew he was lying but it made me giddy anyway.

"If I did what would you say?"

"Get out. Stop playing. Shut the front door."

"Is that what you are saying now or what you will say then?" he laughed.

"Both."

"How disappointing. I was expecting a yes. I would even take a maybe. A let me think about it. Even a why did you embarrass me in front of all these people would work," he admitted.

"Considering you are not going to propose, we have no issue."

"Who said I was not?" his tone was serious.

"No matter how you are in front of us you are not really an attention getter. You would not want that much attention. Besides, it is your day. You do not want to mix the two occasions. Keep the main thing the main thing," I advised.

"It will be a combination event. A coming out and engagement party. You are the main thing."

"Naw. I don't think I would be prepared. Besides, what I wear to your coming out party would be different from what I would wear to our engagement party. Not to mention, you said your close friends and family and since mine will not be there that would cause a conflict and a commotion all of its own. You have not met Mama Rose; therefore, you cannot propose. Oh, and the main thing, you have no idea what kind of ring I want."

"Wow. That was a lot. Let me see if I can address all of your concerns. I must warn you, you may want to always wear something proposal ready because you never know when I may propose. This maybe the best time to invite your mother and family. Let me go ahead and kill two birds with one stone. You are right I am not that impressed with attention; so, I am easily able to take it off me and direct it towards you. Lastly, I do believe you have mentioned on several occasions the size and clarity of the rock. All I need to know is the shape and design. If you do not like what I pick out then we take it back and you can pick out what you want. The ring is the least of my concerns. You can have one for each day of the week and every hour of the day as far as I am concerned. Right now the biggest concern is me getting up the courage to ask you and I am constantly praying you say yes."

"You haven't spoken to my mother," I reminded him.

"We will stop by her house tonight. What is your next excuse?"

For some reason I felt the seriousness in his tone. It made me happy and uneasy all at the same time. I asked a series of questions. "How do you know this is what you want? How do you know when you are ready? How do you know it is not too soon? Are you ready to change your life this drastically and this quick?"

He replied, "I have a friend that is closer than any brother. When I talk to my friend, He leads me and guides me along life's narrow way. When I speak to Him He speaks back to me. He tells me what direction to travel. He speaks to me in a still small voice. I have bowed down. I have kneeled and I have laid prostrate. I have spent numerous hours with Him. You are aware of it and my travail has not been in vain. He has spoken to me. He has changed my heart. He has told me the plans He has for me. These plans include you. Danielle, He has never steered me wrong."

He continues, "It is very important for you to understand men have a hard job. However, when it is the right time and the right person it is clear and evident. There is no need in stressing over it. No need in prolonging it. I just need to make it happen. I have to make sure you are ready and have received the same conformation. I am not waiting on me. I am waiting on you. I am ready. We could marry today. Though, you are absolutely correct. I have not to spoken to your mother. I need to ask her for your hand in marriage. I need to do a lot of things. However, I cannot right now. I have to wait for you to grant me permission. Once you do this, all things are possible. Just as spontaneous as I am on simple things is the same way I am on a larger scale. You know me well enough to know how I operate."

"Yeah you do everything big. The city may shut down for the proposal."

"I had not thought of that but I can make it happen if that is your wish," he said. "I was really saying I do nothing until I get confirmation from God. I have prayed and prayed and His word has not changed. You know I am a praying man and I come from a praying family. I have a praying best friend. Why on God's green earth would I not choose the praying woman of my dreams? You are well aware God hand delivered you to me at His house. There is no way in hell I will let you slip away. I will not give you the opportunity to lose interest or for the enemy to come in. No way. He comes to kill, steal and destroy. It ain't happening."

He slowed down, pulled over to the shoulder of the highway and turned his hazard lights on. I instantly got nervous. *What is he about to do?* Years ago, I would have thought a guy was putting me out. Normally my mouth would have warranted it. Right now, I had no clue what was going on. I began to sweat. I felt my hands shaking. I put them under my thighs. My heart was racing. If he looked at me, he could see it throbbing in my neck. I could not speak because my throat welled up. I tried to distract my thoughts. His family was a praying family; little did he know, so was mine to a degree he could only imagine. We somehow managed to keep it concealed. I thought of my parents, grandparents, my Sissie, and my niece. He looked straight ahead. I tried to look at his face. He leaned his head down. I leaned down with him.

"Are you okay?" I asked.

He cracked his knuckles. I took that as a yes. At least five minutes passed. He was so, so weird, emotional, strong, commanding, surprising, sensitive, and Godly. *What is happening? What triggered this?*

The Range Rover shot by us. His phone rang at the same time as mine. I assumed King was calling him and Keith was calling me. He handed me the phones. I did not reach for either of them. They both rang back to back to back. When I looked up lights were approaching us backwards. I reached to open the door. He pulled my arm.

"I got it." He placed the car in park and got out. All three of them were out of the truck. Keith and King were facing me and his back was to me. RJ walked over to the other side of the truck as if he knew it was a grown folk's conversation.

I got paranoid. *Did he tell me all of that to prepare me for something bad? He is not going to dump me or propose right here on the side of the road.* They walked in front of the truck. RJ walked in front too but on the opposite side. I could not see anything. *I wanted to get out too. What was going on?*

He finally came back. Keith leaned over the driver side window, "Are you good?"

I shrugged my shoulders. I did not know what was going on.

"Ms. D I try to let you have a date on your own and then I have to back up on the highway to see what is going on. Do you know how much of a troublemaker you are?" King said.

"Move King," Randall shouted.

RJ leaned over and kissed my cheek. "Thank you sweetie," I said.

"Pick another name for him," Randall said without looking but opening his door as he sat back in the driver's seat.

RJ stretched over me, playfully punched his dad in the head and then pounded him.

"I am not leaving until you pull off. We will be right behind you. Let this top up. Now," King ordered. All three of them walked back to the truck. King did not get in. He stood on the outside waiting on his boss to follow his instructions.

"I heard you," Randall shot back.

"Let it up," King growled

Once he let the top up King got in the truck. He took my hand and laid his head on the steering wheel. "Danielle your pop up today and the soliloquy the other day was confirmation whether you know it or not. I asked God and prayed for confirmation and in no less than two hours later you showed up and confirmed what I was questioning."

"After that there is no way I will lose you. Call me a stalker if you want. All I know is my child adores you. My best friend has given me his blessing and my staff is delighted. Although, I am not sure if they are happy because I now have something to keep my interest and not bother them or if they are truly happy for us. And King." He paused. "Well he is being King. He may seem hard but he is actually challenging you to make sure you are the right one. If you were not you would have been long gone by now. I think you would have jetted if your intentions were ill. I never thought that of you but it is their job to protect me from both seen and unseen danger. That is what I pay them to do."

"You know how I feel about you. You make me weak. I am not sure if I want you to witness me fight. You will definitely have to be seated towards my back. Otherwise, I cannot stand strong looking at you," he paused. "It is no mystery that I will go out of my way for you. You do not have to ask. I do it because I want to. You want to know why I cannot sleep. It is because my mind is wired up thinking about you. Danielle, I cannot live without you. I get tongue tied when you show up. My palms get sweaty. I am jittery. I see your face and my heart melts. The smell of your perfume challenges my strength. Sometimes when I walk into the sanctuary, I cannot contain myself. I cannot think clearly and it is hard for me to focus. There are even times when I do not know what Hunter preached. I find myself worrying about you all day. Wondering if you are okay. If anything is troubling you. Are you sleeping? Are you working? What is on your mind? It crushes me inside. I need you to be with me, beside me, laying with me to take my worries away. Spend your life with me and grow old."

"Wise," I said correcting his old statement.

"Whatever you call it just do it with me. I want to give you the world on a platter. Snap your finger and it is done. That is not you. This challenges me. You could care less who they say I am or how they perceive me. You see ME. You see the Randall underneath the robe, the boxers and the gloves. You see the true me behind the jewels, the fast cars, and designer things. You see me transparently. You know the real me. The person I will be forever. Not the person I am for the moment. You are the only woman I have loved and the only one who has loved me back."

He did this all the time. He said a mouth full. He did not speak sincerely to me often. Most of the time he avoided it and blogged his feelings to the world instead. But when he did, he always laid it on heavy. He did everything big even big conversation.

He was surely someone else when it was just the two of us. Behind closed doors and behind the keyboard, he opened up. He was comfortable being sensitive and affectionate. I loved it. He had no shame and he did not hold back. I knew I wanted to grow old with him too.

We rode back in silence. Once we got to my gate, he spoke, "Sorry. I should have asked before we pulled up. Do you need anything or want anything before I leave you?"

"I am good."

We reached my driveway and he helped get my belongings out of the car. As we walked to the door he asked, "Do you want me to come in?"

I did but I knew it was not going to be good. We both were already emotional. "You better go home. The baby has already asked if you are coming home," I replied.

"Out of the mouths of babes. We will have a talk," he said referring to him and RJ then he shook his head.

"Leave him alone. He is new to this too," I reminded him.

"You sure take up for him a lot."

"Someone has to when you have a mean and commanding father."

"I think that is the definition of father. Thank you again for coming."

"You are welcome." He did not address my comment. I truly thought he was rough on the kid.

"For some reason I feel like it was not for me but I will take it."

"Call me when you get in the car."

He kissed my forehead. "I miss you already. I can't wait to see you in the morning."

"I love you."

"I love you too DJ," he said as he ran down the steps.

Sunday

He called me a little before six. I answered groggily, "Hello Randall."

"Good morning my love."

"Are you at church already?" I asked.

"Not yet. Who do you want?"

Confused by his question, "Huh?"

"Do you want King or Keith?"

"UGH?"

"I take it that is Keith?"

"It does not matter. Surprise me."

"I love you DJ. I will see you soon. Bring all of your things. We will be spending the day together. Work is permitted. I am proud of you for not working yesterday."

"Thanks man. I love you too." I had not told a guy I loved him in so long it felt like foreign words out of my mouth. The feelings felt strange also but they were real. I laid there thinking of him. The thought of the party danced in my head and it hit me. *This means I was going to meet his family and I think he is expecting to meet mine.* Not that I was hesitant either way but I was afraid this relationship was getting serious. Eight hours ago I was spending time with his son and now he was asking me to arrange to meet his parents and for him to meet Mama Rose. *I am not sure this is a good idea. Getting serious leaves room for getting hurt. Been there...done that. I still have the baggage and bruises to show for it,* I thought to myself.

After sulking, I finally got up and got dressed. My home phone rang to let me know someone was at the gate. I did not say hello. I picked up the phone and clicked open the gate as I gathered my things. I had considerably more things than normal. With my bag of clothes, computers and plans in tote, I walked to the front door. The Maybach was waiting as I opened the front door for Keith.

When I walked into the church, I could see him with his back turned in my peripheral vision. I intentionally did not go in his direction but he was like a bloodhound and noticed my scent. Seconds later, I could hear his feet moving in a running motion behind me.

"Ms. Danielle."

"Deacon Washington," I said without turning around.

He caught up to me, "Good morning."

I slowed down, "Good morning," I returned the greeting.

"Do you need an escort?"

"I would love one."

"What about a hug?"

I started giving him a church hug. In the midst, he pulled my waist closer and laid his lips on my neck. I looked up to see who was watching. Then it dawned on me that it didn't matter. He was not married and neither was I.

He held me tight and long despite having seen me eight hours ago. His face was to the wall. He was not able to see the faces staring at our embrace. "DJ," he whispered.

"Yes," I answered.

Barely above a whisper, "You smell good. Let me have you, please."

"You can't. I am taken."

"I am sure I can fight him for you," he said joining into the impromptu role-play.

"Do what you do but I doubt it." He walked me to my seat and left Keith by my side. Ten minutes later, he arrived to his position. He came in from one direction and Trevor came in from another. They always came in together timely. I looked at each of them observing them closely. It was amazing. Randall looked the same every day. He kept the same expression all day. His face was stern and serious. I looked at Trevor and he always looked the same. It did not matter if he was wearing a white tee or a three-piece suit. From joking with his friend to preaching on Sunday mornings, he was the same person. I looked at Keith next to me for so long until he looked back and asked what was wrong. I was making him nervous. He repositioned himself in the chair and looked around the room to see what had me deep in thought. Eight hours ago, King and Keith were on a boat wearing shorts, flip-flops, talking trash, laughing, and having fun. Now, here they stood, expressionless, serious, with their faces cold as stone, on duty and on point. They looked the same as they always did. Not a smile or a tooth to be seen. There is nothing you could do to either of them to expose a smile.

I was in observance mode. Keith asked me again, "Are you ok?"

I nodded. I was busy watching all of them especially Randall and remembering our conversation from last night. I was wondering if I could do this. This was the beginning of his journey. He was going to preach one day. My heart knew it even if his did not. *Will I be able to handle it was the million-dollar question.* I knew this life all too well. I knew it was work and sometimes it did not end well. I watched everyone in the church with this in mind. When service ended, I was still in a zone. I prepared myself to leave then realized I did not have a car. I walked back inside the door. "Keith, I am ready."

"Give me a minute to let them know we are gone."

Sure enough, Randall came running around the bend, "She is riding with me," he stated.

"Not today," Keith said and directed me out of the door with his hand on my back.

"DJ."

I turned my head.

"We have some things we need to discuss," Keith informed him.

Keith was not normally this abrupt and stern. I was glad to see he had it in him. He was serious and he was not about to change his mind.

Deacon Washington walked up to me, "What is going on? What is wrong?"

"I am good," I said. *Was I?*

"Can you wait for me?"

I looked at Keith.

"I am asking you?"

"You can send King with us if you want to do something," Keith said sternly.

He summoned King to come where we were. When King arrived, Keith spoke again.

"We will see you at the house."

I leaned in and kissed Randall on the cheek.

Once got into the car and Keith said, "What's up Ms. D?"

I knew exactly what he meant. "Nothing. I was just observing. A lot goes on the naked eye does not see but I can. I find myself asking is this the life I want to live? A life with you always around? Church is a major principle in our lives. His best friend is a preacher and he could possibly become a minister one day. I am checking out the view. It is a lot to take in when you look at the bigger picture. You do not just get the nice handsome guy. A ton of responsibility comes with him. You two, for example, come too. Along with horrible eating habits and behavioral traits which have been learned over years. Then you have practices, training, and conditioning that is out of the ordinary. This is huge. He is huge. This is on a grand scale. I just want to make sure I am okay with it before I go another further as the old folks say."

"No worries."

"Nothing is wrong. Everything is right. So right. Too right. Like a Cinderella dream coming true. He is my Prince Charming," I said holding back the tears.

King smirked.

I turned around from looking out the window, "What's up?"

"He said something similar," King confessed.

"Extremely similar." Keith co-signed.

"What do you mean?"

"He feels like you are his angel sent to rescue him. Does he call you Angel?"

"No," I answered confused because he has never called me Angel.

King sat back in his calm stance as always reading the paper he brought in the car. "He calls you Angel," he mumbled.

I looked over at Keith surprised. "Yes he does. Now you have referred to him as Prince Charming."

"Right," King mumbled as I turned around. "It's pathetic," he said like a grumpy old grandpa before I could say anything.

"It is love," I barked at King.

"Umm hmm. Love doesn't love anybody but don't listen to me."

Keith looked in his review mirror but King did not look back, "Let's get to business. What was up with last night?"

"I don't know. He wanted to talk."

"Yeah," King muttered as if I was lying.

"King, what's the deal?"

"With what Ms. D?"

"Is he ready? When are you going to schedule? How do you think he will do?"

"Not quite. I could put him in there but he is not one hundred percent ready yet."

"What is he missing?"

"Something I cannot give him, only you," he said seriously.

"I am not giving him that."

"No. Not that. Confidence," King quickly clarified.

"Why do you think?"

"I know it," he stated.

"How do you know?"

"A student is not above the teacher. He who is fully trained will be like his teacher. Physically I would need a week or two as long as I can get his mind where I need it to be."

"So what do I need to do?"

"I need him to stay calm. Keep telling him you love him. Let us know immediately if there is an issue we need to discuss. We are all going to have to work together. This first fight will be the hardest. Then the other fights will be easier. He needs this. He will never admit it but he does."

As we entered the house, "Ms. D do you need anything?" Keith asked.

Me being me, I had to talk trash but ultimately I did not need anything. They stayed for half an hour to confirm I was good. When they left, I laid across the couch and checked emails. By the time he showed up, I had already drifted off to sleep. I heard the alarm but I did not wake from my sleep. He touched my feet to gently wake me. I was excited when I saw him. I thought *I could get used to this life.* He had a few bags when he arrived. *I know doggone well he was not at the grocery store by himself. What was he thinking?* King was going to handle him. I am sure of that. I rolled over, "Hey you."

"Did you tell the ladies dinner tonight?"

I was not sure if I did or did not, "I will text them now. What time?"

"Five. I will be outside. Do you need me?"

"No. What are you doing?"

"Lighting the grill."

I laid right back down as if nothing had happened. At five, the house was full. Considering I did not wake up until about four fifty I was not quite myself yet. I went into the bathroom to change my clothes and wash my face. When I heard the noise from Sade, I emerged from the bathroom.

She wanted a full tour. I could not be a guide because I did not remember the details of the house. We needed RJ here for the tour. Since he was back with his mom, we had to figure our way through the maze of rooms ourselves. When we entered Randall's room, everyone was in awe.

"Why were you in the other room?"

"I think that is my room. I do everything in there. I don't really go in his room."

"Why not?" Leigh asked.

"Umm, it may get dangerous," I replied honestly.

We all laughed.

As we ate, he spoke as if he was making a formal announcement, "I was thinking of having a white party. It will be a white affair. It is similar to a coming out party but more like an announcement party. Sade before you ask, it is a fighting announcement. I have asked Dani and Vickie to spearhead this project but I am sure they will need a committee. My plan is to provide the guest list and write the check. With this team, I do not think it will be that easy for me. Does anyone have any suggestions?"

The masses began to speak. He looked at me and Vickie suggesting we take notes. We had no idea the conversation was going to disturb dinner. We went over the plans for the party. A few hours passed with the discussion. Then King came out with a cheesecake. He brought over my own special piece from Harold and one for everyone else. I knew it was mine because it was decorated with roses just for me.

I looked over at Randall and said, "Your little narrow tail gets on my nerves. You think you are so slick."

"Narrow? I got your narrow woman," he laughed.

"Really?"

"I am two hundred pounds of twisted steel coming at you like a freight train at one hundred and fifty miles per hour."

"Correction two hundred and ten point one pounds," King clarified without ever looking up from his cheesecake.

"I hope it is strong and hard like twisted steel and you bring it like a freight train because the track is delicate and long. You may want to up your weight to gain an extra three pounds." The room went silent.

"Whoa," King finally yelled. "She got you dawg. I hope you can handle it. I think that was the queue for us to exit."

Everyone begin to pack up.

"Two hundred ten point one pounds Danielle. Get your math right," he shouted annoyed.

"I stand corrected. However, is it coming at one hundred and fifty miles per hour, hard, long, and strong? On the other hand, it is more like MARTA instead of a freight train. Refurbished steel going at a maximum speed of thirty five miles per hour making frequent stops."

"The bed is just a few steps away Danielle let's go see and you can publically report back. That is if you can walk that far afterwards."

"Why we got to go that far." I moved everything off the table to the floor with one sweep of my arm. "Here you go."

"Kids are in the room," Leigh said while Keith confirmed.

"Y'all need some bad," Sade said shaking her head as if we disgusted her.

"Bye, we are gone," Paige kissed me on the cheek, which was unusual behavior for her.

"Handle your business Uncle Hooks," Sade replied and gave him a high five.

"Uncle Hooks and Auntie D better pick this paper up off the floor and let that be that," Paige said sounding like my mama.

"I will be standing outside the honeymoon suite waiting on the sheets and if they are thinking about it I may not leave now," King exclaimed.

I looked at Randall, "Is he going?" I abruptly asked.

He smiled a confirming smile while I rolled my eyes, "Baby we will talk about it later. King, you and Keith can go stand right outside this door. Will a table cloth do for now?"

"Bye man. Leave her alone," Keith said. "I have a chastity belt attached so I am not worried. She is an angel now and she better still be one in the morning."

King looked at me and pointed directly in my eye as he backed out the door. "I am watching your levels. Let one rise. I am kicking both of your tails. Mark my words."

We lay on the dining room table and talked as we listened to 104.1. We fell asleep arm in arm. After two hours or so, I woke up and nudged him, waking him from his sleep. "Are you ready to take me home?" I asked.

"No, I was hoping you would move in and that way I never have to leave you."

"You know Trevor will not allow that."

"Do we have to tell him?"

Now, he was going so against the grain, "Yes silly," I laughed.

"Let me handle Trevor."

"I think you will lose."

"Do you and Vickie need anything else from me other than a check?"

"I will view everything tomorrow and update you."

"Are we good for Saturday?"

I had no idea, "What is happening Saturday?"

"The party."

"Boy stop," I bared rolling my eyes.

"What?" he asked.

"You know this cannot happen Saturday. Don't push me," I said calmly.

"You can do it for Saturday?"

I rolled my eyes at him a second time.

After dropping me off he called Trevor. "Tre, what's the deal for tomorrow?"

"Nothing I can think of. What's up?"

"Can you and first lady roll with me tomorrow?"

"Let me check with her. What's up?" he asked again.

"We will talk tomorrow."

He then called Sade, "Hey baby girl. What are you doing tomorrow?"

"Is this a trick question?" She asked with suspicion because everyone knew Sade did not have a real job. She was like Tommy from Martin.

"No, meet me at the gym at ten."

"Cool." He must not know I am single and ten is too early for me. I will try my best.

"Do not tell DJ," he stressed.

"It will cost you for me to lie to Auntie."

"I am not worried about the cost. Besides, I did not ask you to lie. I said do not tell. There is a difference."

WEEK 24
Monday

At five AM, my phone rang. I reached for my cell but realized it was my house phone ringing. "Hey," I answered.

"Babe, are you still sleeping?"

"Yeah, I guess I was."

"Are you sick?"

"No."

"What is wrong?" he asked instantly panicked. "Do you need me to come over?"

"I stayed up late trying to figure out all these details for your party. Now my head hurts."

"I thought something was wrong with you. Call me once you get situated." *Girls* he thought.

"Babe, I love you."

Her transparency and confession melted his heart. This was the reason he planned today. The love was mutual. "DJ, I love you too," he felt his heart racing as he spoke the words to her.

In my car, I checked my messages to see what the day had in store. I arrived at work by the time I finished checking all of the voice messages. I called Randall from my office.

He answered breathless, "Babe, I am still running. I will call you in a little while. I have an extremely booked schedule today."

"I will see you at the gym," I said. I could not help but to feel as if he was blowing me off.

"Have a good day," he ended the call. When ten o'clock arrived, surprisingly, everyone was prompt. They all parked in the back of the gym. "Let's meet in my office. Vickie can you get everyone what they need." After everyone was settled with coffee and water, he took a seat. Keith, King, Sade, Trevor, and First Lady were all present.

"I guess you want to know why I called you in today," he sighed nervously. "We have a big shopping day ahead of us. I think you all are fully aware of how I feel about Ms. Rose. I have known her almost six months. During the majority of this time, I was legally married. I know that does not seem like a long time but I have known her long enough to know how I feel about her. I think my feelings are obvious to everyone. She drastically and completely changed my life. I cannot explain it. I know it is too soon but I want to be prepared. I want to show her how much I love and need her. I want to marry her. No, I am going to marry her," he corrected himself. "I do not know when but I am. Honestly, I have no idea what I am doing. You take me to a car lot and I can pick her out a car. I can hit the mall and pick out a pair of athletic shoes for her but I am not sure I can pick out the perfect ring. I want to look today and get ideas. I thought all of us together would be a perfect combination. I am nervous and excited all at the same time. I have no idea how much to spend. I need help," he said looking at Gabe. "This is a secret and it should not leave this room. What we do today will remain with us until she receives the ring," his tone was authoritative.

"I do not plan to propose tomorrow but I want to be prepared when I do. If it takes me a month, six months, or a year at least I will have the ring. If I have to carry the ring in my pocket every day, I will. This may sound silly, stupid, or premature but indulge me and do not judge me. I may not buy anything today but I do want to get an idea of what I should be looking for and what my budget should be."

"You are setting a budget?" Trevor asked as if it was unheard of.

He answered reluctantly, "I do not know what to expect."

"Money should not be an object RW if you love her," First Lady said and glanced at Pastor. He got the message loud and clear. He disagreed but was wise enough to pick and choose his battles. This was one he decided to pass on.

"RW, what I think she is saying is the cost is nothing compared to the rewards. Yes, we want to be mindful of the cost but you want to make her happy within reason while remaining a good steward."

"I do not think Uncle Hooks will have a problem there." If it were left up to Sade, Danielle would have a diamond mine on her finger. What she could not understand was why Uncle Hooks thought he could trust her with such a large secret.

The room was quiet for a second. "Do you all think I am crazy?" he asked.

"No, not at all. We know you are insane," King replied laughing at all the nonsense.

Randall looked around the room and made eye contact with everyone there. "I am ready when you are." They went to the mall looking at sizes, clarity, shapes, and brands. They looked at Cartier, Verriao, Scott Kay, Tiffany, David Yurman, Tacori, Simon G, Christopher, Michael B, and more. They left the mall deciding she might be interested in a one of a kind design or something from the Apparel Mart so they headed over there and then to Solomon Brothers.

The consensus was to purchase something she could take back if she did not like it. "If she tells me what she wants we can always have it made. For now, I think we are only getting ideas. If I run into something I am crazy about I will get it today and return it if I have to. If I see two or three maybe we will get them all and make a decision later," *or keep them*. He thought to himself.

They all knew he had no control with his spending. This was going to be an interesting adventure for him. They could see his enthusiasm. It was as if he was purchasing a car for himself. Most guys dislike this part of the ordeal. They have to try to figure out what the girl wanted and then spend their life savings or finance a piece of overpriced jewelry before the privileges came. First, a guy had to ask her parents for her hand then nervously and anxiously determine the right time to propose. So many choices. Picking the right time, choosing the right location but most of all the right words and sentiments. Then they would hope she says yes.

He had not thought that far in advance. All he wanted to do right now was look. He had a lot of things going on in his life but he still wanted to be prepared for the moment. Everything was going good and he prayed it continued. He really felt like this proposal was going to be spur of the moment. Not the way he preferred. He would like to have the ring baked in the cake or lasagna for the memories but he knew he was not going to be able to do it.

It was now late afternoon and Sade asked, "Uncle Hooks do you plan on feeding us? If not I will be in the food court."

"Thank you baby," First Lady said.

"You all know who we are with. You have to be prepared not to eat," King stated.

"Sorry, I forgot I was with the humans. What do you all want to eat?"

"I will take a fried bologna sandwich right now. I know Pastor loves those," First Lady Gabe said with Pastor and Sade high fiving.

"Dang, y'all. It is not that late. Pick something my treat," he said with annoyance in his voice.

"You are definitely treating us. I had to get up early this morning, lie to Auntie, and then hang out with you all day looking at jewelry that is astronomically high, gaudy, too shiny, and you thought you were not going to feed me? And you are going to gas up my car and please know I am turning in overtime if we go past five o'clock buddy."

He looked at First Lady Gabe and asked, "Do I have to take the niece too?"

She laughed, "RW, they do not go anywhere. You get them too."

"Tell me about it," Pastor said.

First Lady was always quiet, meek, and reserved but today she snapped her neck, "Watch it Tre."

"Baby I am just saying. Sade and Danielle are practically the same person. So RW had better get used to it. It is funny to me."

"Yeah, Trevor," Sade said sarcastically. She knew she was out of line calling him Trevor. "Everyone tells us we are just alike. Twins to be exact. I do not think so. She is a nerd and so is her boyfriend and now I am stranded with him, his best preacher friend, his sidekick, and King Kong. First Lady let's hit the food court."

Randall pushed Sade like a little kid, "What do you want to eat girl?"

"Can you go to Benihanna's?" She asked Hooks while looking at King.

"I think we will be fine," King said.

At lunch, Randall's phone rang. He motioned shh. "Hey babe."

"Hey. Did I catch you at a bad time?"

"Never a bad time. What's going on?"

Sade motioned, "Ugh."

"Ugh," Dani moaned.

He laughed aloud.

"What's funny?"

"Hold on babe," he muted the line. "Sade she just said the same exact thing and I bet she made the same motion and facial expression you did."

Unmuting the line, "Okay babe. What's wrong?"

"Nothing. It's a manic Monday."

"What can I do to help you?" He stood up to walk away from the table with King walking behind him.

"Fly me across the country to make sure this Hotel is what I have envisioned before they prepare for an opening. Otherwise, nothing babe. How is your day?"

"Honestly babe, I am covering a lot of ground but I am not sure I am making any progress."

"How can I help you?"

"Marry me and tell me what ring you want so I can go pay for it."

"Ahh rings. No single solitaires. I am not found of round stones and I do not care for the vintage look either."

He ran back to the table quickly and quietly got everyone's attention. Then he repeated her, "So you do not like single solitaires, round stones or the vintage look? What do you like?"

"I like colored stones, big, huge, white gold or platinum. I like three stones and I love the Halo look. Three stones are nice and tension settings are always good. I am sure Tiffany's has something I would like. There is nothing greater than getting a blue box."

He repeated it. He motioned for Sade to write. "I was just kidding. Nevertheless, let me make sure I have this straight. You do like colored stones, big, huge, white gold, platinum, three stones, whatever the halo look is, tension settings and Tiffany's. Did I get all of that?"

"Yes you did. Good job. Are you taking notes or something?"

"So basically, I need to cut what I am doing short and head over to Tiffany's?"

"No you do not have to do that," she giggled.

"Just out of curiosity should I know what tension or halo means?"

"Good question. Tension is just that. The stone is protected in what they call a tension setting. Most of the settings at Tiffany's are Chanel setting where they sit on prongs. Tension will not sit on a prong. Halo is a huge stone surrounded by smaller stones. You are so nice and funny pretending as if you are interested in this stuff."

"I am interested."

"About as interested as a pig at a luau."

He gave up my laugh, which always made me happy. "Really. I am seriously interested. I have to run. Can I call you later? I need to make a few calls quickly."

"Great. Thanks."

"For what?"

"Cheering me up."

Everyone at the table was looking at him. He shrugged his shoulders, "What did I do?"

"You laughed. It makes me happy when you laugh. I know you are happy."

He dunked his head and smiled from ear to ear. He spoke very soft, "I love you D. I hope your day gets better."

"I love you too Randall. I will see you later."

She hung up but he was still in motion as if he was talking. He finally barked orders, "Sade get Leigh on the phone right now." He called Vickie.

"What's wrong?"

"Do what I told you to do," he thought of Dani. *Am I always telling people what to do?* Sade rolled her eyes but made the call. "Vic, get a pen," he barked.

"What am I asking Leigh?"

"Can she talk right now?"

"Yes, Sherlock. What am I asking?"

"What hotel is Dani upset about?"

Sade asked Leigh and then replied, "The Smyth Royale."

"Where is it?" he asked Sade. Then responded, "Never mind," to Sade but ordered, "Vickie please call Leigh at Danielle's office right now. Make sure she can talk." He counted, "Make reservations for eight to arrive there Wednesday night. DJ, Leigh, King, Keith, Paige, Sade, you, and Me. Find out what the problems are and the hotel's agenda. Call me back. We are at the mall right now. Tell me what I need to buy. I have no idea how I am going to get her away from work much less out of the country for three days. I may have to have Sade pack a bag for her. Call me back with the details. Leigh and I will have Danielle and everyone else will follow."

"Leigh, Vickie is about to call you. Uncle Hooks wants her to make reservations for us to travel." She hung up the phone and said to Hooks, "Sade is not doing any more of your dirty work. You are on your own." *It was a stretch for her to keep this from Auntie.*

"That is fine. You can stay here without us," Hooks replied.

"You make me sick."

"I thought you would change your mind."

"What's up with the hotel Deac?" Hunter asked.

"She has two that have been a problem. One is complete. She has not arranged to travel there because she did not want to interfere with my fighting announcement. I think I am going to surprise her and take her. I know she will not leave work without Leigh or the kid. I guess the kid tags along too."

"You need some home training Uncle Hooks. I am not a kid," Sade clearly stated before popping a shrimp in her mouth.

He mean mugged her back this time. "Let's get back to business. Now if I had asked her those details last night I bet she would not have answered. What do we have?" he asked. "Read them back. Please." he said in a calm voice trying to minimize his reputation of barking orders and commands.

Sade read the details back. Now they had specifics. "I know she likes wide bands. And I think we all know she likes everything Texas style."

They all laughed. Not that it was funny but it was true. "Well, the first stop is Tiffany's. Her exact words were there is no greater gift than a blue box. Let me go get my baby a blue box. We can look at the rings there based upon the specifications."

"You two are sickening," Sade exclaimed.

"Whatever. Let's look at the pictures." Earlier Hooks instructed Sade to take pictures of all the rings they narrowed down. He wanted to see if he could quickly make a decision based on the photos.

Just then, Sade's phone rang. "Shh," she said nervously.

"It is Danielle," Randall confirmed recognizing her ring tone.

"Hey Auntie. What's going on chick?"

"Nothing girl. Working. What are you doing?"

"About to get out of the bed," she said having no choice but to lie.

"That is lazy, trifling, and ridiculous Sade."

"Okay, I was just playing I am at lunch with Uncle Hooks, First Lady Gabe, and Pastor."

Pastor almost choked and Hooks jumped up almost knocking the floor-mounted table over.

Danielle scoffed, "Shut up Sade."

"Well then," Sade spoke as she threw her hand up to the table. She knew her Aunt would not believe her. This way she did not feel like she was lying to her. "You know where your Boo is honey. How is work?"

"It sucks today."

"What is going on? Do I need to come up there? I will swing by and pick up King Kong, Uncle Hooks and Pastor. We will roll up."

"What kind of tag team is that?"

"King will set them up. Hooks will knock them out. Pastor will pray over them as they lay on the mat defeated."

"What are you going to do?"

"I am taking names."

"You are a sick child. Where did we get you from?"

"Mama Rose said Daddy Rose generated me in a test tube in a foreign country then left me on the door step in the middle of the night. At least that's the lie y'all keep telling me."

"That is not quite how I remember it." It made me think of my father and her father. It made me sad to think Sade and I only had Mama Rose and Sissie to rely on all of these years. We talked for a little longer then hung up. I continued working thinking about Daddy Rose and my childhood. The sudden depression made me decide I was calling it a night at early.

Only a few blocks away from me they went back to the mall as planned. Hooks bought a present from Tiffany's. He had a hard time deciding on a three-row diamond bangle bracelet, a necklace with a diamond heart or a diamond key. He choose the diamond heart with the key attached. The note read 'You hold the key to my heart'. They all agreed upon four rings. Since he could not make a solid choice, he planned to buy them all. Then First Lady stepped up, which is exactly why he invited her.

"RW, let's get the stores to hold them and sleep on it then we can come back on Wednesday to purchase the ring you feel is the perfect one. You are not proposing tonight right?"

"No, definitely not."

"Then let's wait baby. This is so cute. You are so excited. I am excited for you. I want to stop off on the way back and buy you something."

"Great. You know I love you and I am so glad I have you and Trevor's support." They left the others and walked off hand in hand.

They went back to all of the stores. He requested pictures, prices and a copy of the certificates. He was Randall "Hooks" Washington. The stores would have allowed him walk to out with the rings and bring the money back later if he requested. The money was not an issue. Everyone knew that. He wanted to make sure he was picking out what she would like. His desire was for her to be able to look at that ring and recall a magical moment. He wanted this to be the most special event she has ever encountered. This proposal was a onetime chance. He was not going to be able to redo it. This ring had to be the ring of her dreams. He could always change it, upgrade it, engrave it or size it but he wanted it to be right from the moment she saw it. He wanted her to love it. He really wanted to take them all home, look at them himself alone in the dark, and decide. He contemplated asking the jeweler to turn off the lights so he could see what they did in the dark.

At six PM, he realized the humans might want to eat again. He did not realize this would turn out to be an all-day event but he was glad it did. This proposal had to be right. Surprisingly, he decided before they ever left the mall which ring he was going to buy although he did not share his decision with the others. He wanted to call the insurance company and find out about insuring and call Schlossenbloum to inform him of the huge purchase he was about to make. The cost was another reason he did not purchase the ring in front of everyone. He did not want anyone to be able to slip up and tell and he definitely did not want anyone to count his chips and make any mention of the cost. He was about to spend a lot of money. A hundred times more than what he would have spent if he were just Randall Washington instead of Hooks. He tried to rationalize in his mind and justify the cost. Then he made it clear to himself. He loved her. He could afford it and there was no limit to what he was planning on spending. In fact, his budget increased in his head since he left home this morning. The Lambo he desired was now further in the distant. Its allowance was being spent on diamonds or colored stones. If he could spend that kind of money on a car he drove occasionally then surely he could spend that much for a ring for the woman he loved to wear daily.

They sat down for dinner. He thanked everyone for coming and expressed how his mission was accomplished. He did not think he could have pulled off everything within one day without them. He apologized for holding their day hostage but for him it was well worth it. In the middle of his speech, he paused then said, "I knew I loved her from the moment we meet. When she opened her car door and flashed me I knew right then. She knows me and loves me in all three persons, Randall, Hooks, and Deacon Washington. She has helped me to identify them and differentiate between them. She has brought so much light and life to me it is unbelievable. I will never be able to repay her."

After dinner, they stopped by Barnes and Nobles as First Lady requested. Suddenly, all the nerds came alive. Even the ones who would never admit to being nerds, Sade and King. Everyone had a book or two in their hand. First Lady wanted him to pick out a journal so he could capture his thoughts. He seemed to write really well when he blogged. She knew this proposal was important to him and wanted to give him a way to make this a moment for him to remember. Hooks was her friend, her husband's best friend and a man of God. He had been miserable for a long time. She wanted him to be happy. Of all people, he deserved it. Not only did she want to see him happy but also she diligently prayed for his happiness for as long as he had. She was thrilled to be a part of this journey with him and it made her feel special to be included. Along with the journal, she also picked up a copy of The 5 Languages of Love for him. It was another great library addition and a must for his new life.

***

I arrived at the gym around seven. Randall was nowhere in sight. In the meantime, I hit the track. It had been a long day. I put my iPod on and walked as fast as I could. I wanted the troubles of the day to disappear before I saw him.

After two hours, he still was not there so I figured it was time to go home. I packed up and ordered a smoothie on the way out. I drove home in silence feeling somewhat down and thinking about Rose. I went straight to the shower. After I got dressed, I laid on the bed and closed my eyes. As soon as my eyes relaxed, my phone rang his ringtone. "Hello."

"Babe, I missed you?"

He asked a question he knew the answer to. I responded anyway, "I missed you too."

"No, I missed you at the gym."

"You said you had a lot to do today and I was not sure if you were coming back or not."

"I know," he said glad she was gone when he arrived. "Can I come over? I need to see you."

"Sure."

"Open the gate."

"I should have known," I said laughing. *He is always so close yet so far.* I opened the gate. Before I made my way to the door, he was ringing the bell. When I got to the door, I did not see him. Reluctantly and with my hand on my watch, I opened the door. He was standing on the side of the door with his hand held out. There was a single blue box in his hand with a white ribbon.

I leaned on the frame of the door smiling, "What is this?"

He looked at his hand, "A blue box."

"I can see that much."

"You will have to open it to see what is inside."

"Why is it in your hand?"

"Because you have not taken it yet."

"Why do you have it period?"

"You have not because you ask not. Give and it shall be given unto you, good measure, pressed down, shaken together and running over, shall men give into your bosom."

"I did not give you anything."

"You have given me more than you will ever know. Are you going to take the present?" he asked.

"Are you going to come in?"

I took the box out of his hand as he entered the door. *I desperately wanted him to do this every day. I wanted him to come home to me daily. Not just to bring me gifts but to be with me.*

He leaned against the wall after putting the Tiffany's bag down and placing his hands in his pockets. He did everything so effortlessly all while looking sexy doing it. I could not resist. I hugged him. He did not move so I pushed back. I realized I was too close to him. Immediately, he took his right hand out of his pocket. I could hear his bracelet moving. He wrapped his arm around my waist.

"I missed you too. Why didn't you wait for me?"

"I waited for two hours. I did not want to look desperate."

"You would not look desperate," he mocked me.

"Besides, you would not have come over if you saw me at the gym."

"Yes, I would have. All you have to do is invite me or tell me to come over."

I took his hand out of his pocket and held it as he stood in front of me while we stared lustfully at each other.

"You know we have an event tomorrow at the VA hospital?" he reminded me.

"Yes I know. It is on my calendar," I sighed internally.

"I have another thing I want to ask you?"

I had no clue what was next.

"Can you change your schedule to travel with me on Wednesday?"

I did a laugh that sounded more like a choke. "What?"

"I need you to accompany me on a trip Wednesday through Saturday. I will have you back for church on Sunday. I promise."

"Where and why?" I asked.

"You can bring Leigh if you need to. Work is permitted."

"I don't know if Leigh can arrange her schedule. What is this about?"

"Come on DJ. Think about it. It is only two business days. I need you on this."

He convinced me right then. My answer was going to be yes regardless as to what was on my schedule. Although I did need to check my calendar and with Leigh. His words made me weak. All I could reply was, "I'll think about it," I said trying to play it cool. We talked for a few more moments then he departed. I called Leigh and mentioned it to her as soon as he left. She was pumped.

"Sure," she said without giving it any thought.

Why is she so excited? We do not even know where we were going.

Tuesday

I woke up and I knew he would ask again if I could travel with him first thing this morning. Sure enough he did. It was five in the morning and I was already in the car headed to the office. I could not sleep. I was too pumped to sleep. "Hello Randall," I answered. "You are on time as always."

He did not beat around the bush, "Did you speak to Leigh?"

"Yes, I did."

"Have you made a decision?"

"I need to look at my calendar." I am sure he knew I checked it already.

"Great. Let me know so I can make the flight arrangements."

"Hey, where is the destination? What is the weather? Why are you inviting me?"

He let my laugh go. "Well," he stuttered. "The temperature is hot. The destination is unknown to me at this time. I am inviting you because I love you and it is important to me that we go together."

It was no surprise he did not answer any of my questions. But he said it was important for us to go. Maybe he really did not know. I may need to call Vickie and find out where he is going. "Let me check with Leigh and see what she can arrange."

"Would you please?"

"Only for you sir."

"Thank you Mrs. Washington."

I laughed at the sound of being called Mrs. Washington. "You are welcome Deacon Washington."

"Bye sweetheart."

"Will you call me later?" It was a question I asked but more so a reminder since he was not used to dating.

"I always do."

I made it to the office. A dozen things crossed my mind. *There were a few things on my calendar for the rest of the week but nothing urgent. The guys will be glad if I did not show up to the jobsite on Friday. Instead, I thought about asking Sade to deliver donuts in my absence. Then again, that could be a disaster getting her to deliver them at five in the morning. I may have to ask Mikey to make the delivery instead. The most important thing on my calendar for the rest of the week is my stand-in hair appointment. There is no way I am going to be able to make a hair appointment unless I go tonight or leave work early tomorrow and sneak in before bible study. That is going to be difficult to achieve because I need to get my suitcase together before service. Randall knows I do not do this last minute stuff. He is working my nerves. Most of all, I do not even know where I am going.*

When Leigh arrived, I barked like Randall. "In my office now. We need to talk." He was rubbing off on me. I do not know why he did it but it worked for him.

Leigh was antsy. *What does she know?* "Yes ma'am," she replied as she came in with her iPad.

"Okay, what is the deal?" I looked her in her eyes to intimidate her into telling me what she knew.

"I can go. I will accomplish my personal errands tomorrow so I can be packed and ready after service."

"CRAP," I mumbled.

"What?"

"I was hoping you would say no."

"Why friend?"

"I don't know where I am going. This is last minute and I need to tie up some loose ends here."

"Like what?" she asked sincerely.

"The Smythe Royale is still having a hard time getting their Certificate of Occupancy. I need to find out why. I want to dive into this. This place needs to open. They are losing money every day they cannot. Besides the selfish part of me is ready to see the final product."

"You can do all of this over the phone and via email which is why I am going. I will be there to help you. It will be just like we are working from home but home will be next to a pool I hope and nowhere near snow."

"I need to call Vickie," I mumbled.

"For what?"

"I need to get some details from her since he has none. I am sure she is making all the arrangements for him."

Instantly, Leigh shot Vickie a text.

> Danielle will call you. She is trying to get
> information on the trip. Avoid her if you can.

"I'm sure he has no clue. All he knows is to show up."

"Easy for him," I barked.

"Relax D, it will be fun. Besides, you know we could use a vacation."

"Not quite my idea of a vacation considering I do not know where I am going and I will still be working."

"I got you girl. Chill."

I worked all day. I could not get a hold of Vickie and managed to avoid him for as long as I could. He was relentless and called again, "Dani Ro," I answered.

"Hey babe. How are you going to answer once your name changes?"

"I don't know. I will cross that bridge when I get there."

"Get ready."

"Whatever," I rolled my eyes as if he could see me.

"How is your day?"

"It is cool. I am trying to get in touch with Vickie for details about the trip."

"Like?"

"The location for one."

"I do not know the name of the city. The flight leaves at eleven PM tomorrow. Thursday there will be a showing and viewing all day. I do not see why you could not wear whatever you wanted. Something comfortable is acceptable. Friday there will be numerous press conferences so you will need whatever professional suit you choose to be filmed or photographed in. Keep in mind it may be televised. Later that night there is a formal event and I want you to be the star of the show. You are the star of the show," he corrected. "Saturday, we will chill; hang out at the pool and jet whenever you all are ready. I think my business will be done Friday night."

"Humph," I said under my breath.

"What was that for?"

"No reason."

"Yeah it was."

"No it was not."

"We do not keep secrets remember," he reminded me.

"Yeah, I know." *I had a feeling we were going to Vegas and he was publically announcing his return to the ring. If this was the case why was Vickie and I planning this huge party?*

He felt her skepticism but knew it was because of her lack of control. He emailed Vickie right then. Contact Danielle. We need to coordinate a response. I do not want her to have ill feelings that you are avoiding her because I am keeping a secret from her. *I just told her we did not keep secrets and here I am keeping a secret. He felt like crap.*

"D let me have Vickie contact Leigh. May I come take you to lunch?"

"No need. I will see you at three."

"I feel horrible. Let me come."

"No you are good. Everything is okay," I said dryly.

"You did not say whether you would go or not."

"Oh, I am going. We are going rather."

"Great. I am happy to hear," he expressed excitedly. "The trip would be wasted without you. I do not think I would go," he confessed.

"Leigh and I are going," I tried to repeat his excitement.

"Awesome."

"Now where am I supposed to be at three?"

"I will pick you up."

He was prompt as always. His timing today was a little too soon for me. I stepped in the elevator still working as we headed to the Veterans Hospital. I had all my computers and plans with me to continue with my day. Upon our arrival we walked in like a clan coming to war more so than a group trying to encourage the Veterans.

I did what I normally tried to do until he summoned me. I sat in the back working. He gave a nice speech. *Who wrote that?* I looked up a few times and noticed he did not appear to be reading from anything. *Did he memorize this speech? He did not sleep so he had plenty of time to do so. I realized he is a great speaker. I do not get to see this side of him as often as I would like. I could so imagine him in the pulpit. Why doesn't he acknowledge his calling?* After his thirty or forty minute speech, the staff began to bring in boxes of workout equipment.

The guys there were overjoyed. Their reaction touched him. You could see it in his face. No matter where he was in the room, he managed to find me and make eye contact. It made me feel good every time I looked up and saw him watching me. If he was not watching me, I watched him.

I hoped no one else sparked his interest and attention ever again. Then I hoped the same for myself. I did not want to be interested in anyone else. Randall 'Hooks' Washington was the completion I needed.

In the middle of equipment being brought in, he made his way towards me still holding the microphone. While he was speaking, he paused to look me in my eyes and whisper "I love you" then walked away. They could have gotten the defibrillator at that moment because I know my heart stopped.

As his team showed the guys how to operate the new machines, he came and sat next to me and held my hand. I stopped what I was doing and gave him my undivided attention. Surprisingly, King came back and gave us two waters without smarting off.

King asked, "Are you okay man?"

"Yeah, I am good. I am going to stay back here with Danielle. I will let you all work this out. We will be up there when they are ready for autographs."

He held my hand as if I was the one who gave a fabulous speech. "How do you do that?" I humbled myself and asked.

"What?"

"Two things. How did you find me and secondly speak without notes."

He laughed loudly. "Well, I have thought about this for a few days. I did write out a speech. Vickie has it prepared on my iPad but I have it prepared in my mind. Then; of course, I would be able to find you anywhere. It is easy when you love someone. Tre says it is difficult for him to see everyone's face when he is preaching. There are too many people, too much movement, and too many lights. Nevertheless, he knows what location to look for his regulars. Once he spots them, the familiar faces, then he can concentrate. He is no longer nervous. He can continue to flow even if he feels stumped. If he feels like he is not understood he looks to his regular faces and they encourage him with a nod or smile. It is the same thing for me. Once I locate you, I am good. I can keep my concentration," he said as he squeezed my hand.

Why did he always melt my heart? After the autographs, we all piled back up in the Tahoe and left. They dropped me back off at my office. He wanted to stay and ride with me to the gym but King reminded him he needed to train.

Although I knew King was only doing his job, it still upset me. *Was the Champ ever off duty?* I knew Randall was pissed off when he punched the truck at King's order. *He has a problem with those hands punching objects. I am going to ask him if he has he ever hit his wife. Sorry ex-wife. Yeah, I draw and doddle a lot. It is what I do. I guess the same was true for him. However, hitting was different. My question was did he hit people? More importantly, did he hit women?*

I arrived at the gym, walked in and threw my hand up without speaking. King had his back to me as I started up the steps.

"Humph," Randall said.

King thought the same thing, "Ms. Danielle, cat got your tongue?"

"Shut up talking to me," my tone was beyond hash.

Everyone stopped. King and I bickered all the time but they could tell from the tone that this was not our normal bickering moment. This was serious.

"What's with her?" King quickly asked Hooks.

"Damn," Randall said side eyeing King and sighing heavily. "Unwrap the gloves," he demanded in a soft tone.

I heard them both and yelled, "You are my problem King."

Innocently King inquired, "What did I do this time?"

"What don't you do?" Hooks barked at King playing coy.

"Dani, I thought we had a good day?" King said trying to smooth it over.

"You are not paid to think," I roared back.

He was just as startled as everyone else, "What did I do Ms. D?"

"Nothing out of the ordinary," I yelled down the steps as Randall was coming up the steps.

"Why are you mad?" King asked in a tone that suggested he cared.

"You need some home training."

"What do you suggest?" He was sincere as he stood behind his boss in the safety zone.

"Charm school. You need to learn some etiquette. When to speak and when not to speak. Learn how to deal with people and especially people of the opposite sex," I added.

"Sign me up but only if you go too," he mumbled. "Freaking charm school."

"You are so obnoxious and rough around the edges. You need to be polished. Everything in life is not a fight."

He cut me off before I finished, "It is not?" he giggled.

King was ruffling my feathers and he knew I was getting irritated. Randall guided me behind the closed door. "You do understand his decision?"

"No I do not," I shouted in tantrum mode.

"We left a place where there were cameras, reporters, fans, and unfortunately some people whose mental state maybe disturbed for various reasons. One of the reasons is the result of serving our country and another one is from the medication they are put on to cope with pains they have encountered while serving our country. King's job is to make sure no one has a clever idea to follow and harm me. In hindsight maybe it was not the best place to go today." I pouted. "You know it is going to be like this every day," he admitted with regret.

"What is? I am left to be the target?"

He walked away, "King get in here now," he yelled.

"What now?" King asked solemnly.

"Danielle has brought up a major problem."

As sarcasm took over his voice, "I can't wait to hear."

"We left a venue today and protected me and all of us while we were together but we dropped her and Leigh off. We left her unprotected."

King looked at me.

"We can't do that again. Someone could have easily decided they cannot get me so they get her instead. We do not want anyone to be harmed. Definitely not Danielle."

"I am on it Hooks. It will not happen again. Did something happen Ms. D?"

"Oh you mean other than you?" I asked sarcastically.

Randall cut me off and gave me a look which said do not start. "No. It is handled. Thank you King." He knew that was not the original reason for her disappointment but she did have a good point, which needed to be addressed.

"Lace me back up," he said to King as they went down the steps and left me there to throw my temper tantrum alone.

Wednesday

This morning he called at four thirty eight AM, "Hello."

"Hey sweetie."

"Hey babe."

"Are you up yet?"

"Not quite. I am about to get up," I lied.

"Did you sleep well last night?" he probed.

"I must confess I did not."

"Any particular reason why?"

"No, not really. I guess anxiety of being gone for a few days. I am not sure." *I knew why. I did not confess to him but it suddenly laid heavy on my mind that we would never be alone. Yes, we had a few dates without a crew but in actuality how many would we really have? It stressed and troubled me greatly. What if we ever got serious? If we married then what? If we had kids? Did I want to live like this? It was not the paparazzi troubling me. It was his guys. What was going to happen when the paparazzi got involved? How terrible was it going to be? I really did not know what I was getting myself into over the weekend. Was the paparazzi going to be involved? Would I be a key player or remain in the background? Up until this point, my life has been low key. I managed to stay under the radar all these years. I tried to keep everything in my life on the lowest level of drama. I was concerned and worried about this relationship. Right now all I could do was sit back and wait to see how things played out.*

I was deep in thought when I looked at the itinerary and repacked my bags again. It is hard to pack when you do not know where you are going. How do you know what you will need? My itinerary read a formal event. Is that long dress, cocktail dress, or royal gown? I did not know what to do. I had more than I needed in swimsuits although I was not planning to get in the pool because I knew there was a formal event. However, I was surely going to relax by the pool. I packed several suits and television ensembles. I did not know what I needed for his press conference.

I was more stressed about this rendezvous than I should have been. I was going out of town with him. Truth be told, I wanted to be with him.

Literally, be with him. I was not going to and neither could I, but God knows I want too. This was going to be awkward. How was I going to make it through this weekend without being intimate? He did say we had our own rooms. I am sure he will not be able to leave the room without the secret service hot on his tail. This is going to be difficult knowing we are sleeping only a few doors away. I desperately craved and wanted his body when he was across town. How am I going to make it being so close to him? The only way we would ever get close enough to be intimate is if Hooks could pull one of his disappearing acts like he seldom does at church.

It's early and I have gotten myself worked up thinking about him. If I did all of this then how many other women feel the same way I do who and they are not the ones in a relationship with him. Women who see him at the gym, at church, at the grocery store, and at RJ's school. It made me wonder. I hoped to God that he was faithful to me. It would devastate me if he were not. I would never let my guard down again. I pondered on this for longer than I needed to. Then I went back to thinking of just him. My thoughts of him in a suit, him in jeans, him in his pool, him in the ring with no shirt on, him sweaty, him with his arms around me, him on me, and mostly him inside me.

"I have to shake this loose," I said aloud. I took a cold shower. If we were not traveling, I would have placed my head under the water to cool my body down. I needed to lay back down but I could not. I had to go the office.

Leigh had the day off. Therefore, I was on my own and I promised I would not call her. I was going to make it alone until I saw her in-flight then I would bombard her while in the air. I made a heavy assumption that it would be a long flight and I could work. I knew I would have to leave work early today for bible study and I did not foresee him letting me skip even if I was taking off work to support him in his endeavors.

Not to mention I had a lunch date with Mama Rose. I was going to be spread thin today. It was going to be an intense and long day. All I could do was mentally prepare while I drove into the office.

I left before noon to meet Mama Rose. I called Paige on the way. I was trying to get a gauge on Mama's temperature. How was she handling this? Possibly not well.

Paige did not lead into it. Which gave me the assumption Mama was tripping. Then she politely informed me that she and Sade would be picking me up and transporting me to church so they could say goodbye before I left. You would have thought I was going away for a year the way we all acted. It was just a few days.

He called while I was on the way to meet Mama, "Hey Randall."

"Have you left work?" he asked.

"No."

"I just called you."

"I am on my way to lunch."

"What? Is there anything wrong?"

"No, I'm meeting Mama Rose for lunch."

"Can I come?"

"Negative."

Insulted, "What do you mean?"

"I think you are the villain right now. I do not want to subject you to the torture," I answered.

Confident he replied, "I am sure I can handle it."

"Get in the ring twelve rounds and throwing punches is nothing like having lunch with a girl's mama. Her baby girl nonetheless. Umm no."

"Okay, I will talk to you after you finish your lunch."

"Great," *beat down is more like it. Is this trip even worth fighting with my Mama?*

"Good luck."

"See, even you know I need it." I showed up and Mama was already seated. We ordered, engaged in small talk, then she did what she does. She slammed me.

"So who is this character you are going somewhere with?" she asked in that tone.

"Randall Hooks Washington."

"Do not be a smart a**. I know his name. Who is he?"

"He is a friend."

"A friend?"

"Yes ma'am," I said looking down stuffing a piece of buttered bread in my mouth.

"Is that all you can call him or all you will call him?" She stressed the word can referring to his marriage and now divorce.

I felt inferior to her question as if I was a side chick or groupie. "That is all I will call him."

"What does he call you?"

"Dani," I answered although I knew exactly what she meant. Now second-guessing myself. I should have invited him and my Sissie to this debacle.

"That needs to be your last sarcastic response. You are clear on what I mean?" I knew better. Mama Rose did not take no junk. My Mama didn't play the radio baby.

"His girlfriend. I guess."

Her brows furrowed, "You guess? So you mean to tell me you are going somewhere. You do not know where. With someone you call friend but you guess he calls you his girlfriend. Who just happens to be a champion boxer? Cut the bull Danielle."

"Mom, you know the answers to all of these questions."

"You do too. Danielle, I am going to tell you what I do know, and that is I am not very happy about you traveling with a married man."

"He is not married any more Mama."

"Umm hmm. I am not comfortable with it and neither do I like it."

"I know."

"What would your father say?" she asked.

It caught me off guard. Whom was she referring to? My biological father, my spiritual father, my godfather, or God himself. "Who are you talking about?" I said answering her question with a question. *Did it really matter what Rose thought? Who cared?*

"When am I going to meet the boy? After you get knocked up?"

"You will meet him Mama. I am not expecting to get knocked up."

"Who expects to?"

"I am not and neither do I plan to be intimate with him."

"Danielle, you are so out of focus. Most people do not plan to do it."

"Thanks Mama." Little did she know I had been mentally planning to do it with Randall since the day I met him.

"Anytime. Let's bless the food so we can eat."

After lunch, I headed back to the office. I still had a lot of work. Thank God for smart phones, email, and laptops. I called Sade and gave her a run down on what I packed.

She calmly said, "I will be over before church. We can check it out."

"Okay," hearing the disappointment in her voice because of my selections.

Lunch messed me up. Mama held back no punches. I left the office early to have enough time to get myself together before bible study. Paige and Sade arrived to go to church with me since I was going to be gone for four days. To us four days was a lifetime. Hooks was excited to see all of us. Leigh was not present tonight considering I gave her the day off since I abruptly asked her to travel.

"Ladies," he said loudly as we walked in the door.

I looked around to see who heard him.

"Paige, Baby, Sweetheart good to see you all." He hugged each of us and held my hand.

"We came to spend the evening with Sissie since you are kidnapping her."

"I will bring her back in one piece. I promise," he held up his hand as if he was in court.

"She better be one person and not two either."

"Huh?" he asked confused.

"No hanky panky," Paige said in her mother tone.

He looked at his watch. "That will not be possible. Her cycle will be on in about four hours. Babe you may want to prepare for it."

"Ugh. How do you know that?" Sade asked quickly.

"I have to keep up with these things," he answered sincerely.

I quickly interjected, "Not like that before you get that mind of yours started. The watch tells him," I corrected.

"What a dumb invention. I cannot believe you fell for wearing that. I need to have a big girl conference with you," she rolled her neck and eyes at me.

He laughed my laugh then cut it short quickly, "May I talk to you please?"

Oh gee, I thought as we walked to his office. "What's up?" I asked.

"There have been a few changes."

My neck jerked.

"Nothing major. There will be more people traveling with us. We discovered this event is larger than we anticipated. I need more security. I know how you feel about it but proper protection is required. This was just discovered this afternoon." He switched gears and tried to lighten my mood. "Vickie requested the hotel to provide fresh fruit, juice, and smoothies for me and grapefruit juice, pomegranate, tomato juice, and roses for you. Can you think of anything else? We can call them before we get there and make the necessary changes or request."

I shook my head no in disgust.

***

Once bible study was over Hunter covered us in prayer. Keith came to the car to gather my suitcases with Deacon Washington. He suspended his normal Deacon responsibilities tonight. He was so excited to the point it started to concern me. *Why is he so excited and I have no details?* As I said my goodbyes to the girls, he stood right there like the head master taking me off to boarding school and never bringing me back. It was an intense departure. You would have thought I was going to be away for years.

"Auntie don't worry. I will be on a plane right behind you. By the time you get your bags unpacked, I will be knocking on your door. Okay?" Sade said sweetly to cheer me up.

"Okay. I wish," I mumbled.

"I will see you in a few hours," she repeated.

Finally, we left the church heading to Hartsfield Jackson International Airport. I was shocked he did not charter a flight. Keith and King should be proud. I was carrying a zippered cross body bag. My computers were zipped in a cross body messenger bag. I did have my heels on but I had my drivers in my bag and I tested the heels to make sure they fit in my bag in case I had to change. I made sure I did not have anything to cause suspicion at the security checkpoint. I obeyed all the 'transporters' rules.

However, no one gave me a limitation on bags. Therefore, I had quite a few. I had one bag with after five clothes and one bag for shoes. I will pay for my extra bags that is the least I can do. I am sure I will get my hand slapped for pulling out 'my little card'. I remember him saying that the first day we met when he bought me a CD of service.

I didn't talk much on the few minutes of police escorted ride to the airport. Although I did think the escort was a bit much but what else did I expect from him? He was such a humble person but everything he did was way over the top. I held his hand in the car. He laughed and joked with JJ while I sipped a bottle of water.

They cut up the entire ride. Is this what I have to look forward to all weekend long? Leigh was busy texting and checking emails. As soon as he gave me the eye, a text came through with Leigh's name on it.

Are you okay?

Yeah.

Are you sure?

I think the police escort is a bit much and I have no clue where I am going or why?

D, Chill. Live on the wild side sometimes. Let him do for you what he wants to do. A lot of preparation has gone in this spur of the moment trip. ENJOY. It will be well worth it. Trust me. Trust him. He really loves you.

She snapped a picture as I was reading her text. She makes me sick always having that camera. I knew this was going to be a long weekend. Suddenly, I could not remember if I told Mikey I was leaving. I nodded at Leigh in acceptance of her texted request and called Michael.

Before the line rang, I was amazed again. Then again, he never ceases to surprise or amaze me. Randall was truly my knight in shining armor. I saw why there were police escorts. We pulled directly to the tarmac. The guys checked the jet way. Once given the clearance, our bags were loaded under the aircraft and an Airline representative spoke to Vickie, JJ, and King as they exchanged paperwork, boarding passes and identification. The armed officers stood at the car doors. I looked at Leigh and thought *what in the hell have I gotten myself into?*

Everyone exited the car except me, Randall, Leigh, and Keith. Once we were given an all clear, they herded us out and up the steps quickly. Leigh was still taking snap shots while Keith took my bags. *If I had known this, I would have dressed cuter and not comfortable.*

There was some controversy about seating arrangement. Keith was assigned to sit next to me and King with Randall. Or so they thought. Randall shoved them both out of the way sat next to me. I am sure this was King's bright idea to split us up.

"Man go sit down somewhere," Randall said. "You two are tripping if you really think I am going to sit by one of you."

They both looked befuddled. I swear the plane was moving before I had my belt buckled. King and Keith were not even seated and now the two arguing about who was sitting by the window.

King and Keith talked trash during my favorite point in flight, takeoff. It is like a roller coaster to me. It was a cheap high.

"Are you okay?" he took my hand.

"Yes, thank you. Are you okay?"

"Anytime I am next to you everything is perfect."

I smiled, "You are so amazing."

"You have not seen anything yet," he winked.

Out of curiosity I asked, "What is that supposed to mean?"

"You will not let me do the things I want to do for you," he said as he stared in my eyes.

"You do not have to do anything. You have done enough." I closed my eyes with my head laid back on the seat and whispered to myself, "Perfect."

Confused he asked, "What is perfect?"

"The way the pilot gradually increased speed with perfection to lift this Boeing 747 to her purposeful destination. The sky."

"You know about planes?" he sounded surprised.

"I am an engineer." *Duh* I thought to myself really thinking of my father.

"I thought you built buildings."

"I actually do not build anything. I design them. I almost went to work for Lockheed Martin or Boeing to design aircraft. That is where my father worked. He built planes. I thought about NASA too to design space shuttles but the designer inside my heart decided I wanted to design buildings. Planes and shuttles take years of work. I can design a building right here in the air and be done. I can do more with buildings. I can design it, decorate it and re-modify it. A plane is a plane. Once it is done it is done."

"So tell me what you know about planes."

Now he was speaking my other language. The language my father taught me. "This plane in particular is called 'Queen of the Skies'. She is a massive piece of machinery." I went into elaborate details about the aircraft.

"You are the amazing one."

"No, most of it is useless information. Stuff I learn during late nights on the internet. You do know that is what you do when you don't have a life much less a love life."

I spent four years learning whatever I wanted whenever I wanted. The internet was the greatest invention in the world if you ask my opinion. I remember having to use encyclopedias. In fact, I still have them at home. I have my set, Mama's set, Daddy's set, Paige's set, and Sade's set in my office. I always wanted to learn more. Especially when I was broken hearted. While broken, busted, and disgusted all I did was learn. I took this fifty-gallon drum I call a brain and loaded it with five hundred gallons of knowledge. It was either that or go on a drinking binge to ease the pain. I did what I thought was productive. I think it paid off. I have more now than I did four years ago. I am not speaking of possessions. I have more tolerance, patience, long-suffering, and wisdom of who He is and who I am. I have a very different life and I am a completely different person. Because of my years of solitude, it awarded me to be here staring in the eyes of a man I love. In addition, most of all, he loves me back.

I was deep in thought when he spoke, "Hopefully a day will come where you and I will both go to bed instead of staying up all night."

"Yeah, I hope so. Like Hunter said tonight, go to sleep. Stop staying up worrying. I think he was speaking to the two of us. He is such a traitor. Hunter is beginning to be like comedians. They use their friends as punch lines. I swear he is using us as a sermon. Go to sleep," I said sarcastically.

"Together," he squeezed my hand.

Trying to ignore his go to bed together comment I handed him the other half of my earpiece and turned on my iPod. We listened in silence. I realized I still did not know where we were going. I decided I was going to ask him again. I missed the rolling destination on the check in gate since we didn't check in. We missed the announcements from the pilot. I was clueless. I felt like everyone knew except me.

The pilot exited the cockpit and came right over to us. Randall was such a charismatic gentleman. He stood as if he knew exactly where the pilot was coming. I assume he was used to this.

"Good evening Mr. Hooks."

"Good evening. Thank you for transporting us. I have been learning about this aircraft and the takeoff procedures from the love of my life here."

"Great news."

"Danielle Rose this is Pilot Harvey."

"So you know a lot about aircrafts?" he asked.

"Not much. Just a little."

"I hope you two enjoy the flight. Again, Mr. Hooks we are pleased to serve you and your crew these next two flights. Your continued business is greatly appreciated. We should have clear skies and an excellent flight. Let me know if there is anything you need. Good luck to you Mrs. Rose. Enjoy your trip. I hope to see you on the way back home."

"It is Ms. and thank you."

"If Mr. Hooks is as wise as I think he is it won't be Ms. for long."

Even the pilot knows more than I do. I was so unaware. I leaned in, "Sweetheart," I whispered as my lips and tongue touched his ear.

He shivered and squeezed my hand, "Yes babe?"

"Where are we going?"

"You will see in just a few hours. Relax," he said after he got himself back together.

I put my lips on his ear again very seductively and said "Randall, sweetheart, baby, love of my life."

"I thought we discussed this DJ."

"We did."

"So what is the problem and why are you doing this here?" he asked weakly.

"We also said no secrets." That did it. He was officially weak.

He looked intensely into my eyes. "No. Wait. You will not do that to me." His voice trailed off. "It is cheating and a cheap shot. We are on a plane. You are not going to have me messed up the entire flight. I will lay you out right here in the middle of this aisle and make a XXX rated video." He put his lips on mine. "Do you understand me?" He kissed me passionately. "Say DJ?"

"Stop it," King yelled so everyone on the plane could hear him.

Leigh jumped up with her camera snapping photos.

"Danielle?" I still did not say anything. How could I? He was kissing me. "Do you understand me? Behave. We will be there soon. I love you." He took his hand, covered Leigh's lens, and tried to shove his tongue down my throat.

JJ stood up, "Separate," was all he had to say.

King and Keith were amused to death. Randall moved at JJ's instruction unbuckling his seatbelt. JJ never had to speak to him more than once.

"Sit here Leigh," Keith ordered.

"Take five," JJ said. "We can't allow you two sit on a plane without acting like two rabbits in heat," he barely mumbled annoyed.

"We are," Randall admitted.

"Marry her then and you can do what you want to do."

"I am. I do not want to hear of this from Tre either."

"You will hear from him. In the meantime, why don't you propose?"

"I am."

"Do it now," King instigated.

Next thing I knew they were chanting. "PROPOSE. PROPOSE. PROPOSE." They have no home training.

I took my earpiece out to hear clearly what was going on. What in the world? We are on a plane. They were all uncouth. They have no sense at all. He came back up to his seat. "Thanks Leigh. I am good now unless you want to stay right there."

"You can have your seat back friend. Don't listen to those jerks."

He lifted his hand and flicked them off. It included all that were on the plane if they were paying attention.

"Behave," I said in a motherly tone.

"Yes ma'am. Are you going to speak to them about their behavior?"

"All I can do is concern myself about you. I am not worried about what they do." He liked that. It was a statement a mother would say to her child.

As soon as I reached for my laptop, he took his earpiece out and said, "Not now DJ."

"I want to show you something."

"Can it wait until later? No work. Remember we are on vacation."

"You said work was allowed. Besides, as soon as we land and the paparazzi greets us at the gate you will be working."

"No I will not. This is not a work trip for me." He was shocked she still had no idea of what was going on. He was surprised she had not tried to GPS herself to figure out where she was headed. It pleased him to know he could surprise her.

I was a little confused about his response. I pulled my laptop out and loaded up anyways. I looked out of the window while it started up. I could see we were over water. *Dang it. What body of water was this? Why wasn't I paying closer attention? Because King and Keith were busy acting like two year olds.* I do not think I would have been able to figure it out anyway since I didn't know which gate we left from. I bet I could have if I had paid attention to the runway markers. I was not on my game. I must confess this little boxer guy did it to me.

I began showing him some designs I was working on. He asked, "Can you design houses?"

"Can I? What kind of question is that? Do you jump rope?"

"Like a leap frog."

"Alrighty then."

"Let's design one. We have time," he was being slick. He wanted to see her taste without outright asking. He knew the house she lived in. It was a nice house for a single none gold digging woman. Truthfully, it was a real nice house actually. However, if she could have anything in the world what would it look like? He wanted to know. One day this was going to be a topic.

We began to work. I explained as he made request and solicited my opinions.

"What are you two doing?" Keith asked.

"Building a house."

"I do not see any Legos." King sneered.

"Don't respond DJ."

"It is virtual jerk face."

The pilot turned on the seat belt sign. The flight attendants began to take their landing position. I leaned over Randall. "Excuse me. Can you tell me where we are?"

He put his hand over my mouth. "It is a secret to her. Do not tell her please."

"Will do Mr. Hooks. I am sorry ma'am I cannot say."

"DJ, please be patient with me. We are here. You will soon find out. Behave babe."

"Put your hand over my mouth again and see what happens."

He did it again. I licked his hand and kissed his fingers until he had no other choice but to move it. "I thought so," I said with a mischievous grin.

He gave me a look like when I have the opportunity I am going to wear you out. I responded to his nonverbal comment. "I can't wait." He gave up my laugh as I smiled dreaming about it. "This will be the last time you all will kidnap me."

"Kidnap?"

"Yes."

"No one kidnapped you," he replied with conviction.

"Oh yeah. Well what do you call it?"

"I asked you and you said yes. Besides, Leigh is with you so how is this kidnapping?"

"You kidnapped both of us."

"Oh no ma'am, Leigh came of her own free will."

"With you no one has free will. Nevertheless, I am firing Leigh first thing tomorrow."

He laughed, "Leigh gets fired more than anyone I know."

"If you knew like I knew, you would fire King too."

His voice was playful yet stern, "I am not firing King and neither are you firing Leigh." I swear the landing gear was barely on the ground and King was already on his feet. "Let's go."

The flight attendant stood up and opened the door. King was holding my hand. King went down the steps first as everyone else followed. The captain came out and spoke to Randall. I could see them talking when I looked back for him. King rustled me to the limousines that were parked waiting on us. Randall was still on the stairs talking. Leigh got in the car with me while King went back and waited with Vickie to make sure all the bags were loaded and for Randall to complete his conversation.

I could tell Leigh was nervous, "Let me go make sure all of our bags are in the car. I will be right back."

I was sitting in the car by myself. I could see Keith standing next to the window. I cut my phones back on and waited for the emails and texts to come in. Finally, I texted Sade and Paige. To my surprise, they did not respond right back. Then I called Mama Rose and she did not answer. That was strange. I was getting nervous. Maybe they went to dinner. It was unusual for none of them to respond.

Finally, Randall ran to the door and jumped in, "Hey babe."

"Hey."

"I am so excited," he exclaimed.

"Why?" I asked, my voice shaking. I didn't know where I was or my family was at this point.

"I do not know."

After what seemed to be thirty minutes we pulled off. I tried to read the signs to determine my location while GPS was taking an extremely long time to register. Finally, it provided coordinates but no city locations.

My phone changed to the local time confirming it was late in the night wherever we were. I could not see as much as I wanted in the dark and with the tinted windows. We finally reached a strip full of scenery. My face was plastered to the window. I saw a building ahead that looked very similar to a building I designed. It got my attention. Suddenly, we pulled in.

"OH MY GOD! OH MY GOD! OH, MY GOD!"

The sign read:

THE SMYTHE ROYALE

"OH MY GOD! OH MY GOD! OH MY GOD!" I looked at everyone in the car. I could not hold it before the tears streamed down my cheeks. I rolled the window down and rode up to the entrance like a puppy. "Give me your camera," I barked at Leigh out of excitement.

King spoke into the radio in his wrist, "No one is to move until I say so," he instructed.

There was red carpet and cameras at my door. The sign read:

Welcome
Danielle Rose
Of
Sanders, Carmichael, Morrison and Shwatz
The Architect of
The Smythe Royale

GRAND OPENING

I was now sobbing. I could not get it together. Leigh removed her camera from my hand and took the shots for me. I was soaking Randall's shirt with my tears. He didn't move. Keith handed me a bottle of water. I barely lift my head to take a sip.

"Give us a minute please," he said softly dismissing everyone from the car.

Everyone exited on the opposite side of the car. No one stepped on my red carpet. I could see the roses on the carpet lining the walkway. Each member of the staff stood outside waiting with a single red rosebud pinned to their lapel.

"Take as long as you need," King told him. "This is her event. Let her relish in the moment. I am on one side and Keith will be on the other side."

They closed the door. I laid my head in his lap. He rubbed my hair. I could not speak. I tried. Hours ago, this is not where I would have imagined spending my weekend. I must have been hyperventilating.

"Are you okay?" he asked.

All I could do was nod my head. My face was close to a part of his body that it should not have been. When I nodded my head, I felt a nod back. I lifted my head quickly.

"You felt that?" he asked in sheer embarrassment.

"YES," I managed to laugh.

"That was not me. I promise. It is doing it on its own. We surely cannot get out of this car now."

We both laughed. It lightened the moment. I was so full I could not speak. I was glad he was embarrassed just as much as I was surprised. "Randall?"

"Yes Danielle."

"Why did you bring me here?"

"You wanted to come."

"You, Vickie, Leigh, King, Keith, and everyone else went through all of this trouble for me?"

"It is no trouble darling."

"This is such a wonderful surprise."

"I would do it again and again and again just to make you happy."

"You do not have too. Just being with you makes me happy."

"I want to share in your victories the same way you share in mine."

"I never know what to expect from you."

"No you do not. I want it to remain that way."

"Are you trying to make me give you some?" I asked in a seductive tone.

"No, I am trying to make you marry me so you will have to give me some."

Right then and there, I straddled him. He moaned and I knew why. I grabbed his face and kissed all over it. I kissed his left ear and then his right ear. His eyes were closed. His mouth was open and his neck was on the back of the seat. The erection that went down was back up again. "Open your eyes." He shook his head no. "Look at me," I insisted. Looking into his eyes I said, "Randall, I love you so much. I need you in my life. You make me better. With you I am great."

"I know you love me Danielle Jade Rose. I love you more. I need you too. I cannot imagine living without you ever again. Be my wife."

I kissed him. He did not move other than fidgeting in his pocket. I took control. Actually, I did not want him to move. He laid back and allowed me total and complete control.

He could not physically take it any longer. I could have cared less that there were fifty or more people waiting on me on the other side of the door. Who cared? I waited over a year for this place to be complete. They could wait an hour.

He threw me down on the seat and thrust his body on top of mine. "D. It is about to get real ugly in here. It is getting extremely hot. The windows have steamed."

"So."

"The LORD is my shepherd; I shall not want. He maketh me to lie down in green pastures: he leadeth me beside the still waters. He restoreth my soul: he leadeth me in the paths of righteousness for his name's sake. Yea, though I walk through the valley of the shadow of death, I will fear no evil: for thou art with me; thy rod and thy staff they comfort me. Thou preparest a table before me in the presence of mine enemies: thou anointest my head with oil; my cup runneth over. Surely goodness and mercy shall follow me all the days of my life: and I will dwell in the house of the LORD forever. Psalm 23," he whispered.

"Champ."

"Don't push me Danielle because I'm real close to the edge."

"Okay, let's go," I whispered.

"We cannot right now. Wait a minute. I have to get myself together. I cannot step out of this car like this." He took my water. Then we rolled onto the floorboard of the car. He clicked his radio. "King I need a water and Leigh."

There was plenty of water within our reach; however, neither of us had the mental capacity to think that far. King opened the door and shook his head. Leigh looked in and snapped the camera.

"You both are fired," he shouted.

She went crazy snapping.

"What's wrong?" JJ asked.

"I don't get it," King honestly admitted. "They need to have sex and get it over with," he made an ugly face.

I said, "Get in Leigh and put that damn camera down."

"Yes D."

"I have no makeup or anything. What do I look like?" I asked panicked.

"Like you have been making out in the back seat of a car," she answered fumbling in her bag mumbling words. Randall slid himself back on the seat and re-adjusted his man parts.

"Can you do that somewhere else?" Leigh asked embarrassed and appalled at the same time.

He was just as embarrassed as she was, "I have no other choice right now."

Leigh handed me eyeliner, mascara and lip-gloss.

Once he was physically able, he exited the car. He leaned in. "D?"

I looked over feeling like I had just made out in the backseat and was trying to get myself back together before Mama Rose beat me.

"I love you. This is your weekend. The sky is the limit."

"Thank you. I love you too."

"I will be waiting for you on your side."

Leigh managed to get me back in half way decent order although my face was still puffy and my eyes were bloodshot. She rolled ice and bottles of cold water to take the puffiness down as quick as possible. It worked a little.

"Ready?"

"Yep."

"This is what you have been waiting on. I am so proud of you."

"Of me? No way. I could never do this without you. This is our deal. I know I fire you once a week but I am only able to make all of this happen because you walk with me. You are the greatest sidekick, partner, and best friend a girl could have."

We hugged. She took my bags and exited her side. I tapped on the glass. King stood on one side of the door and Keith on the other side. King reached and opened the door without moving. The cameras flashed. Leigh was in front of all the other cameras. Keith handed me his hand without moving his body. I stood up from the car. Randall allowed the cameras snap as he stepped up and took my hand.

Theodore Smythe himself presented me with a huge bouquet of roses and kissed both cheeks. "These are for you Ms. Rose."

"Call me Danielle, Mr. Smythe."

"It's Ted."

"Thank you Ted for the roses and welcoming us to your beautiful hotel."

"No thank you for making my vision come true and gracing us by being our first guest. We have not allowed anyone to check in until you arrived."

"Oh my God. Let's check in." I shook his hand and the cameras snapped wildly. So many pictures were taken for the local reporters. I was the first to check in.

"Can you please sign our guest book Ms. Rose?" Ted asked. Surely, I did. Then Randall signed right behind me. He signed as Hooks Washington.

The other guest were now allowed to check in while the staff was giving us room assignments and loading the luggage.

"Ms. Rose our penthouse floor is Rose Hall. We have made your accommodations there."

"No. I can take a regular room."

"You will do no such thing. You and your family's stay is on us. You are our guest. Enjoy."

"What I would like to do Ted is take a tour from top to bottom."

"We already have it arranged for in the morning."

"It is morning. Right." I said knowing full well it was the middle of the night. Maybe after midnight but I was insinuating I wanted the tour now.

"Calm down babe." Randall tried to lower my excitement and take me back to DJ and get me out of Dani Ro mode.

"Let's offer you a snack."

We walked into the bistro area next to the check-in desk. I did not order a thing yet plates of food were brought out to me. We were busy snacking when I heard someone call out "Sade," over the commotion. I paused.

What did I just hear? I got up and walked the few feet back to the desk. There was no doubt, I knew that voice anywhere. I peeped around the corner and low and behold, Mama Rose was there. I looked back at everyone sitting at the table continuing their conversations as if they didn't have a clue. I watched the lobby then looked back at the crew. Everyone was texting, talking, reading, and drinking as if nothing was going on. I looked closer and there were the partners from my firm. I looked back again. No one moved. I cleared my throat. No one responded. I cleared it again. I swear everyone I knew who should have been in Atlanta was standing in the lobby. I saw another face in the crowd, which looked very familiar. "I HATE ALL OF YOU JERK FACE LIARS."

I walked right up to my mama not saying a word. "My Rosey."

I raised an eyebrow at her.

"Auntie, I told you I would be on the next flight."

I held one finger up to her. By now, Randall had his hand around my waist. I raised an eyebrow at Paige who, up until now, cannot keep a secret. She threw her hands up. I looked at my crew from work. No one said a peep but rather they let the Ambassador speak as she was placing her identification back in her Chanel wallet.

"Did you think I was going to let you travel with some boy I do not even know? If so, then you are crazy hell. Ain't no way my baby was going to come all this way to receive accolades without me here. The devil is a liar."

"And so are all of you," I barked.

He whispered in my ear, "You didn't tell me to call you Rosey."

"How do you know?" I turned quickly and asked.

"Your mother told me."

"When?"

"We met."

"Come on baby show me to my room," Mama said without looking in anyone's direction. Therefore, I started to walk. "I was talking to the boy," she said to me, which let me know I had her approval. "Bring a few of those handsome little boys with you too. Rosey, you and Sade stay with your sister. You are working. We are going to have fun," she said and winked her eye.

I shook my head. Mama Rose was Mama Rose no matter where she was. As soon as they were out of sight, Paige, Sade and I jumped around as if we had not just seen each other a few hours ago. "Let me show you all around," I said excitedly.

"How are you going to show them?" Leigh asked. "We have been right here for the last hour."

She was right. "I designed the building. Everything should be where I placed it. If not we have a problem."

"Ms. Rose, Mr. Hooks would like for us to escort you to your room now," a well-dressed woman said.

They all looked gorgeous in their immaculate uniforms. The ambiance was perfect. The roses were beautiful. I looked down the hall but he would not make eye contact. "Randall?" I called out.

He did not look but spoke, "Huh?"

"Look this way."

"I am good."

"I thought so party pooper."

We all entered the elevator. A key was turned to allow access to the penthouse. As soon as the doors opened, there was a beautiful sign, which read Rose Hall. There looked to be about four suites on this floor. I was for certain we were about to occupy all four of them. My ladies and I would occupy one suite. Randall and his immediate crew in another. His secondary crew in a third and my firm in the fourth suite. Somehow, this worked out perfectly.

We were shown to our rooms, which were perfect of course. Thirty minutes later, I received a text from King.

> Meeting at the elevator in five minutes.

Everyone convened by the elevator. JJ gave instructions on the do's and the don'ts. There were way more don'ts than do's. Mama started to walk off.

"Where are you going Mrs. Rose," King asked in his annoyed tone.

"To my room. I am not interested in this foolishness."

"I need for you to stay here and listen to these instructions ma'am."

"The only way I am listening is if they are an infomercial on Lifetime. Good night hoodlums."

"Did she just call me a hoodlum?" Randall whispered in my ear.

With her back turned walking down the hall she answered his question. "Yes, little boy, you are the ring leader of this hoodlum clan. The garbage my girls bring home. I wish I had a nickel for each one like you they have brought to my doorstep. This time she brought one who thinks he is worth something. Fighting in the street for your hood is the same things as fighting in the ring for a few million. A typical roughneck. Does he really think he is a good guy? You are not fooling me behind the Deacon title with these reject disciples you got trailing along. Y'all enjoy. Good night." She never turned around and all we saw was the back of her St. John and Ferragamo's.

I hope that was a clear picture of where Sade gets her expressive conversations and soliloquies.

"I am going to need back up," King said as he did a three hundred sixty degree spin. He looked disgusted and defeated. "How did I get stuck with three of them?"

"Baby you ain't seen nothing yet. Wait until I get a few hours of sleep. Sade," Mama Rose yelled, "Come on honey."

Sade walked backwards and threw the deuces up. She was now with her partner in crime.

I pressed the elevator button. "Where do you think you are going?" Randall asked. There was too much going on right now and the guys were losing control.

"She is grown. Where ever she wants to go," Mama informed him.

Everyone laughed. It was amazing how she could hear from such a far distance.

"How do you do that?" he said with his fist clinched.

"I am not dealing with this Hooks," King threw a quick tantrum giving up.

"That's fine. The airport is still open," Mama said and slammed her door.

"I warned you," I said to him smiling.

Agreeing, "Yes you did," Randall admitted.

"The apple doesn't fall too far from the tree. I see where you get it from," King said highly annoyed.

The elevator opened. "Not tonight DJ. It is late."

"Okay," I replied. We walked back to my door and sat on the floor in front of it.

"Do not leave this floor," Keith commanded.

We talked for another hour. I told him how grateful and surprised I was before we went to our individual rooms. It was either real late or real early depending on which way you preferred to look at it. I took a shower, threw on some workout clothes and hit the hall. I went down the elevator with my phone, iPod, and room key regardless as to what they instructed.

I wondered around the lobby, looked through the restaurant, and peeped in the Spa. I checked over the bar, observed the gift shop, and took note of the indoor and outdoor pools. I went in and played around in the game room. Then I fumbled with the conference room and business services. I walked through each ballroom, meeting, and event space. I admired the children's area. Finally, I made it to the fitness center. I hit the television, found the iPod connection and hooked up. I was reflecting on the art, the décor, the roses when Sade texted.

> Mama said get your hot tail back in this room.

> I am working out.

> Yeah I bet.

I heard commotion before I responded. Sure enough, it was the wrecking crew.

"Danielle," his voice rang.

Oh great! I knew I was in trouble.

"Do you hear me?"

"You know she hears like Mazilla."

"King did you just say something about my mother?"

"I thought you could not hear us."

"I will F you up about my Mama."

"I think it can handle its own?"

Did he just call my mama an it?

I got off the treadmill before Randall ran up and tackled me. Without saying a word, he escorted me back to my room.

"Do not leave this room until breakfast. I am going to run." He walked in the suite with me as if he was locking me in.

"Fine."

Responding to my sarcasm, "I love you too. You have a big day today."

"Do you have any more surprises?" I asked.

"Maybe," he kissed my nose. "Danielle please follow instructions," he pleaded. "It is only for three days. Three days Danielle," he reiterated. "I have faith you can do it," he said as he gave more kisses this time to my forehead.

I could not follow instructions for three days. Didn't he know I didn't follow orders and how rebellious I am? In addition, I hated secrets and surprises. "Okay fine."

"Lay down. I will text you once I am done."

Thursday

There was no noise in the suite other than Mama's television. I showered again and laid down across the bed of the hotel I designed. I did not realize I had fallen asleep until I heard my phone alerting me of his text.

> Gather everyone for breakfast in an hour.

All I needed was a reason to make some noise. I started opening the curtains then I heard my phone chime again.

> Come to the door.

I ran to the door as I did when I was fifteen and the captain of the football team; Reginald Timothy Sawyer, was there. This time it was better. I was grown and the Champion Boxer of the World was at my door. The boxer who planned a surprise trip for me which included my family and my office. The best part of all was the fact he wanted nothing from me in return. He asked for nothing. He expected nothing. I gave him nothing except my emotions.

I opened the door. He kissed me and ran down the hall. I stood there watching him run away like a teenager.

We all gathered for breakfast. I was so excited to witness people checking in. You would have thought it was my hotel. I walked back and forth from the dining room to the front desk looking and observing.

After breakfast, everyone did an assortment of activities. Some toured the city; some took advantage of spa services while others relaxed. Me, I was only interested in touring the hotel. I walked every inch of the hotel from breakfast until lunch. I think I wore Keith out. King and Randall would appear to check on us and then disappear. I think King and his team also searched the place from top to bottom. There was not a closet or room they did not sweep. It was his job, which he was good at if I must admit.

After lunch, we all chilled in between the pool, theater, and game room. It was a fabulous day. After dinner, I snuck back downstairs eventually sleeping in the lobby. I wanted to see all the people coming and going. There was a little side office off from the front desk they allowed me access. I went there and prayed.

Friday

JJ was furious when he entered the lobby. I could tell from the way his brows moved. He was not as harsh as King but he was firm. Sometime in the middle of the night, Randall came to order me back upstairs. I refused. Therefore, he stayed in the lobby with me.

"You two should lay down every night in a bed. Hooks it is time for conditioning."

"Good morning J. You are correct," Hooks knew better than to argue with him. "Let's go D." They escorted me back upstairs. When we got off the elevator he said, "Lay down. I will knock for breakfast when I am done."

"I love you."

"Me too."

Later he and I spent the entire day at the spa where we were treated to a couples' day. It was very difficult, weird, and strenuous. I was in the room with the man I loved. Holding hands with him majority of the massage. Lying naked next to him and I could not look, touch, or feel him. Although I wanted to badly. I needed it. My body desired his desperately. No matter how hard the masseuse worked, I remained tensed. If I could not do anything else could I at least stare, look, or take a little peek? This was a bad idea and rather difficult. Why was doing right always so hard? I squeezed my eyes so tight until my head hurt.

It felt as though the massage was taking forever. I wondered if he experienced the same thoughts and feelings I was having. My physical and emotional thoughts were running high. I could not block him out of my mind.

The black tie dinner event was at six. I brought so many dresses to choose from which made the decision difficult. At one point, I was going to call him in and ask which one he preferred. I finally settled on the long black and white gown with the removable dark pink bow, which tied in the back. Everyone in our crews left ahead of us except for King and Keith. I took my time leaving because I did not want to cry in front of everyone.

"You look beautiful." He smiled like I have never seen him smile before. He knew I was going to cry; therefore, he placed his finger right under my eye to catch my tears.

"Thank you handsome."

"Whenever you are ready."

"I do not think I will ever be ready for a time such as this."

"You will be fine. This is the easy part. The fight is over and now this is the parade."

"You would know," I paused. He was always so encouraging. No matter what I was faced against or how negative I was of the situation, he kept me lifted. I knew behind closed doors he prayed diligently and fervently for my well-being. "If I haven't told you, I am so glad to have you in my life. You are the best thing that has happened to me. You lift me up."

"Oh Danielle," he got emotional. "You mean more to me than you will ever know. I have your back. You pulled me out of the gutter and placed my feet back on solid ground."

We opened the door to the room where King and Keith were waiting. They came in and redressed me. *I did not understand why King and Keith could see me half-naked and touch me but Randall could not. I really knew the answer to the question. However, I had to be difficult and ask while they secured all my security gadgets to my waist, both thighs, and ankles. What do they think is going to pop off?*

"Randall are you wearing all of this stuff too?" I yelled in the other room. I could see him pacing back and forth.

"Yes babe. It is precautionary. Get used to it," he said with his hands in his pockets fidgeting. He seemed nervous suddenly.

"Do you need to give her anything before we leave?" Keith questioned. *That was strange*, I thought.

"No, I am good. Thanks for asking," his tone was harsh.

"Oh, I was expecting a necklace like in Pretty Woman."

"You are wearing a necklace already."

"It is costume."

"She is wearing a ring too," Keith said.

"It's real," I stated. "Do I need any more 007 gadgets? If so, get Sean Connery in the room to assist me please. I would much rather have someone sexy and professional to dress and undress me than you two."

"That is all. Follow what I tell you to do Ms. Rose," King ended the verbal fight Randall and Keith were having.

"Yes sir," I knew he meant business this time. We were way out of our zone. Anything was possible. I needed to be on my best behavior and I willingly planned to do so.

We made it to the elevator. King was on his left side and Keith was on my right. He was holding my hand. Squeezing it rather. He was more nervous than I was. We walked down the corridor hand in hand.

"Are you nervous?" I asked.

"No."

"You are lying."

"So what if I am?"

"Why are you?"

"I do not know. Maybe I am excited for you."

"Call it what you want. Relax it is no big deal. It is dinner, that's all."

"So you call it."

"You will be fine."

The elevator doors opened. I instantly smiled. As we approached the lobby all eyes were on us. I was not expecting the hotel to go from the Bates Motel to a full house overnight. The people were not looking at me. They have no clue who I am. Instead, they were looking at the fighter, Hooks. We stood in front of the ballroom door. It read: Royale Rose Ballroom. King spoke in his wrist. He paused. Once he got a response back, he looked at Keith. "Let's do it." He transformed. He went from trainer, head security to The Terminator. Anyone around knew not to try him.

"We are on," Randall said.

I nodded. King and Keith opened the doors. I was behind Keith and he was behind King. Once they separated so we could see the room, he squeezed my hand. His grip was painful. I tried to wiggle it loose. *Why is he so nervous? I am sure he has done this thousands of times.*

The room was beautifully covered with roses everywhere. I walked on the rose petals lining the newly carpeted floor. I wanted to make sure I asked how they got the stems to grow so long and how did they get the others to droop like buttercups. I have never seen anything like it. Not even in my daddy's greenhouse where we grew all sorts of beautiful roses, flowers, and greenery. The room was packed. A few hundred attended. I was surprised again. I thought it was just the owner and us.

King and Keith stopped in front of us. King was a very different person right now. He was in his element. This is what he liked doing. He loved training Randall. He loved getting Hooks ready to fight but I would guess he preferred protecting him more than anything else. I made a mental note to always respect him and obey his signs and commands under these conditions. These conditions only. At the gym, it would be a different story.

Theodore Smythe spoke, "Please join me in welcoming our guest of honor. The person who made this beautiful hotel possible. Who took my dreams, put it with her creativity, and designed The Smythe Royale. The woman who happens to be many many miles away but the instant you meet her, you do what she tells you to do because you know it will be spectacular. I present to you the beautiful Danielle Rose."

Cameras snapped. Leigh's went off first. King made it known ahead of time that no one was allowed to snap until Leigh got her shots in first. I was not expecting an introduction. I thought I was just going to go to my table and eat. I see why he was nervous. I spoke through my teeth. "Did you know about this?"

"Nope. Smile," he backed off to let me have the moment alone. He and the other two stood at attention. I do not understand how King did it, but I am willing to bet he knew every face in the room. As if on a swivel, his eyes moved around constantly. The noise level in the room increased when the wait staff began to bring in the dinner trays.

King spoke in his wrist, "Stop them until she is seated. No one moves from their places. They need to come out of the one door where the metal detector is." He held his hand up for the cameras to stop. He stood back in front of me. King, Randall, Keith, and I stood in one solid line. "Secure these doors." Once all the movement stopped, he stepped to the side and allowed the cameras to move again. Leigh was on the floor in her gown. She was getting the pictures of us lined up. It looked like we were about to do a step show.

King was serious. He was no joke at what he did. You would not know a few hours ago that he was the person calling on Jesus to help him deal with Mama Rose. I had no doubt King could take this entire room out by himself with his bare hands. With his crew, he could demolish this hotel and exit with his entire group intact and unharmed. The thought was scary and so was he.

Finally, he stopped the cameras. I gave him the signal. Randall stepped right up took my hand and escorted me to my seat. He kissed my cheek as he pulled the chair out. He was such a gentleman.

Dinner was served. I looked at the table and noticed mine and Randall's plate was different from everyone else. I looked down at Vickie. She knew exactly what I meant. She made special arrangements for our dinner. Our plates were scanned and laid in front of us by Sol and Jon Jon.

Randall looked up as if to confirm they had been scanned. Jon Jon flicked a device in front of him. He nodded. After we ate, they took our plates and started preparing to bring dessert as the program began. I was not expecting a program.

"Come with me," we stood up. "Excuse us," he said as he took me into a closed room. He hugged me tight. Keith was outside the door. He asked King to step outside of the room as well. He was acting so weird. I was concerned about him. He laid his head on my forehead.

"Randall."

"Yes."

"Sweetheart are you okay?"

"I need to sit down."

I pulled up a chair. Instead of him sitting in it he sat me in it. He kneeled at my feet. "Danielle, I am so proud of you. I am overwhelmed and overjoyed. I hope this place is what you expected. I hope it is what you envisioned. It is my desire from this day forward you have everything your heart desires. I pray all of your needs and wants are supplied and fulfilled. I hope God continues to guide you and bless you. I pray we spend the rest of our lives together," he laid his head in my lap. He was so nervous. After what seemed like ten minutes, I lift his head.

"I should be getting back. I am sure someone is looking for me."

He stood then I stood. His eyes were teary. It was not my first time seeing them like this so I thought nothing about it.

"Thank you for bringing me here. This means more to me than you will ever know."

"It was nothing. I love you and I will do anything for you."

I started to walk off, "Are you coming?"

"Give me a minute."

I opened the door and King jumped as if I startled him. "Everything fine?"

"I think so."

"Are you sure?"

"Yes."

"Do we need to discuss anything?" King confirmed.

"No," I said reluctantly.

"Wait right here," he barked at Randall. "Hooks let me walk her back.

Stay put. Do not move from this room."

King and Keith walked me back to my seat. Then King said the same thing to me. "Stay put. I will be right back."

"Is everything fine?" Keith asked.

"Yes," I said.

"What was that? A quickie before dessert," Sade smarted.

I rolled my eyes as Mama tapped her hand. You would have sworn she slapped it so hard it was about to bleed. They both would swear that. They were always in cahoots together.

"You didn't answer D."

I rolled my eyes at her again.

"I take that as a yes. Mama it is disrespectful to leave during dinner." As always, Mama said something to me.

"Danielle behave. Do not leave this table again."

I moved my lips at Sade so Mama could not see. "B***h."

"Mama," Sade squealed.

"Stop it Danielle," she said without looking in my direction. "Watch your mouth."

I laughed. How does she do that? In one smooth motion, I flicked Sade off.

"Girls," Mama said in between her teeth as if we were four and she had had enough of us.

King arrived back at the hospitality suite to find Randall prostrate. He picked him up and put him in a chair. He was sweating. King gave him his handkerchief. "I could not do it. As bad as I wanted to I could not. Not because I was nervous but I am afraid she will say no. The words would not come out of my mouth," he sobbed.

"It's okay. You have plenty of time. I do not foresee the troll going anywhere anytime soon."

"I need to go back to the room to put this ring in the safe."

They did and he arrived back in the dining room just as they were about to present me with a gift. My name was called. Everyone at the table stood. He escorted me to the podium. The crowd was on their feet giving me a standing ovation. Somehow, I think the ovation was more for the Champ than for the architectural engineer. Who really cares about who designs the building? Housekeeping is more of a care than the architect is once the building is occupied.

I was not prepared. I did not know I had to make a speech. Nevertheless, like clockwork Leigh was on point. I made a mental note to take care of her as soon as I fired her. I looked on the podium and on my letterhead was a thank you speech. That little snot.

Theodore Smythe spoke first. "Ms. Rose, you have graced us with your presence which is the exuberance and radiance of this grand Hotel you assisted us in developing. You did not draw the plans and run. You worked with us day and night just as you did with our Belize and Dubai Hotels years ago. You made phone calls. You ordered material. You found us cheaper pricing. You helped us in the permitting department. You collaborated and negotiated with suppliers, contractors, the city, and with me. You freely gave us your ideas for the decor. Explained in detail what you thought the Royale should look like. We have worked hard under your supervision. We hope we have pleased you as much as you have pleased us. We have tried to duplicate every idea you gave. You are the foundation of this structure. We could never thank you or repay you. We made sure you were the first to experience your vision. We are grateful you graced us with your presence along with your friends, family, and staff. I will never build another structure without you. That is a promise. This city has just seen the beginning of Smythe and Rose."

"At this time we would like to present you with a Gold Master Key to the Hotel. This key unlocks every door in the place. We hope it means as much to you as it does to us."

I took the key. It was on a beautiful rose and diamond keychain. I do think they were diamonds and not rhinestones. Lord, this was going to have to go in the safe once I got home. It was real gold. I could tell by the weight.

I looked over at Randall. He nodded as I took the podium. I looked at Leigh who was snapping directly in front of me.

"Thank me later," she whispered.

"I am a little shocked. I am not sure if you all know but this has all been a surprise to me. I did not know I was coming here this weekend. From the last conversation Ted and I had, he did not receive his Certificate of Occupancy. I am sure I owe an apology to quite a few people in the permit department. Maybe even the Mayor."

"They are both here tonight," Ted laughed.

"Great. I do apologize and I will personally get around to telling you how sorry I am for yelling all last week. Once I arrived, I was surely not expecting my family, firm, and friends to arrive. This has all been orchestrated to perfection."

"It was purposefully done Ms. Rose. Perfection is the level you operate on," Ted spoke.

"I was not expecting a gift much less the key to the Smythe Royale. I am at a loss of words." King smiled for the first time all night. "I think I should make mention of a few people who have assisted me. First, I have to thank God Almighty who has made all of this possible by giving me the talent. I would like to thank my wonderful assistant, Leigh, who covers me from front to back day in and day out. She keeps up with my fast-paced mind, my hectic schedule, and me. She does it patiently, calmly, and effortlessly. I would like to thank the firm and partners who have allowed me to be me. They let me be as eclectic, eccentric, contemporary, classic, modern, traditional, stubborn, rude, and as hardheaded as I choose to be. They believe in me. To Mr. Smythe and those here who permitted me to combine my vision with their vision. To my mother who let me draw on the walls, the sidewalk, the furniture, and anything else I could get my hands on as a child. My father who saw my talent and taught me the basis of drawing and design. To my sister and my niece, thank you for being there and being my best friends. To everyone who travelled with me. To the King of the group all the way to the Queen of the group. Lastly," I turned and looked directly at him. Taking my focus off the crowd and Leigh's speech. "I have no other choice but to thank a very special person. A person who understands me and the desires I have to do what I do. A person who trust me, believes in me, and loves me whole-heartedly. A person who expects nothing but gives me his all. A person who has taken my heart and reconstructed it. He made my broken heart pump again. He has made me stronger, wiser, and better. So much better. He is the person my fairy tales consisted of. The fighter in him brings out the fighter in me. He could not be any greater even if I designed and drew him myself." I turned back to Mr. Smythe and lightened the tone. "Thank you for this key. It means so much to me. Before I leave, I plan to check to make sure it works in every lock. So do not be alarmed if you hear sounds at your door later tonight. It's just me checking the key." I looked at Leigh to make sure I did not missed anything or anyone. I did not read any of her words. I mentioned all the highlighted names. At least I think I did. She nodded in confirmation. "Thank you again, enjoy, and God Bless."

I walked to the edge of the platform. His eyes were red again. He was the hardest sensitive man I knew. "You did not have to do that."

"What?"

"Say what you said."

"It was all true."

"Danielle, you are turning me into a punk."

"When you are weak is when I think you are the strongest."

We sat back down at the table. "Nice speech Leigh wrote for you Auntie."

"Mama, ask Sade not to talk to me."

Leigh took her seat. "What am I going to do with you Ms. Lady?"

"Just doing my job," Leigh smiled behind the camera.

"Not so. You have gone above and beyond as you do every day. I love you girl."

"Not now D. Not tonight. No mushy stuff please. You have already said fru fru stuff about Ali over there. That is all I can take," Paige said as if it was going to make her puke if I said one more sensitive thing.

We had our after dinner beverage and the party was over. Or shall I say the formal one was over and the real party was about to begin. We all went back to the room to change clothes. Everyone re-joined in another ballroom with music and dancing. Everyone was having a good time. Randall and I stayed on the couch outside the room talking.

"DJ, it is late. I think I am going to call it a night. Please enjoy the rest of the night and go to the room and not the lobby to go to bed," he and King abruptly left. I hesitantly went back to enjoy the party.

Once they got to the room he told King, "Let me consult with myself."

King had been with him long enough to know what that meant. It was a long day. He needed to kneel and pray in order to process everything. Currently, his strength was being tested physically, emotionally, and mentally. He needed to regain himself. He started to pray, "For the joy of the Lord is my strength."

After all the festivities, I did everything in my power to go to the room. I really wanted to continue to walk the hotel. The only thing convincing me to do so was the fact that all the ladies and I would be together. I invited Vickie to hang out in our room and do it Rose style. We did what we always do on vacation. We ordered room service. We had an array of everything on the menu from lobster to cheesecake. Then we chilled. I did not hear from him. I wanted to talk to him to say good night at least. Therefore, I put my slippers on and walked to the door.

"She is ditching us. It's boo time."

"Shut up Sade."

"It's girl's night," Mama yelled.

"It's intermission. I will be right back."

I slammed the door. I am sure Mama was heated. I walked down the hall and rang the bell. JJ opened the door. I stood there as if I was at a married man's house and his wife answered. He stepped to the side and let me pass by without saying a word.

"Hey D, what's up?" Keith said.

"He is asleep. You are killing me softly," King mumbled behind a remote controller playing the Black Oops Game.

"Children should speak when spoken to." I point in the direction to see which room he was his. Keith nodded.

I opened the double doors, to my surprise the lights were off, and he was under the covers asleep. I could not believe it. He really sleeps.

I walked out of the room and back down the hall to get Leigh's camera and a tube of Mac and my master key. "Be back." I used my key this time when I got back to their suite. They were all drawn on me when I walked in the room. I kept it moving ignoring the heat like nothing was going on.

"Damn you Danielle," King yelled. I guess I disrupted his game.

I went into the room and took pictures of him sleeping. He will swear he was not asleep. I wrote on the mirror with my tube of lipstick a heart with a rose going through it. As I was exiting the main room, I took pictures of the guys. King mumbled more nonsense as I threw up the deuces behind me.

I walked back into our suite just in time. Mama was pulling the popcorn out the microwave and the Coke Cola was topping the ice cream floats. Vickie was in for an all-nighter.

Saturday

At five, my phone was ringing. I jumped up, took the phone and moved away from the group. "Hello."

"I got your message."

"You were knocked out."

"No I was not. I saw you."

"Liar!"

"I'm at your door."

I ran to the door and opened it.

"Good morning," Mama said.

He looked startled. I stepped aside. He looked in and shook his head. "Ladies, what is going on here?"

"Uncle Hooks. What's up?"

"I am trying to figure it out?"

"Girls' night," Paige said with enthusiasm.

He looked at his watch. "It is five AM ladies."

"Carry over," Mama said.

"What is all of this?"

Vickie began to explain every food and beverage item literally.

"This is ridiculous. All of you all are going to be sick. We travel in a few hours' ladies."

"We will be ready Uncle Hooks."

Keith and King leaned in to peek as he kissed me. "I will be back once I am done so we can go for breakfast. Unless you all have already eaten breakfast."

"No. We will be ready. Have a good run." We had been up all night but you would have thought it was six o'clock in the evening. No one moved. I went right back to my original spot on the couch and we picked up where we left off. Vickie fit right in. Not to mention, she really did not have a choice. She was the only girl from their crew.

After breakfast, he and I spent some quality time together. We walked the property. He was patient while I looked and observed the details. King and Keith followed closely behind us. Everyone else found adventurous and fun things to do. Me, I wanted to enjoy the place, the scenery, and the ambiance. I did not know when I would be back again so I had to enjoy it while I could. They did not have a location for a ring and spectators so I didn't see another visit anytime soon. Vegas would probably be where I spent a lot of my vacation, which was just fine with me.

I loved the way he allowed me to be me. He did not rush me. He didn't criticize my need for sentiments. I observed the place as if I was preparing to purchase it. I wanted full confirmation it was exactly what they envisioned and what I designed.

As we walked, I went through and explained to him as much as I could in the time allotted. King and Keith actually hung on to my every word. We viewed the mechanical and electrical rooms. We maneuvered through the kitchen and once we arrived at the server/technology area, the roles changed. He had his opportunity to tell me how everything there worked. It was great listening to him.

Before I knew it, it was time to get in one last spa visit and head out to the airport.

Mr. Smythe never left us the entire stay. I didn't want to leave him either. If I could, I would admit I enjoyed being away and not working. I did not work since our arrival. As we checked out, I gave the front desk my card and walked away. I really did not want to see how much the total was going to set me back. It was going to take a week to figure out how to expense this. I was planning to give accounting the bill and say 'figure it out.'

Randall politely took the card from the attendant. In return, he handed her his card. It seemed like three hundred sheets of paper printed and she went directly to the last page and asked for his signature. Vickie was next to him as he signed. He gathered his things and came back to my side to wait for the car handing me my card with his normal smirk.

"What is that?"

"The bill."

My eyes bucked. He gave up my laugh. *This was the last trip the ladies will attend.* I thought to myself. *I hope they counted this as our annual family trip.* I continued thinking while he winked at me. He turned, went, and sat next to Mama instead. I put my ear buds back into my ears and closed my eyes.

He scrolled to the last page of the bill. The total read $ 2,331.00. He stared at it knowing there were zero's missing. Was it correct? He was for certain what the ladies ordered from room service last night was more than the entire total. Just then, Mr. Smythe came over to say his final goodbyes and inform us the cars were ready.

He spoke to Mr. Smythe with his back turned to us. I let him handle man business. He thanked him for his gracious hospitality and offered to cover the cost of everyone's stay and accommodations. Mr. Smythe would not allow it. We all rose and followed orders back to the limousines awaiting us out front.

We rode to the airport in complete chaos. It was a different ride this time. One the way I had no clue where I was going. I had no idea my family, firm and friends would join us. Now here we were all going back home together. Being nosey, I wanted to know what Randall and Mr. Smythe discussed since he was still deep in thought.

The hotel covered the entire cost for everyone including food and beverage. He did not take the time to figure out the $ 2,331.00. He did not care. He covered the airfare for nearly thirty people. It was nothing to him or his pocket. However, he knew it meant so much to her. He would do it repeatedly to see the smile she currently had on her face. He blessed her, her family and friends and in return, the hotel blessed him. He stared at her knowing he had gotten off cheap and easy. He knew he was blessed to have her in his life.

The flight back was quiet. I think we all slept. As we hit the runway, he was fidgeting in his pocket again.

"I want to thank everyone for taking the time out of their busy schedules at the spur of the moment to enjoy in Danielle's achievement. I hope this is the beginning of future excursions. I pray she has many more places for us to join her in celebrating. Again, I thank you all. This meant a lot to Danielle to have you all here. I want to invite you all to my home tomorrow for Sunday dinner if you can. I am also extending an invitation to join us at service tomorrow morning. If you cannot we will understand. But dinner you will not want to miss."

He was still fidgeting. I tried to reach for his hand. He scolded me instead. "What is in your pocket?"

"Nothing."

"Stop it."

"For those of you who are debating on dinner tomorrow it will be real treat. Mama Rose is cooking." he continued to fidget.

"What did he say?" Mama asked.

"You are cooking tomorrow," Sade instigated.

"No hell I am not. Do you all really think you are going to have me working and slaving over a hot stove tomorrow like I am a short order cook?"

"Yes," the majority of us said at one time.

"Hold your breath."

After the luggage was placed in the respective cars, we all hugged and said our farewells. I was sitting in the limousine and he and the boys were discussing who was about to be assigned to who. He continued to play in his pocket.

I texted him.

> What is in your pocket?

He looked at the text and slid the phone back in his pocket without responding. He came back to the car and once I realized what was going on I could not stop laughing. King was assigned to make sure the ladies got home. Including Mama. I rolled my window down and yelled, "King." When he turned around, I laughed as hard and as loud as I could in his face. Furiously he flicked me off. Randall was sitting next to me and Keith was in the front with the driver.

"Do you want to touch it?"

"Huh?"

"My pocket?"

"Yes, I'll touch it." I needed to figure out why he continued to fidget with it.

"Not on your life." We wrestled in the back of the car.

"Hold it down before I come back there," Keith said as if we were children. "Seatbelts."

It was still early when we arrived at my house. Keith took Randall's things and left after he gave us a responsibility lecture.

After I got my bags put up, clothes in the wash, computer, iPads, iPods charging he asked, "Are you hungry?"

"I do believe I am."

"Let's go," he said.

We went to Mikey's first. He knew me a little better than I thought. He knew after a few days I missed my best friend. I had an appetizer and he had fresh vegetable juice. We left there and I knew he was not going to be able to refrain from stopping. We stopped at the gym and then the restaurant. We ate again at the restaurant. I ate rather. He had his meal in a glass as usual.

We were in the car heading back towards my house, "I can drop you off."

Without thought, "Nonsense," he said.

Curiously, I asked, "So what do you suggest?"

"I haven't put much thought in it."

Although he didn't ask me I gave him my thought, "I was thinking maybe you spend the night and I won't tell if you won't tell."

"The only way I can,do that is if you touch what is in my pocket," he said casually.

"You won't let me," I barked. Now I was curious.

"Well that cancels your suggestion. You are so bad," he smirked.

"You ain't seen nothing yet. When I am bad I am so good."

"Not tonight," he said carefree as if the thought had not crossed his mind.

"I tried."

His phone chirped. It was unusual that his phone rang this late. He read the text.

"Is she serious?" he asked.

"Who?"

"Your mother?"

"About what?"

"Sade is texting me her grocery list."

Laughing, I said, "I do believe so."

"It will take me all week to find this stuff."

"You volunteered her to cook."

"I asked her."

"No you voluntold," I corrected him.

"Now what am I supposed to do?"

"Get the stuff off the list."

"Seriously?"

"Yep."

"Suggestions?"

"Two places. No big deal. We will be in and out."

"I am glad you are confident. You didn't even look at the list." He walked me to the steps when we got back to my house. "I am not coming in." He was still fidgeting and it was driving me crazy.

"What is in your pocket?" I demanded.

"Why do you keep asking me that?"

"You keep fidgeting. You have done so all day."

"Nothing. You make me nervous," he partially lied and changed the subject. "Which car do you want me to take?"

"It doesn't matter."

He hugged and kissed me lightly. "Lock up. Get some rest. I will text you in a few minutes. Let me see how fast this toy of yours will run."

"Your ticket. If you crash it you buy two," I warned.

Sunday

I slept like a baby. He called me at four thirty AM like clockwork. I answered the phone, "When did you meet my Mama?"

"What?"

"You heard me?"

"Good morning Danielle."

"Grrr. Answer the question."

"It is too early."

"Your butt is in hot water."

"I am conditioning. I will see you in a few hours?"

"If you don't want to see me in a few minutes you will answer the question."

"I can't recall the question."

"When, how, where, and why did you meet my Mama?" I really wanted to know what did my mama say to you or tell you.

"Girl, you know darn well I was not about to take you anywhere without talking to your mother."

"Okay. One down three to go."

"What?"

"You answered the why. Now answer when, how, and where?"

"Ugh," he mocked my disgust. "Wednesday I drove over to her house. Are you happy now?"

"You drove over to my Mama's house? How do you know where she lives? Never freaking mind." I was livid he did and even more livid no one mentioned it.

"I love you too. I will see you in a few hours."

It was four forty six AM when I dialed Paige's home phone.

"Hello," she said in a sleepy voice.

"Tell Sade to pick up," I clicked over quickly and added Leigh to the call.

"What's wrong?" Leigh answered.

"Are we all here?"

"Yeah," Sade said as if we were disturbing her from something.

"I wanted to say this one time and make sure you all heard me. I hate all of you two-faced traitors. BI's," I hung up the line.

"That was real Christian like," Paige said while she and Sade were still on the line together.

"She will never be a Deaconess," Leigh reveled.

"I'm telling Mama right now," Sade whined.

I arrived at church. The parking lot guy asked me to pull to the curb.

"Good morning," Keith said at the curb.

"Good morning."

"You look nice," he extended his hand.

"Thank you sir." Tim took my car to park it while Keith and I walked in. I did not see Randall. We walked slowly into the sanctuary. As soon as we got halfway down the aisle. I felt a gentle touch on my back. I looked at Keith on my right and quickly knew it was not him. I turned around. It was Randall. He looked strange.

"What's wrong," I said in a panic.

He stood there. He had been weird the last twenty-four hours. *What was the deal?* If I had not been with him the past few days I would have sworn he had done something unfaithful. He took my hand and did a slight bow. My eyes were rolling around so fast. What was up with him?

"Danielle."

"Yes."

"I love you," he dropped my hand and ran away.

I frowned and looked at Keith. "What is his problem?"

Shrugging his shoulders, "You have him tripping."

We got to our seats and I continued to look back observing the crowd. I was looking around suspiciously. This felt like the weird calm before the storm. Was something about to pop off? Was he about to announce he was fighting tomorrow? I was a tad bit distracted when he and Hunter entered.

For some reason you could always tell the mood of Hunter by the way he entered the sanctuary. He entered and jetted up the pulpit steps. This meant he was hyped. Therefore, whatever it was it was not affecting Hunter's mood. However, something surely had Deacon Washington's mind occupied and racing.

I nudged Keith. "What is in his pocket? Why has he kept his hand in there constantly yesterday and again today?"

"Knowing him five hundred thousand dollars or more. Shh," he whispered.

Five hundred thousand dollars could not fit in his pocket. When the offering was taken, he stood directly in front of me while Hunter blessed it. I got extremely close to him. I was so close until Keith moved too. I whispered to the back of him, "Not as much as I love you."

When he turned his head, mine was bowed with my eyes closed. After service, I was going home to change so I could be at his house by the time he got home. He did not know my Mama. He said dinner was at five, which meant Mama would be there at two to start. Dinner at five meant grace was being said at four fifty five and we were passing plates and eating by five whether Paige and Sade were present or not.

As I was putting the car in drive, he ran over. "Hey, where are you going?"

"Home to change. I will meet you at your house once you are done."

"You are going to the store with me correct?"

"Yes, crazy I am." He was still panicking about the long grocery list. If only he knew how many times we have seen lists like that.

It took us under two hours to get all we needed and we were on the way back just when Sade called.

"Yes ma'am."

"You better respect me. Mama said we are on the way."

"So," and I hung up the phone.

He looked at me, "Who was that?"

"Sade."

Then his phone rang, "Hey baby girl."

"Uncle Hooks why did she hang up on me?"

"DJ don't hang up on the baby anymore."

"Snitch," I growled. She was going to pay later.

"We are on the way back to the house now."

We had not unloaded all the bags from the car when the gate buzzed. He looked at me puzzled.

"Sade and Paige are on time because Mama is with them."

"I should have known," he said under his laughter.

Mama came right in talking trash. Did anyone expect anything different? "This is a nice house but show me the kitchen." Randall took her to the kitchen. She ran her hand over the stove. She opened the oven. She checked the refrigerator and the pantry. "Either a damn good maid service or nothing has ever been cooked in here."

"Check the blender and juicer," he said proudly knowing it was well used.

"Rosey please help this boy. Man can't live by liquids alone. He does not adhere to scripture."

He laughed at the comment.

Mama went through the bags taking her time. Once she got all of her ingredients laid out, she looked for a cutting board, Pyrex dishes, measuring cups, knives, and all the other things she required. She checked the lower cabinets before she yelled, "Rosey."

"Ma'am," I shouted back from the other room and ran to see what the issue was. The house was suddenly quiet at her command. You could hear a pin drop. "What's wrong?"

"Come here boy!"

He looked around like he was scared to speak but he knew she was speaking to him and it was in his best interest not to dispute her. Instead, he stood there like a four year old who just broke a dish.

"Were you married before?"

"Yes ma'am."

"Where is she?"

"I do not know at this current moment."

"What happened with her?"

"Umm, she sort of left."

"Did you eat when you were married?"

"I eat now."

"That was not what I asked you. Did you eat solid food?"

"Yes ma'am."

"From where?"

He looked like he did not know how to answer the question.

"Baby, did your wife cook?"

"No ma'am."

"That explains it all."

"What?" Paige asked as if a mystery was solved.

"Why he is so thin. Why he does not eat anything and why he does not have the pot and pans I need. I thought maybe the heffa took them with her. But she probably never had any. Rosey, go take this boy to get some pots and pans if you all want me to cook. Somebody should have told me I had to bring my own cookware."

He looked like *what have I gotten myself into*. "Let's go," he said without hesitation picking up his keys and phone.

"Dani, do you know what to get?"

"What do you need Mrs. Rose?" he kindly asked.

"I have what I need at home," she smarted off. "But you need everything. You need to get stainless, nonstick, Pyrex, Corning, and cast iron. At this point, I will take whatever you bring back. I am going to get started with the little I have here. Rosey make sure you get me a real cast iron skillet."

"We will be back," I sang surprised Paige and Sade did not jump up to join us which meant they planned to be nosey while we were gone.

"Your Mama is going to get me in shape one way or the other. I am going to bring her to the gym and let her whip my tail in shape there."

"Don't think she won't."

Once we got to the mall, we went directly to the home goods section to avoid all the contact and attention. King and Keith would probably pitch a fit if they knew he was at the mall. "What do you want to get?" I gave him an option.

"Everything she told us to get."

"We don't need all of that."

"I am not going to be disobedient. Get what you would want to use or what you would buy." He thought to himself one day these will be the pots Danielle used every day in our kitchen. He surely had no plans on using them. Therefore, while she spoke with the sales person he observed the blenders.

We purchased full sets of everything Mama asked for. He suggested we get another box set of china, drinkware and a set of silverware just to make sure he had enough. The total was freaking ridiculous. We made someone's day. It was either the cashier, the department, or the corporate office. What we spent in one sale was probably more than the whole department would make all week. I was going to pay since he covered the trip but when I pulled out my card, we stood there and argued at the register. The sales person wanted to ask if he was whom she thought he was but decided to wait in hopes of getting his card and reading his name. After we made a big enough scene I let him win. He handed her his card and pinned my hands. She read the card and knew exactly whom he was. She called for someone to assist us and bring the purchases to the truck. He gave the guy and the sales clerk a signed photo.

"Danielle, stop being so damn independent. You do not owe me anything. I took you and paid because I wanted too. If I want or need you to do something for me, I will let you know. Let me do what I want to do. I promise it is cool. No worries," he said as he pulled off.

I did not respond. I could hear the annoyance covered up in his voice. There was never such a thing as too independent. When we walked back in the house, we could smell the food cooking. I am sure his house never smelled like this before.

"Good. You two followed directions," Mama said observing the purchases.

"Yes ma'am."

"Come over here and tell me what you can have and cannot," her tone affectionate towards Randall.

"No salt, no pepper, no garlic, no butter, no oil, no meat, no seasons, and no sugar."

"Plain vegetables?"

"Yes."

"I am cooking yours separate from everyone else's."

"That will be great."

"Now, I do not know how in the world I am going to make you any corn bread. I will have to make you some water bread on the stove. Rosey, I cannot believe you wait this long to get a boyfriend and then get one this difficult. What am I supposed to do with him?"

He gave up my laugh.

"Get out of my kitchen," she said to us.

"Mama," Paige shouted.

"You know his kitchen." My mama had a nice kitchen. I had a great kitchen but this was a chef's dream. Sadly, he cared less.

"It's cool Mrs. Rose. You can claim it. This is the first home cooked meal it has seen from start to finish."

King showed up with RJ. Mama called Randall in there again after she spoke with RJ. "You are starving the baby too?"

"No. He is just thin."

"Not on my watch." She leaned in, "The heffa starved you and now she is starving the baby. I am going to put some meat on his bones. Ain't no hope for you at this point."

"Mrs. Rose, I weigh 210 pounds," most of which was muscle.

"Umm hmm," she ignored Randall.

At five dinner was served. There was a house full. Some kind of way King and Mama made friends. Randall blessed the food before we ate. Dinner was sheer commotion.

After dinner Randall said, "I would like to make a toast." Paige and Leigh got the glasses. He poured sparkling cider.

"Wait a minute. I did not come over here and slave for cider. You all kidnapped me all weekend then worked me hard and you think you are going to give me cider. There is no need in toasting to fake champagne. Rosaley get me some real champagne."

Sade jumped happy to do so. "What kind Mama?"

"It doesn't matter," Mama replied. "All that expensive champagne and high dollar liquor for someone who does not drink. What a waste. I need to go to the liquor store and slap whoever sold this to him. What were they thinking? Alcohol to a fighter. That does not even sound right. This is a dangerous combination. Can you imagine him drinking or drunk? It rings jail time all over the thought. Then he gone bring me over here and I got to do magic in the kitchen for some grape juice. This ain't my last supper. I do not know about the rest of you. He ain't Jesus either."

Mama was good at talking to nobody but addressing everybody. She did it all the time. Spoke aloud to herself but referencing someone or something in the room. We usually did what we all did right now. Let her talk and not interrupt. This is where Sade gets it.

Sade came back with a bottle and handed it to King to pop the top. He poured some in Mama's glass and then went to pour some in his own glass.

"Boy get your own bottle."

"Mama," Paige said embarrassed.

"Fine. I will share this one time."

Paige still talking, "Mama you were on vacation what do you mean you worked?"

She looked like how dare she ask. "I beg your pardon. I worked extremely hard."

"Doing what?" I asked trying to remember her working.

She looked at me like do you really want me to say. I bucked my eyes waiting on a response. "I kept the fighters hands off you. Honey, if I were not there his hands would be all over you like an octopus. You would be knocked up right now if he had his way." He dumped his head. "You can thank me later. I have been your saving grace. I see all through you. It is called discernment. No need in being ashamed Randall. We all can see it. You want her like people in hell want ice water. She feels the same way. Acting like a silly schoolgirl. We are all intervening. You don't have to worry about being weak. We got your back." Now I was embarrassed. "You are going to have to marry her baby before you get the first pitch. Do not even think about first base, second, or third. I am not having it. I may not be a licensed boxer but do not under estimate Mama Rose. And Mama Rose will protect the Roses on the vine. Mama will knock your narrow behind out. In addition, if I cannot, all it takes is one call. Trust me. One phone call."

"I will drink to that," King said.

"Mama," Paige yelled as Mama tilted her glass all the way back.

"In the name of Jesus," she held her glass out to King for a refill.

We had so much fun. We had as much here as we did at the Royale. I was going to make sure his White Party was spectacular since he provided a spectacular weekend.

WEEK 25
Monday

"Good morning sunshine."

"Hey sweetie."

"How are you?"

"Good. Are you running?"

"Yes and thinking about you."

"Of course."

"Do you remember what is on the calendar for today?"

"You are taking today off," I said as if I was correct.

"Never. Today starts a new conditioning regimen. I will send you the schedule, print it off and place it on your desk."

"What is different?"

"Maybe some techniques you have not seen before. Shadowboxing, sparring, weight lifting, jumping rope of course and you and me in aerobics every day at seven except Wednesday."

"Who authorized that?"

"I did."

"I hope it is low impact."

He laughed, "For real. You remember about today?"

"YEP. Y-M-C-A," I sang.

"You are not going to do the dance are you?"

"Will it embarrass you?"

"No."

"Then no fun."

"Get dressed, call me back."

"I love you."

"I love you more."

I was dressed and headed out. Since Leigh worked all weekend, I was not going to ask her to join me at the YMCA. Instead, I was going to instruct her to go home and rest. The day was a lazy day at the office. I think we were all still in vacation mode. Everyone thanked me a million times. I didn't do anything. All I did was draw the building. I did not even know I was going. They needed to thank Hooks. I ragged them all about the surprise. We looked at the photos and the videos Leigh captured. Confirming all the fun we had. I do not think we all have ever been in the same place at one time. How was he able to pull that off? We are all usually spread out visiting different job locations and never able to vacate together.

Overall, today was a good day. Like clockwork, he was standing in the threshold of my door on time. "Are you ready Ms. Rose?"

"I thought I was meeting you there?"

"You were but now I am here."

"So do you want to go on and I meet you there?"

He laughed.

"I was serious."

"I am waiting on you to wrap up."

"Now?"

"Yes, now."

"I thought I had forty minutes."

"You do but we will be in the car for those forty minutes."

"Are you always this demanding?"

"Demanding no. Punctual yes. Are you blowing me off?"

"Excuse me?" I said sternly.

He laughed again, "Wrong choice of words."

"Sure were."

I took my time while he waited patiently. My actions showed I was not happy about leaving early or about being pushed around. I sarcastically handed him my bag and mumbled. He purposefully did not acknowledge.

We arrived at the YMCA. He was there for a few reasons. To speak to the kids, give them boxing lessons, and his gym was hosting a self-defense class. The afternoon was going great. He was such a philanthropist and I do not think he even knew it. This was easy for him and he was so good at it. He was a natural. Honestly, I think he loved it.

While we were there, he broke away from the masses, "Can I speak to you for a minute?"

"What's up babe?"

"What do you think about this place?"

"It looks the exact same as it did when I was here years and years ago."

"You were a member of this YMCA?"

"Yep. We all were. Me, Paige, and Sade. Actually, we still hold a membership.

This is where we came after school, every summer, and Paige used to teach aerobics classes here," along with much more memories I did not care to relive.

"Let's have dinner when we leave."

"Okay," I wasn't sure if it was a question or a request. He had a way with doing that. Most people would probably not like it. Me on the other hand, it worked for me. My independence almost appreciated someone making decisions other than me for a change. If he were not as direct as he is, I would probably veto all of his request. He doesn't give you an option to veto. Like Mama, you are told and it is done.

Later in the evening, we said our goodbyes. It was always tear jerking to see him leave his events. People would grow attached to him in such a short time because he was so charismatic, personable, and caring. He was one hundred at all times. No matter the setting, he remained real and true.

We arrived at dinner. I was surprised he ordered food.

"Danielle, how would you feel about redesigning the YMCA?"

"Oh boy. I would love to do that. It would be extremely challenging."

"Why?"

"Well it is has expanded the width and the depth of the land. It will be difficult. You can't tear the roof off because they have the HVAC equipment there. This means you have to bring in temporary heating and cooling for an extended period of time and figure out where to put it. Unless you shut the building down for months, this task is difficult. I would have to spend some time trying to figure out what I could do."

"How much will it cost?"

"To draw it or to rebuild it?"

"Both?"

"Let's go down to the city and get the current plans and see what we have to work with. The location has always been tight spot."

"How would you feel if I donated an addition?"

"How do you feel?"

"I want to do it but if you are not comfortable with me doing it then I will reconsider."

"Sweetheart, I think this will be a wonderful blessing to the community."

"Can you help me do it?"

"Of course."

"How do we start and where do I begin?"

"First you talk to your accountant to make sure it is within your budget. Meanwhile, you and I will hit the city and see what we can find out. You will get to see what I do." We talked all night about the YMCA and my job. We had a beautiful weekend and started the week with a wonderful day.

He blogged at three eighteen AM.

> The greatest command is LOVE. The greatest treasure is LOVE. I found the treasure at the greatest place of all.

Tuesday

I read his blog then I tried to roll over and fall back asleep but it didn't happen. After thirty minutes of closing my eyes tight, I decided to call. Today I beat him to the call. You would not believe it, but I still got butterflies and felt nervous around him. I felt like a sixteen year old expecting him to answer the phone.

He answered, "My love what do I owe the pleasure?"

Did he ever sleep? He was awake and excited like it was afternoon. His excitement made me even more nervous. I did not speak. Number one, I was blown away by his greeting and number two my voice still sounded sleepy I am sure.

"Sweetie?"

"You know why I am calling?"

"Crap. I knew treasure was going to be the wrong word. I should have said my angel."

"Rand," I did not get his name out.

"What's up?"

"You tell me. What is the deal with the blog?"

"Just what is says?"

"You have been up all day. Why do you choose to blog at three AM?"

"A lot of reasons."

Did he ever answer a complete question? Did he ever speak more than a phrase?
"I'm listening." I recalled Keith and King telling me he calls me Angel.

"The city is asleep. I can think and reflect on the day. I reflect on my feelings. I am at my most relaxed moment. Besides, it brings excitement. People look forward to waking up to see what my blog reads. Scratch that. You look forward to them. So much so you read them in the middle of the morning and call me right then."

He was being arrogant although he was correct, "Maybe you should blog about how arrogant you are as well."

"No, I am not arrogant. I write just for you."

"Why can't you tell me directly?"

"I could but how boring is that? When I blog the world knows. It is no secret. There is no question how I feel. It cures your anticipation and your thirst for my love notes."

"If you say so."

"What does that mean?"

"Yes, someone knows there is a treasure but whom?"

"I have said your name numerous times."

"Not exactly."

"What?"

"Rose does not constitute saying my name."

"If your name is what you want then your name is what you will get."

He was impossible even at this hour, "Goodbye."

"I will send you the guest list today. I know you did not think I would have it complete."

"You completed it or did Vickie?"

"I plead the fifth," I knew the true answer. Vickie.

I was somewhat quiet at work. His blogs made me so blah. I liked them a lot but why did they have to be so public yet so private? Why didn't he just say it to me every night? It was such a celebrity thing to blog and tweet. I guess he fit the bill. He was a celebrity. He would blog and never mention it unless I did. I was paranoid he was speaking of someone else but who would know? How would I know? It was strange to say the least.

Just as he promised, an email came from him with the guest list. I was in the middle of something and didn't look at it. Vickie and I had already covered a lot of ground. We spoke to the DJ, the videographer, the photographer, Mikey, and the dessert caterer. I had the rentals on standby, a date selected and invitations narrowed down to four choices. I was waiting on the guest list to know how many invites to order. How much to rent? How much food to tell Mikey to prepare? How much alcohol to ask the bartender to allow? This party planning was easy thus far but of course, we were at the preliminary stage.

Finally, late afternoon I opened his email. "What in the world."

I immediately rang his phone and JJ answered, "Hello Ms. D."

I humbled my tone, "Hi, JJ. How is your day?"

"We are working hard over here but the Champ seems to be taking it easy."

"Can I speak to him please?"

"Not at this moment."

"Huh?"

"Is this urgent? Are you okay? Do you need something?"

"I am fine. It can wait on my end but it may not be good for him. I will see him when I get there."

"Hooks, you are in trouble," JJ said in a monotone before he hung up.

I printed the list. I changed the format and sorted it. I scanned it and noticed quite a few celebrities. There were some big names on this list. Some of which were not local. After work, I raced over to the gym.

"Hey Ms. D," one of the guys said.

It was funny how I went from the enemy, to Ms. Rose and now to Ms. D. "What's up?"

"Hey babe," he yelled from his standard place where he jumped rope.

"Hey," I said dryly. I felt all eyes on me. I keep it moving heading up the stairs.

"DJ how was your day?" he asked still jumping.

"It started off good."

"What happened?"

"I got some news which changed my day."

"Anything I can do?"

"Yep."

"What can I do?"

I did not respond. As I expected he sent the Terminator. I opened the door from changing and King was sitting there.

"What do you want?"

"What is wrong with you?"

"Nothing."

"Who does Hooks need to take out?"

I laughed.

"What's funny?"

I was on the track walking by now, "Himself."

"I am not touching that with a ten foot pole. Do I need to send him up?"

"Not necessarily."

An hour or so passed and I could hear his soft footprints on the steps.

He came right next to me, "I hear I am in the doghouse."

I did not speak, instead; I cut my eyes at him.

"Say something love."

"Was that a question or statement?"

"Does this have anything to do with the blog?"

"No, we are beyond the blog."

"What did I do?"

"Tell me about this guest list?"

"I did not have all of your friend's names and address. Be sure to include them."

"Please discuss this list."

He was truly unaware, "Sure what do you have a question about?"

"How did the list go from maximum five hundred to a minimum of one thousand two hundred and forty seven?"

"Oh that?"

"Yes that."

"Minor detail."

"In whose world?"

"Just double the food and everything should be fine."

"Double of five hundred is one thousand. Your list was one thousand two hundred and forty seven," I smirked.

"That is why I love you. You are so smart."

"I feel like you are being sarcastic."

"No, you are smart."

"How did the list double?"

"I decided to invite everyone so I do not have any one mad at me."

"Creep." *Now I'm mad*, I thought.

He grabbed me, "What can I do to help? I will do whatever you delegate to me to do."

"Finish making the preparations," I threw the four invitation options at him. "Pick one."

"Consider it done," he was so oblivious.

This increase changed everything. It was almost like starting over. He had me mentally exhausted. I was preparing for bed when he blogs at two minutes before eleven. That was unusually early for him.

> Since you came into my life all the flowers seem to be plain.
> Diamonds do not shine and the candles are no longer bright.
> The moment you walked into my life I changed. Can I call
> Danielle Rose by any other name?

After I read it, all I could say was, "Wow." No one has ever referenced Teena Marie & Gerald Leveret, A Rose by Any Other Name lyrics to me. Did boys really know and remember this song? Did he really know much about

Shakespeare? This was so strange until it was freaky. I wondered if anyone told him it was my favorite song. It was the song I wanted to be my first dance if I ever got married. I called immediately. He answered the phone laughing. "What's funny?"

"I knew you would call."

"Did you now?"

"I sure did."

"Umm hmm."

"Do we have this resolved?"

"What?"

"Who I am referring to?"

"Well, I would have to say yes at this time."

"Now that this is no longer questionable, what else?"

"Since you asked, where did you get that song?"

"Yahoo."

"Why did you choose that particular song?"

"You don't like it?"

He was good at restructuring things in his favor. "That is not what I asked."

"It is your favorite."

"Who told you that?"

"You did."

"I did not."

"Yes you did in so many words. You have it playing in your car, in your house, on your iPod and upstairs. I finally listened to it closely and figured out why you love it so much. I feel like it was written just for us. I like it too. I have listened to it over and over again and it is so appropriate for the things I want to say to you. With you I have been changed."

I laughed. I think it offended and embarrassed him all at the same time. I quickly tried to repair the offense. I was doing what he normally did when he was nervous or caught off guard. The more embarrassed the louder his laugh. "Excuse me. I think I am shocked. I like the response a lot. I was not prepared nor expecting it but glad to hear."

"No need to apologize. That is how you do. A guy pours his heart out and you laugh."

"I was not laughing at you. I was laughing at myself."

"Thanks."

"I am not laughing at you."

"It feels like it."

"Never. Thanks for the blog."

"All of them are for you."

"Thanks."

His tone changed back to the demanding Randall, "Now go to sleep."

"You are the one who will be up all night blogging."

"I think I am done for the night."

"Good. I love you."

"I love you too babe."

Wednesday

"Randall DeWayne Washington, do not argue with me. I sent you the invitations. Pick one of them by Friday."

He knew I was serious when I called his whole name. His government name, as most people would say. He was going to have to do his share also. This was his party and he was not going to be allowed to just write the checks. Especially, since he almost tripled the guest list.

"Tell me which one is your favorite."

"It does not matter. It is your party."

He could easily propose and make it their party. "No Sweetie. This is our party."

"If that is the case then we need to work together and you need to make a decision?"

He quickly changed and tried to half answer, "It does not matter."

"Lamborghini or Maserati?"

"Lambo."

"See how easy it was to make a decision? Now do the same for the invitations. You wanted to have a party. Then you picked all white. Pick an invite."

"Point taken. You manage to find a way to always state the obvious."

"Umm hmm."

"I will see you tonight."

I took a break and made some calls to change the number of expected guest. I was probably making some enemies. First, asking for service for a party in a few weeks and now I am changing the number of guest. I am sure my tabbed substantially escalated. It is his party. He is the star. Therefore, he gets what he wants. Everything, no matter the cost. I hope that it will soon be my party and I can get whatever I want. Our party. Our wedding. On the other hand, was it wishful thinking?

He called a few times and asked me questions about the invitations. I gave him four to choose. I started out with thousands and he couldn't pick one of four. He wanted to know if it would be all right to check with Vickie and the girls for their opinions. I said it would be okay although it was cheating. Really, I knew which one I liked the best and I might go with it regardless of his opinion. I didn't know which look I wanted for this event. Did he want formal, whimsical, plain, simple, or generic?

During Bible Study, I was completely distracted. It makes no sense how he makes me feel. I was trying so hard not to stare but I could not. Every time he looked in my direction, I would quickly move my eyes away. I really do not know what Pastor Hunter taught tonight because I was in Daniville. I knew this was going to be difficult. This is like getting your honey where you get your money. In my book, that is a no-no. I needed to add a new rule. Don't play where you pray. Originally I was thinking how this would feel if it turned sour. Heck, I can't even handle it sweet. I tried with all my might not to stare. He caught me every time.

"Good evening," I said when he walked up to me.

He knew she was distracted about something by the way she made him feel uncomfortable all night. "Hey babe. Let's go to the gym. Train with me."

"What's up?"

"Nothing."

I walked right up the stairs, changed and came back down. Of course, he was jumping rope. This wasn't in my plans for tonight but maybe it would help me to relax.

"Get a rope," he said.

"I can't jump as long as you."

"Yeah you can. There is no such word as can't."

I snatched the rope from Kings hand and rolled my eyes.

"Ready. Jump." We jumped in unison. Every time I messed up he would say, "Go," to start again. He never stopped. He could tell I was not feeling the rope. "D, follow my instructions without the rope. Jump."

Therefore, I did the motions as if I was jumping rope without the rope. "Crisscross. Backwards. Skip."

This was still hard and tiring. I was dancing and spinning. I was doing all kinds of other things to make it fun.

"DJ stay focused."

My eyebrows touched while I followed his lead. I do not know if anyone did the math but twelve rounds at three minutes was thirty-six minutes. Was he expecting me to go thirty-six minutes with him? There was a bell in between each three minute round. "Where is the bell? Three minutes are up."

"No bell, keep going."

After the first thirty-six minutes he said, "Bell." One minute passed and he said, "Jump."

"What?"

"Let's go."

"Again?" He was already jumping. This was as boring as counting grass. I was too hyperactive to do this. Therefore, I made up my own things to do. I danced. I ran in place. I stood next to him but ran backwards. I went side to side.

"DJ."

I stopped playing and followed his lead. It was about to kill me. It was hard and boring. Didn't he know I had an attention issue?

"Time," King said.

I fell on the floor. Right now King was my hero.

"Get up. We are just getting started." Then we got in the ring.

I thought to myself *I should have gone home tonight.* After another two hours of him instructing me, guiding me in punches at one octave away from yelling, I was ready to go. I will say I enjoyed him guiding my punches. He was behind me holding my arms so they swung when his swung.

"Break," King said.

I was so happy to hear King speak. Something I never thought I would ever say. I raced up the stairs and got my keys. I barely said bye and left. Tonight there were no long goodbyes, no hugging, and definitely no kissing. Bye and a peck was all he got. I went home, went straight to the medicine cabinet, and took an Aleve. Something was bound to be hurting in the morning.

His intent for tonight was to get her to his zone. For her to understand what it took to do what he did. For her to understand his solitude and discipline. In order to jump rope, punch, and do the same exercise repeatedly you had to clear your mind. You had to calm down. Which clearly she did not do tonight. He wanted her to relax if for nothing else but to go to sleep. He knew she was stressed. He imagined it was from his guest list. This was something so trivial to him. He worked hard and he trained hard. Now all he wanted to do was play hard and love her hard.

Go to sleep.

Thursday

I checked my phone at three thirty seven. He had called and texted. I texted back.

I called him once I got in the car. You could hear the warden giving orders. "Babe, I can't talk long. Do you have plans Saturday?"

"I do not think so."

"Good be ready at nine in the morning. You will need comfortable clothes and shoes. It may be a long day in tight enclosed spaces."

"Okay. I guess you are not telling me where I am going?"

"You are right. I promise you will love it. Do you trust me?"

"Yes," I said reluctantly.

"Great. I will talk to you later."

I hung up the line. He always had something up his sleeve. I understood why. From all the jump roping, he had a lot of time to think. That is how he was able to blog. Those thoughts are probably ten hours old when he puts them down. I empathize with him after yesterday's experience. No wonder he does not like the track. There was too much going on at one time. Hence the reason they did not have music at the gym. He appears to like the solitude of training and thinking. The sport is definitely a disciplined and mental sport just as much as athletic. After last night, I agree I am too much of a busy body boxing.

A little after ten Leigh and I packed up for a field trip to the city. I needed to get all the information on the YMCA. I pulled the original general contractor and engineer's information and touched basis with them and the others who modified the building. What I needed from the city was the layout of the lot. What space was I really working with? This could be a ten-minute event or a ten-month episode. I was hoping for the shorter. It was going to be a challenge because we have not spoken with the owner. I need to see what we are working with before he goes and offers something, which cannot be done, or it is not worth the efforts.

Today's agenda was filled with Randall, Hooks, and Deacon Washington. All three people had my calendar full. I was also meeting with Vickie to get this darn party on the road. One thing was for sure, I was not jumping rope today. I walked in the gym and he was in the ring shadow boxing.

"Mr. Washington," I said as I leaned over the ring.

"Yes my love. How was your day?" he asked sincerely.

"I have been at it all day. How do you feel?"

"Better."

"Oh really?"

"Of course now that you are here." King gagged like he was going to vomit. Neither of us looked in his direction.

"You don't say?"

"Yep. How was your day?"

"It was busy. We will talk about it later."

"Busy good or busy bad?" he wanted to mentally prepare himself.

"I was down at the city trying to get information on the YMCA."

"What did you find out?"

"What did I find out or what did they find out?"

He stopped for the first time since I had been there. He walked over to rope, leaned in, and kissed me. "What happened?"

"There were a few complications but I think we have gotten them resolved."

"Like what DJ?"

"They were being uncooperative with the information."

"Did you get it?"

"Not yet. I do not have any reservations that I will not get it."

"What did you do?"

"They found out I can act like King."

He gave up my laugh, "What does that mean? And you get back to work," he scolded King who was in attack stance.

"My behavior was not pleasant."

"And mine isn't?"

"Imagine that," I walked away.

"Where are you going?"

"I have an appointment."

"Where?"

"Let Danielle mind Danielle's business."

"Danielle's business is my business."

I held my finger up, "Put a ring on it."

"In your face," someone said. "What are you going to do man?" They all teased him.

I knew he was going to do this. He waited for two hours and then looked for me. I was not where he assumed I would be. My phone was ringing his ringtone. I was going to send it to voicemail but I decided I might not want to do that. "Yes?"

"Are you in the building?"

"I am in a meeting can I call you back?"

"No. Where are you?"

"I will call you back." I know I told him I was in King mode. He had better stay back. Vickie raised her eyebrows as if I committed a cardinal sin by hanging up on him.

It was not five minutes later and he was knocking on her locked office door. "Yes Mr. Hooks?"

"Is my girlfriend in there?"

"Huh?"

"Do not play with me Varden. Is Ms. Rose in there?" he said in his commanding voice. It startled her. You could tell he did not speak to her in that tone and she didn't want to be on his bad side and since I was the cause, I fixed it.

"We are in a meeting Randall. I'll be out shortly."

"Danielle, open this door before I knock it down."

"Simmer down Hercules. No boys allowed."

It wasn't three minutes and King was pushing the door open allowing Randall to bust in. Vickie jumped while I rolled my eyes. "Didn't I say no boys allowed?"

"She is referring to you," King said as he came in looking around like we were fifteen hiding the marijuana and malt liquor.

"There is no place in this building I am not allowed," he folded his arms.

"You just banned yourself from upstairs with your pompous attitude."

"Pompous?" King said with laughter and walked out the door.

"Come back Robin since you and Batman just had to be in here. Have a seat."

"Don't mind if I do," King said.

"What's going on in here?"

"Nothing," Vickie said with hesitation.

"Vickie and I have been assigned to plan a party for a haughty boxer. Now all of a sudden he is bullying us. Since he has disregarded our decision-making skills, privacy, and competency, we will ask for his judgment. Which table arrangement here do you prefer? Then from there we can determine the linens, chair styles, covering, decoration, china, and flatware."

"I have picked out china once this year. I refuse to do it again," he said referring to the china and pots we bought the other day.

"You had to get in this room so yes you will participate." King stood up to leave. "Sit down," I spoke stern and harsh.

He opened his mouth then pursed his lips and snatched the chair to sit back down. I slung the pictures of the table arrangements towards Randall. I was just about sick of his commanding antics. I told him I was in a meeting. That should have been enough. His eyebrows touched in response to me slinging the pictures at him.

"This was your grand idea to have an event. Let's get busy." He looked like he was pissed. He stormed in the room and I was going to make sure he stayed there. "Are you going to be here tomorrow I asked him?" He nodded a confirmation. "Good. Vickie I will meet you at the house so we can walk the area and figure all the decorations we need."

He stared at the pictures as if it was an ultra sound and we were asking him to determine the sex of the baby. "Randall?" He looked up without speaking, "Can you get me in touch with the Pano's and Paul's valet guy to see if he would be interested in working this event? Is it okay for him to have your home address?" I spoke in a polite professional voice.

He nodded.

Being annoying I asked, "Is that a yes?"

"Yes."

"Great. We are getting somewhere already now that you are here. Thank you so much for barging in on us," I said super sarcastically.

"I didn't know you were bipolar," King stated.

"Oh my goodness. I didn't know you knew such a big word and could use it in the correct content," I came back without ever looking up.

"Chill." Randall spoke softly. I looked up over my eyes. "King. That was to King," he clarified.

"I thought so. You decide yet?" This interruption placed me in executive mode. I felt like this was going to be extremely productive. I rapidly tapped my fingers on the desk.

"I do not know," he said partially frustrated and aggravated.

As I knew I would, I made the decision, "Option C Vickie." he flipped the pictures over and over trying to figure out where I got C from. "Good job Hooks. Now, chairs. Which chair do you prefer?"

"Maybe I should not have interrupted," he noticed me calling him

Hooks. I only call him Hooks when I introduce him or refer to him but never directly at him.

"Excellent observation," I said in an upbeat tone as if I was congratulating him. This was strictly sarcasm. "You should not have but too late now. Let's keep it moving," I issued s fake smile.

He was furious. Oh well. This was not his cup of tea at all. He was used to paying and it was done. Well too bad. This time he was participating. Truth be told, he was not paying me. My services were free and if I had to work so did he. King could have killed him for making him sit through this torture. Weather he knew it or not, it was helpful for Vickie and me. We stayed on track and made decisions without wavering. Yes was yes and no was no.

Vickie and I were at a good point. I did not look up, "thanks guy's great job." You would have thought I said the place was on fire. They almost knocked each other over trying to get out of the door.

By the time we thought they were long gone Vickie and I looked at each other and fell out laughing. "Mr. Hooks is going to kill me," Vickie said.

We could not stop laughing. We packed up and left her office. As I walked back through he was barely hitting a punching bag. "Handsome." He turned around not sure whom I was speaking to, "Good night."

"I will walk you to the car."

Tonight was easy and not drawn out. We said good night and I pulled off. At midnight he blogged. This was the second early night in a row.

Proverbs 31

[1]The words of king Lemuel, the prophecy that his mother taught him. [2]What, my son? and what, the son of my womb? and what, the son of my vows? [3]Give not thy strength unto women, nor thy ways to that which destroyeth kings.

[4]It is not for kings, O Lemuel, it is not for kings to drink wine; nor for princes strong drink: [5]Lest they drink, and forget the law, and pervert the judgment of any of the afflicted. [6]Give strong drink unto him that is ready to perish, and wine unto those that be of heavy hearts. [7]Let him drink, and forget his poverty, and remember his misery no more. [8]Open thy mouth for the dumb in the cause of all such as are appointed to destruction. [9]Open thy mouth, judge righteously, and plead the cause of the poor and needy. [10]Who can find a virtuous woman? for her price is far above rubies. [11]The heart of her husband doth safely trust in her, so that he shall have no need of spoil.[12]She will do him good and not evil all the days of her life. [13]She seeketh wool, and flax, and worketh willingly with her hands. [14]She is like the merchants' ships; she bringeth her food from afar.

[15]She riseth also while it is yet night, and giveth meat to her household, and a portion to her maidens. [16]She considereth a field, and buyeth it: with the fruit of her hands she planteth a vineyard. [17]She girdeth her loins with strength, and strengtheneth her arms. [18]She perceiveth that her merchandise is good: her candle goeth not out by night. [19]She layeth her hands to the spindle, and her hands hold the distaff. [20]She stretcheth out her hand to the poor; yea, she reacheth forth her hands to the needy. [21]She is not afraid of the snow for her household: for all her household are clothed with scarlet. [22]She maketh herself coverings of tapestry; her clothing is silk and purple.[23]Her husband is known in the gates, when he sitteth among the elders of the land. [24]She maketh fine linen, and selleth it; and delivereth girdles unto the merchant. [25]Strength and honour are her clothing; and she shall rejoice in time to come. [26]She openeth her mouth with wisdom; and in her tongue is the law of kindness. [27]She looketh well to the ways of her household, and eateth not the bread of idleness. [28]Her children arise up, and call her blessed; her husband also, and he praiseth her. [29]Many daughters have done virtuously, but thou excellest them all. [30]Favour is deceitful, and beauty is vain: but a woman that feareth the LORD, she shall be praised. [31]Give her of the fruit of her hands; and let her own works praise her in the gates.

I did not respond this time. He was shocked. Therefore, he texted me.

Can you meet me in the morning?

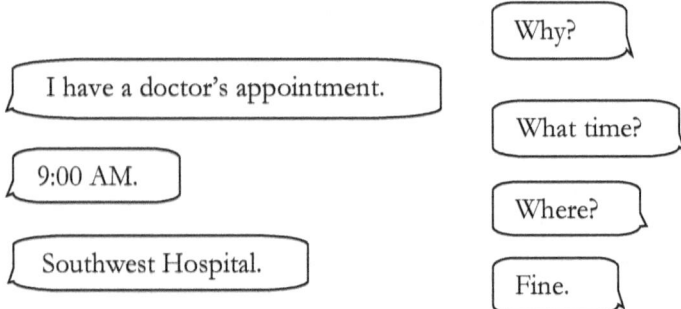

He was confused about the word fine. What did it mean? He got the fact that she was showing up but he needed clarity on the tone.

I rolled over and went to sleep tonight for a change.

Friday

I had no clue why I was meeting him at the doctor. I did not even ask if something was wrong. I guess I will find out in a few hours. I got up on time so I could be in my office by five. I did not understand this city. Nothing opened early and nothing stayed open late. That was the only problem I had with Atlanta. The mall needed to stay open until midnight and Starbucks needed to be twenty-four hours. If Starbucks were open twenty-four hours, I would go to a liquid diet like Randall. My only liquid would be from Starbucks loaded with caffeine. Instead, I fixed my latte at home. A girls got to do what a girls got to do.

It was four fifty seven when he called. "Hey," I answered.

"Good morning sweetheart."

"Everything alright?"

"Why do you ask?"

"Why are you going to the doctor?"

"The association is sending me."

"Is this normal?"

"Yes. Routine. It will be regularly from this point on. Usually less than twenty four hour notice so you do not have time to cleanse your system if you are dirty."

"You may want to lay off the asparagus then."

"You got jokes?"

"I'm just saying. All those liquid vegetables in your system are bound to from an illegal concoction."

"Why are you clowning me?"

"Alright, alright, alright," I said laughing.

"I see you are having a good day."

"You're not?" Although I never really knew him not to have a good day. He laughed, "Yeah, babe I am."

"Great. I will see you at nine."

I beat him to the doctor's office. I was walking down the sidewalk when the truck pulled up behind me. I assumed it was them when the engine slowed down. Without looking over, I said, "Twenty thousand per hour. Two hour minimum."

"I would pay more. You are selling yourself short."

"It should be free," King said as I rolled my eyes.

He, JJ, and King stepped out of the truck leaving Lefty to park. When he stepped out all I could say to myself was *oh my freaking goodness. The man was so fine. He was wearing black jeans, black V-neck, and Jordan's. There was nothing special about his attire. He had on a plain Hanes T-shirt but he looked like a million bucks. I tried not to do a double take.*

We embraced passionately right there on the sidewalk. When I heard myself gently moan and he moan loudly, I knew then it was time to separate.

JJ leaned in over my shoulder, "Enough guys. Break it up."

As bad as I did not want too JJ was correct. It was enough. When he walked in the office, everyone stopped. It was as if time stood still. He signed in and we walked to a seat. Before we all took our seats, his name was called. Being a celebrity had many rewards. He stood up to go back. Two of them stood up with him. He looked back at me and Lefty, "Are you coming?"

I raised my eyebrows. He knew my mind was in the gutter. "Do you need me?"

"Yes please." We all walked back together. The nurse knew there was no way she was going to separate this passé. She dared not ask.

We all stood back as if we were the secret service. They checked his weight, his height, blood pressure, blood sugar, iron, and his temperature. She asked him to leave a urine sample. We all stood behind the door and waited. I could hear the difference in the sound when it hit the cup and the stool. I laughed to myself.

"Mr. Hooks," the nurse said.

"Mr. Washington," he corrected.

She was embarrassed. I squeezed his hand. He knew why. He almost broke mine back. "It is Washington."

I snickered at him trying to correct his harshness.

"Follow me," she said.

We all followed and all four of us went into the examination room. Lefty stayed on the other side of the door. "Undress down to your boxers and put this on." I am sure there was no pun intended. However, there was a lot of pun in the boxer in his boxers.

"Thank you," he said.

"I am going to step outside." I whispered in his ear.

"No chance," he squeezed my hand.

Right then the doctor walked in, "Mr. Hooks."

I squeezed his hand quickly. He got the hint. The doctor introduced himself and gave some basic introduction. He listened to his lungs, checked his eyes, hooked him up to an EKG machine then spoke, "Everything looks good so far Mr. Hooks. We will send the lab results to the Association. Do you have any questions?"

"No. We have done this numerous times." The doctor went into small talk. Finally, he left. Randall got dressed and we all left the room in unison. He walked me to my car. The guards stood back and allowed us to walk hand in hand.

"Thank you for coming."

"You do not have to thank me."

"What are you doing tonight?"

"Nothing."

"Can I come over?"

I wanted to tell him he didn't have to ask, "Of course."

"I will be there by eight. Is that cool?"

I kissed his lips. He kissed me back. I felt like I was out in the middle of the day getting a quickie. Before I went back to work, I stopped and picked up a just because present. I will confess. He blew my mind standing there in his underwear today so I had to buy him something to make me feel lustfully better. I am so glad he was financially stable otherwise; he would have me freely paying his bills. Besides, God loves a cheerful giver. "Earth to Daniville," I said as I misquoted scripture pulling up to Lenox Square Mall.

There was too much to decide from. I had close to thirty items on the counter. I had to make a decision. What should have been a five to fifteen minute decision at the most turned into a dilemma?

I settled for way more than what I went to get. I went for one item. I came out with four. All four for him and nothing for Danielle. It was all good and he was worth it.

I purchased a belt buckle, a leather bracelet, a pair of shades and a dog tag. Nothing said sexy better than a dog tag. I wore them a lot myself. There were more items I wanted him to have but I have done enough damage for one day. Besides, I was thinking of saving something for the party. I had just the right presents in mind. I wish I could purchase him a watch but it would be wasteful since we always wear the James Bond timepiece. He even sleeps in his to record his sleep pattern or lack thereof. I probably should sleep in mine also but that gives him too much access.

I left work a little later than I expected. I wanted to shower and change before he got to my house.

I called him before I pulled up to the house to make sure I did not need to do anything. Keith answered, "Ms. D."

"Yes Sir."

"What's up?"

"Nothing. Is he available?"

"Who?"

"You got jokes too?"

"You two are ridiculous. He is in the shower."

"Ask him do I need to do anything or pick anything up?"

You could hear the background noise. "Does she want to speak to me?"

"She wants to know does she need to get anything." There was a pause. "He said no they have gone to get what he needs."

"Who is they?"

"Vickie left with someone."

"Humph. Okay bye."

"I have no clue Danielle." Keith knew what humph meant and saying Danielle implied no more questions.

I chilled until he showed up. He was looking and smelling sexy all over again. Why was he doing this to me? He came in with bags.

"What is all of this?"

"Date night. Tomorrow is a big busy day. You will need to get some rest."

Date night? I was impressed. "Why?"

"You will see tomorrow."

"Okay tell me what all of this is," we walked to the kitchen. He had peanuts, a veggie tray, and a few kinds of Orville Redenbacher microwave popcorn, bottled water, and a bag of movies. Then he handed me an envelope. Inside the envelope were the four invitations. Each one was marked with a number on the back. I immediately texted Vickie his choice. It was my top choice. I smiled on the inside assuming he had assistance from Vickie which option to pick.

> Can you please order on line for rush and overnight delivery. Text me back the confirmation number. The printer is going to print within twenty four hours and ship them to us so we can get them out starting Monday.

"How many of these are we going to watch?"

"One tonight but we have enough to carry us all the way through training."

"So what are we watching?"

"Take your pick. Old boo or new boo?"

"Huh?" I asked.

"Denzel or TI?" he growled.

"Difficult choice. You did this on purpose."

"I aim to please."

"How about Denzel?"

"What? Thank God." He was surprised by my choice. We watched the movie and vegged out on the couch. When movie number one ended he got up and helped me clean up and said, "Big day tomorrow. Good night."

"Am I fighting tomorrow?"

"You could say that?"

We said our goodbyes. I did not want him to go now or forever. I looked through the bag of movies. Someone went way out tracking all of these movies down. I had to call him.

"My love."

"Thanks for the movies. That was so sweet of you. Someone went through a lot of trouble."

"It is not a problem."

"I wanted to say thank you."

"Good night."

We hung up and I walked back to my bedroom. "Oh crap," I did not give him his presents. I called him right back.

"Hey you must be missing me."

"Where are you?"

"On the highway."

"Can you turn around?"

"Why?"

"I need to give you something."

"Can it wait until tomorrow?"

"It can but I would prefer not." You could hear his engine roar. He took it up a notch and laid on the accelerator.

"Give me a minute. I will be back." He prayed on the ride back. He needed strength. He was cool as long as they were around others. At the gym, he was cool. At church, he was cool. When they were alone, by themselves, is when he could not handle their situation. He has done well for the last few hours. He was not sure he would be able to contain himself and he did not know what he was going back for. *I should have said no.* He thought to himself.

When he rang the gate she thought *is it time to give him a gate code and a key.* "Let me ponder and pray," I opened the door refraining from seducing him. I wanted him badly. "Thanks for coming back."

"You do not have to ever thank me."

"Yes I do because you didn't have to turn around."

"All you have to do is ask."

"Wait right here." I came back with four black David Yurman bags. I requested each present be wrapped separately. It always excited me to open more. I hope that it will excite him also.

"What is this?"

"A present."

"No Danielle," although he was overjoyed.

"Don't dispute me. Open them and enjoy."

He opened each one and stared. He slid down the wall. The same one he always punched. He pulled me over. That is where it went wrong. The next thing I knew we were both breathing hard.

"Thank you DJ," he managed to say during the heavy breathing.

"It's nothing compared to how much I love you."

"Do not buy me anymore gifts. I am supposed to buy you gifts not the other way around. This is too much and too expensive."

We had a few more minutes of heavy breathing. "Don't leave me."

"I don't want to ever but until you marry me I must."

"Don't go," I begged physically and verbally.

"Let's get up from here before we get ourselves into a world of trouble."

"Do we have to?"

"Yes. Do I want to? Never." He scooped me up and looked at his watch. One more movie DJ and that is it. I am serious you need to be rested and alert tomorrow. You need to go to sleep."

When the movie was over, we had another long intense departing.

Saturday

At seven AM, he was ringing my phone.

"Hello Sir."

"Good morning. Get dressed. I just finished running. We will be there to pick you up in an hour."

"Where are we going?"

"Two hours DJ. You can wait two hours."

"You make me sick."

"I know. Dress comfortable. Just to be safe bring an extra set of clothes and shoes. Flat shoes or tennis shoes."

"I am not jumping rope."

He gave up my laugh, "I will keep that in mind."

In exactly one hour, he was buzzing my gate. I could hear all the noise. He did say we. As I approached the door, he was on the step and mini Hooks was behind him. I opened the door.

"My two favorite guys." He had a fresh cut and his face was shaven clean. His skin was radiant. His teeth were beautiful. He was sexier today than he was yesterday. It was as if he had a dial and each day he turned it up and up and up. I was staring although I was trying not to be obvious.

"Ms. D."

"Good morning sweetie."

"Get the bags son." He whispered in my ear, "I'm jealous. I thought we talked about that sweetie nonsense."

"You are sexy when you are jealous."

He licked my ear and neck. "You are sexy all day every day. Get ready. You are the only girl all day. Is this everything?"

"Yes."

"Are you coming back soon?"

"Stop playing and Queen."

"Huh?"

"It's Queen not girl. Make sure the Terminator calls me Queen today." He put his hand on my tail and squeezed it. "Watch it," I said.

"I am as soon as you walk away."

We got to the bus and he was not kidding it was all the boys and me. "Good Morning."

"Good morning Ms. D."

"It is Queen D today," he corrected.

"Did you say Queen B?" King asked rudely.

"Shut up Popeye."

"It's too early kids."

"If I am the King there is no way in hell you are going to be the Queen."

"King size butt hole is what you are."

"Danielle, he yelled at me. "Kid on the bus," he instructed.

"He-Man," King barked back.

"Kids," Randall shouted referring to King and me.

I sat down next to RJ not knowing where we were going. A text came in.

> I'm jealous.

> You yelled at me twice.

It was not thirty seconds later and he was at my seat. "Son enough." RJ got up and moved. I shook my head at his jealousy. He sat down next to me. "Since you will not come to me then I will come to you."

The ride seemed like forever. Finally, we pulled up. I knocked him over to get up. I ran to the front where the driver was. "Hey. Why are you turning in here?"

"This is the destination."

I pulled my iPad and checked the schedule and there was nothing going on here today. *Why were we stopping?* The bus stopped at the request of a security officer.

"Hooks Gym," the driver said to the security guard in the booth.

"How many do you have?"

"Seventeen adults, one child and four boxed trucks."

I looked in his review mirror and sure enough, there were four boxed trucks behind us. I ran back to his seat, "What's going on?"

"Ten minutes DJ."

"Rabbits can't tell time," King said.

"I got your rabbit. Skunk."

We both received an awful look from Hooks. The bus went under the tunnel, stopped, and parked. The doors opened and everybody exited except me. He stepped back on the bus. "What are you waiting for?"

His head was just above the steps. His face shaved clean and his scalp skinned to the bone. "Huh?"

"What are you waiting on?"

"Nothing I guess. Do I need my things?"

"No, but bring your toys if they make you happy."

"What are we doing?"

"We are driving the track."

"Are you serious?"

"Yes."

"Really?" He was now standing on the ground and I was standing at the top of the steps before I jumped in his arms.

"I am glad you are excited babe."

As I got myself together, I realized they were unloading his cars, a rack of helmets, gloves and jackets. I could not believe this. I have walked this track many many times for the Friday Night Drag. I have been in those stands twice a year for years watching my favorite driver drive this track. Never once did I ever imagine I would be driving it myself. I was nervous. Not afraid but nervous. If I knew in advance maybe, I would have been prepared.

This was so fun. I drove around the track a few times. We did exercises in preparation of quick escapes. There were all kinds of timed stunts and tricks. Randall, RJ, and I had the privilege of being picked up, pushed, shoved, and forced into cars, trucks, and vans that sped off before the doors closed.

King and I ended up on a team. RJ was assigned to Keith and Hooks for the day. It was a good team building exercise for King and me. I finally realized I needed to get some footage. If I had known, Leigh would have been here with a tripod on the back of my truck getting all of this. This was better than Inside NASCAR.

Lunchtime was approaching and I requested a turkey leg, dipping dots and a funnel cake. I got the feeling this was not on the menu for today. This was my normal meal here. An hour later a box arrived with twenty-five turkey legs, dipping dots, and funnel cakes. The guys had already begun to eat their prearranged lunch.

JJ spoke first, "Are you sharing Ms. D?"

"No."

"You cannot eat all of that."

"So. I like turkey legs." I sat on the track with the box in the middle of my legs biting the turkey leg as if I was Wilma Flintstone and drinking some of the best lemonade I have ever had.

"You need to share."

"I do not need to do anything. I asked for this. You could have asked too. You have not because you ask not," I said to JJ pointing my turkey leg at him.

They were all asking me to share. Finally, I gave in. "Baby do you want one?"

"I am scared to say yes or no," Randall answered.

"I will give you one."

"Can I bite yours?"

"We have kids here," I replied maliciously.

"One kid," he acknowledged.

"Two including him," I pointed at King with my turkey leg.

Pastor Hunter showed up. I should have known he would. He has a thing for cars too. He likes nice fast cars just like me. Hunter kept his rides clean. Since he was here, I had better behave and share or else tomorrow's sermon would step on my toes. I am sure he had his sermon planned before he left the crib but he will switch it up at the last minute. I loved him for that. It was the faith and substance great pastors were made of.

"RJ?"

"Yes Ms. D?"

"Can I offer you a turkey leg, dipping dots, or a funnel cake?"

"Please."

"Pastor Hunter, may I please offer you one?"

"What is the deal?" Hunter asked observing my food and theirs.

"Well, I asked for this and I received it. Now they are all mad because they got cold sandwiches on some organic bread, vegetable made meat and water. You have not because you ask not," I sang.

"A woman who knows the word and uses the word. Tell them again baby girl," Hunter sided with me.

I said it with conviction, neck rolling, and finger pointing. "Booyah. In your face." I took it there since Pastor approved me to be a smarty-pants.

I handed Hunter, RJ, and JJ a turkey leg and then shoved the box to King. Today was turning out to be a good day. Randall shared my turkey leg although there was enough for him to have his own.

The day was freaking awesome. The guys did many tricks in the cars. You could tell they have done this before. It was all a part of their job to get the Champ in and out quickly if an emergency arises.

It was the best day. I think I had more fun than anyone did. RJ was the only one of us who could not drive. Randall did have his four wheelers on the track for RJ. The motorcycles were on the tracks also. King and the rest of the guys rode me on the bikes. Even Hunter rode his bike.

"Can I speak to you please?" I asked Randall.

"Yes baby."

"I am having a great time. You know I love this place," I said to him.

"This is an activity we haven't done in years and we have never done it here. Since you love NASCAR I decided we should come here."

"This was too much."

"There is no price on safety. Not to mention it looks like you and King have been behaving today."

"Are you about to ride a bike?"

"I was planning on it. Why?"

"You are not going to ride dangerously are you?"

"What is dangerously?"

"Fast?"

"This is the legal place we can ride fast."

"I do not want you to," I humbly confessed.

"You know I am not going to do anything stupid while you and RJ are here."

"Are you admitting that you would normally do something stupid on a bike?"

"Are you admitting you do not want me to ride a bike?"

"Kind of sort of."

"We will discuss this later."

"Promise."

He kissed my forehead, "I love you."

The sun was going down when JJ spoke, "We are going to do a few runs in the dark to practice and then we will call it a night."

As they loaded the cars on the trucks Randall spoke, "Leave the Ferrari out. Dani and I will drive it home."

As we left everyone decided they were hungry so we went to the restaurant for dinner. After dinner, he dropped me off. It was a long exciting day. As we stood on the steps he spoke, "I am not coming in."

"Why?"

"I think you clearly know why."

"I will behave."

"It is not you that worries me. Speaking of behaving, I am proud of you and King. You both did excellent today."

"I think we were both in a zone. We were doing things we like to do."

"What is up with the bike Danielle?"

He called me Danielle. "Nothing."

"Yes it is."

"I do not want you to ride."

"Why? I have ridden all my life."

"I really want you to be safe. I think it is important for your career. A cruiser maybe but the crouch rocket is out."

"I am usually safe."

"Usually?"

"Wrong choice of words."

"Randall I love you and I do not want anything to happen to you."

"I love you too DJ." He kissed me. "I will see you in the morning." He knew right then he would probably never ride his bike again.

Sunday

I arrived at church and honestly, my body was sore. I do not see how Junior, Casey, Jeff, Kyle, and the other drivers do this every week. It is brutal to the body. Can I claim whiplash from speedway practice? I struggled to the door. I walked straight to the water fountain.

I tried to reach in my bag quickly but it was a lost cause. I had to go in the ladies room and sit down to find my Tylenol through all the junk in my bag. I admitted I needed to clean out my handbag. I came out to find Keith at the door not paying any attention to the women who were looking at him. It seemed like you could read their minds and hear their thoughts. He was standing there with a stern look on his face. When they spoke, he did not speak back instead he nodded. He had no clue they were checking him out. Boys are so clueless. If he knew, I do not think he would care. He had no inkling women thought he was sexy.

He opened the door, "Ms. D." All the other women turned to see whom he was calling.

"Yes."

"Everything alright in there?"

"Here I come." A woman can't even be stiff, in pain, and in peace around here. I struggled to get up. I wanted to kick my shoes off and walk barefooted the only problem was my feet, ankles and legs still would have to move. I had the two pills in my hand. As I prepared to pop them in my mouth, he snatched my hand. All eyes were on us.

"What are you taking?"

"What does it look like?"

"It is not birth control."

I looked around to see who was looking. While I did, he took them out my hand. "Hey, don't touch that. I have to take those. I do not know where your hands have been."

He rolled them around and read they said Tylenol. "Let me see the bottle."

Oh no. I am not searching for this again. "I will give it to you when we sit down."

"I will give them to you once you sit down then."

"I will not have any water. Boy give them to me," I said between my teeth.

We walked into the sanctuary slowly. I was not in a position for socializing because that meant I would have to stand. Once we got in the sanctuary, I did what I said and handed Keith the medicine bottle. He turned it around and around and then opened it and looked at the contents and placed the bottle in his pocket. Just as my joints were being acclimated to sitting, I heard a noise in his ear. I knew it was Randall's voice. He stood up.

I pulled his pants leg. He did not move. I tried with all my power and finally stood up. "What does Deacon Washington want?"

He did not speak but motioned towards the door opening. Deacon Washington peeked his head in, smiled, and closed the door as we both sat back down.

"What was that about?"

"He wanted to know where you were," Keith whispered annoyed.

As soon as I got comfortable, it was time to stand. "Help me Lord." Keith took my arm, pulled me up, and smirked as if he knew why I pained.

"It is not funny," I growled.

Pastor Hunter was preaching but I could not quite tell if he was directing his sermon at Deacon Washington and me or if I was being paranoid. With Hunter, it was hard to tell. He was preaching on false prophets. His exact words were, "I did not come here today to tell you what you want to hear beloved. I will not be labeled as a false prophet. I have to call sin - sin. I cannot help you cover up or sugar coat sin. I will not tell you this is a little sin. We do not serve a Piccadilly God. You do not get to pick which commands you will obey. There is no picking and choosing. There is no such thing as a little sin. Neither is there a white lie. Sin is sin and a lie is a lie."

I was trying to go back and figure out if anything happened yesterday to allow him to reference Deacon and me in today's sermon. I could not think of one thing but I surely felt like I was on the hot seat. I felt like Dwayne Johnson in the Tooth Fairy and I needed shrinking paste. I wanted to disappear. I looked over at Deacon and he displayed his normal facial expression. It was one of the qualities I love about him. His expressions were always the same. I have seen him in a suit, tuxedo, jeans, shorts, soaking wet in a pool, sweaty, half knocked out in the ring and his expressions were always the same. It was hard to read him by his body language. I could not tell if he was feeling the heat as I was.

I was already on pins from body ache. Now, I was on pins and needles from this sermon. I made a mental note to never date a person whose best friend is a Pastor again. It was a tough job. It kept us in line. I will confess…if it had not been for Hunter riding us we would have been intimate a long time ago.

I know I would have given in and if he denied me call it seduction or flat out rape. I would have given it a week or so from the divorce being final. I'm lying. If I am going to sit here on the front row and confess privately to myself, I might as well confess honestly. I would have let him have me the night of the pool scene if it was not for Hunter. The spirit will make you confess even when you do not want to. I would have had him on the floor under the desk the night he was approved to fight with Hunter and a room full of people waiting and in the back of the limo at the Smythe Royale.

Thank God for Pastor Hunter. He was a human chastity belt. Every time I felt the urge to give in or the desire to seduce, his face would interrupt my thoughts. Would it be bad to say I hate a pastor? It not only would be bad but it would be a lie. He was fervently keeping us in check. One day I will have a talk with him about all of this. As for now, these are my private confessions.

After the benediction, I ran out. Keith could not keep up. I was half way to my car when I heard a voice.

"Baby."

I tried so hard to turn around. All I could do was stop. He stood in front of me.

"Thanks Keith." Keith nodded and threw him the Tylenol from his pocket. "Where are you running to and why?"

"Hi handsome. Was today's sermon for us?"

"Does Tre have you upset?"

"No. Maybe he stepped on my toes a little."

"It is his job. You will get used to it. Why are you taking Tylenol?"

"My body hurts."

He gave me a look that made me laugh. "Can I rub you down?"

"You can smack it up, flip it, and rub it down." Could he read my mind in service?

He put his hand over my mouth. "Oh no. Go home. I will be over once I am done."

"I won't have anything on."

He laughed and put his finger up to his lips, "Shh."

"Sorry."

"Do you need me to bring anything?"

"I think everything I need comes attached."

"My word. You are still on church grounds young lady. I do believe Tre was speaking to you. Let me get you two or three CD's of today's message babe. What is going on? Anything we need to discuss?"

"No. I guess not. Can't fault a girl for trying."

"I need to check your levels. Something is off balance and I like it."

"Whatever."

He hugged me and whispered his confession in my ear. "I feel the same way all day, every day. I hope I contain it well."

I pushed him back. "Do you really?"

"Heck yeah. I am stopping by the house and I will be on my way. Go take a cold shower."

The way my body felt I needed a hot tub of water filled with Epson salt. Right when my body relaxed and my eyes closed the phone rang startling me. That was it. He was getting a key and a gate code immediately. I really did not want to get up and open the door. I couldn't. My body ached too badly.

He brought food to cook after I told him not to bring anything. He also brought a bag full of movies. We did not finished watching the ones from Friday night.

"What do you want to watch first? A movie, boxing, or me boxing?"

"Do I have a choice?"

"You always have a choice."

"Let's put them in the bag and draw one out. We will watch what we pull."

He drew, "Movie it is."

After the first movie, I said, "Alright boxing."

"Let's watch boxing first and I will commentate and then we will watch me."

Sarcastically I asked, "Are you sure?"

"Yep. Let's see what we learn?"

"Me you mean?"

"No, I am reviewing my strengths and weakness. King cannot say I had a day off. I am still working right?"

"Right, right."

"I have not forgotten I promised you a body massage too."

As bad as my body was hurting all I could think was thank you Lord. Thank you for making me so tired until if he did massage me I did not have the strength to do anything else. I put the fish in the oven. We had corn on the cob and cauliflower. "I am surprised you are eating food."

"I do eat. I choose not to."

"Evander eats."

"How do you know?"

"I have seen him in the restaurant eating."

"Good for Holyfield."

I blew air from my lips. "Floyd eats." He did not respond and gave me a look like how did we get on this subject. I said, "Most people get upset when you point out their flaws."

"What flaw DJ?"

"I have never met a man with an eating disorder."

His voice changed, "Disorder? I choose not to eat."

"Kind of what disorder means."

"I am not purging. I watch my calorie intake."

"However you choose to describe it."

He rolled his eyes and got up and put another piece of fish on his plate to appease me. It worked. I was always concerned about his health. It was one thing to be a vegetarian but he was on a liquid diet the majority of the time.

"Are you happy now?"

"Yes. Thank you."

"Any other flaws you care to discuss with me?"

"Since you mentioned it. I think you have small hands."

"What?" He looked at his hands. "That is complete BS."

"They are small for your size and much smaller than what I thought a boxers hand should look like."

"Hold your hand up." I did. He placed his hand to the palm of my hand. "My hands are twice the size of yours or more."

"I did not say they were not larger than mine I simply said they were small."

"What is this? Insult Hooks today?"

"Is that what you think I am doing, insulting you?"

"You do not?"

"I would never insult you."

"It sure feels that way."

I stood up. I pushed his plate from the table and sat on his lap. I kissed him until he was breathless.

"Let me have you Danielle."

I spoke in his mouth, "I can't," I stood up and walked away.

His head flopped back. "You see why I do not eat? It makes me weak."

"Finish up so we can continue our movie date."

Hours passed. He taught me a lot about boxing. I must admit I did not like watching him get hit. It pissed me off. However, I managed to get through the videos. I purposefully did not show any signs of fear or stress. I think that was the main thing he was looking for. My reaction was the purpose for this exercise. I was actually glad to watch these. I was going to request a copy so I could mentally prepare myself for the real event. This was good preparation.

We changed to another movie and at some point, I must have dozed off.

"DJ, go take a shower. I will wait."

"I am good."

"I know." He gave me a look like go do it and do it now. Right then I realized I might be the only person who disputes his commands. I do not think he knew how to handle it but it may very well be the reasons he liked or loved me.

I was just as stubborn as I wanted to be. I sat there and apparently dozed off again. "DJ! Shower!"

I smacked my lips and got up. I'll show him. He is not going to boss me around in my own house. I took my shower. He continued to watch himself fight. I came out in a sexy ensemble. Not too sexy but just enough to get his attention.

"Okay Danielle, I see where this is going." He gave up my laugh. "Good night. You win." He gathered his phone and keys. He looked at me and shook his head. "I will see you later. Go to bed. I love you dearly. More than you will ever know." He hugged me, kissed my forehead, my nose and left.

He texted me when he got home. Later he blogged at one thirty seven AM. The first time ever. His blog was one word.

TEMPTATION!

WEEK 26
Monday

I had a lot of work and a party planning ahead of me. I was going over the menu with Mikey. He created a few dishes he wanted me to taste. Mikey knew me well enough to know what I liked and what I would appreciate. He knew I was an appetizer and tapas type chick. He knew Randall did not eat much so the smaller the portions the more likely he would eat.

I drove my truck today and dropped it off at the radio shop while the girls meet me at Mikey's before lunch for the taste testing. I was not sure what to do about the cake yet. I had not decided on flavors, styles or shapes. I felt like boxing gloves would be too cliché.

While we were there, I told Mikey I was considering a variety of all white cakes tall, short, round, and square since it was a white party. He sort of did not agree. "Let me sleep on it," he replied which was his way of saying no.

After work, I headed to the gym. I sat in the lot for a good thirty or forty minutes looking over emails. I saw Randall's head pop through the door. "Oh crap." I tried to shut down everything quickly before he approached my truck door.

"DJ what's wrong?"

I barely cracked the window. "Nothing," I rolled it back up and jumped out.

"DJ what is that?"

"Nothing."

"Wrong answer."

"Really nothing."

I walked in the building. He stomped behind me and pulled my arm. I looked back and down with the look of death at his hand holding my arm. He did not budge.

"What is it?"

"A laptop stand."

"A laptop stand?"

"Yes."

"Why do you need it?"

"Because I work a lot and it allows me to secure my laptop while I work in my car."

"Who installed it?"

"The radio place."

"Great. Have it removed tomorrow."

"I will not," I yelled.

"Fine. We will remove it tonight. JJ," he yelled.

"I need it to work."

"No ma'am."

I stomped up the stairs. *Who did he think he was? Who did he think I was? He did not just bark orders and I followed. He was not the boss of me.*

"Let me see your keys," he said.

I kept walking up the stairs. "DJ."

He came up the stairs but I slammed the door safety and locked it.

"DJ open this damn door now," his tone demanding.

I continued changing my clothes.

"I will take it down or kick it off the hinges."

This was not what I came here for. I have to work in my truck at the red lights because I have spent most of the day planning a party for him and this is the thanks I get.

It was at least an hour later and I was in the middle of my walk when he yelled from downstairs. "Danielle."

The next thing I knew Keith was tapping at the door. "Ms. D."

"Yes."

"I need your keys."

"For what?"

"Hooks asked for them."

"Tell him to come and get them if he wants them."

"He is going to have the door taken off the hinges or the truck towed."

"Is this the way he always handles not getting his way?"

"Ms. D please give me the keys," Keith pleaded.

"DJ, do not make me come back up those steps," he said mildly while punching King's hands.

I opened the door and threw the keys down the steps past Keith. They beat him to the bottom. The remote shattered in two pieces and the battery flew in another direction.

"Tell me that was not what I think it was," he said continuing to punch King's hand.

No one said a word. "Why didn't someone warn me? Is this what relationships are made of? Are all women this mean and stubborn? Am I asking too much? Does she not see the hazard in this? Any suggestions on how to handle this? Any help please guys?" No one responded to his request.

After thirty minutes, JJ walked back up the steps and unlocked the door with his master key. He handed me the stand, my keys, walked back out and locked the door behind him. Shortly afterwards a rapid knock was at the door. Now I know someone has a key so why didn't he use the key.

"Danielle open the door."

I walked over, unlocked it and walked away. He came in. "What in the hell is wrong with you? What part of this are you not getting? Have you completely forgotten about safety all together?" He waited for a response. Realizing he was not getting one, he continued. "You cannot drive and work. You cannot work at red lights and stop signs. There are twenty-four hours in a day. Seven days a week. You should be able to get it done in the allotted work period. If you cannot it will wait. The world will continue. Lastly, you cannot throw things down the stairs. It is a safety hazard. You know better. I am shocked at your behavior tonight. If you are not worried about your safety or the safety of others then too bad. I will not allow you to jeopardize yourself or anyone else. It is my job as a man. It is my job as your man. I hope you can respect that. Leave the receipt for the installation. Tell me where to return the stand. We should have a clear understanding. If not I will be on the bag if you need clarification on any of this. Just to make sure we are on one accord you will not have a computer-mounting device in any vehicle. You will not jeopardize your ability to operate a moving automobile. Let me know if you have questions or concerns. Good to see you. I love you," and he walked back down stairs.

"More like on the rag," I mumbled but loud enough for him to hear it.

"I heard you."

I finished what I was doing and went down the steps and exited through the back door. I slid the invoices under the door to his office and left. I said nothing to no one.

I was home, showered, and standing at the kitchen counter working. Standing was something I did regularly since most of my work was done at a drafting table. I would stand at my counter every night and work while I ate dinner. Tonight was an exception. I did not eat. I was too irritated for food. His ring tone rang out. He must have realized I was gone. This is going to be an intense conversation. Maybe even an argument. I answered with an attitude. "Yeah."

"Open the gate please."

I am in big trouble I thought. I opened the gate and he clicked off my line. Oh, I see how he does it. I kept working. After fifteen minutes or so, I looked at my monitor. He should have been at the door ten minutes ago. He must be getting ready for the fight he is walking into.

I checked the monitor again. I did not see anyone. I looked closer. I went to the door. Sitting there in front of my door was four boxes and several dozen roses. I looked around but I did not see anyone. I went back in to get my phone. I stepped back out to the porch, walked in front of the boxes, and ended the call before it had time to ring. There were four dolls. Bratz dolls to be exact. There was a note attached to each of them. He labeled me as Sasha, Paige as Yasmin, Leigh as Chloe and Sade as Jade. All I could do was laugh. *Was he calling me a brat? Was he calling my crew Bratz too?* I laughed because it was true. I was a brat and I did not foresee it ever changing.

There was another note. It read:

It is not about you.

It soured in my spirit. I hated when people used my words on me. That is what I told him and now it has backfired on me. I stood there examining the items. *What did he really know about the Bratz? He had a son. How did this cross his mind?* I must admit this was clever. I redialed his number. Shockingly, he gave me back what I gave him. Although, revenge was not his style.

"Yeah."

"Can you turn back around?"

"I was not planning on it."

"I know that is why I am asking."

"I think I need to let you calm down and work tonight. We have had a rough day. I pray we have a better day tomorrow."

"Randall, can you please turn around?"

"Not tonight Baby. Let's just leave well enough alone."

"Why?"

"I think we both need to calm down and start over tomorrow."

"Oh okay. I am sorry you feel this way."

"I do not want this to escalate any further. Good night," he hung up the phone.

It messed me up. I was not expecting his response. I held the phone like an idiot. Finally, I texted him.

> Thank you for loving me. I am hard working like you. I am sorry it offends and bothers you. It is who I am and what I do. Please understand. I love you.

He did not respond to the text, which was unusual. He normally hit right back or had someone else send the text if he was conditioning. I assumed he was angry. I had not seen him angry since the time he was mad at Trevor the night he found out he was fighting.

I made myself a cup of tea. I did not know how to feel. It was strange. *Were we having a fight? Was this the end?* I was walking to the sofa since I felt a headache coming on. As soon as I touched the keypad to reset the alarm I heard his car approaching.

I went to the door with my mug in my hand. We walked towards each other. He had his keys in his hand. We stood face to face. I slid my hand down my face. I was his height as I stood on the top step. I sat my mug down on the step and hugged him. He did not respond. He leaned down and picked up the mug and said, "Let's go in."

He sat the cup down on the counter in the kitchen and noticed I had everything plugged up and running. "Do you know why I am upset?"

"No."

"I want you safe. Your gadget was not. I know what you are going to say. You want me safe. You want me to eat and sleep. I promise to do better. That is my compromise."

I smiled a weak smile.

"I do not want you angry or think I am telling you what to do. All I am trying to do is protect you. If you feel like you cannot go a moment without working then fine. I will hire you a driver. I have no problems doing so. Then you can work all you want. Whatever you need, ask me and I shall give it to you."

I nodded. I did not want a driver and I did not want to fight with him.

"Work with me Danielle. I have no idea what I am doing here. I have never had a relationship. I am new to this. All I want to do is what is right. I want to be there for you. It is my desire to provide for you. My job to protect you. My role is to be your helpmeet. And most of all I am here to love you."

I gave the weak smile again.

"I can't afford to lose you. I will not lose you."

He spoke his peace. I did not say a word. Sometimes it is best to listen. I did want to give my side of the story but you have to pick and choose your battles sometimes. Right now I would rather be happy than be right. I wanted to give my side to show why I thought I was right. But who cared? He was here with me and I was happy. We lay in each other's arms on the couch until three AM. He said he was going to sleep and he did. He woke up, told me he loved me, and he had to go. He said he would call me in two hours.

"Get in the bed until then."

I wanted to say skip conditioning and lay with me two more hours but sleep took over. I could not speak. He should enjoy this. This would probably be the only time he would see me this quiet.

Tuesday

I walked him to the door. We both realized it was raining. "Are we good," he asked.

"I think so."

"I need more than a think so."

"Yes Randall, we are good," I murmured.

"No working, texting, or emailing while driving."

I did not respond.

"I see we are going to need a written agreement for this. Otherwise, I do not think you are going to adhere to the rules."

"Do you adhere to them or just make them and enforce them?" He did not say anything about twitter, face book, blogging, internet surfing, etcetera. Besides my phone responded to voice command. I should be cool. There is always more than one way to skin a cat.

"I adhere," he replied sarcastically.

"Are you running in this rain?"

"Weather proof," he remarked.

"That is insane."

"A man's got to do what a man's got to do."

"Get sick if you want to. The party will go on without you next week. I am not playing with you and King."

"I am not going to get sick."

"I am serious Randall."

"Babe. This is what I do. I will not get sick. If so, nurse me to health," he said while he kissed all over me. "I will call you in a few hours."

I jumped in the bed and pulled the covers over my head.

When he blogged I knew he was in the car. The argument will be if he was in motion or not. I could get technical and look at my monitors and the time the blog hit and the time he pulled off. His blog was another one word.

This one word was more distressing than the other was.

> HELP!

Then he texted Trevor.

> Hit me as soon as you wake up. I need help.

I swear the hour flew by. I said let me sleep until five. Sure enough at fifteen after four, he was calling. "Babe, I am going to lay here until five."

"Take your time. I will call you back then."

"What is that about?" King asked.

He knew exactly what King meant. It was not that they tracked him to know his every move. It was their job and they knew he was at Danielle's all last night. King had not mentioned it thus far. However, her not wanting to get up was a reason to raise question. "What?" he said nonchalantly.

"What is with the Energizer Bunny? Why can't she get up?"

"Nothing happened. Check our levels. They are not elevated. Actually, I slept. I laid down and went to sleep."

"Don't get slick. Since you slept last night with Danielle how about pulling an extra five miles. Give yourself time in the rain to cool off. Maybe today you won't be as hot headed as you were yesterday."

He knew it was punishment. King knew it was raining. Why was he making this a big deal and requiring five more miles? He was not hot headed for nothing. Danielle was being ridiculous. He did not make a fuss. He did not think twice. It is what it is. It was not going to change and if he had to run an extra five miles because he spent the night at her house then so be it. He would run them with pride. He checked his levels on his watch. Then changed the song on his iPod and checked his phone. He kicked his speed up and took off running.

The rain felt good on his skin. King was right. It was simmering him down. He did not feel hot headed but he surely felt excited and the rain and run was calming him down. It was not a bad idea after all. He was soaked. Nevertheless, he kept moving. When five came, he slowed the pace. He hit the button on his ear and said, "Call Danielle." The phone rang.

"Okay babe. I'm getting up. Thank you. Get out of the rain please."

"I am doing this for you," he clicked off the line.

What did he mean? I thought.

What did he mean? King thought.

He and King went at it until nine. Once they finished the next five miles they went back to the gym and immediately began in the ring. King did not allow him to change clothes. At eleven when they broke, he showered and proceeded to walk out of the door.

"Where are you going?" JJ asked.

"I will be back by five."

"Someone needs to go with you." JJ stated as if there was no choice.

"I will be fine."

"It was not an option."

"JJ, I am going to have lunch with my girlfriend if you don't mind."

"Where will you be the other four hours?"

"I got this. Check my location," he walked out.

"Hard headed," Keith said and shook his head.

"That boy is going to be the death of me." JJ proclaimed.

"Him and the girlfriend," King added. "I am about sick of them. They were together all night last night. Why does he need to go and have lunch with her? This is crazy."

I was busy at my drafting table when there was a rattle at my door. *Who did not know to use my doorbell?* "Yeah."

"Can I come in?"

"Sure," I said containing my excitement.

He walked over and looked over my shoulder, "What are you designing?"

I explained to him what I was doing then asked, "What do I owe the pleasure?"

"Peace treaty lunch."

"I take bribes."

"Peace treaty not a bribe."

"Call it what you want."

"Is this a bad time?"

"For you, never," I winked.

***

After lunch Randall headed directly over to the church. He walked right in and as always Melissa, the security guard, was there. "Hello." She was glad to see him. She was definitely going to put the moves on him today.

"Hello," he said dryly.

"Deacon Hooks, what a pleasant surprise."

"Whoa. That is the same thing my girlfriend said when I showed up at her office to take her to lunch today."

It stabbed her. She could not respond the way she planned.

"Is Pastor in his office?"

"Yes," was all she could manage to say.

He knocked on his door, "Who is it?"

"RW."

"Come on in."

"Hey, what's up?"

"Nothing. What brings you by?"

He plopped in the seat. "I am a hurting man."

"WHY?"

"I have gotten myself into something I know nothing about. Women, relationships, love, and whatever else goes with it."

"What do you need from me?"

"I need to know what to do? I have no clue. I know nothing about how to handle a woman. She was pissed with me last night because I was commanding per her words."

"Were you?"

"I do not think so."

"Did you ask her what leads her to believe you are or were commanding?"

"I didn't."

"Start there. Was it your tone, your body language, the words you used, or who were you in front of? Did you speak to her as if she was a child or an adult? Then from there just an adult, an employee, a girlfriend or someone that means the world to you?"

"I do not know. I did use a few choice words."

"Why?"

"She would not listen and was being stubborn."

"Did she use any choice words to you?"

"No. She really did not say anything."

"We are talking about Danielle right?"

"Yeah. Come to think of it, she did not speak much. She did throw her keys down the stairs."

"Before, after, or during the choice words."

"After."

"Humph."

"What was that for?"

"This is great."

"What is?"

"Who am I right now?" Trevor asked.

"Huh?"

"What person am I speaking to you as?"

"Tre."

"This is great. You picked four years to get a girlfriend and then you get a girl who is not taking any mess from you. So?"

"So? What do you suggest I do? What am I doing wrong?"

"Well son."

He cut him off, "Brother."

"Right. Well brother, you have to treat women the same way consistently. Remember she owes you nothing. You do not possess or own her. She wants to be treated like a queen every day. Not necessarily with gifts but with kindness, love, respect, and adoration. You have to date her and date her forever. For the rest of your life. First Lady and I go out on dates regularly. They can be planned or unplanned. A date Hooks. The gym is not a date. The juice bar may not be a date to her. You will have to ask her and find out what she likes. Even if she says it is okay still date her other than the gym."

"When I say date I mean you and her. We do have some complications with you being who you are. There are places you will never be able to go alone but there are many places you can. She is a smart girl. She loves her job and likes to work. Maybe you can go to Barnes and Noble. You read the sports section of the paper while she reads what she likes. Maybe she likes to work in a secluded area in Starbucks. You do not have to drink coffee. Take your laptops and do what you two do. Alternatively, share one laptop. You can always take her to dinner even if you do not eat. You cannot hinder her from eating. You can go to pottery class, cooking lessons, paint ball, the movies. You both like music. Maybe music lessons or dance lessons. That is one on one and you do not have to be around many people. I can see her and King have a strange relationship. Maybe take JJ or Keith. You should explain to her you can't live without these guys they give you strength and protect you."

"I have explained the group's purpose to her. She understands as much as expected. However, I am sure she wants quality date time. I think I have given her some. Maybe not as much as another guy could give. She and King have a love hate relationship. They have gotten better over the last few weeks.

I really think they like it so I try not to intervene. What is up with everyone and me eating?"

"You don't."

"I do."

"That is not the topic at hand. You have to show her how you feel. Show her you love her. Telling her is not enough. We can say anything with our mouths. Love her out loud."

"I have gotten myself in some mess. I just thought you checked the box and all else was cool."

"That is how it was the last time you dated when we were eight years old."

"Don't remind me."

"Our past, failures, and short comings strengthen us just as much as our successes."

"You are right. Some failures I want to wipe away or redo."

"I think you are redoing now. Do it up and do it right."

"I want to, that is why I am asking for help."

"So what are your plans?"

Hooks did not reply.

"If this applies to you just look straight ahead."

They both laughed. Hunter always used the line in service. It lightened the mood but Hooks weighed the conversation back down instantly.

"If God is willing I plan to marry her."

"Do you know if she wants to be married? What are her views? Her views on kids? Blended families? There is a lot involved other than buying a ring and popping the question."

"Do not forget marriage counseling. I think you have secretly counseled us in from day one. After I ask her these questions and review her answers how do I know when it is the right time to propose?"

"You have to pray about it. You know from experience that marriage will not always be happy. It is not always about warm and fuzzy feelings. There is a lot of work involved. Daily work. Make sure you two are equally yoked. You want to be friends, close friends, and best friends. You want to grow old together. You want this to be permanent. Why do you think you want to marry her? Give me your reasons."

"Trevor, you know where my life has been. You know I was not thinking of anyone when I met her. She just showed up here. Immediately, she caught my attention. I feel like she has everything I want and need in a woman. She encourages me. She challenges me. She supports me. She has my back. She makes sure I am happy. She takes care of me. I love her. I love her family. I respect her. I cannot stop thinking about her. I want to be with her. I miss her when I am not near her. When I am with her we can talk, laugh, chill, or say nothing at all and I am content. She does not let me slip. She holds me accountable. She is patient, kind, and understanding. She worries about me. She is concerned with where I am, what I do, and my health. She is family oriented. She loves me. I trust her. We have similar values and goals. She works hard and I work hard. She sleeps little and I sleep less. As bad as I hate to say it but I want to do right. Sure, I am a man and I have man feelings but I desire in my heart to remain in right standing. My desire is to obey the commands and respect her. I was not and neither am I interested in anyone else."

"Your security girl out there has been very flirtatious lately. I have been here for years. Very few people have ever tried to talk to me. What they say is true. As soon as I get unmarried and involved they all decide, I am a good catch. Not to be arrogant but I could have entertained any or all of them. But I do not, have not, and will not for a number of reasons. One, I love Danielle. Two, I am not interested. Three, it is not my style. I cannot go out like that. It is not the right thing to do then I have to cover you. The last thing I want is people taking my wrong and assuming birds of a feather flock together. I want to be faithful to her. I want her to remain pure and innocent until you have pronounced us husband and wife.

"I refrain from calling her all day. I want to hear her voice. I want to make sure she is okay. She calls me to check in and see if I am okay. She checks in with King and JJ to make sure I am good. I want to give her the world. She has a good rapport with my child. King tried to punish me today and make me run an extra five miles. It was nothing. I would do it over and over again just to be with her. I could go on and on and on. I do not think these feelings will end. I have never felt this way before."

There was a long silence.

"Let me get this straight my security girl has been trying to holler at you?"

"Yes."

"Melissa?"

"You got it."

"I will have a talk with her. Well it seems like you have a ton of reasons to marry her."

"I do not know if that is approval and blessings or disapproval."

They talked for another hour or so. Then he told him he had to leave but thanked him for being a good friend. "I have to get back before JJ tracks me down. I told them I would be back by five. I am sure they have already tracked me to see if I am still with her so they can torture me later."

"Call me later."

"I appreciate you man. I will see you tomorrow."

It was still raining when he left. He wanted to get back and be at the gym when she arrived. He checked his phone. He saw she called and texted. When he looked up again Melissa was leaning over the desk. He quickly hit the send button.

"Hey babe," he said loud enough for Melissa to hear it.

When he arrived at the gym, JJ talked with him first. "Get dressed. We have a lot of work to do today."

"Okay," he replied unbothered.

"What time will Ms. D arrive?"

"In an hour or so."

"Good I need her too."

"Cool."

It was close to seven when I arrived, "Hey."

He stopped what he was doing and ran over, "Change clothes."

JJ cut in, "Actually, you are fine the way you are."

I did not know what was going on.

"Have a seat and do what you normally do," JJ said.

I sat down, pulled my things out and started texting and checking my emails. Twenty minutes or so elapsed. I had all kinds of work scattered out. Instantly, the lights went off. *What the heck* I thought to myself.

"Let's go," King yelled.

It was pitch black. There were maybe one or two emergency lights, which remained lit. I did not move. I could hear and see the shadows moving. I still did not know what was going on. Keith touched my shoulder. It scared the crap out of me. I jumped. "Damn."

"Get what you can. Ten seconds then we need to move."

It was going so fast I could not think clearly. All I knew to do was what he said. I had ten seconds to get my work, which was spread out in the dark. I retrieved what I could. Then he pulled me. I was running in order to keep up. All I could think was *what in the hell is going on?* We ran outside down the sidewalk and to an area where the van was. He shoved me in the van and stood outside. The others started arriving. I was texting, watching, and listening. Finally, I saw Randall's head moving in and out in between the others. Someone handed him a hoodie.

He was laughing and smiling so nothing seems to be troubling him. His hands were still in his gloves. Lastly, JJ came over to the van to rescue me.

"Come on out Ms. D."

King was calling the roll. He was calling people by their first and last names as if he did not know them. He called, "Randall Hooks Washington."

"Here," Randall said.

"Danielle Washington." I looked around. Everyone looked at me. *Why was my name on the roster as Washington?* I liked it but it was not true.

"She is here," Randall responded. However, I do not think he made contact with me. I am for certain he was purposefully avoiding it. He knew I had questions.

My name was the last name on the list. "Good job guys," King said reviewing his list. Vickie was tapping into the gyms security system and rolling back the tape while King commentated. "Alright guys here is the plan. We will head back in the gym and for the rest of the night we will have drills. Plan C has been ran. We will go through all of the plans tonight. Be prepared. Remember when you see the sign go to the proper meeting destination."

I know damn well this was not a drill. I looked at Keith. He gave me the motion to wait even after King dismissed us. Randall stayed ahead. I let all the others go and I fell back with Keith.

"What just happened and why?"

"That was a drill we do randomly to be prepared in case an emergency occurs. You will be taught the individual drills. We will do this again next week at the house to get prepared for the party."

"Why couldn't someone tell me it was a drill beforehand?"

"No one knew it was happening except King and JJ. We prefer people not to expect this. We need your blood to rise to gauge your response."

"You all need help is what you need. How many more of these?"

"About five more tonight."

"I tell you what; I know I did not just run half a mile in my Christian Louboutin's in the rain with thirty pounds of technology for fun."

"Yeah we did. Maybe you will get the point."

"I still don't get the point," I growled.

"The point is you do not need all of this stuff. Wear some flats shoes so you can run. You never know what kind of situation we will encounter."

"Hooks, doesn't like me in flat shoes," I barked.

"But Hooks is in front of the crew right now and you are back here," Keith smarted back.

His response angered me even more. This went on for the entire night. The smoke alarm, the overhead speakers, and some kind of buzzer continued to go off to let us know to go to the next plan. Randall never said anything the entire night to me. It was just like it was normal to him and as if it was supposed to be normal to me too.

After a couple of hours, I was finally ready to go. At this rate, I was not going to be able to accomplish anything. I was trying to put the final touches on his party. "Good night," I said to all.

"Baby, are you gone?" he asked shocked.

"Yep."

He noticed my annoyance, "Wait a minute."

I waited as he came over and hugged me. "I love you," and he walked me to my car in the rain.

"Why don't you get out of the rain?"

"I will be fine."

"At least get under the umbrella." Once he did, he kissed me good night.

At four AM he blogged.

You find out who has your back when the heat is turned up. The heat was on. The festivities began. The challenge she won. She didn't break a sweat. Every obstacle she met. I love this girl. To me she means the world.

Wednesday

He is not allowed to blog. I am going to have to talk to him about embarrassing and blasting me out every night. His late night blogs let me know he is not, has not, and was not sleeping. It was half past four and his ring tone rang out.

"Randall DeWayne Washington."

What did I do? "Yes, my love?"

"When are you planning on going to bed?"

"I went last night."

"You liar."

"What"

"You were up blogging. You were not in the bed and neither did you get in the bed."

"I am busted. I will get in the bed tonight. Will you get in with me?"

"Is that the only way you will get in bed?"

"Yes," he confessed.

"Humph."

"Was that the wrong answer?"

"Yes it was."

"Sorry. I love you. Now get up."

"I can but can you?"

"Low blow Danielle."

I laughed and he hung up the phone. It was raining again today. I was concerned it would rain next Saturday. I checked the weather report several times a day and the results continued to read the same. Rain was not in the forecast. I was praying for no rain. I had a night relying on this prayer. There was a backup plan if it did but it was going to change the entire layout, atmosphere and intent of the party.

It could not rain. This was my thought the majority of the day, "Lord please do not let it rain at all next Saturday." I said hundreds of times.

Nevertheless, work was good. I received a contract on a new project I had been working on. Things were going well. Of course, he called and tried to convince me to allow him to pick me up for church. I declined his offer. I needed to make some calls before I left for Bible Study.

I knew it would happen. I left late and was racing to get to the church. I am sure you could hear me coming a mile away. I had my foot on the accelerator as far as I could. I pulled up to the lot and let up off the gas. The last thing I wanted was to hear his mouth about my driving. I was already prepared to hear it for pulling up five minutes to seven.

I drove into the spot and threw the car in park. I think my shoe was dragging the pavement before I ever parked the car. I was practically running across the lot. I got to the door and bomb rushed it. Sure enough, he was standing there. I was out of breath and disheveled.

"Babe," he said as he looked at his watch. "I am glad you could join us," his tone was condescending.

I rolled my eyes. "Why am I rushing?" I said sassily.

"Because you were working?"

"Yep on a white party," I said as I walked away as if I won the fight. Not quite, I did not win the match but I did win the round. "Guys," I said sharply to the crew. No one responded. It was their job. They were in serious mode.

"Now that you are here let's go," he ordered. Shockingly, there was no back talk about me being late.

Hunter started with his sermon, "I want to remain in the same vein I was in on Sunday. I did not come to tickle your ear this evening. I came to instruct, guide, encourage, and admonish you to follow order. I cannot allow you to run wild. Some of you need discipline. Some need order and direction. You know who you are. If you look straight ahead, no one will know it is you. You need self-control over your bodies, your mind, and your heart. Then there are others who need it over their finances, eating, habits, and addictions. Tonight I want to address those who can't control their minds, hearts, and bodies."

Here we go I said to myself. How many sermons are going to be about us and directed towards us? The point was understood the other day. But no, here we go again.

Finally, he finished. I was planning to have a word with him. I knew I was going to see him soon and have intimate time with him but did I really want to wait that long. No. Therefore, I got in the line to speak to him after service.

"Babe everything alright?"

"Yes."

"Are you waiting on Tre?"

"Yes, I want to speak to him for a minute."

"Do you want to go to his office?"

"No. I'm fine right here," my voice was stern.

"Do you need me to stay with you?"

"I surely do not," my tone direct.

"Oh okay," raising his eyebrows. He slid to the side and motioned for backup. Apparently, he was not leaving until Keith was by my side. Keith was on the other side of the aisle and every time I inched up, he inched up. Eventually, he and I would be at Pastor Hunter at the same time.

My time came. It was as if I was waiting for confession. I extended my hand to show my seriousness. He disregarded it hugged me instead. "Good evening Pastor Hunter."

"What's up D?"

I looked around to see who could hear us. It threw me off. Here I am being professional and he starts with what's up D. *My friends call me D. I thought to myself. My friends do not blast me out and make an example of me in front of thousands of people.* "Pastor, good sermon."

"Thanks D."

There he went again. "Was that directed and intended for me?"

"Are you guilty? Did you feel convicted? Do you have any sin you need to confess. Now is the time. There is room for you here at the cross."

I rolled my eyes and got in stance mode. Keith stepped up closer. I had a real ghetto girl look like how dare you.

Then he pulled the trump card on me like that wasn't enough. "If you confess your sins and believe in your heart, he is faithful and just to cleanse you of all unrighteousness," he extended his hands.

I squeezed my eyes. He smirked a smile like check mate. We stared intensely at each other. I mean mugged him while he smiled at me. A Pastor with a sense of humor. Or so he thought. It would not be the Christian thing to tell the Pastor in the sanctuary of his church right after bible study to go to hell or to drop dead right. My mind kept saying *it would be fine. You can say it. No one will hear you. Just say it.* He had gotten on my last nerve with his antics. I told him on more than one occasion we got the point. Stop driving it home.

I squeezed my eyes so tight and growled. Keith's eyebrows touched. "UGH," I groaned again and walked away.

"D?"

I snapped my neck and turned my head in his direction. "I love you and God does to. Go in peace."

I made a face and threw my hand up. Keith immediately came to my side. "I hate him," I cringed.

He laughed entertained at Hunter and me.

"What was that about," Randall rushed over inquisitively.

"I hate your best friend. Good night."

"Where are you going?"

"Home."

He walked behind me trying not to laugh. It was a cheap sweet victory for him. "Aw DJ don't take it personal. He was not directing at you."

My neck snapped again.

"Us I mean. There were probably many people in the entire

congregation who felt like he was stepping on their toes. Unless this is something you are dealing with."

I stared at him with my eyes practically closed.

"Do you need to confess anything? The doors of the parking lot are open," he extended his hands. King and Keith both turned their heads with laughter. I gave him yet another ugly look.

"Bye," I sat in the car fuming with these so-called men of God.

"Aw DJ, I love you. Don't take it so personal." He leaned down. "Why are you taking this personal?"

I put my face next to his face and whispered in his ear. "Because I am guilty of all the things he stated. My mind, heart, and body are guilty. They are weak. You make them weak. I have confessed and asked for forgiveness of omission and commission. Now back up before I run over your toes," I pulled off.

I drove home feeling as if I was in middle school and my favorite teacher was chastising me. You know I love Hunter. I respect him. He was a G for Jesus. He was a very interesting person. Most of all he heard from God. He knew the word; he spoke it, preached it, declared it, and prophesied it. I had not seen him once do anything out of order. I was praying he never would. He was my shepherd. I loved him and respected him. However, it was not going to go down like this. Hunter was not going to keep getting the best of me. He had the upper hand but not for long. I showered and got in the bed. He called just as I knew he would

"Hello," I answered.

"Hey Babe. Do you feel like company?" he asked.

"I was in the bed."

"Then I guess that is a yes. Now you see why Tre aggravates me."

"Yep, sure do. But two can play that game," I confessed.

"DJ. What are you scheming?"

"Scheming never. Planning or orchestrating?"

"Danielle?"

"I love you too. Good night."

Thursday

It was raining again. I went to bed too early and now I was up too early. I beat him to the punch.

His phone rang. "What is Ms. D doing up this early?" King asked before he answered the call.

He never displayed concern, fear or worry to her but his guys knew him. King sensed it when he said, "Good question." He clicked the button in his ear, "Hey Babe."

"Hey you."

"What are you doing?"

"Thinking about my boo."

He stopped running. "TIP in trouble again," he joked unnecessarily.

"Watch it buddy. I was speaking of a little local boxer. It seems as though he is not interested in a cute little builder. Therefore, I may have to change my thoughts to TIP."

He sat on the curb. "No need." King huffed. "Sweetheart let me go. King is huffing this will cost me six more miles."

"I am sorry."

"It is worth it."

"I wish you would not run in the rain."

"I know."

Leigh and I busted our butts today. I was exhausted. I knew I had a longer night ahead. Vickie and I will be either friends or enemies once all of this is over. She will either think I am about business or an anal BI. I have been giving her instruction after instruction. You can tell she is not used to working with women much less a meticulous and demanding one like me. I swear I am trying to go easy on her. I just want this party to be right. I want everything to be perfect. It is a big night for him. The band and the DJ have to be right. I have a list of the music I want played. I have consulted with him on what songs he wants.

The photographer has a list of mandatory shots. The souvenirs will ship tomorrow. The programs are going to print Monday. The food is selected. The cakes are on order. We have all the rentals reserved. The linen, table arrangements, and guest list confirmed. I have not met with security. I have purchased nothing to wear and I still have not decided on the roses. I am in a tossup of all white roses or some added color.

The rest of my crew walked in while Vickie and I were in my office deciding on roses. There was a lot of props, photographs, and memorabilia Vickie provided for us, which was going to be displayed outside and inside the house.

Everyone had an assignment. I had an email address set up for RSVP's. Paige was in charge of combining these with the reply cards and voice message RSVP's. Sade was putting the photos together and Leigh was working on the slide show. The last thing we were going to do was web search clothes and shoes. I wanted a game plan for shopping. He said he was wearing linen and a white tee. It was not going to be that simple. He was definitely changing more than once. I am sure I would too from sweating and from spilling.

"Ms. D did you order pizza?"

I ordered dinner. I knew it was going to be a long night. "Yes."

"They are here."

I did not respond. I know damn well they are not yelling for me to come downstairs to pay for pizza.

Two minutes later King called me again, "Ms. D."

"What!"

"Did you hear me?"

"I sure did."

"Are you coming down?"

"For what?"

"To pay for all of this food."

"All of you men down there and no one has enough common sense to pay. You men are nothing but a waste of testosterone. Useless if you ask me. I know you are not calling me to stop what I am doing to pay the pizza man. This is freaking ridiculous. I have had enough of you all."

"What do you want me to do?" he asked as if he completely missed my ranting.

"Pay the damn man," I yelled so loud and hard until it rushed to my head. I shook it off and reached for my bag and tried to count my cash instead I gave Sade my card to go pay.

"I guess you heard that," Randall instigated while still hitting the speed bag laughing. JJ roared with laughter while he watched opponents fight on the monitors.

Sade came back upstairs with the card and someone bringing the food, "Someone paid."

I came down the steps, "Babe can you take a break?"

"No, what's up?"

"Are you hungry?"

"Maybe later."

I went back up the steps and came back with four pizzas, a salad, and plates. "Randall."

"Yes," he was annoyed although his tone did not show it.

"I have two individual salads and then vegetables in one container over here for you."

"I will get to them. Thanks."

As I walked up the steps I said, "The rest is for everyone else. Bon appétit." As soon as I bit my pizza and all the ladies had their plates the lights went out. "Not again."

"What's going on Auntie?"

"Get used to it. Safety escape drills. Follow orders. I know King did this on purpose. Jerk." Once we got to the location and the roll was called I looked at King. "Great timing."

Clueless he asked, "Why am I always the one to blame?"

"Because you always do it. I refuse to run in the rain in my Louboutin's again tonight. I am not going to be slipping and sliding across the pavement. As a matter of fact, I am not participating in another drill tonight."

He reached in his pocket, handed me a roll of tape and kept walking. I raced up to him.

"What is this for King?"

"So you can keep your heels on and run without slipping. We have as much as you need. Besides, you have a hundred pair of shoes and tennis shoes in that awful attic of yours. I don't understand why you need them," he mumbled the last part.

I realized it was the tape they used on Randall's hands. "Thanks. Good looking out but I cannot put tape on the bottom of the Louboutin's. That is the whole reason to wear them for the red bottom."

"I will order you non-skid pads."

"There is no way I am putting a pad on my shoes."

"Suit yourself. Then you will run in them."

We had two more drills. The girls and I got a lot accomplished besides the fact. Randall and I had not spent much time together this week. I think I was feeling it. I saw him every day but that was it. I only saw him. I needed some boo time. We packed up to leave. It was later than I anticipated. Thank God tomorrow was Friday. I walked right up to him and grabbed the rope he was jumping.

"You like living dangerously and avoiding all safety precautions?" Inside he thought he was going to blow a blood vessel.

"Get changed. I will see you at my house in a few minutes." He stood still. He did not know how to respond. It did not require a response. It was a command like the ones he normally gives. Sure enough, he gives orders and he follows orders. I opened the gate an hour later while I waited for him at the door.

"Hey," he said not breathless but there was a strain in his voice. "What's up? Anything wrong?"

I leaned up against the wall as he stood in front of me. I stared at him while all kind of thoughts went through my head. Did he have a true clue as to how much I loved him? Hooks, a famous boxer. A person who received and required attention everywhere he went. There he was standing there in the faint moon light in my home asking me what was wrong. I pulled him by his arms and held his face. I kissed him slowly. He was nervous. He was fidgeting again. "I miss you. I wanted to see you. Alone. Away from everyone else. We have been working so hard and I needed to spend some time with you."

He laughed. It was not my laugh. He gave the laugh he gives when he was nervous. "Marry me and this will no longer be a concern."

"Watch what you ask for."

We stood there until we were breathless. He held out an extremely long time tonight. Normally, he was dysfunctional sooner. "DJ, I need to leave."

"Now?"

"Now. I do not want to punch your walls again."

"Please do not leave me."

"Believe me I never want to. Tomorrow we have a date. Be ready after lunch. We have to shop."

"For what?"

"White. All we need is a white tee for both of us and then we can come back here and forget all the rules and kind of sort of box."

"Okay. Get out. Tomorrow after lunch."

Friday

I called him first. I was at the office at four thirty this morning. I needed to get in since I was going to leave early. My plan was to leave at noon. Realistically one or two.

"Hey."

"Are you running in the rain again today?"

"Yep and I earned an extra eight miles," he said sarcastically.

I replied. "Wonderful. How did you earn those?"

"Oh it is easy. I skipped out last night to sneak and see a girl and then I plan to leave early today to hang out with her and I will not be back because we have a date tonight. I hope she has cancelled all of her plans."

"And the jerk gave you eight miles for that?"

"Yep."

"What an idiot. That is well worth twelve miles."

He laughed, "Easier said than done. Please behave today."

"Why? Are they are coming too?"

"All three of the stooges today and Vickie."

"I should have known." "I grimaced. "Where shall I meet you?"

"At the valet at Lenox. I will call you before I leave."

Before noon, I checked my list again. I made a mental note to never plan or host another large function ever again. When you have a list for the wardrobe, it is a bit too much. This was not even my list. It was for him and the crew. I made sure I had everything I thought I might need before I left the office.

Paige was at work. Sade met me and Leigh at the mall. If the mall was involved, Sade was going to be there. We walked in the double glass doors then I had King hold them down. Randall prayed quickly and I gave instructions on why we were there. He raised his hand.

"Yes Hooks," I addressed him.

He blinked quite a few times at the word Hooks as if I said a bad word. "I was thinking I could wear something really simple. Like white tee and AFO's."

"Yes, you mentioned it last night. Thanks for your input."

"I take it you are vetoing?"

"Yes, just as I did last night."

"Let's start at Foot Locker." Leigh stated looking at her list and diffusing the potential debate.

"Umm Danielle. Can I ask a question?"

I blinked at Danielle. Tic for tac. "Go right ahead sir."

"Do you have what you are wearing?"

"No, I do not."

"Why don't we start with you?" the other guys sighed.

"You and I will shop for me tomorrow. Today is your day." I said looking directly at him with a look which said do not dispute me.

"We can get a pack of tees for me, shop for you, and call it a day."

"I was thinking more like five or six outfits." I gave up a fake smile.

"Six?" JJ asked huffing.

"Yes."

"Umm. Not to be difficult but why would I need to change six times? Feel free to change as many times as you wish. I am sure that was your plan anyway." He was blatantly rude and sarcastic. He had his little crew with him so he was cutting up in public. His tone was sincerely wrong. His body language was out of line and his demeanor was unnecessary. He was in the back of the group leaning up against the glass.

"You can come a little closer so we can discuss this one on one. King are we good?" He got my tone that it was not a play date. King and I were jerks to each other but we knew when and how to work well together.

"Yes Ma'am. Just say when and I will release the doors."

"Let's go," I rolled my eyes at the ringleader and mumbled under my breath. "Not today buddy."

I let everyone pass me. I handed the girls a sheet of paper and pens so they could help me with the list. I got behind the crew with King. As we entered Foot Locker, King stood in the door to block and visually scan the other patrons. This was Lenox Square, a busy mall no matter what time of day you visited.

"What's up Ms. D?"

"I need to meet with the entire security group Tuesday night at the house to discuss security issues. Right now, we need to get some uniformed items. They need to all have something where they can quickly be distinguished if something pops off. I was thinking the same tennis shoes and the same hat. Maybe even the same shirt. What do you think?"

"It is your party D."

"Not quite," I corrected. "It is rude boy's party. But there are going to be a lot of people and I need to make sure if something's jumps off everyone is on one accord."

"Auntie what is the deal?"

"They all need to pick the same shoe. AFO, Air Max, I don't care what it is as long as it is the same for all of security. Randall needs to get what he wants, something for RJ and then he should call and see if Hunter wants anything. Then they all need to get the same hat."

He came over after he handed the sales person a few selections. "What is the plan DJ?"

"Get what you need. King and I have the guys under control."

The next thing I knew Randall had ten pairs of shoes on the counter. I looked at the size and they all were his size. Immediately I thought to myself, the number one girl thought. *Big feet plus big hands equals big, never mind.*

I was on a call when Sade came over like a five year old trying to get my attention. I kept moving to let her know not now but she kept trying to get me to look. Finally, I pointed to King for her to get his approval. She had five pairs of shoes in her hand. I did like the black and the silver but it really didn't work with the white theme. King narrowed her down to a pair of Jordan's, the AFO's and the Black Air Max.

As she walked back by me, I vetoed the black. She looked back at King as if they lost a battle. Leigh was typing everything I was repeating to her. Once the call was over, I spoke. "The Jordan's are cool but they have more red and black than I would like. Sade let me see the options again."

"Uncle Hooks got all of these too. Here is the hat for the Jordan's."

"I like it a lot but I am concerned with the color."

"Auntie, you will be able to recognize everyone quickly."

"You are right but I was really thinking on the lines of an Atlanta Braves hat."

"You and these A's. Are you going to make us change to AFO's too?"

"No, you all keep what you have."

"Ms. D, I do not see anything in your hand," Keith said.

"I will get all my gear tomorrow."

"Are you getting the same shoe we get?" Keith asked seriously.

"Tennis shoe?" The store got quiet. Everyone wanted to hear my response. "No. Absolutely not."

"I would prefer for you to," Randall slid in the conversation.

"Not."

"Why?"

"I will not be able to do that." Leigh and Sade laughed.

"What?" he asked unknowing.

"Dani will not be wearing sneakers. If something pops off she will take her chance and loose the shoes."

The sales person came back and said he did not have all the sizes anywhere. I thought to myself, there is more than one way to skin a cat. They tried it their way and now I was able to intervene. "Do you have this Air Max?" He had all but three pair. I could get the other three from Perimeter Mall. The salesperson called to have the other store hold them. We will pay for them here just to confirm.

King threw a hat on the counter. "Add that too," he said arrogantly. "Wait."

King looked like *what?* "I need at least twenty of these hats." He had all twenty. The problem was going to be sizes. Those who were not here may have to settle for the wrong size. And yes, it was an Atlanta Braves hat with a black bib and silver A. It worked well with the shoe. We waited there while they took the bags to the car. I was pleased so far. This may go better than I expected. I was expecting an all-nighter. Then I remembered boys are not hard. Although, the guest of honor was being a jerk. No, he was really being too simple, plain, and humble. That was who he was. However, not on my shift. He had me make all of these arrangements for this party and there was no way in hell he was wearing a tee shirt.

The girls checked the list to confirm we had everyone covered and their size. Once they returned from hauling the purchases to the car, King spoke, "Take your time Ms. D."

Randall looked like *what is up with them.* King knew today was a business day. As soon as we finished business, it would be back on and popping between us. "We can move on to the next store."

"Where to?" Leigh asked.

"Ralph Lauren."

We identified a few white tees. The problem was I needed the emblem on the chest so they could be quickly identified. The emblem on the bottom defeated the purpose. Randall did get his ribbed white tee from there. It cost an arm and two legs but it was his party and he was well worth a hundred and fifty dollar tee shirt.

"What do you think?" Vickie asked.

"I would like to go to Lacoste and then make a decision. Sorry to be a pain."

Randall caught up with me. "DJ, I swear I am cool. I got shoes and a tee so I am good. Let's get you taken care of."

"You are better than good sweetheart. You are great. Right now, we are taking care of the guys. We will get to you next." I leaned in and kissed his cheek. He got the point this was not over. "I think you need a few different looks. One for meet and greet, cocktails, dinner, announcement, dancing, dessert and good night."

"That is a lot. Can I go with two maybe three?"

"Humor me please. It will be well worth your while. You may even luck up and get rewarded after every one goes home." I got close to his ear, "If you know what I mean."

"Enough." JJ said in his serious voice and pulled my arm as we entered Lacoste. Randall stood there like a puppy in heat. I turned back, winked my eye and licked my lips like LL Cool J.

King stood behind him. "God is trying you. I am glad it is not me. That girl is going to make you fail this test. And when she does, your butt is going to be whipped like no other. You will never recover. She is breaking you down man. Breaking you down. Admit it. You are standing here in the middle of the mall and cannot move because she said something in your ear to give you a hard on and now you are functionless. Shake it off man. Get it together. Strip club tonight. First dance on me?"

"Man no. I am not going to a strip club. I cannot move my damn legs."

"We haven't been in years. It will be fun. Think about it. You cannot move because your third leg is rock hard. It is weighing you down. Focus man. Shots on me too."

"I am not going to a strip club. That will be like adding fuel to the fire. What is happening to me King?"

"At least you will get to see some up close and personal. You sure you don't want to go?" He shook his head. "Love and life. Pain and pleasure is what is happening to you. We have all been there or wished we had." King reached in his pocket and handed him a handgrip. "Here. Stay busy. Work out the tension."

"JJ and Trevor will kill us both," Hooks said after taking the handgrip.

"You forgot Ms. Danielle too. I will tell her it was your idea. Yours and Keith's."

"Low blow," Hooks replied trying to focus to relieve the pressure he was feeling.

"She already hates me no need in digging a deeper ditch," King laughed.

"She does not hate you. Loathe is more like the word she would use."

"Are you going to stand there or come in?"

"I cannot move. I think you need to call 911."

"Why?"

"I am dying from epididymal hypertension," King laughs so laugh until he causes attention to them. "Now look at what you have done."

"Hey. Are you two all right? Are you coming in?" I asked from the threshold of the store wondering what they were up to. I was positive one of them was bashing me.

"Yeah. Here we come," King said brushing me off.

"There it goes again," Hooks put both hands over his face and exhales hard.

"How long do you think you are going to be able to do this?" King asked concerned because his number one guy could not move from his body's enlargement.

"Until after the wedding or until it explodes. Spontaneous human combustion. I am not going to be able to do this every day King. Yesterday she wanted to see me one on one. Alone. Some 'us' time. Man I cannot keep doing this. This girl is going to kill me. She has no clue. I can't keep punching her walls or mine." King's eyebrows rose at the phrase punching walls. "Sheetrock walls King. Sheetrock."

"I'm calling Tre."

As soon as he heard Tre's voice, his manhood began to relax. He closed his eyes so he could not see her while this metamorphosis took place. He knew if he looked at her, he would be right back where he started. He could still hear her voice. Finally, he got himself back together, finished his conversation, and rejoined the crew.

I noticed he was acting strange again. I decided I was going to pull up. Maybe I was doing too much and going overboard. The guys picked out a shirt at Lacoste; we paid for them while he remained silent.

"Where to next?" King asked.

I looked to Leigh. "Where do you want to start Dani?" she asked.

"Neiman's," I mumbled. Once we got there, I let him go in his direction and I browsed. He noticed I was not around and searched until he located me.

"Babe, what am I looking for?"

"White."

He looked like duh, "Are you helping me?"

"Do you need my help?"

"Yes, is anything wrong?"

"Why do you ask?"

"You seem a little annoyed with me," he confessed.

"I'm fine. What about you?" I lied. I was pissed with him.

"I'm good," he lied in return.

"Now you don't have to get anything if you do not want to," I said lying again.

"You just tell me what I need. I did put you in charge," regretfully.

We spent the next few hours looking at Sean Jean, Stefano Ricci, Alexander McQueen, Versace, Armani, Dolce & Gabbana and many more. We finally had our selection narrowed down and made our purchases.

"Where to now," Keith said as if he was so over it.

"Gucci and I hope this is it." We spent too long in there but we got all we needed. He needed shoes and belts. I was pleased with his choices. Will it be this easy for me tomorrow? It was seven o'clock. We spent six hours shopping. Not too bad considering we had all of his attire and all the boys'. I hope my day goes as simple as this.

"Do you need to stop anywhere?" he asked still trying to prevent another mall marathon.

"No I am fine. We will do this all over again tomorrow."

"Can we just do it now while we are all here?"

"It took you five hours and now you want to only allocate two to me? The devil is a lie."

He stood directly behind me and moved the hair off my neck. His body was touching my body. "I feel like you should have a present today. What can I give you?" He kissed the back of my ear.

"You are giving it to me now."

"Champ pull it back. I need to see some distance," JJ said as if we were at the prom.

"He just got himself together and he swears it is her. We see who it is." King grumbled thinking to himself he would later have a word with Hooks. "If he keeps going like this the girl is going to be the death of him."

"We need to stop and get ice for him on the way back to the gym. I am going to make his tail sit in it."

"Do you all want dinner?" He gave me the look of death. "Sorry," I said.

"It is fine. They can go have dinner, you and I have a date." he smiled. "Here is the plan." He was back in control. "Leigh is with Sade. Danielle you are going home. Guys, you pick where you are going to eat. I am going to the gym to get my car and then who ever drives me can come back and get you all from dinner. I will be at Danielle's. Sweetie what is the plan for in the morning?"

"I have hair at six. I want to be at the mall at nine when it opens. I think Vickie, JJ, Mikey, Paige, and the rental service will be at the house with whomever you assign. Sade will be with me, you, King and Keith. Leigh where are you going?"

"I will be in between both locations."

"King, I will see you for conditioning at our normal time. Does everyone know the plan for tomorrow?" We all agreed. "Excuse me," he said as we stood in between the glass doors where we started. He pulled me to the side. "DJ, this has turned into more than I was anticipating. You have put a lot into this party. How will I ever repay you?"

"Bribes are accepted."

"I need to make one stop and I will see you afterwards. Order something to pick up. Do I need to bring anything?"

I whispered in his ear, "you," then I flaunted away. "Vickie did we miss anything?" We went over the list quickly and pointed out what was left for tomorrow."

"We are good King."

"All hearts and minds clear?" Hooks prayed us out. He motioned and they released the doors.

I jumped in my car alone and drove home. I pumped my music and opened my sunroof. He made his stop. I ordered the food and headed to the house. What was he going to eat from the Thai restaurant? I wanted to shower and change. I was not sure if I had time. I unlocked the door and took my phone in the bathroom. Sure enough, he called as I was getting out of the shower. I opened the gate. "The door is open I am getting out of the shower."

"Wait a minute can I join you?"

"Don't temp me Deacon."

When I came in the living room, he was fidgeting again. I wanted to say what in the hell is wrong with you? What syndrome do you have? "What's wrong?"

"Nothing."

"You are fidgeting. Are you nervous?"

"Yes."

"Why?"

"You make me extremely nervous."

I was so glad to hear him admit it. He made me feel the same way. It was so random. It was not every day, every hour or every time I saw him. There was no rhyme or reason as to when he made me nervous but he did. His hands were behind his back. I didn't think anything of it. I walked by him. "Do you want something to eat?" He stood there not answering. I walked back in the room. I looked at him and walked over. I seemed smaller since I was not wearing any shoes. "Are you sure you are okay?"

He pulled his right hand from behind his back and there lay a blue box. This always made a girl smile. Then I got nervous. My heart fell. I looked at the box in his hand. I swallowed hard. I knew he heard it. "What is this for?"

"Thank you."

"For?"

"Helping me, being there for me, loving me, encouraging me, supporting me, waiting for me, believing in me, putting up with me, checking me, and caring for me." He lowered his head and extended his hand.

I looked at it.

"Are you going to take it?"

"You do not have to buy me gifts Randall." I hugged him and kissed his face and his neck. "I do what I do because I love you."

"I love you too."

I opened the box. Slowly pull the white ribbon was always dramatic. I wish every present could come in this box. I slid the blue pouch out and dropped the contents in my hand. It was a necklace with a heart and a key. I rolled it over in my hand and observed it.

"Dani you hold the key to my heart."

"You have to stop doing this."

"We have only just begun."

We talked and laughed all night. He asked for hot tea around eleven. I jumped to make it. He never asked for anything. Exactly at midnight he said, "Let me go so you can get up in the morning and King will not punish me." I walked him to the door and he gave a quick kiss good bye.

I went to the bathroom and looked at my neck. He had not been gone ten minutes and my doorbell rang. It scared me as if I was doing something I had no business doing. I looked at my monitor and it was fighter boy. *What did he leave?*

I swung the door open. "Did you leave something?"

"Yes, you," he walked in and closed the door. He sat down and turned the television back on. I sat down too. I had no clue what was going on.

Hooks, what in the hell are you doing he thought to himself. This could easily end badly. I need to do this. I am fighting this battle with myself. I am fighting flesh. *I need to overcome this* he thought to himself. King and Trevor will have to be mad. Tonight I am proving a point. Even if it is to myself. I need to know I can do this. The only way to overcome it was to attack it head on. I was determined to do so.

After two he asked, "Are you ready to get in the bed?"

"I am fine."

"We can get in the bed."

I snapped my neck.

"You on your side under the covers and me on my side on top of the covers."

I was shocked. I was speechless in fact. He seemed to do that to me regularly. I flipped the remote off, stood to go to the bedroom and took his hand. We lay in the bed in the dark exactly how he said we would.

"DJ?"

"Yes."

"If you could have anything in the world what would it be?"

"Easy, a beautiful grand piano. You?"

Her response stunned him. He knew she could afford a piano ten times over. It puzzled him. He answered her question, "You."

It shut me down. I did not say good night before I fell asleep. I think we both slept. At ten until four, I heard him move. He leaned in and kissed my cheek. "You leaving?" I grumbled.

"I will see you at nine. Thank you. I got to run."

Saturday

I could not believe it was raining again.

"Babe are you up?"

"Yes. Are you in trouble?" I asked looking at the clock reading five AM.

"Yes. I will see you later."

King gave him fifteen miles and once they got back, he had to do what King and JJ discussed the day before. They sat him in a tub of ice. The point was to cool him off. It did not bother him. They could have stuck the tub in the freezer if they wanted to. Her love permanently warmed his body.

I left the shop and rolled by Mikey's for a bite. I could not stay long. After I dined and dashed, I headed over to the gym. I knew Randall would be leaving the gym soon so I raced over there to meet him. He followed me to his house. I was glad when I pulled up to the house to see everyone was in order. I loved a well-written plan. Speaking of plans, I drew out what I envisioned and expected. I showed the plans to the group. The valet was there to see where the cars would park on party night. I wanted to stay but I knew I had to get to the mall. It was the only full day I had to shop in between now and the party. I had some ideas based upon what he got as to what I wanted. I was going to hit my favorite stores first and then walk from store to store. If my count was right he had five possibly, six outfits. I was not convinced he was going to change at all. I was certain I would be sweating and working. There was no way I could stay in the same outfit all night.

Some of my outfits should be easy. White wife beater, white skinny leg jeans, white Capri's, and white sundress should be easy it was the two dressy dresses I had in mind, which might be hard to find. I wanted something flowing to wear when he wore his full suit. I was thinking he needed to be in a suit when he made his announcement. Then I wanted a white cocktail dress to compliment his slacks and vest. Shoes were going to be a problem. I convinced myself not to do white shoes. I preferred gold, silver, neutral or multicolored.

The boys cooperated well. They enjoyed me playing dress up and watching me change from one outfit to the next. Even Randall had some input on what he liked and what he did not like. He made a comment on one dress. He said Trevor would have a conniption because the dress was super low in the front and even lower in the back. Sade and I liked it a lot. It was still on the list to purchase and wear at another event. Unless I was planning to be rebellious and wearing it anyway.

It was five PM and we had everything. There were one pair of shoes I was not happy with but I could always bring them back if I did not wear them. I did not have all of my accessories but I needed to go lay my things out to decipher what type of jewelry I required. Randall wanted me to get everything today. I did too but I know they were still at the house working, cleaning, decorating, manicuring the yard, and adorning the trees with lights. This small party turned into a huge event.

We got back to the house and worked while he left to go to the gym. Since he did not go yesterday afternoon or evening I could not dispute with him.

"Will you be here when I get back or will you be home?"

"I will call you."

Sade and I matched up my things with his things. Leigh picked up the other tennis shoes for the security from Perimeter Mall. She and Paige arrived to vote on the outfits. We mixed a few things differently than our original plans. I was glad I was done. This was not me waiting until the last minute. I was going to take his things to the cleaners to have them pressed but instead I pressed them myself. While I was there I pressed mine too so I wouldn't have to take them home and bring it back. Afterwards, I placed them together in the order we would wear them. There were notes pinned to the hangers and the shoes were directly underneath. I belted the pants. The jewelry or cufflinks were pinned to the hanger in a bag also. All I needed was my undergarments and accessories. I was planning to try to have one set of under garments to wear the entire night. Boys were so lucky. They never had to worry about their underwear showing or anything out of place.

He did not call. Which means he tracked me? I heard his car pulling up.

"Hey ladies what's up?" I knew right then I wanted to be with him for the rest of our lives. I had never had this feeling before. I liked him coming in saying I'm home. It brought joy to my heart.

Sunday

When I arrived at church he was nowhere in sight. I went directly to the sanctuary where praise and worship was going on. He came out with Hunter with bloodshot eyes.

"What in the world," I said to myself.

"Humph," Keith said under his breath.

"Why are his eyes red?" I demanded.

He shrugged his shoulders.

Deacon Washington sat up on his knees with his head down. He was not his normal self. He coughed a couple of times. I stared at him. He did not return the gesture. He coughed again. I cut my eyes. Keith sat up in a position to block him from my sight. I slid up to the edge of my seat. Keith slid up too. Some day's Keith was like a mean grizzly bear. Today was one of them. Deacon Washington coughed again.

"Change seats." Keith did not move. I nudged him. He did not respond. I leaned over in his ear. "MOVE." He sat still. "NOW," I said. He squatted down so I could slide in his seat and he slid into mine. I turned my head to the right like a robot. Deacon coughed back to back to back.

I handed King a cough drop. He looked like it was going to be a cardinal sin to take it. My eyebrows rose. He took it and passed it over without looking. Deacon Washington was still sitting up on his knees. He opened the drop, placed it in his mouth then took the wrapper and put it in his jacket pocket. He nodded his head in appreciation without looking. I continued to look at him until he cut his eyes at me and winked.

I told him he was going to get sick. He did not listen. If his butt ate and slept then maybe he would have enough nourishment to fight off this cold. Maybe if he were not running in the rain for five days he would not be sick.

As soon as service was over I looked King and Keith directly in the eyes, pointed my finger and said, "You all are in big trouble." I left and went straight to the store. I picked up orange juice, cough drops, an orange, a banana and a smoothie. I pulled back on the lot and dialed King's phone.

"Send him to my car." He and King both walked out. I handed him the bag.

"Thanks."

"How do you feel?"

"I feel good."

"Oh yeah?"

"Yeah."

"You look like crap."

"I do not feel like it."

"Come straight home."

"I need to?" he asked.

I held my finger up as a warning.

"I will be over."

"Over? I will be at your house waiting."

"Thanks Babe."

On the way home, I stopped by the grocery store to make soup. *I knew he was going to get sick. Why didn't he listen to me?* I got to his house, opened my trunk, took my bag out to change clothes and begin cooking. I was glad Mama Rose forced us to buy cookware. He arrived an hour or so later, changed clothes and started fumbling with everything other than resting.

"Deacon."

"Yes."

"Pick and choose your battles."

He got the tone, sat down, and flipped the remote. He forced himself to eat some soup. He was calling it a full meal. I called it a few spoons. I restricted him to the couch. You could tell it was killing him. He had a choice. It was the couch or the bed. I was at the dining room table working. I heard the noise from the car pulling up. Suddenly, the Tasmanian devil appeared.

"Man what are you doing?"

"Resting. Danielle's orders."

"Not now son we have work to do."

"I cannot today. I am already in trouble."

"Who do you want to be in trouble with me or Danielle?"

"I have to pick and choose my battles wisely."

"Punk, weak one, we still have work to do. Are you letting a little cough stop you? We train in the rain, snow, pneumonia, cracked ribs, fractured hands, stomach virus, and now you let a cough lay you out."

"Yeah man. I can't right now."

"Call me when the wicked witch of the south leaves."

"I heard that."

"I was not trying to hide my comment."

"I got your wicked witch you punk."

"I am glad you know your name."

"You…."

"Aye enough kids. King let me get some rest for a few hours. I will call you after six so we can get started."

"No hell he won't." I said as I heard King's footsteps getting closer to me. "Exit through the pet door please." As he walked by, I licked my tongue out without looking up.

WEEK 27
Monday

"Good morning beautiful."

"Hey handsome."

"How are you?"

"Umm a little overwhelmed," I hesitantly admitted.

"Why?"

"I have so many things to do?"

"Like what?"

"Pay for the champagne, alcohol, finish the souvenirs, pick up the portraits, meet with security, pick up your suit, drop off my dress, get my accessories, make sure the pool has been cleaned, the roses planted, the yard manicured, and the cleaning service scheduled."

"DJ, what do I need to do?"

"I have it all covered."

"Apparently not."

"What?"

"Apparently not it you are thinking about it before five in the morning."

"That was the easy stuff."

"What in the hell else can be done?"

"The DJ needs my list. The photographer needs a list. The cars must be clean. Who is arranging RJ's wardrobe? I have not spoken to Hunter about the prayer, blessing the food, the toast, and presentation. I need to confirm I have ordered enough china, silver, and linen. I can't figure out how this portable dishwasher works or where to place it."

"DJ, calm down. It is not this serious. All I am doing is telling my friends I am fighting."

"Yeah one thousand and eighty seven friends. Not thirty five."

"Fine. King write this down," he yelled. "Text it if you need to. So, I need to tell Tre he is doing the prayer, grace, toast, and a presentation. Check. Done. You do not have to talk to him. This is what he does. He will not need prepping. Next on the list. King we need to get dinner napkins in case we run out of 'linens'. Check. Done. Portable dishwasher? King do you know what that is or why we need it?" King shook his head no. "Fine. Paper plates. We can trash them. The DJ needs a list. How about Michael Jackson, The Jackson 5, Whodini, LL Cool J, Yolanda Adams, The Temptations, Earth

Wind and Fire, and Mary J Blige. Music is covered. Photographer. He just needs to take pictures what would he need a list of?"

"Ugh. I take it this is funny to you. I will handle it." Men were so far from reality.

"If I had known it was going to be this intense I would have suggested a barbeque."

"Oh that is so appropriate for white. Good bye."

He held the phone.

"What?" King asked.

"She hung up."

Call her back. He rang the phone. I did not answer. He called the house phone I still didn't answer. While I was riding in to work my phone rang it was King. "Yes, Sir."

"Are you good Ms. D?" Randall's neck snapped. He could not believe she took King's call of all people.

"Yeah. I am good."

"What do you need help with baby girl?"

"Are you going back to the house?"

"I can if you need me to. We were on the way to the gym."

"Can you see if you can figure out how to make the dishwasher work? It is supposed to connect to any water faucet and power. I need it to keep the china circulating and clean. Then the lawn care service will come today and plant the flowers and the rose bushes. I have marked every place with a pink sheet of paper. Someone will put the lights in and around the pool. These places are marked with green paper. Let me get to the office and I will call you back with the other details. I need to get in touch with Hunter. I know today is his day off so I will call him tomorrow."

"I will text Tre and tell him to call you. I will be at the house and call you with questions," he said jumping off the highway to go in the other direction. 'Now what do I need to do for the DJ and the photographer?"

"I need to get the photographer a list of important people he must photograph. Like Randall's parents, RJ, Hunter, First Lady, you guys, etcetera."

"I am sure Vickie may have something. I will give her a call. What else baby girl?"

"I will call you back once I am at my desk."

"Okay. Be safe. Let me know what you need. We will have it taken care of. No worries."

Randall had his back to the window, "What was that about?"

"I am the peace maker."

"That was BS."

"No it was not."

"How dare you call and she answers and you two have an amicable conversation after she hung up on me."

He rang my phone again. Three times in a row to be exact. I still did not answer.

King laughed.

"Why won't she answer me?"

"Learn how to treat your lady man. I am not brutal all the time."

"What is going on with you two?" He was starting to get suspicious. They were acting kinder to each other. "What's up King? What's going on with you and Danielle?"

"It is not just Danielle. I know how to treat all the ladies," he mushed Hooks' face in the window. They stopped at the red light and RW jumped out and ran the rest of the way home.

At ten o'clock, she still would not take his calls. He was either calling Leigh or showing up. He did not understand the problem.

"Dani Ro."

"Hello beloved."

"Hey Pastor Hunter."

"Did I catch you at a bad time?"

He noticed my tone, "No. Great timing."

"King said you wanted to speak to me."

"Yes. I am making the seating chart for Saturday and I have RJ on one side of Randall. Then you and First Lady on the other side. Is that cool?"

"Yes, I am good with that."

"Will First lady be good with that? If not she is more than welcome to sit at the first table with me."

"I think she will be fine."

"Then I would like to ask you to bless the food, give the prayer to cover him, and the presentation of gifts."

"Not a problem."

"Great."

"What else do you have for me?"

"I think that is it."

"That is all? You don't need me to help prepare for anything?"

"No, I think Vickie and I have it covered."

"Great work Danielle. I really appreciate you taking this task on and making it a perfect night for him. I appreciate you encouraging him to get back out there. I do not think he would have done this if it wasn't for you?"

"Done what?"

"Any of this. Fight again, force the divorce to happen, and he never would have had a party. It is not his style. Thanks Danielle you have changed my friend. You have made him make himself happy. You have given him what none of us could."

I was speechless. These kind words from his best friend and Pastor meant the world to me.

"Hold on Danielle," he clicked the line, "What's up RW?"

"Man, remind me to never date again."

"Why?"

"I have done it again."

"What?"

"Gone and pissed her off."

"Who?"

"Dani."

"She is not pissed."

"How do you know?"

"I am speaking to her on the other line."

"Ain't that some BS? She will not talk to me but she will talk to you and King. I just called her and she didn't answer."

"She is fine. She has put a lot of work into this party."

"It will be the last one I ever have."

"Oh no it won't."

"Oh yes it will."

"How are you going to marry her?"

"I am going to evite everyone to church when I propose and you can do the ceremony right then and there."

"I don't see her going for that but good luck. And no proposals in my sanctuary. I do not want to start a trend. Besides, you know I am hard-core when it comes to marriage counseling. You have to make it through before I deem you ready to marry or pronounce you husband and wife."

"You should have been the preacher for my first marriage."

"You should have waited. Now it cost you twelve years of Hades. Marinade on that," and he clicked over.

"Forgive me beloved."

"Not a problem Pastor. I know you are a busy man. I will not hold you any longer. Do you need anything from me?" My line clicked. I did not even look to see who it was. Then my desk phone rang. It was Randall again. "Pastor," my tone was strong.

"Yes beloved."

"Were you speaking to him?"

"I'm sorry."

"Don't push me cause I'm close to the edge."

"Oh you use my line on me?"

"You can let my Pastor know I pay close attention and I am speaking the word he teaches us."

"Go answer your phone and get off mine. What am I going to do with the two of you?"

I ended the call with Pastor and answered Randall's call, "Dani Ro."

"Sorry, I was an insensitive jerk."

"Who told you to say that?"

"No one. I said it on my own."

"Humph," I mumbled dryly.

"You asked the last time we had the party at the restaurant to give you time to plan. I thought I was giving you much more than enough time. I do not know why I expected anything less. You do everything to perfection or as close as you can get it and this party is no different. Thank you for all of your help."

"You are welcome."

"What can I do to help?"

"You are the guest of honor you cannot do anything but show up and not be sick."

"Can I at least pay?"

"You are paying. Believe that," laughter rumbled from the bottom of my belly.

"Do I even want to know how much this is costing me?"

"No you don't."

"I take it that means the earnings from my first fight."

"I hope you win."

Tuesday

Today's agenda included meeting with King, Keith, and the rest of the security group. We gave them their shirts, shoes, and hats. The rules, what was expected, what was not going to be tolerated, the guest list, and the tentative schedule for the party was discussed.

"Ms. D. do you know you have an appointment tonight at six?"

"No."

"Yes you do."

"Thank you for telling me."

I texted Randall. He texted back he was waiting to call me once the meeting was over. Why would he schedule something when he knows I am trying to get ready for Saturday? Whom did he schedule with?

He called, "Babe, this was planned. I will pick you up at five."

I had no idea where we were going. I rode anyway without asking questions. We walked into a dance studio. "What's going on?"

"I figured since this is a big huge event I may need to learn to dance since you are making me get up in front of people."

"I am making you get up in front of people? I do not think so. One thousand and eighty seven people to be exact." I put a lot of emphasis on the numbers. The lesson was two hours. It was full of fun and relaxation. We had a blast. We agreed we were going to continue the lessons. I needed them for the exercise and to prepare for the wedding I hoped would come one day or a scheduled date night at the least.

Wednesday

He called me at four thirty AM, "Hello."

"Let's play hooky tonight." he joked.

"What?"

"Let's skip service."

"Why?"

"So you can hang out with me. We never skip. Live outside the box."

"Call Trevor."

"And ask him if I can skip? Yeah right. That will not fly. I want to spend some time with you. Just me and you without anything on the agenda."

"Agenda is free tomorrow. We have service tonight," I said sternly.

"No fun Danielle. We never go against the grain. We have busted our butts all week. I promise just this one time."

After all the talk about skipping service who was on the altar? Altar boy. Maybe that is why he was trying to avoid going so he would not be laid out. I pray he is all right. On the surface, everything looked good but you can never tell. The last time he was on the altar his divorce was final. There is a pattern here. If only I can figure it out. I sat back and waited. The only thing I came up with was he was a praying man, he prayed hard, and when he prayed it came to pass. Pastor Hunter lay with him. It was as if he knew the routine and ran with it.

Keith brought me a bottle of water. "Let me take you home. He is going to be awhile."

"What is a while?"

"The party is Saturday. I would say it will be an all-nighter." You can find him here until conditioning time. I will drop you off, come back, and relieve Tre and King."

"Keith can I ask you a question?"

"Yes Ma'am?"

"What is this about? Should I be concerned? Should I leave him?"

"You said one question. No, you should not be concerned. Unless you want to stay up all night then yes you should stay. Otherwise, go home and get some rest. You have a big weekend."

"That was good but you skipped the first question."

He leaned in and whispered. "Ms. D. you will learn. Anytime anything bothers him. If he is worried and need answers. If he has something on his mind or if something big is coming up then he takes this position. Remember his friend is a Pastor. He has picked up on a lot of what Trevor does. This emulation is good. Saturday is a big day. He will be announcing to the masses and then to the world his plans to fight. He is getting confirmation. He needs to know he is on the right track. He needs guidance we cannot provide. Once he makes this announcement, there is no going back. It will be a done deal. Then he has a girlfriend. He has never had one before. It is a lot for us. You are a lot for us," Keith confessed.

I punched his arm. Immediately, he grabbed it, "Aww."

King and JJ were standing still. I do not think they even blinked. Hunter was truly a good friend to him. This was not pastoral duty this was friendship detail. He lifted up and said something to Hunter. He stretched out to touch JJ's leg. JJ and King both leaned down. Keith pushed me. I looked back with the look of death. King motioned for me to come. Keith pushed me again.

"Stop clown," I mumbled.

Deacon reached for my hand as I kneeled down, "Go home. I will call you later."

"I'm staying until you are done."

"Go home."

"You need to include me in this."

He held his head up. His eyes were blood shot red. "Danielle." He said in his commanding voice even through the red eyes. "Trust me. Go home. Leave me to pray please. I will be able to talk to you about it later. I need this time. I know you need me too but this is something I have to do. It benefits the both of us." I was still. "I told you let's play hooky anyway."

"I love you."

"Thanks Danielle. I love you too."

"Jerk," I said as I picked up my things next to Keith.

"Yeah he is," Keith said.

"I was talking about you," I said to Keith.

Thursday

He called me early. I could tell from the echo and empty space that he was still at the church. I could also tell he was in the same place he had been all night from the hoarseness in his voice. I asked him was there anything I could do or anything he needed from me. In his humility, he said no as I expected he would.

From what I could tell, he spent the majority of the day there. When I arrived at the gym, he was still running which lead me to believe he had been on the altar all night and all day and his training was just starting. Everyone looked exhausted. They had been taking shifts on the watch. They were all accustomed to it. I was not. I was new to this. Too new to understand.

When he arrived upstairs, I was working. He quietly lay on the floor while I worked. This confirmed he was exhausted. Once I was done and packing up to leave he escorted me down to the car, went back in and lay on the mat all night.

Friday

Today I woke up with butterflies in my belly. I felt like an upset stomach would follow me all day. I was not my normal self. I did not know if I was going to vomit or experience bubble guts. Either way, nothing ever happened. I rather wished one of the two did. Instead of the feeling of anticipation caused by nerves.

Was everything complete? Did I forget something? Was everybody on payroll going to show up as expected? Was there a typo or misspelling in any printed material? Lord, please do not let it rain. I had so many thoughts in my mind. This was the results of being a control freak. The consequence of always trying to be a perfectionist.

So what, I kept telling myself. It never helped. *Who would know? I would.* I had my iPod on all day trying to calm myself. It was some of the slowest music I have ever listened to back-to-back-to-back.

After work, I headed to the nail salon. I am usually decisive but not today. I could not decide on a freaking color of polish. *What is happening to me? I need a break. This has overwhelmed me. I can build a thirty story-building, pick out wall paint, carpet colors but now I cannot decide on a color of nail polish. How insane.* I got angry with myself and drove home ticked off with no one other than me.

My music was pumping when his ring tone rang out, "Hello."

"Babe what's up?"

"Nothing honey." I was lying. I was a basket case. One small thing may send me over the edge or into a crying frenzy.

"I haven't heard from you all day. Is everything okay?"

"Yes, perfect."

"D?" his voice was strong and filled with concern.

"Yes."

"You are lying," he paused. "But what in God's name are you listening to?"

"Don't disturb this groove by The System."

"What do you know about that?"

"I know all about that."

"You were a kid when the song came out."

"Whatever old man."

He took mental note. *He had not heard that song is years. Where did she pull it from?* "You amaze me."

"Why?"

"You just do."

"And you know what else," I said while thinking, "that was a hot car in the video."

"It is a classic. Would you drive an old car like that?" he asked surprised.

"You can't call that an old car. You said it right the first time. It is a classic." Our conversation relieved me for the remainder of the night.

Saturday

You would have thought he would have given today a break. No, he surely did not. I was at the hair salon at six then I went to Mikey's and cheered him up with his favorite sweets. Afterwards I headed back to the house. He arranged spa appointments at ten for everyone. If I were thinking, I would have done this the other way around. Spa first then hair. Oh well. This is what he wanted to do. It was over twenty of us that showed up. You could see the paranoia on the spa staff's faces but also the excitement of wondering who would have the privilege to give Hooks a massage. It did not matter to me. I am not insecure. He asked if I wanted to do the sauna with him and I had to decline because of the fresh hairdo. After much needed relaxation, we enjoyed tea and scones before heading back to prepare for the festivities. It was necessary for me to go home to get my mind right.

Keith picked me up from my house and drove me to Randall's house. I think everyone was there except me including Mama Rose. It was mandatory that I have some me time before it was all about him. I wondered if Tameka would show up. Today would not be a good day for her to do so. She did not receive an invite. Besides, there were no worries. No one was allowed in who was not on the guest list. I hope I made myself clear on the instruction. The instructions were to contact King or me only. Every guest had to be on the list no matter who you were.

It was time. I was getting nervous for the first time. We were both dressed. I was having second thoughts about the dress I was wearing. I knew I would. Therefore, I purchased a second choice and was ready to change. I took one look around. Everything was perfect. I felt like I needed a Coca Cola, Amp, Dr. Pepper, Latte, or Starbucks. I needed an extra ump.

Randall was nervous too. He was sticking very close to me. Every move I made he was right there hand in hand. Everything seemed to go rapidly. The guests began to arrive. We greeted almost every one of them. One thousand people seemed like a huge number but after they began to arrive, it did not seem so intimidating.

The guests included, all of his staff, his fellow Deacons, a host of auxiliaries from the church, others on his payroll like his doctor, accountant, broker, lawyer, tailor, barber, his entire family, my firm, my family, my crew, disc jockeys, local celebrities, and Atlanta's local fighters.

I went and changed into short dress number two. This was not in the original plan but I was not feeling the first one as much as I was in the store. He and I stuck close. More like we were guests and not the hostess and honoree.

As soon as we greeted the next round of guest Sade was calling, "Official wardrobe change time." We both headed to change. He changed to his white linen pants, wife beater, linen shirt, and AFO's. I changed to a long low cut top in the front and back, leggings, and sandals. I should have walked this route with these shoes on in advance to make sure they were not slick and I would slide across the pavement. As we entered side by side, everyone was seated. Dinner was ready to for serving. We had to pass everyone to get to our table. I should have had our table backwards. We walked in hand in hand, sweating, our fingers locked, and his other hand in his pocket fidgeting. I wished for a pocket for my other hand. As soon as we got to the table, RJ pulled my chair out. Randall popped his hand. Some people laughed at his chastisement. RJ whispered in my ear, "You look nice Ms. D."

"Stop looking son." Then he looked over at me and said, "That top stays here. It is not allowed to be worn anywhere else again. When is the next wardrobe change? Otherwise we will not make it through dinner."

I laughed to break the tension while the cameras continuously snapped.

Hunter clicked his glass and stood along with Randall and RJ. I focused to look out at everyone. They all looked so nice and on one accord. It turned out to be a beautiful party. As Hunter blessed the food, I looked around the yard. It was a white wonderland. The roses were immaculate. The lights and decorations were awesome. Everyone and everything was lovely. I was pleased. It was a job well done. I looked at security and I was so glad they were wearing those hats. It made it very easy for me to identify them. I wanted to go out front to see the cars lined around the sidewalk with the flowers, candles, and lights. I texted Leigh, Sade, and the photographer to get those shots too.

Was this thanksgiving? Was pastor going to stop praying? I was glad. I needed the extra time to observe the view. Randall reached down for my hand. I put his up to my face and kissed it. The cameras snapped until I lost focus. "Amen," Hunter said. "Enjoy."

Dinner was served. Everyone ate except the guest of honor. I felt like this was going to be the last peaceful minutes of the night. Sade texted.

Wardrobe change.

We all stood. RJ and Hunter were coming too. The entire head table was moving. This is where the night was going to begin.

"I need a drink," he whispered over my head. I reached for a bottle of water and passed it to him on the way back in the house. "No a real drink."

"Yeah right."

"I am so serious."

"There is no need. You will be fine. These are all of your friends and family."

"I should have gone with my first instinct and recorded my speech just in case I felt nervous. I would play my speech right now while I am not out there."

I pointed to RJ, "Get Uncle Tre." Tre came in the room half dressed. I left to go get dressed. I returned a few minutes later to find him prostrate in half of his white suit. JJ stood him on his feet. You would have thought he just finished the twelfth round. JJ shoved water down his throat and dressed him. Right now, he was not himself. He was truly nervous. When they finished with him, he looked like Ricardo Montlban from Fantasy Island. *Damn!* I thought to myself. I wondered if he would wear a suit every day. Right then I felt like I needed a panty liner. He was wearing all white; white pants, vest, jacket, shirt, and tie. The only color was on his shoes and belt. His cufflinks were blinging. His face was shaven clean and his scalp was lickable. I watched him closely while King was strapping on my leg band and JJ was readjusting his tie. The cameras did not stop for a moment. I looked over at Hunter and RJ and they looked like a million bucks.

"Two minutes," JJ said and they left us alone. He had his hand in his left pocket. His right hand was holding a bottle of water. He looked awesome. Nothing could take me away from this man.

"You look handsome Mr. Washington." I walked around him. He did not move. JJ knocked on the door. "Five minutes," I yelled. I extended my arm around his waist. He did not moved. He looked down. There was a black box in my hand from my other favorite store. He took his hand out of his left pocket, handed me the water and took the box. He opened it to find a diamond dog tag from David Yurman.

"You do not have to buy me gifts."

"It's your day."

"Our day. Every day is our day."

I was still behind him. "I guess you don't want this one either." It was a blue box.

He gave up my laugh. "Can I please have the box?"

"I didn't think you wanted it."

JJ knocked on the door again. "Not now," I blurted.

"Give me a few more minutes J," he said much more calmly than I did.

"DJ, may I please have the box?"

"I thought you didn't want gifts."

"I changed my mind."

I handed him the box. He gently pulled the white ribbon. It hit the floor. The top followed next. There was nothing in the world to me like pulling the ribbon off a blue box. There were three items in the box. I prayed and prayed and prayed about this gift. I hoped to God that I was doing the right thing. Now, I was nervous. More nervous about giving him this gift than I was about the party.

"Danielle, what is this?"

"I think you very well know what it is. I hope it means as much to you as it means to me. It means a lot to me. I do not know what else I can say. I am proud of you. I love you."

He turned around, dropped the box and the contents. He touched my face so gently. He kissed my hand, my neck, and my ears. He kneeled down to my ankles and he kissed my feet. He slid his hands under my dress touching my skin. I moaned ever so sensual. *Yep, I needed a panty liner.* JJ opened the door right when my hands were on his head. The look was probably all wrong. However, common sense would have said look at the time. There was not enough time to have done anything wrong.

JJ cleared his throat. He was so cool. I think King would have yelled and Hunter would have lost it. "Get up please and let's move now." He entered the room this time. "I can't leave you two alone and stand outside the room for ten minutes."

Randall took his time standing up. "I hope I did not wrinkle your dress. This was not what I was expecting. I love you so much. It means more to me than you will ever know. Danielle, I want to kiss you but I don't want to mess up your make up."

I leaned in and kissed him. I just gave him all of me in a blue box and here he was worried about my makeup. It was a passionate and intense kiss. We both moaned. He extended his hands out as if he was trying to pull away but could not. JJ opened the door and cleared his throat. He threw up his hand. When he pulled his hands down, he grabbed the back of my neck. I kissed him soft, slow, and then I stopped. He leaned his forehead on mine and gathered himself. He gave me my lip-gloss from his pocket and bent down to pick up the contents and the box. JJ came over to help him and saw what it was.

"I take it this relationship just went to new level?" JJ asked.

I gave him two Tiffany key rings. One with a monogrammed key, which held my house keys. One with a Mercedes Benz emblem, which held keys to all my cars and the last item was the gate access cruise card. I never needed to buzz him in again.

"I think so," he said as he looked at me smiling.

"You look nice Ms. D. You have beautiful teeth. You two look great together." He grabbed Randall's face as if he was a child. "This is what you have waited for." He leaned his forehead to his. "A second chance and a soul mate. It is your time boss. I am going to do everything in my power to help you succeed. It feels right." He tapped his face dearly. "Go get em' Champ. You are not alone. We are all here behind you."

He turned back to JJ serious mode. "Get ready for lights, camera, and action. It's on. He opened the French doors leading to the veranda and sure enough, the cameras flashed. Hunter walked out in front with RJ and Randall and I walked in side by side.

"I feel like we are getting married."

"We can. The guests are all here. The Pastor is here. We have everything we need."

"We are missing a ring and presents silly."

"I just got my present and I am sure there is a ring out here somewhere we could use." Little did I know there was one in his pocket?

I let go as he approached the head of the table. Leigh stood beside me snapping. He reached for the microphone from the DJ.

"Are you okay?" she asked.

"I need a panty liner."

She laughed and snapped my picture. "Do we need to go to the ladies room now?"

"No just cover the puddle on the ground when I move." Leigh laughed causing attention.

"Good evening. I am so glad to see all of you. You all look beautiful." He stood there alone. But not really. RJ and Hunter were on the sides of him. Black and Lefty on the sides of them and JJ and King in the back moving like robots. There was no way anything could jump off unless a bomb or a shooter came down from the sky. "Give yourselves a hand. If you all are going to look this nice, I may have to have a black party next weekend. It is a shame a brother has to have a party in order to see and talk to some of you. Just look straight ahead. You know who you are. No one else will know it is you as long as you look ahead. I wanted to take a minute to say thank you for taking the time out of your busy schedules to spend an awesome evening with me and my family." He noticed I was not next to him.

He motioned for me to come. I did not move. "Danielle, do we have champagne?"

I nodded yes. It was passing around now if he could just hold off for a minute or two until everyone had a glass. I spoke in my earpiece. "He needs to slow down. The glasses are being passed out."

King stepped up and whispered in his ear. "Great. Babe can I get a glass please?" I motioned for a glass of water to be handed to him. Black handed it to him. He looked at it and stated, "I think I deserve a glass of champagne. Real champagne please," he winked at me.

We all looked shocked. I handed Black my glass. We did not have time to scan. Black did what the cupbearer would do, smelled it then he took a sip. He waited to see if he fell out then passed it to Hooks.

"Thank you," he said. "Does everyone have a glass in their hand? It looks like everyone does. Danielle I am not feeling good about you being over there and me being way over here." I stepped up closer but not too close. "Again I wanted to thank you all for coming. This means so much to me. As most of you know me, you should have known something was up my sleeve when I sent a party invite. You all know parties are not really my style. But I wanted all my friends and family here with me at one time when I announced Hooks Washington will be fighting again."

The crowd went wild. RJ almost knocked him over. He tried to contain him but I think he was more excited than anyone was. He was trying to ask questions. "Wait son," he laughed. The level of excitement everyone gave thrilled him.

"I want to say thank you to all my staff who helped me get to this point. Doc, JJ, King, Vickie, Hunter, my friends, my family, God, and the love of my life," he pointed towards me. "Without you all I could not do this. I am sorry for the names I did not personally call out but you all have been a major source also. If I called all of your names, we would be here all night. I have not scheduled a fight yet. We will begin working on the options Monday. He turned and looked at JJ for confirmation. We will see who takes the bait and then make the decision of who we want to start with."

"I am excited and pumped. I am in good shape, mentally, physically, emotionally, and spiritually. JJ thinks I may be ready. If not you know he and King will get me ready or kill me trying to do so," he laughed. "Enough of me. Have fun and thanks for coming."

The DJ was playing the theme from Rocky in the background. He passed the microphone to Pastor. He took my hand placing me on his left and RJ on the right. "Cheers." Hunter said and Randall turned up his cup. Pastor Hunter made sure he did not have a cup so no one would mistake him for drinking an alcoholic beverage.

"What awesome news. I think it is befitting for us to cover the man of God. In the book of Matthew around the eighteenth chapter and the twentieth verse, the Bible reads for where two or three are gathered together in my name, there am I in the midst of them. We have gathered," Hunter began to pray.

"Dear Heavenly Father," Randall squeezed my hand. "We come before you boldly and humbly this evening lifting up Randall Hooks Washington. We ask you to cover him. That you strengthen him. Please give him wisdom to know when to fight and who to fight. We ask that you cover his crew. Please keep them safe from harm. Cover them from danger seen and unseen. We pray he is protected mentally, physically, and emotionally while he trains in the ring and in his daily walk with you. Lord, we pray today that you cover him with your hedge of protection. He is always equipped not just with his gloves, trunks, and boxing shoes but with the whole armor of God. Inside the ring, outside the ring and every place his foot treads. Keep him focused and stayed on you. As long as he is with you and you in him, we know he is a winner. He is a Champ. Give him wisdom in the ring to know when to duck, when to dodge and when to punch. Father God, we ask today that you continuously remind him he does this not by his strength but by your might. That he always knows where his strength comes from. And if he should ever feel weak to know, he can always look to the hills which cometh his help. We all know his help comes from you."

Trevor had his hand on Randall's head. "Just as Jesus had the disciples, Father God, who covered him and walked with him, we pray that his crew does the same. We thank you for them and all of their hard work and all that they do. We ask you to bless them. Cover them. Give them wisdom beyond their years, their skills, and their ability Father. Father, just as you gave Adam a helpmate," he touched my forehead. Someone held the microphone for him so he could touch both of our heads. "We ask that if it is your will unite him and his helpmate. We thank you for her. We hope she is blessed to be a blessing. Walk with her continuously, Father, so she can walk with him. Father, we thank you that she rises early and prays for her house, her family, and her friends. She helps us cover him and, Father; she covers him late in the midnight hour. When he has expressed the trails and stresses of the day to her, we pray she takes his hand, kneels with him, and prays. We pray she has no shame because she is a woman of God. It does not disturb her when he lays prostrate before you. She knows enough and cares enough to lay there with him. She gives him quick earthly strength and, Father, you provide him with everlasting eternal strength. As long as they both know, all they need is faith the size of a mustard seed they know there is no battle he cannot win. No fight will he loose. He will win and ways will be made. He will conquer the enemy just as Saul, David, Sampson, Joshua, Barack, Gideon and so will Randall Hooks Washington. He does not need a belt or a title to know he is victorious. We know with you the battle and the fight are already won. We ask these things in the matchless, mighty, and miraculous name of Your Son Jesus Christ and everyone who agrees with this prayer say Amen."

"Amen."

Elder moved the microphone while Hunter continued speaking into our ears. Elder spoke. "I bet you all did not know you were going to get a word today. You know how Hooks does it. Anything goes. Especially when you have a fighter whose best friend is a mighty man of God it all goes hand over fist. Now you all have heard the word. You know some of you all will not step foot in the church all year. We at Victory will bring the church outside the four walls of the sanctuary to praise Him. I see it only fitting we take a minute to congratulate Hooks and have a praise party." The crowd erupted. This is why Elder was Elder. He stepped right in. This was not on the schedule, agenda, or program. Elder got their attention again. "Continue with your dinner and afterwards the party will begin."

Hunter was still blessing us. He kissed Randall's cheeks and forehead then mine. He hugged us deeply together and separately. I did not look up but I am sure Hooks' eyes were wet. They had to have been because mine were. King, JJ, and Keith came over and rushed us out. It was wardrobe time.

The photographers decided they wanted pictures of us dancing in this attire so we had to go back and dance. Both of our eyes were blood shot red. They took the photos anyway. And to think I was paying for pictures I knew I would not like.

It was dessert time and we were changing into our jeans and wife beaters. It took him forever to come back out. I finally opened the door. He was on his knees and they were around him. "I'm sorry. Is everything alright?"

"I think so Danielle," Hunter said. He looked at Randall.

"Babe give me two minutes. Please."

He was too freaking emotional. A few minutes later JJ opened the door and told me, "Come in."

As Hunter walked out, I spoke, "I need to speak to you immediately."

This time I stood outside the door. When he came out, he looked sexy in his jeans. His look was very different. He was wearing jeans, a wife beater, his boxing shoes, and the belt I had given him last week. He was a different person. He was hyped. I was wearing my skinny legs jeans, my wife beater and a chain belt. He grabbed my hand as we walked back outside to join the party. As the cameras snapped, he let go of my hand and threw his hooks and jabs. Hunter and I walked back to the table together.

"Did he tell you yet?"

"Tell me what?"

I leaned in holding his arm, "I'm pregnant." Hunter stood still while I kept walking dying laughing on the inside. I told him I would get him back. He came to the table and almost knocked it completely over. "Is there anything wrong?" I innocently asked. He rolled his eyes at me and swallowed his entire glass of water and the one next to him. He was so preoccupied by my statement he did not even acknowledge First Lady.

Randall came to the table, "May I have this dance?"

"We need to talk," Hunter said abruptly.

"Not now? Photographer said pictures," Randall looked confused.

I walked around the side of Hunter, put my hands on his shoulders and whispered. "Don't worry we already went to the justice of the peace. We are legal. He will announce it in just a few minutes. We still love you."

He almost flipped the chair over standing up.

Randall and I danced. People talked to him and took pictures with him. We danced the normal party dances. Old school, new school, step, Cha Cha, then once the slow music played we hit the floor first before it was time to change clothes again.

Hunter finally got to Randall. I told Leigh to make sure she captured this conversation. Randall searched for me. Just like in church, he found me instantly. He stood still for a long moment. Then he must have answered Trevor's question. "No. Not true." I folded my arms and waited for Trevor to scold me. I laughed from the other side of the pool. I pointed my finger and said, "Check mate," as if they could hear me while Randall jabbed him.

It was time for Hunter to do the presentation. I noticed he had a lot of his memorabilia lying around. It was not framed or in a trophy case or anything. One of the things that confirmed Tameka was not into what he did. Otherwise, this stuff would have been preserved better. Therefore, for the presentation, I had most of it framed and hung on the wall but the items we could present outside we did. Hunter told him there was more in the house. He looked at me and motioned let's go.

I took him and showed him where everything was hung. We took pictures and of course, he thanked me again. There was no need to thank me. It was the right thing to do.

Sade tapped her watch. It was wardrobe time again. We both slightly changed. He added a shirt and changed to the Gucci shoes and belt. I changed tops and shoes. We did not wait for help. We were both ready and came out on our own.

"Are you enjoying yourself?"

"Thanks to you," he replied.

As soon as I stepped outside Hunter jumped me. "Payback is coming. You just wait," he threatened.

"I love you too Pastor. I told you I would get you back. If I recall correctly scripture says an eye for an eye and tooth for a tooth. Watch it. Next time I am going after a tooth."

We all laughed, mingled, had fun, split up, and rejoined. I had a great time. The night was winding down. I was finally able to enjoy myself. I hung out with Mama Rose and his parents. I danced with RJ then Pastor and I led the cupid shuffle. The night was a blast and worth all the headaches.

"Last change," Sade said.

"Remind me to never change this many times again." This time we changed into our Khakis. He put on his V-neck tee and AFO's. I added a strapless top and chain belt. We mingled and socialized with the guests. The night ended quickly or so it felt. It was close to midnight. We started saying good night to the guests as they were preparing to leave. They were cleaning the place. Sade said last change but I changed into a sundress instead of the original plan. The party was practically over. We began paying everyone and I started helping with the cleanup.

"Leave this. I am taking you home," the guest of honor commanded.

"I need to make sure all of this is done before I leave."

"We paid an arm and a leg to have all of this done, cleaned, trashed, and back to normal silence by morning. Let me take you home."

I opened my mouth to speak and he put his finger to my lips, "Let's go." He walked away and went to his bedroom. He came back with a suit and a bag. "Does everyone know what we are wearing in the morning? Good. Get this place cleaned up. Do not expect me back. I have a busy night planned. It just got started. If I am lucky, we can both say 'no' tonight. Great job everyone. This was a beautiful party. We love you all. Have fun stay as long as you want but be on time in the morning. Do not call us we will call you. Somebody is in charge of RJ," he pointed at him. "Behave. I mean it. Goodnight."

JJ spoke, "Where do they think they are going?"

"To D's house," Paige acknowledged.

"I am a grown man," he blurted.

"Someone needs to watch them," JJ warned.

"On it," King said and jumped right in front of me and took my bag out of my hand.

"It would be advantageous and in your best interest to move," I said mildly.

He looked past me in a joking manner and said, "Did she say advantageous?"

"I think she did," JJ instigated.

"Go to bed RJ," his father said firmly.

"I think she threatened me too," King said as if he was stunned and afraid.

"What's up with that?" JJ asked. Hooks and I both threw up the deuces.

"They are going to do it," Leigh said like a ten year old.

"It looks that way," Paige agreed.

"Break him down Auntie. Break him down," Sade encouraged.

I turned and winked. It had to be the one glass of champagne talking to him. He knew dog gone well he was not about to do anything but turn the television on and watch himself until it was time to get dressed for church.

We were walking to the car. King jumped and made it in front of us. He was serious now. He had back up with him. Keith and JJ were in tow. "What's going on?" King asked.

Hooks yelled, "Nothing," sounding fed up.

"Good, I am riding with you for safety," King smirked

"It is a two seater King and you are not riding."

"Are you coming back?"

"Eventually."

"JJ say something," King shouted requiring help.

He rolled down the window, "I will call you when we pull to the lot in the morning."

"No you will not. I will pick you two up bright and early," King slapped the roof of the car as he yelled, "Randall."

I had half of my stuff. It was no big deal. I would get it later or Sade would bring it tomorrow. We drove to my house in silence. It was a wonderful party. I had a great time and I hope he did too.

"You are in big trouble," I said referring to him, King, and JJ.

"I know," he laughed and grabbed my hand. "It is worth it."

"Oh ghee. Hunter will probably be at the door when we get there."

Sunday

I was glad last night was over although I was still hyped when we arrived at church. A ton of work went into his party but he enjoyed himself and that was what mattered. He was off duty today even though he did not know what off duty meant. All of the boys were in black tee shirts, which read Hooks Gym and black pants.

Pastor Hunter was wearing all black and a black V-neck tee shirt too. He was also wearing the thirty-year-old ring he and Randall have alike. Then I felt like crap because Randall's was still in my drawer.

Before we walked in, King, JJ, and three strange guys escorted him to the men's room. He pulled me inside with him. I went in and turned my back while he stood over a urinal and deposited into a cup. They pricked his finger and shaved his private area. I hoped the one glass of champagne did not have negative results. If it did appear in his system, he admitted he indulged the night before. Once he was done, we made our way to the sanctuary. He sat next to me in Keith's seat and Keith and King sat together.

Hunter was preaching on the payoff faithfulness. "God rewards faithfulness." Then he said, "I do not know if some of you all have heard but our very own Deacon Washington announced he is going to fight again. It was an announcement he made last night at a small private party." I thought to myself *small*. "He did have a few reporters there but there was no press conference. With that being said you all are the first to hear the formal announcement from him personally."

"It looks like we have medical staff and persons from the boxing association here to make sure he is keeping himself pure, clean, and on target. We do not have to worry about it because we know he is clean and on point. Nevertheless, they are doing their jobs and we respect their positions. Have you all handled your business?"

Deacon Washington nodded.

"Great. It looks like they are going to worship with us this morning. This is a blessing. Right now, what we are going to do is cover him corporately. We are going to touch and agree. We are going to pray for his safety. We will pray for his health, training, family, for him mentally, physically, emotionally, and spiritually. We are going to make sure we have him covered in our prayers while he is out running, battling, and training in preparation for what is to come. We want one of our own to be blessed, covered and to win."

"Come on man. Get up here. I present to some and re-introduce to others. Deacon Randall Hooks Washington."

Randall took the microphone. "Good morning beloved. It is a blessing to be here today. It is an honor to be able to inform you that I will fight again. I am not quite sure when at this time. However, you all will know and will be present at fight time. I will personally make arrangements. I made the formal announcement to my family and friends yesterday and today to the other half of my family here at Victory in the house of the Lord. This is my formal press release right here in the sanctuary. Hallelujah. Glory to your name Father. I give God all the glory, honor, and praise. I would like to take this time to give special thanks to those who have supported me and helped me get this far. Of course Pastor Hunter, my oldest, closest, dearest, and best friend. By the way, he is older than I am. Thank you for your love, support, prayers, and guidance. To my training staff, thank you. Without you, I am nothing. To my gym, my family, my son, and last but not least to Ms. Rose the love of my life without you I do not exist." Melissa was at the security booth watching the monitor cringing. "God Bless you all. You are everything to me. I do not do this for me. I fight for all of us. I represent all of us once I enter the ring. I do this always in decency and in order."

He turned around, "Oh Lord. I see how you all are doing it today." Hunter removed his suit jacket. "Pastor Hunter is wearing my last championship belt."

Hunter said, "We are going to pray for Hooks now."

Deacon Washington brought everyone up in his crew. He and I are side by side and we kneel at the altar. RJ is behind us. Pastor Hunter prays and covers him.

Afterwards, we had breakfast, food, and pictures at the church. I did not arrange this. It must have been Vickie or Hunter's work. Either way I was glad. It was very nice, thoughtful, and elegant. Deacon Washington truly appreciated and deserved it.

WEEK 28
Monday

Keith showed up to my office. He was always in serious mode but today was different. He was serious, about business and not taking any mess from me.

"Ms. D something has happened. A shift has taken place. The relationship you had last Friday was changed. His life changed and so will yours. We have to make sure you are ready and prepared. Every day this week, I will follow you from place to place. You will go nowhere without me. I will talk to you starting off from my cell phone to your cell phone and then as we progress we will go to the security earpiece."

"I will give you distinct driving instructions and route changes. I will test and challenge your memory and observation. We may or may not be alone. I may have King or one of the other people with Mr. Hooks or me. He may be set to be the distraction or to give the instructions. He may call you in the midst of me giving instructions. He may ride with you. There may be seven of us in seven different cars. This is serious and since you will not allow Mr. Hooks to provide you with a driver we have to make sure you are covered alone." He paused to observe my body language, "Are we clear?"

"HUA. HUA."

He smirked. He did not like my sarcasm. He was talking to me forcefully as if I was a prisoner or in the military so I gave him back a military term.

Heard, understood, and acknowledged. I was having a hard time fitting in here with this brood of vipers. Maybe I was not the right one for him. He needed someone much more subdued, transformable, mousy, reserved, less expressive, not so opinionated, not so independent, helpless, and not as stubborn as I am. "How long is this going to go on?"

"Until we say so."

I felt my eyebrows raise and touch. "Until Mr. Hooks says so," I said for clarification.

"Basically, the suggestion right now is to roll with this or take the driver?" he nodded.

"Let me sleep on it."

"It was not an option."

"Yeah it was. Do what you say or take a driver. It sounded like an option to me."

"I will be back to pick you up at five." I got ready to speak. "I will wait until you are ready. I need to observe this building from top to bottom any way."

This is a shame. Everyone knew I never left the office before five unless I was summoned. Like clockwork, Keith was there at five. I walked him through every floor and every stairwell. He met with security. He wanted access to floors that did not belong to us. He schooled security on the laws and safety in reference to the locked doors, dark stairwells, missing fire extinguishers, smoke detectors, and exit lights. Finally, I said, "I will meet you back in my office. I think you are doing fine on your own."

"This is for your safety," he reassured.

"I am neither the President nor the First Lady and neither are you the secret service."

"Not yet," Keith was always so stern and serious.

"Not yet what?"

"Neither."

"Do you plan on going to work for the secret service?"

"No. But you will soon be the First Lady."

"First Lady of what? All I know is I am assigned to an annoying person who is making me paranoid."

"I am making you aware of your surroundings."

I laughed. That is what I always tell Sade. Be aware of your surroundings. "Have you ever worked for the secret service?"

"No. I have only worked for Hooks."

"Oh ghee."

"What is that supposed to mean?"

"What do you need from me?" I asked annoyed.

"Nothing. Continue. I will meet you back in your office."

Keith arrived giving a full report on his findings. He studied the building thoroughly. He laid out escape plans and routes for me. It was intense. There were different routes for different scenarios. Then of course, he wanted me to practice them. If I had known, I was going to be sweating and running I would have changed into my work out clothes. I was getting exhausted and ready to go. It was late when we left my office. I wanted to go by the gym but I was too exhausted.

Keith said, "It doesn't matter to me. I am following you either way."

As soon as we pulled up to my driveway, he gave me instructions and then pulled off. By the time, I got out of the shower Randall was calling. I swear he had video surveillance inside my house. We talked until I could not any longer. Then we said good night.

Tuesday

Today they had him running all day. It was as if he did three marathons back to back. When he called me, he sounded so pitiful. "Anything wrong sweetheart?"

"Yeah Babe. My feet are killing me."

"Are you on the way home?"

"I don't know. I was going to chill here. Do you want me to go home?"

"Yes. I do so you can lie in the bed and get some real rest. Babe you know better. Treat your body right. The same way you train and eat is the same way you need to wind it down and sleep."

"I can't sleep."

"That's fine. Lay down. If you lay there long enough, you will fall asleep. Even if you don't your body will unwind and relax which is what it needs."

"Fine DJ. I will go home."

I heard the attitude in his voice. I did not care. He gave me orders daily. "I will be over to make sure."

He was not expecting my response but it prompted him to do what he said he was going to do. This time when I arrived I did something I had never done before. I used my own keys and let myself in. He was shocked yet happy. I earned some points in his book. I called out. He did not answer. I called his name again.

He looked up from what he was doing on the couch as if I was disturbing him, "Yes."

"Bed," I said. "Let's go."

He stood up mumbling. I guess I was supposed to be intimidated. I surely was not. He got in the bed as if it was painful for him. I pulled some cream from my bag, "Let me see your feet."

"Why?"

"Number one because I asked for them."

"You are right," he pulled his feet from under the cover. "This does not contain Lidocaine does it?"

Really? I handed him the tube so he could review the contents and the ingredients. He gave me back the cream and I walked out of the room. "DJ where are you going?"

"I will be back." I came back with his food scanner. I squeezed some in my hand and said, "Here scan it."

He did. "I don't think it works like this."

"Try it."

We waited for the results. It showed no signs of danger. "Can I proceed?" I asked.

He laughed my laugh, "May I proceed?"

He was correcting my grammar now. "May I proceed?"

"Yes babe."

I did not stay long. Maybe fifteen minutes at the most. His feet stopped hurting. I do not think he noticed it until I asked. When he walked me to my car, I realized he was no longer limping as he was ten minutes ago.

"Thanks for taking care of me D."

"You do not have to ever thank me."

"Yeah, I do. I think I need to thank you frequently for everything.

He blogged early:

> Meekness, modesty, lovingness, caring, are all the things she is and all the things she displays to me.

Wednesday

Each day his training got harder and harder and longer and longer. It became more strenuous and rigorous. The harder it was for him the harder it became for the rest of us. We all worked as long as he did and some of us just as hard as he did. The more he trained the easier it became for us. The more he needed me and the more I had to give him. The more tired he was the less we thought about our physical needs, attractions, and desires.

They worked him hard today and all week. When I saw him, he looked horrible. I wanted to cry. I could not. I had to be strong for him and with him. His eyes were blood shot. Bruises covered his body. He moved as if every part of his body ached. You could easily assume his eyebrows, teeth, and toenails hurt. It pained him to stand and it pained him just as much to sit. You could see the exasperation when he moved. I felt bad for him. Normally his claps were like gunshots. Today he could not muster up enough strength to get his hands to touch. His hands were battered, bruised, and swollen. His knuckles were unidentifiable. It looked like someone placed hot coal on them. I wanted to ask him to step outside the sanctuary but I assumed asking him to move an inch further would be asking too much.

I nudged Keith. "Is he alright?"

He nodded.

"Are you sure?"

He relaxed his body in the seat as if he was confirming yes.

Deacon Washington sat in the seat with his bottom barely touching the chair with his back arched over. Tonight he never opened his bible. The pen never touched his hand. In fact, the bible remained under his seat.

He needed a haircut and a shave. Typically, his face is like a baby's bottom with his head skinned to the bone. Today was a different story. He was clean other than missing a shave and a haircut. He was immaculately dressed as always. His shoes were on point. His teeth sparkled like diamonds from his mouth being slightly open. The cuff links he wore tonight were crystal clear. His bracelet was blinding. However, his disposition was deadly.

As soon as Hunter said, "grab your neighbor's hand," for the benediction, I almost knocked Keith over. I took his hand gently not wanting to hurt him any further. "Let's go."

"Give me a few minutes," he said with all the breath he could produce.

I gave him a look, "I am driving you home now."

"I can drive."

"Get your things and let's go."

"I'm fine."

"Yes. I know you are." He was so exhausted he did not get the pun intended. He took my comment as sarcasm.

"Let me speak to Tre."

"Call him in the car," I ordered. We walked to the vestibule. "I'm taking him with me. Someone take his car."

"She is ruining you man," King snickered.

"Whatever Bluto."

Randall did not say a word. He followed my lead. I opened the passenger side door for him. He moaned as he stepped in the car. I probably should have taken his truck and left my car. He laid the seat as far back as it could go. I pulled the seat belt over him.

As we approached the highway he spoke, "Take me to your house please."

I looked over at him. His head was back with his eyes closed. I went in the direction of my house. When we got there, I got out and opened his door. "Are we home?"

It was like music to my ears. I wanted to say yes. However, technically we were at my house. We had separate houses. Instead, I pleased us both. "Yes baby. Let me help you out."

We got in the house and he went straight to the bedroom and lay on the bed fully dressed. "Please let me help you take something off." I took his shoes off. He was so tired he did not even attempt to help me. "Can I take your shirt off?"

He did everything in his power to lift up. When I realized he could not and he was leaning up as best as he could I struggled until I got the shirt off. I had been around him enough to know he liked vegetable juice. I did not have the time to juice vegetables. I popped open a V8. I put a straw in it and took it back to the room.

"Can you drink some of this please?" I put the straw to his mouth and he drank without hesitation. I could tell from his wife beater his abs were rock solid. No wonder he could not sit up. They were always to die for but today they were like a nineteen year olds preparing for a video shoot. Ripped. What I did not know was those sexy abs were covered with quite a few contusions and broken ribs.

"Thank you DJ."

"For what?"

"Taking care of me and making me lay down. I really need it."

"Do you need anything? Bengay or Tylenol?"

"No babe. I am good."

"I will be in the living room if you need me."

I went and made me a bowl of cereal and started to work. I checked on him periodically. He did not move an inch. I took a shower and prepared for bed. I laid on the chaise lounge in my bedroom. I was still going at it and figured I better stop. It was three o'clock when his paraffin hands touched my face. My eyes popped open.

"Good morning sweetheart," he rubbed my cheeks and kissed them. "I need a car."

He transformed in those six hours. I wonder if he understood the difference sleep made for him. The light was off in the room but I could see his eyes were white. "Take whichever one you want."

He went to the bathroom with the facecloth and new toothbrush I laid out for him. When he came back out he was back fully dressed, face washed, teeth brushed and most of all, alive.

"Come set the alarm. I love you and I will call you in two hours."

I did not move. I called out the code so he could disarm it. I heard it rearm once he made it to the garage.

Thursday

My phone was ringing. Two hours passed quickly. It always did when you wanted to sleep. "Good morning my love."

"What a pleasant greeting," Keith said. "With that in mind I guess I should inform you we have a date tonight at the church. What time can you be there?"

My other line was ringing, "Hold on Keith."

"Let's try this again. Good morning my love."

"What do you mean by again?"

"Keith called me and I answered him the same way thinking it was you."

"Are you in trouble with him?"

"No."

"Am I?"

"No, he said he and I have a date tonight."

"The devil is a lie. I will get to the bottom of this with Keith. You get to work."

"Randall," I could hear the movement from him running,

"Yes," he said real quick and short. Not to be rude but full of excitement.

"I am glad you feel better and got some rest. Can you promise me you will do it often?"

"I feel better. I do not think I have a choice in the promise."

Smiling, I said, "Great job. Thank you for your cooperation."

"Call me later."

"I love you babe."

"I love you too," he whispered.

"Ugh." King yelled. He ignored King just as he always did.

No one informed me of a change in plans; therefore, I did what I was told to do and showed up at the church. Melissa was at the desk when I arrived.

"Good afternoon. I am sorry Deacon Washington is not here."

No, she did not. I know doggone well sister didn't get cute with me. Lord help my bridle my tongue. I do not think I gave him time to answer my prayer. "Good evening. You are absolutely correct. Randall is not here tonight. I am fully aware of where he is," checkmate. "But he is not who I am here to see," I snarled and continued to walk.

Keith walked me through the entire church including the women and men's restrooms. He showed me all the exits, escape routes, panels, cameras, and more. I take it I needed to know this in case anything ever jumped off. We spent a few hours there and then we headed to the gym. It was getting late but I wanted to get a few laps in. To be honest I wanted to see Randall. I was going to work out and seeing him was the consolation prize.

He was so handsome even when he was tired and sweating. He managed to break loose when I was leaving and walk me to my car.

"You know I have to stay here tonight."

"Not all night?"

"No, not all night but I do need to stay here and finish since I didn't come back yesterday. Now you are aware that since I slept at your house I cannot come tonight."

"Who makes these rules?"

"As you know I don't."

We said good night. I was not happy about the rules but they were in place for a reason. He was not happy with them either but to keep the peace he was obedient. He had a hard job. His main job was to fight. Then he was stuck with the task of trying to appease a lot of us. There was no way he could make all of us happy at one time. He tried hard to do so and was never willing to give up the idea that he could not.

Friday

Today was full of press conferences, appearances, and cups of urine samples. I was tired. How did Beyoncé do this day in and day out? You have to love what you do. We went from television station to television station. Then we went from radio station to station. He appeared at athletic gear stores to magazine interviews. If Vickie handed him one more sheet of paper to review and if he car changed one more time I was going to cut the day short. It seemed like every stop there was someone there with a cup. The problem I had was who was watching the cup.

Finally, I asked. JJ was impressed I noticed and agreed it was an issue. He informed me he stays with the cup. Everything is tested right there in the restroom and the results are mailed out. He called me in to show me how they seal the cup then JJ signs, Hooks signs, the requestor signs, and a witness signs the seal. I signed as a witness. It would be too much trouble and too hard to reproduce all of the signatures. It was not impossible to do but a lot of work. I had to love a guy to sign for his urine. This was amazing and a lot of detail went into his daily routine. Not only from his end but also from the association, his medic staff, and others.

I didn't need to earn any brownie points with JJ but I did. Which in turn meant I earned more with the fighter? He was taken aback to see me in the restroom when he came out with a cup of clear liquid which I questioned.

No one's urine is that clear. When you do not eat food this is what you get. Crystal clear. I took the cup and held it in the light. It was spotless and clear. "Don't ask me to pee in the cup for you. You will be busted immediately." You could not even tell anything was in the cup it was so clear. The liquid was clearer than the plastic. I swear this was water. It felt weird holding his bodily fluid and the need to examine it was even stranger.

"What is she doing in the men's room?" he asked as if it was completely unheard of.

"Witnessing."

"Oh?" he said surprised.

"Yes. She is concerned the facilitator has an opportunity to contaminate the sample."

He raised his eyebrows impressed.

"No hard feelings," JJ said to the facilitator. "Therefore, we will relieve her thoughts by inviting her in. I am sure this guy would not do anything illegal. There was no amount of money that would convince him to be dishonest. Who wants to do jail time over urine? What do you say to your cellmate as to why you are serving a dime? I switched pee. Not cool. You will become someone's," he paused. If I were not there, he would have said the B word. "Desire. Quickly and all day. For some reason I see urine involved."

"J," Randall shouted and laughed. "Enough with the prison body fluids. You are putting a lot of thought into this. We got to roll," he grabbed my hand. He got in the facilitators face, "Dude, bottom line is if you switch the cup, after I reconfigure your face, put your left arm on the right side and remove both of your legs in one snap, you go to jail. It is not worth it."

Saturday

Today Keith took me through a series of escape routes at Randall's home. It was way too much to take in. The thought of even needing this was scary enough. Was all of this necessary? I assume so since they had routes in place. I have designed many buildings with escape routes. A security firm of course, casinos, and government facilities but never an individual's home. Not even my own.

Why would anyone ever want to hurt him? I suppose to be malicious. Get a grip Danielle. People hurt people for no reason or the least little reason. Maybe a competitor would want to hurt him. Come on D. Do not forget the real world. A lot of money rides on these events. Think about it in real talk. Street talk. If the fighters are getting fifty million plus how many street dollars are involved. People take this sport serious. It should not be used as a hustle and gamble; but real talk, I am sure it is.

Someone could ask Randall to throw a fight. The winning or losing of a fight could cause him harm. A number of things could be going on for all of this security to be in place. People also try to test people in the strangest way. Like why in the world would anyone street challenge Dale Earnhardt Jr. That is what Jr. does for a living, drive. Do you really think you will win in a Too Fast to Furious car when he is used to driving special made super charged vehicles day in and day out.

What idiot would challenge a fighter? All of them. Especially a drunk one. Come on man, it is his job. He fights. You are aware he will kick your a** with one blow. Better yet, kill you. This would be like me scripturizing Hunter. There is no way I would ever go toe to toe with Hunter on scripture. For the record, I know scripture. However, it is what he does. Likewise, I hope he never goes toe to toe with me on drawing, building, or designing. All Hunter better try to design and draw is his sermon. Otherwise, I will chew him up and spit him out like cud. That goes for anyone who is not in my field. Don't play with me. Get belligerent and I will break you down and draw you again with the correct specifications. Do not play with me.

Sunday

When I arrived at church, I thought he was on speed. He was zipping and zooming like the place was on fire. He was back to the old Deacon I first met. The brief conversation he had with me was a blur. He said so much so fast I missed it all.

When they walked in the sanctuary, I could see the solemnness in everyone. Hunter, Elder, King, JJ but Deacon Washington was still pumped up. I have watched Hunter and Elder long enough to know something was on the rise. The problem was you never knew what it could be. Elder looked back. He made contact with Deacon Washington. Deacon stepped up to the pulpit and Elder spoke in his ear. I made eye contact with him. He was still pumped. Hunter looked back. He summoned Deacon Washington. He stepped up. They had a long conversation with backs turned. He stepped down and went to his seat. I am sure he knew I was on edge. Therefore, he winked. Keith stepped up to block my view. I stepped up too. He probably could hear all of the whispers in his earpiece that I could not hear.

Hunter spoke to Elder. Elder stepped off the platform. This was unusual. Deacon Washington followed behind him. King gave motion that he was out and he left too. Mere seconds passed and Hunter stepped down. JJ changed gears and followed. Keith hit his wrist. "What's going on?" He leaned in to me. "Are you going to be alright?"

"Yeah. Is everything and everyone okay?"

"I don't know." He summoned Black from across the room. Black stood in his spot on guard for the entire room. He was searching the positions and post. Did everyone leave? I wanted to look and search too but since there was so much commotion going on, I did not want the congregation to get worried. My praise team friends were eyeing me like what is the deal. I kept on praising. I hoped all it was just an upset stomach. Then I thought better. It did not take all of them for one person with bubble guts. Unless Elder and Hunter both had bubble guts which could be possible. Maybe they ate the same breakfast.

I was stressing. Something was going on. Whatever it was my Deacon was calm but it had my Pastor and my Elder uptight and I did not like it. Why didn't I have my phone or my earpiece? From this day forward, I was wearing my earpiece every Sunday whether they liked it or not.

They all arrived back at the same time. It looked like eight left and twenty came back. They harbored around Hunter. I looked around the room. I did not see a threat and apparently neither did Randall he was still animated. Whatever bothered them was not bothering him.

By now, praise and worship was at the highest level. I do not know how many songs we went through. Hunter, Elder, and Randall's hands were lifted. I was on observance alert. Hunter was full. He took the microphone and stood behind the book board. He froze the praise team. He opened his mouth but nothing came out. Time stood still. It was like trying to help a person with a speech problem. We all were thinking get it out but nothing escaped from his mouth. He turned his back then fell to his knees.

Deacon Washington let the cannons off. He clapped so loud. He gave motion to the musicians to take it back up and the praise team continued to sing. King and JJ were at full attention inches from the platform. Deacon Washington's demeanor changed slightly. He was more alert and concerned because his friend was down. Normally, he was the one on the altar.

Hunter's arms were still stretched. His back was to the crowd. I immediately thought oh no not him too. Here we go. Pastor Hunter was trying to contain it. It did not work. Suddenly he hit the deck. I knew then he was gone. I looked at Elder. His nose was flame red. He looked like Rudolph. Before I had a chance to start praying I eyed Randall who eyed Elder informing him he was on. This did not happen frequently but it happened enough for us to not be troubled. Thank God we were a house that knew how to suspend and press past protocol. Hunter was down so Elder was tagged in. Problem one, Hunter was laying on the microphone. I could see Deacon Washington motioning for a microphone as I was bowing my head to pray. Elder stood in motion until another one was brought to him although he really did not need one. They were taking too long for Deacon. I felt him breeze past me to go get one.

Elder stepped right in and preached the word stepping over Hunter when needed. After the word was given and the doors of the church were opened, Randall motioned for all the Deacons to line the platform. Hunter was still laid out. He had not moved an inch. King and JJ were trying to lift him. Randall stepped right in and picked his boy up without any help as they all followed closely behind.

"Stay here," Keith said. "Do not move."

It made me think they might have had many wild college nights where they both had practice potato sacking each other. I hated to say it but somehow I felt it was more Trevor being carried than Randall. Not to discredit Pastor any. He spoke of his club days himself. However, I didn't think Randall deviated much from his quirky eating habits much less getting slizzered.

After service I followed orders and waited right there until Keith arrived.

"Go home Mrs. W. I will meet you at your house in a few hours. Hooks will call you when he gets Tre together. No worries. Everything and everyone is fine. It is Hunter's day today."

"Okay."

"We have a long and busy day ahead. Depending on how this goes you may get off easy."

I was getting my things. It was cool outside this morning. Keith helped me with the lightweight coat over my suit. Just as I got ready to make a step, I saw feet running indicating my knight in shining armor was arriving. He hugged me extremely tight. "Oh," I said shocked.

He sighed heavily but he was still smiling when he let me go, "I got it Keith. I will meet you back in his chambers. Hey babe."

"Hey sweetheart. Interesting morning. Are you okay?" I asked.

"Yes."

"Are you sure? I can only take one of you all down at a time."

"Yes, I am fine."

"Is Pastor okay?"

"He is great. He will be just fine. I do not know if realizes we moved him."

"Use him Lord," I mumbled.

"Thank you for your prayers. We love you."

As we walked through the sanctuary, everyone stopped him. He was so pleasant with the largest smile exposing those beautiful teeth. If something were wrong, you would never know it by his attitude and demeanor. This guy was filled with charisma. He gave candid responses to each person. "The Spirit has moved. The Spirit touched our Pastor this morning. He is full of the Spirit and the Word. God bless your obedience and ability to shift gears. To God be the glory." His responses to people were to say he is human and this is normal. He feels like we feel. He has bad days and good days too. He cries out also. Today we all witnessed it. We got to my car barely without interruption. "I understand you are cheating on my today," he stated with jealousy.

"Yeah. I was told."

"Yeah, and I was told to stay out of the away. I cannot see you today."

"Oh really?" My hand went on my hip annoyed at whoever gave him those instructions.

"Yeah. That is what I was told. I will see how your day goes before I ask any questions. I really wanted to hang out with you but maybe all of this has worked out for a reason. Now, I need to stick with Tre. If he is not functional after a while, I am going to call First Lady and take him home. I will give him a few hours. I do not want to disturb him right now."

"You are such a good friend."

"I try to be the same friend you two are to me."

"Will I see you this evening?" I snuck in.

"If I get permission."

"You are so disciplined. Why do you follow the rules all the time? You can be radical and rebellious sometimes."

"I would love to. Whether you realize it or not I disobey the rules for you all the time. You have gotten me in more trouble at thirty than I was in at fifteen. You know King and JJ want to kill me and ban us from seeing each other weekly. They offered to allow six hours per week."

My face frowned instantly. I must learn to control my body language.

"They love you DJ," he quickly diffused the potential issue. "I love you. They love me and they have a job to do. Their job is to ensure I am in the best condition. They are to block me from all danger even if it is from myself. For the record, you are a danger to me in many ways. If I worked on Wall

Street, they would care less. The job I do is all about discipline. Most people think it is about boxing. As you know most of it is mental. You are aware you have my mind messed up. They have detox and reprogram me daily. Overall, it is a good thing. I think they are all glad to know I love you. However, there are rules. I must remain in the confines of the rules. Otherwise, I am likely not to succeed. Enough of this. I am preaching to the choir."

"I love you."

"I love you too," he said with sincerity.

"Call me later."

"Sure thing," he declared.

He was kneeling down on the side of my car, "Are your knees on the ground?"

"One."

"Man there you go on your knees again," A man said as he passed by.

"I know man. She keeps doing it to me."

"Tell Pastor Hunter we will be praying for him."

"He is grateful for your prayers." Then he turned his attention back to me, "Babe. Please behave today," he begged.

"I'll try. It is Keith only, right? Because I can't promise if King is involved."

"I love you," he kissed my lips and ran away.

"Hey," I called out. He turned around running backwards. "Stop running."

He stopped the motion but his feet kept moving in place. As soon as I passed him, I looked back and he was running again.

***

My phone rang from the gate. Sure enough, it was Keith. He instructed me to get my things and put on comfortable shoes. All I could think was *what are we about to do now?*

"Are you ready?"

We got in the car and once he got to the edge of the drive way and he said, "Where to?"

"Huh? This date is starting bad."

"Let me see your list."

I held my hands up. I did not have a list.

He looked like I failed to follow instructions. "I didn't give you the list did I?"

"Nope. No list."

"My bad. All right, here is the deal. We are going to places you frequent. The salon, spa, nail shop, Starbucks, grocery store, gas station, bank, mall, where you pick up dinner, Mikey's, Paige's, your mother's, and anywhere else you frequent."

"Today?" I panicked.

"Now," his voice was still calm.

This was not what I was expecting but whatever. We started with the closest destination. He observed the parking lots. We went in and looked around at the exits. He wanted to familiarize himself. He got the address and business cards from every location we stopped so if I said nail shop he knew where I was. If I said post office he knew which one I frequented. Then we hit Mama Roses.

"Hey Mama."

"Rosey. Did I know you were coming?"

"Nope. Pop up."

"You all will get enough of popping up on me. I have a man and a life."

"Mama we have company."

"Randall ain't company."

"It is not Randall."

She flew around the corner, "Who is it?" She looked and realized she has seen his face before. "Hey baby. Does Randall know you are out with his girlfriend? I do not want any mess."

"Mama," I shouted while laughing.

"It was a simple question and all I want is a simple answer."

"Yes ma'am. I am on duty."

"You better be. You have a terror on your hands."

"I seem to agree Mrs. Rose. She is stubborn and hard headed."

"You ain't seen nothing yet," I contributed to the conversation they were having about me.

"Well, sit down. Let me fix you a plate."

"No ma'am I am on duty."

I was shaking my head, "Don't ever say no to food at Mama Roses." She pulled out the meatloaf, creamed potatoes, collard greens, fried corn, lima beans, cornbread and peach cobbler. I started fixing my plate. Before I was finished, I saw some person fixing them a plate. The person who said no thank you quickly changed his mind.

We stayed and laughed with Mama. She was happy for the company. I was glad to be there. I got the impression Mama really, really liked Randall and was happy I was being watched since I was out too early and too late per her words. I woke the sun up and reminded the stars to shine so she thought. She wanted me to leave in the daylight and return in the day light. I don't see how that would happen unless I drive the car pool.

On the way back Keith spoke. "Let's call it a night. Thanks for dinner at your mothers."

"She is a character."

"Mother like daughters. All three."

"Yeah, yeah, yeah." Because of Sade's age people always classified the three of us as sisters although she was not our sister.

"Good job today Ms. D."

"Thank you."

"Anywhere you need to stop before I drop you off?"

"Other than seeing my baby no I think I am fine."

"You saw him this morning."

"Doesn't count."

"I don't know what to tell you."

"I guess I do not either. I better get used to it."

"I think you should. Your life will revolve round J and King's schedule. King James as I like to call them."

"Thanks for the day."

"We will reconvene next week. Go in and lock the door. I will tell Hooks you miss him."

"I miss him much," I said and closed the door. It was still early enough for me to work and work out. I had to get the slices of meatloaf off before it hit my thighs. I heard my alarm buzzing. *What the heck,* I thought. Then I pressed the buttons on my phone to show danger. I heard the feet approaching. I was not in a position where I could move, arm myself, or view my cameras.

"DJ?"

I peeked around the corner almost knocking him over. "What are you doing here?"

"This is not the welcome I was expecting."

I kissed him, "I didn't think I would see you today."

"You saw me earlier but a message was sent stating you missed me and since you were on good behavior and I have been on good behavior I was allowed a few hours of leave."

I stopped everything I was doing and chilled with him. A lot of work went into allowing him to break and see me. I texted Keith.

> You big teddy bear. There is a heart in there somewhere. Stay away from King. He will ruin you.

Right then both of our phones rang at the same time. "Hello," we said in unison.

"Why are you signaling danger?" King barked.

"Crap. Because someone was breaking in. Why did you take so long to call me back?"

"Are you in danger?"

I looked at Randall marking King in silence, "No."

"Turn it off then and if you are going to press buttons send the fighter back to work."

I marked him again, "Are you done?"

"Not until the watch is off."

I made sure it was off, "Am I good?"

"Yeah."

I clicked off before King not giving him a chance to hang up first. Randall was still on the line. He looked at me, gave me a bad look and pointed his finger. "Tell her this will be her last free surprise visit," King hung up on him.

Randall looked so sad, "What's wrong?"

"King said I have to leave since you hung up on him." I think tears formed in my eyes. "Just kidding. Now behave," he gave me a nuggie and kissed my forehead.

WEEK 35

Monday

Time was passing quickly. Almost two months had gone by. We all busted our butts making sure he was ready. Every part of my body was sore. I have jumped rope. I have been in the ring. I have been on his back for pushups. I have punched and been punched. I have walked and been forced to run. I am sure all of us were in the best shape of our lives physically if nothing else. Hefty Smurf and I had been working together every day. We were almost a tag team. We conversed to give each other instructions on what to let him do and what not to let him do. He was not fond of our tattling. However, he was glad King and I were cordial and he knew it was for his good.

Since I had been obedient to King and JJ's request and worked in conjunction with them, they allowed us more time alone. He was allowed a date night every week. Even if they killed him for hours before and hours afterwards he never complained. They allowed him his personal time to keep his mind healthy, to pacify me, and to give them a break. Some nights all I could do was rub him down with liniment and ice. It did not matter as long as we were together. Other nights we watched movies or went out. Then there were nights he flat out went to sleep on me. We spent quite a bit of time with Mama Rose. She always had something up her sleeve. Recipes for fat free vegetable biscuits, pancakes, and other items that did not sound delectable to me. Zucchini biscuits and cauliflower pancakes were not something I desired. How do you make vegetables rise? Who knew? Who cared? She was doing it all to accommodate my new boyfriend. Press conferences, guest appearances, photo shoots, benefits, and a booked calendar had us all exhausted.

He was so concerned about my reaction to him in the ring on fight night. He should have been more concerned with me surviving his preparation before the fight. The way I felt I might sleep through the fight. It will be the first moments in sixty days I will have some real sleep. Dating was way more work than I remembered. However, for him, it was all worth it. I loved him and there was no question, he loved me.

The time came. It was the Sunday before our departure to Las Vegas for the week. The checklist was like Santa Claus' list. Who lives like this? This was over load. If Vickie sent me one more check sheet, one more reminder, and if one more item populated my calendar, I was changing my email address. The sad part and the best part of all of this was the Champ was the calmest of us all. He only had to do what he was told and be ready do what he is trained to do. After these two months, I felt like I needed to get in the ring and knock the person out myself on general principle. I was tired. From sun up to sun up again someone was always working on his behalf.

I use to think all you do is jump some ropes, punch some bags, and go knock a guy out. Wrong! There was a science to boxing. Either this group made it rocket science or it was rocket science. A lot of work and a crew of people worked hard to get him ready. King and JJ were just the front row people. Vickie looked like she had been in the ring. Trevor was working day and night. He was meeting him every morning for prayer, running with him, and supporting him as a friend and a Pastor. I was going to scream if he was asked to pee in one more cup. I felt like he needed a catheter so at the end of the day he could give them a bag full of his drug free urine.

It seemed like this day would never come. The job would never end. There was so much to do and so little time to do it. The MGM Grand was sold out. They were forced to open more seats than they would normally have available for a fight. It is not like a concert. You cannot schedule a second show. It was crazy. His guest list was a mile long. With all the other seats they opened up, I felt like we would be sitting in the ring. This was surely going to be a Ringside fight for me.

I was not sure I knew what to expect or how to act sitting so close. This was going to be challenging. All I kept telling myself was it was only an hour or so. I could close my eyes if I wanted to or needed to. It was not working. I was already panicking on the inside.

Sunday

I was trying to figure out how I was going to stuff my final suitcase. This itinerary was deep. There was no way I could stay within the suitcase minimum. I heard my phone ring. It was Randall's David. I let him in the gate. I was at the front door before he was. He opened the truck and brought in box after box.

"Here is everything you need. If you need anything else call Vickie or Hooks," was all he said before he left.

There was a copy of the itinerary including the attire for the week. I skimmed through it. It did not look much different from the one I already had. I could not wait to get in these boxes. One thing was for sure, it was not jewelry or shoes. The boxes were too large. To my surprise, it was Louis Vuitton trunks and luggage. I was dialing him before I finished opening the boxes. There were presents for the girls also.

Fight Week

WEEK 36
Monday

After we arrived in Vegas we got the official Hooks Gym rules. Or shall I say JJ laid down the law. I had a feeling this was review for most and lesson one through ten for me and my crew.

Rules:
1. Always travel in pairs or groups along with someone from the security team.
2. Destinations must be approved if outside the hotel.
3. No food or drink unless scanned.
4. No adult beverages.
5. No smoking.
6. No gifts, food, candy or the like will be accepted from anyone outside the group.
7. Ear pieces must be worn at all times. If you do not have an earpiece you must travel with someone who does.
8. Cell phones shall be with you at all times. Therefore no swimming.
9. If you have a locator it must be worn and on at all times.
10. Everyone will be issued Zoombak.
11. No fraternizing and socializing.
12. We will eat every meal as a group daily.
13. We will all be present during training and arena time.
14. We will all train together. Be prepared with workout clothes.
15. No heels. (He said as he looked at me)
16. No big handbags, cameras bags, laptops, etcetera.
17. Those designated to take pictures will be the only ones allowed to have cameras.
18. Carry as less as possible.
19. No gambling.
20. Do nothing to cause attention.
21. We all will be required to all watch practice tapes.
22. We will have sitting time in the arena to get the feel, learn where the emergency escape routes are, and the plans of action.
23. When the fight is in progress no one will move. Not for concession or restroom. During the fight you will be allowed one bottle of water each.
24. No tweeting, blogging, Periscoping, Instagraming or Facebooking to providing information of what we are doing.
25. Here is the laminated list of everyone's phone number, email address and radio station.

"Are there any questions?"

I wanted to ask can we breathe or do we have to get permission to do that too. There were no ground rules about showering and using the facilities. Did I need a partner to do number one or two? I could get in the pool and relax. All he said was no swimming. Did I arrive at boot camp, concentration camp or prison? What did he mean no gambling? We were in Sin City. Gambling was the main reason people came to Vegas. I was putting my coins in those slots machines regardless of what anyone said.

For me and the ladies, Vegas was the life and we planned to live it up. I may go for not leaving the Hotel but the other things I was not going for. Shopping was not mentioned which meant it was allowed. I did not foresee Paige being here a week and not having her daily night cap of white wine, red wine or if they make it in blue as long as it is wine she will drink it. And if they really thought Sade was not going to check the club scene out they were sincerely misinformed. This was the first time she would have been here as an adult too. There would be no stopping her.

I knew right then some rules were going to have to be changed or this was going to be a long week. I was going to have to go to the source and get a hall pass or permission; otherwise, we were going to check in down the road until Saturday. No one told me there would be all of these rules. I would have stayed my tail at home until Friday. Any other time he complains I work too much. Now, I guess work is all he wants me to do. I mean this beautiful hotel was a nice place to be locked in but I felt cabin fever and it was only day one.

We broke. The question was what were we supposed to do and what could we do? I felt like I was the hired help and not the girlfriend of the Champ. I knew from this point on I was going to be like Trevor and show up a day or two before. They won't trick me again.

It was after breakfast when me and the ladies went back to our suite and worked. I wanted to call Vickie instead I emailed her.

Vickie,

I would like to meet with Randall privately. Today if this is possible. Please let me know if this can be arranged.

Thank you,

Danielle

I felt like Ted Turner when he was married to Jane Fonda. I did not want to end up like them. I did not want to ever get to a point where we only communicated via assistants, meeting requests, and post-it notes on the bathroom mirror. It saddenes me I had to do this but I would not dare let him know it bothered me.

She did not respond. Instead, we all were summoned to the arena. It seemed so large without the people there. The ring seemed one hundred times larger than the one in his gym. He got in the ring. He threw punches. One of the arena security people guided us. He showed us where we would sit. Where we would enter from. He gave us a rundown of the building.

We left there and went for a late lunch. He ate twice in one day. It seemed so backwards. I would have imagined he ate all while he trained and then when he arrived here he would be too nervous to eat. What a strange concept.

We were given two hours of free time so the girls went back to the room. I really anticipated Vickie spending more time with us but she was in full work mode.

Maybe twenty minutes after we arrived back to the room there was a knock. Paige went to the door with Leigh following behind with her camera ready.

Keith stepped in, "Ms. D, come with me please."

I felt like I was on the last walk and this was the green mile. I got my Zoombak, my phones, iPad, and bag before I left the room. I had my iPhone in my hand and the bag across my body as we walked in silence.

We rode down the elevators to another floor. We walked down the hall and then through a door which looked like a room. Instead, there was another hallway. He used a door key and a key card once we got to the second set of double doors. There was another corridor. As we approached I could see the guys standing at attention. Keith opened the last set of doors and motioned for me to go in. The room had a couch, a television, and a table set in the middle. Roses were everywhere. Randall was standing in front of a window. I am sure King was not aware of this or would have approved of him standing in front of a large window. There was no rule but I am sure it was considered dangerous even at this height. I looked around the room. It was picture perfect. I realized this was a secret wing of the hotel and this was arranged from my request to meet with him.

"Hey babe."

"Hey," I said reluctantly still standing across the room.

He extended his hand, "You wanted to meet me privately?"

"Yes. I did."

"Here I am. I am all yours. For two hours at least."

I raised my eyebrows.

"Conversation and then you never know what will happen from there," he winked.

"Oh."

"Is there anything in particular you want to talk about?"

"Well yes."

"Great, go ahead," as he reached out to hug me.

"How do you want to run this?" I asked.

"Run what?" he frowned.

"How are you going to explain our relationship?"

"Just as it is."

"And?"

"You are the love of my life. My everything, my all, my heart, and my love interest."

"How do you want me to respond?"

"Tell them to see me unless you want me to respond differently?"

"No. That's not what I meant."

"Why are you concerned?"

"I do not know."

"Has the question been raised?"

"No."

"Good," he was unconcerned and unmoved by my concern.

We sat at the table. "So what else is on your mind Danielle?" he looked intensely.

I had all of his attention. It was weird how he could change gears and become a different person. "The rules."

He sighed like he knew this conversation was coming. "Okay. Which one in particular?"

"Almost all of them. I can't ask the girls to not have an adult beverage. I can't ask them to be cooped up here all week. We want to shop. Enjoy some of the fun the city has to offer. Maybe catch a show. Have dinner other than banquet served meals and room service. Come on Randall. I would be getting my own room at another hotel if it were me."

"Anything else?"

"You know Sade is not going to obey the do not party rule. I am going to put my coins in those slot machine and flats are out for this entire week. You can hang the thought up."

"You mean swipe your card in the slot machine."

"Whatever," *don't correct me at a time like this.*

He poured water in my glass put some fruit on the plate in front of me as if I had not said a word. I didn't know how to take it. After the fruit he extended his hand for mine and led me over to the couch in front of the television. A Denzel Washington movie came on. He really put some thought into this meeting. He or someone did. But he didn't respond to the reason why I wanted to meet.

We watched the movie. As soon as it was about to end the doors opened. It was ddinnertime. We met everyone in the banquet room. After dinner he went back to training while videos played of his fights, his opponent's fights, and other famous fights. We all watched. We were not required this time but what else could we do?

At eleven they called it a night. His time was up for the arena and it was the opponent's time. As we were leaving out the opponents entourage was coming in. It made me nervous to pass them. Randall spoke. They talked for a minute. The fighters were civilized. The security and trainers were the ones acting like wild beast with the Tasmanian devil in full effect.

We got in the elevators and it stopped at the same floor we were on earlier. Keith and King got off before he pulled me out.

We went back to the area we were in earlier. They fed him a mixed blend of fruit and vegetables. He tried to get me to drink some. I tasted it but I had no desire for it. I preferred to chew my food. We danced to a few slow jams then we laid on the floor and watched movies until they escorted us back to our individual rooms.

Tuesday

It was before four AM. Keith scared me standing over me waking me up.

"What?" I said discombobulated.

"Wash your face. He wants to see you."

I came into the living area of my room where he was standing. I ran up to him and hugged him as if I had not seen him a few hours ago. "What's wrong?"

"I wanted to give you this," he reached in his pocket and handed me the contents. It was a Black American Express card with my name on it, another American Express card with my name and Hooks Gym, a Bank of America card with my name, four MGM casino cards and a list. He stepped to the side displaying a case of white wine and four bottles of Champagne.

"All the rules still apply. You cannot go anywhere that is not on the list. You do not leave this room without Keith. Your devices must be with you and working. Are we clear?"

"Yes."

"Good night again. I will see you at breakfast in a few hours."

I stood on my toes, hugged and kissed him. "Thank you. I love you. This means a lot."

"Yeah," he said as if it was something he really did not want to do. Then he decided to back paddle. "Not as much as it means to me," he grumbled. It was easier to keep the peace. And right now, he needed as much perfect peace as he could get.

He left as if it was a dream. I got back in the bed with the cards and list in my hands. I wanted to wake the others up and tell them. They would not enjoy the happiness now anyway. It was too early for all of them. I shared it all by myself.

"You have not because you ask not," I spoke to myself and dozed back off to sleep.

After everyone woke up I screamed, "WE GOT PERMISSION TO LEAVE THE CAMP! Keith has to come with us. And Paige look a here look a here," I said holding up the wine. "From the words of Wilma Flintstone and Betty Rubble, CHARGE!" I said as I held up the cards. "We going shopping. We going shopping." I looked at Sade. "Before you even ask clubbing and gambling has not been discussed or approved. One thing at a time Ms. Lady.

Until it has been approved you are stuck with the rest of us." I gave a fake smile.

"That's fine. Our first stop this morning will be Christian Louboutin. Compliments of Uncle Hooks and Auntie D."

"I think we need permission for a shopping spree. Get dressed, breakfast, training, and then the strip. YEAH BABY! Now this is a vacation. Laptops, crack berries, Droids and iPhones are off limits today."

They all looked like I had officially lost my mind. I had. Therefore, I made a correction. "At least until we finish our girl's day."

Wednesday

We still had to follow the rules. We had to be at training and have breakfast. Well actually, they had breakfast. Randall, King, Keith, JJ, Vickie and I were at press a conference. The conference went much longer than I imagined. First round was Randall speaking alone. He changed for the second round. He and the opponent went toe to toe for round two. The third round was he alone after the group conference. Then the fourth round was in his boxing gear.

I looked at my watch. We had been there a long time. The good news was the mall was not open yet so I was still calm.

When he was alone, there were many personal questions. Will your wife be joining you? How does she feel about your return to the ring? And a host of other questions he never really answered and no one ever really pressured him.

***

Back in Atlanta, Reginald's phone rang. "Yeah."

"Hey Reg."

"What's up?"

"Are you watching ESPN?"

"It's on but I just stepped out of the shower. I am not paying much attention. What's up?"

"Do you know where D is?"

"What is up with the twenty questions?"

"Keep watching ESPN and call me back."

He watched the replay three times. He even TIVOed it. He dialed the number back, "Man, what am I looking for?"

"Did you see the Hooks Washington interviews?"

"Yeah why?"

"D is in the picture."

"Why would Danielle be in the picture?"

"I don't know. Hence the reason I am asking you?"

"Let me watch it again." Sure enough, Danielle was right there next to Hooks Washington. Why? What business did she have there? Maybe she was designing a new MGM grand. Otherwise, she had no business in Vegas and surely none with him.

He called her phone. It went directly to voice mail. He called her desk phone. It stated she was out until Monday. He zeroed out to get Leigh's desk. Her phone said she was out too. They had to be together. He called Leigh's cell phone. It went to voicemail. He waited another hour, caught the replay again and could not figure out why she would be there. He called Sade and Paige's phone. Why was everyone's phone going to voicemail? He did not leave a message. His last resort was going to be to call Mama Rose. He did not want to if he did not have to. He poured himself a drink. It was too early for spirits for the average person. Nevertheless, like they say, it was after five somewhere in the world.

We were still at the press conference. All phones were turned off and left with security outside the door. It was a shame our country had gotten to this place but we had to follow safety procedures. They might as well have stripped us down before we went in rather than take our communication devices.

This was the press conference where the fighters sit side by side, criticize each other and throw mud. I found out so much dirt on the guy and tried to get Randall to slam him but he was too nice of a person to do so. It was actually a civilized discussion. They interviewed each fighter separate, then by a panel and then together. The fighters changed clothes three times, which gave the look and feel as if it was different days. Television is so clever.

He looked so sexy in everything he changed into. He was full of sex appeal and swagger. I was so engulfed in him I missed most of the conversation during the interviews. Randall definitely did not look his age. He looked like a little boy getting ready for T-ball, first day of school, and then Easter Sunday.

After all the interviews, he was back to the real business. His training, videos, security, and the arena. Finally, we were done. I could not get out of this suit quick enough. I would have gone to the mall in it if I had too.

We broke free. I felt like an inmate being released from the penitentiary. The girls and I were on a mission. At five, we broke for dinner. We were allowed to go to the rooms at five thirty and be back at the elevators at six forty five. This was a time strict schedule. As soon as I was able to get to Vickie and Keith, they were giving me a new set of instructions.

Like clockwork, we were back as planned. We all shoved on two elevators. We convened in a beautiful hospitality room. It was marvelous. There was a huge projection monitor and a few recording cameras. We were all talking and socializing. I was working when he came over and said, "Not now please. Give me two hours. I will greatly appreciate it." It was not quite his usual commanding tone but two steps away from it.

Promptly at six fifty nine, the monitor came on. Victory Hope Greater Faith Church appeared on the screen. Then the sanctuary showed. Oh, cool. We were watching via streaming faith. I loved it. A man after my own heart. Whoever organized this was really on point. All he did was sit back and did what he was told. Everything rode on him and he was so calm. Nothing was bothering him. He was about to check out his best friend at bible study as if he was in overflow. His life had not been interrupted. Nothing changed for him. His environment changed. His surroundings changed. He changed location but his attitude and demeanor remained the same.

Praise and worship began. We all acted as if we were there. We were in the spirit. Hooks was wearing a polo and jeans. Pastor was in his jeans also. Hunter was wearing Hooks last champion belt again.

He spoke to the congregation. Then he said "Hooks, its Pastor Hunter. How are you feeling?"

We were all seated. I was in a side chair next to him. A table was in between us.

"I am feeling blessed."

"We are here with you and wish you the best of luck brother. Your church family wants to pray for you." Hunter prayed. The camera floated back and forth from Hunter to Deacon Washington.

Once the blessing was over and we all said Amen he spoke, "I receive it in the name of Jesus."

"I think Hooks has a surprise he would like to share."

"I want to let you know you all will be with me when I fight on Saturday night just as I promised. The fight will be televised at the church. Popcorn, chips, candy, and water will be served. Bring a friend."

The crowd roared. They showed glimpses of the children in children's church. The kids were making banners to support Hooks. Some of them spoke. The Deacons spoke. The police chief spoke, the Mayor spoke and there was a recorded speech from Hunter. He started, "Hooks, it's me Trevor." He specified Trevor letting him and those listening know he was speaking to him as his best friend right now and not his pastor. Trevor gave him some wonderful and personal words of wisdom. He did not hold back. "I will see you soon man," he ended and went into bible study.

Once bible study was over JJ surprised us with the announcement that we were training until Hunter's flight arrived. Once his flight arrived, we had free time for the remainder of the night. It was going to be way after midnight before he arrived. They purposefully planned a late arrival hoping the crowd in the lobby may die down

I got closer to Keith. "Can we leave the compound?" I asked. He gave me the look he always does. A look of no. This meant he would check. He almost looked like he wanted to leave also. We all knew Randall and Trevor were going to be like two eight year olds so why not let the others free for a few hours.

Hunter arrived Wednesday night with RJ. Randall was pissed because JJ would not let him ride to the airport to pick them up. He wanted to be there to see them both but JJ said no. Training was more important. They did not need him for the arrival. He was so excited. It was like once Tre got there the festivities could officially begin.

When Trevor came down the corridor his appearance, his swagger, and his security entourage demanded authority. The press outside the hotel was having a field day. They knew Hooks' best friend flew in after preaching bible study in Atlanta. One thing was for sure, Pastor Hunter never left his congregation. He was a faithful man of God. He will bail on us for Bishop, for First Lady, and occasionally for himself. Other than that, he was there every Sunday and Wednesday. On occasion, when he did leave us, he left someone who was thoroughly equipped to echo him.

I was sitting in eyesight of the door. You could tell from the way I leaned back that I was looking at something or someone. The entire room noticed I was distracted. JJ stood up. Leigh grabbed her camera and raced in front of me to take photos. Randall stood, took my hand and blocked everyone except Leigh and JJ. Everyone was standing like Hunter was entering the sanctuary or raised his hands instructing us to stand. King and Trevor came down leading the pack. I see what the press meant about Pastor Hunter's Security. He had the remaining of Hooks' men with him. *Was it that serious?*

He walked in just like one of the boys. "Hey. I was not expecting everyone to be up this late. I just came to escort Randall Jr. I am out."

"Why man?" Hooks asked sounding pitiful and giving him a man hug.

"Man, I was just kidding." Then he let off a laugh like Randall. It caught me by surprise. I do not think I have ever heard him laugh so heartily. They embraced again as if they didn't just see each other three days ago. It was not a manly embrace. It was as if his second help arrived. You could see from the hug his weight was lifting in mid-air. It was amazing. He seemed so calm to be preparing to enter into his first fight after four years. But at this moment, his level of peace intensified.

"Why are you all standing?" Hunter said looking around the room as if we were all dorks.

Little did he know we were all waiting for our dismissal. I had my clothes laid out on the bed ready. Once we ate and slightly participated in a little conversation, Randall looked over and said "Babe will you be alright if I hang out with Tre and RJ?"

I said as pitiful as I could, "Yeah."

Then we were dismissed. Trevor, RJ and Hooks remained in the hospitality suite on our floor. They were equipped with enough food, games, and movies to keep them busy. I looked at Sade and remembered when she was the kid we left behind. The crew who had been here all week was given the night off and the arriving crew was on duty.

JJ and King were in rare form once we hit the strip. The gamble was on and so was the trash talking. All I was waiting for was the fingers of scotch. The music was bumping; therefore, we danced until the slow songs came on. It was about time. I was sweating and my knees were just about to start aching. I went to the bar and got water for the group. Then someone yelled, "SHOT TIME." I was hoping shots did not hit the agenda but they did. We had one shot in unison. King was out of control. I saw a side of him I have never seen before. Lord, keep him in the Word with the Word; otherwise, he is going to be a mess. King always needed discipline. I may be wrong but if it was not for boxing, there is no telling where his tail would be. He and I may have travelled the same paths at some point. We will have to discuss this next week when all the stress of this week is behind us and the dust of the win has settled. Not to mention when he is sober.

Yeah, I said win. I am confident Randall is going to win. I was speaking life right there in the club. Out of nowhere, I felt heavy. I needed to pray. I got Keith and Black and raced to the restroom. I pulled Keith in and told Black, "Watch the door. Don't let anyone in."

"What are you two about to do?" Black asked like a concerned child.

"My tampon is stuck." That would make him think for ten minutes and then be grossed out.

"What's up Ms. D?" Keith asked laughing at my response to Black.

"Nothing. I feel heavy." We walked in and of course, it was a five star restroom. A room clean enough for me to kneel. I asked God to cover him and protect him. Keith was checking the stalls before he realized what I was doing. He stood with his feet directly to my back watching the door. My head was touching the floor. I guess from the sniffling he knew that I was crying. He moved to pick up the box of Kleenex and nudged me with them to pass me a few. When I finished I laid there on the marble floor. I heard the door open a time or two and on the last time I heard whispering.

"Let's go baby girl," he picked me up.

He pushed through the door and when I saw JJ's face, I spoke. "Put me down please." I turned my back to the group. "I need to go wash my face."

He got Black's attention so we could go back to the restroom. "Man on deck," Keith said before he entered.

I turned the water on and splashed my face. Keith handed me a hand towel. When I moved the towel from my head, JJ was in the room. "What's wrong?"

"We got it."

Ignoring Keith, "Ms. D. what's going on?" he said sternly disregarding he was in rare form ten minutes ago.

"I said I have it J. She is having a personal moment."

He stood in between Keith, "Is this too much and me Tell me what's going on now."

"Nothing. I wanted to pray for him. I felt he needed the intercession."

"Do you always pray after shots of Patron?"

"Umm, it was one shot but yes. I always pray after shots. The prayer used to be, Lord let me make it home. Then, Lord let this stay down. Then after I have prayed to the porcelain God, I prayed again. Lord, let that be all of it. Lord, please do not let my head bang tomorrow. Just then, I would upchuck again. When I finally would stagger to the bed the final prayer would be, Lord if you let me make it through this I won't ever do this again!" It would not be twenty four hours and I would be back at the same altar with the same prayer."

"Good. Since you know the routine and have the prayers down let's make it shot number two. This is a celebration. My fighter is about to be the heavy weight of the world again."

I think JJ had more shots than I knew about. After the second shot, someone was calling out for a third. *OH NO.* What would the purpose of being with security be if they were slizzered?

I finally made an executive decision that it was time to go. Just because the inmates were free for the night and the warden was with us we were still there on business. In a few hours the business we came for was about to begin. I almost had to drag King and JJ from a card table. It was pleasing for the shoe to be on the other foot for a change. I was able to tell them what to do for probably the first and last time. It was a struggle. If I act anything like they do then I was horrible at following instructions.

We were walking down the block when I realized they had fallen behind. There were only a few places they could be. I had to pay a high dollar cover charge, get patted down, and hit on by a female security officer before I found them up front with a glass and a lap dance. Dang that was quick. Tricks move fast in Vegas. I told her, "Girl I ain't hating on you making your money but these two have to leave. Pay the lady and let's go."

The back talk started. I pulled out my phone. I went directly to Pastor Hunter's name. "Do I need to hit send?"

"He is not coming in here," King said with confidence.

"I was not asking him to come in. I am asking him to pray you out."

"DAMN," King said. He touched the woman and rubbed her in a way he should have been paying for. I slapped his hands and pulled him up. I took JJ's snifter out of his hand and set it on the table. I snatched the hundred dollar bills out of his hand and tried to figure out where to put them so I decided to put them in her hand.

"Girl be safe out here. Be blessed and remember God is all you need."

"What the hell?" King said. "Who let Mother Theresa out? Aye girl, I'll be back when you get off. I got something for you," he said flashing a couple of stacks.

I shoved them out of the club. When we got outside the crew was waiting.

We got a few feet down the strip and I noticed JJ taking a sip. He brought the glass out. I took it directly from his mouth and spilled half of it on him. "Damn," he slurred.

"Come on," I said exhausted to Keith. I ran back to the topless bar, went in, and before I could get two feet in the door the bouncer spoke.

"No in and out."

Keith rose up. They were like two pits at attention pulling the chains waiting to be let loose. This was my first time seeing Keith aggressive.

"Take this glass punk. Before the weekend is out you will regret this conversation. Big mistake. Big huge mistake. Saturday night we will make it our business to take our business elsewhere. Door boy," I said while he and Keith mean mugged.

I was pissed off by now. I am trying to bring your funky glass back and you talking trash. Then I was pissed at myself because he took me there. The club scene, two shots, and the strip club took me back to the old me in a matter of minutes. A me I did not want to remember or want to come back. I surely did not want anyone especially Randall to know that person. I would walk away from my church home and the love of my life before I let Randall meet the old me.

We walked back into the somewhat quiet lobby and changed it from quiet to obnoxiously loud. Once we hit the floor, the noise level was so loud until while Randall called JJ's phone, which he did not hear.

"Your phone is ringing drunk man," Sade said.

He prepared to rebuttal but decided she was a kid and he was probably close to drunk. "Yeah," he answered the call.

"Are you on the floor?"

"Yeah it is us."

Randall opened the door. He looked at all of us as if we did something wrong. We smelled like smoke, alcohol, and some of us smelled like badussy. He observed each of us one by one. Everyone was scared to move.

"Get dressed," he yelled. "We are all training now. No one goes to sleep. Was this all you had to do?" he sounded disappointed. He pulled me into the hospitality room. "What went on tonight?"

"Everyone is fine. Nothing went on. I think everyone was stressed and found a way to relived it. We danced, partied, and had fun. It's cool. No harm, no foul."

"No it is not cool. I didn't send you all out to come back inebriated."

"I do not think anyone is inebriated. We have all drank the same thing. Maybe others can handle it better than the rest. Relax. You did send us out. Right?"

He was pissed, "Get dressed," his tone commanding.

"It is not that serious."

He ignored me and opened the door. "Vickie," he barked. She entered the room, "Never again," he said to Vickie while staring at me.

"Yes Sir."

His tone lowered, "I want everyone back at this elevator in twenty minutes," he slammed the door practically in our faces. I scowled at JJ and King, "Look at what you've done," I mumbled and cursed my way out of the suite.

Thursday

I switched clothes and was the first one back at the elevator. Steam was coming out of his ears as he stood there with his ears plugged pacing the corridor. We were all in the doghouse. RJ and Tre were the only two he was pleased with at the moment. I am sure our behavior was an insult to him. The reason we were here was for him and in the midst, we decided to go out and celebrate which was authorized. We messed up making too much noise upon returning.

All he could do was look at me. I did not know if this could be good for him to get a little angry or bad. I needed to talk to King, JJ, and Tre once the two of them sobered up. My calendar was full today. I needed handle some unfinished business. Fixing this problem was not on my agenda.

I leaned my head in his chest. He rubbed it. "We are sorry."

"I know. I am being too harsh. However, they give this treatment to me. I got to give it back when I can." He made it sound like he was not mad at all. It was the principle involved.

"Are you angry?"

He ignored the question, "Did everyone behave?"

"Yes. No trouble."

"That's all that matters. You all had fun, behaved, and now we are back to business for the next seventy two hours."

"That shoots my question down."

"I'm glad because the answer is no."

"You didn't let me ask the question."

"Are you the spokesperson for the group? Did they sucker you because you sucker me?"

"The question wasn't for the group."

"Who is it for?"

"Just us."

"No DJ. Not right now. I am still in training. I do not want to exert too much energy," he joked.

I punched his arm. He gave up my laughed and pulled out his phone and hit the alert for danger to cause them to rush to his rescue. Tre and RJ were coming down the hall. The others had not surfaced yet. "I was wondering if we could leave the compound today."

"Who is we?" he answered stern and harshly? "The answer is no."

"Me, you, Hunter, and Randall Jr. You know, can you date me?"

"I don't know Danielle. My main security is drunk."

"They are not drunk. Keith and everyone else are fine. It is just the two competitors who wanted to out drink each other. Lay off. They have your back all day every day."

"Yeah and now here we are at the moment of truth and they are f'ing up."

I could feel the tension. I raised my body off his chest since Hunter was approaching.

"Good morning." RJ stood extremely close to me. Trevor stood next to Randall. It was like a face-off between the two of us.

"I see you didn't partake in last night's activities as the others did." Pastor tried to sneak in.

"I think everyone has worked extremely hard and celebrated slightly early. Trust me, everything is fine and under control."

Hooks was dialing King's phone. "Get on this elevator now or go home. I do not have time for you to re-cooperate."

I was shocked at his tone. RJ and I stood there holding hands as if we were both scared to speak. I dialed Leigh's phone. "Let's go. You all are not excluded." I could hear Sade talking in the background. "Tell her I said get her a," Hunter gave me a look. "She better be at this elevator before it opens." She was still talking trash in the background. "What she say baby?"

Suddenly, I heard the room door open. The boys came from down the hall like a brigade. You would have never known twenty minutes ago that they were close to wasted. It was back to business as usual. I had to do a double take.

"Now that everyone has finally joined I have made the decision to skip breakfast today. We will work out until lunch." Mumbling commenced. "Let me know if you have questions. Are all hearts and minds clear?" he paused. "Pastor Hunter will lead us in prayer." We formed a circle holding hands while Hunter prayed.

After he finished JJ pushed the button for the elevator. Once we all entered two elevators, he spoke again, "Leigh, let me see your camera."

I started to pray. Leigh please have used your head this time. Please, please, please. She handed him the camera. The pictures from an hour ago were not there. She was wise enough to change cameras. Thank God!

He was serious. We did not eat breakfast. Fruit and some water was brought into the room. We were all starving but no one dared to mention it.

I made an executive decision and asked RJ if he was hungry. He said a little. I asked Pastor and he said he was fine. He was following in the footsteps of the leader. The good was suffering with the bad. I took my phone, called the Hotel's room service, and asked for two big breakfasts to be delivered to the arena. Then I called the DJ and told him I was ready to review the playlist whenever he was.

When breakfast arrived, I sat RJ down ringside and told him to eat. I motioned for Hunter to get out of the ring and come eat. When Randall noticed, he barked.

"RJ where did you get food from?"

My back was facing him. "It was scanned."

"That is not what I asked," he screamed.

"I ordered it," I barked back which ended the conversation. He was clearly getting more and more furious with all of us. His fury was displayed by the way he was punching King. Did he really think he was seriously not going to feed the kid?

The DJ and I had a lot of work to do. We measured step by step from the location he would be starting from all the way to the center of the ring. We had our iPods and beats on. No one else could hear the music. We walked the route repeatedly until it was perfect. Next, I called the lighting and pyro crew in. They needed to know when to start the lights and the fireworks. This was intense coordination.

I asked Vickie if she wanted to check this entrance out. She said no she had her hands full and Hooks trusted my decisions. Leigh was figuring out her best angles and how far or close she needed to stand ringside to get the best and clearest shots. She was also taking into account most shots would be in motions with quick movements. This was a huge task. After she mentally made note she went on the photo platform and worked from there. Sade was on social media alert to test the signals. Everyone had a job. We were all busy. However, he did not waiver. His no was a no. We stayed there all morning. When I looked around after eleven, he was gone.

As soon as I let the DJ and the dancers go Keith walked up. "Let's go."

I got up without saying a word. I knew when to run it and when to hold it. Today was a hold your tongue day.

Quietly Keith escorted me back to the rom. "Be dressed in thirty minutes. I will knock on your door."

"What am I wearing?"

"Whatever you like."

That was weird. I did what I was told. I was standing at the door pacing when he knocked. Keith, Nate, Sol, Hunter, RJ, and Randall were standing at the door. "Hi," I said as Randall took my hand and led me out of the service entrance directly to a car waiting for us. We drove across town to a restaurant for lunch. We left there and hit a few stores on the strip. Then we went to an empty theater and watched a movie.

In the middle of the movie he whispered, "Don't say I never do or give you what you ask for. You asked for a date. Here it is. We have done all the things you like to do. Eat, shop, and movie. Did I miss anything?"

I smiled and laid my head on his shoulder. The guy was amazing. It was true. He came through on everything I ever asked of him. He even picked up on the things I did not ask for.

When we got back to the floor he said, "I want to rest for a while. I will see you either at dinner or at eleven." Eleven seemed like such a long time. I knew I had work I could do in between now and then. I could check some emails, draw some buildings, but I really wanted to rest with him. Hunter was there so resting together was out of the question.

"You are not coming down for dinner?"

"No, we may stay up here. I plan on whipping RJ on a few rounds of Hooks Mania."

"Okay," I sounded sad.

"It's okay. You and I will have an intimate dinner tomorrow with a few hundred people. Babe, it is almost over. Give me sixty hours. Then I am all yours again. Always and forever."

He made me feel as if I was being selfish.

The others were by the door. "I will be in there in a minute," he yelled. He looked at me deeply and passionately. Words could not express how I felt but the tears in my eyes showed it.

"DJ come on. Don't do this."

I looked up and tried to fight back the tears. He held me so tight.

"Why are you doing this?"

It was real. All of this got real. It hit me. I was not here on vacation. I was here preparing to witness the **Ringside** *view of my boyfriend fighting in a championship heavy weight fight. This was deep. My throat was full. I could not speak.* "I'm okay."

"No you are not. Tell me why you are crying."

"Because I love you so much. Because I am so happy. Because we have upset you. Because your whole crew is here to support you and my entire crew is here to support me. Just because."

He sighed and squeezed me harder. My head was buried in his chest. I could not breathe because my nose was smashed. He laid his chin on my head. "Oh DJ. You make me weak. I do not know why you love me but I am grateful you do. More than you will ever know."

"I don't want to upset you further. Go and relax. I will be fine. I will see you later tonight I hope."

"I am not leaving you."

"Sure you are. I am good. I need a few minutes alone any way," I admitted.

"It has been a long week. None of us has had any personal time. We have all been together for almost a week, every day, all day, and every meal. You need some me time. I will make sure everyone leaves you alone for the next few hours. I love you," he walked off leaving me.

I slid down the wall to the floor and sat with my hands over my face. He entered his suite and pointed at Keith. Technically, he is supposed to be with me anyway. He came down the hall and reached for my hand to help me up before we walked back to the hospitality room alone.

I cried myself to sleep with my iPod in my ears while Keith chilled on the couch across from me dozing also.

Randall called Sade, "Hey baby girl. What does DJ have to wear for tomorrow night?" They conversed before he told her he wanted to make a change. "Originally I was going to wear a suit. I think I want to go formal. Can you handle this for me?" he asked her.

"Yeah, Uncle Hooks. I guess you want me to get up now?"

"Yeah, Vickie is coming with you all."

"Does anyone sleep around here?"

"We are on a mission. If I don't sleep, then you all don't sleep?"

"Where is Auntie? Is she going?"

"She is sleeping."

She threw a tantrum. "Why does she get to sleep?"

"She needs it."

"Umm hmm. Because she is doing the boxer. Which is probably why. I am sure it is hard work. Work hard, play hard."

"Watch your mouth."

"Okay. Fine. Little man."

He thought to himself *what did she just call me. Little man? The nerve of her. How did her mouth get as jazzy as her Aunt's? He was not going to take it from both of them.*

"What are we buying?" she said disregarding her last insult.

"I think I want her to be sexy tomorrow night."

"Nothing stripperish I assume?"

"Careful."

"Yeah. Yeah. Yeah."

"I want all the attention on her."

"Uncle Hooks she is not going to go for it. It is your night."

"This is the reason why I did not ask her and I am asking you. I want to give her a present. She has been a good sport this week. I owe her dearly. I will shine in the ring. My night is Saturday night. I could care less about a sit down dinner, which I am not going to eat anyway. Why do people continue to invite me places involving food," he digressed. "I want all heads to turn when she enters the room including mine."

"A dress ain't going to do it. You should have bought the Tiffany's diamond I showed you. How about a Phantom? If turning heads is the effect you are looking for."

"I have a Phantom she can have."

"Uncle Hooks do you love my Auntie?"

"Wow, you Rose girls sure know how to blindside a man. Your question is probably the biggest blow I will get this weekend."

"Answer the question," she demanded.

He issued another smart remark while knocking on the suite door. Sade opened it, rolled her eyes then hung up.

Looking directly in her eyes, he answered her question. "Yes, I love her. I hope she knows it. I hope you know it. I want the world to know it. It gives me concern that you needed to ask."

"Well I think you do. I know she loves you and I do not want her to hurt again. It was painful for us. It took us a long time to get through it. We cannot do it. I will not tolerate it ever again." She spoke as if their pain was one pain. As if, what hurts one hurts the other. She spoke as if they were one person.

"I would never hurt her purposely. You that is another story. Now here is the money for a dress. Sexy. Reminder, the next time you choose to speak you may want to watch your tone and definitely leave out the height remarks," he said as he covered her head with his hand. "I am still taller than you."

"Uncle Hooks can you handle her sexy?"

It was a good question. One he did not answer because he knew he could not.

I didn't know how long I was asleep. I looked up and Keith was knocked out too. I didn't know if I should wake him or let him rest. I texted Randall.

> Hi.

> Come down to the arena when you feel like it. We will have dinner when you get here.

When Keith and I entered the arena, everyone was doing his or her own thing. I felt energized from my nap. I jumped right in talking trash. "Hit him again King and see what happens."

Everyone heard King say to Randall, "She is not going to be ready tomorrow,"

"She is ready," Randall said back softly.

King hit him again. It looked like he wasn't fighting back. I realized he was not. "King I am not playing."

"It's cool babe," he yelled.

King punched the crap out of him. Before I knew it, I was under the rope pushing King. He turned back and put me in a headlock. Sade jumped in. Then RJ jumped in. It ended up being a family-wrestling match. We were all in the ring laughing and rolling on the mat.

JJ spoke, "Let's get back to business guys. It is late. Or early whichever way you look at it. "Let's wrap it up," JJ said. We all headed back to the rooms.

As soon as I laid down and fell asleep Keith was standing over me. They needed to not do that. It was dangerous. Scary and dangerous as a matter of fact.

"Ms. D come with me." It sounded so harsh. Like they were transporting me to prison somewhere.

I got up and started moving like I was trying to find something to change into. "Wash your face and brush your teeth. You are fine the way you are."

I was too sleepy to ask. The next thing I knew we were headed to the roof. Rose petals and long stemmed roses lined the stairs and there was a candle on each step. I did not know what was going on but I liked it thus far.

Keith pushed the door and Randall was standing there with his back turned. He heard the door open and faced me. He had one pink long stem rose in his hand. He leaned in and kissed me. I was mad I was not dressed for the occasion. There was a table set right there on the roof. It was beautiful. It looked like God set the moon right over the roof. I do not know who was joining us but there was enough food for a group.

For him to be a guy who had no clue about dating he sure knew how to melt my heart. He knew all the right things to do. If we could truly be alone I would give him some. Probably right here on the roof. I confessed to myself that I wanted to give him some. The atmosphere was right. The mood was right. My mind was right. My body continuously said it was right. I wanted to but I knew I could not.

We enjoyed each other's company until it was time for him to do it all over again. He still didn't eat much or sleep much which continued to bother me.

Friday

We were called into a meeting room. JJ laid down the law again. The time was nearing. There were many ground rules that needed discussing. These next twenty-four hours were going to be more intense than the entire weeks and months of training had been.

The remainder of Hooks' guests would arrive today and the television crew from church would be preparing and setting up. They were filming the next twenty-four hours. There were press conferences, weigh in, the last words from the fighters, and then the formal dinner.

I cannot explain how I feel. I have never felt this way before. He was still calm. I could not read his mind. I wished I could. I needed to know what his thoughts were from A to Z. I knew if I asked him he would not reveal them to me.

In the middle of the ring he, Trevor, and RJ played around. Trevor held his feet while RJ sat on his lap while he did crunches. Then RJ lay on his back while he did push-ups. The next thing I knew Trevor and RJ were both on his back.

When he stood up and removed his shirt, I think we all had the same thought. *OMG.* I could not even be mad at the girls for looking and drooling.

"LADIES," JJ said. "May I please have your attention? RW please put your shirt back on," JJ half rolled his eyes at all of us.

He was so naïve. He had no clue what was going on or why he was told to put his wet shirt back on. He looked very different dressed opposed to half way undressed. Dressed he looked thin. He did not look buffed and ripped. On most days, he looked like any other guy. However, underneath his clothes there was a completely different story was going on.

He came and practically sat on my lap. Vickie motioned he needed to change for the first conference. Pulling my arm, "You are coming too."

This ordeal was a lot of work. The conferences and interviews were not long but one after the next after the next. He finally got tired of changing his entire suit and changed his jacket and tie only. Originally, he insisted on changing the entire suit, vest, cufflinks and tie. After a few rounds, he was fine with the decision to cheat the media. He may not ever admit it but today I discovered he liked the attention. It proved no matter how flashy he proclaimed not to be truthfully he really was. I noticed he was not wearing his GPS device on his wrist but the watch he was wearing was a conversation piece. A conversation I was going to have with him and then later with the girls. It looked to contain fifty carats of diamonds nested in platinum.

The girls hung out watching the conferences before they hit the strip without me. Once he finished the last press conference, he called for lunch ringside. Thank God everyone was present and on time. Even the family members who travelled, the rest of his staff, accountant, lawyer, publicist, and a host of others were present. Hunter spoke or preached I should say during the meal. JJ went over the rules and expectations again. King went over security, emergencies, and potential danger. Vickie stressed the time-scheduled agenda. Keith went over logistics, technology, and a list full of other things. Then we broke. Well not really. The majority of us went to the spa. If I must confess, we needed it.

I worked harder this day than I have this entire process. Vickie shuffled me from one thing to the next. I thought she was going to be kicked out while we were getting our massages because the entire time she gave me instructions. She directed me on what to lay out as far as my clothes, what I needed to compliment his attire, which side I needed to stand, and what to expect at each interview.

By the time I was finished with my hair, nails, and feet it was time to get ready for dinner. The six o'clock dinner required him and me to be there at four. Which meant weigh in was at three. Actually, he went ahead of me. He respectfully gave me a little time to whoosa before dinner. When I arrived to weigh in it was turned all the way up. *Was the fight today and no one told me?* I guess this was the street fight before the organized fight. I was stunned from the moment I walked into the room. There was security, bodyguards, uniformed officers, none uniformed police officers, the state patrol, sheriffs, and hired security companies; therefore, no one dared jump in the middle of this mayhem. I could not tell who was battling, the fighters or the crews of the fighters. The verbal attacks were atrocious. I did not know Randall had this much aggression in him.

After a day of pampering and heckling, this was not my expectation. My face hit the floor. He was no longer Randall. He was Hooks and Hooks was in rare form. They were like two raging animals. His team pitted upon the other guys team while the two warriors were at full attention. I called his phone he did not move. Cameras were everywhere having a field day with this. Trevor stood at the back of the stage with his arms folded. *You have to be kidding me. This was the reason he let me come alone. He wanted to act a fool. Not on my shift. Finally, it calmed down.*

He could see the anguish on my face. He looked squarely at me and laughed as if this was a joke. I found nothing funny. The opponent weighed in first. Hooks stood next to Tre, King, and RJ with his headphones around his neck bouncing up and down and side-to-side as if nothing had just taken place. Once it was his turn, he gave all pocket contents to Trevor. He handed RJ his music. He took his shoes off and gave his pants, jacket, and shirt to Vickie. He walked over, took his chain, bracelet, and watch off and gave them to me ignoring my facial expression.

"All in a day's work babe. If you get the enemy riled up, they lose focus. They cannot perform to their ability. It is a part of the job. Get ready. It's show time."

He was a different person. What did they give him?

***

When I arrived back to my room, a knock on the door followed me. The gatekeeper; Paige, opened the door. There stood a man with boxes and bags. Sade took them and signed.

"It's time Auntie."

OMG. The dress was beautiful. I brought a dress with me. From what I understand, dinner did not require formal attire. I looked the dress over. "Has he seen this?" I asked. I didn't want the cleavage and back out to upset him. Normally, I would not have cared. I loved the dress with all the cleavage and back out but I didn't want the man of God to send the wrong statement. The statement that he was here with the flavor of the week.

"Yes, it has been approved."

I called Vickie. "Is he okay with this dress?"

"He said he liked it. He wants the attention on you."

"It certainly will be. Did Pastor see this?"

"I am not sure."

"Oh boy," they were setting me up.

Randall, Keith, King, and JJ showed up at my door at a quarter till five. We arrived at the banquet room at five on the dot. This was the first time I was able to talk to the opponent. He was not intimidating although this morning's meeting was hostile. The press wanted it like that. It pumped excitement for the fans. All the other meetings Hooks had were calm. Earlier he was a person I have never met before. Now they were both calm, social, and friendly people.

You would never know they would battle in a few hours. My stomach turned knots. His competition was a nice guy. Subconsciously I did not want to be here. I didn't want to be in the middle. Luckily, I didn't have to pick sides. I was clearly on one side. I felt bad Randall was going to kick his butt tomorrow night. I suddenly felt bad for the guy and wished I had not met him.

I did not know Hunter was the keynote speaker for this evening. I loved how he switched gears. He spoke on discipline. He addressed both fighters then he wished them both luck and safety. This was a hard task to do. Tonight, he had to be a pastor, a speaker, and not take sides, which he did eloquently and Godly. However, he knew what side of the table his bread was buttered. He knew where his largest love offering came from so before he closed he spoke directly to his friend as a leader, as his spiritual father, as his brother in Christ, as his best friend, and as his biggest fan. He blessed the food then dinner was served.

Hooks managed to escape the table to avoid eating. "Excuse me and Ms. Danielle please."

We went and sat right outside the room. It gave photographers time to take pictures. They went crazy snapping our shots. This time Keith did not stop them and neither did Randall. The cameras made me even more nervous. "Tell me how you feel?"

I confessed right there, "I feel like I am about to suffocate."

He was stunned, "Tell me why?"

"I can't believe the time has come. I am nervous. I cannot breathe. My stomach is a pit of knots. My thoughts are scrambled. My heart is beating five times faster than it should. I do not know if I should laugh, cry, or pray. I am scared. I do not know what to expect. I am a basket case on the inside."

"You are hiding it well. Why are you scared and nervous?"

"I do not want anything to happen to you."

"It is only a fight. I do not think I am going to the electric chair or the gas chamber. I have done this before. Many times in fact. The only difference is I didn't have a beautiful woman supporting me before," he tried to encourage her. "It is about an hour and a half of dancing and punching. I plan to do most of the punching. If it will be easier for you, I can give my hardest and best 'hooks' to hurry up and get it over with so we can get back home."

"You can't be missing your bed," I laughed trying to cover my fear. "This hour and a half will be the longest in my life."

"I want to hurry up and get you and everyone else home so we can get to church Sunday morning and I can get Trevor back." He knew it was coming. She was calm yet afraid.

"Yeah and I ain't never scared but right now I think I am."

"There is no need. I promise you. You have seen him train this week. He is not ready for me. I do not doubt he is a good fighter but he needs to be great. He needs to be the best. There is no need to be scared sweetheart. We got this. We are trained and ready. Remain calm and all will be well. Babe, give me thirty to forty hours and this will be all over until the next time."

"You are so confident. What is your plan? What are you thinking?"

His plan was to bring her here to privately ask for her hand in marriage. He was nervous and fearful. However, she did what Danielle does. She managed to change his plans by telling him she was frightened. He took a deep breath, "I'm glad you asked. My plan may change in between now and when I get in the ring. It may change from what JJ and King instruct me while I am there. I am going to roll with it the first few minutes. I need to dig the scene first. He may come hard in the paint. Then I have to do what I have to do. I hate to come out of the gate hard because I do not want to overexert myself. However, if he is weak then it may be my best time to take him down. I just have to see how it flows. It is not too bad. You will be amazed and impressed when it is over. You and I may be the only ones in the building who thinks it goes slowly. Others will think it went too fast. They want the replays to see how fast and hard the punches come. In less than two hours, months of training will be gone and over. Millions of dollars will have been spent. Let's see what happens tomorrow this time."

"How do you feel?"

"Confident, loved, and blessed you are here."

"Don't change. Stay that way. As long as you stay cool, I am good. Help me help you."

"You are helping me by being here. Are you ready to go back in the circus room?"

I laughed. We walked back in the ballroom and danced all night. It was his way to avoid the explanation of why he was not eating or socializing. For him to be a highly charismatic, talkative, and social person he was still reserved and could care less about the limelight. All he wanted to do was fight.

We talked and laughed the entire time we danced. He did not eat and neither did I. "I will get you something to eat once we leave," he whispered as the cameras continued to snap.

It was cool. I did not think I could eat anyway. My stomach was turning flips. At dessert he stood and motioned, we were leaving. He threw his hand up and waved good night to the crowd. As we were shuffled back to the floor like cattle I was brave enough to ask a question, "What are we doing?"

"Can you date me? Or do you have plans?"

I laughed. He asked so sincere and waited for an answer. I really wanted to take a Tylenol PM and wake up on the flight back home. I could not back out now. *Girlfriend up. All you have to do Danielle is sit in a chair. You can close your eyes if you need to. You are not the one dancing around in some rhinestone shorts avoiding hits.* "Yes. I can date you," I finally replied.

"Hell, I was getting worried," King said awaiting my answer.

"Not you Nemo. I am sure you are worried when you ask a chick out. Who would want to date you? You have the personality of a brick. When was the last time you had a date?"

"Talk to your boyfriend. I cannot date because I am too busy babysitting your disobedient, contrary, mean, feisty mouth. I have a girl I am so interested in but I can't find the time to take her out on a date."

King and I went back and forth until we got to my door; "Get dressed" Randall said interrupting my argument and kissed my lips.

I kissed his cheek, "Sorry you have lipstick and glitter on your lips and cheek. He turned the other cheek. I put my cheek up to it and kissed it too before he ran off.

Thirty minutes later, he was back at my door. I was dressed. I texted the girls to let them know we may leave the compound. RJ stayed back with Hunter while he studied. Randall and I went and saw a show. I was not expecting it. This was his week but he was surprising me. I did not know who was schooling him; Hunter, Vickie, Paige, Leigh, or Sade, but someone was giving him great dating tips. After the show, we made it back to the hotel where he rented an area of the hotel and casino for all of us. He called everyone down except Hunter and RJ. They all gambled as I hit a few slot machines. The girls hung out with guys while I looked around. I found a small shop where I bought him a gift.

Before midnight he sent us all back to our respective rooms. I asked if I could see him for a few minutes before we retired. When we were alone I gave him the box. It was a pair of shiny blinged out dice with a note. "I bet it all on you."

He smiled and rolled the dice in his hand. It was sinking in. The fight was less than twenty-four hours away. He was starting to feel it. His eyes welled up. His tears were hot as they hit my face. As usual, he hit the deck. JJ and King rushed over. They summoned Hunter. This time I was not leaving. RJ came and from his disposition, he was not leaving either. Eventually, he was going to see his father like this. It was not a bad thing. His father was praising God. Mr. and Mrs. Washington arrived. The room was full. Keith prodded me to leave. I finally screamed "No. Leave me alone and leave him alone. Please."

I was out of breath panting and heaving. It was not an option. King picked me up and took me back to my room.

"Give her a Tylenol. She is going to have a head ache in the morning," King commanded as he laid me in bed.

"What is wrong with her?" Paige demanded as he arrived with me thrown over his shoulder like a sack of potatoes.

"She is fine. Hooks is down and it is making her nervous and scared. You two can come if you want to but she is not allowed. He will go off if he finds out we let her stay."

I showered and took the Tylenol. They all left me. As I lay there with my stomach growling I realized I had not eaten. I called room service and fell asleep on my laptop and a movie.

It was ten till four and Sade was just walking back in the room at the same time he was coming down the hall.

"What are you doing out here this time of the morning?" he questioned.

"Did you think I was coming to Vegas and not partying?"

"I will handle you tomorrow. I need to see DJ and where exactly are you coming from?"

"I didn't say. You need to check your girlfriend."

He was furious with her. He could not handle her right now. "Don't take my meekness as weakness. Tell her to step outside please."

Once I got to the door, he spoke, "Come with me. No phones and no laptops. Let's talk. Tell me what you see, how do you feel, what do you think, and what is on your heart. We can turn back right now if you want to. You say the word. How are you? What is on your mind? Real talk."

We talked until the sun came up. King was furious he was up but not running. He said he could not sleep. That is what I was there for if I recall correctly. They got him ready physically and I prepared him mentally. He could not sleep but he did not say and I could not figure out what was on his mind. With Randall, it could have been something or maybe nothing at all. He was a few hours away from a big event. None of us would be able to help him. This was it. I understood his insomnia. I felt it too.

Fight Saturday

Everyone laid low. We all hung out on the floor. The food was brought up to us and all the entertainment was there. He ran but other than that, he was not leaving the floor until it was time to go to the arena. At noon, he sent for me.

"I am about to find my zone. I will be out of commission until this is over. First, I want to make sure you are good."

"I am fine. I wish I could read your thoughts right now."

"They are not important. All you need to know is how much I love you and appreciate you," he smiled.

"If it makes you feel any better this is stressful for me mentally too."

"Thanks."

I left his room. When I walked into our suite, it was quiet.

"I will pick you up at seven," Keith said. "Everyone needs to be ready. We will all go down at the same time."

This was going to be a long day without talking to him or seeing him. To pass the time I slept. The girls left me alone. At six o'clock, they woke me up. I struggled to get dressed. I decided to go with the skinny leg tuxedo pants, sequined tank with low cowl front and back with the tuxedo jacket. My outfit was low key but still formal and nice enough to be ringside. I could put my jacket on to cover up then take it off later for the full effect. My 'girls' were standing at attention. This was two nights in a row. Tonight was a little more risky than the dress he picked out last night.

When Keith arrived at the door, I knew he was not happy with my choice of shoes. I followed directions. Just because I found a loophole in his instructions for my shoes. I was wearing peep toe stiletto booties. It did not give him the option to be pissed.

"You better be able to run if we have to. I am not picking you up."

We entered the area where he was. He was sitting in a chair with his head back and his eyes closed. Time was moving closer to leaving the holding room.

He spoke to me, "It's almost time. How do you feel? Anything I need to do or can do?"

"Be blessed and be safe until you are on the other side of the ring. I will be right up front."

"DJ stay calm. Relax. There is no need to be nervous or scared. Do not squirm. Don't curse," he calmly snickered.

"If you need my help just tag me in," I said with extreme confidence.

"As long as you stay right where I can see you. I have everything under control. Thanks for the offer. Behave and you cannot get in the ring under any circumstance. Please do not get me disqualified. Please watch her. Pastor, watch them," he pointed at all the girls. "Don't let them start any outside fights," he pointed directly at Paige, Leigh, Sade, and me. "My name is on the marquee out there. I am the only one of us fighting tonight. Period. And it will be with my fist not with my mouth. Keep your hot temper cool. Pastor is sitting next to you for a reason DJ."

He redirected his attention back to me, "Remember what I told you. People are going to cheer for me and some may boo me. I will probably be hit. I may get tired. Please remain calm. This is not my first rodeo, as you would say. We have done this before. I can handle it. Keep praying that both guys fight fair and safe. After this first one you will be a pro. Last but not least, tell me you love me."

He quickly gave me a lecture on how to act. I was the only one who got a lecture. Was this good or bad? "I love you."

Hunter said, "Let us pray."

After he prayed King spoke and then JJ. They gave him intense words of wisdom. The heaviness in the room was thick. It was a different weight. They all turned into different guys. The level of seriousness was much different from the norm.

"Baby girl do you wish to say anything," King asked.

It caught me off guard. "Randall, you once said to tag you in. I want to express to you that you may not be allowed to tag King, JJ, Hunter, or me in. Nevertheless, there is someone in the building waiting on you to tag Him in your time of need. If at any point you need help call on Him. He sent you the comforter. He is your help in time of need. Just call on His name. If you feel tired, stressed, over powered, as if you are in a losing battle, or weary call His name. If you stretch out your hand to your help, He will step right in. Pastor Hunter has set the atmosphere. Our Father is in the building. He will never leave you nor forsake you. He is in the ring waiting for you to ask Him to help you. Just as you have done in other times of need do it again today. The same way He helped you then He will help you now. He is the same God today as He was yesterday. Whether you are up against the ropes or on top of the opponent. If you are in the sanctuary, your private spot, or in what we refer to as Sin City in front of millions, He is still the same God. You may not be able to tag us in but He desires you to tag Him if you need Him. He is in you, with you, and all around you. Keep your mind stayed upon Him tonight. Know down in your knowa that He has you covered. If you keep Him as your center and your focus you can say to this mountain move to yonder place and nothing shall be impossible to you."

"If for some reason you are too tired, you can't muster up enough strength to call Him tap your hand, your foot or even your head one time and we will call on Him for you. Stretch your palms up and wait from Him to pour the strength back in you. Whatever you do, do not give up. Do all the things you, JJ, and King have diligently practiced. Keep your mind clear. Listen to your guys. Do not worry about what is happening on the other side of the rope. Do what you do. Do not worry about pleasing us. Sweetheart, do not worry about me. We love you no matter what happens. Fight a fair and safe fight. To me you will always be the Champ whether you ever get in a ring again."

By the time I was finished his arms were around my legs and my hands on top of his head. He never rose from his knees from when Hunter was praying. Leigh and Sade both had a camera and a recorder in my face.

"Danielle, tell me right now how you feel? In your heart, in your mind and in your soul? If you want to turn around, we will right now. There will be no hard feelings. I can walk away. I can forget it all. The money. The fight. Please speak. It all rides on you. Just speak the word." He spoke to me but glared right past me to King and JJ. "I want to be happy spending my life with you. I hope you understand tonight will change our lives forever."

"Randall. I love you. You are my Champ." I tried to walk away but he was like a two year old being left at school for the first time. I didn't want him to misunderstand the tears in my eyes. He was attached to my legs. I could not move. I looked at King's expressionless face. I looked at Hunter. "What are you looking at me for?" I asked Hunter with the tears running and streaming down my face. This was much more emotional than I imagined.

"I feel like I need to give you a love offering."

That was the icebreaker. Hooks let go but fell right on his face. King, Hunter and I all got down flat with him. I listened as King spoke to him. He had his glove on my hand. King was stern with him every day but right now, this was a very different King. He was brutal. The heat was turned all the way up. His fighter was not going to go in unprepared even if it meant he coached him all the way to the last minute.

"Do what we have practiced. We did not come this far and work this hard for nothing. Stay focused. Keep your head right. Its twelve rounds. You can do it. I know you can. You know you can. We all know you can. You are ready. You are the better fighter. Keep your feet moving. You did not claim the name. You earned the name Hooks. Go in there and give this guy all you got. I am not asking for a knock out. I will take it but what I am asking for is a win. Come out safe, fight safe, and give us a victory. Listen to me when I speak to you. Do what I tell you to do. I plan to only tell you once. I do not want to have to tell you anything twice. Do not dispute what I say. I do not want to and do not put me in a position where I have to call the fight. Whatever you do stay on your feet. I know we will be good. We will be celebrating in an hour. The next time we all convene together, we will still be with the HEAVY WEIGHT CHAMPION OF THE WORLD!"

JJ was sitting on his back the entire time massaging his shoulders. He was whispering in his ear so softly I could not hear what he was saying.

When King stood up, he was confident. JJ was ready. Hunter was on point. However, the fighter and I were still on the floor. Keith scooped me up and stood me to my feet then he stood Hooks up. When I saw his face, he was not the person I knew. A metamorphosis, a transformation had taken place. He was now a fighter. He was not a father, a friend, a deacon, or my boo. He came for one reason, to fight, and right now, a fighter was who he was. Fire was in his eyes. I really didn't know what to say. However, I liked who he became. It was who he needed to be at this time.

I will confess. This person freighted me. I didn't know this man. They put his robe on him. Covered his head and placed his cross around his neck. He took his charm bracelet off and put it on my ankle. He pounded everybody in the room. Leigh, the photographer and the videographer were working hard. As we all got it together, JJ spoke.

"Remember the rules. Do we have any questions?" No one spoke. He gave everyone one water as he said he would. He marked the glass bottles in case someone tried to change them. They were glass for a reason. In case anyone quickly needed a weapon and because the bottle could not be punctured.

Hooks laid his head on mine, "I love you. I will see you in sixty minutes. Are you still okay?"

"I'm great." I was lying. I was nervous. My stomach had butterflies. I felt like I was about to wet my pants. My knees were knocking. My hands were moist. My armpits were sweating. I could feel the heat rising on my upper lip and nose. I swear my voice was strained. My legs felt like spaghetti. I wanted to cry and fall out all at the same time. I needed my daddy. This strange person pecked my lips.

"Let's go," King said with authority.

He kissed me again passionately until J separated us. You had to love his crew. "That's enough," JJ said.

"I have never kissed anyone before a fight," he said still kissing me. We all looked like *what*? "What? Why are y'all looking at me in that tone? Do you think they will start the fight without me?"

"No they will not but right now Danielle is a distraction," JJ said sternly. "You need tunnel vision and Danielle is not in the damn tunnel."

"Maybe not but if you untie my hands and give me and Danielle eight minutes I promise I will knock him out by round three."

"I tell you what; if you knock him out period, I will give you and Danielle all the time you need to do whatever."

"The devil is a lie," Hunter blared out. "Let's go now!" he yelled.

The ice was somewhat broken. I felt a little better. Not much but at least I could move my feet now.

The arena security was knocking at the door letting us know it was time. I spent a lot of time with the crew there to make sure this entrance was on point. This was another anal perfection moment for me. King and JJ walked in front of us behind a massive number of local police protection. Hooks and I walked down the long corridor side by side. This better be perfect. I practiced this walk all week. I flew my own DJ out to make sure the beats went just as I wanted them. He could have cared less about how he came out. However, it was important to me. Music is the way to get to peoples soul. Tonight's musical selection was from Atlanta's finest. The dancers were in place. They were male and female dancers I flew in from ATL also.

The mix started with the theme from Rocky as expected. Then TIP of course with *Bring 'Em Out* blaring through the arena. The bass hit from JD with *Welcome to Atlanta*. *Peace up A town* down Usher screamed with Luda and Lil Jon. Next Ciara's *Gimmie Dat* was mixed in the soft and low tone of *I been gone for too long I think it's time I bring it back*. The lights flicked with laser hooks and photos all over the room. The crowd was going mad crazy. You could tell the ATLien's from the A's thrown in the air. I could see the monitors flashing the ringside celebrities whose music was being played.

Then Jeezy jumped in with *I Put On For My City*. Soulja Boy hit with *Crank Dat*. Then Travis Porter boomed with *All The Way Turned Up*. CC came back with *I been gone for too long I think it's time I bring it back*. The DJ was scratching. The light show went off again. We could see the light at the end of the corridor. The beat faded out then the mixes came back in. TIP, Jamie, and Justin flowed in with *You Know You Looking At A Winner*. TIP was next up with *Big Things Poppin*. Ciara again with *I Been Gone for Too Long* with a little more volume.

He played the same set of hooks three times and as soon as we hit the end of the corridor, the lights flashed. Fireworks shot off. Monitors showed filmed clips of Hooks and live footage. Finally, Ciara yelled *Gimme Dat Base*. The monitor showed Russell next to Ciara standing to her feet on the side of the ring crunk. Hooks; on the other hand, was calm as ever. I broke off quickly to my seat although I was hyped. The music made me ready. The DJ went crazy. He earned his keep. He rolled the set over scratching and mixing. He killed it.

Hunter looked at me, "I know who was in charge of the music."

"ATL's finest baby. Don't act. You from da SWATS too." I looked him up and down reminding him, he was wearing a white Armani tee, Gucci belt, and Tim's. "Dude, don't let me check your iPod. Wait until we win." I am sure Hunter's iPod was loaded with crunk music.

Randall's face was serious. It was as if he didn't see the people. He didn't hear the music. His tunnel vision was on. God knows I was praying. He was not as hyped as I thought he would be. I have seen him much more crunk. I almost tensed up. Then the beat came back and relaxed me.

He pranced around the ring. King and JJ were in there with him. His father was standing close. Doc and a few others lined the side of the ring. A lot was going on. I didn't feel comfortable with King in the ring and all these people out here. I was beginning to panic. I tried to keep focused on the music the DJ was playing. I hoped he knew I wasn't paying him for all of this extra. He was putting on now. I tried to look around as much as possible. I didn't see anything weird. Cameras were snapping, people talking, laughing, and having fun. I tried to get my bearings together. I needed to see where my folks were. I eyed in on the exits in case of an emergency. Leigh and Sade were standing taking pictures. I think Paige was tweeting. Everyone had a job except me. Hunter was praying. Vickie was documenting on her iPad. His publicist was being interviewed. RJ was chilling and I was panicking.

I did not think it would be like this. I wanted to yell, 'let's get this show on the road'. *What are we waiting for?* We are building up excitement. My head was heavy. It was not hurting instead cloudy and heavy. I could see all the security. Keith was directly in front of me. I could reach out and touch him if I needed to. This one time I needed King. I needed safety and security. Honestly, I was scared.

The arena was a little tighter than it was a few hours ago. The house was packed to capacity. The fire marshal came in several times this week inspecting and approving the maximum capacity. Because of the high volume, this was turning out to be the largest fight ever. They added all the seats the fire marshal allowed. Randall offered to give our seats up to allow us to remain in the box. None of us went for it. We all remained Ringside.

The Master of Ceremonies came to the ring. He had the referee, the commissioner and a few others in tuxedos with him. The voice of boxing began to speak as the microphone travel down from the ceiling. The show we all waited for was about to begin.

Hooks was moving lightly. He looked directly at me as if he did not know who I was. I tried so hard to smile. It took all I had. JJ looked my way and reassured me.

There was so much noise. Maybe it was because of the security piece in one ear. As I listened closely to my ear, there was a lot of miscellaneous talk between them until I could not keep up. I had my earpiece for my cell turned on in my other ear to try to distract me.

The MC asked us to stand for the singing of the National Anthem by Monica. I stared at him the entire time. I must have been as stiff as a board and as pale as a ghost when RJ came and held one hand while Trevor leaned in to whisper in my ear.

"He is going to be fine."

For some reason it was the confirmation I needed from the right person. I knew Trevor witnessed every one of his fights. Even the ones before he was Hooks. I relaxed a little but not much. The referee held them in the middle of the ring going over the rules. We could hear the first set of rules and then the microphone retracted in the ceiling and we could no longer hear what he said.

The two fighters placed their heads and gloves together. I should have taken a valium, a Percocet, or anything that would have numbed me. Right now, I would have gone for a Zoloft or Prozac. I wanted to announce does anyone have anything in here I can buy. I needed something to take the edge off and all I had was a damn bottle of water.

I looked to my right and saw Hunter. That was the ticket. I had who he had, Jesus. I began to call His name. At the name of Jesus, every knee must bow. It calmed me and soothed me but the fight had yet to begin.

They banged gloves. It was seconds away from beginning. Hooks took the opponent, hugged him, and spoke into him. *That was odd*, I thought. He spoke into him before the fight. The cameras went crazy. *What a mighty man of valor. I wondered if it was too late to say 'STOP'. I don't like it.* I convinced myself *I came this far. I had to keep going.*

He came to the side of the ring and leaned on the ropes. He stood there like a statue. His father climbed up and spoke to him. RJ ran up and Hunter took the oil out of his pocket and rubbed his head. He made eye contact with me. I was standing but I couldn't move my feet. He didn't motion for me so I stayed where I was. He extended his arms. They took his robe off. He was wearing his cross. He held his head down and King removed the cross. He kissed it and King passed it over the rope to Hunter who gave it to me. I placed it around my neck while the media was capturing every moment. He stood there directly in front of me ready and prepared to fight. My face and my expressions were the last he would see before the bell rang. My heart was pumping out of control. I tried hard to smile. The tears were in my eyes. Paige took my hand. Leigh and Sade were trying to get a shot of the two of us at one time but decided one should get him and the other got me. The crowd was ridiculously crazy.

I didn't recognize this man looking at me. He looked like Deacon Washington. He stood like Randall. He was shaped like RW. His expression was solely that of Hooks the Fighter. Neither of us moved. Keith was speaking in my earpiece.

"Relax. Calm down. He can sense your fear. Force a smile. Take your time. Ninety minutes and all of this will be over. Let me know if you need to leave." JJ and King moved which got my attention.

Randall gave me the nod. A nod he has given me thousands of times. The nod, which started all of this in Hunter's sanctuary. A nod that said everything is going to be all right. It calmed me instantly.

I smiled. He smiled. I blew him a kiss. He whispered I love you. I gave up a large smile and bowed. The photographers were being held back by the guys. They were still snapping and yelling to Hooks. I am sure the gossip columns will be filled with my photograph tomorrow.

It was on. When he turned his back, he was no longer the man any of us encountered. I leaned over Hunter, "RJ, are you good."

He was so excited. "Yes ma'am." He was sitting on the edge of his seat.

Meanwhile on the home front the church was packed. Overflow was filled to capacity. Vickie arranged free popcorn, Coca-Cola, water, and Chick-Fil-A sandwiches for everyone.

The kids were in children's church making banners, posters, and cards to present to him when he arrived back. He and Pastor recorded a message earlier to show at the viewing. I hoped they did not trash the church in Hunters absence. The cleaning service had no other choice but to clean it tonight for service tomorrow. If all worked out we would be in the house. I think Vickie expected a big crowd and requested a section of the sanctuary blocked off tomorrow. I knew my office was there tonight and I think they were all planning to be there tomorrow.

The restaurant was packed. We spoke to them earlier. They were freaking out unaware of how to handle this large crowd. The last time he fought, he did not own the restaurant. This was new to them too.

Hooks was sitting on a stool. The closer the clock got to zero the harder my chest pounded. JJ and King were in his face and so was a camera. All he did was nod. He looked like the five year old he often looked like. He calmly listened intently. They greased his face. One of the guys forced water down his throat. Checked his shoes and gloves and then left him alone. You knew he was taking these last thirty seconds to pray. He stood up and looked back. We all encouraged him. He and his opponent stood in the middle of the ring with the referee. They tapped gloves. Some quick bantering took place between the two of them, which no one could hear. The voice of boxing said the magic words.

"Let's get ready to RUMBLE!" The bell rang.

Oh sh*t. I thought to myself. *This is it.* I closed my eyes. I could not stand not watching. *Was I the only person in this entire place nervous? Did he know what he was doing? Did he understand the magnitude?* The crowd made too much noise. Not one single punch was thrown in the first thirty seconds. I immediately freaked out. *Why are they scared to get this party started?* Then I thought *they have eleven more times to do this. It is okay Danielle. Chill.*

Finally, the first punch was thrown. The other guy ducked. He responded. My stomach growled. *Of all the times to get hungry.* A series of punches went on from the both of them. Then a harsh blow was taken. I closed my eyes. I felt my watch pinch me. I took it off and put it in my clutch.

Seconds later a sound came in my ear. I couldn't hear it clearly. JJ and King both were yelling from the ringside. Hunter leaned in, "Put the watch back on."

"Huh?" Then I realized what he said. I looked for the paramedic. *Was I having a heart attack?*

Keith pushed Paige over, "Put the watch back on."

Who is recording levels? I looked down the row. It had to be Vickie. Why? I guess they were going to take me out if they needed to. This was insane. He was in the middle of a fight and still stalking me.

"No need in hiding your levels. They have been high for the last two days," Keith encouraged.

"It was pinching me."

"I know." He motioned to one of the guys confirming I was all right and said, "Give it to me."

I did and he put it back on my wrist. The bell rang. *Thank God.* Round one was over.

"Not bad," Hunter acknowledged.

So you say I thought. Then here came these skimpy heffa's walking the ring with the signs to inform others it was going to be round two. *We know what round it is. Sit your narrow tail down somewhere eat a meal and put some clothes on. Who deemed they were necessary?*

I could hear Keith but I couldn't understand. He turned around, "Good job. Keep them just like that." He was referring to my levels.

I could hear King's voice. It was strong and powerful.

The bell rang again. *Help me Lord* I thought. Sade pranced over.

"Hey Auntie," she said as if it was her eighth birthday.

Was I the only one freaking out? Were they all on something and no one offered me any? Were we all at the same event? I was looking and talking to Sade when I looked up at the wall and noticed the second round was almost over. *Thank God.*

The bell rang. He had a little more life in him this round. It seemed like the one-minute break was over by the time he sat down. I stared at him so hard. He did not know because his back was to me.

"You are doing well," Keith mumbled trying to keep me calm.

I felt like a woman in travail. I was breathing in and out. I am sure Hunter could hear me. He was sitting on the edge of his seat. He was tweeting and communicating with Elder. At one moment, I think Hunter was broadcasting live to the church. I could hear him greeting the congregation.

Round three Hooks moved a little more freely. He was finding his position. Both fighters began to get comfortable. The hooks were coming quickly from my fighter. The crowd made a lot of noise after every punch. Good noises and bad noises. You couldn't tell from the noise level who the crowd was cheering for.

"DAMMIT." He was hit. My squirm meter went up. Even Hunter made a noise, which made my head snap. Keith looked back. I was sliding down my chair. He took a hard punch. It pissed me off. I didn't like this one bit. At the house, I would have been all over dude with a Louisville Slugger. Instead, Hooks came back hard in the paint. I sat up on the edge of my seat. My adrenaline was pumping differently now. It seemed like one hundred punches were thrown. The guy was on the ropes. *How in the world can someone just take blow after blow? Who in the world would want to?* I just knew he was going to hit the deck. The bell rang.

"What the hell," I yelled out. King and Hunter both laughed. Paige was on her phone. Sade and Leigh were hanging off the rope taking shots as soon as he sat on the stool.

I never saw him sweat like this before. He was sweating like no tomorrow. King and JJ were hyped. They were ready and encouraging him. If he only had a few more seconds in the round, the fight would have been over. Now we were forced to go another round.

Hunter was speaking into his phone to the congregation. My DJ was playing a different mix. He was getting the party hyped. He knew music was my passion. It actually calmed me. When I looked down, I had sixty-seven texts. Church friends, work friends, and all others were blowing me up. The skimpy chicks came back out again. Round four.

In the top of the fourth round, he came out fighting. The momentum changed quickly. The guy struggled to stay on his feet. He kept his balance by leaning on the rope. The crowd was going wild. I was on the edge of my seat. This had to be over. He lost his balance. He hit the mat. The referee counted. He was up right as the bell rang.

JJ and King were still calm. They were trying to see if the fight was going to be called. The other guy's team said he could still go. He was not done. The referee and the medical staff checked him. They agreed the fight could continue. I thought it was over. My boxer was sweating but he was still calm. This gave him a few more minutes to rest.

"What in the hell," I said loud enough for Keith to laugh, for RJ to look over Hunter, and JJ turned around. *That was some BS. The fight was over. What in the world is going on? You mean to tell me I am actually going to have to wrestle through more rounds. The devil is the father of lies.*

I looked at Hunter, "This fight is over," I declared. "The most we are going to do is walk around this ring two more rounds then dude is going to have to fall down. He has no choice but to give up the ghost." Hunter looked like I spoke a foreign language. I was serious.

The bell rang. Hooks stepped up as if he was just as furious as I was. Old boy snuck him one. One good one. Hooks bobbed. He shook it off. Then it was on. It was hook after hook after hook. Left, right, right, right, left. I could not tell which one was the most powerful the left or the right. They were coming so fast. The opponent was up on the rope. He would have hit the mat if Hooks stopped punching long enough to give him the opportunity. The DJ started playing. It was evident the fight was over. Everyone knew it except the winner. He was still hitting the man.

No one pulled him off. JJ and King were both standing on the ropes waiting on the okay to come in. The guy was barely hanging on. The bell rang.

He hit the deck. The referee counted but he did not move. His team entered the ring to assist. Everyone in my immediate section stood and cheered. I bowed my head in my seat.

It was sheer pandemonium. I think the team was much happier than the fighter was. I do not think Hooks was out of his zone yet. He stood there very defensive. He was pulling back and being defensive if anyone touched him. They tried to get him to sit. They went for the mouthpiece. They reached for his gloves. Then I realized he was looking up at the board trying to read what it said. He was waiting for it to read something. He had to be the only person other than the loser who was not aware this fight was over. Four years off, half a year of training, in four rounds, and twenty-eight minutes it was over. I was exhausted although I was happy. It was just like the woman in travail. Once she sees the prize all else is irrelevant.

The commentator spoke, "A unanimous decision has been made. The winner and heavy weight champion of the world by technical knockout is Hooks Washington!"

There was uproar like I have never heard before. King picked him up JJ took his mouthpiece out and shoved the water down his throat. He looked like a five year old at touch football. He had no clue what just happened. I now understood why he watched himself so much. He really didn't remember. "What did they say?" as he exited his zone.

"YOU WON."

"I won?" He threw his hands up. I put my face in my hands. It was all I could do not to cry.

He was still not excited. He was calmer now than thirty minutes ago. He was like Sade when she used to compete. Calm as ever. It was all in a day's work for him. The rest of us were overjoyed. RJ was trying to get in the ring. I called on my earpiece, "Help RJ please."

My mix started playing Kanye West, *Amazing*. TIP, Jamie Fox and Justin Timberlake, *Winner.* Monica sang *Still Standing*. Flo Rida, *The Club Can't Handle Me Right Now.*

The ring was packed. I could not even see him. I heard the crowd taking it down. A reporter asked, "Hooks what did you do different for this fight?"

"Nothing physical. Mentally I had Ringside help. The sixth man. God almighty. The love of my life, my pastor, best friend, my Son, my team, my family, my friends, and church family. To God be the glory. What more could a man ask for?"

"Don't get all spiritual on us Hooks."

"It is what it is."

He spoke into a few cameras before he went to speak to his opponent. He was such a good sport. As soon as he stepped out of the ring, he searched for my hand. Paige shoved me forward. Backstage he continued to speak with all of us extremely close by. I was attached to him like a shadow. Finally, we were left alone. Hunter prayed.

He looked at Hunter and said, "You are getting on a plane now." Hunter wanted to dispute but he kept quiet.

After they got Hunter situated he came back. Everything was moving so fast. We were in my room. As soon as the girls and I got there, we immediately popped a bottle. I was cool all the way to the room. Then I let go when the tops started popping. I got buck wild. I became unglued and turned up. Trey Songz rang out and I sang at the top of my lungs. Who cared how I sounded? My boyfriend was still the Heavy Weight Champion of the World. Do you know how big that is? I could sound as horrible as I wanted to. Those who didn't like it could shut up or put up. If not I had someone who could shut them up. I sang. "Bottoms up. Bottoms up. Pass me a cup. Tell security we bout to tear this room up." I was enjoying myself. We worked hard to get here and it paid off. He was the Champ. We clicked glasses, sang, and danced. I noticed I was the only one dancing and singing all of a sudden.

I turned around with the champagne bottle lifted to my mouth and there he was leaning in the threshold of the door. His hands were in his pockets. King, Keith, Black, and JJ with him. They all looked surprised. I let my guard down. All I could do was smile and put the bottle down.

"Can I see you please when you are done?"

Those heffas. I thought to myself. They did not even try to warn me. He was not Hooks any more. In a matter of minutes, he was back to Deacon Daddy. We stepped outside to talk. Now he was nervous. *Was he bipolar?* "Get dressed. I need you at the formal press wearing all black."

He gives me a present from his pocket. I was too hyped to take a present right now. He was still calm but fidgety. I opened the box. Here it was he just fought his heart out and he gives me a present. The box contained a diamond cross like his. It was on a much smaller scale but exactly like his.

I jumped on him. He moaned and closed his eyes. "I am so sorry. Are you hurt?"

"My body aches. This is nothing compared to how it will feel in the morning."

"I am so proud of you," As I view his tatted face I broke down and cried. He cried tears of joy with me. We stood there in worse shape with him as a winner than when he was training.

"We have ten minutes," he let me go and walked off.

In exactly ten minutes, he was back at my door. Didn't he know ten minutes was not long enough for a woman to change clothes much less take the excitement level back down to a normal level? He had his game face on. I was not ready. I heard the heavy sigh from all of them, him included.

"What?" I yelled. He was calm and now I was cocky. "You all have pushed me around all damn week. Told me what I could do and what I couldn't do. What I could wear and what I had to wear. When to eat, pee, and sleep. He had me locked up in this hotel as if it is San Quentin. I am malnourished, tired, and sleepy. I have neglected work. I had to bail the two drunks out of trouble. I have prayed as if tomorrow wasn't coming. I had to sit still for a fight, which seemed to last four days. I know damn well y'all ain't rushing me. What? Are they going to hold the press conference without him? I think not. They will just have to wait. Get used to it. Just because you throw on a suit like it is a breakaway doesn't mean everyone else can. Get over it little buddy."

While I was ranting and raving, the girls were mimicking me. I continued, "I have had just about enough of all of you all. I am ready to get home to my bed and my desk honey. I got him straight now I got a job. I got work to do. Money ain't free around here. I got to go get it. You too Leigh." I was so hype and crunk until I did not know what I was talking about. I think I was nervous talking.

Next thing I knew King was standing in the door. "What are you whining about?"

"You all are getting on my nerves. Oh no Terminator. I am not wearing it. I draw the line." I slid my foot across the floor making a line. "Hooks, Help me. I am not fighting with the Tasmanian Devil right now." I snarled at King.

"She wears it or she stays here. I prefer here."

His posture was so calm and cool as he entered the room. *Did he know what just happened? Was he there? Did he know he was the Heavy Weight Champion of The World? Was he on something?* He leaned on the doorframe. He was suited up, vest, tie, and all. I was half-dressed. I think this was probably the first time he had seen me in this state. He stared. King threw it at him and said, "Handle this. You have five minutes. We lost five with her ranting."

I stood in the mirror applying makeup. He stood leaning on the door. "DJ."

I looked up. I noticed he was fidgeting again. "I love you so much. What happened tonight means nothing compared to what you mean to me."

My brush dropped. The tears welled up. *Here we go again,* I thought. The next thing I knew we were rolling on the floor. We knocked something over and the passé rushed in. Leigh snapped her camera and Paige clapped her hands.

"Not on my watch. Get up and out." Paige demanded.

"She will be pregnant before the week is out if they keep going like rabbits in heat," Sade said with confidence.

Paige pleaded, "King, JJ, help me."

They picked him up. My legs were wrapped around his leg. When they pulled him, they pulled me too. He stood up still calm as ever. He brushed himself off. He brushed me off. He looked JJ flat footed and spoke, "You promised me if I won I got all the time I needed with the love of my life. It starts now." It was not a question. He kissed me and preceded out the door, "Sade and King help her put the vest on."

"Why?" Why are we wearing bulletproof vests?

"Because I said so," he reconsidered his remark. He came back in the room. He unbuttoned his jacket, vest, and placed my hand on his chest. "We all are wearing one." He clapped his hands. The gunshots rang. "Now, let's do it baby." This was the most excitement he displayed all day.

King put the bulletproof vest on me so tight I felt like I was wearing a Body Magic. It sucked the life right out of me. We headed to the elevator hand in hand. As soon as the doors closed, I leaned up to whisper in his ear. He barely moved his head down. "I am so proud of you."

"I know," he said. "You are beautiful. Thank you for everything. We need to talk."

I laid my head on his shoulder. King looked at me in the mirror and gave me the nod of acceptance. The moment was awkward. I broke the silence. "Guys you all have done a good job getting this victory. I am very proud of all of you and I love you all. You too King," I grumbled. "I feel like one big happy family."

"Thanks Ms. D. We are family. We love you too. We really appreciated you being here and being a part of this." Randall squeezed my hand. "It has meant a lot to the group and even more to the fighter. You made training easier. Even when we have had to crack down on him, it was still easy. Your presence has been much appreciated. I am not sure we would have gone this far, this quick, and this successful without you. You have made a strong impression upon us. He is blessed to have you and I wish you many more great and successful years together," JJ kindly said.

Randall was fidgeting again. He was shifting his weight and moving his hands in and out of his pocket. The tears were rolling down my face. King could see them in the mirror.

King looked at JJ, "Speak for yourself." The doors opened. Vickie was right there with the others from the security team. He raced off the elevator as if something happened. King took out his handkerchief and wiped my tears, "Are you good?"

I nodded my head.

"If not we will stay here until you are."

I melted down. King closed the elevator door. "You are messing up your make up and heaven knows you need it."

It made me laugh as I got myself together. "I think I am ready."

"I love you baby girl."

"Thanks King. It means a lot to me."

"You mean a lot to us and to him. And all the stuff JJ said was true."

When the door opened, we were laughing and holding hands. Randall's eyebrows rose. He extended his hand. "Should I be jealous or concerned?"

"Enjoy the moment. With King and me, it will not last long. See what you have done?"

"What?"

"You made the two of us mushy and friendly. That should never happen."

It was press conference after press conference. He said just enough words to move on to the next destination. He never said one word that was insulting or disrespectful to his opponent. In fact, he presented it as if it was a close fight.

We made one last stop before we officially checked out of the hotel. Randall, King, JJ, and I were escorted into the vault along with Khrittyleberrg and Schlossenbloum. Everyone stood as Hooks entered. He pulled out a chair on the empty side of the table and motioned for me to have a seat. Schlossenbloum and Khrittyleberrg were on both sides of me. He, King and JJ were behind me. They went over the numbers. *OMG. I was not expecting the amount of money that was being discussed.* They asked him if he agreed and if so to sign for his payment. He asked a few questions and once they were answered to his satisfaction, his accountant showed him his figure, and he signed electronically. They hit a few buttons on a computer. The wire transfer was complete. They handed his accountant, his lawyer and him a printed copy.

"You can give it to my future wife." They passed me the agreement and the transfer confirmation. He shook hands and we left. I glanced at the sheet. All I saw was zeros and transfer confirmed. My mind could not quickly comprehend the figure.

We met back up with the crew. Vickie signaled time was up. It was late. We had a few more stops to make and a flight to catch since he refused to be seen by a medical professional until he was back in Atlanta. He agreed to make an appearance at a few clubs because people he knew owned them. Sade was determined she was coming along. We stayed in each spot briefly. Long enough for pictures to be taken and the DJ's to announce Hooks Washington was in the building. One DJ announced he was buying the bar. This was news to Hooks. We were on the way out the door when it was announced. "They will figure it out," he said.

A few hours ago, I was ready to leave Sin City but right now, I wanted to stay forever. The plane was waiting for us. It really had no choice. There were over thirty of us together. It was in its best interest to wait.

While we were in route, I sat in between Randall and Randall Jr. His phone rang. He looked at it and immediately passed it across me to RJ.

"Hello," He paused and passed it back to his dad.

"Yeah. What's up?" he sounded annoyed. Everyone in the car got the tone. "Yeah I fought tonight. You need me for something." We were holding hands. My hand began to slip. The entire time we have known each other I have never known her to call. He pulled my hand back and squeezed it. "Tameka I am tied up right now. I need to get Danielle, RJ, and my family on a flight. Son do you have your phone?"

RJ leaned up and said, "Yes sir," and held it up.

"Aye, you can hit RJ back on his phone," he clicked the phone off.

Before I knew it I said, "What was that about?" None of us had ever heard him so discourteous.

"She asked me a stupid question. Did I fight tonight? DUH. What other Hooks does she know? Is she the only person in the world who did not know I was fighting tonight? And to think I was married to her."

I squeezed his hand then I pulled my phone out and texted him.

> Don't ever say anything ugly about her in front of him gain.

He read it and replied aloud. Why did I think he would not?

"Yes ma'am. You are correct. I was bad mannered." What he had a problem with more than Tameka calling was Danielle pulling her hand back during the call. He needed to understand why.

When we arrived, we were shuffled out of the car before it was in park. King ran up the jet way, checked the plane, and summoned us up. The luggage was loaded and as we entered, the sleepy passengers heard the intercom announcing the Heavy Weight Champion of the World was entering. They stood and gave him a standing ovation. The pilot came out. Vickie did what she does. She pulled out the glossy's and began passing them out. None of us slept the entire way back home.

RJ was a good kid. He played his game and listened to his iPod the entire ride when he was not in the cockpit with the pilots. He reminded me of Sade. Well, when she was a kid. He entertained himself. He may have been listening to the adults but he knew when to be a kid and when he could join in. I could call him stepson. He was mannerable. I was not going to have to put in work with him. I liked the kid a lot. He was a boy so he and Sade didn't have to compete and he was young enough until she may not even care.

"Since I can't get the lemon or lime what about a Bugatti Veyron?"

"Don't try me Champ."

Just because we were back in the A did not mean we were off duty. We were all required to be in service in a few hours. We got word Hunter's flight landed; he was home safe and expected to see us all in the morning.

Sunday

When we arrived at church, they had signs out and the kids had banners and posters lining the driveway. He is so humble. He cried. I am glad we arrived early because it was thirty minutes or so before he exited the car.

We were all wearing all black again. Black was not a color he normally wore a lot. He usually wore just as much color as I did but this week black was his theme. He sat me down and people were trying to congratulate and speak to him but he was as modest as can be. It was as if nothing happened. To him it was a normal Sunday. The only difference was his body ached from head to toe more than usual. He ran back to walk in with Pastor Hunter. We were all asked to stand. Security was lining the aisles. The band played the theme from Rocky while Deacon Washington and Pastor Hunter came out. Hunter was wearing his belt from last night.

Hunter was off the chain. He took off his suit jacket off. He was singing and directing the choir. I am not sure who was more excited. Hunter, the crew, or the congregation.

Hunter preached and tore the church up. I was off my feet the entire service. My whole family and office was there. Hunter preached on perseverance, obstacles, trials, and determination. How your blessing may be one-step away. How you never know when or where it will show up. "For Deacon Washington it showed up right here at church when he least expected it." He was talking about me. He closed out his sermon and opened the doors of the church.

The announcements began to play. He stood up. He asked Keith to stand. He did. He kneeled beside me. They showed clips from the fight. Mama Rose leaned in and said, "I love you Rosie."

"I love you too Mama."

The church was clapping and celebrating. Then the film made a noise demanding your attention. Hunter appeared on the screen and said, "This broadcast has been interrupted by a special announcement."

"Thanks Tre. Thank you for all of your prayers and guidance. I would like to thank God because it is through him I am able to fight. I would like to thank my team who prepared me. I need to thank my son for believing in me and my family for their support." He was on his knees next to me.

His tone changed up. "To you Danielle, my Rose. The love of my life. I cannot thank you enough. I love you and I need you. I cannot go another day without you. Will you be my wife?"

I was looking. I was waiting on the next part of the film. Then I realized Sade and Leigh were standing over me taking pictures. I looked like a deer in headlights. The congregation's whispers ceased.

I looked at him. He had a blue box in his hand. Tears were flowing down his face. I looked at Keith, JJ, Paige, and then King. "King, what is going on?" I asked in sheer panic.

King kneeled down on the other side of me. "I think you know. This is it baby girl. The moment we have all been waiting for. It is all on you."

I took his hand. I dropped my head. The tears were streaming. I took one hand and covered my face. I sobbed. I could not breathe. He took my face.

Keith gave me a bottle of water.

"Danielle listen to me. I love you. I need you. Will you please marry me?"

"Did you ask my Mama first?"

"Yes, I asked her, Paige, Leigh, Sade, Mikey, Hunter, King, Keith, JJ, RJ, and God. Do I need to ask anyone else?"

"What did my mama say?" For the first time in a long time, I wished my father were here.

"She gave me her blessing. Anything else?"

"Yes."

"Yes what?"

"Yes. Yes, I will marry you."

"Oh My God."

Hunter leaned in, "What's wrong RW?"

His microphone was still on. Randall spoke and when he did, it was right in his mic. "She said yes."

"SHE SAID YES," Hunter announced. He then said, "You all were the first to get the press release that he was fighting and witnessed his victory. You were present for the proposal and invited immediately after service for the first of many engagement parties. Breakfast, cake, and punch will be served. I think there are souvenirs also. Please do not leave until we can properly congratulate Deacon Randall Hooks Washington and the Future Mrs. Danielle Jade Rose Washington."

Who told Hunter my whole name and who allowed him permission to use it?

We had breakfast and an engagement party right there after Sunday morning service. We also had a photo shoot and videos made to commemorate the event. It was all moving too fast for me. Just when I thought the fun was over he brought the spice right back.

We had not had time to be alone from the week, the fight, and now this. I needed to talk to him alone. I needed to speak to him as my Champ and now my future husband. Right now, all I could do was look at this monstrosity on my hand. This ring was too big to be real. Unfortunately, I knew it was.

The day was a very long and unexpected day for me. I had to respond to the ton of phone calls, posting, and blogs. It was funny how quickly news travelled. I do not think he expected the press would get this information so soon. Vickie spent most of her day responding to them along with Leigh and Paige. I think the parents and grandparents sat around proudly. While the future bride and groom panicked from one minute to the next. This was surreal. It was very unexpected for me. I could not calm myself mentally or physically. The more my mind raced the more my heart raced and so did my inner hormones.

Once the evening was ending and we walked everyone out. We both stood on his front step filled with emotions but not knowing what to say. I think each of us avoided eye contact. It was too much. I needed to go home. I had not had time to think and digest everything. We had not been alone to enjoy the moment. The day went so quickly until I wanted a replay. I had not had time to review the proposal video. Mentally, I stood there exhausted. Physically, I stood there excitable.

"Come," he said in that Hooks tone which only requires one word. He placed his hand on my waist and guided me back in the house. When he closed the door, our eyes met. Passionately and aggressively, he kissed me. My body heated upon contact and from the way his body parts touched mine his did too. Within seconds my breasts were exposed and his mouth touching them. Left to right then right to left again. Even at this intimate moment he still did everything disciplined and in order. My internal thermometer was at fever level to the point I had to squeeze my inner muscles tightly to avoid the pulsation. Our breathing was intense and audible. I needed him to touch me. To touch inside of me. As soon as I had the thought, his hand rolled down my legs and before I could blink, my skirt was over my waist and his hand was gradually touching the lace on my underwear. I could feel the moisture cool yet hot prepared to trickle from its hiding spot. He needed to stop. My heart was racing. I didn't know which was worst the pulsation I was receiving internally below my waist or the ones I was feeling in my chest.

I tried to open my eyes and focus. The room was spinning. I could easily be having a heat stroke or heart attack. Something was happening. Something we promised not to do but I loved every second of it and evidently, my body did too. His hand made its way underneath the lace. He caressed me soothingly. His mouth rapidly and aggressively going from breast to breast and then back up to my mouth. I was beyond distracted. I could not think clearly. I was overly excited. My body was experiencing too many different physical pleasures at once. It was overwhelming.

He softly inserted his finger. I gasped for air. *What are we doing? Just a few more seconds and we will stop.* I could feel the moisture being exposed. *HELP.* My mind screamed. *CONTINUE.* My body demanded.

He purposefully took his time. He was waiting on a no. A request to stop. A do not do this. A reminder of the promise. The more he fondled the less of this he could endure. He knew he was pleasing her. She did not have to tell him. Her body and face told it all. This was a feeling and a look he longed for. More than wanting to please himself he wanted to please her. He waited as long as he could for her to reject him. She was going to have to be the stronger one tonight. He was the weaker of the two. She never gave the impression she wanted him to stop. He took the foreplay until he was throbbing and lightheaded. With one hand, still caressing her he unzipped his pants. His body released like an untamed animal being uncaged. He tried to rationalize with himself. He could not do it. He immersed himself inside her. His plan was to be soothing. However, as soon as their bodies met his body took control.

"ARGH," she gasped arching her back and sliding down the wall. His body stayed with hers. As they met the floor, she continued to display her emotions verbally as he kept his to himself. He watched every movement and facial expression. He knew this was pleasurable pain for her but right now it was something both their bodies both needed and what better day than on the day he proposed.

Before it was over, I awoke from the dream.

WEEK 37
Monday

I arrived at the gym so we could make the parade. I was trying to hop in the van with the others when JJ informed me I was in the wrong car.

"Ms. D why are you here? You need to be in the car with Hooks."

"Why?"

"So you two will be together when we get to the entrance point."

"For what?"

"He wants you to walk with him."

"JJ will you please let John know that Jackie will not be walking with him. She will be on the sidelines," I said referring to the Kennedy's.

"I do not think it was an option."

"I do not think I was giving him a choice either."

"Next car please," JJ said like not today. "Do what I tell you to do."

"I do not have on shoes to walk down Peachtree." Needless to say, I walked down Peachtree. Thank God Cole Hahn teamed up with Nike, which was my choice of shoes for today.

A local reporter reports, "It is confirmed the female companion accompanying Hooks Washington is Danielle Rose of Atlanta. She has been with him recently under the assumption she was in his entourage. We were informed she is not an employee and he and his entourage refer to her publically as his love interest. There were separate suites booked for this past fight in Las Vegas. A group of friends who arrived and left with her and Hooks accompanied her penthouse suite. The MGM Grand has confirmed the bill from her penthouse was combined with Hooks Gym's bill."

"They have been spotted at benefits, dinner, and we are told she spends quite a deal of time at his gym. The hand gesture they display you should see on the bottom of your screen is a peace sign and then a hook representative of the name Hooks. We have a reporter at the courthouse currently who reports his divorce is final. He was married to his high school sweetheart and the mother of his only son Randall Junior. During his career, he has remained out of the public eye. We have not seen his son until Saturday's fight and today at this parade. It looks like his love interest is not camera shy. We hope to see more of them in the future. Maybe wedding bells are in the making. Congrats to Atlanta's own Hooks Washington, who continues to hold the title of the Heavy Weight Champion of the World. Reporting to you live from Downtown Atlanta."

The parade was nice. Vickie was in full force deciding whom he could speak with and whom he could not. I think the next thirty days were booked with interviews. I did not see him doing a ton of interviews. It was not his style but for some reason he agreed.

We headed back to my office. Mikey prepared brunch for us there. My phone was ringing from the office at the same time the elevator doors opened. I answered, "Dani Ro."

"Quick! Reginald is here!"

At the same time he was saying it, Reginald and I made eye contact as soon as the elevator doors open. King, Keith, JJ, Randall, and I were on one elevator. Leigh, Sade, and the rest were on the other elevator coming up behind us. "Thanks. Can you contact my assistant immediately?"

"You see him I take it," the mailroom person confirmed while hiding behind a column.

"Yes. Thank you. We will be in touch."

"Hi," I grimaced. "I will be right with you." I went to unlock my office door. I let King, Keith, and Randall in. Leigh was calling, "Yes."

"I am trying to get up there as quick as I can."

"Thanks."

I went back to Leigh's desk, "Follow me please," I ordered as I led him to the executive conference room. We walked in and I closed the door behind myself. We stood there in silence. I was confident. I was ready. I felt no feelings for him. It felt good to feel like this. It may have taken four years but it was well worth it. I rolled the ring around on my finger for added confidence. I shook my wrist as the rose and hook charms clanked. I felt like saying WHAT IN THE HELL DO YOU WANT.

He did not say anything. In fact, he looked at me as if I did something to him. I finally folded my arms. I realized he wasn't going to speak. So I did, "What can I do for you today Reginald?"

"Dee?"

"Yes," I said abrupt and annoyed.

"Is this how we greet each other?"

"What do you mean?"

"You greeted me like a business associate."

My eyebrows rose.

"What is up with that?"

"Last time I recalled this is my place of business."

"I assume the other company you were keeping is business also," he said referring to Randall.

"Assumptions are like assholes."

"Watch your mouth Danielle."

I laughed. Everyone seemed to always want to tell me to watch my mouth. They hadn't seen potty yet. My mouth used to be horrible. He of all people should remember.

"For some reason I do not think he is here on business."

"No one asked you to think."

"Is there a reason why I am getting this attitude?"

"You tell me."

"Let's take it down Dee." He tried to hug me. I did not move or respond. Immediately there was a rattle at the window. Reginald closed the blinds.

The door swung open slamming into the wall. It was Keith. "Ms. D, are you good?"

"Yes. Thank you."

Keith stepped in and opened the blinds back up. JJ was standing outside the window.

"What is that about Danielle?"

I scowled.

"We are better than this."

I raised my eyebrows again and slid my hand down my face.

"Can I not speak to you in private?"

"Not really."

"Not really is not a response. It is a yes or a no."

"Evidently no."

"So you spend your time hanging out with boxers now?"

"I have hung out with worse rift raft before. You should remember."

"Are you calling me rift raft?"

"Street thug is more like it?"

"What's going on and why are you doing this?"

I was confused. *Dude the last four years you did you. The four years before that you did you. Where was this coming from? He was happy and content knowing I was single but now that I was not he was about to blow a blood vessel. I was being sunburned from the heat he was radiating.* "I am really not clear on what you are asking, why, or where it came from?"

"I am asking what is up with you and the boxer."

"You were just face to face with him why didn't you ask him?"

"Maybe I should have. However, my business is with you. I have no business with him. Your loyalty is to me."

"LOYALTY! LOYALTY! Did I hear you correctly? How dare you barge in here after four years and ask me about loyalty. If my memory serves me correctly you know nothing about loyalty." I closed the blinds. "You know nothing about faithfulness, love, honesty, relationships, or communication. Do I need to go on? You have some f'ing nerve."

"You need to lower your voice. It does not require all of this."

"You know what, you are absolutely correct. A conversation with you does not require anything at all."

"Do you want to tell me about you and the boxer?"

"As a matter of fact I rather not."

"Are you in a relationship with him?"

"It appears to be that way," I smirked.

"Is he married?"

"I think you should know me better than that. Either way it is my problem. And it would not be any worse than the things you have done to me."

"That is not what I came here for Danielle."

"What exactly did you come for?"

He lowered his head. "I guess this means there is no room in your heart for me any longer," his tone changed.

I didn't respond.

"That was a question."

"Actually, it was a statement. You left my heart vacant years ago. The vacancy has been filed."

"I hate that Dee. I wish you would reconsider." He walked up to me real close. "Please reconsider. Do not do this to us. We had some good years. We have a history together. Do not let four years, some quick fun, and fame destroy us. If I recall correctly your dream boy spent four years lying low too. Why? Think about it. There is a reason."

"I am sure you know a lot about quick fun, strip clubs, private parties, easy money, street power, and hood fame. What was your reason?'

"You know where to reach me."

He opened the door. They all were standing there. My back was turned. I heard King speak. I was so glad he was there. He was the most brutal of them all and I needed the extra reinforcement.

"Good day," King said in the harshest voice I have ever heard. It was more like leave and leave now.

"Mr. Hooks," Reginald said in a conquering and intimidating tone.

"And you are?" Randall said back as fierce as he was addressed extending his hand.

"Reginald Sawyer," he stated with pride and snide.

"My pleasure. Pleased to see my appearance gave you reason to surface after four years. Thank you for the visit."

I looked like damn. Are they going blow for blow? This is going to prove interesting.

"Same here. Four must be our lucky number. Nice come back. Double victory. You take the belt and you take my girl. How long do you think it will it last? Nevertheless, congratulations are in order."

"Thank you. Danielle is absolutely a prize and four years was worth the wait. Your disappearance has been much appreciated and will continue to be. Do not worry I did not take either the win or Danielle. I worked hard for them both unlike one of us. Besides, I already held the title."

"Don't get too excited."

"My sentiments to you. What you are thinking right now is only just a dream. I am the Champ. We thank you for stopping by to congratulate us and formally say farewell. Our blessings are with you."

I closed my eyes. Leigh stood off in the background watching and listening. I am sure she was recording this somehow as my entire office watched this performance.

"Mr. Hooks your brutality is more appreciated in the ring."

"There is a difference between brutality and honesty. Truthfully," he said with both fist balled up. "I have earned the right to be as brutal as I want when I want. Mainly when it involves Danielle if you get my drift. I hope we have a clear understanding."

We were at the elevator. Randall pushed the button. The tension was heavy. You could not cut it with a machete. I do not know who was standing closest to me, King, JJ, Keith, Black, or Randall. Randall was so close to me until we could have been Siamese Twins. Keith was on my right. King was on Randall's left. JJ was behind Randall and Black behind me. It was a true standoff. Reginald stood directly in front of us smiling. I wondered if Reginald understood what congratulate us comment.

Once the elevator arrived, Reginald spoke again. He always tried to have the last word. "We will see what your next fight looks like. It maybe sooner than you think."

King moved as if he was getting on the elevator with him. Randall pushed him back with one arm. "Put your money where your mouth is."

I reached my left hand inside and pressed the button so this tit for tat could cease. Reginald saw the rock on my finger. He grabbed my hand. I snatched it back. My bracelet with the rose and the hook dangled in his hand. Randall made eye contact with him and smiled with his hand resting on my waist.

"Checkmate," as he threw up the deuces his identical bracelet dangled in mid-air. The elevator doors closed.

PREAMBLE TO CONFESSIONS OF A BUILER AND A BOXER

My head was spinning. Saturday was still fresh on my mind. I remembered every punch. Then Sunday's proposal was a complete shock. That is how humble Randall is. It was his day and his time. He worked hard and deserved the attention. Instead, he threw it all off on me with a beautiful proposal. We will not even discuss this monstrosity of a ring on my finger. Then today's parade, interviews, and Reginald's surprise visit I was a little overwhelming. I didn't have time for Reginald's interruptions and antics. I needed to clear my head. I was determined not to entertain Reggie.

Tonight I confessed. I was feeling stressed, confused, and annoyed. I began to think. *Why did he show up? Maybe he really loved me. Maybe he needed me. Was all of this right? Were Randall and I moving too fast? Was I supposed to be with Reginald? I needed answers. I needed help. Twenty-four hours ago, I was sitting on top of the world with the man I loved. Now I was sitting in the middle of my floor questioning myself.*

This day was supposed to be one of the happiest days of my life. All of a sudden, Reginald did what he seems to be good at. He jumped in and changed my life in a matter of minutes. Why do I keep letting him do this? Why would he not get the drift and go away.

Lord help me I cried out!

STAY CONNECTED

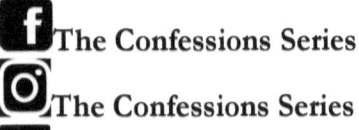 The Confessions Series

The Confessions Series

@ConfessionsSeri

www.confessionseries.com